I0645322

Driftdead

"*Driftdead* is as canny a book about the uncanny as you would want to read. Past and future stream; our catastrophic present is registered with hallucinatory clarity: haunting characters from a small Aotearoan town speak the rapsodies of their passing from a dreamland where beauty and horror orbit each other in the eye of an incorrigibly domestic storm. It is disturbing and salutary in equal measure; philosophically astute; a slow burn which generates terrific supense. Mike Johnson has written a classic."

\- Martin Edmond

"*Driftdead* is a small-town saga that rivals García Márquez *One Hundred Years of Solitude*. It is Mike Johnson's *War and Peace*, or perhaps *Gormenghast*, because in many ways the tone of his work is more reminiscent of Mervyn Parker's late, baroque masterpeace. It's a major novel, written by a consummate artist at the top of his form."

\- Jack Ross

Driftdead

Mike Johnson

Press

Published by 99% Press,
an imprint of Lasavia Publishing Ltd.
Auckland, New Zealand
www.lasaviapublishing.com

Copyright © Mike Johnson, 2020
Cover design © Jennifer Rackham, 2020

This book is copyright. Apart from any fair dealing for the purpose of private study, research, criticism or reviews, as permitted under the Copyright Act, no part may be reproduced by any process without the permission of the publishers.

ISBN: 978-0-9951398-3-1

Author's Note

A work of this length, and the years spent in its gestation, mean that it has woven in and around the lives of my family and my colleagues, and to them I owe a debt of gratitude. There were times I thought it would never be finished. My first debt of gratitude however should go to the great filmmaker George A Romero whose zombie movies became so much a part of my imagination. Thanks are due to Leila Lees who listened to me reading it aloud, and made lots of useful comments. Thanks also to Rowan Sylva who read an early version of the novel and made some crucial suggestions, and to Martin Edmond for his kind comment on the novel. Further thanks are due to Jennifer Rackham for her wonderful original cover artwork and design. Last but not least are the proof-readers who had their work cut out for them: Janscie Sharplin, Neil Sonnekus and Odette Wards.

Mike Johnson, August, 2020

Contents

Strangers in Keatown

Book One

Sirocco

The first person to notice the arrival of the driftdead in our forgotten little town was a kid called Sirocco Cornet, who liked to get up at dawn, sit beneath the crab apple tree in the yard and draw shapes in the sandy dirt with his favourite stick while the sun came up.

That's what he was doing when he noticed the wind. Or maybe it noticed him because, as he later described it, wriggling currents of air drew their own shapes in the dirt and tried to burrow up his nose as a baby will do with its fingers when it's trying to find out if your face pulls apart. A hesitant, cheeky, infant wind.

Then he saw the woman, the woman who couldn't be there, crossing their hot, weedy, tussock-ragged property as if gliding over a cool marble floor; in her hand, a large rose as fresh and pristine as the moment it was cut. And a voice. A cool silvery murmuring voice. Like the moon as it fades into an autumn dawn, gathering in its threads. If the moon had a voice it would sound just like this one: distant, faintly metallic, elusive, inaudible. He didn't like the voice because it made him want to follow it. Hard lessons he'd learned in the desert under the guidance of Lizard, learning not to follow the voices of shimmering mirages.

Of course, everybody knows that Sirocco Cornet is a pretty odd-looking runt with his funny little wizened face and strange habits, like getting up early and drawing circles and stars in the dirt with his stick as if creating the universe anew every day. Sirocco Cornet isn't even his real name, but was given to him by the woman who adopted him, Gypsy Cornet.

As the story is told, Gypsy Cornet had a dream in which her mother had left something for her in the desert way to the south. Gypsy was spooked as her dead mother had never come to her in dreams, so she sought the advice of our local wise woman, Akona, who told her to go to the desert and find what her mother had left for her. She loaded a backpack with provisions enough to last for four days and headed off south, leaving her bemused man, Scale, behind.

She didn't find what her mother had hidden there, but she did find Sirocco wandering the desert in the company of a lizard. He couldn't remember his name, where he came from, or how he ended up in the desert with only a lizard to talk to. At first he could hardly talk at all, just bits and pieces of language, as if he'd found these phrases and fragments lying around in the desert like the scattered bones of some undreamed creature.

So nobody gives him much credence, although I always listen carefully to what he says, believing there is more sense in his nonsense than people generally credit. Some people find their appearance prevents them from being taken seriously. Sirocco is one of those.

However, the story about the woman with the rose can't be true because there are no roses in Keatown, except for Grandmother Gaunt's, which are as dried and withered as she is, and there hasn't been a decent dew fall for as long as the old timers can remember. Many little streams that once trickled down from the mountains have dried up. If you believe them, those old timers could remember back several hundred years to when dew fell every morning, covering the town in diamonds and pearls that glittered like a debutante's necklace, and streams threaded the land like the veins on the backs of their hands. But the crowning impossibility is the woman herself. There are no such women in Keatown, at least not any longer, certainly not grand ballroom ladies with big piles of gold hair who might grow roses in their spare time. And just happen to have a freshly picked one handy.

It is generally agreed that the runty Sirocco with the raisin face spent too long in the desert and was still subject to hallucinations. He fried his brains out there. Pretty soon he'd forget he ever saw her and everything would go back to normal. Yet he persists in his story.

The way he tells it, he was sitting under the crab apple tree, as usual, minding his own business when, it seemed, a warm finger stroked his cheek the way a tender parent might stroke a sleeping child. At that touch he felt a great sadness envelop him, as if the tender parent wanted to cry at the impossibility of such a love. With that sadness there came a yearning, but it was a yearning without object, for something unseen and unrealised.

As he sat there with his sadness cupped in his hands, a ground-hugging trickle of air from the east, the seaward side, wriggled and squirmed over his symbols, demolishing their outlines, turning circles into waves and stars into particles and particles into nothingness. Just dirty sand. Leaving nothing but the smell of seaweed and something rotting, putrid and rotting.

Above the crab apple tree, the sky wheeled in a well-worn vacant circle. The ocean, just down the road, was a collection of familiar sighs, exhaling the predictable smell of salt and composting fish. As always, Keatown sat quietly between the mountains and the sea doing pretty much what Sirocco was doing – minding its own business. Everything was very normal. Soon Orlap the Viking and his fishermen would be arriving at the wharf and the chuff of the trawlers would be heard as they set out for the day's work.

He drew again, with determination. A deep circle. A ridged star. The wormy air returned, from the west this time, from the mountains, as if having forgotten something, and casually obliterated his pattern. This wind smelled of ice and rock and something bitter, like loneliness.

He spat it out and tried a third time, third time lucky, but the wormy air returned again, sticking close to the ground, this time from the south, from the desert, and it smelled clean and arid, like a night sky full of stars, and it smudged out his sand drawing with apparently deliberate intent. It made him think of his lizard days in the south. Here was a snake wind, capricious, elusive, with the touch of the malicious in it.

Why stop at three? What was so magical about three? Just because in fairy tales everything seems to happen three times was no good reason to give up. So he tried again for a fourth time, just to show who was boss. Here's a circle, here's a star, and here come the wind worms wriggling along the sandy ground like invisible snakes. This little wind from the north got up his nose and nearly choked him with some chemical particulate matter, thick as smog and heavy with the smell of coal smoke.

He coughed and spat and coughed again and gave up. There'd be no circles or stars this morning; day would have to break over the crab apple tree without them.

That's the way he tells it.

He was about to get up and seek breakfast when he saw something that couldn't be there, couldn't exist, at least not in the world he knew: a stranger, walking sedately across their tatty yard, a woman with a fancy hair-do piled up on top like a meringue, regal in a long, darkly flowing skirt and gauzy white blouse, glancing neither right nor left. She carried a pink rose held out before her like a beacon, like a tiny rosy-tinged dawn. It looked fresh and alive, still dressed in ruby dew. And she was singing. At least, and on this Sirocco grows a little vague, there was a voice in the air about her, an airy voice, but distant, just beyond the shape of melody or words. A voice that belonged to night and the moon.

Caught in the first fragile light of day, she faded to pale and disappeared around the side of their paint-peeling, weatherboard house.

Sirocco Cornet's Rose Woman.

A creature of air; a wind shape.

A woman made of light and dust.

A star being.

He'd never seen anything like that before.

That's the way he tells it. With flourishes. Hand gestures to shape the creature of air, a wide-eyed expression for the star being.

Naturally he follows her. There is something about her he can almost place: the way she walks, the way she holds her head, the way she disdains to look right or left. He's seen these things before somewhere, in another time, before the desert, before Lizard, before Gypsy Cornet found him. A time of random things being thrown into suitcases, slamming doors and shouting voices, violent motion inside the guts of stinky, throaty machines, the sound of gunfire like pepper in the wind, the taste of iron on the tongue. A woman walks across a ballroom in a shower of rose petals and shrapnel. Pauses to take a bow. There is music playing. There are couples holding each other in their arms, dancing cheek to cheek.

Sirocco doesn't know where these memories came from, but it isn't a memory he follows across the Cornets' raggedy backyard. It's a real person, just strange looking, that's all. Someone who doesn't belong.

As he follows the woman around the side of the house, Scale appears at the back door, dressed as usual in a black singlet and baggy trousers. The same black singlet and baggy trousers. He yawns, scratches his crotch and gives Sirocco a bleary eyed look. Sirocco is not sure what holds this unprepossessing, hairy little man together with the raven-haired, somewhat exotic Gypsy, but they seem to work okay, most of the time. All that happens when Gypsy gets tired of him is that she turns her Arabian Rasta music up to full bore and so drives him, and anybody else around, out of the house and far away. When that happens Scale will go off drinking with Blade, a buddy of his, and they'll talk endlessly about their jobs at the fish shed, and how much the mayor might be making out of their labour, or how much diesel Captain Orlap is siphoning off the boats to sell at inflated prices to farmers who, for one reason or another, want to avoid going to Flay's

Garage.

'Did you see her?' Sirocco yells. He's reluctant to stop, to lose sight of the woman even for a moment, but it would also help to have a witness, because he knows that nobody will believe him. They'll just say he's spent too long in the sun.

'See who?' His voice is thick and phlegmy.

'The woman. With the rose.'

'You been pokin' too many holes inna ground with your stick. Funny stuff comes out.' He always speaks like that, as if his utterances were leftover bones he could never quite fit together into a skeleton that made any recognisable creature.

'Come with me. I'll show you. Quick!'

But Scale doesn't do quick, not at Sirocco's command anyway. He's never entirely trusted, or even liked, the little desert rat Gypsy dragged in from one of her southward rambles. Picking up bits and pieces is one thing, all the rumours about the random stuff in the Cornet house are true, but taking in waifs and strays quite another. At the same time, there is something else behind Scale's hostility Sirocco has never figured out.

'If you don't come now, you'll miss out.'

Scale looks up at the morning sky, silver as a fish's belly.

He can't see that he'd be missing out on much.

Sirocco is in time to catch the woman at the wire fence bordering the side road they call Beauty Parade, which runs east, up to the mansions.

What happens next is curious; she doesn't clamber through the wires, but rather bumps against them, losing all fluidity of movement, suddenly aimless, confused, following the wire up and down as if blind.

After a few trips up and down the wire, no more than a dozen paces each way, she stops and kneels and wriggles through the wires like a child. There isn't much left of her dignity, but her rose is still intact as she gets to her feet, quite smoothly, and sets off for the other side of the road with the same serene grace as before.

When he gets to the fence, the woman has disappeared into the beechy scrub on the south side of the road, but he finds tiny filaments of sand scuttling down the wire like ants, and a faint sound, like something left over in the sky after thunder. At the edge of hearing, a woman's voice. Putting an ear to one of the worn wooden uprights of the fence, he hears, through the telegraph of wood and wire, the same echoey sound, still far off, wire-sliding all the way down from the mountains.

The whisper of sand along wire.

The rumour of a wind that walks.

a moment at the gate

Sirocco Cornet is not the only soul in Keatown who enjoys getting up early and pottering about. It might have been a coincidence that on this very morning our herbalist and wise woman, Akona Kāmaka, while welcoming the dawn, decides to visit the spring known to her as Wai-O-Tapu, or sacred waters, but which most of the more ignorant inhabitants simply call The Spring, just as they call the river that flows from Wai-O-Tapu Rocky Creek, whereas it is known to her as the Wai-O-Tapu river.

She regularly visits Wai-O-Tapu, not only for the pleasure of dipping her feet into the deliciously cold water surging up from below, but also to assert, if only to herself, her right to place her feet on that land, in that water, to visit her people's taonga, and call the spring by its true name. This taonga was a part of her tribe long before the Johnsons and the Kensingtons arrived with their guns and their white skins and their sibilant language. She can hardly think of the deep pure waters of Wai-O-Tapu, and its role in her whakapapa, without thinking of Bob Kensington and how he betrayed her and the Kāmaka family with his dirty deals.

And worse.

Bitterness doesn't sit well with her dawn-welcoming ritual, which should clear the mind for the day's challenges, not muddy it with the dark past. It should have no place at all, but it is always only a thought away. Dispossession, a word that hisses like a snake. Betrayal, a word that brays like a donkey. Regret, a word that hides its face. All of these things, only a word away. Words in a language not her own, and which sometimes stick in her throat like dead birds.

Having saluted the four directions, and greeted the spirits of the air and the earth, she sings in her high, now croaky voice, a song she made up from some old melodies her mother used to sing. Pop songs. The song doesn't mean much. It is just a series of sounds that make her feel good about the dawn and the early world, and banish some of those dead-bird words. Once she joked with her nearest neighbour, Cherrie Lamont, that she sang to her garden to make the plants grow, but she should have known better than to say things like that to the fluffy-headed Cherrie Lamont, who already believed that Akona had magical powers, at least when it came to her garden.

Cherrie Lamont – who really hadn't been such a good schoolteacher after all, being far too fanciful for impressionable young minds, at least in the opinion of their parents – claims to have heard Akona chanting magic spells. She will make such claims, and others, in a special shocked whisper, as if the idea that Akona is a witch was new to everybody, or that one might be shocked by the notion of an old woman talking and singing to her plants.

All this is a source of amusement to Akona, who, in one of her many visits to the library, confessed to the librarian with a giggle that her famous herb garden owed its virtue to her composting toilet. She read once that in ancient China the very poorest folk would sell their pee as a fertilizer, and was very impressed. As for her chanting, what the feather-brained Cherrie Lamont has heard is Akona trying to sing some of the pop songs current when she was young. Her mother would turn up the music and dance. 'Never forget to dance and sing, taitamaiti,' she would say. She always called Akona taitamaiti, but the child grew into the venerable Akona, who, while she has never forgotten how to dance, could never learn to sing, and whose unself-conscious warblings could be mistaken for chanting, even calling up the spirits. As for talking to plants, plants are her friends. They like being friends with humans and grow better when they get to know the gardener – there is nothing hocus-pocus about that, it's just plain common sense. No reason a garden can't be a friendly, chatty place.

For the librarian, the matter doesn't end there. The old woman, the librarian perceives, is very good at hiding behind her little giggle and her bright-eyed common sense, her innocent chattering to plants. It was her researches into Akona, and the Kāmaka family, that led the librarian to begin her Chronicles of Keatown, a general history and account of the town, including present events, all written in the present tense in order, as the librarian put it, to put the past and present on a level playing field. I was unconvinced of the logic of this, and remain so, but have let it pass. After all, as she has pointed out, she is the one who has to do the hard yards. It's all very well for me to come in like some visiting dignitary, but I should keep my nose out of 'operational matters'.

Instead of going to the garden when she finishes her song, Akona returns home to make ready for her journey up the Makurutanga. As usual, the marae is quiet at this time of day. Her secretive companion, the Man in Black, will be around somewhere, but he tends to stay away from her in the early hours, to give her room. She appreciates his thoughtfulness, although there are times when she would prefer to have company, even the tall, silent man.

Akona is not sure what she thinks of the librarian's studies into her family background. She isn't sure she entirely trusts the inquisitive woman who seems to love only her books and her precious Chronicles of Keatown. Once she suggested that the librarian should look to her own whakapapa and leave Akona's alone. Such studies are just an excuse for people to go poking around in other people's business. In reply, the librarian made quite a little speech about history and the importance of it, and how valuable contemporary records can be for future generations, and even went on to suggest that Akona was secretly pleased that someone was taking an interest in her history.

That suggestion made Akona grin, and she grins now remembering the moment because, for a second or so, the usually discreet librarian thought she might have put her foot over the line. Akona's reply was suitably tart, suggesting that perhaps the nosy librarian should look carefully at Bob Kensington, and the sneaky deal he did with Brian Fairweather, the so-called baron, over the Wai-O-Tapu spring. And the librarian should also, in her precious Chronicles, stress the fact that the blood of Ellen Johnson flows in Akona, just as it does in the snooty Bob Kensington.

She doesn't have to elaborate. The librarian knows that history as well as she does. In the most famous scandal ever to hit Keatown, Charlotte Kensington, the whitest of the white, granddaughter to the pakeha dowager Ellen Johnson, became pregnant to a local Maori man, albeit of high standing in his community, a chief by the name of Nōpera Kāmaka. There was no joyful union of the two families, but the blood of both ran in their children and grandchildren. Even now Bob Kensington, who fancies himself as a large landholder, refuses to admit the family kinship with Akona and always looks the other way when he sees her. She always says kia ora just to spite him.

More than this, Akona is made uneasy by the idea that sooner or later the librarian will stumble across Akona's own tragedy, that which her mind can only touch briefly and lightly; you can't hold your hand too long in a fire. There is a huge hole in her heart, barely bandaged by her compassion.

Having placed in her kete some dried beef strips, wild seed bread and a salad consisting mostly of nettle, parsley and cleavers, she sets off across the marae heading for the back gate and the path to Makurutanga. She doesn't linger too long at her garden, although she is pleased with how things are coming along, and how other women in the community are coming to help. Even Melissa Tonguestone, who took the Kensington side of the argument, and was no great friend to the Maori, has been turning up with her gardening gloves and her garden fork. It's taken Akona and the Man in Black a long time to build up the soil on this rocky promontory. In the early days they dragged many tons of kelp up here. The potatoes and the kumara are doing particularly well. Nobody, even a Kensington, will turn down food if they are hungry, no matter the caste or colour of the hand that feeds them. Hunger is the great leveller.

When she reaches the back gate, the highest point on the marae, she instinctively turns for a look back over the garden and the low cluster of buildings, and beyond to Keatown, just waking up to the light. The marae is on a promontory, the highest point in the village, which gives her a view second only to the mega-views to be had from up mansions. All quiet and familiar. A little wind ruffles her face, as if having just discovered her. It has a smell she doesn't know and finds hard to characterise. A faint greasiness in the air. Something cloying.

In their stall, her two goats, Nanny and Lusifā, bleat thinly.

They feel it too, she thinks. A disturbance in the etheric. A restlessness among the ancestors. She shrugs as she closes the gate behind her.

Whatever it is, it will soon show its face.

Keatown: the sun in the eighth month

Bemused, Sirocco climbs through the fence and wanders out onto Beauty Parade, listening to the grumble of his stomach. He already believes he was dreaming when, still half asleep there under the crab apple tree, he saw the Rose Woman. That was much more likely than seeing such an apparition. Sometimes he gets up before he wakes up, and sometimes he gets a little confused between past and present;

the present tending to catch up with him in small bursts as it did in the desert, where time became compounded, the past and present hammered into a single piece of polished bronze. More likely that his Rose Woman walked into his world from the mirage world of the desert.

Sirocco looks west to see if the mountains have anything to say. They don't say much, but they are noble creatures that change their colour to reflect facets of the sky; surely the heaviest things ever fashioned, yet they harbour the secret of floating, which they share only with the snow.

Sirocco looks east down Beauty Parade to the beach. He likes the mountains for their superiority in all things wind-blown, but the nearest peak, which Akona calls Irirangi, which means spirit voice, is a good two days' walk over the foothills, however close it might look. The ocean is disturbingly and intimately near, slapping and sucking at the eastern beaches like a lover too long denied.

Sirocco doesn't look at the sky for too long. It reminds him of the desert where there was nothing much but sky. A hard-blue sky often filled with noises, crackling and fizzing like lightning and thunder. Sounds that might have been coming from his own head, like Little Sanyo's tinnitus.

He doesn't like the idea that the Rose Woman is a dream or hallucination. He did plenty of hallucinating in the desert, when he had no choice. Without the guidance of Lizard he would never have found his way through the landscape of tussock, sand and bare rock where there were once farms. Polluted streams still soured by nitrates. Everything drying up in front of his eyes.

In something of a daze he walks down Beauty Parade to the roundabout and looks up and down Highway 6. South, towards Flay's Gas and Annanda's Sunshine Supermarket, and beyond them, south, into that very same desert as far as the mind can travel. North, where the road skirts inland to avoid the rocky beginnings of the pine-clad peninsula called Pine Point, the wandering coastline beyond, and the unseen cities he'd heard lie further north beyond the inlet. North. Where the trucks come from, when the trucks come.

This is it. Keatown. A piece of Main Road squeezed between a harbour and the foothills. Mostly a scattering of houses along Highway 6 and up Beauty Parade. Some are made of brick and glass, and at one time must have been pretty flash, like pretend-mansions, with Sky TV dishes on their roofs. Others of timber with hardwood pallets for foundations and maybe plastic sheeting for windows. The Cornets live in one of those.

At the very centre of the roundabout, where he pauses, some local government wag installed a steel signpost that had pointers to London, New York, Tokyo, Shanghai, Rangoon, Ragnarok; grandiose, fabulous places known only by their names. The pole was still there, the metal place-names twisted and bent. London was down through the earth and Tokyo was up in the sky. It was from this pulpit that Mayor Bronzy would preach to us his optimistic philosophy that one day soon the Long Emergency would be over, travel to wondrous places would be restored, and, like a dizzy roulette wheel, the roundabout would spin once more to the flow of eager commerce.

The mineral opera of sky, sea, mountains and rock brings Sirocco to his senses. There is no Rose Woman. No snake-wind with a grudge against his primitive art. Everything is quiet. And still. And normal.

But it isn't. In Keatown, a coastal settlement butting up against the wide Pacific, there is always some kind of wind, onshore, offshore, chill from the mountains, warm and salty from the sea; always some sounds: the rattle in the corn in Akona's garden, a chromatic whisper in the pines on Pine Point, the grunt of a fishing boat rubbing against the wharf. The pan-pipe grief of seagulls. It wasn't normal to be this still and quiet, and for the ocean, which he could see clearly from the roundabout, to be so flat and apparently lifeless.

Shortly, he is joined by his buddy called Sad Toof, after a recalcitrant molar of the same name. Sad Toof read a lot of AA Milne when he was young and over-identified with the lugubrious donkey, Eeyore. The town has librarian, who first put the Pooh Bear stories in his hands, perhaps bears some responsibility for the boy's adopted persona. Sad Toof is the sad sack of the mokopuna, with a gloomy outlook on life, the universe and everything.

This celebrated molar is the everlasting fire of his great throbbing. His martyrdom. And he is very attached to it. Once everybody offered to remove it, but he defended it with a bitter tenacity. Akona, the nearest we have to a doctor remaining in Keatown, suggested wrapping it with catgut, tying the other end of the gut to the door handle, and, by slamming the door, ripit out of his mouth. That'd fix it big time. But he wimped out and protected it as if it were more precious than his own life, so we gave up. It is his pain, after all. He has a right to protect it. It's his identity. He believes that one day the Tooth Fairy will come and take it right out of his mouth while he sleeps. He'll wake up one bright and miraculous morning and there will be no pain. This one little crack of idealism in his normal gloomy cynicism is his undoing as far as getting rid of his pain is concerned.

Sirocco realizes that there is only so much you can know about people's lives. You know about their teeth, how they smell or how they whistle; you hear how they find their way through words. With enough patience you can worm your way into their dreams, but Sirocco isn't that interested. In the beginning there were stories, stuff people made up, a pastiche of impressions that became a town called Keatown. To make it official, the mayor put up his own sign at the roundabout: Keatown Welcomes Investment. The mayor had put his own money where his mouth was and bought the fish shed and put people to work. That's how he became mayor. No one knows where he got his money from and no one asks.

Sirocco begins, 'I saw…' and stops, not knowing how to say it. Sad Toof waits patiently, pulling at his jaw in the locality of his pain. '… a fancy woman carrying a rose.' The word fancy made it fanciful, laughable, so he gave a little laugh as he said it.

'I seen her too,' Sad Toof says, minus the embarrassed laughter.

'You don't say.'

'I seen her.'

Sirocco has to believe him. Sad Toof, never one to mistake an empty glass for one half full, is generally too sad to lie, too stubborn for fantasy. He gestures south, as if his mouth is too weary for words. 'She wiz traipsing through peoples' backyards.'

'Did others see her?'

'I dunno.'

'Y' dunno much.'

'You c'n say that again.'

'Why should I?'

Satisfied with this ritual exchange, they prepare to start the conversation from the beginning, because Sirocco can't quite believe it, and Sad Toof can sometimes be as slow as he looks – but they are distracted by the antics of Lucifer, the goat. He is approaching them with odd sideways movements, Nanny following up a respectful distance behind. Goats can be graceful creatures, in a ruttish kind of way, purposeful in their movements – Lucifer, certainly, always knows where he is going and most people learn how to get out of his way – but not this time. He trots aggressively forward for a bit, stops… looks around confused, ears flattened, head raised, before pacing forward again like an antsy horse. He pauses to look at Sirocco and Sad Toof, yellow eyes with their vertical black slits. A magnificent animal, with his sturdy legs and straight back, his coat pure white but for a circle of black between his eyes.

You don't play with Lucifer. He is too sceptical of mankind to be a good playmate, with a twin set of horns that curl around in the classic manner, their business ends pointing forward. Sirocco and Sad Toof regard him warily, aware that he seems to reserve a special contempt for the mokopuna.

They might have stayed that way forever, eyeballing each other, when, just to the north, the pine trees on Pine Point let out an enormous exhalation, as if the peninsula finally breathed out after holding its breath for centuries. Branches creak and snap as they strain upwards. Pine needles reverse themselves and stand upright. Lucifer gives one of those thin, colourless bleats goats have, shows them his rump, and makes off as if all the trolls in creation are at his heels. Nanny bleats once at the boys, apparently scolding them, and runs after Lucifer.

Sirocco and Sad Toof look at each other.

'What's that all about?' Sad Toof says, pulling on his jaw, tugging at the old tooth, giving it no rest.

'I dunno.' Sirocco says,

'You dunno much.'

'That's for sure,' Sirocco says.

'It doesn't look good to me.'

'Nothing ever does.'

They speak mechanically, just going through the motions of their banter; even Sad Toof's despair lacks its usual conviction.

Who's going to believe that a huge lump of rock with some trees clinging to it let out a great big breath?

Flay with shotgun and spanner: a still life

Meet our resident petrol-head, with shotgun and spanner, the second inhabitant of Keatown to encounter the driftdead. Flay. Flay the hard-arse. Owner of Flay's Gas, and a man of power. He has the goodies. The good oil. Liquid power. Seven years of muscle power in every barrel is the figure he loves to quote to people who might otherwise object to paying the prices he gouges for the resource he is sitting on. He and his shotgun. And his boys, Pinky & Co, the petrol mafia. And Pinky & Co get to sniff all the petrol they want at Flay's expense.

Flay's Gas isn't exactly the thriving centre of the town it once was, but Flay is always at his post, standing astride his hoard, watching the road or tinkering with some vehicle way beyond its use-by date.

He isn't just a man of power, lording it over everybody with his underground tanks of gas, but a man of rare skill, a community asset; he can repair just about anything, even the ethanol and homebrew straw-alcohol engines he despises. There are lots of things he despises. Everybody he has power over, for a start, which is just about everybody who uses an engine of some kind, which is just about everybody in town.

He's the only one who can deal with the cranky diesel motors of Orlap's little fishing fleet, and supply the filthy stuff that powers them. Or repair the dozen or more generators that put precious electricity nto people's homes. Without him the town would be heading downhill a lot faster than it is.

Rumours that the cadaverous Flay, the last of the true petrol-heads, has endless gasoline if you can pay for it, aren't entirely true. How long is a piece of string? A lot longer than what is left in his tanks right now. As the resource gets scarce, the price goes up. If the payer can pay. What he is going to say to Orlap the Viking, leader of the fishermen, when he next turns up for diesel, is what's bothering Flay on this bright, harmless-looking spring morning. Three, maybe four more fishing trips before the diesel runs dry, even cut four ways to hell with home-brewed ethanol.

Flay can never tell them that he's running dry. It is all going to be smoke and mirrors and money until the last drop is sucked up.

Orlap would take over Flay's petrol tanks in the flick of a Nordic eyelid if the fishers got a whiff of the truth; Captain Orlap is starting to take this Viking bullshit seriously, letting his hair grow everywhere, getting delusions of grandeur, thinking the whole world revolves around him and his silly little fleet, thinking of Flay's stock as his own private store to be tapped on demand. The last time Orlap turned up, he'd brought his first officer, Butch, who thinks she's tough and cultivates a sense of menace around her. Flay isn't a man to be intimidated by the likes of Butch, he's seen plenty worse than her, but her manner was suggestive, and while she may not be as tough as she thinks, she is smarter than Orlap, which is a worry in itself.

The only advantage Flay has is psychological, with a bit of shotgun thrown in. He let it be known that he'd booby trapped his underground tank, and those who tried a little looting would end up fishing in the ocean for their vital parts.

Nobody can accuse Flay of being a deep thinker, but that doesn't stop him from making a careful, if prejudiced, analysis of Keatown's economy. In a word, fucked. A cheap little town like this never was much more than a petrol fart at the end of a long road, always hungry for tourist dollars, always looking to the rich cunts in the mansions to drop a few coins, and those who worked for the rich cunts to drop a few more coins. Keep that Indian fairy across the road in his supermarket smiling, keep Flay smiling, keep the mayor smiling, keep everybody smiling their faces off. Enough smiling to make you sick.

And vehicles! Vehicles of every shape and size from desert-exploring Humvees to fat sedans to camper-fucking-wagons, Flay didn't give a toss as long as they guzzled gas. And there was always that lovely rich spicy smell of exhaust fumes in the air.

Then it had all turned pear-shaped. The rich cunts, having built their zillion-dollar mansions and enjoyed their zillion-dollar views for a few seasons, hopped into their helicopters and fucked off, most of them anyway. When they decamped all the hangers-on and bottom feeders disappeared along with them. The tourists melted away, just like a fucking dream at dawn, like the sound of a six-cylinder twin cam roadster fading into the distance, like a fucking ice cream on a hot day.

It was as if some fool pulled the plug and all the money drained away. Down the gurgler. No point asking where all the money went; it never existed in the first place. It was just debt built on the promise of future payoffs. Flay knew people in London who tried to pull fast ones like that, fancied themselves slick talkers they did, dressed in suits. Flay knew how to deal with them.

So did the banks. At the height of the boom Keatown boasted three banks. Managers with suits and smiles and offices with skinny computers. Fancy city tarts as cashiers. ATM machines and Wi-Fi. Hauling the money in. When the guts fell out they pulled away overnight leaving gaping empty shop fronts and a hollow feeling. Now Keatown gets a once-a-week visit from an armoured car, generously described as a mobile bank, which comes down from the north to do business for a day, bringing money in and taking money out, restocking a mini cash machine at the Sunshine Supermarket and picking up any deposits left in the supermarket strongbox.

It worries Flay that the mobile bank has missed a couple of weeks. Not because he has a lot of business to do – he keeps cash in his own strongbox thank you very much – but what it might mean. He's visited the supermarket a couple of times to check his account on the fairy's two public computers just to make sure his money is still there. A dead hole like Keatown could easily fall off the map altogether. At the rag ends of the earth, with only the hard core left, like Flay himself, the bare rock, those with nowhere else to go or who just hung on for no better reason. Sometimes, he's heard, when civil authorities evacuate a town or city in the face of a disaster, there are always a few who refuse to go, who take their chances, who would rather die than run. Fair enough. Flay is past running himself.

In the boom days Orlap's little fishing fleet was only for show. A bit of window dressing for the whale watchers and other idiots with more money than sense. A bit of local colour. Orlap, without his shirt, posing on the bow of his quaint little fishing boat while pale-faced Asians snapped pictures. Butch in a black tank top bending over the bulwark. It would make you sick if you weren't smiling so hard.

But after the bust, that same little fleet suddenly becomes a core part of Keatown's economy, such as it is, helping to feed the town and generate a bit of cash flow from the remaining celebs, and traders from the north, little better than car-boot hustlers most of them, with no-questions-asked goodies to swap for smoke-cured fish. Orlap turns into the golden-haired boy, and his plucky little fleet is much admired by fish eaters and other pansies. It is enough to make you puke.

People go for the fish all right, but not Flay; he prefers fresh venison, or even dried venison jerky, or even goat meat, to smoked fucking fish. The new currency, the mayor had declared it to be, which might well be since he owned the fish shed and the attached smokery. Gasoline might've become the new currency too, kinda did in a way since Flay has done all right out of it in cash and tradeable items, but the fact is that, despite his mechanical genius, there is a declining number of motors in Keatown, a declining demand, slow but sure. After all, engines fuck up eventually. A cracked head is only good for the scrapheap. Batteries go flat and won't charge.

The long-term outlook for Flay's gas is shit. The short-term outlook is shit.

He stares at the landline he's got hanging on the wall the old-fashioned way. He's got a fancy cell phone but it doesn't do jack shit. The cellphone tower to the south of the town blew over in a storm and now the network's down. The landline is more reliable, but what's the point in ringing when all he's going to get is, 'Thanks for ringing Horizon Oil. Your call is important to us. Please leave your contact number and we'll be back in touch as soon as possible.' That was a joke. Back in touch!

His fingers curl around the barrel of his shotgun. Fuck them. He could shut up shop and sit on what was left until hell froze over or he ran out of shotgun shells.

He wanders outside where his petrol pumps sit in silent vigil. Diesel might be short but he's still got half a reserve tank of regular 91 petrol. Most of it would trickle out to those with generators and a couple of farms to the south that kept tractors running. Oh, and let's not forget the mayor's private BMW, which hasn't been further than Southbridge in the last ten years. The mayor is very proud of his BMW and will polish it up to make it shine. He is a great believer in keeping a well-polished car, Flay will give him that. So Flay hates to remind the fat man that BMWs get rust just like a cheap Toyota. Even a fancy car without gas is just another piece of scrap metal. All you have to do is look past the shine. Cars are a bit like women in that respect, which may be why Flay has never had a woman around for too long. He's got plenty of cars, why should he bother?

He glances north, as he does countless times every day, the direction any tankers will come from. Sooner or later they will get here, and the golden piss will flow. He's up to date with payments, all made online in the usual way. Bankcards seem to work; eftpos seems to work. There is a big world going on its merry way out there, money being made and lost, it just seems to have forgotten Keatown, a bit like one of those pokey little towns that dies when a main road is replaced by a motorway a couple of kilometres off. Tinpot little garages just like his going broke with the roar of passing traffic not far off.

The big rigs would come, the brightly painted rigs, stinking of beautiful petrol, because where there's muck there's brass. They'd come because the drivers knew he'd have something special for them, little titbits and teasers he'd saved – a piece of South Island greenstone a hundred percent pure; perfectly preserved starling's eggs in their original nests, one of nature's great works of art; a miniature dinosaur in kauri gum; frozen or smoked salmon fillets or blue cod, ready to eat, courtesy of Orlap and the fisherfucks; a complete set of Arnold Schwarzenegger's action movies; an eclectic range of Blu-ray porno; some plonk locally distilled by the famous Och Arglin, guaranteed to be lethal. Even some old books the librarian sometimes chucks out – books have become something of a currency too.

He's a bit of pack rat, is Flay.

We catch him looking up and down the road as if he's just missed something. And he has, but he'll have a second chance. There's nobody but that little runt Sirocco and the tall goofy guy they call Sad Toof, lurking around Annanda's Sunshine Supermarket opposite.

Flay hates being beholden to anybody, so dependent on one source of supply of one product. Like a fucking junkie with only one pusher in town. Flay prides himself on being a tough, independent bastard, a bastard people don't mess with. He wears a purple singlet that says, in faded yellow letters, Petrolhead Apocalypse, totes a doubled-barrelled shotgun slung casually over his left shoulder plus a heavy spanner swinging idly from his right hand. Enough to give any fucker pause for thought. Any sensible fucker would vanish before you could say 'turn the screw'. The only one turning any screws would be Mr Screwdriver himself.

He is so tough he can test a battery by grasping both wires in either hand, quickly like a gunslinger. The jolt he gets tells him lots about the health of the battery. Every time he does it, and Pinky the Pimple happens to be there, Pinky cracks up laughing. And when he laughs, his sidekick Tony laughs too. The two of their m giggle like a couple of girls. Deadpan, Flay wants to know what's so fucking funny. Punks like Pinky and Tony are a dime a dozen, or used to be; he's dealt with them all his life. They'll crash whatever car they get to drive, screw whatever woman they get on their gear lever, and snort whatever powders they can find. He doesn't need a belt of electricity to tell him this.

Flay prides himself for being tough and knowing the score. But now he sees the weakness of his position, and it's giving him some ugly thoughts. He's only a tough guy as long as cheap gas is flowing like mother's milk and the rubber is hitting the road; when the gas stops flowing, he's little better than a fucking pansy. Even that Indian fairy across the road in his ridiculous Sunshine Supermarket has been able to diversify, turning his supermarket into a fucking flea market, filling his freezers with venison brought down from the foothills by hunters, turning himself into a big wheeler-dealer.

What's Flay to do, start selling flowers?

For all his tough exterior, Flay has a heart of pure petrol fumes. He remembers stuff. London. Now there was a town! Cars and chicks for the boosting. Chicks in cars. Flay is of the old school when it comes to screwing chicks; if you couldn't screw them in the back seat of an alfie, with the stereo up and the smell of fancy vinyl in your snozzle, they weren't worth screwing. That approach worked wonders in London, with the posh tarts, but cuts no ice in Keatown where there are no posh tarts, except rumours of them up mansions, and the smell of fancy vinyl is no more than a wet dream.

Parked at the pumps, as if about to fill up, is Flay's own precious alfie, an Alfa Romeo, one of the fanciest cars ever built for the gas-guzzling elite, especially those with a taste for a bit of style with their speed. For the sporty kind, was the alfie. Great for driving around London. Nice liddle chick magnet. Those days are long gone, 'cos Flay is smart, see, and knew when to get out, with the alfie, still on the road, a fact Flay likes to demonstrate from time to time by driving the warhorse up and down the main highway and around the roundabout a few times, tooting the horn in triumph and burning up some fucking gas!

The age of the automobile is not dead yet, by god. Not as long as there is an alfie on the road and a Flay behind the wheel, even if it is the last alfie still snorting gas this side of nowhere.

There's a saying that every drink you have accumulates in your nose; looking at Flay you know that's true. Amazing what the body can withstand. The nose tells its own story. Flay's snozzle, with its massive crumbling edges, like that of a mashed-up Brixton boxer, is a legend. Flay himself is a legend. Once, Keatown rumour has it, a 1956 Rolls-Royce Silver Ghost passed through town, whispering like an angel. It stopped at Flay's Gas and some mysterious transaction took place between our cadaver, with his overalls falling off his bony shoulders, and a sleek sea-lion dressed in a Savile Row suit smoking black Russian cigarettes.

Flay is a man of connections. But his connections won't be worth jack shit if the tankers don't come.

He gets his second chance when he sees a dude walking in from the north carrying what has to be a petrol can. He looks a bit like a tired, pissed-off tourist whose holiday isn't working out so good. Maybe an even more pissed-off tourist wifey waiting in a car up the road. Great to see some action on the road, even this sad sack.

Maybe Flay can offer him some help with that empty petrol can.

The sad sack, however, walks right on by.

Doesn't take a slightest interest in Flay or his gas station.

'Hey!' Flay calls, but his voice is pulled apart by a little bitching wind.

Like a deaf man, the sad sack keeps walking. Silently, doggedly.

'It's a long way to next station, buddy.'

A sand snake whispers around the base of his petrol pumps. He pulls the nozzle from its holder and hears the pump clatter into life. A reassuring sound.

It's a long way to the next fucking station.

you can't hustle the wind

Across the road from Flay's Gas, Annanda Patel, owner, manager, checkout counter attendant and delivery-boy at Annanda's Sunshine Supermarket, is also a man of power but as dependent on the next supply truck as Flay. Well... not quite true. Annanda is able to do quite of lot of local trade on the side, just as Flay has noted. People need food; growers need outlets. Annanda has freezers and solar power. Annanda is the man. He can provide the place, the space, the face. He understands that while ordinary dollars still hold some sway, sometimes other currencies are just as good, or some item of barter, whatever people put their faith into at the time of the transaction, and further grasps how he might make a little something for his efforts. Compared to Flay he's quite a visionary, although he wouldn't see it that way. Having an eye for the main chance is in his genes, coming, as he does, from a long line of street hustlers. Lucknow, India, is to Annanda what London is to Flay. He got out of India to escape the street hustle, but, as the Buddha would have it, ancestral habits die hard. Or hardly die, as his old dear friend Suneal would say.

The empty mini cash-machine in the corner is a handy reminder of what can happen, and what local resilience might mean in the long run.

Annanda has set up everything to look like a real supermarket, with mini aisles and checkout counters and sexy signs advertising things he doesn't have, like camera film and cigarette lighters and deodorants and just about everything else – except for some Chinese bootleg DVDs and cell phones prominently displayed. His own office overlooks it all from the glass-walled mezzanine of which he is very proud, where he does business with all the gravity of a man with an empire to run. Suneal would be impressed.

He is very proud of the large sign, supported by a firm steel frame, the logo of the mega-corp that distantly owns the image and makes sure the trucks keep coming: a Disneylike sketch of a friendly corner-store grocer holding out a bag of groceries with beams of yellow sunshine radiating from his shoulders. To his mind far more stylish than Flay's dreary Flay's Gas sign.

The stylish logo reminds Annanda of the high hopes he had when he came to Keatown from the sweating streets of Lucknow. He told Suneal, dear Suneal, that he would make a large fortune and return to India. Suneal just listened to him and smiled sadly. Annanda often thinks of that smile. Perhaps Suneal knew better than he did what would happen. When business was booming he was too busy making money to return to India, and when business declined, well, he couldn't leave, could he? Suneal understood, but his emails dried up and finally ceased.

Still, business is not good. Worse. How can you hustle when nobody comes by? You can't hustle the wind. Annanda knows in his Lucknow street bones that Keatown has well passed its use-by date. He and Flay are of one accord there. These humble premises, his supermarket, had once, during the construction of the mansions, been overflowing with customers, centre of the local economy, serviced by vast truck-and-trailer units chugging dirty bootleg diesel and guarded by paramilitary in black thermals bearing evil-looking weapons.

In the heyday of the mansions, the rich and famous would sashay half-dressed down Beauty Parade on their way to the beach. The roads were alive with whale watchers and backpackers and rock climbers. The trade he did in sunscreen alone! And ice cream. The trucks couldn't keep up with the ice cream so Annanda had to sell some locally made stuff on the side.

Back in the day!

We find Annanda sitting at one of his empty checkout counters in his worn grey suit and red tie gazing blankly at the dimly lit, mostly empty shelves. All those high hopes – where are they now? Beside him, on the blank face of the cigarette cabinet, he has pasted a picture of the monkey deity Hanuman blithely holding up a mountain with one hand as he trots across a river and its plain. He is wearing a red wraparound open at the chest and has a curvy bow slung over his shoulder. Hanuman was the first and greatest superhero of all time. You can forget about your Superman and Batman. Hanuman performed prodigious feats of strength and courage in the god Rama's war against the demons – the Rakshasa. It is that strength and courage he looks to now on this dreariest of mornings.

The local reverend, known as the Reverend Stickman, with a fine nose for Polytheism and Paganism, once questioned him about it, and Annanda had to patiently explain that he did not worship Hanuman but rather admired him for his qualities. These he listed for the Reverend's benefit. Hanuman is not only strong enough to carry mountains with ease – his body itself resembles a golden mountain – but is also one who has complete control over his senses, and who is the repository of all virtues and good qualities. One could hardly object to such a paragon. Not only that, but Hanuman excels at the literary arts as well, being the ablest sentence-maker of his age, scholar in nine schools of grammar.

Besides, Hanuman worships the god Rama, who is a manifestation of the god Vishnu, so how can he be a god himself? Does a god worship another god?

The reverend was not convinced, so Annanda had to smile and let it pass. It is clear in his mind. Some people are never satisfied until you think exactly the way they do. Right now he is in sore need of a little of Hanuman's strength.

Syrupy Indian music from old Bollywood hits oozes softly from the ceiling. Ah, Suneal, I forgot myself. I should have come back for you. Together we could make it through the hard times. Alone, I'm not so sure. Perhaps I should become a Sadhu, a wandering mendicant, and renounce the world. His grandfather did that at the age of sixty. Left his wife and home and set off into the world as poor as a beggar. Before he left, he said to his grandson, 'The world may be made for us, but we are not always made for the world.'

That tricky little bugger Sirocco Cornet comes weaselling in, accompanied by his mournful sidekick, the shambling Sad Toof, always on the hunt for pain-killers.

Sirocco mockingly brings his palms together in front of his chest and bows slightly.

'Annanda...' he begins cheerfully.

'Mr Patel to you.'

'Mr Patel, have you seen any strangers around?'

'A tourist bus?'

'A woman. Dressed like a lady.'

'I see no ladies. There are no ladies. Why should I?'

'I saw one. She wasn't from here.'

Annanda makes a dismissive gesture. He doesn't like Sirocco.

Sirocco has a face like a walnut and a mind like a lizard. And nobody knows exactly who he is or where he came from. They say Gypsy Cornet found him in the desert. She should have left him there. Too kind, is Gypsy Cornet. Prone to picking up waifs and strays.

Apparently bored, Sad Toof begins to wander down one of the aisles, loitering near an ageing stack of sardine cans.

'I know you mokopuna, how you work. The Sirocco keeps me talking while the Sad Toof steals things.' Annanda is deeply suspicious of all that little gang of in-betweens and leftovers Akona affectionately named the mokopuna, and the name stuck.

'What things?'

'Everythings...' He makes a large gesture to the largely empty shelves. In his mind's eye they are elaborately stocked with all kinds of stealable items. He is about to elaborate when Hera, the acknowledged Queen of Keatown, enters the store, the fabled Baby slung across her chest.

Behind her, across the street, Annanda sees, to his amazement, a stranger. No fancy lady of Sirocco's babble, but a tired, dusty looking man in a rumpled suit carrying a petrol can who walks right past Flay's Gas as if it didn't exist. Annanda stares. What would Suneal say? That this dusty looking man is a Rakshasa? As if Annanda can just think them up and manifest them.

'Good morning Mr Patel,' Hera says politely.

Annanda claps his palms together and bows. 'Mother Hera,' he says, 'you look radiant today. And the Baby too.' Although he can't possibly see it, snuggled as the Baby is against Hera's chest.

'Only today, Mr Patel?'

Annanda blushes, and succeeds in looking suitably shamefaced.

'Of course, you are always radiant. How could I think otherwise? Radiance does not admit to degrees. It is an absolute quality.'

Annanda always creams on like this when he is about to make a sale. The old street-hustler wisdom holds good even in the case of the magnificent Hera: there is no woman born impervious to flattery.

But he has a point. There is something truly grand and superior about Hera, although not everybody fawns on her the way Annanda does. There has to be a woman, resplendent, to shine, and shower blossoms with her smile in the royal manner; there has to be a woman in this town made sad by miscarriages, stillborn babies and cot deaths, to have a baby clean of limb and pure of eye.

When he tries to picture Sita, Rama's consort, it is Hera who appears in his mind. In a place where everybody is dusty and tired, Hera looks fresh and new. Her breasts engorged with springtime whatever the season, Hera is full in form and large in spirit, her clothes all voluminous, lusciously coloured – and always clean. Many fear her because of her laugh, which, like Hera herself, can sweep you into an abyss. According to popular legend, it was by choice that she came down from the mansions to live with us in shabby Keatown. Trapped by her wealth and status as a celeb, and an eternal sterile, Botox youth-hood, she sought the mortality and humility of Keatown, choosing to live alone in the red-brick ruins of the Bay Motel, the lower reaches of which are already under water, as a penance for her godlessness. Her devotees have uncovered photographs of her on the covers of old magazines, looking like a princess, a big-screen celeb.

But not everybody buys into the legend.

Reverend Stickman hints darkly that she was once a whore, flown in by chopper on a night of feckless revelry and thrown down from the mansions the next morning, despoiled and discarded. So, she made the best of it, passing herself off among us as a celeb. What rankles with the reverend is that it should be Hera who has given birth to Keatown's saviour child, and not a more godly woman, like Mother Smiley, or the young Melissa Tonguestone, or any of the good women of Keatown yearning for a child to hold in their arms, women far more worthy of God's grace and favour than this hip-swinging slut. But who cares what the reverend says, since he is not a real reverend any more than Mayor Bronzy is a real mayor.

Besides, there are, equally, rumours about the Reverend Stickman too. That he got his name not from his sticklike frame – everybody is skinny in the Long Emergency – but for his skill with a billiard cue and a pack of cards. A low-life barfly card sharp and snooker snapper. He doesn't completely deny the rumours, a concession he considers puts him on a higher moral plane than the harlot, since she will admit nothing. All he will say is that he was a pitiful atheist and rationalist who was playing poker, a variation called five-card-stud, when he picked up a new hand and God was in it, peeking out from behind the Ace of Spades. God, the joker in the rationalist deck, trumps everything, trumps the game itself. He likens himself to Saint Augustine and Paul the Apostle, sinners redeemed.

Whatever his background, or his opinion of Hera, she can't help but walk like a queen, talk like a queen – and cast her glances in an imperial manner. There is something about her eyes; you can't look at them.

They are just too blue. Bluer than the sky, bluer than heaven. They are either drop-dead gorgeous or just plain drop-dead. In contrast, her throat plays rough and tumble with words, sounding like the gravelly riverbed of a whisky-drenched nightclub singer.

Mayor Bronzy spends a lot of time clearing his throat when he is around her.

'You flatter me, Mr Patel. Ah… I see the mokopuna are here, what are you up to today, Mr Cornet?'

Sirocco doesn't know which way to look. Nobody calls him Mr Cornet, yet he can detect no mockery in her voice. For some reason as mysterious to him as Scale's antipathy, Hera has never treated him with anything less than respect. She'd be pretty much the only one, at least among the adults.

Annanda throws them a dirty look. 'They are up to no good, as usual Doubtless here to rob me blind. Dishonesty is also, I fear, something of a fixed quality.'

'Surely not,' she says. Gently she begins to unwrap the scarf that protects the Baby's head. A pink snubby face appears, eyes peacefully closed.

Annanda is disgusted to witness the sycophantic bow Sirocco gives Mother Hera. What is she going to think of his establishment if he tolerates these mocking urchins on his premises? All they do is drive away good customers.

'Mr Patel, you might have noticed, is given to hyperbole.' When speaking to adults, Sirocco always uses a high, querulous voice and quaint phrasing, as if it were a foreign language he is talking. People always grin when they hear it, much to his frustration since they are often too busy grinning to listen to what he is saying.

At the sound of Sirocco's voice, the Baby stirs, lifts his head from Hera's breast, fixes his large eyes on him, and, unclasping a tiny hand from Hera's blouse, waves. Feeling obscurely shame-faced, Sirocco wriggles his fingers in reply. The Baby bares his gums. Sirocco smiles back, having the advantage of teeth.

The Baby gurgles. Either he is laughing or the sight of Sirocco's teeth has given him indigestion.

Annanda is deeply unimpressed, saddened even, by this pantomime but he is as much enthralled by the Baby as everyone else. He has to be. This is the fair-limbed wonder, the focus of all hopes, and ultimate symbol of faith in a town of empty bassinets. The women say the men are running short of sperm and firing blanks. Like the fish catch, the sperm count is down. And the little sperms left are bent and deformed. Nothing left to fertilise the ocean, or the women. The Baby is a real baby; Hera's sceptre; the jewel of Keatown.

The question of who the father is has worn out wagging tongues, and remains Keatown's best-kept secret.

Mr Patel sighs with due reverence. 'And how can we serve you?' he says, apparently addressing the Baby.

'Safety pins,' Hera says. 'I thought you might have some hidden away somewhere.'

Annanda's face lights up. 'Of course, please watch these scoundrels while I'm gone,' and he scurries away, delighted to do business. Any business. A sale is a sale.

'Do I need to watch you so closely?' Hera asks Sirocco and Sad Toof.

They shake their heads. The Baby gurgles and waves at Sirocco again. He gives a silly little wave back and the Baby gurgles some more.

'The baby likes you, Sirocco,' Hera says.

He demurs. He blushes to the core. He pretends he doesn't know himself.

'Would you like to hold him for a moment?'

The very idea brings him to the edge of panic. The light, supplied by generous skylights, becomes preternaturally bright. The muted sounds of the supermarket break with a horrible sharpness. His arms start to tremble. Hold the sacred Baby? Take him from the baby-bearer? Sirocco, the runt of the litter if ever there was one? No number of lifetimes spent in the desert could prepare him for such a moment.

'Ahhh...'

'It's alright,' Hera says with great gentleness. 'But I think the Baby would like it.'

He is saved by the bustling return of Annanda who would certainly not have approved of the thief Sirocco holding the Baby. I won't be such a coward next time, Sirocco tells himself.

'Here we are!' Annanda says, placing a package on the counter with a flourish. 'Just what the doctor ordered.' He pulls open the snap-top fastening to his plastic bag and proudly pours out some of the contents. Tiny safety pins the colour of gold, although some of them are a little tarnished, glitter on the counter.

'I'm sorry, Mr Patel, but these are too small. I need them, you see, for his nappies.'

'Nappies? Yes, I have nappies. Lots.'

'No. These safety pins are too small.'

Annanda's face falls. 'You just use more,' he says brightly. 'Instead of one big pin you have lots of little pins...'

The door slides open and another of the mokopuna appears. This is Orchid, or the Orchid as she is sometimes known. To Sirocco she could well be the flower itself, having taken human form. She is the oldest of the mokopuna, perhaps about fifteen, although Sirocco is not good at judging ages. Her youthful beauty is famed throughout Keatown and beyond, but it has little effect on Sirocco. Sad Toof, however, always blushes and hides himself away when she is around. Apparently the sight of her makes his toothache worse.

Behind Orchid, in her shadow, comes Typhoid Mary with her spiky hair, her pock-marked face and the eternal grey scarf she wears around her neck. Typhoid Mary is not renowned for her beauty, far from it, but the sly one does have a certain mystery to her as nobody is quite sure when she turned up or where she comes from. Sometimes it seems to Sirocco as if Mary has always been there, just unseen. There are desert creatures like that; you never see them until they let you.

As soon as she sees Hera and the Baby, Orchid hesitates. Hera, however, greets her warmly with an awkward hug. The Baby looks at the girl with a cosmic stare.

'Perhaps you'd like to hold him,' Hera says. There is gentleness in her roughhouse voice.

'Oh no.' Orchid takes a quick step back. A look passes over her face he can't identify but which she covers up immediately. Revulsion, perhaps. Or a struggle with desire. Mary gives Hera the evil eye, and is about to spit with contempt when she notices Annanda's eyes on her. She offers him a vacant smile.

Ignoring her, Annanda says, 'Miss Orchid, can we be helping you today?' Annanda is polite but alert. These girls may be older, but they are still urchins, liars and deceivers. Orchid hesitates.

'Do you have any ciggies?' Mary says. She's assumed a casual attitude, one that would fit the flourishing of a cigarette.

'I would most certainly not sell them to you,' Annanda says, a little shocked at his own emphasis. He did in fact have some homegrown tobacco said to be of good quality, and is not one to pass up a sale.

'Oh, I didn't mean to buy,' she makes the whole idea sound beneath contempt, 'But I thought you might like to buy. Proper ciggies too, imports in cellophane packets. The most perfect nicotine delivery system ever devised.' From a pocket in her overalls she produces a packet of cigarettes, just as described, all gleaming and new. Like a conjurer doing a trick, or perhaps someone undressing a lover, she slides off the cellophane, flips open the lid, slips out a cigarette from the pristine row, savours it between her lips while she pretends to search for a lighter. 'I thought you might like a little sample,' she says.

'You're not lighting that in here,' Hera says.

'I wasn't going to light it. I was just demonstrating. Who knows, perhaps Annanda might become a valued customer of mine.'

Annanda looks ready to choke, but it is his turn to hesitate. If indeed this scabulous girl could obtain such a quality product, an American import by the look of it, Annanda might certainly be interested. In this day and age you can't afford to pick and choose who you do business with. He feels doubly uneasy when he discerns that the desert rat seems to know exactly what is passing through his head.

'Never name the well from which you will not drink,' Sirocco says solemnly.

The door opens behind them and the Reverend Stickman appears. He has short, mousey hair on top and a straggle of thin hair down his shoulders. Everything about his face is long, from his elongated forehead to his descending chin. Above a prominent, sharp nose, two very blue eyes seem to look through rather than at the world. A vertical frown appears on his vertical forehead when he sees Hera.

'Ah, the good reverend,' Annanda says, 'How can we make your day a little better?'

'That's a question indeed.' The reverend looks around the supermarket shelves without much hope.

Sirocco takes a step back, attempting to merge into the environment the way Lizard taught him. 'Learn how to make yourself invisible,' Lizard counselled him. Not so easy in a supermarket where he can't just hunch down in the sand, but worth the try; the good reverend has little love for humanity, and even less for a desert rat with pagan tendencies.

But the reverend has no time for the mokopuna right now, although his disapproving eye notes the presence of the Orchid and her nasty shadow. His attention is focused on Hera, and the tiny life that dozes contentedly at her bosom. 'Ah,' he attempts a show of goodwill, 'I see our Baby is safe and sound.' His effort to smile reveals a set of long, yellow teeth. He often said 'our Baby' because he considered that the child belonged to the whole town. As well as to God, of course. 'But when will he be named? Baptised.' He puts great emphasis on the last word. 'In the name of the Lord.' For the moment he looks tall and commanding, the way a reverend should look – full of the holy presence.

'All in good time,' Hera says. Her voice is mild enough, and her tone pleasant, but the reverend detects a note of insouciance. A stubborn will. An infuriating indifference to the needs of the child's soul.

'A child with no God given name wanders in the wilderness, bereft of God's grace.' As he says this, his eyes slide across to Sirocco, another nameless creature from the wilderness. 'Feral,' he says.

'I don't accept any of that crap,' Hera says. If her voice had elbows it would be making room for itself right now.

'What is crooked cannot be straightened; what is lacking cannot be counted.' The reverend speaks half to himself but everybody understands.

'Get over it then.' Hera turns back to the counter where Annanda's tiny gold safety pins still lie in a bright scatter. She appears to consider them deeply, her chest rising and falling.

'You may have no regard for your own blighted soul. That's understandable. But to happily doom your own child...' the reverend shakes his head as if such evil was beyond human comprehension. 'You have no idea the torments that await you.'

'I have plenty of torments right now, Mr Stickman. I mean of the human kind.'

'And what of the father? He who comes and goes in the cloak of night. He who is too ashamed to show his face. Let him now step forth.' He looks enquiringly around the supermarket as if the wretched offender might make a shamefaced appearance. There is nobody but Sad Toof peering from behind a row of shelves with some trepidation.

'That's telling her straight, Rev!' Mary says, clapping her hands.

'And what right do you have, you miserable excuse for a human being, to judge the actions of others?' Heat is creeping up into Hera's face; the Baby stirs restlessly.

'I have God behind me. And right beside me.'

'Do you think he would stay my hand if I were to slap your face?'

Everyone is quiet. Orchid stares at the Baby while Sirocco stares at the floor and Annanda sweeps the tiny safety pins into a pile. Mary's face is suffused with pleasure as she pretends to chew gum.

'As the Lord wills.'

'Okay.'

The slap makes a thin, bitter sound. She doesn't hold back. A clawlike shape appears on the reverend's face. After a stunned moment it is not to her that he turns but the Baby, who is peering at him wide-eyed.

'For he cometh in with vanity, and departeth in darkness, and his name shall be covered with darkness.' He speaks with all the force of an oracle. Or perhaps the wicked fairy who pulls down a curse on the newborn.

'I'll tell you one thing, I'm not going to be spooked by a creep like you, Mr Stickman. Don't think I don't know how you would earn a nickname like that.'

'Ah ha!' Mary says to Orchid, Sirocco and Annanda, Sad Toof still being in hiding somewhere in the vicinity of the sardines, 'She's onto him. How she plays hardball.'

The reverend tries to add to his height by lifting himself onto his toes. This way he towers over the woman, and everybody else. 'I have never pretended... mine was a misspent youth lived around the pool tables...'

'Stickman, stickman, stickman,' Hera chants, spitting in his face, 'watch your left kidney,' at the same time producing an imaginary knife from beneath the Baby's frontpack, and taking a quick stab at the reverend's right kidney. The action is so assured and fast, Sirocco is convinced he can see the knife, a narrow curved blade. The reverend twists as he leaps back, protecting the kidney; at the same time his right hand flashes across his body to his left hip, where there is no longer a scabbard holding a knife, a feral snarl in his throat. He freezes, his right hand still hovering over his empty left hip.

'He's outed!' Mary shouts with glee. 'Quick with the stick is the stickman, but the queen is quicker.' She turns to Annanda, 'Mr Patel, do you have any real knives? Hunting knives perhaps. Something for skinning carcasses?'

Annanda does indeed have such items, albeit second hand, but he has other matters on his mind. 'Where is your moral leadership?' he says. His question is directed at the reverend, but takes in Hera by implication. His voice is low but trembling with indignation. 'You, sir, claim to be a religious man, yet you get into a brawl with a woman on my premises. People look up to you, both of you, the queen and man of god. Each of you needs to be... resplendent, yes. That's the word. You need to be what you appear to be, otherwise, as you are so fond of saying, all is vanity.'

For a moment Sirocco sees the pair as Annanda sees them, or would like to see them. Hera, queen of the earth, and the fecund powers of the earth; the reverend, king of the air, and the powers of the spirit, walking hand-in-hand through Keatown, inspiring confidence and strength in its suffering inhabitants. If men and women cannot become gods, then gods cannot become men and women, and the world falls asunder.

Hera says, 'You are right, you shame me.' She glances at the reverend to see if he too is shamed, which he is not. 'Mr Stickman is not the only one to have had a misspent youth. But when he comes to the Baby,' she glances now at Orchid, 'when it comes to this child,' she strokes his head, 'I will not see him baptised in the name of a god who knows only how to curse and smite.' So saying, she sweeps out the door, Orchid and Mary in train.

As they leave Mary turns for a parting shot. 'You've got some fancy moves there, Rev.' She blows Annanda a kiss and is gone.

Just to the south of Annanda's supermarket there is a huge structure composed of steel girders, staggered, bare and windswept. A rusting tribute to somebody's commercial dreams, a warehouse perhaps, or factory in the making. A brief march of steel. Huge uprights with sloping peaks in place for a roof which never happened. Walls which never happened. We just call it the girders. When storms get up, it howls like a demented organ.

Sirocco and Sad Toof pause nearby – they don't like to get too close – and Sad Toof pulls a slightly rusty can of sardines from his pocket. He grins at Sirocco, affording him a rare view of the sad toof itself in all its putrid glory. They look up and down the empty road, north and south. The sky is as clean as a licked plate, but there is a faint rumbling as if somewhere far off, on the other side of the world, a storm is brewing.

Abruptly, out of the silence, the girders give a loud moan, a single iron cry of agony or pleasure. The boys move back out of range, but nothing happens. There is no encore. The morning stays quiet.

Sad Toof snaps open the tin of sardines. Nice and soft. The metal winds up like a Dead Sea Scroll.

He doesn't offer Sirocco any but turns away and sucks at the tin noisily.

a balcony with a view

There is one denizen of Keatown who hates rising early, if you consider the mansions to be a part of the town. True, most of the super-rich and the celebs have already jumped in their choppers and flown away to their fastnesses in other lands, but not Baron Brian (Brainbox) Fairweather, at present standing legs firmly apart on the concrete ramparts of his mansion home, looking east at a view to die for. Or pay the earth for.

A hawk's-eye view of this cluster of mega-houses would reveal fortress-high greywacke walls, sequestered courtyards and elaborately arching roofs or chopper pads. A clutch of grandiose dwellings with 180-degree views built into the rock on high promontories overlooking the bay, like the eyries of fantasy birds of prey. Too grand to be called houses, some of the mansions are thrust forth, lording it over the coast and humble town below, while others are hidden out of sight, the bulk of them buried in the rock itself. From below, you can't see much of the baron's establishment but the semicircle of the curved balcony on which he is standing and a slice of the flat roof behind.

What the baron sees, his view to die for, is one great glittering morning of ocean, with, in the foreground, a tufty little rock that is Pine Point and a miniature wharf complete with corrugated-iron fish shed, looking very down-home, and a few quaint fishing boats bobbing up and down in the light. Here's a view with bells and whistles; here's a view that's a work of art, a vast composition of sky, sea and rock. Here's a view his Shanghai buddies can't buy, at any price. All his.

The only blotch on the canvas is scrawny little Keatown itself, a straggle of decaying houses, a pathetic little gas station and a tin shed that calls itself a supermarket. There is nothing picturesque about it. It looks the way half-abandoned things get to look after a while. Ready for a giant broom. One that sweeps clean. These dog droppings that call themselves a town are admittedly tucked away in the foreground, but a blotch is a blotch, and at times he stares at it through powerful binoculars as one might study a virus in the Petri dish. Pitiful lives he does not pity, aimless comings and goings, coupling and decoupling. Sometimes he imagines a nice cleansing tsunami sweeping it all away, the rude scratchings, returning the bay to the tabula rasa of its natural forms.

Occasionally their scurrying lives offer some amusement, such as when, around the time of the exodus, they contrived to lay cables and illegally hook into the main line that feeds electricity to the mansions. Quite assiduous and clever they were, working at night, tunnelling, showing a certain rude skill in syphoning off the juice and creating a mini-grid that fed either directly to their dwellings or into the lines already there. The whole village was in on it. Enterprising little insects. The most amusing part was their clandestine bustling, their pathetic belief that they were getting away with this, that nobody knew, whereas the baron monitored the whole operation, noting carefully how much juice they ended up stealing.

It amused him to do nothing about it, to allow them to go on thinking they were getting away with it and feeling very pleased with themselves, and it still does. It amuses him even more to know that he has the power, just a switch away, to shut down pretty much the whole town. Given the fragile state of their economy, the baron has it in his power to deal the death blow, to turn off the lights once and for all, to kick Keatown back into the Stone Age. The idea amuses him, and keeps amusing him as long as he doesn't do it; once he's done it, it's all over. Do it, and he loses the pleasure of anticipation; only when it stops amusing him will he do it.

The same applies to the spring that the old woman who talks to herself insists on visiting, even though the property no longer belongs to her or her family. When he bought the property off the stupidly greedy Bob Kensington, he planned a large development on that site. A kind of convention centre at the top of the world where the 0.01% could meet and, like the gods of old, rule the four horizons. Everything as far as I can see is mine! His engineers advised him that the spring could be destroyed. It would take an enormous amount of rock and rubble to block it up, but with enough brute force it could be done, with the upsurging water being driven back underground. He'd got as far as planting explosives all around the spring in accordance with the engineers' design. Enough to do the job. When the Long Emergency began, he dropped his plans. The 0.01% had scattered and nobody was sure who ruled the world any more.

He hasn't dismantled the explosives. Just knocking out their electricity might not be enough to destroy Keatown, if that's what he wants. It would make their miserable lives more miserable, but they would cling on, because that is what they do. They'll cling on when all hope is gone. But if he knocked out the stream that fed them, that would end it all. Again, there was pleasure in the thought, a pleasure that would be destroyed as soon as he pressed the button, which was right here in his house, a few steps away.

In the meantime, he lets the old woman go up there to pray or wash her feet or whatever she does, but he's starting to send out his guard dog, Manny, to make his presence felt, maybe even scare her off. Manny's good at that sort of thing.

Why she bothers rankles the baron more than a silly old woman should. The Brainbox made his fortune understanding algorithms, and the financial implications of fractals, but he is buggered if he can understand the logic, or illogic for that matter, of most of the events, what he can see of them, in that same pathetic excuse for a town. He would have to understand, completely, fully, the capricious individual motivation of each virus fragment – Fibonacci eat your heart out! – if it weren't for the most choice fish, provided on agreeable terms by the indomitable Orlap the Viking, who has an unaccountable loyalty to the town, and the clandestine visits of Flounder Phil with his flounders, the baron would have wiped it off his mind-screen long ago. Especially that ridiculous and pompous person who calls himself the mayor, and who tried to brown-nose his way into the baron's good favours by offering his services as general pimp and procurer. Still, fresh flounder in black bean sauce, or grilled snapper, compensates for all sorts of defects.

Behind him stand the mountains, as solid as a Swiss bank account. It comforts him to feel them there, like allies protecting his back. No enemies creeping up on him from that quarter. On the patio immediately below him Fraulein Zhenhua, a tall woman of mixed German and Chinese decent, and his ever-faithful ally, is teaching the new girl, Orchid, some intricate dance steps. Contemplating the exquisitely slow process of turning this village orphan into a rare flower and mansion whore gives the baron shivers of pleasure in all the right places. Feed her dainty foods, give her baths and massages and sweet things to rub on her even sweeter skin, teach her how to dance and sing, make her the centre of the most beautiful world an urchin girl could imagine, full of fine clothes and noble people – like the baron himself. A slow but sure corruption, every step of which the girl gratefully receives, until she is ready to join one of the more private parties the baron enjoys from time to time, and the ripe fruit of that corruption will fall into his outstretched hands. All his.

A glad light falls on the patio below. The red-haired Cherry Blossom, the blue-haired Blue Zither and the platinum blonde Sun Petal, his goose girls, are sweet and have got their moves off pat, but they cannot compare to even the most amateur efforts of Orchid. They are indeed goose girls dancing with a swan. Watching Orchid now, so graceful, quick and apparently artless, makes him realize just how tired he has grown of them. I should have left with the others in the general exodus, he thinks, not for the first time. It was sheer perversity to stay. Discovering Orchid has certainly been a compensation, but not without a bitter taste, for his delight in her has merely highlighted just how dull his perfect life has become. Somehow this girl shows him up, and that's a new feeling for him.

The source of her fascination is that she can somehow be both innocent and insolent at the same time – and he's looking forward to exploring both aspects, especially the insolence, oh yes!

Just how Fraulein Zhenhua found this rare flower is something of a mystery, which makes Zhenhua herself something of a mystery despite the years he's known her. She glances up at him and smiles; she always knows when he is observing her. That reminds him of his first glimpse of her standing in the doorway of his hotel room in Hong Kong or Singapore or wherever, the highest of high-class call girls with a price tag to match, wearing a slender, close-fitting dress, very classy, very much like the one she is wearing now. What impressed him was that she didn't appear at his door with a phony, professional call-girl smile on her face, the kind of smile he'd seen many times before on the faces of even expensive girls, but rather with a protracted, and potentially sensuous scrutiny, letting her eyes linger on the details of his face. And, when she looked into his eyes, with a frankness that bordered on wisdom, he was hers no questions asked, no awkward conversation required. It might just as well have been telepathy. More than just hotel sex took place in that room that night, and by the morning they were welded into an unstoppable team. Partners in crime. Closer than a marriage, he has always thought.

Of further interest, there is another girl out there, hiding just beyond his walls, waiting to meet Orchid when she chooses to return to Keatown. A sneaky girl the baron has glimpsed from time to time. Sooner or later he will find out about her. Zhenhua will bring her in. He assumes she is some urchin friend from the town. At present Orchid comes merely to do dancing lessons, but is already starting to linger afterwards. This trap is best gradually sprung. When it comes, her enslavement will be voluntary. Perhaps the sneaky girl is shy and wants to join her friend.

At that moment there is a rustle of movement and he is joined by his dog, Manny, who likes to get out and around and patrol the area. He is panting gently. Nothing happens around the place without Manny knowing. He drops one hand to negligently fondle the dog's ears. It is Manny he has to thank for discovering the sneaky girl, locating her hiding place in the scrub on the northern side, a spot that affords her a view of the very deck he is now standing on. Being the intelligent, well-trained dog he is, Manny did not attack but merely barked once to alert his master. The Baron, for reasons obscure even to himself, pretended not to see her, and Manny did the same.

Clever for a dog, but then, Manny isn't quite an ordinary dog. A pitbull Rottweiler mix with selected pig genes thrown in for intelligence, the pig being the smartest of land mammals, and octopus genes for good measure, the octopus being one of the smartest of the sea creatures. It is true that Manny is a laboratory creation, a splice of the best genes on the market, but he is a real dog for all of that, and enjoys having his ears fondled.

'What am I still doing here?' he asks the dog. 'Why didn't I leave with everybody else?' A good question with no obvious answer. Certainly, since everybody's departure, he's found himself talking to his dog, and even his bronze reclining Buddha. Terry and Joe, his security, were not hired for their conversational skills, and Zhenhua has never been given to idle chitchat or casual socialising. If it's sex he wants, Zhenhua or the goose girls will oblige, but companionship? Not exactly.

Manny of course doesn't answer, his dog jaw is not built for speech, but that doesn't mean he can't understand. He can look up at his master with his overlarge, disconcertingly pink eyes, and sympathise. If he has a wall to support him, he can rise up on two legs more gracefully than a dog should, almost as if to assert a kinship with his master, which is touching.

Baron Fairweather resists the temptation to go into the hangar bay and take a look at his long-range, diesel-burning, Turboshaft 300 – his ticket out of here when he needs it, the very best helicopter money can buy. Lately, he's taken to popping into the hangar every so often just to take a look at it and stroke its sleek sides, as if he has to reassure himself that it is still there. That's as worrying as talking to his dog or his reclining Arya Tara, mother of all buddhas. If he starts talking to his helicopter he'll know it's time to leave.

Maybe it was time to get the Turboshaft 300 up onto the landing pad on the roof and ready for take-off. Maybe the time has come and he doesn't even know it. Time to shut off the electricity, blow the spring and fuck off out of there.

A harsh cry cuts across his meditations. Harsh and unwelcome. 'Kea! kea! kea!'

'I thought we'd got rid of those bloody birds,' he says to Manny, who's looking alertly towards the north.

'Not over there, dummy.'

He sees it now. Mockingly close, it is. Dull green body. A cheeky flash of orange under the wings. It fills him with fury. Some fool named the town after these malicious birds.

'Kea! Kea! Kea!'

It sounds like a warning. Or a judgment.

The kea was the world's only alpine parrot, Zhenhua informed him once, but the baron didn't care. He and his Mosin Nagant rifle, a precision killing machine, had other ideas. The irascible, destructive birds had once attacked his Turboshaft 300m, attempting to rip the rubber off from around the doors. So he started shooting them at every opportunity. For all their bluster, they died just like any other bird. Pretty soon he'd cleared them out, or thought he had.

Now one has returned to mock him. It sits on a rock uphill, northwest of him, and seems to have him under steady observation. Where is his Mosin Nagant when he needs it? There was a time when he never stood on this balcony without the rifle within reach, just in case any unauthorised living creature, like the kea, should happen by.

As the thought crosses his mind, the bird lifts off its perch and takes to the air with several sharp cries, seemingly directed at the baron, and soars back up towards the mountains.

While watching it, he's distracted by a movement to the north. The foothills stretch several miles north in a series of folds, escarpments and valleys, until giving way to the great shingle plain of an extended riverbed. Two folds to the north he can see tiny figures moving south. At first he thinks goats, maybe wild sheep, but the binoculars show him three human forms, making hard work of it, for they are not following any walking path. Even the binoculars can't show him much at this distance except that they are definitely humans in a place it makes no sense for humans to be, heading in a direction it makes no sense to head, across the grain of the land.

Manny whines, just like a real dog; he can see the intruders too.

The baron considers sending his two bodyguards out to have a look. He has Joe, a Samoan and a magnificent male specimen, a black belt in Brazilian jujitsu and as strong as two men. Since he is also a spectacular addition to his private parties, the baron has had ample opportunity to admire his physical prowess in quite a different field of endeavour. Then he has Terry the Ukrainian, not quite as big and broad as Joe, but who makes up for it in viciousness. To each their own special gift.

Deciding against that, he turns for the house, thinking the scope on the Mosin Nagant might be stronger than his binoculars. Be nice to see these people come up on the crosshairs. Just the fact of them being there makes him feel a little less safe, as if his allies, the mountains, have somehow let him down, let the enemy in the back door. On his way through his swanky living room he notices his flat-screen blinking softly – message waiting.

There'll be time for that later. Time for all sorts of things – later.

return to the mountains to be cleansed by the winds

Akona's feet soon find the familiar trail that leads to the Makurutanga, and it's not long before she hears the sound of water rushing over stones, a sound she has known all her life yet never tired of. The nature of her mission is somewhat obscure, even to herself, but she doesn't mind. Return to the mountains to be cleansed by the wind, her mother used to say. Although how much closer to the mountains a morning's walk will take her is doubtful. A benefit of age, perhaps, she can follow her inner promptings without having to explain, even to herself.

It's the spring, Wai-O-Tapu, she thinks. It just calls to me from time to time. As it must have done for her great grandfather, Nōpera Kāmaka, who once trod this very path to seek the blessing of Wai-O-Tapu for his marriage to Charlotte Kensington. This was a marriage the Kensingstons would make sure the couple regretted. The marae was a thriving settlement then, with over ten families, and Nōpera was their leader.

As Akona arrived at the river, she felt close to Nōpera. Perhaps that's what getting old means too, getting closer to the ancestors, getting ready to join them. Have a little chit-chat about old times and air old grievances.

The path to Wai-O-Tapu is a gentle climb westwards, following the river into the lower foothills of Mt Irirangi, skirting the fortress of rock that houses the mansions to the north. As she climbs, she stops from time to time to test the temperature and energy flow of the river. To bring maximum benefit, the temperature of river water should not exceed four degrees above freezing, she has learned. Four degrees is optimal. Warmer, and water opens itself to greasy choking slimes, pathogens and plagues. Once, when the mokopuna called Little Sanyo asked her why trees always leaned out over the water, she said that the trees sought to keep the water cool, but he hadn't believed her. They leaned out like that to catch the sun, he told her. That's right, she said, but he didn't understand her. Akona, the name means 'teach' or teacher, but she's never had much success with it.

The water feels just right. A coolness she can breathe in, and taste what the early world was like. This is the taste of childhood for Akona. She takes for granted that the Wai-O-Tapu River can merge with her mind, and carry it along, down to the sea, where it might break apart in the huge, careless generosity of the ocean. That happened when she was a little girl. The river swirled in and out of her sleep and her waking without impediment. And still does.

She learned, soon enough, to keep that hidden. The world might be made for tasting, but only secretly. Adults didn't understand it. And still don't.

Keeping things hidden was ingrained in Akona at an early age, and has made her a reclusive adult. It amuses her to think that Bob Kensington is even more reclusive than she is. Probably squatting like a broody hen on his pot of gold, looking at the land he no longer owns. He's gone and dispossessed himself, the fool. Like Akona, Bob Kensington has no children, no one to inherit except his niece, Orchid, so why not sell the land to the mighty baron for a mighty pot of gold? Akona doesn't think that way, but Bob Kensington would. He'd cut off his nose to spite his face, then do the same to her.

However, as she gets older she finds she cares less about what other people might think of her and more about the long slow dreams of the land. Cherrie Lamont spies on her all the time, and Grandmother

Gaunt, in a false show of the sisterhood of crones, will turn up at the marae door in order to snoop and pry and carry off some little titbit of gossip. That used to bother her. Nowadays she just offers the meddling, nosy old woman a cup of tea and nods politely, or better still, gets her working in the garden. Every so often the Reverend Stickman will issue a proclamation against witchcraft and herbalism, instruments of the devil. These accusations are usually made after she has cured an infection or brought down somebody's night fever. Such fools believe her herbs work magic rather than simple chemistry. This talk once infuriated and worried her, but now she sheds it like water from a duck's back. They might whisper behind their hands, but they still come to her when troubled in mind or body. As for the reverend, he might rail against her as much as he likes, but praying to his god doesn't work half so well as her cures. Really, she reprimands herself, she only stays hidden now out of habit.

She paddles upstream in bare feet for a while, enjoying the cool rush on her sweaty legs and the fresh air of moving water on her face. In the tumble of water, it's too easy to hear voices and fall prey to memory. Moving water is full of voices. Right at this spot, where she likes to paddle, she is prone to hearing the voices of her grandmother, Naira, and her grandfather, Lawrence. These two wonderful people had raised Akona as their own when her parents were killed in a landslide when she was little.

Naira, forged with the fierce sense of independence that ran in the veins of both the rebel Charlotte Kensington and her Maori Chief Nōpera, repeated history by marrying a foreigner, Lawrence, from off the ships. Her voice was sharp, from all that yelling at the kids. Lawrence-from-off-the-ships, being from Canada, didn't really care about the high and mighty Johnsons and Kensingtons, or the touch of the tar brush, or the equally proud Kāmaka family. His voice was quiet and blurry.

She remembers her grandfather Lawrence because of his soft chamois drawstring bag with little nuggets of real gold inside, gold he'd found south of the desert. If they asked him nicely he would bring it out and show it to the children, rattling the nuggets around so they could hear the dull clunk. 'That's the sound of real gold,' he would say. Some of the more malicious tongues suggested that Lawrence had wooed Naira with that bag of gold, but the young Akona had not been impressed. The gold looked as dull as the sound it made, ordinary and impenetrable. It didn't sparkle like mica in rock, and it didn't glow with the colours of the forest, like the piece of greenstone Naira sometimes wore around her neck, where it sat prettily on her olive throat. It didn't have the scent of dawn or dusk. There was no poetry in it, as with diamonds and emeralds. It looked ordinary and prosaic, just rather heavy.

Grandfather Lawrence, who lived to a ripe old age, never did cash the bag of gold in, even when times got tough. She thinks of that gold when she reaches the private-property sign Bob Kensington put up when he realized that Akona treated the land as if she had a right to it. The sign, old and worn now, he'd put up specifically to remind her that she, and the Kāmaka side of the family, had no legal claim on this, their ancestral territory. A point he had rammed home by selling the land to Brian Fairweather for a nice little pot of gold, and Fairweather left the signs untouched. Not nuggets as in Lawrence's chamois bag, but just as dull and meaningless. Childish, to be sure, but she always spits on the sign as she passes it, and today is no exception.

Also, whenever she passes that sign she feels as if there are eyes upon her from the hills and rocks around. It would not be hard for someone to stay hidden and spy on her, not impossible that Fairweather had placed cameras everywhere to keep an eye on his investment. This feels more like the alert scrutiny of a predator than the cold, impersonal eyes of a camera, however. Whatever it is, this uneasiness, it takes a moment for her to reconnect with the land beneath her feet, land the Kāmaka family and their forebears walked for many hundreds of years. Every step she takes, the land welcomes her feet.

When she gets to the rapids, which spill from a deep pool, she sits and dangles her legs in the water, almost getting right in, enjoying the rush of it across her skin. You don't have to be a witch to appreciate such things. However, once people have decided she is a witch, everything she does, even the most normal thing in the world like going for a paddle, is assigned some witchy purpose. It's enough to make a cat laugh.

She wades out a bit to feel the roughness of the chill water on her legs and feel the crunch of stones underfoot. Near the middle, right where the river air rushes at its coolest and the river is at its loudest, she feels a wind on her face that doesn't belong there. It is not a clean wind, the mountain kind that might do some cleansing of the soul. It is not rich with scents and echoing the agate voices of the earth, but a dry, desiccated wind from a dead zone, a place with no life or voice. A place where the last murmurs have died. She wants to brush it off her face and hair as if it were made of cobwebs. The briefest shred of it is enough to open a crack in the air through which such voidness might creep, such overwhelming absence, a place of deadness and dust, dun-coloured, like moss, but without the glow of the moss, without its silky calm. The smell of tombs. The smell of enclosed spaces. A smell that has no place here in the wide open, before the pristine slopes of Mt Irirangi.

'Don't tell me I'm losing my marbles,' she says aloud. She's heard that the sense of smell is the first to go with dementia. That would give Cherrie Lamont something to cackle about. Sometimes she's imagined her mind dying just the way clouds will dissolve back into the sky, vanish away without fuss or bother. Still midstream, she looks up to see Grandfather Lawrence slowly and patiently crossing the river from north to south, just below the boulders that form the bulwark of a deep pool. It's not the most sensible place to cross, since the water there is rough, but it doesn't seem to deter Grandfather Lawrence, who's concentrating on putting one foot in front of the other. He's dressed in a dark suit, the one he called his Sunday Best, though it was the only one he ever had – and it wasn't really for Sundays but for weddings and funerals.

Her first thought is that she is having a vision. As she gets older, her visions increasingly arrive this way, without preparation or warning. She has learned to be patient. Sometimes the elementals will speak to her in images and smells. But this is not a vision, and the figure of Lawrence is not an elemental. If anything, it is the negation of all things elemental.

'I didn't really need those marbles anyway,' she says to the rushing river. Birth, marriage and death – the three-cornered game of life guaranteed to knock out your marbles. But there it is, staining the abrasive edge of mountain water, something dark and slimy and sludgy, something that doesn't belong, either to the fizzy air or the intense mineral spaces of the earth.

The figure she can see that looks like Grandfather Lawrence is not really him at all, but somebody who might, at a glance, be mistaken for him. The way he puts his head on one side when looking down. Naira told the real Lawrence that he would ruin his neck muscles if he kept on doing that. Or the quizzical way he looks about him, as if he's not quite sure how he came to be where he is. It's not her marbles she's losing but her eyesight! That is, if you don't count the minor matter of

Grandfather Lawrence having been dead for a very long time with no business wandering around the Makurutanga.

An almost warm clammy touch on her leg, and the sudden guttural sound of the river, tell her there must be something very wrong with the figure that looks like Lawrence. He's not even a man, let alone her grandfather. Where a person should be stands an emptiness, a vacuity. This is not true emptiness, which is infinite, but simply a lack of anything, of everything – a blind, creeping lack. Since this creature is standing in the river, a part of him has merged with it, despoiling it, poisoning it. And she is standing a little downstream in bare feet!

At that same clammy touch, she is hit by a lightning bolt of grief. No storm precedes it. It comes out of nowhere, as it always does. She doubles over as it hits her in the abdomen, stumbles and nearly falls over. Ari! Ari! You cannot be dead, Ari. And I cannot be lying here, raped and broken. This time she does fall over, and water covers her, hard stones beneath. Now the water is fresh and clean again, and it heals her mind and body once more, just as it had on that night years ago. But while the healing waters of the Wai-O-Tapu River can touch that darkest sore like a balm, it can never heal it.

Time has not healed it either. Time has just made it worse, the memory more bitter. She should have surrendered to her blood and murdered the Kensington boys where they stood, but she was too steeped in the philosophy of aroha, that great and impossible love, to take revenge. Yet she has never stopped dreaming about it. Once her great-great Grandmother, Beatrice, mother of Charlotte, came to her in a dream and assured her that her revenge would come when Ari's body was found. Then and only then would her aroha and her revenge merge in a final, satisfying act.

She trusted this prophecy, and still does, despite Beatrice being as white as driven snow, daughter of the stern Victorian dowager, Ellen Johnson, and despite her marrying Alfred Kensington. She hasn't told the librarian that Beatrice's own daughter, Charlotte, told her daughter, Naira, that Beatrice's marriage was not a happy one, and that the gentle Beatrice came to hate the brutal Alfred who was determined to make her life a misery.

She stays in the water, letting its chill tumble over her head and shoulders and down across her body, wishing it could carry off these memories and lose them in mother ocean, but it doesn't work like that. Not unless she opens her mouth and fills herself up with the waters of life to overflowing – and she's not ready for that now.

Or ever.

finding a gate made of wind

She hastens right on out of there and quickly puts on her shoes. She can't see him from this southern side, but knows where he will land. There's a bit of scrubby bank up which he will have to scramble. She makes her way there with all due speed, wondering again why anybody should choose such an awkward place to cross. He's creepy, this un-man, this not-man, but she wants to see more of him, having never seen anything of the like before, certainly nothing that belongs to her familiar world.

He must have moved faster than she thought, because she doesn't see him, but she hears a voice, a dry whispering voice from that dead place. A voice without words, of no more substance than the rubbing of dry reeds against the wind.

What wind whispers here?

She looks upstream towards the spring, Wai-O-Tapu. Except for the Man in Black, her family, her tribe, are now scattered to the four winds, but she knows that her Maori ancestors used to come to Wai-O-Tapu to hear prophesies in the voice of the waters. The librarian found a reference to it in the diaries of Charlotte Kensington herself. Perhaps the waters of Wai-O-Tapu had some message for her today. There is no other reason for her to be making this journey.

Once more she sets her course for the spring.

a platter of sand and sky

Little Sanyo likes the beach and the beach likes him.

The soothing sound the ocean makes on the sloping sand he likes most of all, because it drowns the dull ringing in his head that began the day his parents were killed and has never left him. The librarian gave him a book about it, and gave it a name, tinnitus, a word that sounds a bit like the pinging of rain on a tin roof. The book said that the sounds he can hear inside his head are pitches he would never hear again with his actual ears, since the tinnitus means he is slowly losing his hearing.

Here on the beach, especially with a bit of wind in his ears, and especially if the sea is a bit rough, he can forget about the tinnitus and the soundless world he is slowly approaching.

Upon occasion, the beach gifts things to him as if in compensation, offers them up on a platter of sand and sky. A barrel of whisky, a dog in a bamboo cage, a wooden god of an unknown land, an intact dinghy, an empty dress suit. Sometimes he gives the things he finds to Scale, who's a bit of a pack rat but doesn't have the concentration span to be a good beachcomber and find stuff for himself. Doesn't have the eye for it. Little Sanyo does. He can find treasures where others just see an empty beach. Once he found a perfectly good garden fork he was able to give to Akona in return for intermittent board and lodgings. The most precious thing he ever found was a gold bracelet with some tiny sparkling stones set in the centre. Sometimes he imagines the slim arm that might wear such a bracelet, and blushes at the thought. He can't save the stuff he finds because he has nowhere to live. He has a couple of stashes along the southern beach but he seldom visits them. What's the point in digging stuff up just to look at it? The thrill is in the finding.

And that thrill is on him now as he heads towards a distant curved shape in the sand. He's south of the wharf, working along a series of beaches and rocky headlands that continue apparently forever, vanishing into the obscurity of distance, a devastation of rocks and whitecaps. It's one of his favourite spots as he always seems to find something. He's got a theory that the ocean currents tend to wash things up along this strip of beach. Once, when a woman threw herself off the wharf and drowned, her body washed up here.

The shape in the sand isn't anything he immediately recognises. That's what having a good eye means – being able to see anomalies, the shape of something that doesn't belong. Little Sanyo's parents had been very rich, almost celeb status themselves, or wannabe celebs. They knew how to drink champagne and drive fast cars. They bought Little Sanyo all the high-tech gear he wanted, and he was barely out of his nappies when he rewired the security system to the house so he could get in and out unseen. He'd get out to escape the rowdy parties and go to the quiet beach where there was nothing but stars and thin lines of foam glowing in the dark. He was a prodigy, a little Einstein in the making, at least so his parents thought, but all that came to an end when they were killed in a car crash in a wave of booze, cocaine, steel and glass.

Nobody wanted Little Sanyo with the hurting noises in his head. Nobody cared. He was just a leftover kid at the end of the party. His parents, it turned out, didn't have friends, just party buddies and fuck buddies who melted into the mist when the good times ceased to roll. The pampered little high-tech kid had to learn to fend for himself, make himself useful where he could, and sleep under houses because he feels comfortable with the great bulk of a house above, like a hen protecting its chick.

Little Sanyo is one of the urchin mokopuna. Another of the ragamuffin crowd. Some of them he likes, Sirocco for example, who's always kind to him, and Orchid, who has a kind of lazy magic to her; and some he doesn't, like Rasputin, who gets all religious, and Sad Toof, who can be wearying, and sneaky Mary. But, whatever their shortcomings, they are his crowd. He is one of them. He likes to be with them – except when he is beachcombing. That he can only do alone. When there's nothing but himself, the beach, sky, the sea. And things to be found. Some of them very tiny, like a narrow ring with three diamonds embedded in gold, like the three stars of Orion's belt. Such a thin little thing. He has to admit that he found it by accident, but then again, when he's on form, lots of such 'accidents' tend to happen. It's all to do with the play of light on things, he has decided, being of a scientific turn of mind. He's still got that ring in one of his hidden stashes. One day he might find somebody to give it to. That's what his parents did, he remembers. His father was always giving his mother rings and bracelets and things. Things that glittered.

He's drawing closer to the mysterious shape, and it doesn't look so mysterious any more. He feels a stab of disappointment when he realizes that it is a dead fish, a big one but still just a dead fish. Once, he heard, the cutters in the fish shed found a gold coin in the gut of a tuna. For some reason that made everybody laugh, but Little Sanyo couldn't see what was funny.

He squats down beside the bloated body of the fish, little more than a wide mouth hopelessly agape, full of sharp, slender teeth, and a distended gut. A big creature, almost the size of Little Sanyo, it is freshly washed up, its huge black eyes still blank and glistening.

From the tight bubble of its skin, he figures that it was a creature of the deep, never meant to rise into the terrible air above the water. The air is too light for it. Too tight for it. Come too close to the quivering surface, with not enough weight of water above, such creatures will fill up with air – and sometimes explode. Something has driven it up from beneath, he reasons, or it was borne by a rogue current. Now gulls circle.

Little Sanyo peers into the gaping jaws. He likes to see everything up close, as if he were short-sighted, but really just to make sure of its existence. Like these teeth, marvelling at their sharpness, their clever pain. Briefly, he thinks of rounding up the others. Sad Toof would be chuffed to see such clever, happy teeth.

The sea darkens. It has a deep, oily quality, yet the sky is a bright, hard blue. The surface of the bay shivers. Some wind, running counter to the gentle onshore wind. It lifts the hair at the back of his head. Blows dry sand into the mouth of the fish. Little Sanyo imagines that deep in the minor chords of the ocean another wind is blowing, a swelling bass line, swirling the strangest creatures up out of their weighty element.

There is the sharp hiss of escaping breath and a sudden putrid smell as the sea creature deflates.

Little Sanyo pulls back, suddenly fearful that its unholy breath could breathe sickness into him, and watches the deep-sea creature flatten as if some invisible foot were stepping on it. Its mouth looks bigger with the body deflated, cold and lipless, the colour of dull pearl. All the fearsome musculature of the body contracts to that still, wide, pearly mouth. The rest is just scaly sand, already growing wind ridges.

Sand grains flick in and out of its mouth like myriad ants. He wishes Sirocco were with him. Sirocco knows things. But could such a desert rat, even with all the wisdom of his lizard behind him, comprehend this creature from the far deep? Or know why it strayed so far from its territory?

Gulls glide above, criss-crossing one another as they slide back and forth, cocking their heads hungrily from side to side. Little Sanyo watches them for a bit and they watch him, waiting for him to move. There is an augury in the pattern they weave, if only he could read it. He's afraid of birds, dating from the time a gull dive-bombed him out of nowhere. He was certain he'd been nowhere near one of their nests. Since then he's been a bit superstitious about gulls, reading all sorts of meanings into their actions. Getting spooked, even in the middle of the morning on an empty beach.

A sudden slap and surge of water among the rocks beside him draws his eyes back to the ocean to see if some vessel were passing, creating a wake to slosh against the rocks so, but the expanse of ocean is lidless and empty. He edges closer to the rocks and looks down into the blowhole below where waves make quick animal movements, heaving and gurgling with an inexplicable, salty passion.

The surface of the sea begins to ruffle with an odd, contrary wind coming in off the land. Looking towards the sandhills and the town beyond, he can see the coarse marram grass stirring as the wind funnels through, burrowing from the land towards the ocean, bred somewhere between the mountains and the sky, smelling of yellow mountain gorse, of the open sky, the nakedness of empty tussock, the loneliness of ice. Behind the silence there's a rustle, like spider legs, or the swishing of long skirts, and here they come! Waves of dry sand are spinning out of the dunes and heading seaward. The onshore breeze falters; the lips of the sea darken. Wisps of sand flicker over the waves and hurl themselves into the purple swell. As the errant wind picks up, the sand forms into long filaments – sandsnakes, he thinks, savouring the new word – that weave across the beach towards him with what looks like intent, writhing vortices of sand which appear to lift their heads and look about like sentient creatures. When they reach Little Sanyo they tickle and sting his legs. There's a little slap in that wind.

As he makes his way north, back to the town, the wind quickens and the sandsnakes move faster. Their writhing forms cover the whole beach, turning it into a silent frenzy of twisting, interlocking shapes from which there emerge larger, more ominous sheet creatures that undulate towards the ocean. They make a sizzling sound, like distant static. A new noise for his head.

Fractious gulls move in, screaming in the flying sand.

He stops briefly to look back. Already the skull of the creature from the deep is no more than a tent of cartilage and bone, the eyes no more than stringy sockets. There is a dead thing looking at him from the architecture of bones.

Little Sanyo runs for it.

To get back to the main road he has to pass through Nightshade Track, a path that dips into a mass of the purple-green vegetation that gives the track its name. Here this stinky green plant, with its tiny, black, poisonous berries, has defeated the lupin and marram grass. He doesn't like the place; the nightshade with its maggoty white roots gives him the willies.

He's in the dip, where there's the least wind, when he sees a girl, not much taller than himself, appear out of the nightshade, heading south, briefly crossing the track, looking neither right nor left. She's a stranger, not one of the regular mokopuna girls like Orchid, or Mary, or the twins. She has dark hair and is wearing a severely white blouse and a black skirt that just reaches to her knees – and her legs are so pale Little Sanyo can barely believe them. It is as if she has just stepped in front of him, freshly dressed, out of a sunless world. She moves with a certain wistfulness, and is carrying a piece of paper rolled up like a scroll.

She passes close enough for him to reach out and touch her.

He wants to say something, to ask her who she is, where she's just sprung from, what she is doing here and where she is going, but there is something about her that forestalls him. Perhaps it's the way her big dark eyes fix upon the southern coastline as if she were moving through a different landscape altogether from his, and although she is close enough to touch he is afraid to try, as if his hands would encounter nothing but empty air. Maybe it's the way her head turns, kind of swivels without her body changing course, and how her eyes pass over his face as if it weren't there. As if he weren't there. Or maybe it's the way she moves, unhurried and sure.

Or maybe it's just her silence.

As he steps back, as from the strange and unknown, he feels something brushing his body like the current of air a fast-moving river will make. And there is a sound, like singing, a distant chorus, calling from the other side of the wind. From the other side of the whistling inside his head. Calling him.

Without stopping or even hesitating, she passes into the greenery on the south side of the track, her body slowly dismembered by the bracken and the sharp shadows thrown by the nightshade.

Little Sanyo doesn't stop running until he gets to the roundabout.

The inside of his head is screaming.

Mother Smiley and the slutty girl

Keatown might be a lonely place, might even exist at the edge of space, seemingly far away from floods, droughts, cyclones, die-offs, and all the rest of the world's burden, but it's not a mysterious place.

An ordinary fishing village with fading tourist pretensions, its concerns are practical, with a little casual superstition thrown in – find a pin sure to be good, pick it up and stick it in wood – but no aspirations towards the supernatural. You'd be hard put to find a single person in the town who believes in ghosts, except perhaps Madame Cherrie Lamont, who once taught with the librarian at the now deserted school, but as she is French she doesn't count. Akona, who speaks to her plants, doesn't count either; after all, plants are not ghosts. Nor does Gypsy Cornet, who has a fanciful imagination and a taste for a tall tale. Some of the women claim to hear the sound of pipes echoing in the foothills from time to time, like pan pipes, and Och Arglin sometimes spins a story or two about what lies beyond nothing, but he's a gin-soak and nobody listens to him.

The librarian believes that the no-nonsense, practical nature of the locals is due, mainly, to a strong Puritan streak in the Presbyterian settlers from the Scottish Lowlands. The Puritan god was very much the god of no nonsense. A cold south wind moaning in the eaves is never anything more than a cold south wind moaning in the eaves. Those worthies kept the gothic at bay with large doses of common sense and a stern faith. I trust the librarian on this; she has done the research, compiling all kinds of information for her Chronicles. She has investigated the old families of Keatown, tracing their roots with loving care and attention. She will tell you that this rich vein of Puritanism is now largely played out. The old stone church built by the descendants of Ellen Johnson and her nine daughters is so bleak and forbidding even the Reverend Stickman won't go there, let alone hold services there. The Reverend Stickman, the town's self-appointed Jeremiah, the informed librarian will go on to tell you, has no credentials, either from God or any church; he is nothing more than an itinerant preacher, not so much a keeper of faith but a mere remnant of a faith no longer kept.

The reverend has one great theme, his only theme really, and that is the vanity of all things earthly, of all human strivings. He's travelled far and seen many things: vain posturing, most of it; vanity and foolishness; the blind leading the blind; the self-deceivers and unbelievers. Those cruelly deceived by the whims of the heart. Belief in ghosts is just another expression of vanity, and the Father of Vanity the Puritans named Satan.

As we descend from heaven to earth, we discover the reverend, standing in Mother Smiley's backyard, listening to that good woman's sad and vain complaints. He'd heard many complaints from Mother Smiley, particularly about her husband, Flounder Phil, but really... a ghost girl?

'Some slutty girl. Sprang out of nowhere.' Mother Smiley is a big woman with lank, mousy hair, a big mouth and lots of teeth, just made for smiling. But she isn't smiling now.

Everybody is familiar with the failings of Flounder Phil, particularly his problematic visits up mansions to sell his fish to some super-rich overlord, but this latest story is a hell of a stretch, even for the gullible and credulous.

'And he just followed her?'

'That's right. Carrying his little hand-net. And off he went after her. Trit-trot.' Mother Smiley looks as if she were about to puke.

The reverend is not the only one having trouble with this. Even Mother Smiley's staunchest allies in her ongoing battle with her useless, no-hoper husband, her sister Jolene Smiley and the ever-vigilant Grandmother Gaunt, are looking a bit queasy. Our little town may have many virtues and natural attractions, but has a chronic lack of slutty girls to go running off with. Where the grizzled Flounder Phil might find a convenient floozy with whom to abscond, not even the Reverend Stickman, well marinated in the devious ways of sin, can tell; nor can the women of the town well used to keeping a weather eye on each other – and their men. Keatown might have its little secrets, like all places, its midnight comings and goings, but it is no Sodom or Gomorrah, the reverend would concede.

'What did she look like?' The reverend keeps his voice mild, like a man of sympathy who is yet to make judgement.

'What do you think? Like those kind of girls look! Red hair all over the place, stockings with holes, a skirt no wider than a hem – and high heels.' Grandmother Gaunt, no stranger to the perfidies of men, is silent. Everybody's silent. Everybody is trying to imagine such a creature, here in Keatown.

'She was wearing high heels?'

Mother Smiley looks about frantically, as if said girl might appear out of some bordello in the sky.

'No! She was carrying them! Like a sneak!'

To the reverend's recently adopted acolyte, Rasputin, this sounds a bit too crazy to be made up. Rasputin, one of the mokopuna, so named for his black hair and flaming dark eyes, likes to stand in the shadow of his master and pay careful attention to his strictures on the nature of vanity, while, in turn, the good reverend himself is not so far above vanity that he doesn't enjoy the attentions of an acolyte. Sometimes Rasputin wonders how this happened, and if he doesn't just enjoy the flow of the reverend's language, most of it derived from the Old Testament. Somehow he never tires of hearing how the appearances of this world are nothing more than the red paint on the lips of a harlot, or hearing the words of the great Ecclesiastes, poet of doom, in the Reverend Stickman's reedy voice, 1:6 The wind goeth toward the south, and turneth about unto the north; it whirleth about continually, and the wind returneth again according to his circuits.

The young Rasputin can feel that wind now, that fickle wind of the world tickling at his ragged, Huckleberry Finn jacket.

Mother Smiley takes a deep breath and starts again. 'I was in the kitchen, thinking about breakfast. I was looking out the window.' She points to the kitchen as if everybody had forgotten where it was. 'From there I can see his shed.' She gestures accusingly at Phil's garden shed, the source of all iniquity. There it stands accused, an ordinary looking shed with two dust-encrusted windowpanes. A man-cave. Rasputin glances at it sceptically. It doesn't look like a den of iniquity or a house of whoredom, but one never knows. 'Phil came out, and then this girl appeared from behind the shed, right by the door she was, mincing along, and Phil just followed her, like a dirty dog, right across the yard and through the fence.'

'He's one sick puppy,' Jolene says.

'From up mansions.' Gaunt says, working her jaw with the effort of so much thought in the face of such improbability. 'They have sluts up there, of course they do.' She nods fervently. Jolene Smiley, with a sisterly, but firm grip on Mother Smiley's arm, nods in agreement. 'Of course they do,' she choruses.

This improvised support doesn't comfort Mother Smiley. Maybe said out loud like that made it sound unlikely to her too. It's one thing to think, another to say out loud. 'She must be somebody's child! She was young enough, Christ knows.'

Briefly, the Reverend Stickman meets Rasputin's enquiring look. As the Prophet said, there is no new thing under the sun. As long as there have been wives, husbands have been deserting them, and as long as there have been husbands, wives have been deceiving them. What they are dealing with here, the good reverend's look to his acolyte implies, is hysteria of a particularly female kind.

Rasputin is not so sure. The woman is as puzzled as she is angry.

'Why didn't you stop him?'

'I just stood there with my gob hanging open.'

Not an image to dwell on.

'Most likely he'll come back,' the reverend says in reasonable tones, and not without kindness.

'He'd better not.'

Jolene has a stroke of inspiration. 'What about that mokopuna girl, the pretty one, she goes up there, doesn't she? She might know.'

'Yes!' Gaunt is jubilant, 'and that ratty sidekick of hers.'

Attention turns to Rasputin, who blushes. He always blushes at the mention of Orchid, 'the pretty one.' It's a sensitive topic. Her visits up mansions is an even more sensitive topic. For Rasputin, the baron is a semi-mythical figure with dark powers at his command, powers he would wield over the heedless Orchid. It might all be vanity but it can still wound the heart.

'I can ask her,' he says without enthusiasm.

'I'll ask the little baggage myself,' Mother Smiley says. But she is not mollified. So what if Orchid knew the girl? What does it matter, this bit of baggage or that, they are still gone, her Phil is gone and deep in her stony heart Mother Smiley knows he will not be back, even as the reverend is suggesting that everybody pray for Phil's safe return, 'I said in mine heart, God shall judge the righteous and the wicked: for there is a time there for every purpose and for every work.'

'It was devilry,' Mother Smiley says with some cunning. There have been times when the reverend has doubted the sincerity of Mother Smiley's faith, her honesty before God, and rather suspects an opportunistic form of faith that would evoke God to suit some very human and likely venal purpose. Such 'faith' is mere vanity, of course. But in this case he is starting to suspect more than female hysteria might be involved, that something else might be afoot. The reverend has a fine nose for devilry.

'She's probably murdered him and hidden the body,' Mother Smiley says. She grins like a death-head.

Taking her sister more firmly in hand, Jolene says, 'You can't know that.' Jolene doesn't look anything like her sister, no big mouth and lots of teeth, and her hair is not lank but a rich dark, which was once full of what she called raven lights.

'That's right,' the reverend says swiftly. 'Let's not have the devil run away with our thoughts.'

'You're an expert, are you?' Grandmother Gaunt says. She's turned having a thin mouth into a fine art. 'He's probably too lily-livered to come back and face the music.'

With a quick touch on the back of his master's hand, Rasputin slips out from under the conversation, out of Mother Smiley's benighted yard and into the God-given open air.

Finding Orchid and asking her about this is not a bad plan, if he can bring his cowardly heart to heel; if he could face the girl, he might be able to face God.

the liddlest of the liddles

Sometimes little Witch Hunt dreams of having a daddy, just like Miranda. Miranda is lucky to have a daddy, and Witch Hunt is lucky to have a friend like Miranda. It seems that having a mummy is not so important if you already have a daddy. Of course, having both is the best, so Miranda is doubly lucky since she has both, which makes Witch Hunt doubly lucky to have Miranda as a friend because Witch Hunt doesn't have a mummy either. Not a proper mummy anyway – the details are a bit vague in her mind.

Witch Hunt is the littlest of the mokopuna. They call Little Sanyo 'little', and so he is, but he's not as little as Witch Hunt. Witch Hunt is the littlest of the littles, as Miranda, dear sweet Miranda who can sometimes be a little cruel, likes to point out. Actually, what she says is 'the liddlest of the liddles.' Right now Witch Hunt is busy being just that, tagging along after Miranda, who is tagging after Orchid and Mary, who are tagging after Sad Toof and Sirocco, who are, in turn, following Little Sanyo who's got something to show everybody. Which is just like him. Last time he had something to show everybody, they all had to go down the south coast to see a live dog in a bamboo cage. Apparently – little Sanyo had it all worked out – the dog had been tossed off a ship, or tipped off in a storm, and had survived because the bamboo floated. Little Sanyo was very excited, but the dog looked beyond caring. Sirocco had solemnly let him out and fed him some fish scraps the dog ate faster than anybody had ever seen in their lives. That dog is still around, somewhere.

As they are making their way up a zigzag trail that leads to the top of Pine Point where Little Sanyo's something-to-show-everybody is to be found, Witch Hunt is preoccupied with a serious problem: how is she going to tell Miranda that she has seen her daddy? Has actually seen him. Because dear sweet Miranda – who can be cruel sometimes, mostly out of thoughtlessness – might sneer and jeer. Might even bite her. Witch Hunt loves Miranda, totally and without reservation. She would be offended if someone suggested that her love was tinged with envy, which made it all the more hurtful when Miranda did her sneer and jeer. And her biting, the hurt always going deeper than the teeth marks. The last thing Witch Hunt wants is hurt. That awful heart-hurt.

But she saw her daddy. Of that there can be no doubt. It was just this morning, in fact, with the sun still low on the water making the light jump about. She had been at Miranda's place looking out the window. They'd just got out of bed, and Miranda had been grumpy, the way she usually is when she gets out of bed. Witch Hunt always goes very quiet when Miranda gets grumpy, and does all sorts of unobtrusive, innocent things like looking out the window until Miranda gets even grumpier and instructs her to 'stop creeping about like a frightened little mouse.' How can she when that's what she is – a frightened little mouse? This time, when she looked out the window she saw somebody. A man. Her daddy. She knew it was her daddy because he was carrying a briefcase and looking very important, heading off to somewhere very important, not looking right or left, and his lips were moving as he repeated very important things. If he had just looked to the left, he would have seen her there, standing at the window, but he didn't because he had important business. That's one thing daddies always seem to have. Like Miranda's daddy, who's called Blade, always has to be going off to the fish shed where his blade flashes and the creamy red guts of the fish spill out.

Maybe it would be better if she blurts it all out and just says, 'Miranda, guess what, I've just seen my daddy,' and Miranda would turn and give her a pretty smile to go with her golden curls and her turned-up nose and everything would be lovely. Or it might be better if she led up to it by saying something like, 'Guess who I saw this morning out the window?' and Miranda would say 'Who?' and Witch Hunt would then say 'My daddy' and everything would be lovely.

One way or another, everything would be lovely. And there would be no biting.

They have reached the top of Pine Point now and are moving through the mysterious pine trees. Witch Hunt always finds the pine forest quite spooky, although she doesn't tell Miranda that as Miranda might laugh at her and call her a scaredy-cat. But a pine forest has a special kind of silence it's hard to ignore, and the dead pine needles have a funny way of whispering when you walk on them. In bare feet, they can make a tickle prickle. That special silence of the pines is a secretive kind of silence, which suggests to her that maybe it would be better not to tell Miranda about seeing Daddy, since no matter which way she approached it, Miranda might not understand and might accuse her of making it up, and making things up is a bad thing to do, even though Miranda does it all the time. Sneer-and-jeer doesn't like liddle liars. Liddle liars get bitten.

The pines counsel silence, and Witch Hunt is inclined to listen.

Little Sanyo has led them through the pines to a rocky headland overlooking the steep northern face of Pine Point, and further north to the great shingle fan of a riverbed with rocks as white as bones.

Little Sanyo stands proudly on the headland and points triumphantly down.

He says, 'There! Look at that!'

the prophecy of the waters

The waters of the Wai-O-Tapu spring come clean and strong out of the earth. The sound it makes is unique, between a rush and a roar. As soon as Akona hears it, she pauses. The spring is now just ahead, beyond a lip of rocks from which the Mak flows, and she needs a moment to compose herself, to quiet her turbulent heart, even put aside her sadness, before facing her tipuna, her ancestors. They have a way of appearing at the spring when she is there, and her vision, if that's what it was, of Grandfather Lawrence, was like a eclipse of the moon, full of portent.

Preparing herself for such a meeting means gathering herself into a fine point, like the sharp tip of the five-finger leaf, for there is no way of meeting these ancestors without bringing forth her own warrior. Her tipuna are a dark and formidable bunch, and don't meet just to pass the time. They always test her mettle.

When she comes within sight of the spring, she pauses again. Here it is, not much larger than a pond, looking as if the water were boiling out of the ground. From a distance it might look small, but she can feel the trembling of the earth beneath her feet, and the agitation of the air above. Her grandmother Naira once told her that the spirits of the air mated with the spirits of water as the air hungry water broke from the ground, and Akona doesn't doubt that now, as she stands before it. She can taste the ecstasy in the air.

She doesn't approach the spring directly. That's no way to approach a sacred spot, Naira would say, when the child Akona just wanted to bounce right on up to it. She edges around it, moving from the east towards the south, keeping a respectful distance.

There will be a point of entry, like a gateway to the sacred, but it changes all the time, shifting through the points of the compass. There is a significance to which direction it might open, but Akona has forgotten much of what Naira told her, except that it can only be found through the heart. 'You must open your heart to find the gateway, taimati,' Naira would say. 'Otherwise Wai-O-Tapu is nothing more than some water coming out of the ground.'

She passes through the south and southwest, but there is no sense of opening. 'The threshold is hidden,' she says to herself, 'hidden in the air.' But you need a humble heart to sense it; the tipuna grow angry at mortal arrogance, preferring their own, immortal kind. She passes through the west and into the north west. Still nothing. Still no sense of easing. At the same time the wind doesn't feel quite right to her. There's a faint odour, the musty smell she noticed downwind of the Lawrence figure.

It isn't until she gets past the north to the north east that she feels the air give a little, and the opening is there. With her head lowered in prayer to those who came before her, she steps across the threshold. One step closer to the spring.

As soon as she does so, her diaphragm expands, her lungs open, and she sings in a voice she hardly recognises as her own.

'The north wind caresses my body,
carries a fond past –
I mourn
in sorrow for my kin
lost to me in the spirit world.

Where are they now?
Where are those absent friends
who once lived so well?

The time of separation has come,
leaving me desolate.'

A long silence follows. Her voice disappears as if into a deep well. The wind dies away. It feels as if the silence itself is rushing up from deep within the earth. She waits patiently, looking around her, happy to connect with earth, sky and sea.

Up here she can't see Keatown, which is hidden by a foothill, and she can't see the mansions either, although the ridge along which they are built is clearly visible to the north east. She could be alone in the world. To the west stands the noble Irirangi, clear and proud. To the east, the ocean. These things look eternal, but she knows that they are not. Mountains can crack open. The sea will go sour, unable to breathe as it gets too hot. Coastlines will dissolve like clouds in the blue air.

She takes another step forward, and another until she is at the edge of the spring. She watches, fascinated, as the water rushes up from the earth. How mysterious it is, at heart, for who could say what drove it, such a mass, against the force of gravity. It is nothing less than an upwelling of life, and she bows her head before it.

One more step and her feet are in the water, feeling the tingle of it all the way up her body. She can't take it for long, it's too cold, but it gives her a rush of energy, a strength that comes from deep in the ground. Up through the soles of the feet it comes, up through the bones of her legs. When she finally pulls them out her legs will ache like hell, but it's worth it.

'Why sing of dispossession?' a voice says quietly. It is her great grandfather Nōpera Kāmaka. A proud man by all accounts. Proud and brave, prepared to suffer at the hands of his own family for his love for the lily white Charlotte Kensington. His father, Ihake Kāmaka, being the head man of the marae, had banished the couple from the tribe's ancestral land. Nōpera knew as much about dispossession as anybody, but had never lost his gentle touch.

'I feel it in the wind,' she says, pulling one foot out of the spring. She was aching to sit down, but she didn't want to show any disrespect to her tipuna.

'What is in the wind?' This is another voice, Nōpera's mother, Te Ao, wife of Ihaka. They are all crowding around now, her Maori tipuna. 'What's wrong with the world?'

'Everything,' Akona says. 'There's a foulness in the wind.'

'You must prepare yourself,' a new voice says. This is Taika. Ihaka's father, her own great great great grandfather. He doesn't often appear because he doesn't understand the land under the sway of the white invaders. He still dreams of hunting moa and eating the brains of his enemies. He is held in great reverence by the other tipuna, who are silent, in case Taika should want to say more. He doesn't, and the wind blows over Akona's cold feet.

'Prepare myself for what?'

'What you will have to do.' This is Naira now, her grandmother. 'Where is your vengeance?'

There is a rustle of agreement.

The memory came stabbing back. Because of what happened to her own daughter, Manaia, Akona's mother, Naira, despite her kindness, died bitter and resentful and stayed that way.

'You remember.' Naira says, a touch of cruelty in her voice. She knows Akona hates to remember, because Akona's soul was almost destroyed the day her parents died. 'It was an act of war, you remember?'

Akona prefers not to remember. To remember is to open old wounds.

'The woman is a coward,' old Taika says with contempt. The women of his generation were real women, women of power, women of strength, women who walked with pride and mana.

'You have a burden,' Nōpera says quietly. 'One day you will put it down.'

Taika snorts. Nōpera had been hopelessly compromised by the missionaries, as far as Taika could make out. Better to put out your enemy's eyes.

'The day of the Christening,' Nōpera says. 'That will be the day.'

'And it can't come too soon,' Naira says, 'but will she be prepared for it?'

'Your blood runs in her veins.'

They are fading now. Before they leave, she catches a brief glimpse of their physical forms. Taika, the tallest of them all, dressed in a magnificent moa feather cloak, seems to lift into the air. Naira, her face like a thundercloud, seems to sink into the earth. 'The children of sorrow have come,' she says.

And Akona is alone. The waters of M continue to bubble. As she pulls back, her lips begin to form the words of the song she sang when crossing the threshold. Particularly those lines,

Where are they now?

Where are those absent friends
who once lived so well?

She doesn't know why she should have chosen this lament for land stolen by the white invaders, nor does she fully understand the prophecy, except that it might have something to do with the Baby. Like the nostalgia it celebrates, the song itself must be borne away on the waters of the Wai-O-Tapu. And it will take the children of sorrow away with it. She doesn't know who the children of sorrow are, but they are close, as close as the songs of the dead, as close as the illusions of the living.

She sits by the spring until the afternoon turns pale and it is time to return to Keatown.

Time to prepare.

a most peculiar couple

By the time Rasputin locates the others, and catches up with them at Pine Point, he finds the mokopuna gathered at a vantage point overlooking the northern coastline.

Trying not to immediately look at Orchid, Rasputin is well aware of the odd status the mokopuna, as a group, have with the good folk of Keatown. They are leftover kids, the outcasts, casualties of the early days of the Long Emergency, who run wild and, in the eyes of the inhabitants, have grown half feral. Rasputin himself is exactly one of those, left in the care of the reverend by parents who had grown tired of being parents and always poor, who left him in the care of whoever would take him, which in the end turned out to be the goodly reverend himself.

Orchid had a father, still does, in name at least. When his fortune went down he took to patrolling their property armed with a machete, hunting for trespassers. Orchid left him when he nearly hacked off the arm of a young fisherman who came for a midnight visit to daddy's little girl. She went and lived with Hera who was strong enough to brave down the machete-mad father, who subsequently went into retreat and has hardly been seen since.

Then there is the strange case of the inscrutable runt, that desert creature they call Sirocco, who used to be called Age until he changed his name. Apparently Gypsy Cornet found him wandering in the desert talking to himself. The Reverend Stickman didn't like Sirocco from the start, doesn't trust him. 'He's a pagan, he worships a lizard god,' the reverend counsels him. That makes Rasputin curious, as he's never met a real pagan before, unless you count Akona whose composting toilet might qualify her as one, but Sirocco eludes him, eludes them all, slips like a lizard from one rock to another when he moves, blends in when he sits still. If he worships a lizard god he never says anything about it. The sands of the desert have long since obliterated tracks any parents might have left. It is said, with some cruelty, that maybe his mother was a lizard because of the way his eyelids hang halfway down his eyeballs.

And the rest of them, godless Sad Toof, stuck permanently in the Slough of Despond, who stays mostly at the marae because his parents gave up on him and moved north looking for work; the freak Little Sanyo with singing in his head who sleeps under people's houses because his parents got killed in a car crash; the snivelling Witch Hunt whose mother stays drunk all the time and whose father left one day and never came back. And Typhoid Mary who turned up one day out of nowhere and attached herself to Orchid. A secretive girl with a pock-marked face and a grey scarf she always wears around her neck, she never speaks of any parents or any background at all. She jumped out from behind a toadstool, is what the reverend once said about her.

Of the mokopuna, only Miranda boasts a full set of operating parents, although none of them envies her having Jolene for a mother. Or Blade for a father for that matter. 'Mum tries too hard,' Miranda once said, 'and dad doesn't try at all.' When she was very little he would try to feed her and she would try to bite his finger off. He soon gave up.

These are Rasputin's friends, the crowd he runs with, the souls he would one day, according to the reverend, lead to God. I have to find God myself, first, he tells the reverend. Don't worry, the reverend says, God will find you.

God may not have found him yet, but Orchid has; as rough as a tousled-haired tomboy one moment, as graceful as a Psalm the next, Rasputin has no defence against her sly beauty. His heart blazes in his chest, which is not a pleasant feeling, whenever he sees her. Vanity, vanity, sayeth the Preacher. He both welcomes and dreads the opportunity to talk to her about Flounder Phil's disappearance and Mother Smiley's slutty girl. He welcomes the prospect of her eyes on his face, which might with its lock of dark hair across his wide forehead be considered handsome, yet dreads the thought of blushing in front of her. Vanity, vanity! And how's he going to talk about slutty girls without blushing? Does God have any idea what he does to us?

There's no opportunity to broach the subject immediately anyway, the others are too preoccupied watching something. At first he can't see what they're looking at as he looks down the northern slope of Pine Point. Then he does. Not far below them an aged couple, man and woman, toil up the slope, weirdly coming up the steepest part instead of detouring a little inland, around the peninsula, where the slope is easier and a trail to be found. Or they could have just followed the road, the most sensible option.

'Look at them! They haven't stopped once, not even for water,' Little Sanyo says to Rasputin.

'Not even to take a breather,' Miranda says.

While the couple climb together, they neither speak nor look at each other, choosing their separate ways as if the other does not exist.

'They don't look at each other,' Orchid tells Rasputin. She's in tomboy mode in floppy dungarees with a loose flannel shirt rolled up to slender elbows and opened at the front with careless calculation. With her elfin grace and her straw-tousled hair she looks like a scarecrow brought to life by a cruel witch for the purpose of tormenting hopeless fellows like Rasputin, with his lock of dark hair escaping from his theology, and his dark eyes hunting about for somewhere else to look. Somewhere God says it's okay to look.

The man is silver-haired, well preserved and urbane, in a white shirt, black bow tie, a neat, formal suit with a long-tailed jacket, looking as if he's just stepped from some official reception, or dropped in from the mansions, carrying what might have been an iPad. The woman is in old baggy jeans, a shapeless T-shirt top and a dirty apron which hardly hides her floppy tits, looking like the cleaning lady on a bad day.

'I don't believe this,' Orchid says. She turns to Sirocco. 'I don't like them.'

'Where the fuck did they come from?' Mary says. She has a habit of tugging at the scarf around her neck, as if wanting to loosen it.

'That's what we'd all like to know,' Sirocco says.

It seems that Typhoid Mary can never open her mouth without some profanity emerging. Rasputin has no time now to spend disliking Mary, an unsavoury, cunning little deceiver with a spiky hairdo, a pock-marked face and a nasty tongue. How Orchid can be best friends with her is beyond him, beyond any mortal reasoning. Truth is, Rasputin can see something about Mary none of the others seem to see, that she has an agenda, a purpose, and that includes Orchid in some way. Rasputin doesn't know what the agenda is, or what Mary has in mind for Orchid, but sooner or later he'll find out.

They are innocent in many ways, these mokopuna, Rasputin thinks. Even Sirocco, the lizard worshipper.

Rasputin gets the feeling that Sirocco doesn't like Mary much either, but maybe not for the same reasons as Rasputin: vanity, before God; jealousy, before God. Nothing he can feel proud of.

'What're we going to do?' Miranda says. There's a bit of a wail in her voice.

Rasputin sees that at moments of crisis, especially when the twins get upset, Sirocco the pagan becomes the de facto leader of the mokopuna, the one who should know what to do. What qualifies the runt, as the adults call him, the desert rat, to this role is a mystery to Rasputin. Maybe it's because he just seems to know things sometimes.

'They look like… pilgrims,' Rasputin says. He's not sure why he says this. It's certainly not how the couple are dressed. More likely it's the way they never look back, or how steadfast they are in their labour. Unhurried and unflappable.

The strange couple are not far down from the watchers now. If they looked up they would easily have seen the curious faces looking down at them, but they don't, not once. They just keep climbing, steadily, patiently, concentrating on the next step.

'Hello? Hello there!' Sirocco calls. The couple take no notice.

'I don't like them,' Orchid says.

Everybody feels the same way; nobody can quite put it into words.

'They won't answer,' Little Sanyo says, as if he knows something the others don't.

'They're not doin' anybody any harm.' Sad Toof says.

'I can hear something,' Sirocco says.

'Like singing,' Orchid says.

'It's just that funny wind,' Little Sanyo says. It's not as bad as it was on the beach, but it hasn't gone away, that funny wind. Every now and again they hear it in the uneasy creaking of the pine trees around them.

'They don't look dangerous,' Mary says to Orchid, who doesn't look convinced.

'How can y' tell?' Sad Toof says. 'They might be comin' up here t' kill us.'

'Nice one, Sad Toof,' Mary says. 'Go suck your tooth.'

Sirocco finds that the odd couple reminds him of his Rose Lady, but he doesn't know why.

'They're creepy,' Orchid says. Tiny gold hairs are standing up straight on her pale, freckled arm.

Nobody disagrees.

Witch Hunt holds Miranda's hand, and Miranda does not shake her loose.

There are never any strangers in Keatown, not now. Everybody knows everybody, even if just to say hello to.

The mokopuna draw back as the couple clamber over the last rocks. They don't stop to relieve an aching muscle or take stock of their new position, or congratulate themselves on their successful climb, they simply pass right on by, looking only ahead, apparently not seeing the cluster of silent mokopuna.

'When Lot's wife looked back she was turned into a pillar of salt,' Rasputin says, not quite knowing why he was reminded of that text. 'In the Old Testament story, Lot and his wife were fleeing the city before destruction rained upon it. But they weren't allowed to look back. Lot's wife does.'

'So what?' Mary has little time for his biblical allusions.

'Maybe they can't look back,' Rasputin says. There's a horror taking shape at the back of his mind. Some awful visage. He tries to banish it but it comes back again. It comes back again and it knows his name. It knows him and he knows it, and if he's not careful it will swallow him whole, like the whale that swallowed the disobedient Jonah.

'Hi there!' Sirocco calls, breaking the hushed, eerie silence of the pines. 'Can you hear me? Who are you?'

The man seems to hear, for he frowns and half turns his head as if there were something he would like to remember. The woman takes no notice. They look as if they have been hypnotised.

And they keep walking. They don't for a moment pause.

Rasputin feels his stomach begin to crawl, as if it were full of maggots. The way they walk, looking only in front of them, the way they ignore everything around them; there is something profoundly wrong about them. Something horribly unnatural, despite their ordinary appearance. 'Godless,' he says aloud. It was as if they weren't properly alive at all.

'I hate them!' Miranda screeches. 'They're horrible.'

'Calm down,' Mary tells her, but Miranda has hit a nerve. For all their unassuming manner, there's something relentless and implacable in the unhurried way the couple move. And there's an aura around them, as if they were sleepwalkers, and that goosebumpy tickle on the skin is telling you that if you get too close to them you might get swept up into their nightmare. Their eyes betray nothing of their feelings. If they have any.

'They're not going to hurt you,' Mary says, tugging at her scarf. 'I don't think they know you exist.'

'You don't know that,' Sad Toof says.

'I wish you'd shut the fuck up,' Mary says to him. 'What do you know about it anyway?'

'Not much,' Sad Toof confesses.

'Maybe they're deaf,' Witch Hunt says brightly. 'So they can't hear us.' Witch Hunt herself was once afraid of going deaf. That's when she was sick and couldn't hear anything.

'They're not bloody blind,' Mary says, 'yet they don't see us.'

'You don't know that,' Sad Toof says.

'That's right,' Little Sanyo says. 'They might see us but just not care.'

'That's right,' Sad Toof says, 'I mean, why should they care?'

'I still hate them,' Miranda says.

'Christ!' Mary says and shakes her head. She takes out a packet of cigarettes, perhaps the same packet she showed Annanda, and ostentatiously lights up using a fancy looking metal lighter. She blows the smoke into the air like a circus performer exhaling flames.

'I'm with Miranda on this one,' Orchid says, and gives the younger girl a rueful smile, momentarily gladdening Miranda's heart. She loves any attention she gets from Orchid.

The couple are negotiating the pines just fine, not bumping up against them. They look so small and ordinary, plodding along. This is it, Rasputin thinks: I bear witness to the destruction of everything. To the opening of the floodgates. For that most terrible of all things, the withdrawal of God's grace from the world. Might as well snuff out the sun.

The blood drains from his face and he feels dizzy, nauseous. He finds a pine stump and sits down. He tries to find a prayer but there are no words. Luckily everybody is too busy watching the plodding couple continue their methodical way, steering between the trees, to pay much attention to Rasputin.

'Let's follow them,' Little Sanyo is saying, as if they were all on some kind of fun picnic. The others don't need much encouragement and straggle off.

Orchid doesn't though. She lingers. Joins Rasputin. For the first time in what seems like forever to Rasputin, they are alone.

the feet of a famous dancer

'Are you okay?' she says when the others have gone.

A smile would be a nice reply, if he could manage one. Someone told him once that he had a nice smile, one that showed his lovely white teeth. But he can't manage one, even for her, because God is pouring revelations through his head too fast for thought. Images rushing by in a torrent of the destruction of Keatown and the rise of the Pilgrims. All he can do is sit helplessly and watch. Death will come one way, or another. It will walk on stilts or it will slither in the night. And it will have one face, the face of the Pilgrims of Darkness.

Orchid sits beside him and takes hold of his arm, which is trembling, and holds it gently. He draws strength from that, strength he needs to face God's unwelcome news. What does God want of him? To become Keatown's very own prophet of doom, perhaps. As if the Reverend Stickman is not enough with his constant cries of vanity, vanity.

Despite all this, and God's best efforts to keep his attention – for there is more to come – he finds it overwhelming to be with Orchid, alone, no Mary in attendance, and his heart feels as if the devil himself were squeezing it, and he is painfully aware of her slim freckly arms and open shirt. She doesn't help by moving up closer to him, their knees touching. There was a time, before the arrival of the Baby, and Mary, and God, when he and Orchid would have the run of Keatown, giving cheek to Akona, or throwing stones on the roof of Flay's Garage and running away yelling when Flay came after them swearing and waving his shotgun. Her sitting beside him now evokes that childhood togetherness, but it is not that. It is far from that. Tomboy doesn't come anywhere near it, not anymore.

It is all different now, and here they are, trembling in that difference, or at least he is. Surely his feelings must be an open book to her, as they are to God.

'You don't have to talk,' she says.

But he does. It's the one thing he has to do. It is his duty before God to find the words for the horror he sees in front of him, the great creeping death these sleepwalkers are bringing with them. He just doesn't want her to be the first to hear them.

Orchid squeezes his arm in sympathy. Her hands are small and smooth and pure and unbearably vulnerable. Slowly, he says, 'God's pilgrims always keep the Holy City before them, no matter what. A shining vision.' He has to pause again. The words are a long way off. He has to search to find them. 'If Satan had pilgrims, their eyes would be fixed on the Gates of Hell. No matter what.'

'You're a deep one, aren't you,' she says. Her eyes are a moody, ocean blue. Dark one moment, full of phosphorescence the next.

He blushes. He knew he would. It was just a matter of time. And his pale skin is a dead giveaway. He tries not to look at her. 'Those two are just a sign.'

'A sign of what?'

He shrugs. There is much God has not revealed to him, much there is to happen.

'The doom of Keatown.'

Orchid drops her tomboy mask. Her face grows serious – and more beautiful. He sees the woman she could become, might become, and there is nothing more glorious in the sight of God. 'How do you know?'

'I can see it. I don't want to see it.' Suddenly he just wants to get away as far as he can from God's terrible presence.

She nods. 'We have to think about what we can do,' she says, mostly to herself.

'What can we do?' As Rasputin sees it, there is no way around the judgement of God.

'I don't know.' She smiles. 'You never know what might turn up.'

Of course, something always turns up.

Rasputin smiles in return. He feels much older than her, even though he is not. Such naivety! Such a touching faith that things will turn out right in the end.

'You never know,' he says, surprised by the gentleness in his voice. After all, that's what the grace of God is, something turning up. 'Have you been visiting some of the mansions?'

The question takes her by surprise, but she doesn't remove her hand from his arm.

'I'm taking dancing lessons with a wonderful teacher called Zhenhua. She said I could be famous one day, with my dancing. We could do a tour of Europe.'

Her sudden enthusiasm, and the light in her eyes, makes him feel hopeless and sad. How frivolous it all seems – vanity indeed! – with the Pilgrims of Darkness at their door and God breathing down his neck. But it is not frivolous to her. A tour of Europe, fame and fortune on the stage and before the cameras! What urchin girl from Keatown might not dream, and in that dream be ensnared?

'Is that likely to happen?' He isn't trying to be cruel; he really wants to know. Perhaps this Zhenhua person can wave a magic wand and make it all happen just the way Orchid imagines it. The Reverend Stickman has often spoken of the 'dark arts' practised by the super celebs up mansions: witches who live by breathing air alone, dogs with devil genes, drugs that can transport the user to the underworld, a bronze statue of a female demon that could talk, an infantile genius who can think in mathematics... and Rasputin thought he was exaggerating, even to the point of chiding his master for falling into superstition, reminding him that God is our only bulwark against such superstition. Now he begins to wonder if the reverend were not speaking the literal truth.

To his gratitude, she takes the question seriously. Her enthusiasm fades. 'There are... other things to take care of.' She looks down at her feet. They are still there, bare and urchin like. The feet of a famous dancer. One day. She rubs them against the prickly pine needles.

He doesn't ask what these 'other things' might be; he will learn about them soon enough.

In the rustling, pine-tree silence that follows, they hear the shouts of the others. Orchid takes hold of his hand and interlaces his fingers with hers. Happiness spreads through his body as if God himself has touched him.

how the driftdead got their name

By the time Rasputin and Orchid catch up with the others, earning a dirty look from Mary, Little Sanyo is about to conduct an experiment. He is waving a stick like a band conductor.

'I'm going to touch them with this stick. Then we'll know they really exist.'

'We know they exist now,' Sad Toof says. He often has problems with Little Sanyo's logic. What difference is touching them with a stick going to make?

Little Sanyo is dancing along beside the couple, poking his stick at them but not getting too close. Sad Toof trudges along behind him, shaking his head. Sirocco, looking worried, runs to catch up with them, and the twins run to catch up with Sirocco.

'I'd be careful if I was you,' Sirocco says to Little Sanyo.

'Maybe we can only see them and hear them, like ghosts,' Little Sanyo says. Maybe they don't exist, Little Sanyo thinks, except in our minds, like memories we thought we'd forgotten, like a little girl with impossibly white legs crossing Nightshade Track.

'They're not ghosts,' Sad Toof says. 'Any poor galoot can see that.'

Little Sanyo pauses to inspect his stick. It's a piece of pine, dried and old, wouldn't hurt a fly. 'I said like ghosts. I'm going to touch them anyway.' Maybe on touch they will deflate, like the belly of the dead fish he saw. Or pop out of existence like soapbubbles.

'Then shove that stick between their legs. See if they fall over.' Sad Toof laughs at what he sees as his great wit but nobody joins him.

'That's a silly idea,' Sirocco says. 'You don't know what will happen.'

'Do not provoke the Pilgrims of Darkness,' Rasputin says solemnly.

The others all stare at Rasputin. They have stopped now and have formed a rough circle. The strange couple continue their unhurried progress. Little Sanyo finds a better stick. Not so dry. Stronger. 'I have to know,' he says.

'They might eat you all up,' Witch Hunt says.

This time nobody laughs at her silly comment except Mary.

'I have to know,' Little Sanyo repeats, and takes off after the couple. The others follow. When he reaches them, he dances around them, ready to take flight at any moment, and taps the man lightly on the shoulder. The man doesn't take any notice. Little Sanyo hits him a bit harder. The man takes no notice of that either.

'He feels solid enough,' Little Sanyo reports.

'That doesn't prove anything,' Sad Toof says.

'It proves they're not an illusion.'

'No it doesn't.' Not that Sad Toof thought for one moment that they were illusions.

Little Sanyo says nothing. He's learned that once Sad Toof starts on this line of thought, nothing can ever prove anything about anything except how sad and unfair and toothache-filled life really is.

They have stopped again and stand around, not knowing what to do.

'I wonder if we could kill them?' Little Sanyo is thinking aloud again.

'You're a sick puppy,' Miranda says admiringly. She likes that phrase. Her mother, Jolene, uses it all the time. According to her, everybody is a sick puppy if you look hard enough, and long enough.

'The thing is,' says Sad Toof, pulling at the sad side of his jaw, 'could they kill us?' The idea seems to give him some pleasure.

Nobody says anything to that. Silently they accompany the strange pair who continue their methodical way, steering gently between the trees. It hits Rasputin that while these two might be travelling in the same direction, south, at roughly the same speed, they are not travelling together; their being together is no more than a coincidence of time and space. At any point he might take one path and she another. Each walks their own path alone.

'But who are they?' says Witch Hunt. At first she thought they must be friends of her daddy, at least the man since he looked grand enough, but now she's not so sure. The man doesn't look like a friend of daddy's, or anybody's. And the woman with the apron won't even look at her. She clings closer to Miranda who for once doesn't seem to mind. 'And where are they going?' They have to be going somewhere, so intent and tireless their movements. Everybody's going somewhere.

They can find no resting place, Rasputin thinks, those who must travel through inconsequential worlds, doomed to trudge forever through the Dark One's illusory dimensions.

'We shouldn't follow them,' Rasputin says, and stops.

The others hesitate. Little Sanyo jumps from one foot to the other.

'Why not?' Sirocco asks.

'Because they are Pilgrims of Darkness, and you do not want to become their fellow travellers.'

'But I want to see where they go,' Little Sanyo says, about to run off after them.

'They're going to the Gates of Hell, that's where they're going. And you don't want to be of their company.'

'I won't follow them that far,' Little Sanyo says.

'They're zombies,' Witch Hunt says. That's what her daddy is, now; that's why he didn't see her. And that's why she is becoming so afraid.

'Zombies chase you, silly,' Miranda says, but she doesn't sound too sure of herself. She's a bit vague about zombies, but she knows they want to eat people all the time. This pair aren't interested in that. Or maybe they're just not hungry yet. But zombies are always hungry, aren't they?

'Naw,' says Little Sanyo. 'They're the driftdead.' He's already moving away, through the trees, following the couple that aren't a couple. Sad Toof follows him.

Like the storm stuff thrown up on the beaches he scours, Little Sanyo has found a word, coined a term, and that word is to stick, despite all the best efforts of the Reverend Stickman and others to replace it with zombies or hellspawn or the Godcurst or even just the strangers. A new word is born.

The driftdead it is. Not alive. Not dead. Drifting. Drifting between the worlds of aliveness and deadness. Drifting, inexorably, towards the Gates of Hell, the City of the Damned, if you were to believe Rasputin, who will always think of them as the Pilgrims of Darkness. Satan is calling these Pilgrims to him. He has wiped their minds clean and replaced them with a simple imperative: come to me. And so they come. And more will come.

Come to me! Rasputin hears the call. It comes from far off, but at the same time it's horribly close. 'Whatever you call them, we shouldn't be following them,' Rasputin says, but he is too, along with the others. He's following after Little Sanyo. Yet he can tell Orchid agrees with him by the way she turns her face towards him.

They can't do much more following anyway, as they have by this time tracked their way back over Pine Point and have nearly reached the southern cliff face.

'I'm going to see what they do,' Little Sanyo says and races off.

The others straggle behind with varying levels of unwillingness.

'They'll fall off the cliff and die,' Miranda says to Witch Hunt, who very much wants to see that. She wants to see them walk blindly over the cliff and drop. She wants to see them very dead, not just pretend-dead. While Witch Hunt pulls Miranda along after Little Sanyo, and Sirocco and Sad Toof keep each other company behind them, it is Rasputin, Orchid and Mary who bring up the rear.

Rasputin can't talk to Orchid with Mary around. The connection is fragile enough. Orchid seems to feel the same as she keeps a moody silence, wrapped away in herself and apart from both of them, her moment of sympathy for him gone and forgotten, he thinks. Now she is the way she's always been. Unapproachable. Unreadable. A keeper of secrets.

Mary says to Rasputin, 'So what do you think this is all about?' She finishes her cigarette and grinds it beneath her heel.

So rarely does she address him, Rasputin is taken aback and immediately on the alert. Ah, she is inviting him to make a fool of himself, to look stupid in the eyes of Orchid. Then they can both laugh at him and despise him. Then he'll be what the pock-faced Mary wants him to be for perverted reasons of her own, an object of derision, someone she can grind beneath her heel.

He has to search in that difficult place to find the right words. The wrong ones just won't do, and will have the taint of lies about them. Once he's found the right words, whatever they are, and given them shape, it won't matter if they despise him or not, it won't make any difference. At least to the outcome. The right words are like a bridge which will take him across the chasm, the great chaos of unmeaning that is the real enemy of God. But not now, not for Mary. 'I think you should pray,' he says.

At the south side of Pine Point, where the cliff drops sharply towards the sea, Sirocco stands with the others watching the retreating couple Little Sanyo has called the driftdead, toiling uselessly down the rocky promontory, which scours deep into the land, helping to create Keatown's mini deep-water port. It's a silly way to go, since there is a track that leads around the cliff edge to an easy descent to Highway 6. It's even sillier because they can only get so far, to a point where they either retreat or throw themselves into the sea.

'They'll throw themselves into the sea and drown,' Miranda says.

'Maybe they won't drown,' Sad Toof says, getting a dirty look from Witch Hunt. He's always been a meanie. Miranda explained once that it was his sad tooth that made him like that.

'Wind's blowing in the wrong direction,' Sirocco says. He can smell the desert in it, a smell that shouldn't be there since it is coming in from the sea. It should smell of the sea, not of tussock and rock. He remembers the wind thrumming through the wires down from the mountains, clean and cold and strange, like an omen of the Rose Woman's passing. His Rose Woman, the first of the driftdead. Lizard is here, he thinks as he stares into the past and up towards Mt Irirangi. He's back. I just can't see him yet. Sooner or later he'll show himself.

Little Sanyo jumps up and down in excitement. 'It must be stronger down there. Look, it's attacking the town.'

It is a colourful way of putting it, but nevertheless true. Up on Pine Point they can barely feel it, just a rubbing on the skin, but below, columns of sand have crossed back over the sandhills, over Nightshade

Track, and are tearing up the town. They stream in long sinuous lines, wreathing the roundabout and fingering up towards the houses. The adults are swarming around like a cluster of disturbed insects, trying to mount a defence of the town with shovels and sandbags. The mayor, our impresario, is a man who knows when his moment has come, how, in the face of adversity, to rise above common humanity into true leadership. Even from Pine Point the mokopuna can identify his unmistakable figure strutting at the forefront of the defences, directing this and misdirecting that, dashing about importantly.

Then it all gets blotted out in the fury of the sandstorm. Great columns of sand writhe into the blue air as if to a snake charmer's flute before bending over and hurling themselves down onto the town.

'Look!' Only Witch Hunt cares that the two driftdead have thrown themselves calmly into the ocean and are dog-paddling into the heaving bay. Where they will drown. They have to drown.

The wind coming off the ocean is mixed with salt and sand, flecks of foam, the musk of seaweed, darker scents from deeper down – and spiders, tiny spiders from the marram grass tunnelling helplessly through the air. Some rise so high they float past the mokopuna on their spiderweb cushions, buoyed by the churn of the sandsnakes below.

The pine trees start to scream.

Sirocco does what the desert taught him to do in a sandstorm: hunker down and make himself as round and as smooth as possible. In such storms, Lizard has the remarkable capacity to merge into rock and become a part of its grain. Little Sanyo runs back into the pines. Sad Toof looks for a pine tree to hide behind; he finds a tree but can't work out where 'behind' might be. Witch Hunt and Miranda grab each other and start screaming in each other's faces.

For Rasputin it's far worse than anything like that. The godforsaken wind blows straight out of the Gates of Hell. There is the stench of the fiend's curse in it. It howls through his mind, demon-driven, surging up onto the peninsula and lashing Pine Point with foam and sand.

The mokopuna scatter like clumps of spinifex.

Rasputin feels the hand of God descend and snatch him up. Just in time.

TEMPEST

Book Two

but always it moaned

For many days the wind blew from the ocean, freighting in a great bulk of sand to pile up against every available surface, tempering corners with an insidious softness and sifting down from eaves and ceilings. Walls, streets, fences, roads, all vanished into the general, implacable undulation. Sometimes it was quiet, constant and forever, or quick and violent, but always it moaned. From a simple rustle to a chainsaw roar – there was never any true quiet.

Sirocco's infant wind had grown into a serious adolescence. It might obliterate the town just as easily as it obliterated a few marks in the dust under a crab apple tree. Turn the library and all its books into an underground tomb forever. Another twenty-four hours, we weary inhabitants might have abandoned Keatown to its fate and moved on – but few had anywhere to go, and there is a bitter, backs-to-the-wall grimness in the inhabitants' battle with Little Sanyo's sandsnakes.

The battle began outside, defending doors and windows, but soon moved inside where, as in some child's book, floors turned into beaches, furniture into driftwood and ceilings into drizzly skies. Cupboards squeaked with dust, porridge turned granular and words turned into clogged syllables, grit and spit. We became a village of spitters and hoickers because the sour taste of the sea was in our mouths, and our tongues were too dry and salty for talking. People hacked out only the most necessary communications, such as who had only sand left to eat, who needed digging out and where the cleanest water was.

The sandstorm clogged the river, but the Wai-O-Tapu spring continued to flow, pure, from underground; without it Keatown would have died – as Akona never tires of pointing out. People did their best to hold onto their lives, sealing food down under plastic covers and sweeping out their houses until their brooms ran out of faith. The men knocked themselves out trying to dig protective walls in a shifting ocean of sand. In the end most of them, except the most obsessive, gave up. Even the mayor concentrated on sealing up his own place nice and tight.

We all got around with scarves or handkerchiefs across our faces, looking like bandits or medical attendants. The vanishing of Flounder Phil was quite forgotten, although to the general indifference, the mayor named Reverend Stickman chief in charge of the investigation.

This didn't mean much, since Reverend Stickman was tied up battling for the integrity of his plumbing; the sandsnakes had discovered the septics.

Sometimes wind toyed with us, dropping to no more than a few whispering whirlpools below sound. People would come out of their houses, shake the sand from their hair, look at the sky, or rather where the sky should be, and stare at each other. During these brief interregnums the air did not clear, but remained clogged with dust and what smelled like coal smoke. This was not good clean sand flying around but some dirty mix that had everyone coughing up black spit. And the wind had not gone away, it had just turned cunning, playing dead, getting ready to spring – or sidle, or slither...

...before returning with all its fury, turning the air opaque with stinging sand. Houses and streets were buried, uncovered, and reburied at whim. Keatown vanished, reappeared and vanished again in the space of a day. The Girders looked like a steel Stonehenge one moment and were denuded to their concrete foundations the next, at which point they would groan ominously. The crab apple tree in the Cornets' backyard was, at one point, completely covered in soft, undulating sand. Sirocco could walk on top of it. He dug down until he found the top branches, just to reassure himself that it was still there. The next morning it was back again, quite unfazed.

Mother Smiley sat alone and watched the wind bury and unbury the image of her husband, scouring an imaginary grave clean and filling it up, dressing and undressing him. She made a vow never to smile again.

The storm got into our heads. None of us could sleep. We dreamed on our feet. Our ears were carried away by the wind. Our bodies shook. That same wind insinuated itself into our waking dreams until we couldn't distinguish ourselves from our memories.

the House of Books

The librarian gets up from her computer where she has been working on her forever unfinished Chronicles of Keatown and walks around the library thinking about the duties and obligations of the historian. This is her library. The House of Books. The House of Singing Paper. A museum of words, although she hates to think of it that way. Being housed underground in an abandoned wine cellar, a series of connected cellars, the House of Books is largely immune to the storm and the depredations of sand. Yet, with the solid outside door tightly shut, and towels on the floor to block the crack, sand grains still make their way inside like insidious, scuttling insects.

She's having a hard time finding herself. Once and still a spinster. Once a school-teacher. Once a historian. Once a student with literary ambitions who stayed up all night worrying about the world and avoiding sex. Certainly, she is concerned for her books, her precious books. It cost her much in time, effort and connivance to secure this space for the books and written records, and set up a steady flow of electricity, a good computer – everything she needs to complete her Chronicles of Keatown. A good thing that she got all this set up before the mayor's woman, Mavis, turned up, looking for a site for a brothel. These underground chambers would have suited her perfectly. Sighs and whispers.

It is unthinkable that it might all be wiped out by a vagary of nature, if that is what we are facing. More than a vagary of nature would load the dice, tip the scales, upset the apple cart in a manner she doesn't quite understand but which makes her fearful. She is comfortable, burrowed away underground with her books and her dance of the past and the present tenses. She doesn't want the world burrowing in after her, not now, not ever. Whatever else happens, the Chronicles of Keatown must be finished, the story of Ellen Johnson and her descendants must be told. For example, before the storm she was working on the life of one of Ellen Johnson's sons-in-law, who constructed what was arguably the first building in Keatown, Stanley's Drapery, the first shop in the country to sell Indian fabrics. Fancy building a town around a drapery. Of course draperies were where women went, and it was the librarian's thesis that women played a much larger role in the development of the town than generally recognised.

Thinking about her work brings her some pleasure but doesn't alleviate her fear of this seemingly unnatural storm. The face at the window didn't help. That was scary enough, like those Goose-Bump books the kids used to enjoy. But the thought that this is not just an ordinary storm out there, that it is peopled with creatures, storm creatures, is even scarier. This is the way it happened. Beside the main door, which leads to a covered courtyard and access to her house, there is a window, starting about waist height, looking out at the courtyard. It is the only window of the library, much neglected and dust-filled. She was standing by it, listening to the glass rattle, trying to get the sense of the wind direction and intensity of the storm, when a human hand appeared on the window, followed by a face, the face of a woman, a complete stranger. She was maybe in her fifties with lank grey hair and a thin face. She put her face against the glass until her nose went squishy and stared in with eyes as blank as milk. The hand on the glass began to close, turning fingers into claws.

It is all too ridiculous really, in the memory. Her mind flounders around for literary references to which she can cling. The atmosphere is Edgar Allan Poe, the territory is the Twilight Zone. Not bad. The Frights provided by Lovecraft, picked up by Stephen King by way of Charles Dickens. There are literary references galore without having to start on movies, she can go on making them up forever, but none to which she can cling for longer than the passing moment. It's all a big laugh when safely bound in the gothic section of the library, something else again when it's loose and wandering around outside like Mary Shelley's monster, peering into windows with eyes like blank slates, the same chalky grey.

It is not clear that the woman saw her, or saw anything with those chalky blank eyes, but the librarian was searching for something. And a creepy little voice at the back of her mind is telling her that the creature was searching for a way in.

The librarian is not one to jump at a mouse. She is made of sterner stuff, and besides, she's read too widely to get stuck in some tawdry horror story, standing by a window, heart beating wildly, while that thin face pressed against the glass and the hand turned into a claw – it is simply not her style. She prefers Virginia Woolf, a touch of Janet Frame perhaps, and certainly Barbara Kingsolver. She prefers her reality, literary or otherwise, to display at least some sensibility and not resort to crude and gaudy special effects or gratuitous plot twists.

Nevertheless, she saw what she saw and there is no getting around that. She is too much of a realist to deny the reality, but, it seems to her, that reality itself is making certain... well... genre choices recently. Flounder Phil, apparently led astray by an unlikely girl never seen before in isolated little Keatown; Akona apparently seeing the ghost of one of her ancestors up Makurutanga Creek; the prettiest girl in town taking dancing lessons up mansions, lorded over by a mysterious dark baron; Sirocco having visions of a woman with a freshly cut rose passing across the Cornets' backyard. While these events make for fine gossip, they are not of a genre, or mix of genres, that hold any appeal to the librarian, whose tastes are classical and who prefers Jane Austen to Emily Brontë. Moors are all very fine, but when patrolled by a Heathcliff or a Woman in White they become, well... kitschy. The same could be said of windows, fine in their place, but not with a witch scratching away at the glass.

It doesn't have to be a witch. More likely a woman from the village that the librarian didn't recognise, lost in the storm and wandering about. In which case, where is she now, and why hasn't she sought refuge in the library? Despite her misgivings, the librarian refuses to be like one of Daphne du Maurier's wimpy heroines who begin to doubt their own experience, or let a man talk them into doubting their own experience. The last time that happened to the librarian the man got the short goodbye. The librarian has learned that the best way to deal with relationships is not to have them. Who needs a relationship when you've got a library? Much more fun to read about a relationship than to have one. Safer too.

The same applies to friendship. The last friend she had was Madame Cherrie Lamont, who taught with her at the school when schools were still possible, but Madame Lamont became so carried away by her New Age trips that she seemed to forget that other people existed. And since she has stopped all reading on the grounds that too many words would pollute her brain, and no longer drops by the library, even for a chat, the friendship has fallen away.

The librarian pauses in front of a shelf of books, the beginning of the D's. She likes D for its solemn tomes of Dostoevsky and Dickens, solid Nineteenth Century prose, prose to get lost in. But it's not these weighty gents that catch her eye, rather a more modest My Family and Other Animals by Gerald Durrell. Light humour is not exactly her genre either – except for a sneaking regard for PG Wodehouse down the other end of the alphabet – but the title says it all. The librarian has long since left her family behind, and she's never had much success with other animals.

She takes out the book and weighs it in her hand like a merchant with a loaf of bread. She is puzzled as to why the face at the window should spark this line of thought, and decides it has something to do with loneliness and pathos – there's Little Nell just a few volumes away. The librarian has never considered herself to be a lonely person, but the face at the window made her feel like one, for it was a face shorn of all human connection.

She puts Gerald Durrell back on the shelf, where he sits with his older brother, the weightier Lawrence Durrell with his massive Alexandria Quartet that no one seems to read any more. Looks like the younger brother got the last laugh. She picks up The Alexandria Quartet and tries to recall the story. Four intersecting stories, reality retreating behind subjective points of view, but surely it has something to do with sex and brothels.

One way or another, it's sighs and whispers all the way down.

holes inna world

The mokopuna don't have much of a life during the siege. All work and no play, and most of the time they go hungry. At night they find their refuges, a safe place to hole up in the storm.

The twins separate since Miranda has grown tired of Witch Hunt sleeping in the same room, the same bed even. After all, Miranda insists, they aren't really twins, just friends, and besides, Miranda looks nothing like the plain Witch Hunt with her straggly looks and rats-tail hair. Miranda is too pretty to be Witch Hunt's sister, and she's going to grow up to be prettier than Orchid one day, so she tells the mirror. After all, Orchid isn't that pretty. Well, she has those almond-shaped eyes which make her look pretty, but her hair isn't as pretty as Miranda's. And so on and so forth. At one point, when she's very involved with her prettiness, Witch Hunt annoys her so much she bites her on the arm, deep enough to draw blood. That would teach the ugly little worm. Witch Hunt screams, bringing Jolene running to find out who's been murdered. Witch Hunt covers the bite with her sleeve, but Jolene's had enough. The upshot of all this being that Witch Hunt is sent out in the storm to her camp in the abandoned school building nearby where she has a snugly sleeping bag and can settle into her memories of the librarian, with her gentle mouth, who would read aloud books like Little House on the Prairie, and she and Miranda would play games based on the characters. Sometimes she thinks of her real mother, who lives somewhere on the outskirts of town, practising her drinking. Witch Hunt has a vague memory of visiting a woman who promised to beat her 'within an inch of your life' and went ahead and did it. Witch Hunt would have died from that beating if Akona had not got wind of it, scooped up what was left of the little girl and patched her up as best she could. She got a scar on the cheek and a crooked eye out of that one.

The schoolhouse camp is not such a bad place, all things considered, and Jolene, in a fit of guilt or sympathy, has supplied her with a bag of food. Good food. Nuts and dried fruit as well as smoked fish.

Sad Toof is in a similar position. In his case, his parents did the best they could for him before deserting him with the hollow promises that they would return, but there is something irredeemable about Sad Toof that, in the end, erodes compassion – why won't he get rid of that toxic tooth and buck himself up? For the duration of the storm, Sad Toof has chosen his second home, an abandoned hut on the marae, with Akona's tacit permission. She even leaves soft foods for him sometimes, like roasted kumara, which is his favourite food in the whole world. Little Sanyo, the only true orphan of the mokopuna, likes to crawl in underneath houses to sleep near the earth, but since the invasion of the sandsnakes, he's had to bunk in with Sad Toof, a mutually discomforting arrangement. Sad Toof is a noisy sleeper, even in a storm. He sleeps with his mouth open because, he says, his Sad toof needs lots of air.

Little Sanyo doesn't sleep much anyway because of his tinnitus, and now, in the general cacophony, he can't sleep at all but lies awake thinking up circuitry for all the devices he will never get to invent.

Since the storm began, Rasputin, with the Rev Stickman's approval, has gone into retreat in the old colonial church, built in stone by hardy pioneers, the good Puritan children of Ellen Johnson and her daughters. Rev Stickman has held vigils in this sturdy monument to faith, but its chilly Protestant interior is too much even for him, leaving it mostly empty with nobody caring if Och Arglin sleeps it off on the nave floor.

Rasputin is shacked up with God, Sad Toof says to Little Sanyo. He's sleeping on a stone floor and praying all the time. It can't be good.

Sad Toof is equally downbeat about Orchid. When the storm hit, she turned up at Hera's place and resumed her old role of nanny to the Baby and assistant to Hera. The old Bay Motel, right on the waterfront and already subject to rising sea levels, had to be abandoned. Hera and Orchid took the Baby to an empty house near the school and set up camp there. Then... Mary turned up. Sad Toof says that in a voice which tells you that it can't be good. No good ever comes of Mary turning up. And so it turns out to be. Mary, whispering in Orchid's ear all the time, even with the storm booming around the empty house. Then – Sad Toof likes saying then, mostly long and drawn out with a dramatic pause at the end – after a couple of days Orchid and Mary vanish into the storm and haven't been seen since.

However, it is Sirocco who has the hardest, if not the loneliest time of it. He spends the first two days cowering on his bed, fixating on Gypsy as a mother figure and trying to regress to infanthood – but with no success. He can wind back time, but only as far as the desert. And the desert is a labyrinth, its walls made of wind. At night he dreams of it, his own garden of forking paths, except it is not a garden but a wasteland of rock and tussock, sand and gravel.

'A labyrinth is not a maze,' Lizard says to him in his dream. 'Have you forgotten everything I've taught you? Look for the pattern.'

But every corner he turns brings him back to the same place, the same piece of rock washed up in some ancient deluge. It's a hard dream to wake up from, for whenever he wakes up he's in the same place, and the wind hasn't stopped tearing at the sky. Like Theseus, who escaped the Minotaur through a labyrinth by following thread laid down by Ariadne, Sirocco lays down thread to help him find his way back out of the desert. Thread doesn't work in the desert so well. It takes him around corners while appearing to go in a straight line. It sews up the seam between sleeping and wakefulness so that he cannot wake up, cannot return to sleep.

After two days of wandering the labyrinth looking for the pattern and finding only shards of memory split open by the desert sun, he decides to rise from his mattress and join the land of the living, to move from the hard illumination of the desert sun to the gloom of the Cornet house. It's all very well for Lizard to discourse wisely on the nature of the labyrinth, and how it is not a maze, but he's not stuck where Sirocco is, as if between lives, nowhere to turn.

Against the conventional wisdom that filling a room up with things would make it look smaller, the Cornet lounge, created by knocking out half the internal walls of the house, is made larger by its clutter. Its piles of magazines, odd bits of furniture like the curved liquor cabinet with leaded windows, even its two large indoor rubber plants, are but landmarks in a much greater territory. In the middle of the room, a table has become the semi-permanent home of a number of strange objects, including a birdcage made in the shape of a standing bird, a hawk perhaps, some bird of prey with a suitably sharp beak. Inside the cage someone has placed a Barbie doll with black skin and shiny black hair. That was probably Scale, who thinks things like that are clever, like the little statue of the Madonna encased in a condom which stands outside the birdcage like some unlikely threshold guardian. Hilarious. This little scene is watched over by a soft toy, a rather large and round-eyed teddy-bear with tattered yellow fur. It looks like a childhood relic, but Little Sanyo the beachcomber found it and offered it to Gypsy, who took a fancy to it because it reminded her of something. A tall lamp, gracefully curved, carved from a single piece of wood, towers over this tableau. It doesn't work, at least as a lamp, but it looks impressive, the queen of the table bric-a-brac.

Around this table, the rest of the room arranges itself, seeming in this dim light to shade off into indeterminate distances. One of the old bedrooms survived the gutting of the house, but the door to that room is always closed. This is Gypsy's special room where she keeps her most precious things, her personal memorabilia. 'Photos and stuff,' Scale said once, somewhat dismissively. Another time he joked about a 'magic mirror' with a mother-of-pearl back she kept hidden in her room.

'It won't make you look any younger,' he once jeered at her when she took it out.

'It was a gift from my mother,' she replied with impressive dignity. And, she might have added, it does make me look younger.

When Gypsy brought him in from the desert, she didn't quite know what to do with him, and lost interest in him. She rummaged around and found a mattress, old but not too uncomfortable, and some wooly army blankets left over from some war. She threw the mattress onto the floor, in the northeastern corner. Not exactly five star, but luxury enough for a desert rat.

Now she hardly takes any notice of him. Sometimes she pats him on the head while thinking about something else, and sometimes she'll talk to him just because he's there, and talking to him enables her to talk to herself without feeling odd about it. Rescuing him was one thing, having him move in is quite another, and Scale agrees. During the storm she does her best to pretend that he isn't there.

Scale and Gypsy sleep in the southwestern corner of the room in a large and comfy bed. It's diagonally opposite Sirocco's corner and, with the table in between seems a long way off to Sirocco, but the feeling of privacy is illusory. Sirocco snuggles down into his army blankets and covers his ears when the couple make their old bedsprings creak, and Gypsy starts to sing in a wailing voice.

'To mammals was given the gift of ecstasy,'Lizard once told him. 'For lizards it's different. Our only heat comes from the sun.'

The arrangement, however, has had one great advantage; it got him out of the desert and into the company of others, of humans. The desert can follow him only in his dreams. He has never minded that, never minded waking up on his less-than-comfy mattress to find the desert no more than a fading image. A huge relief, in fact. Perhaps one day it will swallow itself up and he could forget it completely.

Now it seems to him that the wind has tracked him down with the aim of taking him back again, or bringing the desert to him. Taking over the township completely. That's a desert wind he can hear scraping at the house, scraping on his sensitised eardrums. Scraping against the side of the world. That's a wind he never wanted to hear again.

But it's that wind that shakes him out of his lethargy and gets him on his feet. Now he's up and about there's not much for him to do, however. He can help Gypsy keep sand out of their food supply, or prepare their less-than-lavish meals. Mostly he just wanders about looking at the assembled objects and wondering about their history, or delving into a pile of ancient National Geographics which showed the world as it once was.

While the electricity lasts, there is at least some light in the house, and Gypsy can play her favourite Arabic reggae as she dusts her broom and endlessly wipes surfaces with a weary cloth. To begin with, she dances as she cleans. She loves to dance to that chicka-chicka-boom-boom stuff, those long, twisty, echoey female voices undulating in from the desert, while rotating her hips like an Egyptian belly dancer. Sirocco loves her hair, so long and thick and black and lustrous and pagan.

On the second day, when the storm shows no sign of abating, and there is more sand than dusters or brooms can handle, Gypsy breaks out the Och's Hock, the world's most vicious alcohol. She pours a generous portion for herself and Scale, who seizes it with two trembling hands and the drinking starts. Scale finds some old, dried up tobacco leaves, home grown, and the smoking starts too. It's as if the smoking and drinking can keep out the world and all its storms.

When, towards the end of the third day of the storm, the power goes down and the light goes out of the world, there is nothing to hold back the endless scrape and moan of the wind; the dust goes out of the broom and the weary cloth lies on its back saturated with sand. Gypsy sits down at the table with the air of someone who never wants to rise again. Sirocco busies himself by pouring her one and sitting with her to drink it. And, with the fastidiousness of the half-drunk, rolls cigarettes for both of them.

Gypsy gestures to the dark figure of the yellow teddy bear. 'I guess we'll just have to sit it out, teddy,' she says.

The teddy's amber eyes gleam.

At that very moment Scale decides to get cabin fever. At first he took the storm as a personal affront, expending himself each day uselessly shovelling sand, lying exhausted on the bed afterwards, aimlessly tugging at his black T-shirt as he studied the sandsnakes crawling across the ceiling. Then the manic energy deserted him, but it returns from time to time in bursts of useless, hoch fueled activity.

Scale spends a lot of time sweating, as if he has a real fever, and scratching himself as if the sand has got under his skin. Staying home drinking is all very well, but Scale would rather be at work with Blade and others, joking and bullshitting and gutting fish. He's a bit too crazy himself to have the world go AWOL on him. He's the kind of man who needs the earth to be steady beneath his feet, otherwise holes open up everywhere. Holes in the world, holes in the bottom of the glass.

He jumps off the bed, where he has been lethargically lying, and circles the room at a quick trot, holding his hands up, palm out. At the same time he begins to yodel like a cowboy singer.

'What's happening? You got ants in your pants?' Gypsy says, all grumpy. She wants him to calm down without having to be told.

'It sneaks through holes inna walls,' he says, 'and inna floor. I never knew so many holes. You can't see 'em, but they must be there.'

He is right of course, all that sand is filtering in from somewhere, but Gypsy just gets more irritated. 'Holes in yer head,' she says.

That's pretty unkind. There are those who say, behind their hands, that Scale is one circle short of a star – but I'm not so sure. In the fish shed, his apparently clumsy hands can scale fish faster than any other; he's a model of speed and efficiency. After all, that's how he got his name. And, if he's scruffy, he keeps himself clean and washes his black singlet, the only top he wears, at least once a week, and his khaki shorts, the other half of his attire, every other week. The librarian has no idea of his lineage, suspecting perhaps a Croatian or Serb ancestry, and that his odd English has more to do with some immigrant background than lack of smarts.

Right now, however, he doesn't look very smart, circling the room, pushing at the air here and there as if he could push the wind back through the invisible holes. In fact, he looks pretty stupid, but that doesn't explain why Gypsy is becoming so irritated with him; that has to be the cabin fever building up inside her, Sirocco decides.

'Do something useful!' she snaps. 'You're not pacing around the room all day, so you can forget about that.' She sucks hard at her cigarette and throws back what's left in her glass.

Scale stops by the door where he earlier left a shovel, picks it up and looks at it.

'Whaddya you think you're doing?'

He looks at her quizzically. It's a familiar expression. Sometimes he thinks the world is the way it is because he says so. If he says it's sunny he won't wear a raincoat, even if it's actually raining. You could say he has a problem with cause and effect. Yet sometimes, in his look, Sirocco catches some deep puzzlement, as if he knows something is wrong but not what, and he'll look at Sirocco or Gypsy as if about to ask a question. A question that never quite makes it into the world.

'You're not shovelling sand in that wind.'

This apparently reminds Scale of something, as he grabs the shovel, opens the door, letting in a blast of swirling sand, and steps out into the maelstrom. Sirocco and Gypsy rush to the window. 'He's got a bee in his bonnet about something,' she says.

'It's the wind,' Sirocco says. He can't see very far, just to the crab apple tree, which looks like a grey ghost in the shifting densities of air.

Scale hasn't gone very far. He's down on his hands and knees, poking around in the sand one moment, on his feet digging furiously with the shovel the next. Then he bangs the shovel down as if hitting at a dodging rodent.

'What does he think he's doing?' Sirocco says.

'He thinks the wind is coming up through holes in the ground,' Gypsy says. Her irritation is melting away. She is going into a listless, dreamy state. The cigarette has gone to sleep between her fingers.

'Holes inna ground,' Sirocco says in good humour.

Gypsy nods. 'He's trying to find the holes and push the wind back into the earth. Crazy bugger.'

'He'll get over it. It's just cabin fever,' Sirocco says. 'And the wind.'

A bulky figure looms out of the murk close to Scale. A big man, naked to the waist with sloping shoulders and a large round belly, almost knocks Scale over as he passes, heading for the east side of the house. He is completely indifferent to the stinging wind.

Scale leaps back and flourishes the shovel as if it were a serious weapon.

'Did you see that?' Sirocco turns to Gypsy, suddenly feeling the comfort of the woman's presence, her big, bold face.

'See what?'

'A man. A big man. Just about knocked Scale over.'

'I don't think I saw that,' Gypsy says. Her face is set at neutral. She's not going to change her expression whatever Sirocco says, so he says nothing.

The door bangs open and Scale blunders back inside, slamming the door behind him. 'There's some kinda people out there,' he says.

Gypsy joins him and starts to brush the sand from his hair and clothes. 'You've got to stay inside,' she says, all calm and tender.

'I don' wanna,' he says, reaching for his drink.

Looking at them both, from one back to the other, Sirocco wonders about love, and under what strange and hostile circumstances it might thrive. If love were a life form, how tenacious it would be, like those super-bugs Little Sanyo says can live inside nuclear reactors, or in the holocaust spume of deep-water volcanoes where gravity is twelve times the surface level. Make life impossible for love, and it mutates. Love is hardwired into the circles and stars, he thinks. It never misses a chance.

on second-guessing God

Despite the storms and the dangers, the librarian decides to leave her fastness and visit Akona at the marae. The librarian loves her books, but doesn't wish to be buried with them. In the shifting topography of the storm, the old wine cellar that is now the House of Books could be buried under tons of sand.

The librarian would be the last to admit that she was driven from her precious books as much by an oppressive sense of isolation as by some rational urge to seek higher ground. With all her books, she tells herself, she can never be alone. How can she be alone with all the great voices of mankind at her fingertips?

This is a rhetorical question, but it is directed at me. Just as Sirocco talks to his lizard, and Akona will talk to her ancestors, and the baron talks to his Arya Tara, and Annanda will talk to his absent friend Suneal, and Flay will talk to his shotgun, the librarian talks to me, or thinks she does. In her mind I am this shady, sovereign character she calls The First Person. However she imagines this 'me', it is always a projection of herself, slightly wild-eyed and frizzy-haired. And I of course refuse to come out of the shadows just for her. Why should she get any special privileges?

Akona and her goats welcome her. Akona has brought Nanny and Lucifer into her place where she can reassure them and keep an eye particularly on Nanny. Without Nanny's milk the baby could well die, and Akona doesn't want her to dry up. Nanny going into fright at this storm and losing her milk would be a catastrophe, so Akona is prepared to put up with the stink and the inconvenience.

The marae is not protected from the wind, which rips and tears at it, but does not receive the full brunt of the sand. A few other women, including her old airhead friend Cherrie Lamont, have sought refuge there, but the librarian, in her pride, has been loath to think herself one of them. After all, she has no need to seek refuge. She is only here because she didn't want to end up buried alive like an Edgar Allan Poe character.

For once, Cherrie Lamont is not rattling her mouth off but, white-faced and silent, her hands gripping her chair, is staring from one woman to the other when they speak, wide-eyed and uncomprehending.

Melissa Tonguestone is on her knees, head bent in fearful prayer. The devoted young woman is one of the reverend's closest supporters and a true believer in her own eyes. Her husband is a fisherman who works on Orlap the Viking's boat. For many months now, the reverend has been blessing their union in an attempt to encourage or perhaps cajole the Almighty into blessing them with a child. The blessing, if there was one, went astray to land on Hera the Harlot instead. Little wonder that the distressed woman should turn to Akona for some helpful herbs, perhaps, or even a little spell or two – God wouldn't mind if it were for a good cause, like getting her pregnant.

Usually a quiet, meek sort of person, her eyes as she fixes them on the librarian, are livid. 'This storm is God's punishment on us,' she declares.

Cherrie Lamont whimpers. She wouldn't be surprised if God were waiting right outside the door with more punishments in store, like a Father Christmas without the ho, ho, ho – and a sack full of nasty surprises from storms to zombie invasions.

Here we go again, the librarian thinks, the same old superstitious madness, generation after generation. To subtly separate herself from the others, the librarian moves closer to the goats, taking up a spot beside Nanny sitting quietly chewing away on some dried grasses. Lucifer gives the librarian a suspicious look. Quite a misanthrope is Lucifer.

'Punishment for what?' Akona says as she unobtrusively puts together a herbal mix for a relaxing cup of tea for everybody. Lots of chamomile and kawakawa.

'For harbouring the Child of Jezebel.'

Ah, this is a new twist on the town's icon. The librarian wonders, just for a moment, if Melissa would appreciate the irony that the biblical Jezebel was associated with the worship of Asherah, goddess of motherhood and fertility, she to whom many a goat was sacrificed. Probably not. A little learning can be a dangerous thing.

'That's a stupid thing to say, excuse me,' the other woman says. This is Margot Hamlin, a supporter of Hera. A kind and practical person, and a true Baby lover. 'You can't blame the child.'

'Children are not innocent, you know. Babies are not born innocent. They are born with the stain of sin on them.'

'What rubbish. The stain of sin indeed.' Margot looks to Akona and the librarian for support, but Akona is busy preparing tea. Her manner is calm and steady. The librarian, however, nods in agreement. Like Margot, she has no truck with the doctrine of original sin, which she sees as a source of great evil and suffering in the world. It's like being born with an unpaid debt, she said to her First Person.

'Everyone is very agitated,' Akona says. 'Wind can do that. Especially a wind like this.' She remembers something her mother said. Like the rain that pelts down upon the roof, the lips of women move below...

'There is no innocence,' Melissa says with monotonous insistence. Her eyes are glazed and fixed. 'Man is not innocent. Nature is not innocent. Nature fell from innocence when Man fell from innocence.'

The librarian recognises the tones and inflections of the Reverend Stickman. People run to faith when reason fails them, she thinks. The toxic old doctrines.

Margot paces about, looking from one of us to the next. 'So what would you do? Murder the child in the arms of its mother?' Her eyes linger on the librarian. The librarian knows what she thinks but as so often in these situations she has to hold her peace.

'Baptise the child in the name of the true God,' Melissa snaps back. 'Baptise the child and drive the Devil right out of him. Baptise the world and drive the Devil out of the wind. Drive out the devil wind.' The young woman's face is flushed, as in a fever, her words falling over each other.

'Akona is right,' Margot says. 'It's the wind. Storms are scary.'

Cherrie Lamont buries her face in her arms and makes the sound of a person who is very scared.

'It's not just the wind,' Melissa says, her voice heavy with significance. Having won the first round, she is more than ready for a second. 'There are things out there. Things that look like people.' She begins to rock back and forward in her seat.

'That's rubbish,' Margot says.

'No, it's not.' Akona says. 'I've seen them too. Perhaps the storm brought them. They can come in the guise of our ancestors.'

Melissa is beside herself. 'Yes, yes. Yes, yes,' she yaps like a dog. 'The storm brought them. Out of the past. Or they brought the storm. Under the cloak of the storm, God brought them, to wander among us and haunt us...' (the librarian tries not to remember the face at the window, looking in), '... under the cloak of ignorance. The wandering ignorant. What am I saying? Why am I babbling like this?'

The room is silent. They all have some ideas, but nobody is prepared to speak them out.

Nanny bleats quietly.

Akona pours the boiling water over the tea and covers the pot with an ancient crochet tea cosy her mother used. She knows it's silly, but the tea doesn't quite taste the same without the tea cosy. Patience is now needed while the tea steeps for just the right length of time.

'Sing,' Cherrie Lamont says abruptly to Akona. 'You know these magic songs that keep away the dead, I know you do.'

Akona sings. She's never had much of a voice, so nobody is likely to recognise the old pop song 'Are you Lonesome Tonight?' as sung by Elvis Presley, a song her mother never tired of playing.

By the time she is finished, Cherrie Lamont is staring glassy-eyed into the distance, and the tea is ready.

'We should pray!' Melissa says as Akona pours the steaming tea into the cups.

'I'm sure we're all doing that,' Akona says.

'We should tear our flesh with cruel hooks!'

'No we shouldn't,' Akona says, although she feels ready to make an exception.

'They have come among us to destroy us.'

'Let's not second-guess God,' Akona says. 'Have a sip of tea.' She does so herself, as if to demonstrate to a child.

'What's in it?'

'Chamomile. Nice and relaxing.'

'I don't need relaxing. I need saving.'

Nevertheless, Melissa takes a sip or two. Not quite the forgiveness of God, but she's not complaining. Praise God for small mercies.

There is a bang on the door. The librarian, nearest to the door, opens it and Grandmother Gaunt makes a grand entrance with a roar of wind and sand. Her eyes are as wild as Melissa's. She fixes each of us with a stare as if having to establish our individual existences.

'I don't know how to say this,' she says.

'Just say it,' Melissa says.

'There are... people out there. People in the storm. Of the storm.'

'They're not people,' Melissa intones. 'They're not people. Don't for one minute call them people. They are insects pretending to be people.' She clutches the cup with both hands.

'They look like people. Just ordinary people,' Gaunt says, although her voice falters. Normally there is no stopping her.

'That's where you're wrong. Yes, they might look like people, but they are... cockroaches!' Melissa looks from face to face, eager to share her eureka moment. 'Once they were people, perhaps, only God knows because he knows everything... Once they were people who woke up one morning to find that they had turned into cockroaches. And what do you do with cockroaches? I'll tell you what you do.' At that point Melissa, who has been sitting at Akona's kitchen table, puts down her tea, gets to her feet and begins a stamping dance. 'You stomp them and squash them. Stomp stomp! Squash squash!'

Cherrie Lamont squeals and claps.

Grandmother Gaunt, who's not yet taken a seat, jumps forward in alarm. Akona, however, gets to her feet and dances along with Melissa. Stomp stomp! Squash squash! Gaunt gets the idea and begins to do the same. Margot looks from one to the other as if everybody has gone mad. Stomp stomp! Squash squash! Even Lucifer gets into the act and begins to bang the floor with his front feet. Melissa giggles. Her stomping and squashing become erratic and random. Her arms flail about. A moment later she collapses into her chair and buries her face in her hands.

'It's not fair,' she says into the heels of her hands. 'It's just not fair. Sometimes I hate God!' Her skin turns bright red with shame.

Akona rustles in her cabinet and produces a small bottle with an eye-dropper cap. She squeezes a couple of drops into a glass of water and hands it to Melissa, who stares dully at it. 'What is it? Rescue remedy?'

'Essence of praying mantis,' Akona says, 'for runaway thought processes. To sever the thoughts that keep taking you back to pain.'

'What do you know of my pain? Are you a witch?'

'Pain from thought is always the worst kind of pain,' Akona says. 'And I don't think God wants you to be hysterical right now.'

'I said... I said didn't I... what do you know of my pain?'

'More than you want me to talk about right now.'

Everybody in the room knows what Akona is referring to. It's not exactly a secret. Melissa's barren womb is a constant torment to her, but nobody's going to say that at this moment. Even Melissa's not going to get started on that right now, although a bitterness passes over her face arising from the corrosive power of thought, proving the very thing she cannot face.

In the subsequent silence, the storm comes rushing in, smashing against the walls and shaking the building.

'Don't worry,' Akona assures them. 'This place is built to withstand the worst southerly storms. The foundations go down into solid rock.'

Melissa puts her hands back up to her face and moans.

Nanny joins her. Cherrie Lamont joins in with Nanny.

Akona makes sure everybody gets their tea.

the history of inconsequence and the Book of Imaginary Sentences

After the failure of his efforts to conquer the wind with his spade, Scale takes to the bed once more while Gypsy, broom in hand, resumes her unhurried sweeping, every now and again shaking her large mass of black hair to shoulder it free of blonde sand. Sometimes, maybe just to break the silence, Scale will say something to her and she will bite back in monosyllables. Other times she will climb onto the bed with him and straddle him as if oblivious to Sirocco's presence. Then they whimper at each other and bury their heads in each other's shoulders. Or they lie, coupled but barely moving, each lost in an exhausted reverie.

Sirocco turns his back on them when they begin to carry on, and escapes into his own reverie. While Sirocco can read, albeit slowly, he has never learned to write, content to draw stars and circles in the earth. In his mind, however, he is writing a book, one that would surely rival the librarian's very own Chronicles of Keatown if it were written down. The words come easily when you only have to think them. His imaginary book contains real sentences, he can hear them rolling through his mind, and his mind is such that he can scroll back through the narrative, seeing it as if it were on a computer screen or unrolling parchment, and pick it up at any point.

Not that there is much of a narrative. Mostly it consists of lists of things and conversations he had with Lizard in the desert. Like the stars and circles he draws in the dirt under the crab apple tree, his book is a series of fragments in search of a pattern. The labyrinth not the maze. He doesn't mind that; fragments are okay with him. One day, he trusts, the pattern will be revealed. The fragments he composes, little blocks and strings of words, might be inserted at any point in the book, which is becoming a series of interlinking branches. It's fun, and he enjoys making up the sentences, imagining that he's talking to the mokopuna, holding them spellbound with his magical storytelling abilities. In his imagination he no longer has his silly piping little voice but resonant tones, rich and redolent with emotion. His special, storytelling voice.

You see, my mokopuna, Gypsy and Scale picked me up along the way, as they picked up a tumble of other things in the most unlikely places: a stray cat or two, a rusty flashlight, a painted feather, a birdcage shaped like a bird, a Marilyn Monroe hologram, a sofa with its innards hanging out, two kitsch Victorian vases in the Chinese style, a box set of Kurosawa DVDs that don't play, a banana-shaped telephone, a Russian babushka doll, a Complete Oxford Dictionary in two volumes in miniature writing, with magnifying glass attached, three crystal flutes of impossible pedigree, a shark's tooth, photos of people long lost to sepia memory, a cobwebby bookcase full of dusty National Geographic magazines, and a fairy in a tutu made for the top of a Christmas tree – our big lounge room is a history of inconsequence of which I am but a humble part.

On this occasion his storytelling is interrupted by an argument Gypsy and Scale are having, their voices rising over the relentless moan of the storm.

'It can't be, it can't be,' Scale is repeating stubbornly, shaking his shaggy head and pulling at his singlet.

'It has to be,' Gypsy says. 'Just admit it.'

'Admit nothin'.'

'That was Fat Freddy wandering about out there. He must've got lost in the storm.'

'It wasn't Fat Freddy.'

'Of course it was, who else could it be?'

Sirocco joins in. He tries to tell them about the Rose Woman, and the couple on Pine Point. And the girl Little Sanyo saw. And Witch Hunt's daddy. Scale nods his head as if he's taking it all in, but he's hardly listening. Gypsy, on the other hand, won't have a bar of it. 'You've got it all mixed up in your brain,' she tells Sirocco. Gypsy is one of those in the town convinced that Sirocco's brain was fried out in the desert. She's overheard him having one-sided conversations with Lizard as if the creature were still about, lurking somewhere.

When he describes the Rose Woman, who apparently crossed over their yard three days ago, Gypsy, who's sitting at their table, holding a broom upright in one hand like a flag planted in the earth, raises her other hand to forestall him.

'That would be Mother,' she says. She takes a long, thoughtful drink. 'Mother wore those flowery things when she was young. Like her feet hardly touched the ground. Mother didn't walk, she swooped. She didn't talk, she sang. She was a lady once, wife of a diplomat, don't you know. Coming to Keatown was like coming to the end of the world for her. A place of exile. A place to die. All we had were these print frocks and dresses from China and India. Annanda had heaps of them in those days. The pattern was always of flowers, mostly imaginary – they never looked like anything real.'

Sirocco recoils from the intensity of her memory. With every hole Scale can find stopped up against the sand, the house lives in a perpetual twilight, elongating the distances. The bed, with Scale lying on top of it, looks like the lumpy shape of foothills. Powdered by a fine layer of sand, the room looks too much like the desert for Sirocco's comfort. No amount of stop-gapping can keep out that wind. Shreds of it sneak in everywhere. In the gloom Gypsy sits, tall and straight-backed, face handsome and solemn, like a totem.

Little wind devils have invaded the house, Gypsy's house, pulling the precious embroidered white tablecloth she'd inherited from Mother, and stirring up the dust behind the sofa. Beyond the bravest broom, they are. Miniature rivers of air, they swirl along invisible channels, leaving areas adjacent untouched. Behind the sofa one mini air demon springs up, whirls the somnambulant particles around for a few moments before allowing them to lapse once more into their old negligence; one corner of the curtain twitches to the paw of an invisible kitten; the bed sheets sigh and ripple.

Sirocco realises with a creeping horror that these windsnakes can get inside people's heads and swirl their memories around, which is what's happening to Gypsy. Those wormy threads are coming up through holes in her memory the same way they are coming up through holes in the floor, making her pupils grow big and dark. Mother died sitting at this very table, she tells Sirocco. She paints a picture of an old woman who sat looking out the window waiting for a life to come around the corner, waiting for a miracle, twisting her hair between thumb and forefinger. And drinking tea. Endless cups of tea. And codeine. She loved her codeine. Coffee and codeine, she'd say, makes a pleasant start to the day.

'Mother didn't die, she floated away on an ocean of pillows. She got the cancer like all the old people. It gets them in the end, you know. She needed lotsa pillows to float away on. The bed was piled high with a lake of cushions. Like candy floss. We made cushion covers out of those flower-print dresses because they were the cheapest material we had. We'd take her pillows and set her up in the market so she could watch the daily life of commerce, and understand the nature of dying and floating away...'

Sirocco remembers this old lady, hag more like it, how she would snarl at anyone who came near her. As the cancer mushroomed inside her, her eyes got smaller and more glittery and she spat out her food. She spat out words, too, in the same way. Chewed them up with her false teeth clacking and spat them out.

'I don't trust you.' was the last thing he remembers her saying before spite and death got the better of her.

compassion and emptiness

Baron Fairweather stands at his favourite post, on his favourite balcony overlooking the bay, watching the siege of Keatown. Manny sits alertly by his side, sharing the view. And quite a scene it is. Since the sea-blown sandsnakes can't get much higher than about halfway up Beauty Parade, the baron has the luxury of watching the destruction of the town in comparative peace. Up here the storm is no more than a stiff breeze ruffling his hair. He takes a peculiar satisfaction in the sight, a sneering delight in the travails of the blighted inhabitants of the pitiful settlement of Keatown. It's as if the baron himself has conjured this wind, like a wizard or god, to bring doom upon his despised subjects. To finally wipe them from the face of the earth. And how much more beautiful the bay will look without them. Pristine, that's the word. Unsullied, that's another.

And there is not a cawing kea in sight.

If the ground-hugging wind should lift its sights to the mansions – well not much would happen. The baron would retreat behind his double-glazed windows and watch it all from the comfort of his lounge with his faithful dog Manny by his side. And maybe the girl, Orchid, too – she and her handy little friend with the pocked face have already sought shelter under his roof. It's a nice feeling to know that she is tucked away in his fastness, a prisoner of the storm rather than his prisoner.

At the same time he can't help but wonder once more if he shouldn't have left when most of the others did. Of the fifteen mansions scattered across several hillsides, only four of them are still occupied, or partially occupied, including his own. The inhabitants meet from time to time for dinners and sex parties, but enthusiasm for both has been waning of late as the survivors burrow deeper into their isolation. Even the Strongbows, always party stalwarts, have been keeping to themselves lately. A pity since the moody Lady Strongbow shares with the baron a taste for dancing girls, while the baron has developed quite a taste for Lady Strongbow . There just isn't the critical mass needed for a really fun time. Excluding the new flower, who isn't broken in yet, he has only three dancing girls left who, if truth be known, are somewhat faded on the vine, a pitiful troupe even given the talents of Fraulein Zhenua, dancing mistress extraordinaire. Truly, Cherry Blossom, Blue Zither and Sun Petal have seen better days; they are running out of hair colour. And, with the Strongbows playing coy, the remaining three households are pretty lacklustre in the partying department. Even with their clothes off these people are bores. Especially with their clothes off. The most interesting ones have already scattered to their choppers.

With these thoughts in his head, he suddenly loses interest in the invasion of Keatown, as if the fate of these people to some freak circumstance were nothing more than a distraction. In some respects he finds his profound indifference pleasing, but he is also disturbed. The 'brainbox' baron, with all his mathematical skills, hasn't counted upon the algorithms of melancholy.

What he finds oddly hard to face, as he returns to his lounge, is the idea that this gorgeous mansion, with all the money he put into it, has passed its use-by date. Its rooms built for mood and taste, like the bedrooms which open out onto astonishing vistas, which are minimalist and modern, walls clean and antiseptic, to his master bedroom, baroque with red velvet drapes and silk galore, mostly creamy white, like a whore's panties. To this huge lounge with its white leather sofas, and open fireplace, a reclining female Buddha in bronze, and Francis Bacon's famous flayed nudes which make perfect patron saints of an orgy. All this, and a vault full of gold ingots, is merely an antipodean outpost, a weekend bach, hardly the centre of operations. His stay has been a pleasant one, but the time may be at hand to remove himself to somewhere a little more secure in terms of supply lines. Time to belatedly join the endlessly anxious, migrating super-rich.

It's one thing to be here by choice, quite another to be trapped here. His mind returns once more to his helicopter, his Turboshaft 300. Since he's made sure he can pilot his own helicopter – he wanted to be rich, not helpless – he could, once a couple of little issues have been sorted out, jump into it right now and fly away, leave Keatown to rot on its own, probably the last of the celebs to leave. The Strongbows will never leave because they are too indolent, the brisk but batty Benedicts are too addicted to the invigorating mountain air, to which they ascribe magical properties. And as for Mrs Watson, the former beauty queen grown so fat she can hardly waddle, she is too reclusive to do anything but quietly eat herself to death up here in the mountains. She isn't going anywhere.

Perhaps he might have already left it were not for lack of diesel for the reserve tanks of the Turboshaft 300... and the Orchid. There is something different about the girl. But there is no reason she should hold him here. He could simply take her with him. He wouldn't have to kidnap her. Doubtless, she'd be more than willing to leap aboard. So why this odd reluctance? He can tell himself that he can do his work anywhere in the world as long as broadband holds up, one of the advantages of being a brainbox. But that's just an excuse to put off the inevitable, and the baron is more used to staying one jump ahead of the inevitable than trying to delay it. He hasn't got rich by denying reality, and the reality is, sandstorm or not, Keatown is finished. All the sandstorm is doing is administering the coup de grâce, a finishing touch to the work of deconstruction. The doom he is wishing upon the place makes his own position here less and less tenable. A thriving Keatown was a cool place to be; a backwater Keatown is a place to flee.

He toys with the idea of asking Fraulein Zhenhua to bring the Orchid to him, and asking her directly if she would hop on a chopper and fly away with him to a better place, but curbs his impatience. Something has freaked her, and it would be worth waiting a few more days to soothe her ruffled feathers, groom her a little more. Besides, there's some kind of resistance in the girl that is erotically interesting, but might be annoying should she prove stubborn. This wild flower should not be made to wear the collar – that would take all the fun out of it. After all, a collar has to be earned.

No need to panic. There will be time for a last grand party, a farewell fling at which he can unveil his Orchid. The Strongbows will come; Lady Strongbow won't be able to resist the lure of some fresh meat.

On either side of him, at a respectful distance, stand his bodyguards

Joe and Terry, also looking down at the storm below. The large Samoan watches impassively but Terry looks agitated, his hands twitching as if he wants to kill something. Maybe the storm is bringing out the best in him. This is what it has come to, this is his world – a couple of heavies and a genetically engineered dog; a dancing mistress who keeps to herself, and some bored girls he can barely be bothered fucking. He got insanely rich for this!

He finds he has wandered back into his lounge. Perhaps he should have taken a wife, one like the good Lady Strongbow, one who shared his perversities, who had no problem with being filthy rich, and who would be sitting in the lounge, having poured his favourite cocktail, ready to exchange inanities no questions asked. Truth is, wives hold little interest for him – except of course when they make themselves available to him, which happens with predictable monotony – certainly not enough interest to rival a good Fibonacci cycle or an Elliot wave, or those cool equations that have added so many zeroes to his accounts. It is difficult to imagine a woman whose figure would out-curve a classic Elliot wave.

The corner of the lounge boasts a bronze figurine of a reclining female Buddha, almost life-sized, a rare and very expensive piece from Indonesia, bedecked in jewels like a favoured courtesan. Quite curvy too, with small but interesting breasts. Head propped up by a graceful arm. He thinks of her as his favourite possession. Arya Tara is her name. 'The truth is,' he says to her, 'I am an emotional retard, incapable of forming a mature relationship. I'm just an overgrown nerd with a taste for dancing girls, orgies and virgins.' Not that his Orchid is a virgin, his male intuition tells him that, which adds the spice of deception to her elusiveness.

Arya Tara doesn't answer, but he detects in her silent serenity an attitude of superiority, as if she has one up on him. He's not sure if he likes that blissed-out smile. Despite the promise of her voluptuous curves, she is as indifferent to him as he is to the hapless inhabitants of Keatown, an indifference he has hitherto found provocative and mysterious, a little like the lure of the Orchid, but now finds as discomfiting as the indifference of the universe itself, the great Elliot wave of creation that honours nothing but the maths.

In another corner, beside his Mosin Nagant still lying where he left it after studying the odd group of people stumbling around on the high slopes – he hasn't worked that out yet – is his workstation, an array of the best computers corruption can buy. The email light is still blinking. Stuff it. What's the use of all those zeroes in your account if you can't ignore your emails for a day or two?

And how can the infantile brainbox do his work without a little stimulation?

He pulls on a silken cord that will ring a silver bell down on the next floor, where Zhenhua and the girls are housed.

'I'd like to see the new girl,' he says when Zhenhua appears.

Zhenhua nods. 'Would you like me to... prepare her?'

'No, no. Nothing like that. It's too soon for that. I want to talk to her.' In fact, he realises, he wants to ask the girl to join them when they leave. To hell with waiting until she has been lured deeper into his trap. She has no reason to turn him down, surely. In all likelihood she has been angling for a place on his chopper right from the start, knowing that sooner or later he would leave.

'Ah.' Zhenhua doesn't miss much. It's a bit scary the way she can read him, but he's got used to it. She read him correctly that very first night in the hotel room and hasn't stopped since.

He's far too self-centred to care, but sometimes he wonders if she ever gets lonely or bored out here at the ends of the earth. He knows she spends a lot of time skyping Yum Yum, her friend from her high-class escort days, and chatting to others on Facebook, but she seems so self-sufficient, self-contained, it's difficult for him to imagine her being lonely. Then again, other people's feelings are not his forte.

While Zhenhua's out of the room fetching Orchid, the baron consults his female buddha once more. Did you really preach that desire is a bad thing, tying us here to the world of illusion? You know I can't agree. It's our desire that makes us human, our lust that makes us real. It's nirvana that's the illusion. After all, we do have physical bodies, you know. He stroked the buddha's sleek flanks. Just like you, bronze beauty.

In that oddly intimate moment, if one can have an intimate moment with a bronze statue, he becomes aware of somebody standing beside him. For a moment he thinks that the buddha has taken flesh. The same slim build. Those same almond-shaped eyes. The same half-smile. The odd mixture of innocence and mockery he'd noted before.

'She's beautiful,' the girl says. 'I've never seen anything like this.' She touches the statue gently on the arm as you might a sleeper you don't want to wake.

The baron basks in her admiration of his favourite possession. 'Her name is Tara, or Arya Tara, although I'm not saying it right.'

'Arya Tara. That's a beautiful name.'

'So is Orchid.'

She looks at the floor. 'It's probably not my real name.'

'How come?'

'My dad, he just forgot my real name and started calling me after these flowers he used to grow. I never liked them much. They have a heavy smell. He cared more for them than me. He called me his Moth Orchid.' She touches the bronze woman again, this time on the forehead, resting her fingers there for a moment. 'Does the name mean anything? Arya Tara.'

'I'm not sure,' he gives a self-deprecatory laugh.

'Only some names have meanings,' she says.

'Compassion and emptiness,' he says.

'What?'

'Compassion and emptiness, that's what the guy who sold it to me said her name meant, what she represents, I suppose. I'd forgotten about that.' Compassion and emptiness, the more often he repeats the phrase the less meaning it has. And the words meant nothing to him in the first place.

'Funny meanings for a name.'

'Oh, the name may not mean those things.'

'It's hard to see how they go together.'

'What?' With Zhenhua, he can always follow her reasoning quite comfortably; with this girl he feels lost, never sure which way her mind is going to jump next.

'Compassion and emptiness. They are different things, aren't they? They don't mix.'

'How come?'

'If you are filled with compassion, how can you be empty?'

'That's a toughie.' It's all he can say. He's way out of his depth with Buddhist theology. Anyway, he never pays much attention to a sales pitch. The guy who sold it could have told him any old garbage.

'I might be leaving soon,' he says.

If the news takes her by surprise she gives no sign of it.

'Will you be taking her with you?'

For a silly moment he doesn't know who she's talking about. 'I hadn't thought about it.'

Orchid places her open hand between the statues' gleaming breasts. 'She must weigh a ton, all that brass.'

'Yes.' Come to think of it, he would have to leave it behind. She can practise compassion and emptiness in an empty house.

He moves away, towards the lounge settee, hoping to draw her after him and away from the disturbing presence of Arya Tara. That eternal Mona Lisa smile is starting to unsettle him. The wave of the world could break over that face and the smile would not change. Orchid, however, does not follow him but continues to stand by the statue.

'I'm going to have to leave everything behind,' he says. 'There's no reason I can't come back, probably will at some stage.' None of the others who left had. Not yet. But it might be better to suggest that he would. 'There are people I want to take, even before Arya Tara.'

He hopes that she'll pick up on his hint, his emphasis, and make his job easier, but not this girl. She just looks at him, not making anything easier. The smile on her face is not that different from Arya Tara's.

'Wow, this is a big room.' She looks around as if noticing it for the first time.

It is true. It was built to fit his ambitions. And he had the most expensive experts in décor choose the muted colour scheme to balance the size with a sense of homeliness or comfort, but it still sometimes feels to him like somebody's dream airport lounge, complete with bar in the corner, which makes him feel, especially alone in the evening having a cocktail, that he's been waiting for a flight for a very long time at an airport that has already closed.

'It looks better with people in it,' he says.

It certainly looks better with her in it. Doesn't feel so much like an airport.

Quite unselfconsciously, like a child, she does a few dance steps into the middle of the room. Recently learned from Zhenhua no doubt. Yet executed with a natural style and grace that trumped any technical perfection as far as the baron was concerned.

'You learn fast. You have a natural talent.' That was the least of it, really.

'Fraulein Zhenhua is a good teacher.'

'I don't doubt that.'

The question is, why did he feel so nervous about this? Like a teenager on his first date. He's throwing her a lifeline, for Fibonacci's sake! Offering her a way out of this cul-de-sac. She should jump at it with both hands. He's the one doing all the favours here. He's the baron; she's nothing. Just a homeless urchin from Keatown! And yet, being with her alone in this big empty room has somehow unnerved him.

He turns his back on her and walks to the window. The light of day is beginning to weaken, as if there were an eclipse, and he realises that the air is filling up with dust and particles from the storm below. His balcony has turned from pristine white to a faint dirty orange. To hell with her. A girl like that is always more trouble than she's worth. He could call Terry or Joe, have her thrown out, back into the storm, and see how she likes it.

'I'm thinking of asking you if you want to come with us, get away from here.'

He doesn't say it to her, but to his own reflection in the window, as if addressing himself. Behind his image he can discern her figure, standing in the middle of the mountains like a ghost of light. A moment later she joins him at the window. She looks out, her young face serious.

'There are certain conditions,' she says quietly, more adult now.

The baron breathes a sigh of relief. Negotiations. That he can understand. For a geek he's pretty good at negotiations. The first thing to do is to sound cautious.

'You're going to have to spell them out.'

'Ok,' she says.

And she does.

And the baron can hardly credit his good fortune.

Sirocco on the move

After an eternity Sirocco decides to leave the house, despite the siege, despite knowing that all outside work has ceased lest the sandsnakes strip the flesh from the defenders' bones. Gypsy and Scale have both got cabin fever worse than Sirocco's ever seen, pacing around in the crepuscular shadows of the house, caught in a whirlpool of their own mind-storm, gesticulating, bumping into each other and groping each other's memories. Often talking and mumbling, as if the room were full of people.

And always drinking.

To lessen the chafing of sand against his sensitive skin, Scale has taken to wandering about naked, skinny as a stick insect but not as graceful. Gypsy has taken to squatting amid the growing sand drifts on the floor – she has given up on chasing them with her broom

– smoothing the sand over, and over. It's a bloody madhouse, and the longer he sticks around, the more likely it is that Sirocco will get sucked into it. Their efforts to regress have been more successful than his, since whenever he tries to rock himself into oblivion, the desert yawns open before him, and Lizard is there with his jewelled eyes fixed on him. Go back, Lizard says, you can't go this way.

So he wraps himself up as best he can – it is a painful struggle to get back into his body, to learn how to move again and be in the world, as if convalescing from a long illness – and leaves the house, the rudiments of a plan forming. Above the township, up Beauty Parade towards the mansions, there is an outcrop of rock and flax called Stag Point, maybe above the storm, or near enough. A place to take refuge. A place to take the mokopuna, if he can find anyone.

Around him, patches of air boil with sand, and the ground heaves with the writhing energy of the windsnakes. Curtains of sand, some of them taller than the girders, drift with eerie, sinuous slowness across the streets and over the houses. Pieces of kelp walk erect, as if possessed of skeletons. Lumps of marram grass do tumbleweed somersaults like circus performers. Spiders surf the air with grim equanimity. There is human stuff flying around too, bits of paper, family photographs whirling like confetti, a sock biting its own tail, a floppy doll spinning spread-eagled limbs, a pair of trousers going helter-skelter down the road with legs of wind, a piece of rusty corrugated iron revolving like a roulette wheel, and over at the marae, above Akona's garden, whirlwinds are doing a potato-and-carrot dance in the air. A tricycle with only one wheel limps in circles. Lumps of timber do dangerous somersaults. Dreamy shards of glass in motion. Like everybody's dreams all mixed up flying about in the real world.

Occasionally he glimpses figures in the murk that are neither villagers doing battle with the storm, nor wind-driven columns of sand, but human shapes nevertheless, seemingly struggling into material existence out of those turbulent elements. He tries to take no notice of them.

Despite the shuffling wind, which does not so much howl as rasp like the sound of sandpaper on sandpaper, Sirocco thinks he can hear the strain of the 'Pan' pipes some of the women claim to hear, but so faintly it could have been a temporal echo. The windsnakes seem to have the power to conjure sounds from the past, ancient melodies, ancient weeping. And the smell of the desert at every turn. Snatches of memory flying this way and that around the vortex of some unsprung, unseen well of being.

The cry of a woman. The cry of a child. The cry of the wind.

There is no way he can curl up and start weeping now.

Sirocco stubbornly makes his way to Beauty Parade, slipping through the same wire fence the Rose Woman had negotiated, and uses that fence to haul himself uphill, glad the wind is at his back. Sirocco never has taken kindly to being trapped in rooms. There's too much of the desert in him, too many open spaces, whirling currents and spinning stars.

He doesn't get very far before he is joined by Little Sanyo, hauling himself along the wire behind Sirocco like a stubborn mountain climber. When Sirocco sees him they exchange determined grins, but Sirocco wonders why the kid didn't stay in his refuge at the marae.

At one point the wind has sculpted a hollow beneath the fence, with both wire and fence posts hanging free, held by the tension of the wires across which they swing, hand over hand. Sirocco is good at being a monkey, but Little Sanyo, not quite so wiry, loses his grip and drops down into the soft sand, willing death to take him, easy enough when the sand is floating up his nose and into his mouth so obligingly. No more sleeping under houses or in culverts. No more scrounging.

However, Sirocco is there, smiling his ageless smile, one hand on the lowest wire, the other held out to him. Little Sanyo reaches for it.

a safe and secure place

Being the oldest women in Keatown may suggest to some that Grandmother Gaunt and Akona are close, or must have a lot in common – but that is not the case. Gaunt is constantly testing Akona's patience, seeming to be, at least to Akona, one of those people determined to learn as little as possible from life, and who largely succeed. The less they learn, the more strident and dogmatic they become. And yet, she has on occasion pitched in at the marae gardens with Melissa, and has proved herself to be willing and hard working.

Work, or the work ethic as she sometimes calls it, is Grandmother Gaunt's guiding star, the measure by which she judges people, and she is great at judging people. It is something of a speciality of hers.

Beware of falling on the wrong side of that judgement, for there be no-hopers and the work shy under every rock you care to turn over. God, with Grandmother Gaunt's approval, takes a stern view of laziness. Mother Smiley's husband, Flounder Phil as they called him when he was around, was a no-hoper because he never did anything but a bit of fishing every so often. So much for him. And there is Gypsy Cornet's man, Scale, who does have a job but is, from what she's heard, a malingerer, quick to let others do the lion's share. They say he's done nothing through this whole storm but cower inside or run around uselessly brandishing a spade. She feels sorry for Gypsy Cornet. Now there's a magnificent woman hitched to a no-hoper and driven to drink – isn't it so often the way? What makes these wonderful women choose such deadbeat men has always been a mystery to her. Men of course, she has often observed, tend on the whole to be lazier than women. Gaunt herself has always striven to set a good example to younger women who, given half a chance, would sit around painting their toenails. Women don't have time to be lazy. Except some we better not name...

And so on until Akona loses patience, for the gossip on which these judgements are built is anathema to her. All kinds of monsters lurk in the shadows of gossip, eager to feed: prejudice, envy, spite, hatred; as far as Akona is concerned there is no place for these things on the marae, where people should come together, meet over their differences, grow food together, eat and drink together, see out the old year and welcome in the new. That isn't too much to ask. Generations have done it in human communities everywhere. They can go somewhere else to tear each other apart.

It takes Akona a moment to realise why the old woman has come visiting, perhaps the same reason that drew the librarian. Like most women on their own, Gaunt is fiercely independent of spirit, and fiercely self-sufficient. It is part of Gaunt's work ethic that she stands on her own two feet and is beholden to nobody but the Lord himself, who will one day recognise her virtue. Now she is here because she is afraid. Too afraid to remain alone.

Looking around her comforting kitchen table, Akona sees all five women with the same expression on their faces. Fear. Not just of the storm, but the unknown it brings with it. It is easy to say that life will never be the same again, harder to sit at someone's kitchen table and face the fact. This is their refuge, their safe, secure place. And they all look to her, Akona, because they think she is not afraid, and because she is their seer and wise woman, their kuia.

Akona takes a bag of last year's broad beans, her seed stock for this year, and empties them onto the table. The best ones she will sort out for a particular spot in the garden she has in mind. The great thing about broad beans is that they thrive in the poorer soils the rocky headland offers. They hate being coddled. The women watch her intently as she begins to sort through the beans, as if she were showing them some kind of magic trick. 'If you keep looking at them they disappear,' she says, but only the librarian smiles.

'How do you know which are good ones?' Gaunt asks.

'Just by looking at them.' She's not about to tell Gaunt that she is testing each seed for its vital essence, its eagerness and capacity to grow. Best say nothing and get on with it.

'What about everybody else?' Akona says in a practical voice. 'Is everybody safe? What about the mokopuna?'

There's no way they can know, but the question takes their minds off themselves.

'The little Asian one can burrow in the ground like a mole,' Gaunt says.

'They say people have gone missing,' Margot says, 'but they may turn up.'

'I heard the Baby crying last night, just crying and crying. He's normally such a cheerful little chappy.' This is Cherrie Lamont, but how she managed to hear the Baby crying in this storm is a bit of a mystery. She's a troublemaker at heart, Akona decides. Even stupid people are capable of malicious intent.

Out of the corner of her eye, Akona catches a movement. It's a spider heading at due speed across her floor. Perhaps it imagines that it will arrive at some safe and secure place. Lucifer notices it too, and keeps an eye on it.

'Probably the storm,' Margot says.

'Probably,' Gaunt says, taking the bait laid for her by Cherrie Lamont.

'What do you mean?'

'I mean probably. That's what I said, isn't it?'

'But you sound like you mean something else.'

'Well...' Gaunt picked up a broad bean and turned it over in her fingers, 'far be it for me to say... but there are those, whose first care is the Baby, I hasten to say, who are concerned at the Baby's living conditions and wonder if he is in the right hands.'

'Amen to that!' Melissa says. This turn in the conversation has perked her up. She has something other than cockroaches to think about.

'Hera is a good mother,' Margot says.

'Oh! Queen Hera is a good mother,' Melissa repeats back into Margot's face.

'I'm sure she is,' Gaunt says. 'Say no more.'

'You've already said enough,' Akona says.

'No she hasn't,' Melissa says. 'There's a whole lot more to say.'

'Then when you next see Hera, you can say it,' Akona says, 'to her face, like an honest person.'

Akona is tired. If only sorting people were as easy as sorting beans.

'If every mother whose baby cried had it taken off her, the world would be full of motherless children,' Margot says, unable to let it go. She and Melissa sit there steaming. Old friends who can hardly look each other in the face. Gaunt seems to be gloating. The librarian is smiling to herself. Cherrie Lamont has gone into a blank space. They've all gone a little crazy, Akona thinks.

'You can see it that way,' Gaunt says, smoothly taking over from Melissa.

'How do you see it?'

'I see a tragedy looming if we don't take action.'

'Amen to that!' Melissa turns on Akona. 'You would put the so-called rights of the mother, the harlot, over the welfare of the child. If that poor unnamed baby comes to harm, you will be to blame. You!'

Before Akona can speak, Margot jumps in. 'Oh! So he's a poor unnamed baby now, is he? I thought he was the Child of Jezebel, with the stain of sin upon him...'

'Which is why he must be baptised!' Melissa is on her feet again in a frenzy. She is ready to stomp on more cockroaches, each one with the face of the harlot. 'Born in sin and unredeemed.'

'You are right,' Gaunt says, 'but you must calm down.' She flicks Akona a grin of triumph. 'Melissa has a point. After all, the child has no name and no father. If he had a mother like Melissa here, a god-fearing woman, he would have a father too. A good, strong father. And he would take his father's name.'

Melissa blushes furiously, but it's all true, every word of it. And Billy would be a good, strong father. A wonderful father. He only beat her a couple of times, when he was drinking Och's hock, and that was partly her fault because she acted uppity and tried to tell him what to do. She lived to regret standing up to him, and has even made plans for escaping south, to get away from him, if need be. All that would change if there were a child. Whoever the father, the Baby would inherit Keatown, Akona thinks. Everything. All the blood lines have dried up. Only the Baby will be left.

Listening to people, Akona decides, is very different from listening to plants. People are louder, for a start. With people you have to get past the words and listen to their purpose. Look at Gaunt. Now that her fear of the storm has subsided, she has returned to her old pattern of trying to take advantage of every situation, winning converts to her cause, her long-standing efforts to get the Baby away from Queen Hera. She can't even say the name without curling her lips. Queen? Ha! After all, the Baby is living proof that Hera is a woman of loose virtue. The reverend has got that right. No angel of the Lord visited her on a night. Some man in Keatown fathered the child. The more time that goes by without the father stepping forward, the more likely he is to be married and hiding his disgrace. How the woman could parade around the way she does, flaunting her shameless breasts and holding her head up, as if she really were a queen, is quite beyond Grandmother Gaunt.

Akona, who has never had a husband, has always been puzzled by the way in which her fellow women will complain endlessly about them, condemn their men on one hand and yet hold tenaciously to them on the other. These worthless, good-for-nothing, no-hoper whoremongers are apparently so precious their wives will scratch each other's eyes out for the privilege of keeping them! The gossips will be right, Hera is protecting somebody – but worrying about what bed a man might be in is a silliness Akona has never had time for. She's been too busy with important things.

Like sorting beans. She has two piles now. The hopefuls and the hopeless. The chosen and the unchosen. She tries not to draw any conclusions as she sweeps them into two different jars.

Conclusions can be very tempting.

Pyjama Pants and Smart Pants

Annanda cowers inside his supermarket, spending his time between apprehensively glancing up at his roof, afraid of the accumulation of sand on the integrity of the structure, which has heavy solar panels installed, and spying on Flay who is working angrily with Pinky and Tony, covering the precious mechanisms of his pumps with thick plastic held down by the largest lumps of metal he can find, creating odd service-station sculptures, but Annanda can see that he is not satisfied. This sand wriggles everywhere, and can no doubt wriggle under Flay's makeshift tarpaulins. Annanda fully appreciates that if Flay's pumps jam with sand, he will have a job siphoning the petrol out of his underground tanks, and he sure won't want any sand to get into his precious storage tanks. Annanda feels somewhat smug that his great sliding-glass doors seal the whole supermarket beautifully. All the windows are sealed too, and the back door, the service entrance, is made of double-reinforced steel. Only the roof is a bother. If only he had Suneal here, who was like a younger brother to him, he could send him up on the roof with a shovel. Suneal was always game for an adventure, Annanda was known as the cautious one.

He gets up and goes to the checkout counter where he has shamefully left scattered packets of tiny golden safety pins. In his mind's eye he can see them prettily stitching up the Baby's nappies, but of course that would take time, and mothers, even the best of them, are so impatient these days. His own mother would have jumped at the chance of getting her hands on such versatile little safety pins, good for everything from pinning up fabric, dresses and the like, to fixing babies' nappies. Of course he hasn't said any of this to Hera, who is a very independently minded woman, a woman who doubtless wouldn't really care what Annanda's mother might have done.

Seeking strength, he glances at the picture of Hanuman on the cigarette cabinet. The monkey god could lift a mountain with one hand easily, whereas Annanda can hardly lift a few tiny safety pins, so heavy is his heart. It is this storm. If only Suneal were here, they could weather the storm together, remember and have a good laugh about old times in Lucknow, the happy times they had fleecing tourists and hustling for their bread. The loneliness and isolation of Keatown, which he welcomed after the hurdy-gurdy of Lucknow, is now eating into his soul.

During the boom time, the beauty of the landscape, its bareness and grandeur, was a bonus. After closing up shop, he could go down to the beach and sit in front of the ocean and think of Suneal, and how it would be when his friend joined him. Annanda had never seen the ocean, had hardly ever left the streets of Lucknow, and the sight of it was an amazement. Now he hardly ever goes there. So empty and huge, it merely serves to remind him how far away he is from Lucknow, and Suneal.

Doubtless, Hanuman would have swum the vast ocean in a few swift strokes.

Annanda sighs, a big empty sigh for a big empty shop. A shop without customers is not a shop at all, it is a museum, an art installation, a morgue. He tidies the safety pins away, and is about to return them to their shelf out the back, when he notices something wrong with the stack of sardine cans. He doesn't have to count them to know that one is missing. The mokopuna! The big dopey one with the toothache maybe isn't so dopey as he looks, using Hera and the cunning Sirocco as a cover.

He's calculating a revenge when he hears a bang from the sliding doors. The sand is blowing hard but he can discern two figures, one side-on shoulder to the door, the other facing him through the glass. Facing him but apparently not seeing him, as if the glass were opaque on the outside. Annanda hurries to the door. Nothing's very clear but it seems there are two women, quite disoriented, banging up against the glass door, driven perhaps by the wind. He doesn't know these women, he's sure of that, which is astonishing. Visitors, stranded in the storm? He pictures a car, a mini-van, a tourist bus! engines clogged with sand. Distressed tourists hungry for snacks. Of course, letting them in means letting in a certain amount of sand, but he can cope with a bit of sand with customers in the offing.

He pulls open the door and the two figures stumble inside. It's not clear they want to come in. The one standing sideways keeps trying to walk forward against the edge of the door, but is pushed in sideways by the force of the wind; the other staggers forward with the wind at her back. Annanda slams the door shut, puts on his most helpful face, and turns to greet his customers. Some fresh spring water, perhaps, bottled locally? The two women, however, take no notice of him or his welcoming smile, but have already found their feet and are wandering, not down the aisles, but straight past the two disused checkout counters towards the southern wall and the baked-beans stand. He follows politely behind, noting that the women are not exactly dressed like tourists. One of them looks like a smart city woman, with a helmet haircut and a cellphone in one hand; a woman with money, Annanda guesses, but a hard one who would try to drive a bargain. He has dealt with such glitzy women before, seldom to his satisfaction. The other is dressed bizarrely in camping boots, pyjama pants and a man's suit jacket, clutching a small teddy bear which she swings back and forward as she walks. For a moment Annanda thinks she could be a leftover celeb, high on drugs; it's the way she walks, oblivious to everything around her; stoned out of her gourd, as they used to say. If it's drugs she's looking for, Annanda doesn't have any. In Keatown's heyday he left that kind of thing to Flay, who doesn't have Annanda's high moral standards.

When they reach the southern wall they grope at it, dislodging a shelf of baked beans, before turning west and heading down the aisle to the back of the supermarket. Smart One walks quite determinedly, as if she knows where she's going. The stoned one, Pyjama Pants, keeps bumping up against the southern wall. Annanda has always espoused the view that one should not impose on customers, or give them the sort of hustle that belongs to the streets of Lucknow, but it is time to say, 'Excuse me ladies, is there something you would be seeking?' Always polite but never obsequious, that is the rule.

They take no more notice of him than they do of each other, but Annanda is not fazed; a customer's mood may change at any moment, from indifference to delight, for example, when they see something they want. Or of course a sale can go cold right up to the moment before money changes hands.

He is about to suggest some items they may be interested in – biscuits, not too far past their use-by date, chocolates and candies still good to go, refreshing soda water, or perhaps some tourist mementoes of Keatown, including miniature rabbit-fur-clad seals, and blue glass whales on stems as slender as wine flutes – when the women reach the southwestern corner, the freezers, at present filled with goat, pig and fish meat, all locally provided of course. They stop in confusion, groping at the walls and banging into each other. Then Smart Woman sets off north, along the back wall, but her gait is now far less decisive, as if she were pushing against some invisible force, weaving this way and that against it. Pyjama Pants tries to follow suit but, showing signs of distress, although she says nothing, hesitates and pushes up against Annanda's freezers before turning and blundering back up the south wall towards the checkout counters.

For the first time Annanda feels alarmed. They could both be drunk or otherwise, as the celebs used to be; he was well accustomed to bizarre behaviour even to the point of ejecting some of his best customers when they grew too frolicsome, but what alarms him is their utter silence, their impassivity. Their wilful lethargy. Perhaps some new drug he's never heard of which renders its victims mute, and maybe deaf too. Who would take a drug like that?

Now he has to decide whether to stay and watch Pyjama Pants making her way back along the southern wall or track Smart Pants. Since he can't see Smart Pants, he goes after her in time to catch her as she reaches the north wall. This time there is no hesitation. She briskly follows the north wall east. With a sinking heart Annanda realises that these space-cases are not going to buy anything, they're not even looking at the displays. It's like they've blundered in here by accident and, like blind rats in a maze, can't find their way out again. Already Pyjama Pants has reached the end of the south wall and is stumbling around, apparently reluctant to retrace her path back north to the door. Smart Pants has already reached the door and is feeling the glass as if she remembers it. Annanda wastes no time, whisking open the door regardless of the sand whisking in and gently propels Smart Pants out the door, not without a moment of regret, watching her as she makes her way south along the display window, buffeted against the wind and the sand, still clutching her cellphone.

In the meantime, Pyjama Pants has turned west again and is walking down the first aisle, blundering from the cleaning fluid on the north side to the racks of toothbrushes in their yellowing cellophane packs on the other. Annanda hurries after her, catching up with her before she reaches the end of the aisle.

'Madam...'

He takes her gently by the arm, just behind the elbow, a little trick he learned in Lucknow, but she hardly seems to notice, and begins to drag him along. When they again reach the west wall with its freezers, the woman stops of her own accord. Her head moves from side to side but her eyes don't shift at all. Clearly the woman needs medical attention, but there is no way he can get Akona down from the marae in this storm. Perhaps he can induce the woman to lie down. He gently pushes a foot in behind her knees, catches her as she topples backwards, and lies her, equally gently, on the floor, making sure he respects her person as much as possible. She goes down unresistingly, but immediately, as soon as she is prone, begins to rise again, getting back on her feet with surprising alacrity. As Annanda again takes her arm, more firmly this time, he wonders if the woman might not be on drugs at all but ill, perhaps contagiously so.

She is largely unresisting as he strong-arms her back down the aisle, past the cleaning fluid and toothbrushes, to the main door, although she keeps leaning south, towards the toothbrushes. Odd that, while he does not find the woman at all offensive, holding on to her makes Annanda feel slightly queasy, like seasickness, like homesickness, as if he is once again walking through the crowded streets of Lucknow, escorting some beggar woman back to the thoroughfare, regretfully, silently evoking the blessings of Rama for her.

Annanda is only too pleased to let a little sand in as he propels Pyjama Pants out. Life can be cruel sometimes. But Pyjama Pants doesn't seem to mind the storm. Annanda has propelled her far enough to be clear of the supermarket, and she stumbles south, soon to be eaten up by the sand.

Before he closes the door, Annanda notices Flay, standing by his besieged pumps like a captain ready to go down with his ship. He flourishes his shotgun at Annanda.

# of crying and forgetting

Jolene Smiley, Miranda's mum, Mother Smiley's younger sister, and wife of Blade, the fastest filleter in the fish shed, is sitting on a box in front of the fireplace staring into it as if a real fire burned there and not a hoax of dancing sand-devils.

Jolene is not having a good day. First Miranda, who finally kicked out that stupid little clinging-vine Witch Hunt, became weepy in the storm and rushed out of the house even while the Devil's own wind was still blowing. Jolene fears for her daughter's safety, but is not about to rush out into the maelstrom on some futile rescue effort. Kids! Then there is her dear sister, the embittered Mother Smiley, who has kind of moved in since Flounder Phil went walkabout, and loses no opportunity for a sarcastic comment. Finally, there's Blade himself, her dear man, sitting slumped in front of the fireplace, hardly moving a muscle, indifferent to the fate of his daughter, indifferent to everything. Blade flourishes in the fish shed, where he can show off his skill and be a man, so he can come home and be a man too, but three days in futile battle against the sand has apparently defeated the knife-wielder.

Truth be told, she has sometimes wished for the wind to be taken out of her husband's sails, the grin wiped off his face, because his idea of being a man at home does not always accord with hers. Yet, to see him stricken like this, somehow defeated, brings her no satisfaction. She gets up and makes tea on an old Russian samovar she inherited from her ancestors, for her real name is not Jolene – the name of a song – but Anastasia, and her earliest memories are of this very same battered samovar, and the dark shape of her mother bending over it just as she's bending over it now, although thinking about such things merely adds to her burdens. There must have been a time, she thinks, when I was really happy. That thought does not make her happy, for any magic moments she might have had are buried so deep in the past they only surface at odd moments, and indirectly, wrapped in nostalgia. Moments that now lie out of sight, around the corner of memory.

She pours tea into his favourite cup and takes it to Blade who receives it mechanically, without looking at it, and places it on his lap. Jolene has come to understand Blade pretty well. Not a complicated man, or given to introspection. His only vice appears to be a taste for Och's hock, the vilest bootleg liquor ever, courtesy of Keatown's wild mountain bootlegger, Och Arglin. Yet the famous Blade, King of the Fish shed, doesn't know who he is or what to do when he isn't working. He works and eats and sleeps and sometimes lies on top of her and discharges his manly duties to his own satisfaction. And occasionally hers. She has no cause for complaint. He has a favourite cup and a favourite knife. Sometimes he pats his Miranda's goldie locks with vague affection. At least he doesn't beat them, despite her mother advising her that all men get drunk and beat their women and children. That's the way it was in Russia.

Not the sharpest Blade in the drawer (ha ha, there's an old joke), but an honest one, as far as men can be honest. There was a time when he took to visiting that Lamont woman, and that wasn't exactly honest, but Jolene understands that men can be attracted to flipperty women like the so-called Cherrie Lamont who are all fluff and flounce, and it didn't last very long. Blade is the strong, silent type who doesn't appreciate chattering women, and Lamont never stops jabbering in that phony French accent of hers. It was only a matter of time before it all faded away. Jolene didn't waste any time or words on the issue. She didn't have to; he knew well enough. Her silence stuck deeper than words.

The one thing, however, she's never had to deal with is this sudden withdrawal, this frightening abstraction from everything, this horrible indifference even when the storm shakes the house to its foundations, their daughter rushes out in a tizzy, and sand sifts down from the rafters. Looking at him, one would imagine that he would be a pillar of strength in this situation, but no, all his will seems to have drained out of him.

Mother Smiley is standing to one side with a conflicted smile on her face, watching Jolene tend to her man. On one hand, Flounder Phil's desertion has convinced her of Grandmother Gaunt's contention that all men are either faithless or fools or both. Blade, with his self-indulgent behaviour, getting her sister to run around after him making him cups of tea while he goes broody, is typical. On the other hand, she's jealous that her sister has a man to run around after, and recognising that she's jealous makes her nasty. She's supposed to be making one of her famous soups, her key ingredient being her magic stone, which she found on a dried riverbed sparkling with all the minerals and flavours of the mountains, but she's lost concentration. Besides, without a few flounder bones, and a generous sprinkling of herbs from Akona's garden, her soup loses much of its lustre.

Jolene, making sure the tea is secured in Blade's lap, meets her sister's sardonic smile with one of her own. Yes, a woman has her cross to bear, but at least she has one, so her jealous sister better go eat worms. They're locked in that wonderful sisterly moment when Blade begins to lean sideways. His favourite cup tips over, spilling hot tea on his lap, before falling to the floor and smashing. He bends over, picks the cup's handle from the shards, ignoring the rest, and stands up. It is like he is asleep. He shows no reaction to the hot tea in his lap or the loss of his favourite cup. He tries to walk through the door without opening it, as if he's forgotten what the doorknob is for.

'What are you doing?' Jolene says.

He doesn't answer, but blindly finds the doorknob and stumbles outside.

'Where're you going?' Jolene says with sudden fright.

She and Mother Smiley make a rush for the door and collide. Jolene pushes her sister aside and, after a deep breath, steps outside. All around her are columns of moving sand, like ghosts, driven by the wind, disintegrating around buildings or crossing the street like eerie pedestrians. One of them is her man. Heedless, she grabs his arm and screams into his face, but he takes no notice of her, just keeps plodding, dragging her along, still gripping the cup handle. She soon lets go. It's too frightening out here and Blade is suddenly more frightening than anything else because she no longer knows him, his face no longer animated by any echo of feeling she can recognise.

When she gets back to the house, Miranda and Witch Hunt have returned, bringing along with them the goofy one with the tooth, the geeky kid, and the runt Sirocco.

'Where's Dad? Miranda says instantly.

'Gone,' Jolene says. A small word with a long sound. A long, empty sound.

'Gone where?'

'I dunno... I'm tired... maybe to help with the storm. He was going a bit stir-crazy around the house.'

Nobody says anything. Mother Smiley snickers.

'He'll come back,' Jolene says. He always comes back. Like after a binge on Och's hock. After all, where else can he go?

'Which way did he go?' Sirocco asks.

She gestures south. 'He'll come back,' she says.

Sirocco nods gravely. Miranda bursts out crying. Witch Hunt joins in.

At that moment the house moves, as in the Russian tale where the witch's house stands on chicken legs and runs around. The crying turns to screaming. Mother Smiley is shouting. Jolene buries her hands in her face and prays fervently to the Stickman's god. Any god crazy enough to take responsibility.

The pesky runt is pulling at her arm. He's saying something. '...up to Stag Point... out of the wind...'

She nods. It's a good idea. Probably many have already done it. But of course she can't leave. Like generations of Russian women before her, she has to stay and tend the samovar and wait for her man's return. Men always go away, sometimes to war, sometimes to work, and sometimes to whores, and the women wait for them to come back. They wait and they weep. The image of him returning and finding that she's deserted is too much to bear. When she meets Sirocco's earnest gaze, she sees something calm and lucid, as clear as a desert night sky.

'Take care of Miranda,' she says, unable to believe that she is handing the care of her child over to this enigmatic little leader of the group they call the mokopuna. A nut-case, in the opinion of most people, who claims to have been guided out of the desert by a talking lizard. But it won't be for long. Just the duration of the storm. Miranda will be safer with her friends on Stag Point until after the storm. Then Blade will come back and everything will return to normal.

Sirocco nods with the same gravity as before.

Behind him, Sad Toof bares his wounded gums at her, melancholy but benign, and takes Miranda's hand.

'Go to safety,' Jolene says, 'while I wait here for Daddy.'

Miranda understands. Somebody has to wait for Daddy.

'You can wait for my daddy too,' Witch Hunt says. 'I saw him, you know. He was carrying his briefcase.'

'Spare me!' Mother Smiley says. Thank God she and Phil never had kids!

As the mokopuna troop out the wobbling door, the two sisters face each other. No way will Mother Smiley be deserting her sister in her hour of direst need. The sisters are bonded now; both have seen their men walk away. All they have is each other. But something is bothering Mother Smiley.

'There really was a slutty girl,' she says.

As the mokopuna leave, the house groans and shakes, pounded by sand waves which rise and fall beneath as if it were perched on some great copulating beast. It is hard to tell if this is an effect of the wind or an earthquake. It feels as if the wind is in the very earth itself, right down to the rock.

'I don't want to leave Mum,' Miranda says, twisting around to take a last look at her place as if she might never see it again.

'We'll come back,' Sirocco says, 'when the wind stops.'

Miranda nods but is not convinced. What if the wind never stops? What if Dad never comes home? What if she gets stuck with Witch Hunt forever?

'How can a body just walk away like Blade did?' Sad Toof says.

'I think they just forget who they are,' Sirocco says.

Sad Toof doesn't ask who he is talking about. Maybe he understands. 'How can you forget who you are?'

'Easier than you might think,' Sirocco says.

# of prayer and prophecy

After three days of ecstatic communion with God, Rasputin arises from his thin, tatty mattress on the old church floor, cleansed and purified. God has made a number of things clear to him, and gifted him warnings and prophesies. He, Rasputin, will become a leader and saviour of his people as God's darkness falls upon them. Just who his people might be, God did not explain, but when God showed him that his master, the Rev Stickman, would soon stray from the path of truth, Rasputin understood that it was not just the mokopuna he must lead, but all living souls remaining in Keatown. But would they accept him, a mere mokopuna, as their prophet?

The rapture is under way, God assured him, but not quite the way fallible man imagined. First, the souls of the wretched would be called to Hell by their dark master. Rasputin is right to think of the driftdead as Pilgrims of Darkness, for that is what they are, the Legions of the Damned, already stripped of soul, each one a walking emptiness. And God made them visible so that everybody, even the most craven, could see the truth, and cleave unto the true God. Their dreadful pilgrimage is an object lesson to everyone. Only after the legions have passed, and they will pass, God assured him, would the Holy Spirit come down upon the worthy, the chosen that remained. Those who survived the call of Darkness would be transfigured, just as Christ himself was transfigured.

On Pine Point, where he sat with Orchid, God showed him the driftdead overrunning the earth. In this bleak stone church, God has shown him his own difficult path.

Stretching his muscles and pacing around the now sandy floor of the old church, getting the feel of his body again and increasingly aware of the snicker and lament of the wind in the eaves, he sees just how strewn with obstacles, like roadside bombs, his path will be. God has given him no directions as to how he will become leader and saviour – that he must do for himself. And he has to face, not only the dereliction of his master, but his own errant feelings for Orchid. God showed him that Orchid's soul had already fallen under the shadow of a dark power that lives in the mansions, Baron Fairweather, a creature of evil, and much danger lay in that direction for Rasputin.

The danger was that in trying to save her soul, he would succumb to the pull of the flesh and in the process hideously deceive himself as to his true purpose – and the Devil would have his soul just like that. In a finger-snap. Then there is the question of the reptile worshipper from the desert, Sirocco, as they call him, and his odd power over the mokopuna. God hasn't revealed anything about Sirocco, but Rasputin can follow the dots for himself. Sooner or later he will cross paths with the pagan and he needs to be ready.

He goes to the door of the church, opens it a fraction and peers out into the storm, which has, like some mad artist, reduced the world to shifting patterns of illusion. Shapes come and go but don't resolve themselves, and sounds echo and get snatched away with no telling which direction they are coming from. Rasputin is not fooled by the storm, and so he is not afraid of it. It is the Devil's Veil, masking the arrival of the Pilgrims of Darkness. Once Satan's use for it is over, the storm will drop and zombies will come en masse. God has revealed this future to him. And God said, everywhere you look you will see them, the Pilgrims of Darkness, mere bodies without souls, and the world shall fill up with them, and there will be no end to them, and those who have dreamed of a zombie apocalypse will get their desires.

But now that his ecstatic communion with God has ended, Rasputin feels bereft. Would that God walked with him every step of the way! His three days with God have already become a memory, and memory, God has shown him, being mother of the imagination, is easy prey to distortion and fabrication. He must not rely on memory, but live in God every moment lest his prophecies become rote and he fall into illusion. It is up to him now. This is not God's burden; God has no burdens. This is his.

He is not surprised when, through the shifting patterns of the storm, he sees a straggle of mokopuna heading up Beauty Parade, led by the diminutive lizard worshipper. God, without a trace of irony, is showing him his flock, at least the first of it, this unpromising material, the outcast and the forgotten. Maybe forgotten by man but not by God. He is filled with gratitude. Thank you, Lord! The world might fill up with the Pilgrims of Darkness, but it is God's love that fills the greater void beyond. He knows he has to be strategic. He cannot simply announce himself the saviour; that would not be well received. Better to join them and let God show the way.

Be humble, God says as he steps out into the storm.

a brave little Witch Hunt

The least and most humble of that courageous little band must surely be Witch Hunt, the plain, battered little girl nobody cares about except maybe Miranda – although Miranda seems to mainly care about herself – so Rasputin attempts to join her and walk beside her, for even the very least of us are blessed in the eyes of the Lord. Now that the scales have fallen from his eyes, and he can see the world in all its divinity and terror, he understands that Witch Hunt is driven solely by her love for the more fickle Miranda. The force of it disturbs Rasputin. He's not sure that the Reverend Stickman would approve. But the reverend is not God, merely a frail emissary, and Rasputin now has to walk with God every living moment.

If Rasputin had tried to explain this to Witch Hunt he might have been surprised by her answer. The little girl who doesn't talk much well understands the nature of her feelings for Miranda, and would hardly describe it as love. Miranda is kind to her, mostly, and sometimes lets her stay over and sleep on the same bed as her, but her devotion to the older girl is more like the love of a dog for its master than between two people. Miranda holds her hand, pats her on the head and sometimes even kisses her cheek, which makes Witch Hunt pant with happiness, but would not describe her feelings as love – rather fear. Fear that one day Miranda would turn and walk away from her, and she would be left alone in the world. She can easily imagine it, her friend's figure getting smaller and smaller, never turning her head once to look back.

She grips Miranda's hand for dear life. With every step the sting of the sandsnakes grows crueller and the air more opaque. How can she be sure the world is still there, the way she remembers it?

She closes her eyes and every step becomes interminable, the warm hand she is holding her one link to the world. She thinks about her Daddy. The one she saw from Miranda's window, the one with the briefcase. All he had to do was turn his head and he would have seen her. Why didn't he?

When Rasputin joins her, she doesn't take much notice. After all, he has never bothered with her before, having eyes only for the prettiest one, the Orchid, apparently oblivious to the existence of the least and plainest. Then he smiles at her. She's not to know that Rasputin is trying out his new God smile, and it warms her heart. She tries to smile back.

She's nothing if not a brave little Witch Hunt.

At that moment the straggling column falters. Sirocco, who's leading the way with Sad Toof and Little Sanyo, has stopped and is pointing to something. As Miranda, Witch Hunt and Rasputin join them, other figures materialise around them, passing in front of them, crossing Beauty Parade heading south. The way they move, their indifference to the storm, reminds Witch Hunt of the strange couple they saw on Pine Point.

'Driftdead alert!' Little Sanyo pipes, dancing from side to side.

Rasputin draws his breath in sharply. 'Yes, Lord, yes!' he says.

Then the driftdead are among them. A big woman in a nurse's uniform is bearing down on Witch Hunt with a baby's feeding bottle in one hand. Her face is large and round on a thick neck and her bulging eyes are fixed on some point way above Witch Hunt's head. For a terrified moment Witch Hunt thinks it's her mother coming to beat some sense into her, and that the bottle she is carrying doesn't contain milk but sickly liquor, the woman has that same heedless, oblivious look. Witch Hunt screams as the woman blunders into her, knocking her down, and curls into a ball, waiting for the blows and the force feeding of liquor. They don't come. Instead Rasputin is kneeling by her side, his hand in hers, his face turned ecstatically to heaven. She feels tenderness in his touch, but also trembling, the fear. Sand fills her mouth. Miranda stands beside him, looking down at Witch Hunt.

'What are you doing?' she shouts at Rasputin. 'She'll get buried in the sand!'

As Miranda and Rasputin pull her to her feet, Witch Hunt keeps her eyes closed. When she opens them the woman is nothing more than a fading shape in the soupy air.

girl on the roof

While none of them is enjoying the conversation particularly, except perhaps Grandmother Gaunt, they are loath to let it go. Without their gossip, there is nothing to keep out the storm that shakes the walls and rattles the windows. When the wind drops away, there is nothing but silence, and that is worse. Then there is nothing to do but stare into their empty teacups.

Melissa is gabbing away about the mysterious nature of the seclusion Hera went into when she was pregnant. Of course the woman would be ashamed to show her face, that was understandable, but to refuse all visitors and well-wishers seemed excessive. Why, the woman wouldn't even let Akona examine her or the Baby. Her only attendant was that slip of a girl Orchid. Seems like the woman was trying to hide the Baby away from the sight of the Lord himself.

With Gaunt's encouragement, she is developing that theme when Akona holds her hand up for silence. There's another noise, apart from the knocking of the wind. They can all hear it.

'It's on the roof,' Gaunt says, clutching the table. 'The wind doesn't wear boots.'

Cherrie Lamont jumps up and hides her face in her jumper.

Nanny struggles to her feet and Lucifer pulls at his rope. Akona gets up and puts on a coat. The spider she saw on the floor is now halfway up the wall.

'You're not,' Gaunt says.

'I have to,' Akona says, 'There's something on my roof.'

'Maybe it's a branch or piece of debris. There's all sorts of stuff flying around.'

The banging on the roof repeats.

'No,' Akona says. 'Not a branch.'

Melissa grabs her sleeve. 'Don't go out there. Please, just don't go. There are creatures out there. Demons. We're safe in here.' The woman looks fearfully around the room, 'They can't get in here. You don't want to go out there. Truly you don't.'

'That's life,' Akona says. 'You end up doing things you don't want to do, seeing things you don't want to see. Hearing talk you'd rather not hear.' She pulls her sleeve free of Melissa's clutching fingers and makes for the door. Melissa turns to Margot and grabs her arm. Her fury gone, replaced by fear, Margot becomes her trusted old friend again, one who can stand with her in the face of the unknown.

Outside, Akona finds the storm jerking from one extreme to the other. Almost calm one moment, slamming into her the next. It is gusting off the sea, but there is a contrary wind, like an echo, a bounce back off the hills. Doing her best to ignore it, she moves away from the house a little to get a view of the roof. She's not afraid of the wind blowing her over, it's not quite that strong at the moment, but she has to watch for flying debris, dust and sand.

There's a young woman on her roof. Looks like a city person, dressed in tight jeans and a T-shirt with lettering on it. In one hand she is holding a stone which glows a ruby red in the fitful light. Akona can't make out what she's doing or how she got up there. She seems to be clumping aimlessly about. Akona considers shouting something but knows it'd be useless, and not just because of the wind. So this is what they are all afraid of, she thinks. Akona is not afraid. This young woman reminds her of a not particularly bright animal who can find its way into a trap but not out of it. Having found her way onto the roof, apparently at the northern end, she is now facing too deep a jump at the southern end and doesn't have the sense to retrace her steps. A bit like silly Nanny who will twist herself around a tree to the point of choking to death.

Akona's first thought is how to get the poor woman down. She has a fold-out ladder that might work against the southern side of the house. She's fetching the ladder from the lean-to on the northern side, where she keeps her gardening tools, when Gaunt joins her. The severe woman is dressed in a bright red mac. 'What are you doing?'

'Getting that woman off my roof.'

'That's not a woman.'

'Whatever it is, she can't stay on my roof.'

There's a sudden lull in the storm, at least where they are. Not too far off they can see columns of sand moving through the air like half-dematerialised statues. They can hear a sighing close by, while further off a distant thrumming as the wind plays the girders like a giant musical instrument. Akona takes the opportunity to haul the ladder around the side of the house.

Gaunt follows her. 'You don't understand.'

'What don't I understand? And why are you so frightened?'

'You have to kill it.'

'No,' Akona says as gently as she can. Frightened people are dangerous. You have to be careful with them.

'But you have to kill it. It's unclean!'

Unclean. You could say that. Akona remembers the thing that looked like her Grandfather Lawrence and the stale wind that blew off the river. You could call that unclean.

Gaunt gestures to the curtains of shifting sand. 'They're out there. This wind has brought them in.'

'What do you think they are?'

'Horrible things pretending to be people.'

As she places the ladder against the wall, Akona tries to get a focus on the young woman who's pacing back and forth along the south side of the roof. This creature is only able to see certain things, she decides. Much of the world she can't see. The question now is, will she be able to see the ladder and understand how to lower herself onto it? Whatever else she might be, she doesn't look that bright, maybe not as smart as a chimp who would certainly understand the ladder and seize the opportunity. As would a cat. Sometimes she opens a window to let out a bird trapped inside, only to have the bird banging up against a closed window right beside it. It is all to do with awareness, what a creature can and can't see.

'You're not going to bring it down.'

'What else am I going to do?'

'Kill it!'

'How?'

'Shoot it!'

'I don't have a gun.'

Gaunt groans with frustration, bending over double as if she has a pain in her gut.

The young woman does see the ladder, but since it does not come all the way up to the roof but hits the wall a little below, getting onto it poses some problems. An agile child would have no trouble. Suddenly the woman seems very awkward. She sits on the edge of the roof with her feet dangling, looking at the ladder below. She can't see that she has to turn around and lower herself that way, Akona realises. Instead she just skids forward on her bum over the edge of the roof and down, her feet connecting with the second rung but not holding, and a moment later she is pitched head first into the sand.

The ruby stone gets thrown forward.

Gaunt shrieks and throws herself to one side.

Akona observes closely as the woman pulls herself upright. It isn't a long fall, but it would have been a jarring one at best. Possible to break an anklebone or an arm with a fall like that. But she shows no signs of trauma or distress. She didn't make a sound when she fell. She just gets up, not even bothering to brush the worst of the sand off her front and her face. She looks as if she is about to set off but instead she pauses, her body goes rigid except for her head which swivels slowly in Akona's direction, like a mechanical device.

Gaunt screams and jumps backwards, shoving her fist into her mouth.

Akona waits. When the creature's eyes catch up with Akona's face, its head ceases to move and its gaze locks in on her. Nothing. Not so much emptiness as vacancy. Imagine a clear night suddenly void of stars. A book from which all the words have fled. An indifference that is not cold, because it doesn't recognise either heat or cold. Akona is not even sure if it sees her, or what exactly it sees. Slowly she moves out of its line of sight, but the creature continues to stare into the empty space Akona has just vacated.

A moment later it bends over, picks up the stone and swings away south, not looking back.

Gaunt's mouth is hanging open. She's beyond words. 'It...it...it...' she says but can't finish the thought.

Akona finds it hard to think of the young woman as an 'it', to strip her of the last vestige of her humanity. A creature, but not in the usual sense. If she were no longer fully human, she had once been a person, a woman, with a life, and not that long ago. It is as if she had just put down her humanity and walked away.

It is a temptation, Akona can feel the force of that. To leave behind the bright pain of being alive. To walk on with eyes wide shut. And to keep walking. Away. Away from the world.

Akona can feel the pull of that.

Manny shows himself to the mokopuna

Bit by bit, the mokopuna make progress, the sting of the sandsnakes growing a little less with every step and there are swathes of calm in which everything seems to be happening as if through soundproof glass. Then the wind will return in all its fury. There are no driftdead around, and Witch Hunt feels safe enough to let go of Miranda's hand to make it under her own power. The incident with the large driftdead woman with the baby bottle has left her feeling embarrassed, screaming the way she did, and she doesn't want to appear such a sissy, a silly sissy.

With a show of independence and bravery, she gravitates to the left side of the road. Miranda merely glances at her, perhaps relieved to be free of her burden for a moment, but Rasputin follows her, and when she looks at him, questioningly, he gives her that same God smile again, only this time it does not warm her heart. This time it makes her feel uneasy.

She looks up to the mansions, now looming closer, visible through momentary patches in the storm. Like many of the inhabitants of Keatown, Witch Hunt is superstitious about the mansions. There are whispers of hidden laser weapons, robot guards, black helicopters with noiseless rotors, dogs with forbidden genes, not to mention the tales of feasts and orgies, and most of the good folk of Keatown are afraid to go beyond a certain point: the point at which the shadows of the mountains grow too long for courage.

Witch Hunt is too young to understand what these things are, and what they mean, but the strangeness and the menace get through. She's heard the adults talking, Miranda's mum Jolene and Grandmother Gaunt and Mother Smiley, and their tone of voice is enough. In a world without fairy tales, forbidding mansions with evil wizards and doglike monsters are just what the imagination ordered for a girl who's never read much, although she has heard the librarian reading aloud from the Little House on the Prairie.

She is still looking upwards at the legendary homes of the super-rich when her feet stumble on something in the sand, and she almost falls over again. She gropes about to see what tripped her. Something round and smooth. With a hole. Two holes.

She recoils and lets out a big long sissy scream. The others crowd around. Little Sanyo gets on his knees and begins to dig, slowly revealing the skull, and the skeleton beneath. The wind tears at his fingers and the sand rushes back in even as he digs.

'It's been buried standing upright,' he shouts.

Miranda comes up behind Witch Hunt and puts her hands on her shoulders. Witch Hunt refuses to cling to her friend but feels, despite the horror in front of them, a surge of pleasure when Miranda squeezes her. When she realises that in this case it is Miranda who is grasping her for support, she doesn't feel like such a big sissy anymore.

'There's no clothes,' Little Sanyo says.

'Probably rotted,' Sad Toof says.

The wind keeps shifting direction, forcing them to turn their faces first one way then another.

Mary squats down beside Little Sanyo. She's wearing a hoodie and doesn't look at him. 'Could it be Flounder Phil?'

'Too old. Years old.' Little Sanyo gets right up close to stare at the body's grinning teeth. 'Just like the fish,' he says, but nobody takes any notice.

Staring at the skeleton's now revealed hand, leaf-curled in death, Witch Hunt wonders if it could be her daddy. But he would never let go his briefcase, not even in death.

'We have to go,' Sirocco says. We need to get out of this wind.'

Nobody disagrees. But nobody can tear their eyes away from the sight of the skeleton being dug out, not only by Little Sanyo but the wind, which is now seems determined to help him.

'Look!' Little Sanyo points to the back of the skull. 'Murder by blunt force trauma,' he shouts triumphantly.

Nobody asks him what he means so Witch Hunt says nothing. To be a sissy is one thing, to be a silly sissy is another. Her mother, if she were her mother, once told her not to be a silly sissy when she was pouring liquor over the girl, with the plan to set her on fire. She would have too, except the matches wouldn't light, having got soaked in liquor, the little pink heads dissolving into a smudge. When she told that story to other adults, so that she could get to stay with Miranda, she received a most satisfactory response, with general cries of outrage. Grandmother Gaunt was particularly incensed and patted her on the head and said that this kind of child abuse was the worst crime in the world, and she never had to return to her mother again. After that, Witch Hunt likes to repeat the phrase worst crime in the world whenever she thinks about it. It looks like here there is a worser crime.

There's nothing they can do but move on, although little Sanyo would have loved to take the skull with him and add it to one of his stashes. If he still had any stashes.

They pass under the jutting bower of a mansion deck, heavily reinforced with steel and concrete, a semicircle wide enough to land a helicopter, supported by massive yet crumbling pillars of concrete. They pass near elaborately thought-out gardens, tiered to work with the slope or expensively bulldozed. Most are neglected, or hastily unkempt, but here and there Sirocco catches a Zen glimpse of paradisiacal garden vistas, trimmed by the shears of angels, and like some pornographic image, waxed to the point of martyrdom.

Somebody is still getting paid to tend to the aesthetic. The mansions still live, albeit in hibernation. Perhaps some faint flicker in a far-off stock market brings them back to life from time to time, Sirocco thinks. He's read about stock markets in some of the magazines the librarian keeps, and while he doesn't understand exactly what they are, he does understand that before the Long Emergency, even since then, people could make or lose a lot of money on these markets.

They go down between finely shaven faces of rock and come up through a riot of broom and gorse. The scent they give off in the spring is heavy and yellow, redolent of dreams. The rocky outcrop, called Stag Point for the tall, sharp flax that flanks it, is a little too close to the mansions for the comfort of most of the villagers. One of the lower mansions looms not far above; the rubble displaced by its sloping ramparts has almost engulfed Stag Point, and piled up on either side where the flax now grows.

Mostly the mokopuna are not bothered, although none of them would care to venture up this far at night alone. It's scary enough though, with the rag ends of the wind tearing at them and the flax snapping like scissors. Behind the rocks, which form a rough battlement, there is a small flat protected space into which the mokopuna tumble, breathing hard and long.

It is the fourth day of the storm and the shadows of the mountains grow around them into twilight, breeding shadows in the mansions above and pouring darkness down their ramparts. A serene last light touches the ocean. However, as they gather at the rocky edge and watch the siege of Keatown unfold below, the ocean looks far from serene. It is in turmoil, roiling with dark and clay-yellow colours like a diseased limb, while the waves themselves are horribly unnatural. For, rather than crashing in parallel to the beach as waves should, they are tunnelling in at right angles, corkscrewing manically through the sand, tearing up Nightshade Track, by this time heavily burdened with sand and shell, rock, salt and spray, to expend the last of their energy on the roundabout. The manic onshore wind picks up the sand and debris stirred up by these water cannons and dumps them on the town.

They can only catch glimpses of the town through the gaps in the storm, those patches where the wind unaccountably dies allowing shifting portals on the stricken town. Nightshade Track has been obliterated and Highway 6 buried beneath a single undulating sand creature that stretches from the roundabout to the ocean. That sand creature looks like a great tongue burying itself deep in the land. It has brought with it a strange fruit. Orlap's fishing boat, The Wanderer, with the shark's mouth painted on the bow, now perches on the roundabout facing west as if about to sail off into the mountains or be swept into the air like a magic ship with the next flurry of the storm. It looks as if the whole town will be submerged in one huge lapping flurry. The last of the sand and the spray dashes itself upon the hillside below them, leaving a salty residue in their mouths, and a stickiness in their hair. Around them flax fronds slap themselves silly.

It is like those pictures the kids have seen on the librarian's computer of coastal lands inundated by rising seawaters, except it isn't water but sand, wind-driven sand that has drowned some areas leaving others high and dry, houses with sand frothing at the rooftops while others are stripped to their foundations. Occasionally they glimpse human forms, but can't tell if these are the driftdead or fellow villagers. Certainly any organised defence of the town has long since collapsed. Despite the busyness of the scene, with its hither and thither of wind and sand and scurrying debris, the town feels deserted, as if everybody has either left or died, and only wind-torn ghosts remain.

They all feel it, standing there, looking down, trying to peer through the storm to the town they remember.

As they watch, the gaps close up and the whole town vanishes under a heaving sea of sand and wreckage. This great sand creature squats over the town as if digesting it. Dirty fingers reach up towards Stag Point. Witch Hunt screams and Rasputin attempts to get her onto her knees to pray while she tries to claw his eyes out.

A single sandsnake, thick as a man's thigh, tosses itself over the rocky outcrop. The mokopuna stagger back, rubbing their eyes.

Then it stops, sheer.

Just like that.

From blasting whirlwinds and haunting, suffocating veils of sand – to absolute stillness.

The wind doesn't die, death takes time; it simply stops in mid-air. Ceases to be.

The sandsnakes fall where they are, like people fainting. They keel over without making a sound.

Everything they are carrying drops or floats or simpers to the earth.

The silence is staggering. They've never heard anything like it, even on the stillest day. In nature, there is never complete silence. Not like this.

Below, the new contours of sand grow soft with shadows. As the last of the sun fades to a faint glow behind the mountains, shadows walk in from the east, from the sea. Vast, silent shadows.

The sky is so clear you can see all the way to Andromeda. Fuzzy nebulae. Circles and stars.

Venus hugs the sky bright.

Witch Hunt rubs her eyes. She can't believe what she is seeing, just an arm's length or two away. It can't be there, this dog creature from her nightmares. It's as black as a panther, but its eyes are pink, like a pig's, yet huge and glassy – and it stares at her with an unrelenting intelligence. It doesn't do anything else. It just stares its piggy stare. It's bigger than a normal dog. And uglier. Much uglier.

It's so ugly she can't even scream.

A Soft Beat at the Heart of the World

Book Three

the librarian encounters some narrative uncertainty

In the last hours of the storm the librarian stays in front of her computer attempting to further her patchwork Chronicles of Keatown, a history it is her ambition to leave to posterity – if there is any. A written history becomes a part of that living history, which makes her feel proud. On looking back, later historians, if there are any, will recognise her chronicles as a landmark, an outstanding contribution to the understanding of our town – if there is still a town. And if there is not, those same later imaginary historians might wonder if there ever was such a town, or if there ever was a person known as the librarian.

Her Chronicles were all written from the magisterial, 'invisible historian' point of view, as a good history should be. She only appears very peripherally, in a footnote or two, or when she is uncertain as to her judgment and wants to leave it to the reader. She appears only as a reluctant and shy first person, peeking through here and there. Avoiding the singular 'I' as being too assertive, too loud, she prefers, at such moments in the text, the plural 'we', as in, 'We cannot be sure if Ellen Johnson's only son Victor ever made it to South America, as there is no record of him after he left Sydney in 1888.' The meeker, more inclusive plural allows the librarian to keep herself out of the limelight. A reader would hardly be aware of her mediating presence, which is as it should be. She is not the subject of the Chronicles; the founding families of Keatown are. The Johnsons, the Kamates, the Kensingtons.

Her 'invisible historian' gives her all the advantages of the third person omniscient.

At the same time, ghostlike, she senses the presence of another first person, the source of all narrative authority. In such moments I am very near her. I can hear her short, shallow breaths. She imagines she can hear mine. She imagines she can feel me in the muted clickety-click of the keyboard. A presence very near yet very far, and hence a riddle. A presence that seems to permeate all points of view.

It spooks her, there in third-person land, to feel the breath of a first person. The First Person. Singular, what's more. The First Person Singular is always pre-eminent, after all! Like a potentate, worthy of capital letters. The omnipotence of the third person is an illusion, the librarian has discovered. Something of a false god is the third person omniscient. All those hims and hers are nothing more than disguises. Masks. The hidden presence, the First Person Singular, is no further away than a quick tap on the keyboard. History, always close enough to fiction to make her uncomfortable. If she 'brings her characters to life', as the saying goes, how is she any different from some third person junkie pulp writer?

The expression, 'brings her characters to life,' was used in a favourable review of some sketches she did of Keatown when she first arrived, and the rather hollow phrase had pleased and disturbed her. Disturbed, because she realised that it doesn't matter if the person she's writing about is a real, living person or a made-up fiction – they are all just words on the page in the end. A name dressed in a little description. Always, an emperor with no clothes.

The situation did not improve when she began to write about historical characters. It was very easy to see Ellen Johnson in larger-than-life terms, the heroic pioneer woman who brought up nine daughters. Her husband, Peter Johnson eventually followed her over from Britain, but by then Ellen had established herself as matriarch and dowager. The situation itself was tailor-made for a fairy tale. And what of the blighted love affair between Nōpera and Catherine Johnson? There was a wild and romantic tale of true love and courage and the doom of families if ever there was one. Not her job, she tells herself with some satisfaction. It's her job to be an imaginary fly on the wall, that's all. No reconstructed conversations, no colouring in, no purple-prose descriptions. Just the facts. The facts are fascinating enough. History itself has no voice, however. There is no disembodied, disinterested historical voice, droning away in the ether somewhere. But we can always pretend, can't we? We can always take refuge in the good old third person omniscient and pretend that all is well and pretend there is no partiality. No favours.

And yet she can't help but be aware of herself as observer. The role of historian as witness. The First Person as oracle. I am never that far away.

While these issues prickle at her as she writes, she at least finds comfort in the past tense, the natural tense of history. A soothing quality. In the past tense actions have their proper beginnings and endings, just like the sentences that describe them. A marriage took place. A baby was born. A matriarch died. A town was plundered. Such things are contained neatly in a sentence, the subject cuddled up close to the verb. A completed sentence that takes its place, proudly but not arrogantly, with other completed sentences around it. Everything is settled and secure, rounded off with a nice little dot. A satisfying closure. The sentence settles into domesticity. The paragraph lives happily ever after. The chapter rests on its laurels.

In contrast, the present tense is, like the present itself, unsettling, unnerving, and unfinished. The present tends to go on hour after hour seeking closure but never finding it, like a sentence that can't find its little dot, its full stop, not until everything has been said.

The present hangs suspended above the past, always about to plummet.

The problem is, the closer she gets to the present, and the lives of the descendants, Akona Nōpera and Bob Kensington, the more the insidious first person want to intervene and the more the past tense wants to give way to the present. There is always some discomfort for the historian as the story gives way to the present. She must be close to abdication time, which is why she keeps going back and adding passages to previous events. Writing history is a bit like filling in holes. The more holes you fill in, the more holes appear.

However, even the past tense and its superior air of closure and certainty, cannot banish inconclusiveness, ambiguity even. Doubts widen as gaps open up. Right now, she has returned to one of her early passages and is scrutinising it.

> A number of the descendants of these original families still live in the district.
>
> While many of Ellen Johnson's nine daughters scattered to other parts of the country as they married off, Ellen's third daughter, Beatrice, stayed in the district and married a farmer, Alfred Kensington. Alfred Kensington was a thrifty, industrious man who spent almost everything he earned buying up more property, expanding his holdings. Beatrice gave birth to twins, Charlotte and Thomas. Both children had an austere upbringing, as Alfred Kensington became more miserly as he got older. Thomas married the daughter of a gold miner, Prudence McKinney,

and the couple moved into a farmhouse they built adjacent to Alfred Kensington's property. Their eldest son was Bob Kensington. Their only daughter was Alice.

It was Ellen Johnson's second daughter, the rebel Charlotte, however, who sparked a fierce outcry in the district by marrying a local Maori chief, Nōpera Kāmaka. According to legend the first child of that marriage was kidnapped by Alfred Kensington and one of Beatrice's eight sisters, Hanna. Hanna Johnson had apparently got religion and considered the child to be a 'half-cast abomination.' They are supposed to have taken the unnamed boy out into the desert and left him there to be food for the hawks.

Charlotte and Nōpera left the district to have their second child, Naira. They never returned, but Naira did.

Naira, forged with the fierce sense of independence that ran in the veins of both the rebel Charlotte Kensington and her Maori Chief Nōpera Kāmaka, repeated history by marrying a foreigner, Lawrence, from off the ships. Naira saw that the blood of her father ran strong in her granddaughter, Akona, and dedicated her life to looking after the orphaned child.

The librarian pushes back her chair and gets up. Reading her own work has made her restless. True, she has kept herself out of the picture, stayed in the third person, 'invisible author' mode, and kept within the carefully prescribed boundaries of the past tense – however, even the mention of the still vital and living Akona makes her uneasy. Writing about the woman like this, as if she were already dead, seems disrespectful. She wonders how Akona might feel about it. Especially the bit about her parentage and the possibility that her real father was Joseph Kāmaka, a weak and dissolute man who fecklessly presided over the decline of the marae after Nōpera left. Even repeating such a claim could be seen by Akona as deeply insulting to her mother, Naira.

There are issues too. She had to slip into the present tense to convey her uncertainty about the story of Charlotte and Nōpera's murdered baby. Since she has no hard evidence for the story, she should probably have left it out. Despite their bitter differences the Johnsons and the Kāmaka family closed ranks over the story. So complete was their secrecy that even the birth and brief existence of such a child became uncertain.

And didn't her sentence about the 'high and mighty Johnsons and Kensingtons' somewhat lose its strict objectivity along the way? Of course, she was evoking Lawrence's point of view, but how did she know he felt that way? Surely she was doing a little colouring in here. And the reference to the 'tar brush' doesn't quite come across the way she wanted it to. It was an expression, like 'half-cast' that belonged to the time, the era, so she should be able to use it to typify the attitudes of the time – but it doesn't quite work, she has to admit. She will probably end up editing it out.

'You try and do better,' she says to the First Person accusingly. I say nothing. I want to keep right out of it.

She does not, however, get back to her Chronicles, as she is interrupted by the arrival of the mayor, Big Bill Broonzy and his consort, the red-haired Mavis.

civilization as cargo cult

This is an unusual event as Mayor Broonzy is not exactly a big reader, nor has he been an unqualified supporter of the library, and you can say the same for Mavis and double it. Libraries look backward, to the past, whereas our good mayor is a forward-looking man. As he sees it, the future prosperity of Keatown lies in his hands. His sudden appearance disconcerts the librarian, as if she has been visited by one of the characters from the library, a character from Dickens perhaps, or from Brecht. The mayor would fit well in the world of the Threepenny Opera, just the right mixture of greed and pomposity.

He's a little uneasy with the librarian too, as he might be with a priest. In his mind the Keeper of Books can easily become the Keeper of Secrets. Like many who don't read, he is somewhat superstitiously in awe of books, but he is a man of firm purpose and not about to be intimidated by a female librarian, the mysterious tomes over which she fusses, or the great weight of history and humbug those tomes represent!

His semi-official consort, Mavis, is a lank woman with flaming red hair who rolled into town one day on a petrol tanker and never rolled out again. A fierce, ugly, foul-mouthed woman the mayor treats like a trophy wife, she has the effect of neutralising the power of any female who comes within range, which may well be why he likes to have her by his side. A psychic bodyguard of sorts.

She's particularly cold to the librarian. It turns out she came to Keatown in the last days of the good times, hoping to set up a brothel, and what better place than these underground wine cellars and cask vaults? The thought that this ideal space is wasted on the wallflower librarian and her crusty books returns to niggle at her whenever she comes here, or even passes by. Sometimes she bitches at Big Bill about it, but he does no more than grumble. He calls himself a mayor, but he's no more than a puff of wind.

'Maps,' he says. 'You know, of the area.' He shapes a territory in the air with his hands.

Funnily enough, the librarian does know. It's topographical maps he's looking for. Like many who need to fix the world into sections and certainties, so that it might be shaped to fit ambition, he has discovered that memory is an unreliable narrator. Men argue; nature acts – according to Voltaire – and in this case nature, in the form of the freak storm, has transformed the topology of Keatown to the point where nobody can be exactly sure of the shape that lies beneath the new contours of sand, or where one property might begin and another end. An alarming state of affairs to a man like the mayor.

Inheritance and dispossession, pieces of paper that declare ownership. Signatures and seals and solemn legalities. All of these have become tenuous and pale since the onset of the Long Emergency, and have been made next to impossible by the storm. Ownership has nothing to do with those legalities. In fact, there is no ownership, the librarian realises, just a feeling of affinity with a place, the kind of symbiosis that begins to happen when the signatures fade and seals are long since broken.

She thinks of Akona as she searches her map drawers. Dispossession and displacement. All done with theodolites, plumb lines, set squares and maps.

The librarian finds him the maps he wants, even an allotment map, which he pores over with all the gravity of someone used to restoring order and dignity to the chaos of human affairs, while Mavis strolls along the bookshelves looking as if she were having a mental argument with every book. People like her don't enjoy libraries. In fact, they find them stressful places filled with a disturbing cacophony of voices. Nothing like the soothing sighs and whispers of a brothel.

'Hmmm,' the mayor says, and pulls at the scraggy bit that wants to be a double chin. 'Hmmm, hmmm, ah-hmmm,' he says. With his saggy waistcoat, baggy trousers and faux white shirt, he looks like the mayor of Ragtown.

He's mayor perhaps because he is the only one in town left with a presentable suit, which he keeps packed away for ceremonial occasions. Or perhaps because he is the only man in town to present a belly worthy of the suit, a mysterious girth no one can explain for he is, necessarily, a man of modest appetites. We all are. Maybe he has a secret stash of chocolate, or has some secret pipeline to the mansions, or maybe he is the only person in town left with a superfluity of words.

An optimist by nature and profession, he preaches that one day soon the Long Emergency will be over, the choppers will return, and the roundabout will spin around once more to the eager flow of commerce. And he will be there to take advantage of it. His claim to fame is that he was once a butler up mansions, one of the wealthiest outfits of all, he claims, with several choppers at their command. He talks of choppers as if he has a great familiarity with them, and his hand will flutter in the air to suggest many grand comings and goings. One day, he assures everybody, the Chief Executive Officer will return with choppers, money, jobs - and girls the like of which mortal eyes have not spied in living memory. It is his version of the Rapture, the return of material wealth. The choppers' homecoming.

It is his little cargo cult, and, like the Rev Stickman, he has his adherents. Others are simply amused. One of his initiatives, to erect the sign at the north end of town proclaiming Keatown Welcomes Investment! has provided plenty of fodder for the town wags, as well as the object of some target practice.

His optimism is crowned with a rosy vision of Keatown's former glory and prosperity, the Golden Age when the rich people once swarmed in to build mansions. Said choppers coming in every day swinging packets of Canadian Cedar and Indonesian Sequoia, landing them like insects laying eggs. Hundreds of contractors, workers, mechanical diggers! The air thick with cement powder. Annanda Patel's Supermarket was always full. Our local mechanic, Flay, had more work than you could shake a wrench at. The price of fish went through the roof. Orlap and his fishermen always wore big grins, as if born that way. Mother Smiley's stone soup was rich to overflowing. Then more choppers came – the mayor relished the word choppers, spitting it out – bringing the celebs themselves, the global super-rich with enough clout to build themselves a luxury bolt-hole here at the ends of the earth, in Keatown, of all places! These semi-mythical beings would hole up out of the sun during the day, protecting their precious and well-insured complexions, and swan down Beauty Parade in laughing clusters (which was how the street got its name) to the beach in the evening to swim, flirt, and watch the gentle Pacific Ocean lap up against the old but solid wooden wharfs of the harbour. So retro! So, like, original! So old-world!

Those were the Good Times and everybody lived the Good Life.

Then property values collapsed, the economy had a heart attack and most of the rich people choppered away. But no worries! One day the choppers will return and bring the rich people back. Once more, the catwalk of Beauty Parade will be graced by the rolling hips of legendary celebrities. The Good Times will roll again just like the dice in the mayor's little gambling den. He never tires of pointing out Keatown's attractions: a nice sheer, deep-water port, where the whales would come once more to flip and frolic for the delighted eyes of rich Koreans; mountains in the back for the hardy ones to climb, Germans and Swiss; chamois and tarn for the gun-crazy Yanks; a seal colony up north for the kids and the misty-eyed animal lovers; the seals obligingly bellow their primeval cries and flap their flippers just to amuse you and titivate your chequebooks... Once more Keatown will be abuzz with tourists, whale watchers, deep-sea fisherman with deep-sea wallets, sturdy mountain trekkers in shorts and boots, backpackers galore. Divers with fancy deep-sea watches, watches that can image link with computers and have an app for playing the stock market underwater; and big bad ugly Four Wheel Drives lined up at Flay's Garage like the FBI at a shootout.

I doubt that even a storm like the one we'd just had would dent his optimism. In the mayor's mind, everything must soon go back to normal. The economy, the government, the weather – all just aberrations as far as he was concerned. Pretty soon everybody would come to their senses, even the weather, and everything would get back on track again.

The topographical maps, however, do not reassure him. He keeps running his fingers over the lines as if to feel the shape of the land. His world, after all, is built on the inalienable right to private property.

The right to own property is the cornerstone of his world view, and you'd think it would take more than a little bit of sand to shake it. Perhaps a lot of sand might do it. Dunes where there were once paddocks, the landscape is so altered that even the landmarks like the mansion range, and the big one called Irirangi, seem to have shifted their positions. No one can properly identity what is theirs any more, or how the land even looks beneath them, the shifting sand mocking any stakes they try to plant.

When he's finished staring at the maps and saying ah-hmmm, he looks vaguely around as if considering some deep issue or other, but I get the feeling he's eyeing my library up with more than a little calculation. After all, it is not only Mavis who has her eyes on the library. The house on top is a slightly grander dwelling than the mayor's own, which always gives him pause for thought. Built in a reckless attempt to create a vineyard by a speculator with more money than sense back in the boom times, this silly pink Mediterranean-looking villa pretending to be a mansion, the sort of mansion cheap money could once buy before it became even cheaper, is just the sort of place the mayor would fancy, given his tastes. In that respect he and Mavis are in one accord.

The mayor knows, and, the librarian knows, that some vast and terrifying mortgage lies over the place, but since the owner went bust to a bank that went bust to an economy that went bust, nobody cares too much. Possession is nine tenths of the law, they say. Mavis rubs it in by making a point of looking at certain objects the previous owner left behind which are of scant interest to the librarian, such as a pair of pseudo-Victorian vases with faux Chinese scenes on them, and a wide fireplace with old iron tongs to go with it, things that Mavis makes no bones of coveting. It's the librarian's indifference to this bric-a-brac that really drives her crazy.

'This is the one,' the mayor says, briskly rolling up a map. 'I need to take a good long look at it.'

'I'm sorry,' the librarian says, 'the maps are for reference only.'

The mayor cocks an eye at her.

'Tell her to get fucked,' Mavis advises him.

But he doesn't. He places the map carefully back on the table and decides to nod his head in approval, as if she were somehow carrying out his instructions to take good care of the maps. 'I bet there's no law against copying them. I mean by hand.'

'None at all,' she says, 'but it's a long and tedious job.'

'Just the kind of thing Mavis is good at,' he says.

Mavis snarls something at him about doing his own dirty work, but approaches the table and deigns to study the map.

'She's an expert draftsman,' the mayor says proudly.

close encounters of the driftdead kind

This little scene doesn't play to its end, for the three of them are distracted by raised voices outside. They make a rush for the door, the mayor in front, his belly preceding him, a magisterial look on his face.

Directly below the library, on Highway 6, a number of the inhabitants of Keatown have gathered. At first glance the librarian sees the Rev Stickman, Hera and the Baby, Orlap and some fishermen, the mokopuna, even Flay's sidekick Pinky the punk, sometimes called Pinky the pimple, his mate Tony the tough and a couple of the wharf rats he hangs with. What's flustering them is the sight of a troupe of about forty people approaching from the north along the road and the sandy margins, forty to fifty strangers, which is quite impossible.

That's what the mayor mutters as he strides down towards the scene, Mavis flustering along beside him, 'impossible, impossible,' to the wobble of his jowls.

The librarian has studied the geography of this part of the world using maps left over in council offices when local government withdrew to more distant centres as one of the many cost-cutting, centralising exercises that took place at the beginning of the Long Emergency. There is no settlement closer than 90 kilometres to the north. Past the seal colonies there is a little place called Manitata, once a touristy place like Keatown with a bit more lipstick – no way this group could have come from there. Besides, this is no ordinary collection of people out for a stroll, but a peculiar grab-bag of types and styles. Seen from a distance they could have been a troupe of revellers heading for a party, or travellers making for a train station, or an odd assortment of workers heading for an office building or factory. Or none of these. Collectively, they do not make sense, as if they spring from lots of different fictions. Nothing unites them, except each carries something, some particular object, and all are walking in the same direction – south. They don't really care about the road, which is merely the line of least resistance to their southward path. Together but apart, they walk with a sure, unhurried purpose. Nothing bothers them.

It is only as they draw closer that she notices the strangeness of their separateness. Since none speak or incline a glance at another, their association seems entirely accidental. There are no linking moments. There is no group purpose here, no group in fact, just a blind, common groping southwards.

'Who are these fuckers?' Mavis says.

'The damned,' Rasputin says. Standing behind the boy, his hand on his shoulder, the Rev Stickman is staring at the visitors as if at some inner vision.

When they are still some distance away, the mayor, after a nervous look in our direction, steps forward and calls a greeting. 'Welcome, travellers, to our plucky little township... recently suffered a freak storm. We have a shop, a garage... and...' he tails off as the advancing group shows no sign of response, not even the most minimal acknowledgment that he is speaking to them. It takes the wind out of his sails.

'It is like they walk in their sleep,' Orlap says. He's a Swede who looks like a Viking and who talks in an over-correct, pedantic English. The handsome Captain Orlap is not just the admiral of our little fleet of fishing boats, but its life and soul.

'Refugees,' Hera says, holding the Baby a little tighter. 'They must be horribly traumatised. They don't even know we're here. They must need...' and she too tails off. 'Refugees,' she says again, as if saying it will make it so, that the word itself will turn these creatures into something recognisable.

'Zombies,' the Reverend says nodding his head as if it were made of brass or mercury, not looking at the arch Harlot, Hera. 'The Devil's dead. That's what they are.' He doesn't say anything more out loud, but his scrawny, rooster throat jerks convulsively as he subvocalises the word zombie. He bends over and whispers furiously in Rasputin's ear. Rasputin slowly shakes his head.

Hera says nothing. Normally, the strong rough voice of our Queen would be lifting spirits, getting people organised. Blankets, food, water... the mayor running around pretending that all her good ideas were his. Now, like the rest of us, she just stands and stares.

'They can't be zombies or they'd be chasing after us, trying to eat us. Isn't that what zombies do?' Miranda says, her little voice filling in for the silence of the adults. She very much doesn't want them to be zombies. Zombies turn into biters, or might turn into biters at any moment. The idea of them biting puts her teeth on edge. She's not so much afraid of being bitten but turning into a biter herself. After all, sometimes she bites Witch Hunt.

'That's right,' Sad Toof says, speaking from his wide knowledge of a TV zombie series he used to watch when he was little. 'Intestines are a delicacy to them.'

'And they don't rot,' Miranda says in the same terribly practical voice. 'Aren't zombies supposed to rot?'

'That's right,' Sad Toof says, 'bit'sa flesh fallin' off. Bones showin'.

Melissa Tonguestone, meek and mild no more, pushes her way to the front to stand by the reverend and Rasputin. She is in a trembling frenzy. 'Cockroaches is what they are. They only look like people, but they're cockroaches. They have taken human form to deceive us!' The reverend puts a hand on her arm to steady her. 'It's squash or be squashed,' she says. Pinky and Tony laugh, to the confusion of Melissa, who isn't joking. 'These things will walk all over us,' she says.

'Poor Melissa,' Pinky says to Tony, 'She's got her knickers in a twist over the zombies.'

Margot Hamlin puts her arm around Melissa, who is after all her old friend, even if they are now separated by differences of outlook. 'It's okay to be frightened,' Margot says, looking around for Akona, but Akona isn't there. 'I'm frightened too, but we have to withhold our judgement. We don't really know what they are.'

'They're called the driftdead,' Little Sanyo calls. Nobody takes any notice. Mostly people ignore the mokopuna – except Hera.

'Driftdead?' Hera says. 'That's a horrible thing to call them. Can't you see they're people! Not cockroaches either. Why not beetles or ants or maggots...? They're people!' Tears are coming into her eyes but she can't say why. She seems to see people she knows but when she tries to focus on one the resemblance vanishes.

'Funny-looking people,' Pinky says. He says it with a sneer, the way he says everything, but his eyes are riveted on the visitors.

'Pretty funny,' Tony says, but only for the sake of form. In fact, he's sticking pretty close to Pinky, and doesn't look much like Tony the tough any more.

They come close enough to see them as individuals. The cliché from all walks of life springs to mind, and while that's true as clichés must be, and the librarian finds she can focus on one or another of them, as a group her eyes tend to slide over them as over a shoal of fish. Different as they are individually, there is also a sameness to them en masse, as if they all walked in the same invisible river. They might be characters from fiction. There's one, like Mr Pickwick, with a briefcase. Another, an old man who might be mistaken for Captain Ahab. And there is Madam Bovary in a reverie. Distinctive on one hand, merged with the mass on the other.

Driftdead. The word hangs in the air. It seems just right. It becomes them.

'Where do you folk come from?' the mayor demands, looking from one to the next to the next to the next. They take no notice of him. 'Have you come from Manitata?'

'Where are they going?' somebody asks.

Nobody has an answer.

'Children... I don't see any children...' Hera's voice falters. None of them has water bottles or food, no backpacks, no carts, none of the paraphernalia of refugees. No whimpering kids. All they have to sustain them is their movement, their incessant movement so magnetic to the eye.

And their eerie silence. So silent. Only the sounds their bodies make in the world. The scuffle of feet in sand, the ruffle of air in clothing. That's what spooks everybody. Like watching a silent film – no zombie moans, no greedy gutturals, just soundless, flickery movement. In the flick of an eye they can look like a bunch of ordinary folk out for a walk, yet not one of them stops to take off a jacket, or put one on, or take a swig of water, or wipe a face, or stop for a piss or a picnic. None of them shows any signs of exhaustion. There is nothing aggressive in their demeanour, but there is something in the implacable nature of their forward movement that makes the librarian want to pull back from them, even as she feels an odd pull towards them, the ways she does with certain books she sometimes has to open. Think of the River Styx of mythological fame; you have to cross over it when you die in order to reach the land of the dead, and you have to leave all your memories behind. You have to let the river bear them away. Each one of these driftdead is like a book of blank pages being thumbed from north to south. All memories wiped. Nothing left now but the journey, the placing of one foot after the other.

Suddenly the good folk of Keatown are all silent too, watching them, caught in the rhythm of their movement. They are all moving at about the same pace, which keeps them together as a group, but again this seems accidental, a mere coincidence, and this very fact helps to make the sight of them hypnotic.

It is the mayor who takes fright first and breaks the spell.

'Don't look at them!' he barks, like a sergeant major to assembled troops, 'Don't look at them! They don't exist. They are an illusion.'

'If they don't exist how can we look at them?' Sad Toof wonders out loud. He can worry about a question like that for days.

The mayor is beyond logic. He places himself in front of us, his back to the passing hoard, his arms outstretched as if he could shield everyone with nothing more than his own heroic will, and tries to stare everybody down with eyes popping out of his head. 'Do not look at them,' he instructs us. His eyes are not seeing us, but are fixed on some horrific vision in his head.

The reverend falls to his knees and begins to pray, his eyes firmly closed. Rasputin joins him and Mellissa Tonguestone follows suit. Several others do the same, including Mother Smiley who seems to be in a race to say as many prayers as possible in the shortest given time.

Margot Hamlin begins to cry, but she doesn't fall on her knees. She walks towards the driftdead, tears streaming down her face. The mayor blocks her path. He has to shout in her face to get her to stop, to snap out of her grief.

Maybe none of us perceives the danger the mayor is first to sense. Maybe, like the librarian, each sees somebody in the passing parade that reminds them of themselves. The librarian sees a girl of about fourteen, tripping along blankly carrying a skipping rope, and the librarian wonders if she has been into a library, or liked reading books as she did when she was that age. She wonders if the girl with the skipping rope has a mother or father or a home to go to. The plight of children has always distressed the librarian. Children have no power to change the world into which they are born, and so are at the mercy of it, like this unknown girl, like the librarian when she was the same age.

Somehow her identity gets mixed up with that girl's, and this upsets the librarian.

'Go about your business!' The mayor shouts. 'Ignore them! Let's clear our homes of sand! Let's get on with it. Let's get the wheels of industry turning!' This last is his favourite phrase and it almost never fails to rouse a cheer, except in this case. 'These phantoms will pass like a bad dream.'

They're not phantoms,' Little Sayno says. 'You can touch them. I touched one.'

'That's right,' Sad Toof says. 'You can't touch ghosts,' he adds with the particular relish some people exhibit upon stating the obvious.

'Don't touch them at all!' the mayor roars.

'Maybe they're infectious,' Gaunt says.

'Give you the clap,' Pinky says grinning. He doesn't actually know what the word means but he likes it anyway. Tony claps to illustrate the point.

People draw back at that thought very quickly. Suddenly nobody wants to get within breathing distance of a driftdead, this fear being much more effective than the mayor's strictures. 'Well they might be,' Pinky says. 'They might carry the plague, like rats.'

'Cockroaches,' Melissa intones, still on her knees, apparently praying.

'It's just so sad,' Margot says. 'It's the saddest thing I've ever seen. I could die of sadness right now.'

At that moment a peculiar, and unpleasant, sensation creeps up on the librarian. A disconnect, as if the cogs that mesh her with the world have slipped. The sounds coming from her friends' mouths do not quite match their lip movements, like a film with a delayed sound track. Time goes out of sync, as if the driftdead bring their own time-space coordinates with them, their own time stream, which somehow contaminates ours. Nobody's thoughts quite match their words, or their words quite match their movements, or their movements their intentions. Everything strikes the librarian as pre-rehearsed, acted out but rather badly from an indifferent script, as if they can barely get out their lines and perform their gestures. They can only just play their parts. They have ceased to be believable. They live in a country of empty gestures. A planet of hollow voices. The mayor in particular seems badly played, like an actor who has forgotten his skills and whose character mask is slipping. Strip him of his imaginary mayoralty, his pomp and circumstance, and he is nothing but a posturing cut-out from a comic book. He postures. He poses – badly. He huffs and he puffs and dreams of choppers. He could get those wheels of industry turning on sheer puff power alone. In themselves, his wobbling jowls do a lot of work.

The others stand around as if they have forgotten their roles or babble pretend-conversations with each other. Tony the so-called tough looks particularly out of place, as if he has just walked onto the wrong film set. It's tough being tough when nobody notices, or cares.

He's used to impressing people with his physique and his pugnacious face – he doesn't have much else going for him – but the driftdead are manifestly indifferent and nobody else cares either.

The librarian goes to take a step back in accord with the mayor's advice, away from the driftdead, but finds she has taken a step forward. She freezes, too terrified to take another step in case the same thing happens. One step back for every two steps forward, a stupid voice says in her head. Sirocco is watching her. There is a power in him she doesn't understand, something he received in the desert. Like a gift. Step back, he seems to be saying to her in a gentle voice, step back.

I'm trying, I'm trying, she tries to say. Two steps back for every one step forward.

She's in the way of some of the driftdead who are walking parallel to the road. While some of them can weave quite skilfully along, avoiding obstacles and flowing towards the easiest paths, others are clumsy, hardly aware of objects until they bump into them. A rather large bossy-looking woman bumps into the librarian. It doesn't bother the woman, she just keeps going, but it bumps the librarian out of her paralysis. She screams and jumps backwards. Sirocco is there to steady her. He offers her his small, calloused hand. She tries to grin at him but he just regards her with his solemn monkey face.

'It's their indifference that makes us feel unreal,' she says, feeling she owes him some explanation. He nods as if he knows what she is talking about.

'Just take another step,' he says.

She does it, aware that Hera is watching closely. She doesn't miss much, our queen.

And another step. The next, and she is free, able to move her limbs again.

'What happened?' she asks Sirocco. Her voice comes out in a croaky whisper.

'They pull at you,' he says. 'It's like a song you can't quite hear. You just want to get closer to it.'

'Go home!' the mayor yells. 'Home! Home! Home!'

The reverend and his followers rise to their feet.

'Well Mr Godman,' Pinky says in a falsely jocular voice, the one he always uses to razz the goodly reverend. 'What does God say?'

The reverend has gone very white. It takes him a moment to bring Pinky into focus.

'God told me that you are toast,' the reverend says. 'Very burnt toast.'

Pinky laughs uneasily. He's not used to the reverend making jokes, even of the mordant kind.

Now that she is out of danger, the librarian starts to shake. 'Damn you to hell,' she says under her breath to the First Person. 'You nearly lost me. What if I'd turned into one of them? What would you have done then?'

Of course I can't answer her. It's not my job to intervene. Sometimes she treats me like a deity, the way the reverend thinks of God. I am her First Person, and therefore all-powerful. Of course that is not true. I am not the author of her being. She is. But when she gets frightened she turns on me and accuses me of all kinds of crimes.

She says no more, but I'm not fooled. This issue lies in wait for us further up the plot line. I don't have to be the First Person to see that.

chasing after the wind

A slim, wraith-like woman holding a candle in a candle holder, white dress half torn, showing a small, pale breast, walks between the mayor and the townsfolk right through the mayor's imaginary wall. She holds the burnt-out candle out in front of her as if it were showing her the way.

The reverend steps forth and addresses her, stoutly delivering the lines his part requires. At least he remembers his lines. 'Cover yourself, woman! For shame! Beg God's forgiveness.' He reaches out, as if to adjust the woman's dress but draws his hand back quickly. 'All sins shall be forgiven unto the sons of men, and blasphemies whosoever they shall blaspheme. But he that shall blaspheme against the Holy Ghost hath never forgiveness, but is in danger of eternal damnation.'

He is trying to work himself into full sermon mode, but his voice keeps choking up. He ends up sounding like a bad imitation of himself, and he can't understand that. To his ears, the words of God also sound like vanity instead of eternal truth – a heretical thought.

The woman takes no notice of his tirade anyway, but continues following her candle, and, as he continues to declaim, he finds himself falling in step with her, keeping pace so he can harangue her further, constantly gesturing to her exposed breast and addressing himself to it. 'And she vowed a vow, and said , O Lord of hosts, if thou wilt indeed look on the affliction of thine handmaid, and remember me, and not forget thine handmaid,...' He raises his eyes to Heaven; he's starting to find his pace. 'All sins shall be forgiven.'

The woman says nothing but keeps her eyes on the candle.

The Stickman swings his arm and knocks the candle from its holder. Let the false idols fall! The woman doesn't flinch but carries on with the empty candle holder, unperturbed, the reverend close on her trail.

'Don't follow her.' The mayor shouts. His voice gets sucked into a pit of silence. It's nothing more than a squeak in dead air. There is no sound but for the steady, ghostly rustling of the driftdead.

'Whatever you do don't follow her!'

'He's mad,' Gaunt says, shaking her head.

'He's in love,' a giggling Pinky says to Gaunt.

'He's blinded by his god,' Hera says to both of them. At her breast, the Baby peers out at the world, blinking. Grandmother Gaunt makes sympathetic sounds.

Meanwhile, there are cries from several throats calling out to the reverend to come back. They sound to me like a scattering of lonely gulls on a beach crying at the wind.

'Delia! he cries out.

Then stops.

He stares at the gap that has opened up between himself and everybody else, as if the jaws of hell yawn at his feet. I know exactly how he is feeling. He just doesn't know how to take that step back to dry land, to safety. And the gap is widening every moment.

While the rest of us stare like idiots, Hera runs forward and holds out both hands as if to a drowning man. The mayor stands behind her, his mouth opening and shutting, suddenly quite useless. When the reverend moves, it is with sudden panic, like a late traveller making an unwise jump for a ferry that is already departing. Everybody can hear the gasp of his breath as he staggers back across a distance growing wider all the time, his feet pedalling as in a void.

When he gets to solid land he clutches onto Hera, his arch enemy, as if she were life itself. He is panting like a marathon runner. 'Madness and folly,' he says, 'this, too, is a chasing after the wind.'

'Sure is,' Hera says.

'Chasing after titty is more like it,' Pinky says. His mate Tony and a couple of others laugh obligingly.

The reverend lets Hera go and turns to the mockers. 'Death is the destiny of everyone; the living should take this to heart,' he says.

'I think I'm scared,' Pinky says. 'But's who's Delia, rev?'

The rev turns away. He is not answerable to his mockers.

The driftdead woman continues on her way, her ripped shirt still hanging off her shoulder, her small, pale breast still exposed, the candleholder held forth as if there were still a candle shedding light upon the darkening path.

a long lonely lilting chant

Pinky the wharf rat, who only comes into the library looking for pictures of war and sadism, doesn't usually say a lot because nobody, except his mate Tony, likes him or anything he says. He is a school bully having trouble growing up, a wannabe big shot who survives by undertaking obscure missions for Flay, like transporting Ock Arglin's bootleg firewater to the security of Flay's garage for distribution, to scavenging leftover fish from the fish shed which Flay swaps for rabbit meat. Pinky is a pugnacious punk who sees himself in a world full of pansies and feel-good goody-goods. He despises the fish eaters, Mother Smiley's stone soup, Akona's garden – he most decidedly does not talk to plants – preferring any kind of red meat he can hunt or scavenge: wild dog or feral cat, rabbit, goat, pig, wallaby and deer - and thinks that the mayor and the rev and everybody else, except for Flay who is awesome, are full of shit.

That same rev now bends his eye on Pinky. 'The time of your slaughter has arrived; you will fall and shatter like a fragile vase,' he says, and bares his teeth at them in a grimace that could never be mistaken for a smile.

'Ooee, I better run,' Pinky says, and Tony laughs like a cheap hood from a B-grade TV rerun. These two clowns are Keatown's very own juvenile problem, and have attracted the company of a couple of the younger boat hands and wannabe fishermen. Orlap calls them wharf rats.

'The same destiny overtakes all,' the reverend says.

Made bold by the reverend's impotence in the situation, Tony steps forth to play the hero, grabbing a driftdead man – not too big – by the shoulder, swinging him around and jabbing him in the jaw like a boxer testing his opponent's defences. The man does not register the blow at all, except to reel a little from the physical impact. He doesn't appear to see Tony, or attempt to see him, and his facial expression doesn't change as he turns south and keeps walking. Tony is left looking and feeling a little stupid. 'You can't even pick a fight with them,' he mutters. 'What kind of zombies are they?'

The group of driftdead pass, leaving nothing behind them but the dead candle the rev knocked from the wraith woman's holder. Smaller scattered groups and loners can be seen approaching out of the twilight (when did the day get so old?).

We are about to turn and head for our homes, and the long clean-up job, when the sound of chanting is heard from the south. It is Akona, the healer, standing on the promontory in front of the marae, singing a karakia. We have all heard her singing before, singing to her ancestors, singing the newly dead into the afterlife, singing a welcome onto the marae, singing for joy and sorrow, but never like this – a long, lonely, lilting chant. The sound phases in and out but there is no wind, just the same eerie stillness that followed the storm. Her fluctuating volume threads her voice in and out of time and space, seeming to weave a net to hold the world.

By the time the librarian gets back the to library, the chant is over and the troop of driftdead have vanished south. She sits at her desk trying to work on her Chronicles of Keatown in a peculiar state of tension and excitement, but there is no flow in the words, or even the history itself. It feels like the driftdead are walking across the page with no sense of the delicate order of things, scattering words before them with a simple, mindless brutality. For them, there is no history.

In the face of that she becomes frightened, not because they are physically dangerous, but because they can walk through your head and take your memories along with them. They are the negation of everything that lives, sparks, and shapes intention to the act, and mind to the intention.

It would be so much easier if they just wanted to eat brains.

Is that what it's like for everybody?
'Lizard was my thread in the labyrinth.
Silence was my thread through the stars.'
   – Sirocco, Book of Imaginary Sentences

As darkness falls, and the first light of an old moon breaks out of its cave in the mountains, Little Sanyo tracks after Sirocco, wondering how he's going to say what he needs to say, scary as it is. Wonderful but scary.

Sirocco doesn't help. He seems to be lost in his own thoughts. Keatown doesn't help. Eerie silence reigns over the stilled battlefield around them. Everything has fallen into a waxen trance, but there is no sense of peace or calm. The battle seems simply frozen in mid-motion, as if about to resume at any moment with full ferocity. Houses lie askew at the mercy of poised sand dunes, trees are strewn about at wanton angles, half sunk in sand, looking as if they were about to be sucked under. Orlap's boat, The Wanderer, is surrealistically perched on the roundabout as if on the top of a wave. The conical teeth painted on the prow remind Little Sanyo of the stranded fish he found on the beach, although they are intended to look like sharks' teeth. A few indifferent driftdead pass beneath the painted teeth of its prow, no more than vague, indistinct shapes in the dull moonlight.

Little Sanyo and Sirocco pause on top of a dune and look down at Sirocco's place, where Gypsy and Scale live, and where the homeless Little Sanyo has been known to find refuge for the night. The house is there, and the crab apple tree where Sirocco likes to squat in the dawn and draw on the ground with his stick, but its trunk is half buried in sand, and the house itself is menaced by a circle of sand dunes, as if caught at the centre of a frozen vortex. Should the reprieve end and the storm resume, it could be sucked under in a spume of tin and timber in the blink of an eye.

Sirocco looks up at Venus, which is keeping its distance from the old moon. Little Sanyo doesn't have to be the genius he might have been to know that what Sirocco sees around him is the desert, the desert he once thought he escaped through the miraculous intervention of Gypsy. And here it is. The desert has followed him out of his dreams back into the real world.

Sirocco has that watchful look, the look that never sleeps. The eye of the scorpion. Like a desert person.

There have been times Little Sanyo has suspected that Sirocco, being a creature of the desert, will one day return to it, that his attempts to try being a person living in a town are just that, attempts, and that one day he will revert to form, whatever that might be, and vanish back to his natural habitat.

'You know,' he says, trying to sound casual, 'The driftdead look like ordinary people, right?'

'Hmmm.' Like Sad Toof, Sirocco has been drawn into Little Sanyo's deductive exercises before and is wary of them. They begin innocuously enough but don't stay that way.

'I mean, they don't act like ordinary people but they look ordinary enough. If you saw a photo of one, for example, would you know the difference?'

'Probably not.' But Sirocco is thinking about their eyes. There is something not right about their eyes. They can look at you and not see you. The thousand-yard stare amplified to a million miles.

'Right. So, if they look like ordinary people, they most probably were ordinary people at some point.'

'That's a fair assumption.'

'So if they were ordinary people once and are driftdead now... that means that at some point they turned. It means they...' They can change back again, he wants to say,

'... died on their feet and kept walking,' Sirocco says.

'Something like that. You've already thought of it.'

'Sort of. I wonder about Flounder Phil. Maybe the slutty girl was a driftdead. Then there was Blade.'

'No one else has said anything.'

'That doesn't mean much.'

'The reverend nearly got pulled in just now.' Little Sanyo grins nervously at the memory.

'And the librarian,' Sirocco says.

'I didn't see that.'

'It's all possible,' Sirocco says.

'Which means...' Little Sanyo doesn't finish the thought. If any of them might turn at any moment, what is the use of speech? Better not to think it, even, in case thinking it made it happen. The whole town could empty.

'I'd hate to be the last one left,' Little Sanyo says.

They stand there a little longer, each unwilling to move. In a moment Sirocco will go down the slope of the dune to the house, and Little Sanyo will continue on to the marae, but that moment has not yet arrived.

There is a soft beat at the heart of the world.

'And there's something else, something that's already changed. Since the storm,' Little Sanyo says. Now is the moment. If he can't tell Sirocco who can he tell?

'What do you mean?'

'Have you ever had tinnitus?'

'Ringing in your ears?'

'Yes. I used to have it. Quite badly. It was hard to hear what people said. Not a pleasant ringing, more like a high-pitched whine.'

'You never said much about it.'

'I thought everybody had it. I thought it was normal until I read about it in the library. It's all about hearing loss. It's the sound your head makes when you are losing the world of sound.'

'Why didn't you say something?'

Little Sanyo pouts, as if he were about to cry. 'Didn't want to.'

'All right.'

'That's why I like the beach. The sound of the waves helps drown it out.'

'I never thought of it.'

'Nobody did, except the librarian. She noticed what I was reading.'

'All right.' You have to be patient with Little Sanyo, Sirocco thinks. He'll get there in his own time.

'Well, it's gone.'

'The tinnitus?'

'Just like that. The storm came and took it away. No more buzzing in my head.'

'What does it feel like?' Sirocco says.

'I can hear to the other end of the universe,' Little Sanyo says solemnly.

'And what does that sound like?'

Little Sanyo says nothing.

The silence of the sky envelops them.

'You must be happy.'

'Yes, but I can hear myself talking in my head when I speak, like a great voice booming.'

'It was like that in the desert,' Sirocco says.

Below them, on the seaward side, a few driftdead are half-heartedly ploughing into the slope of the sand dune on which the two mokopuna are standing. One, a stern woman in her late fifties maybe, dressed in fishnet stockings and a tiny halter top, carries a transparent sealed container filled with murky water in which there lurches a live frog, bumping up against the edge of the container and staring out with mad eyes.

'They're not dead,' Sirocco says.

'They're not alive either,' Little Sanyo says.

'They never sleep,' Sirocco says.

'I can sleep for the first time in my life,' Little Sanyo says.

They are both quiet for a time. Under the stars.

'There's another thing,' Little Sanyo says.

'What?'

'I don't dream anymore. Do you dream?'

'Yes.'

'What about?'

'The desert.'

'You're lucky.'

'How?'

'To have a desert to dream about. Is Lizard there?'

'Yes.'

'I wish I could dream about the desert.'

'You wouldn't want to.'

'Why?'

'Because it's empty.'

Little Sanyo thinks about that. 'My head is empty too,' he says. 'Is that what it's like for everybody?'

'No,' Sirocco says.

They are about to turn away when their attention is drawn by some movement south of the roundabout.

There is just enough residual twilight to reveal, as if through layers of gauze, several driftdead heading south across the invading dunes in their usual myopic silence. Pinky, Tony, and a couple of fishermen have separated two driftdead women and are molesting them, making a game of it. Each time one of the women moves forward a giggling hero pushes her back, roughly, ripping off a piece of her clothing, and each time the woman tries again, another piece of clothing gets torn. Back and forth forever, until the women are naked.

The boys are enjoying themselves. The passivity of the driftdead inflames them. They don't fight back!

It is Akona who comes from out of the night and confronts them.

'Leave them be. They are like fish in a stream, let them pass.'

'Get fucked!' Pinky's voice is thick with booze.

'Stop abusing them,' Akona says.

This is no request. Pinky hesitates. 'They don't feel any pain,' Pinky says, prodding one of the women in the chest.

'That's what they used to say about fish,'

'Blah blah! All you could do is sing to them! Fat lot of use that is.'

'I wasn't singing to them.'

Pinky turns back to the driftdead woman who is still trying to move on and pokes her in the chest with a stick. 'See! Nobody home. No sense. No feeling.'

'Then what's the point of abusing them?'

Pinky is too befuddled to think his way around that. He doesn't care. But by this time Akona has spoiled the mood and the driftdead female has moved on.

'They're getting awaaaay,' Tony says. He's so drunk he can hardly get to the end of his last word.

'There's plenty more where they came from,' Pinky says.

'I think you boys need to go home and sleep it off before you fall over,' Akona says.

Pinky stares at her for a long moment. Perhaps he is considering defying her, even bullying her, but drunk and inflamed as he is, he has to think twice. Wherever the old lady is, the Man in Black is never far away, and besides, Pinky is somewhat afraid of Akona, little and old as she is, because there are some funny stories about her, like the man who tried to steal from her and ended up with festering fingers.

'You are not my mother,' he says.

It's pathetic, but it's the best he can come up with.

At that moment another driftdead woman blunders into them. She is prettier than the two the boys have been playing with, and looks like a flower in her summer print dress. For a moment it looks as if Pinky's interest is revived, but the pretty woman is holding a tommee tippee cup, and the sight of it gives him a strange turn. His world goes bright and then very dark.

'Let's get outta here,' he mumbles. He staggers backwards, reaching out for Tony's arm. 'I think I've had enough,' he says.

Keatown, open for business!

Over the next few days, the resilient inhabitants of Keatown begin, with the encouragement of the mayor, to put their lives back together.

The spring sun shines cheerfully, perhaps a little too cheerfully, on the sand, and on the drab town folk trudging dazed and weary through the heavy elements, shifting stuff and clearing what they can. Everybody pitches in. Even Pinky and Tony and the wharf rats. Sand is shovelled away from paths and gardens, houses are restabilised, brooms begin their brisk work on floors and roofs, and, when the electrical lines are cleared and re-established, the chicka-chicka boom-boom sounds of Arabic reggae once more rise up from the Cornet house.

The lower reaches of the Wai-O-Tapu River are cleared under Akona's direction, most of the work done by herself and the Man in Black. The sluggish, sandy water clears quickly and pure water flows. Akona constantly gives quiet thanks to the gods of the earth and the sky, and her ancestors, for the blessing of the Wai-O-Tapu: the water, the sky, the earth, all a manifestation of Atua, the great god. Foolish people, it makes her heart ache to see them, stumbling around in the dark searching for Atua's blessing when there it is right in front of them, all around them, to be drawn in with every breath and exhaled with every thought.

Within a few days wild flowers spring up each side of the cleared stream, forget-me-nots mostly, and the white-flowered wild onion, pushed along by the already summerlike heat. Other delicate grasses appear, and common weeds like burdock, mullein, dandelion, puha, celery and chickweed. All with their uses, to raise the body or the spirit. Fed from the newly cleared stream, Akona's garden goes wild with parsley, echinacea, comfrey and kawakawa.

People call to each other cheerfully and lend their neighbours a hand where they can. There is optimism in the morning and exhaustion at night. Everybody does their best to ignore the driftdead and work around them. To give him his credit, despite his bombast, the mayor seems to be everywhere at once, exhorting and encouraging, as if by sheer will alone he can pull a miracle out of the chaos. The main focus of energy is the repair of the fish shed, the long, thin galvanised iron structure that had its back broken in the siege, and to get our plucky little fishing fleet repaired and into the water. The Rev Stickman always appears, with his young acolyte by his side, where the workload is heaviest, reading soul-stirring passages from the Bible. Hera is everywhere also, letting Baby be seen, for the sight of the child is a great reviver of souls. All he has to do is find a smile or burp to get weary people laughing. Grandmother Gaunt sees this as a PR job, but nobody listens to her. Old Grandmother Gaunt is getting a bit cranky, people decide, and she's got worse since the storm.

People do what they do best and get on with it. The librarian sweeps her house clean before going over the library with a particularly discriminating duster (one that has a penchant for poetry), discovering tiny deposits of micro-sand that have somehow found their way in. Flay unwraps his pumps carefully, as if he were undressing a shy woman, briefly hoses them down and towels them off before flipping the switch. The pumps hum, ready for business. Across the road, Annanda sweeps the pavement outside his supermarket, which leaves a nice clear patch in front of the doors, but he can't sweep the whole street, the whole world. At least his roof has held up. The solar power is still working.

On the wharf, which is still standing, the fishermen face the huge task of reclaiming what they can, most of the boats being deposited on dry land and lying around in drunken disorder, suffering varied damage from gaping hulls to hurt feelings. The long, slender fish shed lies in two parts, as if a fist has pushed up from beneath directly into its spine. The girders stagger in frozen fall, leaning crazily, deserted in mid-flight.

The town looks vulnerable, makeshift, contingent: one casual flick of this storm's tail and you could kiss goodbye to Keatown forever. No more than a few marks scratched in sand, a circle and a star. Just one more flick of the tail, that's all it would take.

Not only do we have to deal with hefting huge quantities of sand, but with stringy groups of driftdead who tend to meander all over the place as they seek their southward path. The mayor continues to exhort the townsfolk not to look at them, to pretend that they aren't there, because they aren't really there at all, and most people take his advice because there is too much work to do and nothing to be done with them anyway. They are just another cross to bear. But, as more come through with every passing day, it is impossible to ignore them. It is common now to see them in groups of a hundred or more, ambling along, taking no notice of anything around them. After trying to give them food, and various other strategies, most of the villagers have given up on them and ignore them, except when they blunder into people's homes or into groups of workers clearing the sand. They seem harmless enough, easy to manhandle out of a house or yard, as if they were big, awkward bumble bees, and direct them on their way south. Annanda has to keep his door closed so he doesn't have to spend this time chasing them out of his supermarket, placing a large cardboard sign, in strong black marker, underlined twice in red, on his closed door proclaiming Yes, friends, we are open for business! Occasionally, someone gets distracted by this passing parade, and will stand gazing at them mesmerised, but there is always a friend or neighbour at hand to pull them back to reality.

Much to Reverend Stickman's chagrin, everybody has adopted the term driftdead, as if it were quite natural – he insists on calling them the plague and the scourge, and the devil's spawn, and zombies, but none of these names catches on. The only other dissenter is Hera, who insists on calling them refugees. 'They are fleeing from some mind-numbing terror,' she maintains. 'They have shut out the world so they no longer see or feel anything. But they are still there, inside.'

Despite all this a certain festive atmosphere develops. People begin to laugh, and laugh too much. They become a little febrile, but it seems to be all for the good. In the general delirium, miracles happen. Food is produced from hidden stashes. Dried fruit guaranteed sand free. Sunflower seeds guaranteed moth free. Even more important, wild wheat still good for bread. In the spirit of generosity, Annanda contributes a case of dodgy-looking canned peaches. Everybody says thanks. There's sex going on everywhere, with the local fishermen doing all right in the beds of the local women.

Flay is not impressed. From the moment one of the bungling driftdead tried to climb over the top of his revered alfie, Flay has developed an itchy trigger finger. There is one sure way of taking care of these useless fucking pedestrians. If this was the end of the world, why couldn't they be drivers, racing south in Ferraris, for chrisakes, or cruising to their doom in stretch-limos? A pedestrian apocalypse? It's offensive.

But he has other problems. They turn up at his door in the shape of Orlap, Captain Orlap, the alpha male of the fishermen, a big wide Swedish grin on his face, and his hatchet man, Butch, who is proud to be a woman and bloke all at once. She's smiling too, just like the Nord, hey! Happy holidays!

Flay does what he has to do, excusing himself quickly, once he has established them on his sacred sofa – sacred because it is liberally patched with cuttings from old leather jackets of arcane badges and patches from petrolhead gangs Flay once associated with. In his garage, he quickly locates a certain discreetly hidden tin and rolls up precious shreds of a mind-blasting hydroponic skunk he's been keeping for just such an occasion. The Nord loves his fucking smoke. Rolling up gives Flay a moment to contemplate, a moment to nostalgically recall London where the streets were so chocca with cars you couldn't fuckin' breathe. That's where Flay had learned to smoke, and drive. He knew about smokers. Kicking off with a spliff would put Orlap at his ease. The Captain would chill out, blow himself up to twice his size and make large, expansive gestures. Flay would have an obligatory toke and then amiable deals would be done.

What's worrying Flay is not Orlap so much as Butch. She'll have a toke all right, but it won't necessarily make her amiable – quite the opposite. Why has Orlap brought her? This is no longer a visit, it is a deputation. And Flay has a horrible feeling he knows what it's about. And if he's right, there won't be any amiable deals, skunk or no skunk.

He plasters the usual scowl on his face as he rejoins them, judiciously leaving his shotgun behind. Not a suitable bargaining tool at this stage.

It all goes as planned. Here a toke, there a toke, everywhere a toke-toke. Orlap relaxes and grows expansive. Butch nails Flay with a paranoid eye. A little codeine would chill her out, but he has too little left to waste on her. So far so good. They talk about the driftdead. Orlap tells him the fishermen have seen them in the ocean, some of them swimming, some of them walking on the bottom of the sea. They don't breathe, Orlap says. Flay doesn't give a shit what the pedestrians do or don't do. He's waiting for Orlap to get to the point.

'The storm,' Orlap says, in his correct but plodding, heavily accented English. 'From five boats we have two operational. All the diesel was lost.'

Flay nods wisely, like an old friend or advisor. He well knows that Orlap's own boat, The Wanderer, is still perched on the roundabout looking pretty stupid with its sharks' teeth gnawing the sand. If Orlap is grieving over that it doesn't show, which is one up to him, Flay figures. If you're going to look like a tough bastard it's best to be one.

'The ocean is not normal. There are fish we have not seen. Some cold water also. But there are fish. And we must fish.'

Flay nods in agreement with logic. When the fish are running, the fishermen must fish. Keatown must eat, and maybe some deals can be made when the trucks come through again. Flay understands.

'We put to sea... but we need diesel.'

Once more, Flay does the maths in his head. Two empty tanks. Blah-de-blah gallons remaining. Would leave him with one more refill of the same before his pumps start sucking air. The freak storm couldn't have happened at a worse time for Flay. Orlap always kept his tanks topped up. Now all that precious fuel has gone to waste. It has to be replaced. This is no top-up. This is a fill-'er-up exercise.

'I'll tell ya what, there's a question in my mind as to how you will pay for the diesel. I'm not like that Indian pansy over the road. He'll take any kind of funny money. Me, I like cold hard cash. Bankable money,' The banks haven't gone down, not when Flay last looked. His bank anyway. His accounts are still good. Flay does not exactly subscribe to the mayor's hopes of an economic revival just around the corner, he is too canny for that, but if you scratched his cynical, oil-soaked hide hard enough, you would find, in the spaghetti junctions of his mind, a rather vague faith that everything is going be all right in the end, just as he believes that the age of the automobile will never end, that vehicles of all shapes and sizes will be humming along forever, with nothing but blacktops and gas stations between here and eternity.

'How about gold?' Orlap asks with a smirk. Butch is smirking too.

'That would do the trick.' Where would these fisherfucks get their hands on gold? Flay doesn't have a lot of time for gold himself. You can't eat it, or even wipe your arse with it. You certainly can't stick it in your fucking gas tank – he can't see that it is much of a hedge against collapsing cash: cash is king and always will be. Nevertheless, other people value it, which makes it valuable. Gold might help him loosen up those tight arses who have been buying diesel and stockpiling it, probably in the hopes of making a killing right about now. He knows who they are.

'Two full tanks,' Orlap says, waving the joint in the air. Flay grabs it and takes a toke. He doesn't really want it, but he hates the Nord hanging onto it, waving it around like a fucking wand, playing top dog to his bitch.

'I get it,' Flay says, 'I'm trying to figure the price. In gold. Wouldn't want to rip anybody off now, would I?'

'One ingot for one tank. I give you two ingots.'

Ingots! Jesus! Flay coughs up some heavy smoke. Where in bitumen would Orlap get his hands on ingots? Flay imagines a bunch of gold bracelets and things he could haggle over. Stuff locals or visitors might have given the brave, handsome sea captain over the years. Never ingots.

'Not just ingots.'

'No? Bells and whistles too?'

'Stamped.'

'What do you mean?'

'With stamp. Seal. US Federal Reserve Bank.'

Flay laughs. It's a strange noise not many people have heard. It sounds a bit like an old lady changing gears in a VW Beetle. He waves the joint under Orlap's nose. 'Had a bit too much of a good thing, have we? Sucked the old brain out the other end, have we?' To Butch, he says, 'Sad to see such a noble mind so fucked up.'

As he reaches into his backpack Orlap is laughing also. Too stupid or too stoned, or both, Flay figures, to get that he is the joke. Well, have a good laugh at your own expense, buddy – no extra charge.

Still laughing, Orlap draws a package from his backpack and opens it up. Lying in his hand is a gold bar. Flay stops laughing, but Orlap doesn't. For him, the joke is just starting. The look on Flay's face is good for a kick-off. Even the stony-faced Butch cracks a grin.

Flay takes the gold bar out of Orlap's hand and turns it over. There it is, the stamp of the US Federal Reserve. This little baby came right out of Fort Knox. Well well, the joke's on me. Never let it be said that Flay can't take as good as he gives. Ha fucking ha. His fingers tighten on the bar as he scratches at it. He's no expert, but this has to be the real thing.

'Where'd ya get it?'

Orlap giggles. 'We found it in the belly of a fish.'

'Musta been a big fish.'

Orlap giggles harder and Butch is fighting for control of her facial muscles. Stoned out of their fucking gourds, but that doesn't alter the reality of the ingot in his hands. Its convincing weight and density. Its approved seal of reality.

'Very big. Some strange fish now...' Orlap tries to nod solemnly, hard when you're giggling like a girl. Flay does it for him.

'Very strange.'

So it's gold for liquid gold. At least someone appreciates the value of his asset. There is only one place the Nord could have got his hands on gold like this. Flounder Phil was not the only fisherman in town to do business with the remaining rich-shits up mansions. There is no law against it. Flay suspects that some of the fresh-produce people with their innocent potatoes and veges do a bit of quiet trade up there as well. Good on them. It just sticks in the craw in Orlap's case, the great hero of the seas returning with the catch to feed the good people of Keatown, many of whom give their labour in the fish sheds and free produce to subsidise the brave little struggling local industry... Give Flay a fucking break! All the time their Capt'n Orlap and his sidekick have apparently been running a nice little racket up mansions for ingots of official gold. It sticks in the craw all right. Good thing Flay has never been tempted to give him a discount. No discounts, no credit. Them's the rules.

Logical as it is, the story doesn't quite fit. Hard to imagine ingots of gold being stored away for any length of time without word seeping out.

Then Flay has his big insight, his grand, stoned moment. There's something more going on here. Orlap isn't paying in precious ingots, however he got hold of them, just to go out and catch a few mutant fish for the poor hungry people of Keatown. There is something greater at stake. He has some other purpose for the diesel. Flay doesn't know what that is. His mind is not large and capable of wide vistas, but it has a brute persistence; he will figure it out in the end.

Orlap reaches out for the ingot and Flay hands him the joint. Time for some fancy footwork.

'Which boat is in best repair?'

Orlap sucks tenderly at the joint, 'The Merry Widow. She suffers the least. We work on her now.'

Flay hefts the gold bar as if measuring it. 'I'll tell you what,' he says, 'We'll half fill The Merry Window, and do a test run.'

'Why just one boat?' Butch says as if she has been waiting for this moment, which she probably has. 'And why half-full? Half full means half empty? You want to kill us?'

'Capt'n Handsome said it himself. The sea is not normal. Anything can happen. We don't want to lose another tank of gas.' Which is very fucking reasonable, and reasonably put, if Flay says so himself. 'And we don't even know if there are any fucking edible fish out there.'

The Nord seems to agree. He kicks back and worries the roach with a flame. Ball in your court, buddy.

'Hanging onto our gas for all we're worth, are we?' Butch says. She nods at the gold bar in his hand, 'Price just gone up, has it?'

Flay grows discursive. 'You remind me of something my dear old mum used to say. Never spent a day in her life out of Brixton, but she knew a thing or two. Son, she'd say – she always called me son, on account of forgetting my name – there are those who know the price of everything and the value of nothing.'

'I know enough to know a chiseller when I see one.'

'You bet your fucking boats I am,' Flay says.

'Never seen a grease monkey who could lie in bed straight.'

'Coming from you, that's a good one.'

'He has a point,' Orlap says ponderously, as if reporting some received truth.

'Of course he does,' Butch says, giving Flay the hard eye. Orlap isn't keeping to the script. Probably got too stoned. As for Flay, he feels just fine.

'I can't make half an ingot.'

'So give me a whole ingot. For safekeeping. If all goes well and you get back, even if you don't have much fish, I top up the tank and keep the ingot. If you lose The Merry Widow, you forfeit and I keep the ingot. I keep the ingot whatever happens. Couldn't be fairer than that.'

'We're not giving you an ingot for half a tank of gas.' Butch looks suitably outraged.

'That's my offer. I don't bargain.'

Butch has hold of the joint now. She sucks on it so viciously that what's left of it is consumed in a few seconds. The smoke disappears into her body and doesn't reappear. Probably a hundred per cent absorbed. 'A full tank for an ingot. That's what I call fair.'

The Nord nods his head. He seems to have finally found his wits. 'A full tank. I don't want to put to sea with half a tank.'

'That's right,' Butch says, 'What if we're blown off course? We have to have a good safety margin.'

Orlap nods again like a fucking Noddy toy with its head on a spring. 'Safety margin,' he repeats.

Flay gets up and puts the gold bar on his chipped Formica table, goes out into his garage and retrieves his pump-action shotgun. He doesn't have to check to make sure it's loaded. When he walks back through his living room he doesn't look at his two guests, or the gold which is still on the table, going straight past them out to his pumps. A few pedestrians are bumbling around. One of them, a big man going to fat wearing some shapeless toga thing and carrying a Xmas-tree fairy in one hammy hand, bumps into his 91 Octane pump, bouncing off it like a squishy pinball. Flay takes casual aim and fires. The blast rattles the loose window behind him. The big man's head vanishes in a cloud of blood; his body keeps walking a few more loose steps.

One less fairy to worry about.

With considerable satisfaction, Flay notes the two horrified faces staring out the window. Whatever floats their boat.

Negotiations complete.

they just keep coming

Annanda hears the shot and looks in time to see the headless body collapse in a gout of blood, and sees Flay turn back inside before the body hits the ground. The other driftdead take no notice of the death of one of their number, Annanda notices; they keep on coming, walking over or around the body as if it were just another obstacle. Annanda is shaken by the blast. Even if these zombie people were the dreaded Rakshasa, they do not deserve such casual and brutal destruction. Annanda has always had his doubts about Flay and his shotgun, never trusted the man's stability, and now it seems his doubts are fully justified.

Word of the deed gets around fast enough.

Hera is outraged and calls it murder. Melissa Tonguestone says it's about time, and Grandmother Gaunt backs her up. Sirocco asks the reverend if the driftdead have souls, and is told they are already gone to the devil. So, Sirocco persists, killing them can't be called murder, right? And the Reverend Stickman has no answer, none that will stick. The mayor blusters on about getting Keatown back on its feet and ignoring mirages. Akona tells Flay that the driftdead are not like fish to be shot in a stream, but are sacred in their own way, and must walk their own hard path.

Flay doesn't give a shit. Pedestrians, sacred? Don't make him laugh. Dammed or sacred, it's all the same to Flay.

Flay's action, however, seems to spark a change in attitude among the good people of Keatown. Up to this point, while spooked by the manifestation, most of our good denizens have been vaguely tolerant of their mysterious but harmless visitors.

Ignore them and eventually they'll go away, is the prevailing attitude.

They are a nuisance of course, but as such have to take their place among the greater irritations of life. Just another cross to bear. Just another tribulation brought upon them by the storm. Many have been influenced by Hera's contention that these are real, if totally traumatised, people, whose humanity is still buried deep within them somewhere. It isn't beyond possibility, Hera says, that one day they might wake up, like the sleepwalkers they mimic, and find their humanity again, find their thirst and their hunger, their joy and their weariness. Therefore, it is important to treat them with forbearance. Hera starts calling them sleepers, to suggest this possibility, a day they might all wake up and come to their senses.

Over days, however, and as their numbers swell – they just keep coming – the people have grown more intolerant towards the driftdead, pushing them aside roughly or bashing them with handy implements to keep them away. If they are sleepers it is time they woke up. But of course it doesn't keep them away. Contempt is beginning to overcome any other feelings people might have had for the driftdead. Does one have compassion for stones falling out of the sky? Or walking corpses that don't rot?

Flay's single shotgun blast sets off a wave of sympathy for Flay, and a wave of revulsion and fear towards the driftdead. Maybe Melissa Tonguestone is right. Maybe the driftdead are cockroaches in human form. Maybe the reverend is right, and these are the legions of the damned trekking through little old Keatown on their way to Hell's Gate.

It turns out that Flay is not the only one to treat the driftdead as less than human.

Pinky and Tony have taken to tracking a few driftdead females south and, out of town and away from prying eyes, raping and tormenting and torturing them to their vile hearts' content, with no Akona around to remind them of their fading humanity. Afterwards, Pinky confesses that the whole thing was a big disappointment. He tries to explain it a bit like this – when you kill an animal, a rabbit say, when you wring its neck, you can feel its pain, you can see the spark of life pass out of it, and there's some satisfaction in that. But these driftdead feel no pain. You can cut off their arms and they keep walking. You can cut off their legs and they fall over. But the stumps are still waving in the air or scratching at the sand until, like an old mechanical clock, they wind down and stop. There's no pleasure in that. Might as well be chopping up shop mannequins. Pinky cunningly suggests that, since rabbits are closer to God than the driftdead, then raping and tormenting and torturing them can be no sin. The reverend has no answer to this obscure theological challenge, but Rasputin does. His eyes glow with god-power, his voice resonates:

'Since the so-called driftdead are the Pilgrims of Darkness, they are lower than the animals and therefore demonic. Intercourse of any kind with demons is an irredeemable sin. Like the Pilgrims themselves, Pinky and company are now beyond salvation. But there is hope for those who remain.'

Pinky gives Rasputin the finger, but the reverend is grateful for this wise judgement, and kneels on the sand before Rasputin and kisses his hand, making a complete fool of himself.

Hera, backed up by most of the women including Akona, the librarian, and even Mother Smiley and her sister, call it an atrocity, and call on the mayor to incarcerate Pinky and Tony and bring them to trial. And Flay too. The mayor calls for calm.

The argument goes on for days. Pinky and Tony go their own sweet way.

Meanwhile, the driftdead just keep coming.

the stealers of dreams

Sirocco has never believed Hera's contention that the driftdead are harmless. Harmless victims, in fact. As far as he's concerned their apparent harmlessness is deceptive. Their bodies are harmless enough, ambulating through town, but Sirocco believes that they can walk in and out of people's heads as easily as they do their houses and yards, without turning a hair. They are not figments of the imagination so much as figments of the world, but he can't explain that to anybody. Even the librarian.

The idea first occurred to him as he sat and listened to Gypsy's account of the death of her mother, how he thought that the wind had got inside Gypsy's head, stirring up currents of memory. More recently Witch Hunt made a comment that set him thinking. Since seeing her father out of Miranda's window, the little girl has stopped dreaming about him. 'I used to dream about him all the time,' she told Sirocco. 'Now I don't dream about him at all. I don't dream about anything.'

Not only can they walk in and out of people's heads, Sirocco reasons, but they always take something with them, a memory or a dream. They are dream stealers. The objects they all carry might be just that, things stolen out of people's heads. And the more that come, the more dreams and images they steal. Sirocco senses that, like Witch Hunt, others have stopped dreaming since the driftdead arrived, that the eerie silence following the storm has followed sleepers into their sleep and silenced their dreams. Sirocco has felt that silence. It eats into the side of his head at night when he is trying to write his imaginary book. It carries all his words away before he can catch them. Nothing emerges from that silence. No meaning. No bright, shiny phonemes. No rolling sentences. Only the blank-eyed driftdead emerge from that silence.

'How do you know? Maybe people do dream but they are just too tired to remember them?' Little Sanyo says when Sirocco tries to explain it. 'Everybody dreams, it's just that not everybody remembers their dreams.'

'Wait a minute,' Sad Toof says. 'How do we know people dream if they can't remember dreaming?'

Little Sanyo is eager to share his knowledge. 'You can see their eyes moving back and forth very fast. It's called rapid eye movement. REM. When REM is happening, people are dreaming.'

'You can't know that,' Sad Toof says stubbornly. 'All y' c'n actually know is that their eyes are movin' back and forth.'

'The only way to really know,' Little Sanyo says 'is to ask people.'

Sirocco doesn't want to do that. People are suspicious enough of him as it is without him poking his desert stick into their heads and stirring up their circles and stars.

'Let's start with you.' Little Sanyo turns to Sad Toof. 'Are you dreaming?'

Sad Toof points dramatically to his sad toof. 'It won't let me' he says sadly, a young man bereft of dreams. 'I jus' get into some nice little dream, the pain comes along and....' He snaps his fingers, or tries to.

'What about you, Sirocco?'

Sirocco is reluctant to admit that he is still dreaming. As soon as he closes his eyes he is back in the desert, with Lizard beside him, talking away about lizard things, such as the right technique for catching a fly. However, he makes an exception of himself on account of Lizard, for these meetings with the creature are more than dreams if less than reality. The driftdead would be powerless over Lizard.

He doesn't try to explain that to the other two, since what tends to happen is that Little Sanyo pulls everything he says to pieces and Sad Toof gets to pick over the remains. One to search and one to destroy. All that remains is the stubborn impression that the driftdead are not leaving town empty-handed, that somehow, perhaps through their very vacancy, they are taking something with them, something they have absorbed. Dreams.

The three mokopuna can leave it there, unresolved, but it is harder for the librarian to do the same, for it forces her to think hard about the nature of the invaders. It is just possible that, if Sirocco were right, it is the suppression of dreaming that enables these creatures of the night, who should belong only in the dimensions of the imagination, to invade our waking life, enables them to walk right in over the border, that now-porous border, between the unreal and the real, the waking and the dreaming, right into town, into people's houses and onto their roofs, and into the Chronicle of Keatown too, over which the librarian has laboured long. It is no comfort to imagine that the driftdead have walked in here through the empty spaces left by people's vanished dreams, and walked into the Chronicles by the same route.

The librarian is disturbed by the implications of this line of reasoning. Invasion by creatures from other dimensions is not her genre, far from it. She prefers good, solid historical fiction, well-researched recreations of the past, stories drawn from the real world, from the world of real, recorded human experience. She's never had the patience for fantasy, believing, in her solid mainstream heart, that fantasy is for children or big kids who never grew up. Simulacrums who belong in dreams but walk into the world through silenced minds are most certainly a fantasy, something Witch Hunt might have nightmares about, but the librarian, like everybody else, must somehow account for her experience. Like it or not, they're here!

do the driftdead rot?

The question occupying Little Sanyo's mind is particular and singular, and yet he is surprised nobody else has asked it: do the driftdead rot? The zombies of popular imagination must rot because they are dead. The flesh begins to fall off their bones, their eyeballs hang out, and they become all peeling and putrid. Rather than the walking dead, they should be called the walking carcasses. The driftdead on the other hand may look muddy and filthy – but none are rotting away. Not that their skin looks healthy, exactly, they have too great a pallor for that, and some have scars or are missing limbs – he has seen one on crutches – but they are not going off. Flies have no interest in them. None look as if they have crawled up out of a grave.

Which brings him to his next point.

'Do they have a circulatory system?' he asks Sirocco as if Sirocco might actually know. 'Are they warm-blooded? Or cold-blooded like reptiles?'

'Blood came outa the neck of the one Flay blasted,' Sad Toof says with relish.

'Which means they need oxygen just like us, which means they have to breathe.'

'But Orlap's seen 'em walkin' on the bottom of the bay.'

'Maybe they can breathe underwater.'

'I don't see none with gills.'

Little Sanyo asks Sirocco directly, 'What do you think?'

Slowly, Sirocco says, 'It's in the desert that you find the juiciest plants.'

The other two stare at him.

Sad Toof licks his lips. 'Mmmm! Nice cactus!'

That's about all his friends have to say on the issue, but it's hard for Little Sanyo to let it go. This tendency to worry a problem into the ground has been made worse by the change that has come over him with the ending of the storm. The hissing, tinging, whining, humming, whistling sound of far-off celestial voices called tinnitus has indeed vanished, as he told Sirocco, leaving his head clean and empty for the first time in his life. It doesn't make it any easier to talk to people. Everything he says booms loudly in his head and makes him forget what he is saying. The single cry of a gull will echo in his head like a prolonged musical note, bent and piercing. Each sound, or medley of sounds, unfolds out of the great silence and folds into it again like a conjurer's card trick. Then there are the sounds that only he can hear: the great clattering of the sun as it raises the horizon; the thin, milky wail of the moon; the hard scratch of a blue sky; the velvety stealth of twilight – sounds that don't exist outside that profound quiet.

The same quiet has similarly amplified his thoughts, which pound in his head the way storm waves will pound on a beach. If the driftdead don't rot, they are not dead, is one such thought. There is a chain of logic to be honoured. Like ordinary people they can be killed; that much is known. Like ordinary people they rot once they are properly dead; the body of the one Flay blew away has attracted enough flies. But, he asks himself, if they weren't killed, would they die like ordinary people? He can imagine them somehow walking on and on forever in a twilight immortality, and as long as they keep walking, the world will keep unrolling beneath their feet.

It is intolerable that so little should be known about the invaders, about their basic physiology. Answers to some very simple questions are lacking. For example, it appears that they do not eat, drink or excrete, so… where do they get their energy from? Or are they perpetual-motion machines that defy the laws of physics? The idea of perpetual-motion machines appeals to Little Sanyo. Sometimes he imagines that he will find one washed up on a beach, but he hardly thinks the driftdead qualify.

And there are other stories. Grandmother Gaunt has a story that a driftdead woman that strayed onto Akona's roof during the storm actually stopped and looked at her. And the librarian tells of one staring in the window at her. They become aware of us, but only very slowly, Little Sanyo speculates.

What is needed is study. Careful study. He needs to test subjects, and a place to do his tests. Somewhere tucked away. He knows the place almost as soon as he has the thought. After all, he has lived as an urchin in Keatown for a good while and knows all the culverts, empty garages and lonely barns. They are more or less his stock and trade. There's an empty barn just south of town. It sits off-road a way, is part hidden by a line of pine trees, and is not locked.

He heads that way, scouting out the land around, getting it figured out. He worries about how he's going to get his test subjects into the barn before realising that they will just walk straight in, more or less. Double doors face east, towards the sea. Passing driftdead walk right by. They are quite passive. All he has to do is escort one inside.

He makes his preparations carefully. A search of the barn turns up a few useful things, including a length of chain, probably used for tying up a dog, and, more curiously, an ancient set of handcuffs with the key still in them. The cuffs had not been used for many years, but with a little oil he was able to turn the lock.

Capturing the driftdead proves as easy as he imagined. He picks younger driftdead, noting as he does so that there are few children among them, the Nightshade Girl having been an exception. Picking them out allows him time to observe that they are not all moving in the same manner or speed. Some are striding confidently, as if off to an appointment, others amble along as if heading nowhere in particular. None of them runs or even jogs. Some are graceful, some are clumsy, but all move with a steady pace.

Watching them is hypnotic, and as he does so, he conducts a thought experiment, a little trick he learned from reading about Einstein. Imagine all the driftdead setting out at one time from one place. Since they are moving at different speeds, and some will pull ahead of the others, the group will become spread out with the faster ones in front. This, however, is not what is happening. Wherever he looks, some are moving faster, some slower, with groups forming of those accidentally moving at the same speed. This suggests that they all set out at different times. Which means that Hera is probably wrong when she says that they are all in flight from a common disaster, like true refugees.

Logic, however, can only take him so far. All will be revealed when he can examine his test subjects.

He needs three, at least, to begin with.

The first he chooses is a boy somewhat older than himself who is walking quite slowly, holding a cellphone. This one he guides by the arm straight into the garage where he quickly handcuffs it to the dog chain, which he wraps around the vice that is in turn bolted into the thick, hard wood of the bench. The length of the chain gives the boy a little movement but no possibility of escape.

The next is an old man, also getting along quite leisurely, carrying a dishcloth. He looks like an easy mark, but pulls against Little Sanyo when he tries to steer him into the garage, as if there is some force pulling him forward. A quick shove, however, and he's in. He doesn't try to escape through the doors, but wanders off into the barn. Little Sanyo wastes no time picking the third test subject, a girl, about the same age as the boy, also meandering along. She's carrying a framed photograph of a woman who might be her mother. Little Sanyo steers her quite gently inside, quickly pulls down the barn doors and locks them. There's a small door on the northern side he can use to get in and out.

He makes his decisions. The boy he will leave chained up. The girl he leaves free to wander around. The old man... the old man has to be killed, if that is the word. He needs to do an autopsy, have a look at the heart, the lungs and the brain. See what he can see. He's no expert but maybe he'll see something. A little perpetual-motion machine where the heart should be. Fungus on the brain. In a locked cupboard in the old school building there are some microscopes. And thermometers. He can examine the blood. See what he can see. Maybe they have tiny nanobots running around in their bloodstream. That would be exciting.

He takes the knife and thinks about his next steps carefully. He suspects that the driftdead are like real zombies in that their brains have to be put out of action to stop them trying to move. He has to put the knife into the brain of the old driftdead, or sever the spine. The quickest, easiest way to the brain is through the eyeball, and while he would do pretty much anything for the sake of knowledge, the idea of sticking the knife though the old man's eye disgusts him.

Furthermore, he wants to keep the brain intact, so he can have a look at it. The best method would be to separate the head from the body. Easier said than done. First he ties both its arms behind it with some greasy rope he finds, and although it continues to struggle weakly, it's immobile enough for him to do his grizzly work. Then he has to get a box to stand on to give him some height. He closes his eyes and rips into the top of the spinal cord as hard as he can go. He's not quite strong enough and has to hack at it several times before the head finally falls forward on the old man's chest, held only by the skin of the neck, and he slumps to the floor, dead by any measure.

There is blood but not as much as he would have thought, and it doesn't squirt everywhere, as you see in the movies, but wells up, slow and dark, from the open neck.

He doesn't ask himself why he chose the old one to kill and not one of the younger ones. It doesn't bother him. He knows that in a subtle way he is treating them as if they were human, discriminating against the oldie because he's already had a life in favour of the young whose life is to come. Except of course none of these three have a life of any kind, either now or to come as far as anyone knows; they have crossed over and have become something else. What they have become he hopes to find out.

'It's all under investigation,' he tells them.

The only explanation he has for the lack of physical degeneration in the active driftdead is that they are not subject to time, and therefore decay, in the same way that humans are. He has the feeling that if they keep moving they will be immortal, not subject to the arrow of time at all. These two young ones he has chained up, eventually their bonds will rot, the garage will disintegrate and they will keep moving south as if nothing has happened. They will not age. They will not change in any way. They will keep walking until the earth falls to pieces beneath them and the stars rot.

At least that's what he imagines. A waxen immortality.

He takes the knife and makes an incision in the old man's stomach. There is no putrid smell, he notes, as there would be if the thing was dead. He locates what he thinks is the liver, and removes it. A floppy, nasty-looking thing, but quite healthy, he surmises. Certainly not decayed in any way. The inside, useless as it may be to them, is as immortal as the outer skin.

He places the liver on some paper on a clear section of the bench.

Now, he suspects, it will rot. Because it will now belong wholly to this universe, to this time stream. The driftdead can be taken from their time stream, piece by piece.

He returns to the body and begins to feel around the sides for the kidneys. A feverishness has quietly overtaken him. He pushes around inside the body as if he were looking for something at the bottom of an old suitcase filled with useless junk. When he finds a kidney he rips it unceremoniously from the body. It takes him a moment to get control of himself. The girl's driving him crazy, constantly banging from one wall to another, as mindless as a fly. And with as little memory.

As quickly as he can he sews the body back up, very amateurishly, but the best he can manage with the rusty sewing needle and thin black thread he finds. The needle has a flattened head, like an arrow, and he figures it was used once for sewing bits of hide together. It makes a mess of the skin, but at least there is no blood.

Logically, he has to acknowledge, because the organs look intact, that it is not impossible that one day these driftdead might turn back into humans again, if indeed they began as humans, but doesn't want to face the ethical implications of that. That would make him a murderer, like Pinky. What if Hera were right and the driftdead were like sleepwalkers who would one day wake up and find themselves back in the world – what would happen then?

He would face it then, that's what would happen. In the meantime there is work to do. He drags the corpse to a pallet he's prepared by covering it with an old tarpaulin. He hefts the corpse up into the pallet, takes his knife, and before he can think too hard about what he's doing, hacks some of the flesh from the arm. This he lies beside the kidneys and the liver. He makes a note of the time with the stub of a builder's pencil on the surface of the wooden bench. Since he's not sure of dates, he will mark off the days with a simple stroke.

Now for the hard part. Using the knife and a hammer, he manages to hack through the skull and locate the brain. He's only seen pictures of the brain –drawings and graphics – so he has no way of knowing if the gelatinous mass he finds is normal or not, but he studies it with interest anyway. Hungry for knowledge, his mind will greedily pick out and store all the details. Eventually, he will have to look at another brain and make some comparisons, although he won't be able to get much further unless he can get a look at an ordinary person's brain and do some real comparisons. He can't see any way that is going to happen.

He does the same with the chest and locates the heart. It looks like an ordinary heart as far as he can tell. Tubes in and tubes out. But the blood looks darker, as if not properly oxygenated. He can't tell what any of this means. He only has his curiosity. At least now he knows that they do have brains and hearts. The illusion of humanness is not just skin-deep, he thinks. I can't expose that illusion with just a knife.

He's reluctant to leave, despite the carnage, as if there might be more to learn. For a while he observes the boy and girl. The boy struggles against his captivity, not fiercely but consistently, pulling on the chain over and over, pushing up against the bench or trying to tug it south, vice and all. The girl bangs up against the southern wall, follows it a short distance to the bench, turns and goes back down, west, along the southern wall to the corner, turns again and repeats the process. Up and back, up and back. Patient, tireless, mindless.

When he leaves he makes sure everything is securely locked. He hides the key to the little side door. He can hear the girl, banging up against the south wall, but it's a soft sound and there's no way anybody in Keatown is going to hear it.

Now he has a chance of finding out what happens if the driftdead can't move south.

And how long it might take them to die.

Or rot on their feet.

she sees me!

Sirocco has gone back to his old habit of rising at dawn, sitting under the crab apple tree and drawing in the sand with his stick, although the tree is half buried in the great dune that now protects their house from the sea. All he has to do is reach up and take hold of a branch, as if he is sitting on sand that has spilled out of his desert memories. This landscape with its new soft curves and rippling edges, its dangerous weights, its weightless sky, makes for a world more of memory than matter. He has to wonder again if he ever left the desert, or if the desert wasn't perhaps following him, chasing after him all the way to Keatown. Lizard warned him once that the desert would not let go easily, that it would follow him in his dreams, but he never imagined that it would actually follow him.

Would that Lizard were here, in this quasi, shifting world, this labyrinth with no walls, to guide him to the other side of mind. He's keeping one eye out. If this is the desert, Lizard will be here somewhere. He'll be on his way or already here, hiding.

In the meantime he's thinking about patterns: circles and stars - his stick draws them, and the thread that binds them, but the loose, restless sand quickly blurs their edges. Still, they seek a pattern. He learned about patterns in the desert. A labyrinth is not a maze. But if you can't perceive the patterns, you die. If you cannot trace the path with your feet, you die. If you cannot find Ariadne's thread, you die. Patterns take you to water and food; patterns take you to Lizard. If you don't find your Lizard you die, at least in the desert you do, where you need every ally you stumble upon. And you have to be able to wait with a Lizard stillness, to polish the silence and hear Lizard's voice, to eat the insect sun and spit out the moon.

He begins with two stars. Flounder Phil, a man who disappeared apparently following a girl, and Miranda's dad, Blade, who just got up and walked out into the storm never to be seen again. Did they turn, become driftdead as Little Sanyo suggested. The whole town could empty. He tries not to imagine the panic that will ensue once people realise that the driftdead are not just harmless walkers. I'd hate to be the last one left. And they don't even have to bite you. Just their presence is enough. Fear will walk among us in the form of the driftdead.

These are all thoughts he has to keep to himself, at least in the meantime. They are nothing but patterns in the sand.

Dawn is breaking and Sirocco has duties to attend. His part in the Great Reconstruction is to take care of the mokopuna, make sure they don't get underfoot and lend a hand wherever they can. Sirocco will get them working as best he can, sweeping out houses and other light tasks. Sad Toof is pretty useless. Give him a broom and he'll sweep the same spot for half an hour. Little Sanyo isn't much better. Give him a broom and he'll start analysing the arrangement of the bristles, developing new designs for improved brooms, or get lost in the rough music the bristles make on the floor. Miranda and Witch Hunt take to any task with a will, although they usually end up squabbling over how best to do it, with Witch Hunt running off in tears, crying out to anybody who will listen that Miranda doesn't love her anymore. Or Miranda bit her arm. Truth be told, a certain steel is entering Miranda's soul. Since Blade did his runner, Miranda has become withdrawn, worried about her mother, Jolene, and increasingly bitter about Mother Smiley and her corrosive influence in the house. Altogether too involved in herself to care too much about Witch Hunt, who is still sleeping in the old school house.

Sirocco has time to think about these things as he places his stick beside the tree and gets to his feet. Scale appears at the door in his black singlet and black underpants. His underpants are baggy and his legs look like pale spiky twigs. He looks up quizzically at Sirocco. He's never really liked, or trusted, this funny-looking runt Gypsy picked up, but that's her business – you can never tell that woman anything. Any bird with a broken wing turns her into sucker bait. Not that Sirocco is a bird with a broken wing. There is a strength in the little bugger. It's just that you can never quite know him, or quite know where you are with him or what he's thinking. He's a bit of an enigma, and Scale dislikes enigmas on principle, as they usually involve deceit of some kind. And that's Sirocco for you. Polite enough, but deceitful. Enigmas are all very well, but you can't trust them. True, his own gypsy woman can be an enigma from time to time, but that's different, that's a woman's prerogative.

Soon Scale will be off to the fish shed which he's helping to repair. Rumour has it that Orlap has done a deal with Flay for diesel and that the Nord will be putting the best of the three boats, The Merry Widow, to sea as soon as possible. That is, after repairs have been made, a process that can't be hurried, not if you value your life on an uncertain ocean. Rumours of the deal, and all the hard work going into The Merry Widow to get her seaworthy, have lent an urgency to the work on the fish shed. The mayor, too, is often there to urge them on. Yes! The fish will flow. The wheels of industry will turn again! Especially the fish shed, in which the mayor has invested heavily of course – but that's hardly the point. We're all in this together!

In turn, Gypsy will head off to join Akona, Grandmother Gaunt, Hera, Margo and a couple of other women to help reclaim the marae gardens, which Akona opens to anybody who wants to put in some work and share the harvest. Being on high ground and rocky, the land is not particularly good for gardening, but years of building up the soil, the Man in Black hauling trailer loads of kelp on the back of a quad bike Flay repaired for them, have paid off, and most of the top soil has survived the storm.

It looks peaceful and normal, Scale standing in the doorway scratching his crotch, looking quizzically out at the morning, but only if you screen out the few driftdead that have found their way up the sand dune to the north and carried on down past the house. People are learning not to see them, to screen them out, to ignore them as the mayor suggested, and to a large extent it works. The driftdead become invisible. It doesn't work when they blunder into the house or bump into you, but they are soon gone and just as quickly forgotten. At least in the meantime.

Scale looks as if he'd like to ask Sirocco a question but can't think of the right one. He's always doing that, is Scale – chasing thoughts that are forever running away, just ahead of him, like the gingerbread man escaping from the cook. Run, run as fast as you can...

'You've got that right,' he calls.

'What's that?'

But Scale doesn't know, or has forgotten, or didn't mean anything by it in the first place. He shrugs and gestures ambiguously towards the sky.

'I'm right about the sky?'

'The fish are running,' Scale says, still looking at the sky as if fish were running up among the clouds.

'Okay,' Sirocco says.

'The children are dancing,' Scale says. He's still looking up, where presumably the children are dancing among the fish and the clouds.

'How are they dancing?'

'First one leg. Then the other.' He takes little mincing steps to demonstrate. He gives Sirocco a cunning look, as if he is deceiving a dangerous enemy.

'O-kay!' Sirocco says. So that's the way it is this morning. Fish and dancing children, or is it children and dancing fish? One way or the other, Scale is in good form.

Little Sanyo appears at the top of the sand dune to the north of the crab apple tree. The day's first mokopuna. Sirocco sighs. So, he'll have to share his breakfast. So what? He wouldn't be too hungry. He'd learned the meaning of real hunger in the desert.

'Scale is very sprightly this morning,' Little Sanyo says as he joins Sirocco.

'Ha ha. Sprightly. Where did you pick up a word like that?'

Little Sanyo inclines his head with modesty. 'I just find them. Like I find things on the beach. Old words that people don't want anymore. Like sprightly, and earnest. Perfectly good words going to waste.'

'The kid can fix my radio,' Scale calls. He's forever asking Little Sanyo to fix his radio, and Little Sanyo is forever telling him that his radio is beyond fixing. This frustrates Scale as he likes to turn the radio up loud when Gypsy is playing her Arabic reggae.

'Just pretend, and he might give you breakfast,' Sirocco says, adding, when Little Sanyo hesitates, 'which will be more than eating half of mine.'

'I don't like to take advantage of him,' Little Sanyo says.

A driftdead woman appears at the top of the sand dune to the north, as Little Sanyo had done. For a moment she looks quite graceful, archetypal even, with a long gauzy outer gown shifting around in the gently moving air, her body outlined against the pink dawn, hair a great golden halo. It takes Sirocco a long time to see what is wrong with that picture. The woman has paused. The driftdead never stop, not for anything, but this one does. She moves her head slowly back and forward, apparently scoping out the landscape.

'Akona saw one that stopped,' Little Sanyo says excitedly. 'And she's looking around.'

'But is she seeing anything?'

'Why stop and look around otherwise?'

When she begins to move again, the woman comes straight for them, passing within arms reach of the crab apple tree. Without the vivid backlight of dawn, the woman now looks quite dusty and ordinary. She's carrying something hidden in her fist. However, as she passes, her gaze fixes on Sirocco. She sees me, he thinks, but isn't sure. She looks at him but he can't say she sees him. As she passes the house, she does the same thing, staring at Scale, who stares back, until her head has to swing back to the front.

'What if they become aware of us?' Little Sanyo says.

Trev duo to Trev uno, cut speed…

Our esteemed mayor, Big Bill Broonzy, sits, ankle deep in sand, hunched at his table, a half-smoked but dead cigar jammed between two fingers, staring down at the map Mavis has fastidiously copied. For all her red hair and her swearing, she is careful and professional when it comes to drafting. Around him are other maps, old tourist maps and the like. Beside him, with one red eye blinking, his short-wave radio lets forth occasional bursts of static. Behind him, on the wall, is a picture of a radiant Elizabeth ll, Queen of England, as she was on her coronation. He glances at it from time to time for inspiration.

He's busy drawing lines on a piece of paper. Mavis is sitting on a couch nearby pretending to read a book she borrowed from the library. She didn't borrow it to read, rather to annoy the librarian who doesn't like her. It's Tess of the D'Urbervilles by Thomas Hardy, and she's struggling with it. Even pretending to read it is a bit of a strain. She prefers maps to literature. With maps you know where you are, quite literally, and with a pleasing certainty. You can put your finger on a spot and say, 'I am here.' Still, reading is better than sweeping sand. Mavis won't go near a broom. As far as she's concerned, the Great Reconstruction can get along without her.

'I bet he's got a chopper stashed away,' Big Bill says. He's staring at the map as if he could look right through it.

Mavis, who's heard this conversational gambit many times, doesn't take the bait.

'I mean, it stands to reason. A man like that, one of the top five richest men on the planet, is not going to trap himself up there in his eyrie. He'll have one of those long-range choppers, one of those diesel jobs. Maybe a couple of them. One for him and one for his fancy tarts.'

Mavis tries not to listen. If she's heard all this once, she's heard it a hundred times. Even Tess is more fun. A very foolish young lady if ever there was one.

'It'll be all juiced up and ready to fly at a moment's notice. With this storm just passed I'm surprised he hasn't gone already.' His tone a classic mix of envy and resentment. Oh, he's had his dealings here and there with the great Baron Fairweather, mathematical wizard, and he was never that impressed. What he won't admit to himself, and what Mavis, revealing an unexpected delicacy, won't point out to him, is that, soon after most of the celebs had bailed, Big Bill did his best to become the baron's go-to man, his intermediary, his agent in Keatown, eager to supply the great man's needs, from cans of caviar to willing bitches like Mavis herself, but the baron spurned him. Apparently he has no need of Keatown's tatty offerings. Until now, that is.

'One for him, and one for you and me. That's what you should be thinking.'

'Easy to think. He's got armed guards, and some weird dog with octopus eyes.'

'To frighten off cowards, the fat and the lily-livered fuck-faces, like you.'

'Thank you, sweetling. To work this one out needs brains.' He taps the side of his head with the knuckles of his right hand. 'Don't you worry your pretty little head about it.'

'Oh thankth,' she lisps. She waves Tess under the mayor's nose. 'My pretty little head is already thretched to the limit.'

'Listen, harpy! If we had something he wanted, it would be a different story.'

'What could the likes of you offer him, for Christ sakes? Other than your fat gut.'

'Orchid,' Big Bill says aloud, hardly realising he'd spoken.

Mavis laughs. 'That fledgling has already had her tail feathers plucked, I would imagine. Anyway, who are you to offer her around?'

'It's a big missed opportunity.' If he'd seen it coming, he might have been able to insert himself into the process somehow, become indispensable. Now it's too late, too late for anything short of incarcerating the girl – and let's not pretend he hasn't thought about that. A hostage to bargain.

'He'd take you up a few hundred feet, high enough for you to make a big splat on the ground. Difficult to cash in on your rat-arse deals when you're spread out over the landscape in little wet pieces.'

He has to agree. Short of besieging the mansion with an army, there is little he can do but fret. There's a lot more he'd like to say on the subject of the baron's chopper, and how he and Mavis could get their hands on it, but he is interrupted by the unwelcome arrival of two of the mokopuna at his door. It's the little Asian kid and the walnut face. He can barely remember their names. Little Toyota or something. None of these pesky mokopuna have real names.

'Well,' Mavis says, 'If it isn't the nerd and his monkey.'

Sirocco and Little Sanyo take no notice.

'What're you two doing here?' Mavis says. It's not that she's got anything particular against the mokopuna; everybody gets the same treatment from Mavis.

Little Sanyo's the first to speak, and breathlessly. 'The driftdead, the zombies, they're changing.'

Abruptly Mavis puts down the heavy, tragic world of Thomas Hardy where, it seems, everybody is doomed from the start. 'What do you mean?'

'They sort of pause and look around, then they keep going. 'We call them pausers.' Having named the driftdead in the first place, Little Sanyo is keen to do the same with this variation, although 'pausers' does not have quite the same ring to it as driftdead.

'They look around?' The mayor sounds disbelieving. He's built his reaction to the invasion around the fact that the driftdead have no relation to this world, the world they are passing though. They have no sensory interaction with the world, and are therefore little better than dreams or illusions. His logic is a bit shaky, but he's stuck to it. It has protected him. His often repeated cry, don't look at them! is based on the belief that looking at them makes them real, more real than they really are. This news is therefore unwelcome and disturbing.

'Sort of... come and see for yourself.'

'No thanks.'

It seems that this variety of driftdead offer no menace, yet are at the same time menacing. And while they may be motionless, they are always on the point of motion. At any moment they may resume walking as if they had never been interrupted in the first place. Later Big Bill himself will see one man freeze in the middle of taking a step, one leg up, remaining that way for several hours before completing the step and moving on as if nothing has happened.

Big Bill is busy trying to absorb the implications of this news, and how it might affect his long-range plans to get himself and Mavis onto the baron's chopper, when his defective short-wave radio bursts into life. A metallic voice echoes through bursts of static, 'Trev uno to convoy, increasing sand dunes...' another rage of static and a second voice says, 'Trev duo to Trev uno, cut speed...' Whatever Trev uno might have answered is lost in a bubbling vomit of white noise.

The mayor rushes to the radio and desperately adjusts the knob. 'There's somebody out there,' he says eagerly.

'I should fucking hope so,' Mavis says.

'A convoy. Somebody's coming! Trucks!'

'The army is coming,' Little Sanyo says.

'How do you know?'

There's nothing more, nothing but screaming static.

'Those voices, they sounded like soldiers.'

'I know what you mean.' Big Bill is all over the idea like a rash. The army! Just what is needed to clear these driftdead away and get Keatown up and running. Restore order. Put an end to this crazy weather. Get the trains running on time.

'Convoy.' Little Sanyo repeats. 'They used that word. It's an army word'

'You're right.'

'South, maybe. From across the desert.'

'Maybe.' Hard to imagine.

'West, then. From the other side of the mountains.'

'We don't know if that road's still open.'

'Well... the north.'

'Yeah, the north.' Big Bill doesn't want to say it. The north is where the driftdead come from. The army should be from somewhere else. To rescue them. Defend the town. If the army was coming from the north it was running away.

Little Sanyo does a sideways dance towards the short-wave. He waggles his Nintendo thumbs and Big Bill nods reluctantly. A number of times the little bugger has tried to get his hands on his short-wave, and as long as it was working, he refused, despite the kid's reputation. Since the storm, however, he hasn't found any short-wave chatter. Until now.

But even Little Sanyo can't coax any more urgent voices out of the short-wave. 'We don't know how far away they are,' he says.

Big Bill hates to agree. They could be just up the road or way to hell. 'We need to put watchers on Highway 6, one to the north, one to the south, just in case.' His mind is working furiously in its most hopeful mode. The arrival of the army, with supplies and the means to repel the driftdead, would alter the balance of his relationship to the baron and the other mansion mongrels, but just how he's not quite sure. Maybe the army was coming to evacuate them, and he could thumb his nose at the richies.

'What the hell are you doing?' he says to Sirocco, who's somehow sidled over to his table and is staring at the maps.

'He's a nosy little bastard,' Mavis observes.

'You have a grand plan?'

Big Bill does, in fact, but he doesn't particularly want to share it with Sirocco. Not yet. But the nosy little bastard has half figured it out.

'A barrier? You want to build a barrier?'

'Something has to stop them.'

'What would you make it out of?'

'We have lots of debris, timber, all kinds of crap. And I know where to find heaps of barbed wire.' After all, it is barbed wire that built this country; now it may defend it. Big Bill has fond visions of the driftdead tangled up in barbed wire. Hung out to dry.

'There's a natural bottleneck at Pine Point,' Sirocco says, staring at the map.

'Quite right. They'll be forced up towards the mansions, or they can jump in the ocean and drown.'

'They don't drown,' Sirocco says. 'They swim. Or walk on the sea floor. I've heard of them doing that.'

Big Bill waves that away. As long as they stay clear of the town. His town. They can walk on their hands underwater for all he cares.

'We make a gate at the Pine Point bottleneck. When posterity, I mean prosperity, is restored, we have a tourist feature: A tribute to the fortitude and bravery of the good citizens of Keatown in their time of crisis.' He sounds as if he is making a speech to a whole crowd in one of the set-piece scenes he likes so much.

Mavis's cackle, like that of Baba Yaga with the Iron Teeth, is heard from the couch, where she is still sitting. It's not clear if she's laughing at Big Bill or the desperate antics of Tess in Hardy's novel.

Big Bill pulls his maps away and rolls them up ostentatiously. 'It's still just at the ideas phase,' he says.

An urgent voice spits from the short-wave, where Little Sanyo is fiddling with the controls, 'Trev uno to Trev duo...Trev uno...'

They all turn to the radio, and wait.

matters of church and state

Sirocco isn't the only one difficult to convince a barrier is going to work. There's no way the mayor can force the weary souls of Keatown into such an ambitious undertaking. He has his wonderful gift of the gab, his ability to paint a compelling picture of how life might thrive behind his barrier, and how life might become impossible without it.

The one person he knows he has to convince is Akona. Hera might be the queen and walk in queenly fashion, but the quiet old kuia up on the marae is the power behind the women of the town, as Mavis, with much disgust, has informed him. 'The real power in this town is a batty old woman who talks to plants,' she told him once. When he pressed her as to how that was possible, Mavis said 'because they are afraid of her. She's mad, but she speaks with the power of a fucking oracle.'

He sets out to visit Akona, without Mavis. This calls for delicate negotiation quite beyond the diplomatic skills of the marvellous Mavis. He's got a lot of talking to do. It would be easier to convince Akona if the army had arrived with reinforcements, but there has been no further spluttering from his short-wave, and the day is already well worn when he sets out to canvass a few people. He has put Akona last on the list, figuring that if he could convince a few others first, it might be easier to convince the 'fucking oracle.'

He starts with Orlap, since it would be the fishermen who would constitute the core of his labour pool, such as it is. Orlap, however, has other concerns.

'Diesel,' he says. 'Flay is holding out on us. You have to tell him.'

'I can say something,' Big Bill says cautiously. He's never had much power over Flay. Big Bill likes to work through appeal to the common good, useless in Flay's case. The row over the diesel, however, intrigues him. Although he may whine and moan, Flay has done pretty well out of Orlap and his fishing fleet, over the years that is. He would have no reason to start holding out on Orlap now. The mayor decides there is more to this than meets the eye, and that sooner or later he will get to the bottom of it.

In the meantime he has other fish to fry, as the saying goes. They are standing on the wharf, which itself sustained little damage, looking at The Merry Widow which Butch and her boys are busy outfitting. Butch gives the mayor a cheeky wave. Big Bill does his best to outline his strategy to Orlap, who hardly appears to be listening. He casts about for inspiration, and finds it.

'Look!' he points to the roundabout where Orlap's own indomitable little vessel, The Wanderer, sits helplessly up on the sand, looking stranded and very much out of place. To add insult to injury, it is crawling with driftdead. Since the line of least resistance for the driftdead is Highway 6 itself, The Wanderer, right in the middle of the roundabout, is squarely in their path. Some go around it, some keep on bumping up against it, and others climb over it. Whatever they do, it's an unwholesome sight. 'Unless we can keep them out, they will be all over us the way they are all over The Wanderer.'

Orlap is forced to agree, but with a grumble. 'How can I get The Wanderer back in the water if I'm building a fence?'

'If we don't build the fence there will be no town.'

Big Bill tries the same argument with the Reverend Stickman, who may himself not do much work, but is vital for the morale of a venture of such magnitude. Being a monarchist by sentiment, the mayor's always thought that church and state should stand together on the grand issues of the day. Besides, he's not insensitive to the growing appeal of the reverend's attitude to the driftdead, who do seem like the damned, the walking damned, and Big Bill is prepared to endorse the religious view of the invasion in return for support for his grand barrier project. If the reverend says that the zombies are all heading for the Gates of Hell, then that's all right by the mayor, who doesn't know what they are, except that they are a hellish nuisance. A little give and take between church and state is all that's needed.

'We have to keep these demons out, right? Hold them back! Build a.... wall of righteousness.'

The reverend doesn't seem to see the deal being offered. All round, the preacher doesn't seem as sharp as usual. In fact, since the incident with the candle girl, the reverend has not quite been himself, as if the stuffing has been knocked out of him. He says, 'But if this is God's work, we will never hold them back. And I will turn thee about, and will lead thee on, and will cause thee to come up from the uttermost part of the north; and I will bring thee to the mountains of Israel, and I will smite the bow out of thy left hand and cause thine arrows to fall out of thy right hand...'

'This has nothing to do with bows and arrows,' the mayor says, hopelessly lost.

'But everything to do with will and intention. The Lord smote these driftdead, and took from them the bow of their will and the arrows of their desire, and set them walking in the darkness, so how can human walls keep them out?'

'With the Lord on our side we surely can. Because the Lord's certainly not on their side.' It's not much, but the best Big Bill can do in a squeeze. This religious stuff makes his head hurt.

The reverend turns to the dark-haired kid beside him. 'What do you think of the plan?'

Big Bill grits his teeth. What does it matter what the bloody mokopuna think? Big Bill has never liked Rasputin much. He finds the kid's intense, dark eyes disturbing, a real God botherer in the making. And God botherers turn into people botherers. As if one isn't enough. He also finds the master deferring to the disciple disturbing; this would never have happened in the old days. It would have been all fire and brimstone. Something has taken the wind out of the reverend's sails.

'There's no staying God's hand,' Rasputin says at last. 'There's no holding back God's judgement with sharpened sticks. Such an idea is nothing more than vanity and vexation of spirit.'

The reverend hangs his head in a shameful display of cowardice. At least, that's how the mayor sees it. A humiliating surrender of power to... to a twisted kid!

The state holds firm but the church has lost its mojo.

It's hard to trust a man if you've never seen him smile

These are not exactly the ringing endorsements of direct action he was hoping for, but with a little spin they will serve. At least he has not met with outright rejection.

As he approaches the marae, a new metaphor occurs to the mayor. Cattle. You don't just let cattle wander everywhere they please, doing what damage they please, you fence them off, fence them in, fence them out – Jesus! Whatever else they might be, the driftdead are human cattle. Maybe they had a lobotomy in another fracking universe, he doesn't care. Here, in his world, in his town, they are mindless cattle, dangerous only in their sheer numbers, but dangerous nonetheless.

He's thinking these thoughts, his mind working in a kind of frenzy, when he is brought up sharp by the sight of a man standing still in front of him. It is obviously one of the driftdead, but he's not moving. He's wearing a pin-striped suit and carries a silver, locked briefcase, and is swinging his head from side to side in an odd manner as if his head were a camera and he was filming in a slow pan from left to right. After encountering nothing but their relentless, inhuman movement south, this pausing to look around should have offered some comfort, been a step perhaps in the direction of humanity, but that is not the case.

It's just as the little geek said. A pauser.

As he passes the man, who could be a banker on his way to work and who might have just realised he has forgotten to lock his car door, or has left something important behind, the mayor tries not to look at him. He still believes that looking at them encourages their existence. However, although he might ignore the driftdead, the man is not ignoring him. Cognisance is there, if slow. The man's eyes are blank but they are staring in his direction. It gives the mayor a chill to see it. It is as if the driftdead really were sleepwalkers and were now starting to awaken.

He hurries on, trying not to think of these matters. Somehow it was better when he could pretend that these things did not exist.

He is less than pleased to find Hera and Baby at the marae with Akona, along with Melissa Tonguestone and Margot Henny. The oracle herself is hard enough to deal with, but Big Bill has always found the presence of Hera disturbing in a way that makes Mavis suspicious, and has never moved much beyond official approval of the Baby. He's not the baby kissing kind of mayor.

As always, he feels awkward going onto the marae. Although Akona greets him graciously, he doesn't know the protocol. He doesn't venture here often; it's outside his comfort zone. And the mute Man in Black puts him off too. The tall man manifests a watchful silence that seems to call the squawking of mere humans into question. It's hard to trust a man if you've never seen him smile. Or heard him talk.

To add to the confusion, the two goats, Nanny and Lucifer, are in attendance, and sniff him over the way dogs do. Lucifer fixes his inhuman yellow eyes on Big Bill, lowers his head and waggles his horns suggestively.

Quite a little welcoming party.

He hovers in the background as Akona and Hera show him the work the women have been doing reconstructing the gardens. Big Bill knows better than to blurt out his business, but does the tour and duly admires what he has to admire. Mostly, his admiration is genuine. Keatown, he thinks, will never die as long as there are women like Akona to tend the gardens. As long as there are women like Hera to swing a baby at the hip. He admires the potato patch and the kumara field, and duly takes note of the traditional food-storage hut up on poles to keep out rats.

'The potatoes and kumara are the vital crops,' Akona explains, although Big Bill really needs no explanation. With fish from the sea, deer and pig from the hills and kumara from the ground, Keatown would eat. This little place has everything going for it, he thinks, possibly for the millionth time. Nobody has more faith in the town than Mayor Broonzy.

'We will weather the storms,' he says, trying to adapt to Akona's oracular style, not necessarily a good move as he ends up sounding bombastic. 'You have done an amazing job here.' He stands back to include Hera in his praise.

Akona smiles. 'Waiho ma te tangata e mihi,' she says.

Big Bill smiles but he's starting to sweat. He's not sure what she is getting at, and besides, Akona knows perfectly well that her use of te reo makes him uncomfortable, even when she follows it with a translation, which she hasn't done in this case. He can't quite grasp why she should use te reo when he doesn't understand it. Unless of course she wants to make him uncomfortable.

'Better you sing my praises than I do,' she says.

Again that off-putting glint of humour.

'I notice you don't get too many driftdead up here,' he says casually.

'Some, from above, from the northwest. Few from direct north bother trying to climb up here. Although some do.'

'There's always some,' Melissa says. She shudders. 'Cockroaches,' she says under her breath. She's said it so often now that people are tired of hearing it, except Grandmother Gaunt who always applauds vigorously.

'They are people,' Hera says sharply. 'They may be blighted in some way we don't understand, but they are still people. We can't forget that.'

'I pray to God every day to lift their burden from them,' Margo says.

Big Bill understands that there is some division among the women on the nature of the driftdead, but can't figure out yet how to take advantage of that knowledge. 'Not having to deal with them must make the gardening easier,' he says.

Akona gives him a quick look.

'Have you ever woken up drunk and wondered how on earth you got there, maybe in a strange bed in a strange place?' Hera asks. The

Baby's head appears and a pair of very bright eyes fix on Big Bill. The Baby seems to be interested in the answer.

'Well... um, ha ha, can I pass on that one?' Hera's question has roused a memory of doing just that, waking up drunk in a strange bed with a wild red-haired harridan riding his morning tumescence. He blushes the colour of Mavis's hair.

'What if the driftdead are waking up?' Hera asks. 'They're stopping now, you know. They are becoming aware of the world around them.'

'Maybe.' And, he thought, maybe that isn't such a good thing. Along with sentience might come wanting. What if they all suddenly woke up with a raging hunger and turned into real zombies, what then?

Melissa says, 'Even cockroaches are aware of the world.' She puts her hands up to her forehead and waggles them around. 'But you still squash them.' The Baby gurgles in appreciation.

'In the name of the Lord, of course,' Hera says.

Like many a true believer, Melissa chooses not to acknowledge irony. 'The Lord never told us we had to love cockroaches.' She is answering Hera but is looking at Akona.

'I thought he did,' Hera says, 'I heard your own Reverend Stickman talk of compassion for all creatures.'

'He did?' Melissa is momentarily taken aback. That doesn't sound like our reverend.

'He said we would all need all the compassion we can muster if the rebuild was to be a success. He spoke from the heart for once. Christians don't have a monopoly on compassion, you know. Even us sinners can know it. Even the most despised can know it.' Hera looks hard at Melissa and Grandmother Gaunt. 'Judge not lest ye be judged.'

'I've never thought of the reverend as a compassionate man. More like a bigot,' Margo says. 'I think when he prays he argues with God. He's changed his tune, has he?'

'I can have lots of compassion for a cockroach, while I'm scrunching it underfoot. Better luck next time, buddy! That's what I say.' Melissa's excited voice further arouses the Baby, who starts babbling away in his own language and kicking his feet out of the bottom of the front pack. Two tiny pink feet, still wrinkled.

The mayor tries to lever his way into the conversation. 'What about a wall to keep them out? A fence. A driftdead-proof fence.'

The women fall silent and look at Big Bill. The Baby does the same.

'Less scrunching to do if they're not underfoot.' He laughs weakly. Trying to joke with these women is something he's not quite up to.

Only Akona is grinning and he's not sure if she's laughing with him or at him. 'This promontory has natural walls on three sides. The line of the terrain guides most of them down below you.'

'That's true,' Akona says. 'My ancestors knew the value of high ground.'

He points north. 'See how the hills come within a couple hundred yards of the road at Pine Point. We could build a fence, a barrier, coming down to the road. Force them onto the beach just this side of Pine Point. Or up into the hills.'

'That's a lot of work,' Hera says. This large, energetic woman looks suddenly tired.

'That's true.' He lets the truth of it hang there. 'But there are more and more of them.'

'First you see only one, then there are a hundred.'

Big Bill refrains from agreeing with Melissa. He much prefers his cattle metaphor. 'Already they're just walking over everything.'

'Swarming,' Melissa corrects him.

Inspired, Big Bill says to Hera, 'If we don't build a fence to keep them out, people will start killing them, as if they really were cockroaches. That's not what we want.'

'Do you think people will really start killing them?'

'I really would,' Melissa says brightly, as if some picnic had been proposed.

'And Flay already has,' Big Bill says, 'and God knows what Pinky and the wharf rats have been up to.'

'It doesn't seem quite real,' Hera says. She falters. 'You're talking about murder.'

'Nothing's seemed quite real since this whole thing started,' Big Bill says. 'The storm, these human creatures...'

Akona kneels and pulled some grass-like weeds out the garden. For the first time he notices some tiny flowers, coloured fluorescent blue, along the edge of the garden. Without thinking about what he is doing, he kneels down beside Akona to get a better look at them. His eyes suddenly ache for that colour.

'They're called love-in-a-mist,' Akona says.

'I could do with some of that,' he says.

'In a desolate land, man is deserted,' she says quietly to him, too quietly for the others to hear. Then, louder, she says, 'Perhaps we do need this stockade you describe. You know our ancestors built villages protected by walls of sharpened sticks.'

'That's what I'm talking about.'

'But those sharpened sticks seldom held back the determined attacker.' She spreads her fingers. 'You can't hold back water with an open hand.'

Big Bill finds himself wanting to bend right over and smell the love-in-a-mists. Or at least see if they had a smell. Good thing Mavis isn't here to see this, he thinks, as he gives way to the impulse. It feels terribly vulnerable to be bent over like this, bum in the air, nose in the dirt. The flowers don't smell but the earth does. It smells of minerals.

'I guess we have to give it go,' he says, sitting back on his heels. 'Otherwise we'll be overrun.'

Their tour of the marae has brought them back to the entrance again. Only Akona and Hera are still with him. Melissa and Margot have continued working, albeit in grumpy silence. It occurs to Big Bill that the onset of the Long Emergency has not changed things much on the marae. Boom or bust, the potatoes and the kumara still have to get planted. Big Bill is a true devotee of progress and development, and this evidence of the superficial nature of it depresses him. Underneath all the whiz-bang, things don't change. Civilisation boils down to the quality of its topsoil. How dull.

The three of them stand at the gate and watch a large, straggling troop of driftdead, a hundred or more of them, working their way along the road.

'Today it's hundreds, tomorrow it's thousands,' Big Bill says. He's not trying to sell his grand plan anymore, he's not even sure that it will work.

'What are they, do you think?' Hera says. She has the palm of her hand cupped protectively around the back of the Baby's head.

'Our future,' Akona says.

does God have a problem with lace?

Among the mokopuna, only Little Sanyo shows any enthusiasm for the mayor's driftdead-proof fence. 'It's a grand plan,' he says to anybody that asks him. It's the grandiosity of the plan that appeals to him – a great fortification stretching from the sea to the mansions, almost. In his mind's eye, it is a wondrous, luminous thing. The Great

Wall of Keatown!

Naturally, Sad Toof joins the naysayers. 'If y' ask me, I think the mayor is losin' it.' The idea seems to give Sad Toof some pleasure. There's something satisfying in the sight of control freaks losing control. Grown men, used to having it their way, grasping at straws, not finding any, the looks on their faces changing from self-satisfied to terrified, that's what appeals to Sad Toof. Of course, nobody is asking him, least of all Big Bill.

The mokopuna have gathered at the roundabout, a natural place to meet even though it's half covered in sand, and The Wanderer lies slap in the middle of it with its shark-tooth-painted prow nosing up Beauty Parade. They are hanging out not doing much after a day helping people clean up their houses and yards.

Everybody is there, even Orchid and Mary, which is something of a rarity these days, Rasputin observes. The old gang is starting to split, with Orchid and Mary spending more time up mansions. The days of the mokopuna are numbered, Rasputin realises with a certain pang.

Without warning, Rasputin remembers how he and Orchid once sneaked up Beauty Parade to spy on the people in the mansions, people the townsfolk seemed to despise and revere at the same time. They were just being a couple of naughty kids, really. Their naughtiness was rewarded by the sight of two fair-haired naked adults sitting in a secluded spot. They weren't doing anything, it seemed to Rasputin, just sitting cross-legged facing each other. The naughty kids couldn't see much, except for the woman's breasts, which looked saggy and somehow pitiful. 'They're doing some breathing exercises or something,' Orchid whispered. He could feel the heat of her breath on his ear. It was exciting but, after a while, when nothing more happened, they made their escape.

He didn't tell the reverend about it, didn't want to hear, once more, about the sinful nature of the flesh. Rasputin did not see sin that day, peaking through the shrubs, just two adults sitting in the sun without clothes breathing deeply.

That seems a long time ago, even more so as Orchid sits down beside him and gives him a friendly smile. He thinks, he hopes, that she has not forgotten their moment alone on Pine Point before the storm. She'd sat close beside him with their knees touching. She spoke then of 'other things' that might affect her dream of fame and fortune as a dancer. It all seems so long ago that such dreams were even possible.

Subtly, she has changed since then. She no longer wears her

tomboy outfit, having replaced it with a pair of slim, hip-hugging blue jeans and a white blouse with a little lace along the hem and down the front opposite the buttons. She's not saying anything, but Rasputin is convinced she got those clothes up mansions, probably given to her by her dancing teacher, or perhaps even the baron himself, the infantile genius of local legend who does, apparently, actually exist. Despite Rasputin's strictures about superstition, the reverend has put it about that Baron Fairweather is in thrall to a demoness who lives inside his bronze statue, and who has given him his amazing mental powers for the usual price. His soul. His sanity first, then his soul.

It's that lace edging on Orchid's blouse that bothers Rasputin as much as anything else. Again and again his eye is drawn to it, and the little taste of flesh behind it.

Orchid appears to be blissfully unaware of Rasputin's agonies, but Mary isn't. Every time he meets Mary's eye, she gives him a knowing, triumphant look and slides a forefinger around the inside of the scarf around her neck in an ambiguous gesture. Rasputin doesn't know where to look, so he pretends to watch Little Sanyo and Sad Toof who have taken to climbing up onto the deck of The Wanderer and leaping off the prow into the soft sand. Sad Toof is making braying sounds that may well be laughter, rarely heard. When he lands hard, however, pretty much the same sound serves as a bellow of pain. Witch Hunt would love to do the same, but she's a bit scared. She can scramble up on the deck all right, but jumping off the prow is another thing.

Since he has the opportunity, as he and Orchid are sitting under the stern of The Wanderer, quite close together, he quietly says, harking back to that Pine Point conversation, 'Well... has anything turned up yet?' A touching faith she has, he'd thought then. It hasn't occurred to Rasputin that Orchid might have had something specific in mind when she spoke of 'things turning up', but he certainly doesn't expect her reaction. She registers shock as if he jabbed her with a pin.

'What do you mean?'

She can't have forgotten, he thinks. Forgotten her fervent hope that everything would turn out right, that something would come along to put the world to rights and set her on the path to fame and fortune – forgotten their moment or two among the pines. That is not possible; she can't have forgotten. Therefore, by looking up at him innocently, as if she doesn't know what he's talking about, and asking her question, she is lying and dissimulating, which puzzles and saddens him. In fact, his question must have hit a nerve.

He remembers the feel of her hand on his shoulder, a smile that was innocent. A touching belief in the ultimate fairness of things. Her naïve trust in her dancing mistress. He finds it hard to account for the obscure, but acute, humiliation he feels. It's just God, he thinks, who seems to require his suffering on an ongoing basis, and seems to have a problem with lace.

'It doesn't matter,' he mumbles. It would be humiliation to have to remind her of a conversation she must remember in the first place.

Now she's acting offended and has gone all cold on him. Pulled away. She doesn't want him following this line of enquiry, and that makes him curious to know what she is covering up.

Meanwhile Little Sanyo and Sad Toof stand beneath the prow of The Wanderer coaxing Witch Hunt to jump.

'It doesn't hurt,' Little Sanyo says. 'Anyway, Sad Toof can catch you.'

Sad Toof pushes Little Sanyo, trying to knock him over, but the little weasel dances out of range. Sad Toof is bigger than little Sanyo, but is a lot slower. Little Sanyo delights in tormenting him. Witch Hunt watches them and forgets about jumping. Little Sanyo gets tired of waiting for Witch Hunt to jump and starts talking about the mayor's planned wall, presenting it as some exciting experiment on a grand scale.

'Just think,' he enthuses, 'we could keep them all out.'

Sitting on the prow looking north, Witch Hunt has a fine view of the approaching driftdead, alone or in clusters, and begins to cry. Between sobs, she says, 'A great big big big big big wall to keep them out.'

'Don't be such a cry-baby,' Miranda, looking up at her, says in a tone of voice usually reserved for dolls and teddies. 'They're bumbling and harmless. They're blind, you know.' This time she sounds like her mother. Miranda is proud of having overcome her initial revulsion to the driftdead. Her fear wore off when she saw that they didn't attack people, or try to eat them. She'd overheard Hera telling her mother, Jolene, and her Aunty, Mother Smiley, that underneath it all, the driftdead are still human. They are not monsters, just ordinary people lost deep inside themselves. 'They live beyond the body,' she said, and Miranda has not forgotten that.

'I don't think that's true,' Sad Toof says, talking to no one in particular. He's given up chasing little Sanyo, and gone into his philosophic mode. Philosophy is his antidote to toothache.

'What's not true?' Little Sanyo has to be forever on the lookout for Sad Toof's sad logic.

'That they're blind. You can't say that for sure.'

'I can,' Miranda says. 'They can't see me, anyway.'

'You don't know that,' Sad Toof insists. 'What about the pausers? They stop and seem to take a look around. I've heard of them looking in windows.'

Witch Hunt gives a wail. 'I don't want them looking in windows.'

'I've never seen them do that,' Orchid says, disturbed by what was news to her. She looks at Mary who shrugs as if to say, pretty soon it won't matter. Rasputin notes the exchange and it puzzles him.

Little Sanyo jumps in, keen to beat Sad Toof at his own game. 'Maybe they look around but you don't know that they are seeing anything.'

Sad Toof looks sad. He's flopped down on the sand which he's running through his fingers as if it contained all the cares and hopes of the world 'That's true. But that doesn't mean they're blind.'

'They are not harmless!' Witch Hunt wails. She's feeling very alone up on the prow of The Wanderer. 'Not like ordinary people.' She can't explain what she means, but she knows she is right. 'They come from a cold place,' she says between gasping breaths. 'They trample over everything,' she finishes, quite lamely.

'That's why we need a stockade to keep them out!' Little Sanyo says in frustration. He loves that word, stockade. He says it over and over under his breath. He's starting to construct a wall of sand, finding twigs to represent the driftdead and seaweed pods to represent fortifications on top of the wall. It's all there in his mind's eye.

As the argument proceeds in this sideways fashion, with the main point being lost at every turn, Sirocco, Rasputin notices, doesn't say anything. He's lying on his back on the sand staring up the sky. Rasputin gets the feeling that the disputants are waiting for Sirocco to intervene, give his opinion, which will, by some alchemy Rasputin does not understand, become definitive. Sirocco will have the final word.

Orchid wriggles a little closer to him.

'The reverend hates Hera, doesn't he?' she asks.

Rasputin thinks this over carefully. The question is important to her, but he doesn't know why. Perhaps because Hera was like a mother to Orchid for a while. Such loyalties can run deep. 'He doesn't believe her. He thinks she lied about her past. That she was a prostitute.'

'Does that make her an unfit mother?'

Another oddly charged question. Rasputin has never thought about it much. The reverend has often vented his frustration that God chose a dubious woman like Hera over some of the more virtuous and deserving women of Keatown, like Melissa Tonguestone for example, but his frustration is as much with God as with Hera as far as Rasputin can see.

'Unworthy, perhaps. Why don't you ask him? Hera is the Baby's mother. There's not much can be done about that.'

'Grandmother Gaunt doesn't think so. She wants to take the Baby away from Hera.'

'Grandmother Gaunt says lots of things. And not all of them make sense.' Rasputin is curious as to why Orchid has brought this up, what might lie behind it. 'You've lived with Hera Served her. What do you think?'

Orchid draws idly in the sand with her finger, a swirling figure of eight. 'She loves the Baby very much.'

'But?'

'It's just that sometimes... she forgets.'

'Forgets what?'

'Where she is, even who she is. Like old people.'

Rasputin gathers she means dementia, of which he has little idea other than in the end the sufferer forgets to live.

This is not in accord with his own impression of Hera, who is large bodied with a larger-than-life personality to go with it. A woman with a laugh that will fill up a room. Whatever her past, Hera has always struck Rasputin as firmly grounded. Certainly no dreamer.

Little Sanyo holds up his hand for silence. 'Shush!' he yells.

Everybody shushes, another word he might have savoured if he had time to consider it.

'Engines,' he says tersely.

Everybody listens, and after a few moments they all hear. The dull snarl of engines to the north.

The mokopuna leap to their feet as the first vehicle emerges from the shadows of Pine Point. Large, squat and olive green. A second follows behind it.

Humvees!

Coming down Highway 6, straight for them.

the game changer

Double-syllabled, double-toned, single-grilled. A strange word that conjures up a dark terror. Hummers. The mokopuna have seen pictures of them in the library, bumping over long desert roads driven by desperate-looking guys in uniforms with desperate-looking weapons.

The two broad, squat, ugly, military-style vehicles, with huge front wheels and armour-plated sides come grinding in from the north around Pint Point like a pair of triceratops, spotlights swivelling back and forth through the evening murk as they bear down on Keatown. A third follows a little way behind. The mokopuna make no move to escape the roundabout, even with the first Humvee coming right at it; they huddle in under the prow of The Wanderer, staring at the medley of harsh lights bearing down on them.

The first Humvee almost comes to grief at the roundabout. For a start it is moving too fast, and apparently not under full control, suggesting that Trev Uno or whoever has been too long behind the wheel. But that isn't the immediate issue. Everybody has observed that the driftdead are mostly adults, because we've only seen adults, hardly anyone under ten. Little Sanyo's Nightshade Girl, maybe. Or the girl that reminded the librarian of herself as a kid. It's likely that Trev Uno had the same experience since, when a driftdead child around the age of four, dressed in a white nightgown, is picked up in his headlights plodding south, clutching some bauble to her chest, wandering over the road, he swings to avoid her into what should have been no more than a patch of sand. The hidden concrete buttress of the roundabout hits the squat Humvee's right front and back wheel, lifting one side up onto the roundabout, and it progresses that way at a daredevil angle around the roundabout before crashing back onto the road once more and revving on ahead with an angry snarl.

The second Humvee, coming close behind, makes no effort to follow the roundabout and ploughs directly into it, sending the mokopuna scattering, and coming to a halt just below the stern of The Wanderer. The dark military vehicle stands spectacularly on its nose for a lucid moment before tipping sideways, landing on its passenger side, motor screaming uselessly, wheels churning the air. The driver's door opens and a man clambers out. He is dressed like a high-altitude test pilot in padded suit and mask. He seems unharmed. In fact, absurdly, he's holding a sandwich.

The mayor and other worthies of the town hurry to the scene, garishly lit by the Humvee's headlights. Hope is written all over the mayor's face. They cluster around with avid faces, but at a safe distance, their shadows billowing huge behind them. Hera is there, the Baby in her arms as wide-eyed as everybody else. Nobody objects when the Mayor pushes himself to the forefront.

The mokopuna huddle together as a group. Typhoid Mary takes Orchid's arm. Witch Hunt huddles up close to Miranda. Little Sanyo is itching to get closer. Sad Toof has a burst of pain in his jaw and has to sit down and hold his head.

'Why doesn't he turn off the engine?' Little Sanyo shouts above the racket to Sirocco, as if Sirocco knew. Actually, Sirocco does know. He doesn't have to explain it. Everybody sees it for themselves soon enough. As soon as the figure has emerged from the cocoon of the Hummer, the driver starts walking south. He doesn't look at anything. He doesn't say anything.

Without a word the crowd pulls back into the shadows to let the figure walk past, their faces agape with shock. The mayor watches him go with increasing incredulity. Melissa Toungestone begins to wail.

'Deserter!' the Mayor roars.

And this is how deserters got their name, but the Humvee driver is not the first. Now Sirocco can complete the pattern. Flounder Phil, Miranda's dad, Blade. And maybe one or two others thought to have vanished in the storm.

'Don't look at him!' The mayor commands. 'You can't look at them!'

As if that were going to make any difference. They are way beyond that; hostility trumps fear. Any indifference towards, or lingering sympathy for the driftdead, drains away like sunlight from a winter afternoon, to be replaced by a cold terror as the realisation sinks in that anyone might desert at a moment's notice. You don't have to get a bite or a scratch to turn you into one of them. The infection, if there is one, is in the air. Nobody is safe. The mayor does not appreciate it right then, but in that moment all opposition to his driftdead-proof fence disappears. He will get his fence, and Keatown will get a crack at survival.

The engine of the upturned Humvee screams itself to death, but the evening's drama is far from over.

As a second figure, also wearing a padded suit and a mask, clambers out of the Humvee, the third vehicle arrives, travelling more slowly, its third-eye spotlight swivelling hectically back and forth, briefly lighting up the faces of the crowd. The driver must have seen the upturned Humvee, for the vehicle proceeds with caution, skirting to the left to stay clear of the concrete buttress. The figure that has just emerged from the upturned Humvee waves furiously at the third vehicle, but it does not stop. Its gears clash and grind as it surges on. With a scream of frustration the figure, slighter than the first and who might have been a woman or an adolescent, pulls out a pistol and fires at the departing vehicle. The bullets ping uselessly against the Humvee's armoured back. The sound of its engine fades into silence.

It's quiet, except for some creaking from the upturned vehicle. Its headlights are still on, throwing their hard light on the mayor and the sharks' teeth that decorate the prow of The Wanderer.

Finally this he or she turns to face us, pulling off goggles and mask, revealing a young man, about eighteen. He waves the pistol wildly around. 'Stand back.'

'It's okay, it's okay!' Big Bill is out the front, doing what he does best. 'I'd say welcome to Keatown, but in the circumstances...'

He tails off as the youth lifts the pistol to his own forehead.

'Wait! Son! Before you do this... please!'

'Please what?' The pistol stays where it is.

'We're cut off here... I mean, where are you going? Who are you?'

'That bastard Lowry, just drove on. Did you see that? Wouldn't stop, not for ten miserable seconds.'

'Where are you going?

'South. To get ahead of the heebies. We heard that they can't cross the desert. They just dry up. That's what we heard. It's safe on the other side.'

'Ok,' Big Bill says in the voice of a man getting somewhere in a negotiation. 'So how far have you come?'

'Look, you people,' the youth gestures with the pistol to everybody standing around. They all shrink back. 'You've got to get out of here. Head south, get across the desert while you can.' There is a hysterical edge to his voice.

The crowd is quiet. Everyone can hear the sea shushing against the land. Little Sanyo can hear the stars pinging in his head.

'What's the rush? Maybe you'd like a shot of brandy, you know, before you...' the mayor gestures to the gun.

'You don't get it, do you? You think there's time to sit around drinking brandy. But more heebies will come, and the more that come, the better chance you have of turning into one. That's what happens. That's what happens to everyone, in the end, don't you see, you bloody fools, we all go the same way. That's what happened to Trev. One minute we were driving along making jokes, he was eating a sandwich, the next minute he was a heebie, just like that! With some it's fast and with some it's slow, but the end is always the same.'

If Big Bill feels a sinking in his heart when he hears this, he doesn't show it.

'Try to calm down a bit, son. Screaming and yelling won't help now.'

'You're right, nothing will help now. I've watched my whole family go, first mum, then sis, then Trev, and I'll be the last one. Ha ha ha. The lucky last.' He pokes the gun barrel into the side of his head as if banging himself awake.

'Wait!'

'I don't want to wait. The longer I wait the more likely it gets, and I don't want to become a heebie. They give me the heebie-jeebies. Ha ha ha.'

'At least tell us how far you have come.'

'From the ends of the earth! Christ! We've been driving non-stop for five days trying to outrun them.'

Hera has joined the mayor. It would be the last time we would see her looking so commanding, standing in the glare of the headlights, tall and calm, the Baby very much awake in her arms.

'You're safe with us,' she says. She cradles the Baby to demonstrate.

'No, no. No. I'm not safe. With anybody. Nobody is safe. You don't get it, do you.'

'I mean, you are welcome here.'

'No. No, I'm not – and you're crazy. All of you. You don't get it. But you will. Then it will be too late. Like it was for us.'

He fronts up to the mayor, who's sweating hard. He lifts his pistol to his forehead. 'Wake up, fatty!' His face pulls into a rubbery grin, as if invisible fingers are lifting the sides of his mouth, and he pulls the trigger. Blood splashes down the mayor's front.

Silence reigns. Even Pinkie looks shocked. He turns to his friend Tony, 'Way to go,' he says.

Grim faced, the Reverend Stickman steps forth and kneels down and gently closes the eyes of the youth's half shattered skull. 'May the

Lord have mercy on your soul,' he intones. He sounds as if he means it, his compassion apparently having got the better of the severe judgment that must come down on those who take their own lives in defiance of God's will. Now was not the moment to rail against suicide.

It takes a while to haul the body of the youth away and approach the upturned Hummer. Everybody agrees that the youth was hysterical, maddened by stress and grief. The mayor talks eloquently about the need not to panic. Right now panic is our worst enemy, he declares, with the agreement of everybody who is not overcome with it.

'It wasn't much of a rescue,' Sad Toof observes. His tooth is giving him hell and it's painful for him to talk.

'There's a silver lining to every dark cloud,' the Mayor says, pointing to the upturned Hummer. 'I bet they had supplies.'

Looting the Hummer is something that takes skittery minds off the youth's wild words. Big Bill makes a big deal out of finding the keys and opening up the door to the rear of the vehicle. Everybody clusters around, staring in, their eager faces lit by the wan interior light of the Humvee. There are all kinds of boxes and packages and bags. Looking like a big, excited kid, the mayor leaps up into the back of the vehicle. He gives a series of excited cries, and begins to toss packages out onto the sand like Father Christmas throwing gifts to kids. There are all sorts of goodies, an odd mix of basic items and luxuries. Toothpaste! When did Annanda last stock toothpaste? Slabs of thick, dark chocolate. Big Bill allows his people to rip open some of the chocolate and feed their faces. There is a sudden hunger to stuff their mouths with something. Anything. There's a crate of wine, the best quality, Big Bill guesses, too precious to be left behind. He allows a few bottles to be opened but puts the rest aside to take to his place for safekeeping.

Then Big Bill strikes gold. With Orlap helping him, he hauls out one of three large metal trunks. They are olive green and look very military. Nobody can find any keys, but Flay soon takes care of the problem with his welding torch. It slices through the padlocks in a few seconds. Big Bill does the honours, and throws back the lid.

Weapons.

Heavy, military-style weapons. Looks like Trev and his mates planned to make a stand somewhere.

The other two trunks contain more weapons and ammo. Lots of ammo.

'Well, that's a fucking turn up for the books,' Flay comments.

'It's a game changer,' Big Bill says. Nobody is quite sure what he means, but they all agree.

It's a game changer.

the algorithms of ruin

Baron 'Brainbox' Fairweather is exercising his famous brain when he hears the distant pulse of engines. At first he doesn't register what he's hearing – the familiar sound of the internal combustion engine. The algorithms of his ruin, no more no less.

It is because of that awful prescience that comes from knowing the numbers and reading the patterns that he has ignored the blinking light on his computer for as long as possible. When he reads, at super speed, inhaling whole pages at time, the graphs and numbers sent to him by a program designed to alert him as soon as certain parameters are breached, he knows what he is looking at, the nature of the beast. This is the 'brainbox' in action and it works holistically on the data, barely registering the details in the search for patterns, trend-lines and emerging algorithms – in this case appallingly easy to see. If you're a brainbox. And what the patterns and trend lines and Fibonacci cycles tell him is that he is toast. Burnt toast.

He, and lots of other people, but he doesn't care about them. Good thing he's got his escape plans well along the way. He has even tested the hydraulic lift in the hangar room and found it working smoothly. No more than half a minute to raise the Turboshaft 300 up onto the roof, ready to go.

'Greed isn't working anymore,' he says to the Arya Tara who patiently hears all his confessions. 'Too many zombie banks falling over.' His choice of words disturbs him. The word zombie seems to be creeping in everywhere: zombie banks, zombie securities, zombie money, robo mortgages – a whole zombie economy marching over the cliff. And then, there are those half-people wandering around out there. They're real, but there's no pattern. His mind switches into places we can't follow, I'm afraid, unless you understand mathematical notation and have solved the five-sided equation that cracked open string theory.

In that case, you might see something like this:

$(a, b) + (c, d) = (a + c, b + d)$

And as a consequence, when (a, b) multiplies (c, d) we get the less obvious

(a, b) x (c, c) = (ac − bd, ad + bc)

Which leads to the possibility of

(a, b) x (a, b) = (a, b) x (a, -b) = (aa + bb, a(-b) + ba) = (aa +bb0)

That is what it's like in the head of Mr Brainbox, who can think faster and more fluently in maths than the librarian can in words. What this maths tells him is that there is an algebraic foundation to consciousness, an ultimate eleven-dimensional equation, but there will be no time to further a potentially lucrative quest for it, because those same numbers, debased into Fibonacci cycles and Elliott waves and coded into the social fabric, spell the foundation of his ruin. This ruin takes place in virtual space, against the spinning roulette wheel of numbers, and his number is up. Driftmaths. It has less to do with chance than with folly, his own. Once set in motion, the numbers erupt at fantastic speeds, replicating and walking over everything until there is nothing but ruination. His fail-safe, fallback positions, with staged automatic sell-offs, vanish in the flicker of a quantum eyelid. It took the Roman Empire three centuries to decline and fall; it takes the Fairweather empire about three nanoseconds. At the same time, there is something in the maths, some thread of logic, hidden but interwoven, that doesn't quite gel with the rest of the less-than-pretty picture. It can't be seen in detail, but shows up in the total picture. Whatever it is, it shouldn't be there, even in a pattern of collapse. Something to be investigated.

His faithful dog Manny wanders in and stares at him, somewhat forlornly it seems to the baron, as if the dog were full of questions he knew he would never get answers to, or would never understand if he did, leaving the animal with a kind of inarticulate yearning. The baron fondles the dog's ears and, quite inconsequentially, remembers Lady Strongbow's hinted interest in Manny's maleness. There are certain things, she suggested to the baron, that she hasn't done yet, and might look forward to doing, in the right, supportive environment of course. The baron finds himself wondering if Manny would oblige. Perhaps Lady Strongbow would bring out the octopus gene in Manny. That would certainly be a dénouement for his final party at the end of the world.

The baron's equally faithful bodyguards, Joe and Terry, stand on either side of the balcony, relaxed but alert – the Mafia's own threshold guardians. What would they do, the baron wondered, if they knew what he had just discovered? Nothing probably – where would they go? He looks to the north, past the shingle fan to the rugged country beyond, and the rest of the world beyond that. There is nowhere to go without a helicopter, and a long-range one at that. He pushes back the thought that even flight might be useless, from one stronghold to another, one fortress to another. He thinks he can talk to people. He thinks he can sort something out. After all, he'll have some strong bargaining chips if that game were still on.

It will take time for the consequences of his ruin to show – what is instantaneous in the virtual world takes time to register in the real world. Like the time it takes from the end of the dream to the moment of awakening. Time to pick up the phone and give certain orders, time to throw one last party, at short notice. Time to again wonder why he has hung in here for so long, playing caretaker to a bunch of mansions. 'Time to murder and create...' his mother used to say as she played the currency trades. As a child he would sit on her knee, spellbound before the lines of numbers she spun across the screen, fortunes made and lost in the span of a fevered cigarette that seldom strayed from the side of her mouth and which bounced up and down when she rattled out numbers.

The pulse of engines. He's identified them before he gets to his favourite lookout point, where he once stood balancing the world on the palm of his hands – as far as I can see is mine! Ha ha! It would be comforting to think that there were boy-racers out for a spin in old jalopies, tearing up the back-blocks for the hell of it, but there is a sense of grim purpose in the way these Humvees approach Keatown that sends a prescient tickle up his spine. There is something he doesn't know.

He's never been one to bother with social networks, but as soon as the drama below is over, he leaves the good citizens of Keatown to run all over the stranded Humvee like a pack of ants, and reactivates his Twitter account. He needs to see what's going on in Tweetland, jack back into the old global brain, feel the pulse of the beast. What began as a retreat from the hurly-burly has ended up with him as a perverted recluse, dangerously cut off from important larger data streams. There is nothing he could have done to prevent his ruination, but what he does now will tell the tale.

He needs to know certain things, even before he lifts the phone. For a start, how widespread these half-people are. It is ridiculous to imagine the whole globe swamped by them, but maybe the ridiculous is now on the table. With some fascination he's watched them inundating Keatown, and is doubtful any will reach the mansions; they tend to take the least line of resistance, but none of that explains what, or who, they are. And what they are, he has to face, is an eruption of the irrational into the rational, empirical world. Like gate crashers to a champagne party. Even his precious Fibonacci cycles and Elliott waves, even the freaky self-generating fractal world, operate on known, mathematically consistent principles. His ruin can be well explained in a rational framework, but the half-people are something else. They are the joker in the deck of reason, and they threaten to bring down the whole house of cards.

His Twitter results are not encouraging. There are enough messages flooding in but they are jumbled and the texts are garbled. Bits of language flying everywhere as if some lexical bomb has gone off in virtual space. Abandoning the search for meaning, he gives himself over to the flow of fragments, their rhythm and direction. They're not just flying off in all directions, and even if they were, there would be a maths to their trajectories. There is a pattern here. There always is. He just has to find it. So he switches from cumbersome thought to maths, and does some mental S-matrix spreads of the data. His state-of-the-art-plus computer could do this but he can do it way faster in his mind. He can sense the pattern the way you might sense a large object hidden in mist, and it reminds him of something, that wriggling sinuous movement of numbers across the vertical plane. All he is left with is metaphor; the way the sand weaves sinuous, snaky patterns, like a spell, over hapless Keatown during the storm, patterns that have manifested in cyberspace also; cybersnakes obliterating the pattern, creating new non-linear landscapes, turning the S-matrix field multidimensional, introducing chaos into the equation at every quantum turn, just the way Einstein encountered infinities everywhere he looked, and invented his famous 'cosmological constant' to suppress them. With that trusty cosmological constant, the universe looked nice and smooth, just the way Einstein liked it.

Unfortunately for the baron, there lies no ready-made equivalent of the cosmological constant on hand to suppress the chaos erupting through the equations, and even if he could invent one, which he probably could, he didn't see the point. He could face what Einstein apparently couldn't: the fundamentally discontinuous nature of matter. Without that trusty cosmological constant, the universe would be appearing and disappearing every nanosecond. Uncreated and recreated almost instantly. The baron could live with a universe that flashed in and out of existence much faster than the senses could apprehend. But what he is facing is that something is happening between the disintegration and the re-creation. The familiar replicating mushroom-shaped fractals were bent out of shape by chaos. Of course there are patterns in chaos too, butterflies with asymmetrical wings, but finding those patterns endlessly complicated the maths, sending his brain spinning out of control, multidimensional equations spinning in his head like a fireworks display.

He could see this new factor at work in the flow of data through social media. Always something of a modern Tower of Babel, the world of social media has pretty much disintegrated, like words falling apart into syllables and syllables falling apart into phonemes and fricatives.

This Tower of Babel has become a tower of cyber-babble, and finally not even a tower. Garbage in garbage out, sure, but in this case it doesn't matter what goes in, you still get garbage out. Mathematically speaking, these are waves of unmeaning, and the baron is moving from fascination to fear, for if Twitter has twittered its last tweet, what is the state of the www and can he trust his ruination alarm?

With more decisiveness than he's felt for some time (fuck! his seclusion has led to lassitude!), he strides back inside, sits at his flat screen state-of-the-art-plus and calls up the net via broadband. He gets in okay, the web is alive, but it is seething like a witch's cauldron. Website addresses refuse to stay stable. State-of-the-art-plus is engaged in constantly loading and reloading apparently random addresses and fighting pop-up pages pushing everything from sex chat rooms to surefire ways of getting rich. He thinks perhaps some diabolical genius, like himself, a super hacker in this case, has come up with a self-replicating worm that beats all the back-room boys, a fucking snake for whose poison there is no antidote. Faster than melting ice, it has spread through the system, creating chaos. He thinks for a moment, with a bunch of fireworks going off in his brain, of complexity theory. The trend line follows a classic underarm rising curve ball; increasing complexity of any system leads to increasing sensitivity of that system to perturbations, and therefore increasing vulnerability. One spanner in the works is all it takes. The whole system blows. Even more pertinent, non-linear complexity can overwhelm subsidiary linear systems. In which case linear thinkers are fucked. Once, he'd read a fascinating theory that the Roman Empire fell because it could not handle the increasing complexity of the challenges it faced. All it knew how to do was build more forts and increase the army.

But his ruination alert is still there, loud and clear and steady in the shifting chaos. Since it doesn't come through the web, but by coded email, he has to trust it. He looks for other emails but doesn't find much, just a bit of Viagra spam, which he finds reassuring. So long as there is Viagra spam, civilisation still exists. Q.E.D. Just about everybody has given up on sending him hellos he never answers. He's so rich he doesn't have to spend a single moment of the day getting richer; that is all taken care of. He can afford to ignore the world. Or rather, he could.

Given that, his inbox still looks suspiciously empty.

He's working on this, his mind flicking in and out of maths faster than a frog's tongue in a swarm of flies, when Fraulein Zhenhua politely enters the room. She stands quietly before him, waiting to speak. Ah, Zhenhua, the woman who has shared so much of his life – and his fortune. Is it only the money that holds her here? Aside from the scenery? Yes, he decides, it most probably is; it is certainly not sentiment. Over the years she's spent with him, at his side, she must have amassed wealth way beyond her escort daydreams. Last he looked she was listed as one of the five richest women in the world. The brains behind the brainbox, they called her. An article in a prominent financial publication suggested that he, the baron, couldn't even tie his own shoelaces, and would never have made it big time without her acumen. A cartoon showed a subservient-looking Zhenhua kneeling in front of the baron tying his shoelaces while he sat in a toddler's high chair with a bib around his neck. Cruel, but with a certain truth, he thought at the time. To be properly cruel, it has to be true.

That's what she has been busy doing, isolating herself with him like this, letting his self-imposed exile rule her life, becoming a rich and powerful magnate in her own right. You don't have to be a famous mathematician to figure what she might do if she discovered that the vanishing zeroes on his account balances might mean the same for hers.

'We've got problems,' he says, anticipating her.

'Yum Yum reports Bao Dae has fallen over,' she says.

The baron has met Yum Yum a couple of times. A woman hatched in the same cauldron as Zhenhua herself, and who has become Zhenhua's right hand, just as Zhenhua is his right hand. He's heard the women plotting away in Mandarin on Skype. Bao Dae is one of their big networks, of which Yum Yum herself is the CEO.

There is going to be no hiding the fact of his ruin from Zhenhua. Sounds like she is ruined too. Time to go back to California and pick up the pieces.

'There's a fortune to be made on the way down,' he says, his mind again beginning to churn numbers.

'That depends on how far down.' She says.

It is axiomatic that people as wealthy as the baron don't go down in financial crashes. They create them. A crash is just a market opportunity to buy at the bottom of the cycle and make a fortune on the way up. The baron can now hardly avoid the irony that the famous 'crosshatch' algorithms he invented in the early days of his genius, algorithms that enabled the development of the nanosecond computer trading applications that made his first fortune, have now come back to haunt him. Those same algorithms are now being used against him, which raises a question. This may be a group of Young Turks who have taken his work and built on it, produced permeations and elaborations even he hasn't seen, and used them against him. A group prepared to crash the world economy just to bring him down, to shatter him and feed on the pieces. It is possible. And if it is possible it is likely. It is not necessarily megalomania to think so. Such things have happened before. The fastest gun alive sooner or later finds someone faster. Or... Or is this a natural effect, an unintended consequence of the maths no one has foreseen? Numbers can do that to you, kick back in unexpected ways; a counter-current built into the direction you are pushing the numbers.

To answer that question he's going to have to do a lot of maths. It's a problem of perception, like those human faces on Mars: artefacts or natural formations? Or a wall with regular cracks: made by man or a natural formation? Somewhere in the maths there will be a signature line or sequence that will give him the answer. There's something I'm not seeing, something I should be seeing. I've become lazy and slow. He thinks of the hawks he's seen hanging over the foothills. They seem lazy and slow too, but they know when the time is right to strike.

'How's the situation in California?'

'Stable. Everybody's using Federal bonds as collateral. CalleTech is circling the wagons. They're paying employees in promissory notes that can be redeemed at particular stores.'

'How do you know all this? Have you had any trouble with your internet connection?'

'There have been some interference patterns,' she says. 'My Skype connection with Yum Yum froze this morning.'

He thinks that over. Part of the reason he asked the question is to remind her once again that he knows she spends a lot of time at her computer, and he doubts she is writing her memoirs. She has her reclusive side too; they are a matched pair. But what is she doing in her room alone in front of her flat-screen-state-of-the-art-plus, or Skyping Yum Yum, is not something he's bothered to think about too much. Yet.

'And these half-people stumbling around, what do you think of them?'

'I think they are asleep. I think they are sleepwalking. In a coma.'

'Let's hope they don't wake up.'

She laughs, and as usual, he's not quite sure if she thinks he's funny, or if she just knows when to laugh. It's just the translation lag, he thinks. After all this time, she still thinks in Chinese.

'How widespread are they?'

'I couldn't tell. But there are other places Yum Yum told me before Skype froze. But it can start anywhere, with just one or two people, and slowly it gathers.'

'You mean people get infected?'

'They join, yes.'

She speaks abstractly, remotely even, as if she were describing some far-off stock-market jitter, but it gives the baron a bad moment. He isn't sure what he imagined. That the half-people just materialised out of nowhere already walking south? No, of course not. Someone somewhere dropped his or her life into the past and, stripped of identity, started walking. Then, because of a copycat, mass-hysteria effect, others started to do the same. That doesn't make a lot of sense unless it's a virus or something. Chemical or biological warfare might do it. A terrorist plot to turn half the world into zombies, that might do it. Terrorism has come a long way since roadside bombs in Iraq.

'We have to leave a lot of things here,' she says.

'Everything.' Maybe even the goose girls, he thinks. Let the meek inherit the mansion.

By stating the obvious, Zhenhua is subtly questioning the move. After all, there is three to four years of food. Art treasures. And gold. When things were humming, he'd stored a lot of gold and selected precious items in the vaults below. All that stuff was put aside as a hedge against the very thing that has happened, the vanishing of zeroes from the computer screen. You don't just walk away from a stack of gold, is what she is saying. Leaving Keatown is like dying – you can't take it with you. Not on one or even a hundred choppers.

'It's not like we can't come back,' he says. He touches the reclining Buddha right where Orchid laid her hand, between its breasts. The bronze is cool and reassuring to his fingertips. He could leave Arya Tara and the goose girls in charge.

'The Strongbows or the Benedicts could keep an eye on the place,' he says, unwilling to discuss who might go and who might have to stay.

Zhenhua doesn't answer, but her silence is answer enough. Having uttered them, he can see how thin his words are. It's true that the Benedicts would never leave, such is their love for healthy mountain air – if they ran out of food they would live on the air alone – but as caretakers they would be quite useless. As for the Strongbows, they would be more likely to break in and loot the food, and get the gold too, if they could. And while it is reassuring to think about returning, it isn't likely to happen. None of the others who left has come back. Of course, he has another mansion and another vault of gold in California, but who knows how many vaults of gold he's going to need before all this is over. There is a big black hole out there, waiting to suck up all his gold, his art collection, his mansions; everything he has can disappear through the event horizon of ruin and debt.

'We have to consider carefully the weight we put in the helicopter,' Zhenhua says.

Ah, so that's what this little visit has been about. His grand plan. Of course, she doesn't know about the more private arrangements he's made, not yet. Just why he is holding this back from her he doesn't know, but nevertheless he is, out of some obscure instinct. Somehow she's sensed it, sensed his holding back, and is now using silence and indirection to probe.

Well he's not going to satisfy her, not yet. She'll just have to wait.

'And the party?'

'We'll have the party.' Oh yes. No sense in letting a little thing like ruination and the end of the world get in the way of pleasure. His hand moves to the statue's cool breast.

Outside, the careless sky goes dark.

The Drudgery of Trance

Book Four

fear walks on stilts

After half the town witnesses the driver of the Humvee turning into a driftdead, and hears the desperate talk of the now dead youth, resistance to the mayor's barrier plan crumbles. The driftdead are nothing less than plague carriers. A plague that turns people into zombies. A plague not spread by a physical agency, like a virus, something inhaled or absorbed by the skin, but by a psychic force, a mental parasite.

There is not a single inhabitant of Keatown who does not feel a keen stab of fear every time they think about the possibility of turning, or that some may already have turned. Founder Phil. Blade. Maybe more, who knows? People are not only afraid of turning, but afraid of even thinking about turning, because the instruction to turn might be carried by no more than a thought.

Everybody is on the edge of panic, and Big Bill has to talk hard to prevent chaos and wild flight. He soon hits upon a line of reasoning that works pretty well. Running away didn't help the Humvee people much, hadn't stopped them from turning, he argues. Since flight is hopeless, it is better to stand and fight. If they can keep the driftdead at bay, keep them out of Keatown, maybe they won't turn. That the townspeople accept this line of reasoning, with the assumptions on which it is built, is a clear indication of the dread that has overtaken us.

Now that the secret of turning is out of the bag, people begin to report all kinds of responses to the driftdead. Some say they can hear them singing a siren song to lure them. Just as Odysseus was lured to an island where men would dream themselves to death, so the driftdead are calling the living into their false, half world. Some say the driftdead exert a hypnotic pull, like the tug of gravity. Others say they can smell a wind, a dead vacant wind, in their vicinity. Still others can feel their skin crawl, as if they were being touched by invisible fingers.

The nights are the worst. There is no keeping out the shuffling sound a mass of moving people makes, and their unnatural silence seems louder at night. Some claim that the behaviour of the driftdead changes when the sun goes down, that they move more slowly, that there are more pausers at night, and there have been further reports of faces looking in at windows, reports the librarian certainly can't dismiss. There is an uneasy, unspoken sense that the driftdead are generally more aware of the world at night, and therefore more aware of people. At night, the pausers seem more like watchers. Their heads move when I move, someone reports.

Cherrie Lamont arrived at the marae in a hysterical state, claiming that a group of driftdead clustered at her doorway in the night, trying to get in. Nobody took much notice since Cherrie Lamont is not the most reliable of witnesses, but again the librarian is reluctant to dismiss the distraught woman out of hand. The librarian knows Cherrie Lamont, remembers her well from their school-teaching days, and is happy enough to acknowledge that her old friend might get the wrong end of the stick sometimes, confused and muddled, yes, with a fluffy mind, yes, but hardly possessing imagination enough to make up such a story.

The idea that the driftdead may be changing, albeit gradually, is not welcome, and slow to take root, but the stories accumulate as the driftdead get more numerous. A farmer and his wife report waking up one morning to find two driftdead standing in their bedroom looking down at them. The couple panicked and leapt out of bed. The driftdead pair continued to stare at the empty bed for the rest of the day before resuming their march south at nightfall. Another farmer reports finding one sitting in the driver's seat of his ute, staring rigidly ahead. A fisherman reports finding a driftdead woman lying on his bed holding up a spiral sea shell. Still another tells of finding his house jammed full of them, unable to move, unable to walk but still going through the motions of walking, lifting up their knees and pushing into each other. The owner couldn't get inside, couldn't clear them, and has had to stay with a neighbour.

These stories, which the librarian assiduously writes down, make her think that these driftdead are looking for a life, a life they can occupy. She thinks they might be still driven by memories, fragments of memories of a once normal life. The man sitting in the farmer's ute had his hand on the gear lever, as if about to drive off. The couple looking down at the bed were nostalgic for sleep.

Somehow everybody has become accustomed to the sheer purposelessness of the driftdead's southward movement. We saw them as lifeless machines we could sort of ignore, but the looming threat of turning, and the changing nature of the driftdead, have become the driving forces behind the frenetic barrier building. Fear and hope, a desperate mix. The mayor can hardly believe the energy and the will, and how quickly the barrier takes shape. People have forgotten how to laugh, make jokes, appreciate ironies. They have even forgotten how much they dislike each other. Their thoughts are fixed on one thing only: the barrier, the driftdead-proof fence. Night and day the frenetic building goes on. People work until they drop, sleep where they fall, and when they wake up they go back to work. Materials, everything from barbed-wire to pine planks, appear as if by magic from backyards and under people's houses. Keatown is gripped by a common purpose.

They have no need of Big Bill's rhetoric to hold them to task, nor the reverend's prayers.

It is certainly an ambitious undertaking, running east to west at the northern edge of the town, from the rugged foot hills below the mansions down to the ocean, the aim being to herd the driftdead upward into the mountains or down along the shore to be drowned or confined to the beaches. The reconstruction of the town goes on hold; everybody's sole focus is on the building of the barrier. Even the librarian leaves her books and her Chronicles of Keatown to come out and lend a hand.

Hera's view that the driftdead are like traumatised refugees, and may one day recover their humanity, is quickly abandoned by just about everybody except Hera herself, and her loyal friend Margo. The question of the driftdead's humanity, or relationship to humanity, is quickly buried beneath fear and revulsion. All kinds of superstitions appear like weeds in a garden. If you don't look at them, you won't turn. If you dream about them, you will turn. If you start seeing your friends and family among them, you will turn. If you pray to the reverend's god, you won't turn. Akona is making a medicine that will prevent people from turning. And so on and so on. Even the librarian is not immune from this kind of thinking. As long as I stay in the library, with the books, I won't turn. Writing she sees as another defence. I won't turn if I am writing. As long as the words keep flowing. We have to keep doing the things that make us human, Hera says. That's all we can do.

Despite that good advice, compassion has become a memory, and Witch Hunt, from her school-room sanctuary, can hear Hera crying at night along with the Baby. Witch Hunt suspects that Hera is using the Baby's cries to mask her own. Margot and a couple of the other women still meet with Hera to keep alive the idea of the essential humanity of the driftdead, but they make hard work of it, and Hera herself begins to suspect that Margot and her friends are holding onto the idea as a form of comfort. If the worst comes to the worst, and they do turn, then perhaps they might have a chance of turning into their old selves once more. This, Hera recognises, is little more than blind faith or pious hope, since nobody has witnessed a driftdead turning back into a human. Not yet.

Melissa Tonguestone feels fully vindicated in her hatred of the driftdead, and her barely repressed desire to kill them all. Now everybody wants to kill them, not just Melissa and Grandmother Gaunt. Not only are they cockroaches, but they are worse than cockroaches. They can sneak in and steal your soul, and so turn you into one of them. She concocts her own theology based on the reverend's gloomy apocalyptic views, in turn based on his studies of Ecclesiastes and the other ancient Hebrew prophets, and mixed with a terrified, and terrifying, vision of the driftdead as the Devil's own plague, sent to suck on the souls of the faithful and faithless alike. Nobody sees them as zombies because they have no interest in eating our flesh, but in fact they are far worse than zombies, with a hunger for more than our flesh. A hunger for that very spark that makes us human. Since it has somehow been extinguished in themselves, they hunger after it in others. Those we called the pausers are actually casting around for their next victim.

From the reverend's point of view, all this hysteria smacks of heresy, but since the existence of the driftdead is itself a heresy of nature, he finds it hard to formulate a position on the matter which would come anywhere near assuaging Melissa's fears, or anyone else's for that matter. What he can't admit is that the existence of the driftdead constitutes not just a heresy of nature, but a blasphemy against God and therefore a challenge to his faith, the very basis of his faith. This is not the Rapture some see prefigured in the gospels, the separation of the wheat from the chaff, the sheep from the goats, as far as he can see. There is no salvation here, either for the driftdead themselves or those remaining. No ecstatic ascension of the chosen from earth to heaven. Rather the opposite, the eruption of hell onto earth. This standing of his deepest belief on its head is too much for the reverend's rigid perception system to bear. It cracks beneath the strain. Holes are opening up in his prayers, and there is no god inside them. All that faith he thought he had was nothing more than vanity. Vanity of vanities sayeth the preacher. All is vanity! He has been quoting these words since the day he put down his billiard cue, but has never understood them, never applied them to himself.

If even finding God is vanity, what hope is there?

Besides all this, there is another force at work in the reverend's psyche which no one, least of all himself, recognises, but which increasingly exerts its gravitational pull upon him, further distorting his faith – but only later is this to become evident. He can already sense it, however, there in the holes between thoughts, like a presence waiting to be acknowledged. Like a memory, but it is not a memory. Like a face, but it is not a face. Not yet. So far there is only the ache.

What it all adds up to is that he is helpless in the face of Melissa's delirium. Rasputin is no help, as immediately after the suicide of the youth from the Humvee, he goes into seclusion in his stone church and hasn't been seen since.

Those who buy into Melissa's panic-driven raving, and who share her urge to get out of Dodge before another single day passes, soon rustle up a couple of cars Flay deems roadworthy. Yes, he tells them, they can get into the cars and rush off with a fart and roar into the dawn, shaking the dust of Keatown from their heels... but, he hates to have to tell them since he would be happy to be rid of them for good, that there is no way they can carry enough gas to get them across the desert, not those cars, which are really just street hoppers and not built for long-range travel. There are of course vehicles that can do it, but those who have them are holding onto them. Nobody is falling over themselves to offer them to Melissa. Perhaps because nobody believes that she and her followers will get any further than some godforsaken strip of road in the middle of nowhere.

Thus thwarted, Melissa's panic turns to madness and she begins to scream uncontrollably – at which point her followers melt away. Akona gives her some calming herbs but they have little effect, and the poor woman screams herself into an exhausted, half-delirious sleep, a sleep full of cockroach dreams. When she wakes up it is with a new resolution. Calmly, she begins to plan her suicide.

Only Hera and Margot care anymore that Pinky and his vile wharf-rat crew go out at night, telling no one what they are up to, but mutilated, dismembered driftdead corpses litter the ditches in the morning from their sport. People hardly pause when Flay's shotgun blasts out over the town. We turn the other way, and we don't say anything except maybe mutter a few curses.

Fear can turn quickly into rage. From cringing to striking out. Under pressure, a thing may turn into its opposite suddenly enough – as love can become hate, and presumably the reverse. From attempted indifference and strained sympathy, the feelings of the townsfolk towards the driftdead change overnight. Good-humoured tolerance, even good-humoured intolerance, become things of the past. Where yesterday they might have pushed a wandering driftdead away, or simply moved to one side to let them pass, they now swear and curse, strike them, even hacking at them with knives, as if that will make any difference. The librarian witnesses some perfectly ordinary, everyday folk beating and kicking the driftdead with all the viciousness of street thugs or disgruntled sports fans. The very indifference of the driftdead to the treatment they receive drives their attackers to further rage and violence. The librarian tries to imagine herself reaching that point, and can't.

Nothing anybody does makes any difference. The driftdead keep coming, larger and larger groups of them. More and more, just as Rasputin saw in his vision on Pine Point. Not only is there the danger of turning, becoming a deserter, but, if they arrive in sufficient numbers, all semblance of normal life will be swamped and all of us swept away like so many ants in a flood.

We don't have to wait long for further evidence of desertion. A now dreaded word. As is turning. We first see it right at the barrier, where everybody is working.

The project has reached a critical juncture. The mayor, who returned to the library, much to the librarian's surprise, to spend some hours consulting any military texts she could find, came up with his stroke of genius, his answer to the inundation. First they dig trenches, then, on the defenders' side of the trench, they erect a line of sharpened wooden sticks in a rough Cheval-de-Frise, bound with number-eight wire and rope, supported by wire fences laced with tangles of barbed wire and bits of metal. However, it can't all be done at once, and since some of the sections are finished before others, the driftdead are herded through the remaining openings, creating bottlenecks where it becomes impossible to block the flow.

Pinky and Tony and a couple of wharf rats are given the job of fending off the driftdead while the defences are being erected, and they take to their work with a will, but it is a losing battle they are fighting; for every driftdead they bash aside, two more take their place, and the ones bashed aside are soon back probing for another weak spot. It happens to Pinky's sidekick, Tony. The one who always laughs at Pinky's jokes and who likes to play dumber to Pinky's dumb. One minute he's there beside Pinky, swinging away at a line of driftdead with a piece of metal pipe kindly donated by Flay, cursing cheerfully, while behind them the fishermen work feverishly on the barrier, the next moment he turns, walks away, blank-faced, within a few moments becoming indistinguishable from the crowd but for the piece of pipe he is still holding.

The work on that section falters as everybody looks at each other and reads the same thing in each other's eyes. If it can happen to Tony, it can happen to anybody.

And it does.

A double desertion. Several fishermen, including Captain Orlap, are busy digging a trench in front of a completed section of wall. They discover that if the driftdead go into the trench, some will tend to follow it downhill and eastward, flowing like water, rather than attempt to scramble up against the barrier from below. A nice deep trench offers the defenders the strategic advantage of high ground. The device works well enough for General Big Bill Broonzy to order as many hands as he can spare to its construction, which is why the fishermen, the strongest males in town, are working on it. Abruptly, two of the men simply peel off and join the driftdead, one of them still carrying a spade.

As with Tony, this happens abruptly and without warning. As Orlap relates it later, one of the men stopped in the middle of a word. A moment later he was gone.

Orlap abandons his post and runs after them, throwing his arms about and shouting as if they were at sea and he was the captain who must be obeyed. To no avail. A couple of others abandon their posts to grab Orlap and hold him back. Then the three of them go into the driftdead stream to rescue the other two.

It is a heroic battle, as against a rip tide, but they finally wrestle the two fishermen behind the barrier. It makes no difference. They can't hold them down forever. As soon as they let go their exhausted grip, the two new driftdead recruits stolidly get to their feet and join the general trudge south. Nobody looks at them as they leave.

Fear walks on stilts, and the work goes on into the night.

the bloodless man and a clash of close-ups

These are the first of the deserters, but there have been a number since, not enough to start off panic but too many for anybody to feel easy. To make matters worse there are different ways of succumbing, either fast or slow, as the suicidal youth said. Some, like Miranda's father and Tony, leave their lives abruptly to join the mindless drool south. Others take longer, grow mesmerised by the flow of upright bodies, the constant shiffle-shuffle of feet and the blind purpose that drives them, and begin to sway, like leaves in the slowest wind, before they succumb. These are the scary ones.

At first, victims may be roused, brought back to life, but soon slip once more into that vacuous state that consumes memories, empties minds, turns them into hollow shells in which nothing else moves but that same blind imperative. They might begin by standing very still, hypnotised by the slow dance of the driftdead. Then, quite suddenly, they will join the throng, step into that deadly ballet and never be seen again. Even putting these people into a locked room doesn't help. They may not be able to see the driftdead but they can hear them shuffling past, sense their passage through time and through the bulwarks of their memories, and are soon bashing up against the south wall of their prison.

You don't have to be a follower of the Reverend Stickman and his redeemed disciple to fear desertion more than death. In terms of terror it ranks alongside being buried alive or incarcerated in a cave full of spiders. If it happens to others it can happen to you. While nobody knows who or what the driftdead are, the suspicion is that, deep down in their psyches, their human selves, who they once were, lie buried, still conscious but helpless. Therein lies the fear. To be a human consciousness imprisoned in an unresponsive body, a body engaged in a single mindless activity. A body you can neither control nor escape. A body that was once your own to command. Perhaps you can look out through that body's eyes and see the world you are passing through. A world that you and thousands like you must pass through. Your ears too might catch the sounds of the world but you can't respond to them.

Nobody knows what the driftdead can see, of course. Maybe they can only see colours but no shapes. And maybe they can hear sounds but not distinguish them. Nobody can know. What people do know is that they don't want to find out the hard way.

Sing or chant all the time you are protected. Parsley prevents turning. Don't meet their eyes or they will snare you with their vacancy. Wear earmuffs to keep their thoughts out of your brain.

For some, the terror is too great. One of our dairy farmers, Pukua Johansson, came in from the morning chores to find his wife swinging from a roof beam, and soon joined her. They were swinging together when a neighbour found them. At the funeral, the reverend warns of creeping despair, and of God's strictures against suicide, but many listen to him in stony silence. Better death than desertion. Melissa Tonguestone has a new set of followers. The suicide club.

For Rasputin with his God-washed eyes, believing the barrier will hold back the driftdead and prevent the whole town from turning is perhaps the greatest superstition of all. There is something ungodly in the fraught faith the townsfolk are putting into this bulwark, and the terrible fury with which they repulse the growing hoards of driftdead. There's no God in it, as far as the reverend is concerned, and Rasputin concurs. And if it is not for God, or of God, then it is futile and doomed to fail. An icon of the mind. A false god, a false hope. Just a wall that will crumble. 'No good can come of it,' the reverend says whenever he stops to think about it. But he doesn't have the stomach for destroying people's hope when it's all they have. He doesn't want their blood on his hands. God, it seems, has plenty of blood on His hands.

The reverend has to face feeling deceived by God, and his cosmology does not include a deceitful god. The reverend's big thing has been salvation of the soul by means of redemption from sin. Pretty straightforward, pretty basic stuff. Be good and God will reward you. Now he can't even tell people whether killing the driftdead is a sin or not, a question Melissa recently asked him outright, and he, with no Rasputin to support him this time, had hummed and ha'd. 'It is certainly no sin to kill demons... if the driftdead are... or perhaps merely possessed... of course you can't kill demons with bullets and blades... or keep them out with walls... on the other hand... if their souls are already given over to the Devil... abandoned by God... their bodies mere walking abominations... on the other hand, you could say... they may be redeemable in the eyes of God... let the fires of Hell consume their own...'

Whatever people believe, what cannot be denied is the effect the driftdead have en masse. Nobody can ignore their collective oblivion, their blind silence, their rhythmic, insistent movements that creep into sleepless thoughts at night and haunt the sleepwalking days.

And, as the suicidal youth predicted, more are deserting. Quietly slipping away.

It is too easy to become fascinated. To stop and look at them. And to look at them is to become something of a voyeur, because the driftdead don't appear to know you are looking at them, they just carry on as if you weren't there. The great diversity of their clothing and styles, and the fact that they all look as if they have been interrupted during some normal everyday activity like getting out of bed or making a cup of coffee, have their own voyeuristic interest. Endlessly varied and endlessly the same. Let's stop and look at them. Let's follow the movement of hand and eye, the vacancy of shuffling, the steady, inexorable purpose, and notice the seductive details: a mouth wide open, eyes cast down, the awkward movement of a knee, the backward bend of an elbow, the sexy hunch of a shoulder – it goes on forever, an endless slide-show. A clash of close-ups. A rise and fall of bodies. Vacant bodies, coming together – falling apart, filled only with a dumb purpose, a blind will.

The whole barrier project is haunted by a fear of failure, a fear so strong that the very possibility is fervently denied. Failure is not an option. The spectre is there every time a section already built gives way to the press of bodies, and resources have to be reallocated to plug the gap, further slowing down progress, which is often marginal. And while men have to sleep, the driftdead just keep coming, patiently negotiating every obstacle, slipping through every wire or banging up against every hastily erected barricade. Even impaling themselves on sharpened stakes. The driftdead don't care if they die, or have to clamber over their own dead. If shot in the head, they simply fall over without a sound or change of expression. If their limbs are hacked off they try to keep walking, on whatever limbs are left, like true zombies, before they fall over. If strangled, they resist, but weakly, as if the deadly fingers were moth wings they couldn't brush away.

A discovery is made which adds to the rising panic. After Tony's desertion, Pinky, whose rage has turned cold, captures a driftdead man, hangs him upside down and drains him of blood, right to the last drop. Then cuts him down. Like a true zombie, he just gets up and keeps walking. That bloodless creature looks ghastly too, made of pale rubber rather than flesh, eyes black in their translucent gel. But still walking.

'This is more like it,' Sad Toof is heard observing.

'I bet that one rots,' says Little Sanyo, who is fascinated and wants to repeat what he calls 'the experiment', insisting that the results should be repeatable – but everybody else is horrified. There are implications. The driftdead may be no more than puppets made of human flesh and an idea that has been waiting in the wings for some time comes to the fore. If the driftdead are not in possession of their own bodies, then who is? Demons or demonic spirits seems like the only answer to those with no other recourse, although Little Sanyo contends that, equally, we could be witnessing an alien invasion, alien beings who can take over human bodies, as in Invasion of the Body Snatchers, starring a sinister Donald Sutherland. Bodiless beings in search of bodies, Little Sanyo speculates. The driftdead are ordinary people whose personalities have been evicted or suppressed by invaders from another realm of being. Whether you go for Little Sanyo's secular version or the reluctant reverend's theological version, some form of possession is accepted as a likely explanation. A bloodless human is no human at all.

These speculations lead to the feeling that when the driftdead look out at the world, it is an alien presence doing the seeing. Behind the apparent blankness of the driftdead stare, something inhuman is observing our world and us. While such an impression may have been almost impossible to verify, equally it is impossible to eradicate. Now the driftdead come to be regarded with as much horror as real zombies might be, more even. After all, real zombies are just dead people walking around with a hunger for human flesh. Our driftdead may be much more than that, much worse: demons, or alien creatures, it is all one and the same, here to gather the whole human race under one dark wing.

All these feverish speculations are a further blow to Hera, Margot and those others who want to maintain what has come to be called the 'humanist' view of the driftdead, maintaining their essential humanity. Bloodless driftdead are one step further removed from humanity; puppet bodies are no more than bodies. The notion that one day they may magically recover their humanity is a pipe dream, and a dangerous one at that.

What Hera doesn't know is that, as yet secretly, and quite unexpectedly, the reverend is sympathetic to her view. He too has an investment in holding onto some idea of the driftdead's essential, and essentially fallen, humanity, for truly, no one is ever abandoned by God, and it is heresy to even think so. An eruption of demons into the world would be a gratuitous act no God worthy of the name would tolerate; senseless, purposeless, and of no moral value – for what lessons might the faithful draw from it? The same might be said for an inundation of abominations. But if they retained even a sliver of humanity, they were redeemable, no matter how deeply the Devil may have his claws into them. No matter how lost they seem. There is no power in the universe that can trump God's grace. Deep in his card-sharp's heart, he knows this to be true.

But a bloodless corpse remotely controlled by demons or aliens? Surely beyond salvation. The reverend can hardly bring himself to believe it. God is not capricious! Nor wantonly cruel. Even to think so is courting blasphemy.

Mayor Big Bill, also, does not like the idea of possession, either by demons or beings from another realm – it gives the driftdead too much mystery, too much power. But after the incident of the bloodless driftdead, he has no explanation. Not even an insane person can walk around without any blood. Still, he stays in the forefront of the defence. His great belief in keeping everybody busy is unchanged. If we all keep busy there will be no time for morbidity. We have more to fear from morbidity than the driftdead themselves. They are no more than ships passing in the night, clouds floating in the sky, brainless dorks. And you don't want to join them. Just concentrate on the task at hand. Sooner or later they will be gone. The town will get itself back on its feet again. And one day the choppers will return.

cross sections

Little Sanyo curbs his impatience and scouts around the garage, making sure that there is nobody lurking around. He doesn't have to worry as everybody is at the barrier working or supplying those doing the work. Nevertheless, he has developed a certain protocol, a ritual approach to the garage he is loath to change. It began as a concern that he was being followed, maybe by Witch Hunt or that creepy Rasputin, someone who was curious about where he goes when he slips away.

His beachcombing is a perfect cover, except he has to return empty-handed.

Not that his results are so amazing. There have been no dramatic discoveries. The roar of flies that greets him when he finally slips through the side door assures him that the old man is rotting in the normal, human way. Putrefaction is proceeding satisfactorily. Of course, Little Sanyo has never sat and observed a disintegrating corpse, but he can't imagine it would be very different from this. Close enough to assure him that the driftdead are not androids with indestructible polymer skin. The stench too, very like that of a rotting sheep, he decides, belongs to flesh, not any synthetic.

He's already decided that the next step is to dissect one of the other two, but that will have to wait until he can get into the library and learn a little more about anatomy. No use poking around inside a body if he doesn't know what he's looking at. More than that, his whole project has been called into question by Pinky's public surgery, and the indisputable result. What use now poking and prodding among their internal organs when, without the need for blood, most of those organs must be just for show. Heart, liver, kidneys, they all have to do with the flow of blood through the body. The next question might be, if you emptied out all their internal organs, throw out the pancreas, the bladder and the intestines for good measure, and sewed them up again, would they still be able to walk, tottering off down Highway 6 on their road to nowhere?

Little Sanyo hardly has the stomach for that, even after everything he's done and witnessed, and besides, he's beginning to suspect that the ground has shifted, and that the real questions won't be answered by dissecting and analysing flesh and bone. Beside him sits the microscope he managed to find in one of the locked cupboards at the school. He's already had a look at two sections of driftdead skin, one fresh, one decaying. He seems to detect some sort of cellular structure, but he's not really knowledgeable enough to know what he's looking at. Those variegated strips could be anything. Same with the blood sample. He can't tell much. Nothing swimming around in there as far as he can see, but he suspects he'd need much greater magnification in order to really see something interesting. He's compared the blood sample to his own, and certainly noticed some differences. His blood is much redder, and brighter, and possibly thinner than the driftdead's blood.

All very fascinating, but what has he learned? A big, fat nothing.

There are plenty of questions of this nature still to be asked. Is the driftdead's blood different because it changes over time after a human turns? He imagines that it might sort of grow tired and change colour because it's not being oxygenated. Lots of questions like this, but Little Sanyo is beginning to see that perhaps the answers are of little use. He sits with his head in his hands and thinks, just like Christopher Robin in the Pooh Bear stories.

While there are lots of physical questions without answers, the real question it seems to Little Sanyo has become: are the driftdead conscious? He has tried to separate this from questions about their brains. He has opened up the old man's skull and had a look at the brain, but, once more, lacked the knowledge to make sense of what he was seeing. Except for an odd greasiness that might be entirely natural anyway, he found nothing he could identify. Do the driftdead exhibit aspects of consciousness? He thinks about this for a long time while he fiddles with the useless microscope, and tries not to look at the driftdead boy and girl he has imprisoned, only to end in frustration. For every behaviour that might indicate consciousness, there is an answer:

> the driftdead appear to negotiate obstacles
>> yes, but so does water
> the driftdead can climb on top of things
>> yes, and so can sand, with enough wind behind it
> the driftdead can pause, and apparently look around
>> yes, so does a leaf hanging from a tree when the wind drops
> the driftdead show signs of clustering
>> yes, so do dead leaves in a cul-de-sac

The unsatisfactory result of all this is that Little Sanyo ends up doubting what consciousness is in the first place. What exactly is he looking for? he wonders. The ghost in the machine. He's heard that phrase somewhere. The point is you can never find it, that ghost in the machine – the harder you look the more it's not there. Worse, Little Sanyo finds himself disillusioned with the whole process of rational thought. If rational thought can deliver such absurdities, what hope is there? There are of course no answers to these questions and that is unsatisfactory too.

Only half conscious of what he is doing, he gets up and approaches the girl. He can see no conscious thought or process in her random bashing up against the south wall. There is as much logic in the random bashing of an unlatched window in the wind. Any self-respecting rat would have found its way out in ten seconds, given Little Sanyo left the side door open. Beside her, the boy still tugs at his bonds, trying to pull away, but makes no effort to untie them or smash them or saw through them. Even a dog will chew through its lead. Little Sanyo deliberately left a knife within easy reach but the boy has made no move towards it. He continues to clutch his cellphone, however, as if his flesh were welded to it.

The girl's actions hardly vary, walking the few paces along the south wall, turning and walking back again, east to west, west to east, bumping against the wall here and there. When he takes her arm and tries to lead her to the northern wall he can feel a resistance. It is not that she fights against him as such, she just seems to grow heavier and more resistant. He concludes that her desire to go south is like the desire of water to flow downhill – no desire at all, hardly even an inclination. Their world just tips them that way. In which case the word desire, when applied to the driftdead, is merely metaphorical and therefore deceptive.

These observations lead him to a memory of a conversation he had with the librarian about the philosopher Descartes, a difficult passage he was having trouble with. 'What Descartes proposed,' the librarian said in her school-teacher voice, 'is that the real world could be replaced by a false world. Since we only apprehend the world through our senses, and our senses can be deceived, some malicious devil could substitute a false world for the real one – and we'd never know the difference.' It was a stunning idea and Little Sanyo thought about it for many days, and decided that perhaps we would know the difference because this false world would be imperfect in some way, contain some fatal flaw, because only God could create a perfect world. And, he now reasons, if that fatal flaw, a mere hairline crack in a good imitation, were to turn into a fissure, then the false world would be revealed for what it is. For us, that fatal flaw has opened our world to the driftdead, who do not belong here.

Holding the girl now, feeling for himself her blundering movements, her incomprehension, he wonders if perhaps the driftdead are caught between dimensions, false or not, where they drift like thistledown in one direction, our physical, magnetic south having nothing to do with it. Deserters are getting pulled towards the other dimension when they turn. After all, there's nothing further south in this world but more of the same, coastline and sea – and desert. He imagines that, to them 'south' is not a real place in our world, but in their world there is someplace they are going. Think of their landscape lying on top of ours. They don't even see our world. They bump into things but don't know what they are.

None of this solves the issue of how cognisant the driftdead are. Since he can't tell from her behaviour, it seems that only catching her eye, catching her attention, can give him his answer, so he manoeuvres her into the south-eastern corner, wedging her arms against the walls and attempting to catch her eye, or at least stare into her eyes. She keeps on struggling but he can hold her easily enough, at least for a while. This close up she smells, not of rot or death as he might have thought, but something faintly sweet; a smell that stands on the edge of his memory like a shadow hovers at a doorway. They don't sweat, he thinks, failing to catch any lingering scent of it. They don't have any body functions, they neither eat nor excrete, nor breathe nor sleep... yet this one smells of flowers.

They may indeed be walking ciphers, but, equally, to be fair to logic, they may retain some residue, some faint trace of their human origins. If that were the case, the eyes would give it away, surely. This girl's eyes are blue, quite deep, and look like normal human eyes. It would be so easy to think that she is looking back at him, for that's what people's eyes do, but she isn't, he decides. He's not even sure the eyes are looking at all. He is examining them when she blinks. He almost loses his grip in shock. Here is a body function still working. We blink to keep our eyes clean and moist, so if she were doing the same, it might mean she was using her eyes. That she needed them.

For the first time he appreciates that the driftdead don't walk like blind people. They might move to avoid an obstacle before they reach it. Water can't do that. He feels quite excited about all this, his thoughts galloping along quite happily once more. He remembers how the man and the woman who had toiled up Pine Point – if the driftdead can be said to toil – wove their way through the pines hardly bumping into a single one. That has to prove something. He also remembers the first driftdead he ever saw, the Nightshade Girl he called her, with the palest skin in creation, remembers how she seemed to begin to turn in his direction, as if dimly aware of him the way a sleeper might dimly apprehend the territory of wakefulness. Little Sanyo can't forget that moment. Another moment or two and they might have connected, even if in some totally tangential way.

He is still thinking of the Nightshade Girl when it happens. The driftdead girl he still has pinned in the corner looks at him. Her dark blue eyes don't just pass over his face as if she were really blind; for a moment she sees him. A distant flicker of recognition. It is just for a moment but it is enough. 'Hello,' he says, sounding and feeling very foolish, even while it occurs to him that if she can see she might well be able to hear. Perhaps this testing for signs of consciousness should include playing them some music, or making very loud noises, to see how they react. If what they see can affect their behaviour, the same might apply to what they hear. In theory it might be possible to establish communication with them.

His faith in rational thought thus restored, he sets about repeating the effect. If she has seen him once she can see him again. Perhaps it will be easier the second time. He feels quite excited. No one else has tried to do this, work with them, break through to them. For a moment he feels like the scientific pioneer he has always wanted to be. In the forefront. An Einstein or a Stephen Hawking. It's in him, he knows it is.

Still pinning her in the corner – his arms are getting tired – he takes a mental step back to consider her. Girls are not really his thing, even the apparently sublime Orchid holds little interest for him, but this one must have been, at one time, quite pretty. Dark hair with a raven's shine. A high forehead, with high cheekbones and wide-spaced eyes. Of course, it takes animation to make a face pretty, certainly not the driftdead vacancy, but it is easy to see the girl who once was – pretty, eager, vital, full of life. He focuses on her eyes, watching them carefully. They do move about, to and fro and around, and these movements are not random or drunken in appearance, or mechanically repeated. This reinforces the impression that the driftdead are seeing something, but just not this world.

Her eyes are passing over his face when they pause on the exact moment they meet his. They stare at each other. She's there; he knows she is. Or something is. 'Hello,' he says again, louder this time. Still holding his gaze, her presence fades. Her eyes are still fixed on his but she's not seeing him anymore. He can sense her sliding away into some other mysterious element.

Contact! However fleeting. Contact!

But there is no proof. It is too subjective. He could be making it up just to satisfy his desire that it be so – how can he know for sure?

He releases her, and stands back to watch her resume her useless pacing of the south wall. No sentience without memory, he thinks gloomily. And the girl shows no signs of remembering anything. If she did apprehend him, it was in a way incomprehensible to him.

He turns to the boy, wondering if he might get a similar response from him, but the heart has gone out of him. This is dispiriting work, no doubt of that. A little better, and perhaps healthier, than chopping and dissecting, but with little more reward than two intriguing moments. The boy will have to wait for the next time. Cuffed to the vice, he's not going anywhere.

Before leaving he wonders if he should clear the garage of the remains of the old driftdead, which are smelling bad, but decides against it.

It might still be interesting to know the exact rate of decomposition.

As he is heading back to the front line, back to his duties on the barricades, he encounters a pauser, standing dead still, as they do, just moving their heads gently from side to side. Two thoughts occur to Little Sanyo simultaneously. One is that the man looks as if he were trying to remember something. The way a person might pull up short, remembering that perhaps they had left the stove on or the door unlocked. The second is that the man could be listening to something, something only he can hear.

Shrugging, Little Sanyo moves on.

the flaw that reveals the falsity

At the height of the building and digging frenzy, Sirocco goes up to Pine Point, and finds the lookout from where the mokopuna saw the early driftdead couple toiling up the slope, and Little Sanyo coined the word. From there he can look north and get the lay of the land... As near as possible, he wants to get a bird's eye view of the town's defences and the approach of the driftdead.

So far so good, but since we last saw him his status has changed enormously. He is no longer just the runt of the mokopuna litter, he is the baby-bearer, the one who holds the town's treasure at his chest – and the librarian has no idea how that happened, or when, or where, or under what circumstances the Baby was transferred from Hera to Sirocco. But there he is, snuggled in his frontpack against Sirocco's chest, staring up at him. And every time Sirocco moves he can feel the weight on his shoulders and knows for sure that this is no dream.

Talking to people has not helped the librarian much. Some look at her strangely when she asks them. Most just take it for granted that Sirocco is the baby bearer. Grandmother Gaunt and Melissa Tonguestone mutter against Sirocco behind his back, just as they did with Hera. When the librarian asked them about Hera, Gaunt would only say, 'the floozy was never a real mother to the Baby.'

She appreciates that when a historian buries herself in the past, there is a danger that the world will have changed by the time she returns to it. Her Chronicles of Keatown swallow her up from time to time, but to think she would miss an event like that hardly makes narrative sense. If such a lacuna were to open up in her historical data, let's say an extra child appearing from nowhere, she would most certainly question the reliability of that data. But you can't question the reliability of reality. Historical records might lie, or be contradictory, or incomplete – but reality can suffer no such limitations. Reality just is. Or at least this is the way she reasons.

The implications for her Chronicles are profound. She always planned to bring the work right to the present day, as far forward as she could, to follow the fate of the Johnsons and the Kensingtons right through the boom years and into the Long Emergency. How is she going to handle this, when the time comes to tell the story of Baby and the coming of the driftdead? By then the reality will have become history, little more than a story. Her reader will turn the page to a new chapter and find that it doesn't connect.

At that point the reader will lose all faith in her authority.

She thinks she must have looked up from her studies to find herself in a different world. A world almost the same, but for this one huge divergence. In this world Sirocco is the baby-bearer. This idea makes her go cold with fear. Goosebumps come up on her arm. Look away for a moment and reality will change itself about. Perhaps tomorrow she will wake up and find herself on a world with two moons or no moon at all. Could reality be so fickle?

No, it couldn't. The truth may be worse than that. The truth is, she is slowly turning into a driftdead. Very slowly. Some go fast, some go slow – she is one of the slow ones. Very slow. It starts with a sense of displacement, the way she felt when they all confronted that first group of driftdead, as if everybody had been pushed out of their lives and couldn't find their roles. As if nobody quite occupied their bodies. And now this, a major disconnect. Two halves of her life that don't fit. Or a big chunk gone missing. Either way, it doesn't matter. The driftdead are invading her mind.

She walks along her bookshelves, running her fingers over the spines and titles. Here they are, all dressed up with nowhere to go. Read me! Read me! they cry. Pick me up! Open me! Admire me! See! I am witty! I am sad! I am clever! I surprise! I give pleasure! I am mysterious! I am beautiful! I am truthful! I am profound! I am sexy! I am compassionate! I am wise! I am terrifying! I am bizarre! I am impossible! I am, above all, a good read! Read me! Read me!

In her mind's eye the librarian sees rows of driftdead passing through the library, each one taking a book until all the books are gone and the library is empty. Sighs and whispers.

Upset, she turns to her deity, me, the First Person Singular, the authority in all matters narrative.

'You kept it from me,' she says. 'You are the First Person Singular. You must have known about Sirocco and the Baby.'

Her faith in my omniscience is touching, but misplaced. If the driftdead have walked through her head, they could have walked through mine as well. I feel I have lost a piece of me to the driftdead march through her Chronicles. That's not exactly omniscience. She should know from looking at all those books that I am many first persons, a whole jumble of them. I am legion.

I wonder if the librarian's Chronicles themselves have become both a vehicle for, and a symptom of, my own growing mesmerised state.

'This is a glitch in causality itself,' she says out loud. Like the reverend, she is getting into the habit of talking to her deity, usually in a reproving voice; and, like the reverend's deity, I prefer to stay out of it.

The librarian continues through the library, touching the books as she goes the way we touch things in the world to affirm their existence – touch the table, smell the dust, taste the air. She is facing not just a hole in the story, but a huge discontinuity that brings the integrity of the Chronicles themselves into question, and the process of its creation to a halt... she is filled with an anticipatory sense of loss and dread, because the construction of the Chronicles, with their strict adherence to the record, has been an integral part of the construction of her identity, her orientation in time and space, and she doesn't want to face what would happen if the book unravelled. She would be better employed up at the barricades fending off the invaders than hiding in the library watching the driftdead walk off with pieces of history.

Her fingers flick over the poets, the philosophers, the scientists and the fabulists, but she doesn't get much of a clue from them. They have all fallen strangely silent, and their cries of 'read me! read me!' have been replaced by a muttered 'don't ask me, don't ask me,' and the busy silence of the library has been replaced by the fusty silence of the tomb. Her books have turned their backs on her. Perhaps they are furiously examining their own stories, looking for similar gaps in their realities.

This abrupt cessation of the roar of words leaves her feeling giddy and ill. It's one thing to stop writing, for her Chronicles to hit a wall, but this sensation of walking through her library as through a forest of dead leaves is something else. Perhaps she can bear her own silence, but the silence of the world staggers her. She is too afraid to pick up a book in case all the words have deserted it, and there is nothing but blank pages. A library full of blank pages, all the words gone south.

In which case, she might as well do the same thing.

I have to exercise my right as the First Person and step in. I have managed to keep out of it so far, but now duty calls. There is a solution, reluctant as I am to suggest it. In her darkest hour, I come to her with my solution. That gap, that bleeding gash in the narrative, she could fill with her own invention. She could make it up. Not just make it up, though, but attempt to reconstruct it the way it pretty much must have happened, given the fixtures and forces involved. If she did it well enough, her patch-over would be indistinguishable from the rest of the Chronicles, at least for the unwitting reader.

She already knows that Grandmother Gaunt is, or was, gunning for Hera, and has her sympathisers, Orchid possibly among them. She doesn't have to make that up. So it's easy to imagine Hera wanting to thwart them. She already knows that Hera has alienated herself from many who have supported her by taking an unpopular position on the nature of the driftdead, and has not quite been her old, bold and beautiful self. It's all there, all the elements needed.

The thought of the unwitting reader, who she would be engaged in thus deceiving, makes her writhe with discomfort, but I don't see any other way, I tell her. Or rather, I encourage those thoughts to come into her head. We all need some supernatural aid from time to time. Even the writer.

The librarian is shocked by the idea. The Chronicles are premised on her integrity as witness and historian; one small patch of dishonesty and make-believe may infect the rest, taint the whole. A reader may not know, but she would know. Her Chronicles would be forever compromised, forever flawed. The flaw that reveals the falsity. It hardly matters if that flaw is hidden deep away from sight, covered over carefully so that nothing shows. It will still be there: a little less than the truth, a little more than a lie.

And yet, she begins to see, it has to be done, a necessary evil in an age of necessary evils and patchwork solutions. The Chronicles cannot stand apart from the events it describes. It cannot exist in some pure space where each thing is possessed of its own absolute integrity, but in the rough and ready world of real things, chipped and broken things, chipped and broken and mended and patched things. Life where the stitches still show, or a scar recalls a wound.

The librarian sits down to the task with trepidation, but a fierce determination. The gap must not be allowed to halt the narrative, or compromise its larger movement, for it is in that larger movement that the history's integrity ultimately lies, she thinks, and, as the first few sentences appear on the screen, the enormity of the task hits her. Not only must she make something up, but must make it so true that, in a sense, it will become indistinguishable from the truth itself, not just a substitute but as good as the real thing in terms of making sense of events, which is the historian's ultimate duty. Without her little fictional insert there is no making sense of real events. Therefore, her deception, if it must be seen that way, must not be merely plausible, rather subject to the strictest probity and the most exacting requirements. It must be built on everything already known about Sirocco and Hera, must have its roots deep in the truth. It must not simply stand in for what really happened but become it, be it.

After a brief, fraught pause, her fingers begin to race over the keys:

a thoroughly unworthy desert rat

Building the defences of the town had just got seriously under way, when Sirocco escaped from his duties and sought the quiet of the beach. Only a few driftdead passed that way; most stuck to the road as the simplest path south. It was late afternoon, Sirocco's favourite time of day because of the odd and beautiful things approaching twilight can do with a landscape, bringing hills closer or taking them further away, deepening a sky or changing the colour of the sea to an unlikely indigo.

As far as he knew, he wasn't being followed by any of the mokopuna. He'd even managed to shake off Little Sanyo. Now he had the space to create another fragment for his imaginary book, his living history of inconsequence. This was a list of the things he'd seen the driftdead clutching. A fresh rose, a scroll, a candleholder with unlit candle, a briefcase, a spade, an iPad (and assorted devices), a goldfish in a plastic bag, a computer keyboard, a light bulb, a book (there were a number of books, titles unknown), a rolled-up magazine, an article of clothing (socks are popular), a knife, a gun, a towel, a paper clip, a broken cup, a plastic bottle of dishwashing liquid (and other bottles of assorted liquids), reading glasses, a sex toy, a range of children's toys from teddies to barbies to snuggy-rugs, from hammers to harpsichords, zips to zithers... This was Scale and Gypsy's living-room writ large. He had often speculated as to why the driftdead, who seemed to have no interest or even awareness of the world, should each carry some item from their pasts, some carry-over perhaps, some clinging reflex in action.

There was one walking with him now along the water's edge, a very old man whose steps were slow and mechanical, dragging himself though the wet sand, each foot coming up with effort, leaving a deep indentation soon to be filled by the next high wave. He was carrying a largish, framed photograph which showed a family group, late colonial, perhaps early 1900s, the women in their stiff white blouses, the men in their straight dark jackets, the photograph composed in that camera-conscious manner of early studio family portraits. It was easy to see the photo because the old man held it steady as if he wanted passers-by to view it. It might have once been very dear to him, containing the secret of his past, or it might have meant nothing at all, just something he had casually picked up before he turned.

As he did many times each day, Sirocco wished that Lizard were with him. Lizard had made the desert possible with his calm advice, and Keatown had become another desert complete with sandhills, only more puzzling and more complicated.

He sat on the sand, up from the waves, and tried to keep his thoughts simple. He picked up a stick and began to draw circles and stars, as he did under the crab apple tree. Simple shapes to clear the mind. Lizard taught him this, drawing these shapes, waiting for the pattern, discerning the pattern, taking action. Don't fight the desert, Lizard told him, or it will kill you very quickly. Be with the desert, then it will kill you slowly, but you won't notice.

As he drew in the sand he saw a figure approaching from the south, which immediately excluded the driftdead.

It was Hera and the Baby. She walked right up to Sirocco and sat down beside him. The Baby gave Sirocco a toothless grin and a chubby wave. From a soft cloth bag she was carrying, she drew a baby's bottle and proceeded to feed the infant. The Baby kept his eyes on Sirocco while his mouth sought the teat. They both watched him for a while. The Baby cooed in the language of babies and Hera cooed back in the same language.

'I never had milk for him,' Hera said.

She said it simply and matter-of-factly, but it made Sirocco feel sad. Hera's magnificence was beyond compromise in Sirocco's mind, forever free of change, of the fracture lines of mortality. And that magnificence had always been associated in his mind with her generous breasts. Because he'd never thought about it, it hadn't occurred to him that something had gone wrong here, or that Hera had some great sadness she didn't show to the world. He had been happy to just admire her and leave it at that.

The Baby didn't seem to mind, however, and took time from his feeding to give Sirocco a milky smile. He'd mastered the art of smiling without taking the teat from his mouth.

'He looks happy enough with Nanny's milk,' he said, grinning at the Baby's evident satisfaction. Perhaps just snuggling up to the regal breasts was enough.

'He's never known anything else.'

Hera sat with the Baby at her breast and stared out to sea. Sirocco checked to see what she was looking at and saw that it was nothing. Two driftdead passed in front of them, one a woman who walked very correctly, as if in church, the other a boy of maybe fifteen who sloped along half bent at the waist, head forward. The boy was moving a little faster than the woman, and their moving together was a mere coincidence of time and their observers' point of view. Neither would remember the moment he overtook her, and the deceptive moment or two in which they seemed to lock step. Sirocco added a bow tie and a bicycle chain to his list of carried objects.

'We'll never find out what they are, who they are,' Hera said. 'Everything we think about them turns out to be wrong.'

'I don't think they really belong in the world,' Sirocco said. It was nice talking to Hera like this, almost as equals. He used to have conversations a bit like this with Lizard.

Hera was sunk in the deepest silence. Sand trickled over her leg, the Baby at her breast forgotten. She kept watching the two driftdead, the boy now pulling ahead of the mincing woman.

'The question is not, who are they. The question is, who are we?'

That struck him as very profound. It also made him uneasy. Or maybe what really made him uneasy was the sense of distance in her voice, as if these questions of identity, of the very nature of being, were only of passing interest – something for the mind to toy with and let go. Her statement, profound as it was, was delivered in a flat, disinterested voice, as if we were no more than they, living humans and the walking driftdead.

The Baby unstuck himself from the teat, gave a tiny cry, sounding like a sea bird, far off and invisible, and banged a tiny fist on Hera's breast.

She took the bottle from his mouth to give him a chance to do some breathing. 'We are lucky to have Nanny and Lucifer. He drank directly from Nanny's teat. Human babies do fine on goat's milk. Gypsy says it's a tradition for babies whose mother has no milk to drink straight from the teat. Such babies were thought to be special.'

'I think our Baby is pretty special.'

The Baby seemed to agree, and gave Sirocco a burpy smile.

'He is.' The touch of melancholy was unmistakable. Not just distance, but regret. Lizard used to say that if you can't learn from regret your muscles become weak.

With another wave in Sirocco's direction, the Baby turned back to the bottle and the teat disappeared. Sirocco wanted to sit alone with Hera and the Baby forever. He felt a thousand feet tall instead of the runt he really was. He felt of some consequence instead of some knobbly-shaped oddity Gypsy found half-dead in the desert. A thoroughly unworthy desert rat. For a moment it was as if he and Hera were equals, and he was as tall as the tallest most magnificent woman in town.

Hera plucked the teat from the Baby's mouth.

'He's had enough, but he doesn't know it. If he keeps drinking he'll get wind, and that'll make him grizzly.'

'Like the bear.'

'Worse than the bear.'

'Life's tough, kid,' Sirocco said.

Hera smiled. It was still a huge, Celeb smile, with enough wattage to blast him off his backside, but the sight of it reminded him that it was the first time he'd seen it in a while.

'Would you hold him for a moment,' Hera said, 'while I arrange myself a bit.' She looked down at herself. Nanny's milk had spilt over her front.

Sirocco blushed and looked away. The etiquette of such moments was quite beyond the desert rat. 'Yeah, sure,' he said, his throat dry.

Without ceremony, Hera plonked the Baby in Sirocco's lap, stood up and stretched her limbs. There was a surge of release that passed up her body, through her arms to the open sky. Sirocco wanted to shield his eyes from the sight, so looked down at the Baby who was quietly studying his face.

'I'll just go to the water and have a dunk,' Hera said. 'It's nice not to have him. He gets heavy after a while.' She flexed her shoulders to demonstrate that unencumbered feeling.

'Yeah.'

Lying lightly in Sirocco's arms, the Baby stared about at the world at large with the space-case eyes that babies have, eyes full of everything and nothing. In that tiny face those eyes were huge and unfathomable. He guessed they were taking in the whole time-space universe at once, and it gave him a shiver. One moment at a time was more than enough for Sirocco.

To get away from those eyes as much as anything, he watched Hera walk towards the waves. Her step was as proud and upright as he remembered it, but there was a weariness in it, a dragging step that reminded Sirocco, unpleasantly, of the way some of the driftdead moved. A weary insistence. A wilful lethargy. When she reached the waves, she bent over and splashed water on her face, over and over, the same movement.

The Baby clutched at Sirocco's breast.

'Sorry buddy,' Sirocco said to him.

The Baby grinned as if they'd just shared one hell of a joke.

'I like your style,'

The Baby gurgled obligingly.

'You two seem to be hitting it off,' Hera said. Her voice sounded distant, as if she were far off, yet she was standing a few feet away watching them. Sirocco hadn't noticed her leaving the sea and coming back up the beach and grew confused. Surely only a few seconds had passed since he'd seen her splashing water on her face.

'We're buddies,' Sirocco said.

'That's good,' Hera said.

Sirocco didn't know why it was good, or why a sudden relief entered her voice when she said that.

The Baby had turned at the sound of her voice and looked up at her, one hand still possessively clutching Sirocco's chest. Hera looked down at him. Without the Baby on her chest or hip Hera, while still a commanding sight, now looked reduced, smaller somehow, less larger than life. More like an ordinary, if handsome, woman. This transformation made Sirocco uneasy. Maybe it was just that, in his mind, the Goddess could not step down off her pedestal. Or maybe her devolution presaged a shift in the alignment of things, and it was that which was raising the hair on the back of Sirocco's neck.

Hera rummaged in her bag, pulled out a short towel, and began to rub her wet hair with brisk movements, as if trying to rub some vigour into her scalp. It was a perfectly natural action, but it just went on too long, as if she'd forgotten she was doing it.

The Baby frowned and waved both arms at Sirocco.

When she had finally finished with her hair, Hera gave Sirocco the bottle. 'See if he'll take it from you,' she said. 'Just give him a little bit. A little top-up.'

Numbly, no longer properly aware of what was happening, Sirocco took the bottle and offered it to the Baby, who snatched it no questions asked.

'He doesn't cry much,' Sirocco said, feeling awkward again now that the Baby was feeding from him. 'I thought babies were supposed to cry lots.'

'He hardly ever cries, almost never,' Hera said, but her voice was devoid of the motherly pride her words suggested.

They both watched the Baby feeding. One tiny hand was curled delicately around the neck of the bottle.

'Without Nanny we might have lost him,' she said. 'That's enough now. He doesn't know when to stop.'

Sirocco was vaguely aware of the arrangement. Nanny and Billy lived on the marae, and Akona supplied the milk to Hera. Sirocco hadn't thought about it much because it hadn't been important to him, or the lives of the mokopuna; now he saw that without that little arrangement the town's favourite icon, the Baby, might well be dead. And there were others too, women with no babies, eager to knit and sew and wash as if the Baby served for each as their own, offering a little satisfaction to their thwarted maternal instincts. Originally, they were named the baby brigade by some sarcastic wit, but it became a title they enthusiastically embraced. This was a world almost unknown to Sirocco, at least until now.

Hera went onto her knees and began fossicking in the bag. Out came a jersey her size, and a provocative pair of shorts she liked to wear to tease the fishermen and annoy the women. 'Nappies,' she said, 'a wash cloth, safety pins way too small, ointment way too expensive...' she was talking to herself, it seemed, but Sirocco was the one listening.

The Baby burped, spewed up a little milk and gave the big wide universe a grin to match. His laugh came as a milky gurgle at the back of this throat.

'He's having a whale of time,' Hera observed, but objectively, as if she were talking about a child not her own.

'You'd better have him back now,' Sirocco said.

The Baby was light in his arms.

Hera stood up and tucked her jersey and shorts under her arm, leaving the cloth bag on the ground. She looked down at him, her face so melancholy it stopped any further words in Sirocco's throat. It was the face of someone who'd seen everything die and couldn't stop looking.

Then she turned on her heel and walked away, north, up the beach towards Pine Point, leaning forward as if against a head wind.

'Wait!' Sirocco struggled to his feet, trying not to disturb the Baby too much.

But Hera didn't wait. She kept walking and she didn't look back.

a win-win for history and for fiction

The librarian quits the keyboard and enters the awkward present moment with a quiet sense of satisfaction, if not triumph. She's done it! She has patched the narrative wound, and has hardly had to depart from the truth at all. It is all built upon fact! Even the driftdead, the old man with the photos and the other two, the teenager and the woman, she had no need to make up since she has seen them with her own eyes. She well knows, as does everybody, of Sirocco's childlike worship of Hera and all her works - and he is not the only one. She is not called Queen Hera for nothing. Nor does the avid historian have to invent Hera's growing abstraction from the world. A creeping indifference. Some, particularly the reverend, have noticed the trend, and for others it will become clear only in retrospect. The details of the baby brigade are also all true. Writing them in makes the librarian wonder why she hasn't already highlighted them in her Chronicles, since they must have grown out of networks of pioneering women. An oversight she rectifies in her little fiction, giving that fiction a firm footing in reality. A win-win for history and for fiction.

She is surprised by how little she had to make up, just a bit of conversation really, what they might well have said to each other. Her little addition will be virtually indistinguishable from the passages of history around it. It will merge in, disappear in effect, be swallowed by the whole. It will remain her little secret. What the reader doesn't know won't hurt anybody.

The First Person has her uses, she thinks.

There are minor blemishes, as one would expect. Sounds of frenetic building activity from the barricade would have carried to them and should have been mentioned for the sake of verisimilitude. Perhaps when she revised the passage she could add some busy, urgent human sounds to the essentially static scene. More driftdead would have drifted by, but they aren't worth mentioning. It must have happened like this, without fanfare or fuss, almost a sleight of hand; it wouldn't have worked otherwise; Sirocco wouldn't have accepted it. He must have been tricked one way or another, as Hera would not have put it to him directly and risk certain refusal.

One side effect of inserting this narrative is that other, related lacunae become visible to the eye of the curious reader. For example, how did the town react to Hera's abdication and Sirocco's sudden change of status, and who showed Sirocco how to change the Baby's nappies and clean him? And how did Sirocco handle it all? How did he handle the fact that, after Hera walked away from him and he stood up, the Baby, who had lain lightly enough in his arms while he was sitting, weighed a lot more strapped in the front pack?

Despite these unanswered questions, the librarian resisted the lure of making up answers, of trying to fill in every little hole. After all, history itself can never be exhaustive, is always selective and riddled with unanswered questions. Far from being the fraught exercise she imagined, the creation of her 'fictional patch' has been pleasurable, seductively so, and for that very reason I hope she will never have to repeat the exercise.

a swelling river, a vast indifferent mass

Sirocco sits on a rock, his legs dangling down, cradling the Baby in his arms. He has learned, since becoming the baby-bearer, to sit down whenever he can and to keep his movements to a minimum. The mokopuna have to get along without him now, mostly. Except for one. Witch Hunt has attached herself to the Baby and won't let go, even at night when she should be retreating to her room in the schoolhouse. She has turned her back on the cruel Miranda and developed a new object of fixation – Sirocco and the Baby, with the emphasis on the Baby. She sits beside Sirocco, legs dangling in imitation, one eye on the Baby, who as yet hardly acknowledges her despite all her best smiles.

Sirocco has not laboured up Pine Point with the Baby on his chest for nothing. As baby-bearer, the strapping Hera had a number of advantages, and swinging powerfully up hills would be one of them. Sirocco is not so physically robust, and he is reminded of it every time he slings the Baby across his chest. He has come up here to get the best view possible of the territory to the north.

Sitting on the overhanging rock, looking north, he sees that the defenders are doomed, and that the naysayers are right. There are just too many driftdead, straggling over the foothills and stony plain. A swelling river, a vast indifferent mass, threading its way across the old riverbed, the threads converging as they approach Keatown, shaped by the steep encroaching foothills. There are so many they've turned the plain into a dark, swirling muddy colour, like an artist's palette after a stormy session. It looks like the whole landscape is on the move, curling and twisting towards the town.

The fragile-looking, driftdead-proof fence is besieged from the highest point, where it nestles in under an overhanging rock, to its lowest point, just up from the road, where the battle to complete it is under way. Some of the sections work well, with the driftdead forced back by the phalanxes of sharpened sticks, but there are weak points too, where the accumulating mass threatens to overwhelm the skinny defences.

The behaviour of the besieging driftdead is inconsistent, Sirocco notes. Sometimes they will move to avoid a barrier, such as a sharpened stick, but other times they will simply push themselves up against the obstacle regardless of the damage done. Already, from this distance, some of the sharpened stakes resemble toothpicks with bits of driftdead skewered on them instead of cheese and pineapple, and some of the stakes have already broken under the strain, further exposing the barrier. The trench is filling up with driftdead bodies allowing others to walk over them.

Sirocco wonders if this difference of behaviour indicates some sort of intentionality in the driftdead, some rudimentary free will, but soon abandons the idea without exploring it further the way Little Sanyo might. Anyone can see that driftdead behaviour is not willed but random. Some do one thing, some another. One will go around a house, another will try to climb over it. There is no significance either way. No choice worthy of the name.

Not that the labours of the town have been entirely wasted. There is some benefit, some signs of success, with fewer driftdead behind the barricades. A small number are coming in from above, but that was expected.

On the lower section of the defences, closer to his vantage point, a cohort of driftdead are unhurriedly working their way through the stakes and wires of the still-forming barrier. Pinky and his boys are trying to hold them off while Orlap and some stout fishermen desperately thread rusty barbed wire along sagging stakes. The mayor is behind them, pacing up and down, gesticulating. He keeps pointing to the road. They are trying to make a gate. Maybe some more Humvees will come by. A gate to let civilisation in, when it arrives in all its glory, but keep the barbarians out.

In the meantime the driftdead are a solid mass on Highway 6.

'Don't look at them!' the mayor screams. His voice reaches Sirocco as a thin, shredded squeak.

'It's not going to work,' Sirocco says to Witch Hunt. 'There's too many of them. They'll overrun any defence, eventually. It's only a matter of time.'

'Don't say that,' Witch Hunt says. She has taken to grazing along the edge of the pine trees where coprosma and muehlenbeckia grow with their juicy berries. Most are not ripe, yet she finds some choice early berries hidden, the muehlenbeckia that are particularly succulent. Some juice runs down her chin, looking like a little moko.

Witch Hunt has come to hate the very idea of time. In Little House on the Prairie there is no time; little girls get sick but they live forever.

And, as she has tried to tell Miranda, there is something scary about the driftdead, their eyes-wide-open blindness, their solitary purpose, even their spooky silence. Sometime she can hear them screaming inside their heads, but Miranda told her off for making that up. 'What if they can feel things but not show it?' Witch Hunt asks, and nobody can answer her. Nobody cares.

The Baby stares up at Sirocco with solemn eyes. Sirocco has had very little experience with babies, but it seems to him that this one is uncommonly smart, apparently understanding everything he says. Too bad, the Baby seems to say in reply. Too bad for everybody.

'Maybe they'll stop coming,' Witch Hunt says. 'There must be an end to them.'

'Maybe.'

'There must be,' she repeats, this time with insistence.

'Must be,' he agrees in order to avoid a tantrum. Lately, Witch Hunt has been rather touchy on the subject of the driftdead. And she has taken to sucking her thumb, which she started while watching the Baby feed, evidently with some envy.

Sirocco gets to his feet, all too aware of the weight of the Baby on his chest and the backpack, filled with baby necessities, on his back. This is how it feels now, to have this burden.

Because of his new status, Sirocco can go where he wishes and do what he wishes, as long as he tends to the needs of the Baby. That is his sole raison d'être. He is sacred ground, untouchable. Anything he wants that can be delivered is delivered. Akona would turn up with a tray of freshly chopped salad consisting mostly of stubborn sage, coriander, burdock and dandelion leaves. A chewy mix. Since this is not for the Baby he guesses it must be for him, to keep his strength up. The Man in Black will sometimes arrive with a bottle of goat's milk in hand. He doesn't smile, but neither does he measure Sirocco up for a coffin.

Once Grandmother Gaunt turned up at the door with a bowl of pea soup, don't ask her how she found the peas, and a bundle of fresh nappies. Sirocco does not count the irascible old woman his friend; she was most outraged when the transfer took place, accusing Hera of all kinds of diabolical plots, almost ripping the Baby from Sirocco's arms, but that does not prevent her from looking out for the Baby's needs – and those of the baby-bearer. Indeed, we can say that to some extent, and evident in her bearing, the old woman feels vindicated in her previous stance regarding Hera, and even triumphant – again only to some extent, for she would never want anybody to guess her uncharitable feelings. Her outrage at the swap is as much for public consumption than anything else; on a one-to-one basis Sirocco finds her quite practical and occasionally even wise.

'Never give a colicky baby cow's milk,' she once says to Sirocco, who finds that quite wise, even though it has nothing to do with anything, the Baby being most decidedly not colicky.

'It's what the Baby wants,' is all Hera will say to those who accuse her of giving the Baby to the wrong person, and Gaunt would be the last to deny it. The Baby is so obviously happy with Sirocco, laughing and gurgling, especially when Grandmother Gaunt is ranting, that the hullabaloo soon dies down.

Besides, people have other things on their minds. There is a war on. There's no other way to describe it. A desperate war, a last battle even. If the cities of the north have not been able to hold out against the driftdead hordes, how is little Keatown going to make it – geography, that's what the mayor is gambling on: the natural buttress of the hills facing north, the mere half a kilometre of fortifications required.

'Okay,' he says to Witch Hunt. 'Do you think you could carry these nappies? It'll make my pack lighter.'

Witch Hunt obliges, but not without the thought that while the baby-bearer can turn up at any house and be welcome, the same does not apply to a bedraggled little girl with nothing much going for her, not even a pretty curl or two. Just dull rats-tail hair hanging down. Staying by Sirocco's side, she can go everywhere he goes.

They thread their way back through the pines. Sirocco's pack may be a little lighter but his heart is not. Never, in his heart of hearts, has he given up on Keatown, his refuge, the place he was led to by Lizard. There must be a way, there is always a way. Now that he's seen them, the endless hordes of driftdead, his faith fails him. The unfortunate Mellissa Tonguestone does not now seem so crazy in calling the driftdead cockroaches. There they are, infesting every nook and cranny in their scuttling migration. No matter how many you stomped on, more come. The town cannot not stand up to them. It will be overrun.

'It's only a matter of time,' he says. I'm

'Don't say that,' Witch Hunt says.

Around him, the pines stand tall and silent. The disappearance of Keatown and its inhabitants will mean nothing to them. Since the storm, the eerie silence that followed has pretty much remained, with an uncharacteristic lack of on- and off-shore breezes to relieve the atmosphere, which is hot and sweaty, like mid-summer. Now, it seems to Sirocco, that the pines are waiting for a sign, as if it were up to some stirring wind to give them meaning. And they are patient. They can wait a very long time.

Witch Hunt pulls closer. 'This is a spooky place,' she says.

'Pines can be like that,' he says.

'The church where Rasputin sleeps, that's a spooky place too,' the girl says.

'You bet it is.'

the secrets of an orchid

On their way down the track that leads to highway 6, Sirocco and Witch Hunt meet Hera, Orchid and Typhoid Mary coming up. Orchid is out in front, moving with determined steps. Hera comes behind her, dragging her feet, her head down, while Mary comes behind her strolling casually along as if out for a Sunday walk, smoke trailing from her fingertips.

They don't see Sirocco and Witch Hunt at first, as they are focusing on the path and not looking up much. Sirocco stops dead still and allows his breath to steady, just as Lizard trained him to do when a desert cat on the hunt appeared, because if the cats were moving, they were on the hunt, Lizard said. And Orchid has the same lithe movements and watchfulness as a young desert cat. It's nice to have a big rock to scuttle under when a cat appears, Lizard said, but all Sirocco has are the soft shadows of the pines.

When Sirocco stops Witch Hunt does the same, and tries to shrink in behind him. Below them, Orchid turns around and says something to Hera, evidently urging her on.

Seeing them together, Sirocco might have mistaken Hera and Orchid for mother and daughter. The older, a beauty falling into ruin; the younger, doe-eyed and slender, smooth-skinned and full of promise. And seeing Mary and Orchid together, Sirocco might have mistaken them for sisters, one spiky-haired and punky, full of attitude, the other with long soft hair full of sweetness.

Sirocco has to acknowledge his fear, that which any prey might feel in the presence of a predator. He grips the straps on his frontpack, and briefly touches the back of the Baby's head with his lips. The Baby goes into alert mode, fixing his gaze on the approaching group. Just why he feels this way Sirocco cannot quite pin down, but he trusts his instincts as Lizard taught him to do. Your body is more intelligent than you are, he once said to Sirocco.

Mostly likely, he is afraid they have come to reclaim the Baby, tell him that it's all been a big mistake and that the Queen needs her Baby, should never have passed him over to Sirocco in the first place, a foolish act committed in the stress of the moment. After all, he is thoroughly unworthy of this most solemn burden, thoroughly inadequate. It's not just others who feel this way but Sirocco himself. Sirocco had a dream in which he and Lizard found the Baby under a clump of spinifex. A big wind came along and sent the Baby tumbling over the sand, head over heals. Sirocco ran after it but was unable to catch up with it. No matter how desperately his little legs churned through the sand, he could make no progress.

Time and again, since their meeting on the beach, Sirocco has wondered what it must be like to give away your child, let it go tumbling into the world. Surely it's an unnatural thing for a mother to do. Many of the women were saying so, not just Gaunt. It would surprise no one if she were to suddenly change her mind and want him back.

And what could Sirocco say? Surely if she asked him, he would have to comply.

The trio has seen them now. The determined, almost grim look on Orchid's face is replaced by a wide, dazzling smile, directed at the Baby, as if she doesn't see Sirocco and Witch Hunt. Mary smiles too, but there is nothing dazzling about it. It is a superior, knowing smile. Hera doesn't smile at all, her face a neutral mask.

Hera and Mary stop at a comfortable distance, but Orchid keeps coming, right up close, focusing entirely on the Baby. Sirocco steps back, but tries to not let his fear master him, and distort his view of things. After all, Orchid spent much time with the Baby after he was born, and with Hera before he was born. Lately, with all that has been going on, she has hardly had a chance to see him.

Orchid comes up close, smiling at the Baby and cooing, only briefly acknowledging Sirocco. Orchid's charms have never worked on Sirocco. He has always been more wary than attracted; there has always been something sly and secretive about the girl. He scared himself half to death once when he read Dracula, one of the more choice items in the librarian's collection, not so much by the figure of the redoubtable Count, but the three female vampires in attendance, all snake-silky and seductive, with mesmeric eyes, and cooing voices that echo down stony passageways long into sleepless nights. Orchid reminds him of one of those – infinitely fascinating, infinitely dangerous. Perhaps it is just her name, the camouflaged flower, and who knows if the hapless honeybee doesn't feel for the smooth petals the same promise of sweetness, the same sickening pull, that Bram Stoker's hero feels for the female undead.

Perhaps Sirocco has never felt it because the said flower has never turned its alluring face towards him, never had any reason to. After all, he's just the runt who runs around with the mokopuna, always there in the background somewhere but of no interest to the budding woman, and whose desert-bitter scent has never aroused the vampire within.

That, along with many other things, has changed since Sirocco became the baby- bearer. Sirocco has become a person of interest to Orchid, and a recipient of her most brilliant smiles. The Baby, it is all about the Baby. After the birth of the Baby – an event surrounded by much rumour and secrecy – Orchid lived with Hera, attending Mother and Baby in every way, as their personal servant. That was before the pock-marked Typhoid Mary turned up out of God knows where, and, perhaps under Mary's guidance, Orchid began visiting the mansions. After that, rumours began to circulate that Orchid had come to the attention of some fantastically rich recluse, some baron or other – whose existence Sirocco at first found highly improbable – who was going to sweep her away into some fabulous fairy-tale existence any vampire princess would relish, let alone an urchin girl without a home in the decay of the Long Emergency. Yet her interest in the Baby has hardly diminished. It is the Baby that keeps her coming down from the mansions, Sirocco realises.

'We came up here to get away,' Hera says, as if she needs to explain herself, brushing something invisible off her face.

Hera looks older. Her chest has caved in and her shoulders have slumped. Her arms hang limp by her side. Her empty breasts droop. She doesn't look much like a superstar celeb anymore. Or a queen. She looks sad and defeated, like a woman who's seen too much. She looks not just smaller but somehow reduced. Sirocco is reminded of how Bilbo Baggins, after he gave the ring to Frodo, became a pale imitation of himself. Hera is like that. Looks like a good wind would knock her over, Sirocco thinks.

She stares at the Baby without expression.

Orchid's face is a host of expressions as she seeks to establish a connection with the Baby, but they all add up to pretty much the same thing: Hi, do you remember me? Yeah, of course you do! Hello there!

The Baby passes his swimmy, cosmic gaze over her face but doesn't return her greetings. Orchid's disappointment is palpable.

'Doesn't he sometimes get heavy?' she murmurs. Her proximity, and her breathless voice, make it sound as if they are intimates having an intimate conversation. Despite himself, Sirocco flushes. Since becoming the baby-bearer he's had to deal with a lot of attention, women with their faces close to his peering at the Baby, but nothing quite so calculatedly disturbing.

'I can always sit down,' he says.

The Baby reacts to Sirocco's voice with a gurgle, as if Sirocco has just made a joke. He grips Sirocco's arm and pinches, while with his other arm he points, not to Orchid but to Mary, standing as always, a little behind Orchid. Mary is looking at Sirocco with cool grey eyes. She is tugging at her scarf, which is the same colour as her eyes. She tries to smile but Sirocco can see that it's a struggle. Smiling is not a natural expression for her. She would just as soon tear his throat out as smile at him, he figures, but he's not quite sure why. Unless it's the obvious: Orchid wants to be baby-bearer, so it's nothing personal – I'll just tear your eyes out while Orchid snatches the Baby. He doesn't want to think like that, but it's hard not to with Mary's snake eyes on him.

'I can always help,' Orchid says.

'I have my little helper right here,' Sirocco says, patting Witch Hunt on the shoulder as the general might a trusted lieutenant. Witch Hunt, whose face grew glum the moment Orchid appeared, smiles radiantly at Sirocco and holds up her little bag of nappies. Orchid's attempted smile quickly degenerates into a sneer. To preserve her dignity, and not descend into tears, Witch Hunt lifts her chin and looks the other way.

'I've had lots of practice,' Orchid says.

'We're boxing along,' Sirocco says. 'There's always Grandmother Gaunt and the baby brigade.'

'Yes. There's always that bunch of nosey-noses.'

'They have their uses.'

'I suppose so.'

She is standing close, her breasts brushing his elbow, which sticks out a bit because of the front pack. She doesn't seem to notice. Mary is watching her friend's every move, and Sirocco's reaction. Watching them as if they are a couple of insects.

He looks over at Hera, wondering if she's brought Orchid up here to engineer some kind of succession rather than reclaim the Baby for herself. He doesn't like it, the feel of it. Orchid's scent is just a little too heady, her breasts a little too soft. He can see himself, in a giddy moment, handing the Baby over to her.

Orchid too is looking at Hera. 'Well...' she says.

'Well what?'

'You know. All those things we talked about.'

'I'm all sung out,' Hera says.

'But you want me to have him, don't you?' Orchid says, sounding like a petulant teenager.

'A last song,' Hera says. 'Perhaps something by Schubert. Something brisk and uplifting. 'To Wander,' perhaps. Das Wandern from Die schöne Müllerin. One of my favourites. I would often do it as an encore.' She begins to sing in a high, forceful voice, like a trained opera singer,

'From the waters we have learned it
From the waters!
It never rests both day and night
Its mind always set on its travels
The waters...'

'Hera!' Orchid tries not to raise her voice. As Hera continues singing, Witch Hunt sees a most unlikely sight. Between two low pine branches a spider is spinning a web, and in its swinging movements it appears to be dancing to Hera's singing, caught up in the deeper rhythms of the world. No one else notices, except the Baby whose eyes get caught up in the same rhythm.

'The stones even, as heavy as they are
The stones!
They dance along the jolly lines
And yet want to dance faster still
The stones...'

'For fuck's sake stop it now!' Orchid is very red in the face, but Mary is laughing. She gives a slow, ironical clap, a cigarette dangling from the side of her mouth in the manner of Flay. 'Our very own superstar,' Mary says.

'I once found Schubert so uplifting,' Hera says. 'Now I can hardly hit the notes.'

'No, no,' Sirocco says, 'You sound wonderful.'

'At least you've got one fan,' Mary says to Hera.

'Me too,' Witch Hunt says. 'I'm a fan.' The little girl seems quite desperate to be one.

'Will you stop fucking around,' Orchid says in a slow, hard voice, as if she's been taking lessons from the embittered Mavis. 'You betrayed me, remember?'

Hera shakes her head wearily, 'I told you. It's out of my hands now. All of it.' She looks down at her empty hands. They look withered to her, old even. 'And I can't sing Schubert anymore.'

'That's a big loss to the world,' Mary says, casually lighting up a cigarette.

Orchid makes a sound like an animal snarling, a dog or wolf perhaps. A flower snarling at a wolf. Doesn't look quite so pretty.

Softly, the Baby begins to cry, snuggling deeper into Sirocco's chest. It is not a cry of discomfort, or even pain – more like the sobby end of a lament.

To Orchid, Hera says, 'I've done everything I can for you. I've given you everything you wanted, and I've done what you asked. Now I've reached the end of the line.'

Orchid holds there for a moment, her body touching Sirocco's, before stepping back. Her hands are balled into fists. 'But you didn't do what I asked. Not that one important thing.'

'Perhaps I have my reasons.'

'Which you're not going to share, you bitch. You don't think I'm fit to be a baby-bearer, a mother, a guardian. That's what this is all about. You would rather see this pitiful homunculus, this burned out desert rat with only half a brain, more or less a simpleton that those who are even stupider follow around all the time,' a poisonous look goes Witch Hunt's way, 'rather than me. And I...' she breaks off as if rage has got the better of her.

'I've already told you over and over. This is what the Baby wanted.'

'Sure, he sat down with you over a couple of gins and said "Mother, I'd rather go with the ugly runt than you."' And you had another gin and said, 'Sure thing."

'I think you've got a little ahead of yourself,' Hera says, with what may be calm or simple weariness.

'You know,' Sirocco says to Witch Hunt, 'I don't think this conversation has anything to do with us.'

'You know,' Witch Hunt answers in the same moderate tone, 'I think you are right. Orchid is saying horrible things.'

'I don't know what they're talking about,' Sirocco says.

'Neither do I,' Witch Hunt says, somewhat relieved.

Mary is shaking her head sadly.

Sirocco holds the Baby tight. He wants to weep. Here is the world, and here is a child – weep! Or sing another Schubert song.

eternity in the human heart

Like an actor in a play who has been waiting in the wings for his cue, the Reverend Stickman steps out of the shadow of the pines, trying to pretend he's just arrived. Everybody goes quiet and looks at him. Even the spider that Witch Hunt has been watching all along ceases its spinning and turns in his direction.

'Uh... I heard singing,' he says, looking suddenly confused.

'I bet you did,' Mary says.

'I was singing,' Hera says.

'Schubert, if I'm not mistaken.'

Hera looks at him with amazement. 'How did you recognise it?'

'My mother...' The Reverend looks lost, like a little boy, 'She used to play it on the violin. That was before...'

'How terrifically sweet,' Mary says to Sirocco, as if they are both engaged in some kind of sarcastic enterprise together. When she pulls a little at her scarf Sirocco is reminded of the way Sad Toof keeps tugging at the source of his pain.

'You know,' Sirocco says to Witch Hunt. 'I think it's time we got going.' The arrival of the reverend has increased Sirocco's unease. He denounced Hera for handing the Baby over to the pagan desert rat, and made ominous noises about taking the Baby away.

'You know,' Witch Hunt says, 'I think you're right. Everybody's being horrible.'

'You're onto it,' Mary says. She's edging closer.

'Reverend,' Orchid says, 'A question for you.'

'Ye-es'. The reverend is wary of questions these days,

'Should this little... should Sirocco keep the Baby?'

In the silence that follows, Sirocco becomes aware of the creaking of the pines, a sound he never heard in the desert, a sound that can easily put him on edge. Those very trees seem to lean in closer, their shadows stretching out before them. Suddenly he seems very small, not much bigger than Witch Hunt.

'That child belongs to God,' the reverend says. 'First and foremost.'

'Don't we all,' Sirocco says.

'Not all,' the rev says. 'Some worship false gods. Even animals. Or reptiles. Crocodiles. Even a lizard.'

Sirocco laughs. But the fear does not go away. The Baby is no magic shield, earning for its bearer an immunity to insult or attack, even if it feels that way sometimes. Lizard told him he had to listen to his fear or he might die.

'I don't worship Lizard, Reverend. I used to talk to him. He saved me in the desert. Saved my life many times. But he's not a god.'

'Saved by a talking lizard.'

'That's a good one, eh Rev?' Mary says.

The reverend casts his eye her way and does not savour what he sees. He approaches Sirocco and peers in at the Baby, who favours him with nothing more than a passing glance. 'I have seen the burden God has laid on the human race. He has made everything beautiful in its time.' He looks from the Baby to Hera. 'He has also set eternity in the human heart.' He speaks with such a sudden and intense melancholy that for a moment the others are stunned into silence.

The Baby turns away from Sirocco's chest to look at him. His eyes explore the reverend's face as if he were looking at the night sky.

'We listen to the voices of time and forget about eternity,' the reverend says in the same quiet voice.

'That's very true,' Sirocco says, wondering what has come over the preacher, and where all this is leading. Orchid takes an uncertain step back. Apparently the reverend's answer was not what she expected.

Tentatively, the reverend holds out a hand towards the Baby. The Baby puts out a tiny hand and grasps the reverend's finger. Tears roll down Hera's cheeks and she makes no move to wipe them away.

'Whoopie do!' Mary says, but she can't break the mood.

With the Baby still holding his finger, the reverend whispers his favourite lines from Ecclesiastes, 'The dead, who have already died, are happier than the living, who are still alive. But better than both is the one who has never been born, who has not seen the evil that is done under the sun.'

'Oh no,' Sirocco says, 'you can't say that. You mustn't say that. You're putting a curse on the Baby.'

'This unbaptised soul needs no cursing from me.'

'But it's true, what you're saying,' Hera says. 'I often wish I'd never been born. Even before an audience, I would feel it – a kind of hollow feeling.'

The Baby lets go of the reverend's finger.

'His true mother is the right person to have him,' the reverend says.

'So that's what this is all about,' Sirocco says.

The path on which they are standing has grown dark. Sirocco can see the sunlight, way off through the trees. He and Witch Hunt look at each other, seeing the fear in each other's faces – and the determination. If they have to, they will make a run for it.

'It's what I've been trying to suggest to you,' Orchid says, as if hating to be the one to break bad news.

'Is that what you were doing?'

'Whoa!' Mary says. 'The little lizard's got a tongue on him.'

'Do not be quick with your mouth,' the reverend says to Sirocco. 'Godless pagan.'

But there is something wrong with the reverend. Despite the requisite, unctuous tone, he can't look Sirocco in the eye, and he doesn't lift up his arm as if to bring down God's non-pagan thunderbolt on the head of the unrighteous. His heart is not quite in it, but he doesn't look like giving it up either. He can't give it up. Baptism is his line in the sand. More, so much more than just a little water on the Baby's brow, or a dunking in the river. 'He must be named and christened and given to the good women of the town to look after.' He straightens himself up, like a man meeting an enemy. 'Or the devil will take his soul.'

At that statement, the Baby lets out a single long wail.

'You see? Even the child knows.'

'I'm not sure he likes the idea of baptism,' Sirocco says, with one eye on Mary, who seems to be shifting to the side and behind him, cutting off his escape back through the pines.

'I don't think he does,' Witch Hunt says, but nobody takes any notice of her. Little Miss Echo, Miranda would have called her if she had been there.

Hera has been standing back a little, her eyes cast down on the prickly pine needles beneath, but in the silence that follows Witch Hunt's comment, they all hear her mutter, 'I'm sure the good women of the town have plenty enough to occupy them – their tongues are busy enough.'

Here again, the familiar friction point between Hera and the reverend. This is the moment when he should deliver his 'Why did God choose a discarded mansion whore to bear the Baby when there are plenty of good women in town?' speech. But he doesn't. Remarkably, to Sirocco at least, he also forgoes the opportunity to add that, since Hera has abdicated her maternal responsibility as might have been foreseen, the Baby should pass into those safe hands and not into the clutches of the pagan homunculus.

One of these good women, of course, is Melissa Tonguestone, whose cause he previously championed. Now that is not possible, not with Melissa and a couple of friends forming a suicide club, having all but set the date for this blasphemy. That is enough to take the wind out of his sails, perhaps, but it can't be all that is bothering him.

It is equally remarkable that Hera, who has her chance right there to get the boot into the man who has slandered and besmirched her, lets it go by, just like that. Surely her tongue must be aching to make some arch comment about Melissa and her little suicide club being a fine environment for a baby.

They stare at each other, mutually refraining from the final bitter dénouement now facing them.

'But why choose him...?' Stickman says.

'I've told you. I didn't choose Sirocco. The Baby did.'

The reverend gives a loud sigh at the impossibility of the Baby having any opinion on the matter, still less being able to express it. God has blessed babies in many ways, but not with powers of choice.

The Baby rests serenely on Sirocco's chest.

'The Baby discarded me. Not the other way around.'

Stickman hangs his head. He doesn't know what to say. He never thought he would live in a world where the dead walked around and babies discarded their mothers. This can't be God's world.

'Man proposes, God disposes,' he says eventually. But can't find much comfort in it. It seems a rather depressing prospect. Certainly nothing to fire the evangelical heart.

'It's okay,' Hera says. 'The Baby is very happy. See. He loves Sirocco.'

'He does, he does!' Witch Hunt says, doing a little dance.

'You should shut the fuck up,' Mary says to her.

'I'm not afraid of you,' Witch Hunt says, and pokes her tongue out at Mary. Mary has eyes as cold as a cat before it strikes.

'Now there's a delicacy,' Mary says, pulling a knife from somewhere and miming the cutting off of Witch Hunt's tongue. At the same time she takes a sly look at Sirocco to see what effect she might be having on him.

'We're just going to leave it there then, are we?' Orchid says.

Hera doesn't answer her.

'Too much bloody talk,' Mary says. 'Many words mark the speech of a fool. Doesn't it say that in your book, Reverend?' To Orchid she says, 'There's two of us and one runt. It'll be quick and bloodless. I could do it myself, with one hand tied behind my back, but it might not be so quick and it might not be so bloodless.' She gives Sirocco a death's head grin.

It's all on, Sirocco thinks, getting ready to fight. He doesn't stop to think about how he would fight with the Baby on his chest. 'Strike fast and sure,' Lizard says in his ear, just as if he was there. 'Take out her eye with your left hand.' As fast and sure as a Lizard's tongue will slip an insect out of mid air. And she'll never see it coming.

'Oh no you don't!' the reverend says, quick as a flash. Some of his old fire is there, the indomitable warrior of morality. 'I'm not going to let the new mansion whore get her hands on the child, not for one moment. Over my dead body.'

Mary looks him over speculatively.

'Better the pagan has him,' the reverend says.

Orchid turns to Hera, but Hera keeps her head down and says nothing.

Orchid screams with frustration.

Sirocco savours it all in a moment of pure pagan delight.

thinking in tandem

It takes a lot to get Flay to leave his garage and walk the few steps across Highway 6 to Annanda Patel's Sunshine Supermarket, which looks as gaudy as one of those cross-dressing pretty boys of Soho. He has to get all his spitting done before he leaves, as well as making sure that his place is secure from wandering pedestrians. While much of the upper side of Keatown is largely driftdead-free, Highway 6 is still thick with them, and under ordinary circumstances Flay would never have left the premises.

It is curiosity that gets the better of him in the end. He has to take out his little brass pipe, which he made himself of course, and have a few hits of his super-skunk before he can see his way clear to doing it. The necessity of doing it, let's say.

I've seen what I've seen, he repeats to himself, the pipe gone cold in his hand. Orlap and that nasty sidekick of his going into Annanda's supermarket. Innocent enough, maybe, but not innocent enough for Flay. For a start it was first thing in the morning with nobody around, and Orlap wearing that backpack that was weighed down pretty heavily. Flay has seen that backpack before and has a pretty good idea what it contains. So the question becomes, what would Orlap want to buy from Annanda that would take an ingot of Federal Reserve-stamped gold? As far as Flay knows, Annanda doesn't have anything worth much of anything, not any more, not since everything is being sacrificed for the defence of the town. Certainly nothing worth a stick of gold.

Flay smells a rat. A dirty, big fat rat. With dreadlocks. And the only way to flush it out is to cross Highway 6 and confront the pansy on his own turf. Ask him straight out. What's going on, buddy? But why should Annanda tell him anything? Flay might have to give a little to get a little, and he hates doing that. He'd just as soon strangle the little bugger, that would get it out of him fast enough, but the situation suggests caution. Stupid to act out of ignorance. First get the information he needs, then strangle the little bugger. Get it round the right way!

His hand twitches towards his shotgun, which is seldom far away these days. Every now and again he blasts a few pedestrians just to show them who's boss, but they don't seem to get it. In this case, he leaves it behind, securely locked up. Annanda is unlikely to appreciate him turning up with a gun in his hand. He doesn't want to frighten the pansy away.

He pushes his way through the pedestrians, kicking and cursing. Pedestrians have always been beneath his contempt, and this lot of braindead are not much different as far as he can see. A bit like the club set at 4am in Piccadilly. Unlike most in Keatown, he has hardly been affected by the general fear of turning, and the frenzy of activity this fear has released. His prime memory of the Humvee incident is not of the lily-livered youth who shot himself, but the weaponry Big Bill quickly confiscated. Flay's pretty sure he saw a 50-calibre in there. Anyway, he's been living on petrol fumes too long to become a fucking pedestrian, for fuck's sake. Would he walk off up the road and leave his alfie behind? Not bloody likely.

The pansy is there, playing with himself behind the checkout counter. He looks up all surprised as Flay comes in, but that's just campy bullshit, because Annanda will have seen him coming, no doubt of it, and will have had plenty of time to compose himself and get the right expression on his pudgy little face, get his plucked eyebrows in the right shape. Back in London, which is surely on a different planet from Keatown, Flay'd dealt with lots of Indians and Pakis; cunning little buggers they were, always on the make, never playing it straight, fiddle you as quick as diddle you.

'Ah... Mr Flay! This is a privilege indeed. Yes, indeed. In these dark times it is good, is it not, to see a cheerful human face...' He takes a quick look at Flay's face '... at least a real human face... with all these Rakshasa around... it's enough to test our endurance... it certainly is...'

Flay tries to ignore the mockery – privilege indeed! – and to concentrate on the issue at hand. He resists the urge to spit on the scuffed but shiny linoleum floor. The pansy sure keeps the place spic 'n span; you can see the fairy-dust sparkle on everything, the pinks and purples. For an intense moment he wishes for nothing more than to be back in the drab, grey realism of his garage.

'Look...' he says. He thought it would be easy and that he would know just what to say, but suddenly, with the expectant eyes of Annanda on him, he can't think of the right words. He shouldn't have had that extra hit of skunk – tied up his tongue at the last minute. 'I've got my interests to protect.'

'Most assuredly. In these dark times our interests loom even larger in our minds. I myself lie awake at night and wonder how it's all going to turn out. I toss and I turn, break into a sweat, but still I am none the wiser.'

Flay doesn't really want to hear the gory details.

'Look around you. What do you see? Empty shelves. Shortages of vital supplies. Surely it must be the same for you?'

Flay's not going to fall into that one. Admit to the fairy that he's running out of gas? Ha ha. But he's not silly enough to deny it. 'I need to know what Orlap is up to. There's a game on the go, and I want to know the whats and the wherefores.'

'Ah! The whats and the wherefores – you put it so well. You know good sir,' Annanda grows expansive, 'on the field of battle my distant ancestor, the great Aranju, found his heart quailing before the battle, and at the sight of the army of the foe before him. At the crucial moment, when he was about to abandon the battlefield, the god Krishna revealed himself to him, and counselled him, and put some steel into his will...'

'Yeah, yeah, hari Krishna.'

'We may need to find that steel in our own wills if we are to win this battle.'

'You've lost me with all this jibber-jabber. Who is we?

'You and I, sir. Pillars of the local business community.'

'Orlap and Butch came here this morning, didn't they? Before you opened even.'

'You saw them, Mr Flay, so that can hardly be a question.'

'What did they want? Were they buying?'

'Not exactly.'

'Well spit it out!'

Annanda stands up. It doesn't seem to make a lot of difference to his height, but it does to his dignity. 'I prefer to keep my business relations confidential, sir, as I'm sure you do. You don't strike me as the sort of person who would be gossiping about his customers, no sir...'

'Just quit the crap and tell me what the ropehead wanted.' Dealing with these people, it always gets down to this in the end, he thinks. It's alien to their nature to tell the truth. They'll only do it under duress. Extreme duress. 'Gold. He had gold, didn't he? Ingots.'

'A rare commodity, especially in these...'

'...dark times, yeah, I get it, but you see, I've got one too.'

'I am begging your pardon. You have what, sir?'

'One of them ingots with the Federal Reserve stamp. You can just drop it into the Feds and they'll give you a bucket of money.'

'Then you are a very fortunate man, sir. You can show it to your grandchildren.'

'I don't have any grandchildren.'

'I am very sorrowful. It is unfortunate for any man of fitting years not to be a grandfather.'

'You do realise that there is only one place that that gold can come from?'

Annanda ponders, as if considering the question for the first time. 'I see we are thinking in tandem, Mr Flay.'

'I doubt it.' There is, he perceives, something obscene in the idea. The fairy is pulling his tit. Another unpleasant idea. 'Whoever is throwing around this gold will want his pound of flesh.'

'The baron has never been renowned for his munificence.'

'If you mean he's a stuck-up, stingy bastard you would be right. But how do you know it's him, exactly? It could be that Strongbow bloke. Or those Swiss nutcases, nudists or whatever they are.' He's heard that the Swiss couple like to run around nude in the snow, but he doesn't believe everything he hears. 'Did Orlap say something?'

'He was saying nothing, my friend. He was keeping his lips tightly sealed.' Annanda demonstrates. Not a pleasant sight. Flay shudders and moves on.

'What did he want to buy?' He can hear his voice grating in his ear, sounding like an old woman trying to change gears. Annanda's voice, on the other hand, is as smooth as oil pouring from a can. Flay is tired of dancing with the fairy. 'What was he buying?'

Annanda considers deeply. Finally, all in good time, he comes to a decision. 'He wasn't buying, sir. He was hiring.' Annanda holds up his hand, forestalling the next grating question. 'He wanted to hire my truck. My delivery truck.' Annanda sounds quite wounded at the idea, outraged even.

'Your truck.' Flay knows the truck, has even worked on it a couple of times. Nothing special. A twenty-foot Isuzu, sixteen tyres, two-hundred-and-ten horsepower – the usual piece of shit. Not like his own old Bedford RL, the beast that never dies and which, to his advantage, runs on petrol not diesel. Bedfords, the mothers of all trucks.

'But Mr Flay, sir, before you are asking your next question. I did not rent out my truck. My truck is not for hire, as I told him. In better days I would use it to deliver all manner of goods to my customers. Now, in these darker times, it has seen loyal service in the battle against the Rakshasa...'

'What did they want with it?'

'This, good sir, he would not divulge. Another reason for not renting it to him, if I may say so. What if he were to exceed the weight limit, for example?'

Flay decides that the fairy is probably lying. Flay can't imagine him turning down a bar of gold for such flimsy reasons. Then again, people do get funny about their vehicles. Flay himself wouldn't let anybody else but himself behind the wheel of alfie – although he might be persuaded with a bar of gold. You can do some wonderful things with greed.

'Let's find out what he wants it for, then.'

'I'm sorry sir, I'm not following...'

'I mean, you should agree to rent your truck to him if he tells you what he wants it for. Then we'll know.'

'But I don't want to rent my truck to him.'

'You don't have to. You just tell him you will.'

'But that is terribly unethical, sir. Not my way of doing business, sir.' He sounds offended that Flay should even suggest such a thing. What a pretender! Covering his arse at every step.

'Well, I reckon we should know what's going on. He and that Butch. It can't be good.'

'But it is his business, Mr Flay. I don't like to be interfering in other people's business.'

'Of course you don't. Unless it suits you.'

Flay turns to go. He's not going to get anywhere. It's like talking to a toffee apple. Everything gets sticky. Flay wants to get back to his garage and wash his hands and have a resuscitating toke on his pipe.

'I will think on what you have said, Mr Flay, because I too am curious, of course; but you remember what they say about curiosity and certain feline creatures.'

'Yeah, yeah. A pansy must've said that.' He's reached the door. The sight of the pedestrians passing no longer looks so bad.

'But just before you go, Mr Flay – I too have a question.'

Flay lingers reluctantly, his hand on the door.

'You too have a truck. A Bedford if I am not mistaken. An RL, a most noble beast. Perhaps Orlap has tried to hire your truck, also.'

That is true. To a point. Flay has the usual arrangement with Orlap to deliver the diesel to the wharf on his RL when the The Merry Widow is ready to sail. The fisherfucks will pump the gas into the boat and Flay take the empty tank away. And Flay will be one gold bar richer. No need to tell the pansy about this of course. Orlap is not exactly hiring his RL.

'Naw.' He opens the door. He can feel Annanda's eyes on his back.

'This is a space we must be watching,' Annanda says.

why does God make it so difficult for everybody?

After the incident with the Humvees, and the suicide of the desperate youth, Rasputin goes into seclusion in the old church once more. He is haunted by images he can't get out of his head. The youth, surely not that much older than himself, holding a gun up to his head. Blood flying everywhere in the crepuscular light. The greedy look on the mayor's face as he hauls the weapons out of the back of the Humvee, while his redheaded harpy screeches at him. The silent, stricken figure of his mentor, the reverend, who is staggering under some burden he doesn't talk about. Rasputin has seen his increasingly frail figure ghosting around the streets of Keatown whispering to himself the husks of Ecclesiastes. Vanity, vanity – it has all come back to haunt the preacher.

Rasputin welcomes the bleak austerity of the church the way a flagellant welcomes the sting of the whip. The unyielding stone of the floor and walls. The brutal simplicity of the rough-cut rafters. It is like a prison cell without the amenities. Emptied of its pews, its altar (if it ever had one), and any kind of furniture or adornment, it is as inhospitable a room as you would find anywhere, which suits Rasputin just fine.

Or, if he prefers, he can sit, unseen, in the shadow of the doorway and look across the road, to the school where Witch Hunt mostly sleeps, and east to highway 6 where the driftdead, unloved by God, go their silent and implacable way. Further north he can just make out the roof of the library, and the Great Futility, the mayor's barricade, on which work proceeds day and night.

Typical of his present state, he cannot quite decide if sitting in the doorway looking out at the world is an escape from his penance or a part of it. Penance? That's what it feels like. The comings and goings of humanity, the vacant movement of the driftdead, even the motion of the stars, may be seen as a distraction, an excuse to tear his eyes away from the terrifying face of God.

As if to prove the point, during his first night in the doorway he sees

Orlap and Butch coming down Beauty Parade, kind of half sneaking along the way people do when they are getting up to something, or just have been. At the same time they are talking intently, like conspirators. This observation reminds him unpleasantly of other things, things his slippery mind would avoid given half a chance, but of course God never gives that half a chance, not on this earth. Speculating on what Orlap and Butch are getting up to is just the kind of distraction his mind is eager for, despite the unpleasant associations. Rasputin wonders if they are sneaking down from the mansions, and, if that were the case, what they might have been doing up there. After all, they don't have any fish to sell.

Why the mind would want to occupy itself in fruitless speculation about the lives of others, rather than face its God and Maker, is one of those mysteries of mind, but not one he now has time for. He's much better off inside, with the stout wooden door firmly closed, upon his knees on the hard grey stone, with nothing but the hard grey walls to look at. Prayer is one of the reverend's gifts to his protégé, how to be humble in your soul and commune with God – perhaps the greatest of all gifts. The reverend taught him how to bare his soul to God, which is perhaps the most difficult thing a human being will ever have to do. To pray takes courage. Nobody told him that until the reverend showed it to him by example, how to face down the inner demons, how to drop the masks of vanity, how to approach God in fear and trembling.

However, he seems to have lost the art of praying, which means his humility is compromised and vanity is still at work in him. Truth is, he doesn't have to look far to find it, for it is there, raging away like Sad Toof's eternal pain. In the face of it, his thoughts are nothing more than thoughts, so immaterial and effervescent as to count for nothing. As for asking God for help, surely, God being God, must see, in his infinite wisdom, that help is needed. Wringing one's hands before God seems craven and gratuitous, and he can't imagine God being very impressed.

Rasputin thinks of his mentor, the reverend, on his knees before the overturned Humvee, appealing for mercy perhaps, or making his abject confessions to God. But the look on his face. Like a man straining his bowels. Rasputin doesn't want to look like that.

This is not the first time he has been at a loss over how to pray, and once sought advice from the reverend. Rasputin said that he was finding it hard to dwell on the image of the Lord, or hold that image firmly before him in prayer, which meant his mind was distracted by every passing thought. The reverend had grown quite stern, even angry. 'Do not make graven images. Even of the mind. They too are vanity. Next thing you will be worshiping a piece of carved wood or a painting. Would you worship a few colours scratched on a wall?' He invited Rasputin to consider the images painted by that sybarite, Michelangelo, on the ceiling of the Sistine Chapel. Grotesque cartoon images of God, which were an abomination in themselves, or, at least, a joke, a perversion.

'You can't think your way to God,' the reverend advised him. 'Thoughts won't do that. You can't paint the face of God. You have to walk there.'

'Why does God make it so difficult for everybody?' Rasputin wanted to know.

'It's not God that makes it so difficult. It's us.'

All he needs to be is quiet and humble and God will gently, and naturally, fill his soul the way dawn light fills up a valley. Sounds simple enough, but when he comes to do it, his wretched heart gets in the way. How can you pray when your heart is in agonies and your being is on the rack – what can prayer be then but a despicable scream for mercy?

The nature of this pain is not the least bit uplifting. It has to do with lusts and desires and tormenting jealousies. His thoughts may strain upward towards God, but his body remains firmly stuck in the muck. Jealousy is a simple word, but the reality is monstrous. It devours everything. How can he humble himself before God when all he can see is the smiling Orlap and Orchid together at the fish shed party, close together, like two people used to being intimate, just how intimate is the question that takes him directly into Hell, the fiery furnace.

He opens his eyes, which he has been screwing shut, and the dim light of the church flashes reds and purples. Does God require eyes shut for prayer? Pluck them out, perhaps.

'Ahhhhhhhh!' he releases a long, animal cry, just like the damned in Hell, but it doesn't help. Of course he knows about his secret feelings for Orchid, his intense self-consciousness around her, but this is something quite different, quite unheralded. No warning. Just a sudden unleashing of feeling. All it takes is a few seconds. Seeing them together as the mayor began unpacking the weapons from the Humvee. Heads leaning towards each other. Like conspirators.

Then he sees it, courtesy of the cruel eye of jealousy. It is not like conspirators. They are conspirators. They are in cahoots, he thinks, drawing some thin comfort from the strange word. Allies. Partners in crime. Now a new question arises. If they were – ah, God help him! – falling in love, then why try to hide it? The women of Keatown have been matchmaking Orlap for a long time now. A procession of hopefuls have tried their chances, but he's spurned them all. Rumours that he must prefer men have come to nothing. Now this. His mind can only touch it the way a hand can touch a fire, briefly and warily. He wonders how come they have hidden it so well, or if they have just started.

He remembers how she reacted as if stung when, sitting under The Wanderer before the Humvees arrived, he asked her, jokingly, if anything had turned up, referring to a conversation they had had on Pine Point when she told him of her ambition to become a famous dancer. Perhaps Orlap had turned up, which is why she reacted to his question. And maybe she was thinking about Orlap on Pine Point, when he imagined she was just indulging in wishful thinking, and had even felt sorry for her because of it. Maybe even then, in her mind, she'd been counting on him.

He remembers the second moment at the roundabout, when she'd talked about Hera and the Baby immediately after her adverse reaction to his question. That was before Hera... his line of thought breaks off as new possibilities occur to him. The timing of these events is suggestive. Hera could have handed the Baby on to Sirocco because she knew something, knew there were moves afoot to take the Baby from her. She could have done it rightly guessing that Sirocco would protect the Baby from... well, not from Grandmother Gaunt, a woman full of piss and wind... but Orchid. Orchid and Orlap. Orchid, who stuck so close to Hera during the pregnancy and afterwards because she wanted, and still wants, to be the mother.

He remembers too much and therefore imagines too much.

Rasputin is way out of his depth. His mind is like a drowning man casting around for a lifeline. He gets up off his knees – no point in pretending he's praying – and paces around the church, his feet hitting hard on the cold stone, and gives himself over to his tumbling thoughts, thoughts that seem to be pouring out of his torn heart rather than his mind. He can't see why Hera wouldn't pass the Baby on to Orchid. After all, Orchid is dedicated to the Baby. And, with Orlap eager to do anything to please his lover, the Baby would have the prospect of a father. No need for Hera to take fright. It all looks pretty good, except... except the shadow from the mansions. The shadow of corruption. It is not Orchid or Orlap that worried Hera, but the baron. Baron Fairweather. His growing influence over Orchid.

It is here he feels the real battle shaping up. Sooner or later the evil power up mansions would have to be confronted.

Knowing Orchid as well as she does, Hera is in the best position to observe the changes in Orchid. Rasputin has already noticed them, felt the air of deceit and corruption around her, so Hera might well have noticed the same – or even more. Further changes that Rasputin cannot see, for the Father of Lies likes to stay out of sight for as long as possible. Hera is afraid of the baron because the baron... Rasputin struggles to make the connection because it is so horrible... wants to get his hands on the Baby for his own hideous purposes, and will use Orchid to do so.

He staggers under the thought, hardly able to keep his feet. It is a vision of evil his poor frame is ill-equipped to handle. Hera of course would be on to it, because the mansions are where she came from. She might even have had some prior dealings with the baron, enough to want to keep the Baby out of his clutches.

A swarm of subsequent thoughts follows. Orchid will use, or try to use, the not-so-smart fisherman to help her, and so together they plot. They put their heads together. Lovers, conspirators, Orchid wittingly or unwittingly the baron's catspaw. It is actually the baron who has 'turned up'. The possibility is that Orchid has been playing the baron, dangling the prospect of the Baby before him. The baron, whose soul was long ago sold to the Father of Lies, now feeds on the souls of others, innocent souls. What a delicacy the Baby would be for such a vampire.

What could the baron offer Orlap in return for handing the Baby over to him? That part is not clear, but he has just seen Orlap and Butch coming down Beauty Parade. It may be possible that the baron has corrupted Orlap also, and that Orlap could be planning to betray Orchid. In a gruesome way, that idea appeals to him; finally Orchid will be forced to see through her false friend, her false lover – there is something pleasing in the idea.

The baron could be manipulating both of them to get his hands on the Baby, setting them up against each other as the Father of Lies will do.

As if struck from behind, Rasputin falls back down to his knees. The horror of it. This thing, this demon of the mansions reaching his reeking hand into the heart of Keatown, plucking what it fancies, toying with its prey.

He tries to give thanks to God for these understandings, to be grateful for them, for the reverend would argue that they are a form of Grace, a gift from God, but Rasputin can't see it that way. More like a curse laid upon his heart. This 'gift' brings no relief but rather infinitely increases his agonies. He clutches his chest as if God were about to rip it out of his body, and he could hold it in by sheer human will, the will of bone and sinew.

His vision is no less than of a damnation that spreads like a virus as the shadow of the demon grows. First Typhoid Mary, the plague bearer, then Orchid, seduced by the baron, then Orlap, deceived by his love for Orchid. And now the Baby. Finally it touches Rasputin himself, even here in his bleak sanctuary, because of his passion for Orchid. He can feel the cold breath of the Father of Lies as if he were right beside him. Hear that spidery voice, spun out of the void, showing him how he could satisfy his desires. The voice twisted a noose around his heart. All he had to do was take the Baby from Sirocco and give him to Orchid and she would be his for the asking

Yes, yes, he can see how that would work.

the genius of Pinky

Living as she does, with the barrier right at her back door, gives the librarian ample opportunity to assess the progress being made. It is, she understands, a work in progress and will be as long there are driftdead to besiege it.

But progress has been made. Some sections of the barrier, the area near her place included, are standing up well, but other sections, particularly near and on the road, are proving difficult if not impossible. The librarian quietly suggests to the mayor that the lower section remain open to act like a sort of safety valve, allow some through and take the pressure off the rest of the barrier. If they enter near the highway they will pretty much stay on or near the road until they clear the town. Big Bill does not dismiss the suggestion, but nor does he seize on it as a sensible compromise. Big Bill, she realises, is so deeply afraid of deserting that he doesn't want a single driftdead passing through Keatown. He believes, with superstitious fervour, that if he can keep all the driftdead out, he can put an end to desertion.

Despite the ongoing nature of the project, work on it gradually falls away as the weary folk of Keatown return to the job of putting their lives back together. Even Orlap has returned to the arduous task of getting The Wanderer back into the water. This means the librarian's suggestion comes about more or less by default. Now that the defence is doing its job, only a small team remains to maintain the barrier and continue work on its weak spots, and there are always weak spots.

This small team is led by Pinky who has, in the process of helping in the construction of the barrier, and his enthusiastic participation in the war effort, been transformed. Pinky has found his mission in life, and has dedicated himself to it to the very last of his energies: to keep back the hoard of driftdead. All that random, violent, bullying energy now has a focus, a channel. Pinky has found his true vocation, has thrown himself into his chosen task with all the will of the fanatic, and, like many a fanatic, he has attracted a small band of followers who share his obsession and bow before his manic energy.

It is not surprising that Pinky has become the mayor's right-hand man.

In the process, Pinky has developed more ways of killing, maiming and generally disabling the driftdead than anyone would have thought possible, astonishing everybody, particularly the mayor, who will now give these hooligans-cum-holy warriors anything in his power to give. One of Pinky's more ingenious innovations involves a trench with a couple of wild pigs, enraged wild pigs, roaming up and down its length. When the driftdead stumble into the trench – slash, crunch! The pigs do all the work, killing, maiming and disabling. This idea works pretty well, at least at first, but after a time even the pigs get tired of rooting in the gore and never develop much of a taste for driftdead flesh. Anyway, there are not enough pigs in the kingdom to make it viable on a large scale. Another stroke of Pinky genius was to construct a kind of cattle-run that leads to a chute that tumbles the driftdead down into an inferno of blazing driftwood. It makes quite a sight, especially at night, with the driftwood flaring all kinds of strange colours as the sulphur in it burns, and the uncomplaining driftdead floundering around in a pit of aquamarine flames. Some, still in flame, step on the bodies of the fallen, make it out of pit and veer off into the dark like the Burning Man come to life.

It works tolerably well, and is very dramatic, but again it can't be applied on a large scale. Even if there is enough wood in the kingdom, there aren't enough hands to carry it, nor enough pits to burn them all, the hordes from Hell. For a while Pinky toys with a scheme of Flay's to build a 'fucking great electric fence and fry the bastards,' but there is no way of getting that kind of electricity. Most of the town freeloads on the mansion cables, and there is no way our ad hoc electrical system could carry that kind of power, no matter how much number eight wire Flay conjured from dim recesses of his garage. Besides, no one knew if the driftdead would feel a bolt of electricity, and no one cared.

Another of Pinky's innovations was based on the idea that simply blinding the driftdead would be enough to blunt their purpose, slow them down mightily. For a while he had his team running around poking burning sticks into their eyes, even training Little Sanyo and Sad Toof to do the same. Again, the device had limited success as the blinded driftdead soon regained their inner compass, and resumed their journey, albeit impaired.

Still, due to their efforts, the barrier holds. Not a hundred percent maybe, not even ninety-five percent, but enough to slow the driftdead down to a trickle, mostly along the road.

That trickle is what holds the librarian's interest as she stands outside the library looking north. A precarious normality has returned to Keatown. The mayor is doing a victory walk up and down the barrier, clasping his hands above his head, shouting out his triumph.

The fish shed is restored and opened! Men can go back to work! Work on The Merry Widow is almost finished, the fishermen will put to sea, the fish will come rolling in, and Keatown will get to its feet again!

Santa Lucia

The day the fish shed opens its doors, Big Bill declares that a party is due, and rolls out a barrel of brandy he's been keeping for a rainy day. Then Ock Arglin turns up, as he is wont to do on these occasions, along with a donkey blessed with a burden of distilled mountain liquor: Ock's famous hock. A somewhat desperate party is held in the fish shed, during which exhausted people sit around and stare hollow-eyed at each other while they get drunk – even the librarian has a tipple or two – or laugh too long and loudly at nothing. Their laughter bounces off the corrugated iron walls of the fish shed back into their faces.

Gypsy Cornet rigs up her miraculously still-functioning CD player and cranks up some Arabic reggae, but nobody has the energy to dance, not even Gypsy, and the music sounds strange in our ears, as if it were from another world, which it is if you think about it – a world without the driftdead, the shadow of whom, even now, passes behind our eyes. The reminder of that other world is a little too poignant for some, and Jolene breaks down and cries and has to be comforted by a maudlin Grandmother Gaunt, who's maybe had one over the odds herself.

The only one who seems to have regained her smile and good humour is Mother Smiley, and no one is quite sure why. Little mysteries. Without them no town would be complete, and the gossipers have nothing to talk about.

Even the normally indefatigable Orlap retires to a corner with a monstrous spliff and seems to spend most of the night watching Sirocco and the Baby with red-rimmed eyes. Every so often the spliff will light up and fade like a third eye opening and closing. Orchid is there, but she sticks close to Hera and ignores Sirocco and the Baby altogether, which suits Sirocco okay. Typhoid Mary is with her, of course, and every time she meets Sirocco's eye she gives him a wink, as if they share some vastly amusing secret.

The reverend is busy shepherding Melissa Tonguestone and her little suicide group, encouraging them to join the festivities and, by so doing, rejoin the community without which the individual must wither on the vine. Melissa, in defiance of her once devout abstinence, recklessly throws herself at the alcohol, then at the men, then she passes out. This is not quite what the reverend had in mind, but a passed-out Melissa can't kill herself – that will have to be faced with the hangover later.

Rasputin accompanies his master, but his heart is not at rest. His revelations in the old stone church are still very much with him. Every time he looks at Sirocco and the Baby he thinks of Baron Fairweather, that powerful agent of darkness, reaching out his hand towards the Baby through those he can influence: Orchid, Mary, Orlap... each with the stain of darkness upon them. A stain which grows with every passing hour.

Thinking these thoughts he can hardly look at Orchid, who looks so beautiful and self-possessed. There is something different about her, something new and disturbing he can't or doesn't want to identify; something that may only come from self-knowledge, but which Rasputin identifies with the evil influence of the baron. Behind this lies a more terrible thought. That she enjoys her corruption, draws strength and identity from it; that she has moved from being a victim to an active participant in her downfall. Stealing the Baby and handing him over to the Devil himself would put the seal upon her damnation.

These thoughts are fuelled by the sight of Orchid approaching Orlap, sitting beside him and talking to him. When she lights up in a wonderful smile, a smile to light the world, he sees, with the harsh clarity that jealousy brings, that she is in love with him. But why secret lovers? Why hide it? This is the one thing he can't understand.

Unexpectedly, Hera appears, dressed in a sequinned gown and, without any accompaniment, lifts her voice in song. The song is Santa Lucia, a Neapolitan folk song made famous by Caruso, if I am not mistaken. The plaintive yet powerful delivery catches everybody up in suspension. Surely this is nothing less than a heartbroken farewell to the world. Her voice recalls a lost richness of tone, but has gained something too, an ethereal quality, as if from the choir of the Order of Angels. It is a voice that calls everybody home and the world to rest. Frail and vulnerable, it is the voice of the doomed. Yet everybody sees, if only for a moment, the star she must once have been.

Afterwards, in the stunned silence, Orlap lurches to his feet and claps loudly while his sidekick, Butch, swears publicly that she will never love another woman. The Reverend Stickman, who has not partaken in any of the intoxicants of course, stands transfixed as Hera sings, his eyes so huge the whites show beneath the pupils, which are as black as the devil's heart.

All along the good reverend has been harbouring a secret resentment he keeps well concealed, even from himself, perhaps even from God. God has seen fit to visit Rasputin and grant him a vision, even touch him with grace, while the reverend himself, who has always believed in Rasputin and taught him all he knows, God has passed over in silence, leaving him with nothing, granting him nothing – he is nothing but the husk of a man who has served only his God.

Now, in this ecstatic moment, he gives thanks to the good Lord, infinite in his mercy, who has finally granted the faithful man a boon, vouchsafed him a glimpse of the infinite in the voice of this woman, who he once despised – and something more has the Lord given, so much more, a glimpse of the infinite: a gift so vast it is terrifying.

A gift he cannot name.

her librarian mask

When Miranda turns up the next morning at the library door, the librarian doesn't assume it is a book she is looking for, but quickly puts on her librarian mask anyway to greet her.

It isn't clear what she wants. She just wanders into the library, looking lost, and passes by the shelves with barely a glance at the books. Her demeanour is so listless that for one sinking moment the librarian thinks she has turned. She has been expecting that sooner or later the mokopuna will start to turn. Why should they be immune? In her darker moments, she thinks that it's only a matter of time before everybody turns, and there'll be no one left to turn off the lights.

'They never cry,' Miranda says, catching at some books with her fingers but not seeing them.

'They never laugh either,' the librarian says.

'But they never cry,' Miranda insists, as if the silly librarian has missed the point.

'Why should they cry? I mean, especially.'

'Because of all they have lost.' The curly blonde girl turns her dry-eyed gaze on the librarian. 'And they have lost everything, except one little thing they carry along.'

'Maybe they don't remember that they have lost everything.'

But that doesn't gel with Miranda. It is too much like adult logic. Miranda knows how she'd feel if she lost everything. And she almost has. First she lost her father, Blade, then her best friend, Witch Hunt, who turned into a clinging little pest, and now, she feels, she has lost her mother, Jolene, to some silly conspiracy being hatched by her and her sister, Mother Smiley, that has something to do with the mayor.

She doesn't like Mother Smiley's new, smiley face. The old grumpy one is more familiar.

You'd have thought that after losing her husband, Jolene would turn to her daughter for mutual emotional support, and that mother and daughter would forge ever-closer ties, but this did not happen. Quite the opposite. Jolene rejected Miranda as if the disappearance of the father erased the daughter from existence. Now Miranda has nobody except the company of those equally lost, like Little Sanyo and Sad Toof. The remnants of the mokopuna.

'I'm afraid,' the little girl says, pale skinny fingers still touching the books as if for reassurance. There is something conclusive, definitive, about a solid, printed book.

'What are you afraid of?' the ham-fisted librarian says. What a stupid question! She could have written something more oblique, with a bit of cunning in it.

The girl answers simply enough, 'I can't cry.'

The librarian has nothing to say to that. Those pretend people, those walking parodies – she hates them for their brute insistence. Hates them for what they have done to this little girl.

'Do you dream about them, have nightmares?'

'No. I don't dream about anything anymore.'

It has occurred to the librarian that some of the Science Fiction stories that Little Sanyo loves so much contain 'portals' that connect one world, or one dimension to another. If the driftdead were coming through some kind of portal between the conscious and the unconscious mind, dreams might be rendered redundant. There are a lot of what ifs when it comes to the driftdead.

'What are the driftdead?'

It's painfully touching, her thinking the librarian would know the answer. The librarian knows everything! Well, she tried. At the beginning of the invasion, she consulted the library on the origin of the term zombie, tracing it back to Trinidad, where men, after being given a voodoo drug that made them appear dead and slowed their metabolism to almost nothing, were buried for some weeks and then dug up, to be used as zombies, obedient workers who never slept, who were alive but in a death trance. The walking comatose.

After the blood-drained driftdead got up and walked, the drug theory went out the window, along with just about all other explanations, from viruses to a plague of madness. Even a virus can't make a dead man walk.

She's tempted to turn to the First Person Singular for some answers, as if the whole thing were my fault. She is deeply resentful and I don't blame her. For her, it is a question of identity. While I can be her, she can never be me, and this upsets her. I must, perforce, know more about her than she does about me. I am the medium in which she exists, and she can never accept that, not quite, just as the skeptical fish might have to be convinced of the existence of the ocean.

'Can I stay here – just for a liddle while?' Miranda says.

The librarian has been dreading this, the library filling up with waifs and strays. Now she is faced with an unpalatable choice.

'Just for a while. Witch Hunt won't come, I promise. I don't feel so afraid here.'

'Why's that?'

'Because once you read us a book that made me cry.' She waves a hand at the shelves of books.

'Which one? I could read it to you again, so you can cry.'

'I don't remember. I don't remember what was sad about it.'

The librarian does not have an iron heart, and can be moved to pity, but what if more come? she asks herself. Mokopuna sleeping all over the place. The librarian's privacy shattered. The library is no place for a crisis resource centre. As long as the library remains sacrosanct – which it has, keeping out the storm and the subsequent driftdead – it remains a sanctuary for the fruits of civilisation. A little place in the world where nothing has changed, and books can go on dreaming the way they do in their eternal past, and the librarian can go on doing what she thinks she's doing.

'Just for a little while,' the librarian says.

'I brought my own food,' the little girl says. 'I won't be a nuisance.'

'You can't sleep here, in the library itself. You'll have to sleep in the lobby, or up in the house.' Anxiety is a lonely feeling. The librarian feels it, Miranda feels it. I cannot help but be touched by it myself.

Miranda nods vigorously. Yes, the lobby will be just fine!

With a heavy heart the librarian leaves the girl where she is, with some books to look at, and goes into the lobby to figure out where she might sleep. A nice little corner somewhere, where she can't readily be seen. Tucked away. The librarian is disgusted with herself but there it is. Not having an iron heart comes at a price.

She's just about figured how it is all going to work, with the minimum of impact on her own life – it will be just as if the girl is not there – when someone enters the main door of the courtyard. It is a girl, older than Miranda, almost a teen, dressed pretty much in rags, but with an attractive walk. She doesn't pause but walks with unhurried steps towards the library.

It takes the preoccupied librarian a full moment to realise what has happened, and a great rage takes hold of her. I can't account for that rage now, for the totality of it, but I can't think of anybody else in the town capable of it. It completely overpowers her. She seizes the spade she used to clear the sand away from the door and approaches the girl, who could have been one of the mokopuna – there is a sweetness and innocence about her. Slicing the spade sideways like a sword, in a single vicious blow, the librarian half-severs the unnamed girl's head from her body. The head hangs down her back where it stares at the world, upside down, while the body keeps walking that same easy, attractive walk before sliding down onto the sand.

Still quaking with rage, the librarian hurls the spade down like a spear, severing the last piece of skin and spine holding the head on. She looks up to see Miranda standing in the doorway watching her and biting her nails.

'Cockroaches,' the girl says in very adult tones.

'Right.' The librarian drags the body to the outside gate. In the past she's escorted them out, the few that found their way in.

Miranda follows her.

'I don't like you watching me all the time,' the librarian says, her whole body shaking. 'I'm a very private person. If you stay here, even for a little while, you're going to need to know that.'

'I know that,' the little girl says solemnly, but she keeps watching as the librarian cleans the bloody gore off the spade by slamming it in and out of the sand a few times.

the last sad orgy at the end of the world

Meanwhile, Baron (Brainbox) Fairweather is carefully undoing the tiny mother-of-pearl buttons that hold Lady Strongbow's silk blouse across her still upright, suspiciously upright, breasts, while they both idly watch Joe, the big Samoan, do a slow striptease as he rubs coconut oil into every ripple of his magnificence.

The baron knows from his long experience of such things that Lady Strongbow's breasts are indeed surgically enhanced with the very best that the best money can buy – Lord Strongbow has been generous to a fault – but that does not stop the baron from drawing them out of their silk cottages, decorated with embroidered flowers, and fondling them, quite carelessly, as if he has every right to do with them as he pleases, every so often casting Lord Strongbow a half-lidded glance. For the baron, much of the erotic kick of it all lies in that assumption of possession and ownership, even, especially, of another man's wife, to be so casually asserted right under the cuckold's nose. It's all about power, stupid!

Lord Strongbow, a big man with an indolent will, hardly cares. He has that supreme indifference to things that only inherited money and lots of it can confer. He will have the pick of the goose girls, somewhat listless as they may be; listless is okay with Strongbow and a delight to be more secretly savoured, with enough cocaine, which Strongbow himself will provide. Terry, the tough-built Ukrainian bodyguard with the hard eyes, might allow Strongbow to lick his killer prick before the evening is out. Besides, his wife's enhanced attributes have long since lost their allure for the lord. Fairweather, an odd sort of a fellow really, is welcome to them.

Lady Strongbow herself is not displeased. Although she's had to suffer a loss of sensitivity to get her breasts looking the way she wants them, she rather likes the way it feels to have another man expose them, and play with them publicly, and so humiliate her husband, if he had the capacity for humiliation, that is – it does take a certain sensitivity. Playing the whore beats the hell out of lying around the house, masturbating, stupefied by boredom. Even the loss of sensitivity in her breasts is not entirely without its compensations, for the baron can pull on them and twist her nipples cruelly, for his pleasure, and all she will feel are distant twinges in her groin, like far off bells ringing. And, like her husband, she has delights to look forward to, apparently, the baron having whispered something about a very pleasant surprise into her pearly ear-drum.

Three others are present besides Joe and Terry. Another couple, Swiss fitness fanatics who stayed behind because they believe, and have the money to believe, that here, in these Alps, the purest, cleanest air left in the world is to be found, and they have no intention of going anywhere else. Purity is their business, this blonde husband-and-wife team who look more like brother and sister, having made their pile in the selling of Pure Products cosmetics. The very air itself, they maintain, has the potency of a medicine – and they should know what they are talking about.

They do a lot of walking and a lot more breathing, and have a similar, public-health approach to the baron's orgies. Lots of sex involves lots of breathing, different kinds of breathing for different kinds of sex, and Frau Benedict has been fascinated to discover, in the course of her explorations, how radically her breathing changes when switching from vaginal to anal intercourse, how the sharp air is sucked deeper into her body, stretching her lungs right out. Her main interest in the orgies is that they offer an opportunity for her to engage in double penetration, which results in an El Dorado of breathing, the jagged peaks and troughs and cross-rhythms of which open up every quivering cell of her body to a great rush of potentised alpine oxygen – the healthiest air on the planet! This Dance of the Double Dong, as she naughtily describes it to her husband during their pillow talk – it excites her breathing just to share those things with him – may well be the key to prolonging her life way beyond the normal human life span.

Her husband, Herr Benedict, is as dedicated to his wife's health as she is, and to seeing that she gets what she wants. He would resent the suggestion that, since she has all the money, his role must hover between that of a lapdog and pimp, because his worship of the mountain air, and its magical health benefits, is as sincere as hers. He is a true believer, and when he hears the blessed sound of his wife gasping and panting and shuddering to the drums of the Dance of the Double Dong, he gives grateful thanks to all those health-giving spirits of the air, and finds his own breath matching hers, his own blood-engorged lungs opening up like a flower in sympathy with hers.

Eventually, they both believe, they will be able to transcend eating altogether and live on nothing but that sizzling mountain air and lots of Tantric sex. They might even live forever.

The final member of the party is Mrs Watson, whose girth and general lack of any charm means that she is often an observer rather than a participant in the evening's festivities, and always stays dressed in a voluminous long-sleeved blouse and equally voluminous below-the-knee skirt – although naked underneath for comfort. Mrs Watson loves to watch. That may well be making a virtue of necessity, but Mrs Watson is beyond caring about the niceties, or whether or not her voyeurism is a natural propensity or the strategy of choice for an ugly fatty. She would come equipped with a fold-out canvas bag, like a wrap-up tool kit, in which is packed, each in its own cloth holder, a variety of dildos and butt plugs. The dildos vary from long thin ones to short fat ones, from the smooth and stylised to a veiny realism: straight ones, bent ones, coloured ones, bendy plastic ones that flop about, wooden ones that don't, hollow glass ones you can see through to the pink flesh beyond: dildos that throb and whirr and wriggle: dildos with knobs on. All kinds of knobs. The butt-plugs vary in proportion from the 'virgin button' size, looking a little like a baby's dummy, to a lump the size of a child's fist. Mrs Watson will settle herself somewhere to the side of the action with a bottle of tequila, her 'tool kit', and happily masturbate her way through the evening, guaranteed to be still going when everybody else has flagged.

Not that she never sees any action. On the odd occasion, Lord Strongbow's desire to test the limits of degradation would overcome his lassitude, and to prove something to the universe, perhaps about the nature of desire, who knows, would approach Mrs Watson seeking a moist orifice, and would be accommodated. Once, his wife, the indomitable Lady Strongbow, herself exhausted from the joys of a threesome with one of the baron's dancing girls and the inexhaustible Terry the terrorist, ordered her husband to attend Mrs Watson, feigning sympathy for the poor neglected fat woman, for no other purpose than that she could order him to do such things, and other even more degrading things too, and enjoy his slave status after other enjoyments have palled.

Hardly a crowd, the baron thinks morosely. Nothing like the old days of a few short moons ago when his shagpile carpet would have been covered with shagging celeb bodies, and the air filled with the glad cries of the fallen. But that's just what they are, the old days, and this is the baron's last, rather sad hurrah. A bit of a let-down really. Those old boogie nights are never coming back, although one can always pretend. Good to know that steps are under way to get his long-range, diesel-burning Turboshaft 300 – his ticket out of here when he needs it, the very best helicopter money can buy – ready for air. He's already done a dummy-run, raising the chopper onto the roof with the hydraulic lift, making sure the doors of the portal are working smoothly.

And he has his passenger list sorted out, quite sorted out in his mind. A few surprises there, ha ha.

He glances over at the final member of this select little group, and she says nothing but lies on her side, propped up on her elbow, watching everybody beneath half-raised, curved, bronze eyelids. The reclining Arya Tara in all her finery does not look out of place at an orgy, except perhaps for a smile that is a shade too enigmatic; she certainly has the svelte figure for it. Being unfazed by the simultaneous unfolding of a zillion universes, why should she be fazed at a little grunting and heaving?

When everything is prepared and the guests are settled, Lady Strongbow's breasts in full view of all and in range of the baron's pitiless fingers, Mrs Watson's hand tucked up between chubby thighs, and the Swiss couple already breathing the medicinal air deep and even, the baron signals Joe to bring his warm-up act to a close while there is still something to leave to the imagination. He doesn't like to let Joe go too far with his striptease, even though the well-built Samoan's splay-kneed campfire dance with coconut-oil hands is a sure-fire way to get the women juicing. Like a good general, or card player, the baron knows how to hold back his best for last, and Joe, when the time comes for some serious hardcore action, is the best on the block.

As Joe retires for the meantime, Fraulein Zhenhua enters with three dancing girls in tow, her celebrated goose girls, Cherry Blossom, Blue Zither and Sun Petal. These are the remnants of what was once a troop of over a dozen dancing girls, skilled in all kinds of dances, from the can-can to ballet to lap-teasers.

Herself dressed in something severe, black and shiny – the baron senses a little shiver go through Lady Strongbow, a quiver through the silicon, her having always been somewhat deliciously afraid of the woman – Fraulein Zhenhua has outdone herself in her costume design for the goose girls. The lavish and intricate finery of traditional Balinese temple dancers, complete with elaborate headgear. The dance she has choreographed is exquisitely sad and slow and hardly erotic at all, at least at the beginning, and when it turns in that direction it does so subtly and tastefully, but is all the more compelling for that.

The melancholy, highly stylised dance relaxes his guests. Lady Strongbow is no stranger to the charms of these particular girls, they hold no mystery for her, but that doesn't stop her from enjoying the slow-motion undressing the dance becomes. Joe and Terry have had these girls too, on a pretty regular basis as the baron understands it – he has little interest in the lives of those who live in the lower floors of his mansion and who serve him – and so they too are feeling pretty mellow. There's nothing here they haven't seen before, but what the hell, the booze is flowing and the lines of cocaine are standing up straight on their mirrored surfaces. There's a pleasing copper sheen to Cherry Blossom's hair, Blue Zither looks interesting in a punk sort of way, and Sun Petal's platinum curls look their best against her darkly pencilled eyebrows.

For the occasion, which he is already mentally calling the Last Sad Orgy at the End of the World, the baron has flung open the double doors that separate the spacious living room and the equally spacious balcony, which now serves as a stage. The night has turned on a spectacular array of stars, a wanton money-shot of suns squirted across the deep black velvet of space. Against this splendid backdrop the goose girls do their endlessly rehearsed dance in which, beginning apart, one on either side of the balcony and one at the back, they are slowly, as if with great reluctance and internal drama, drawn towards each other, towards the centre. When they meet in the centre they link arms in a row and do a series of stately circles, looking, with all that make-up, like three over-dressed shop mannequins come to life, before slowly beginning to undress one another, their movements becoming more languid, their gestures more surrendered and overt.

The audience has thoroughly settled into the show. Lady Strongbow has leaned closer into the baron, her long, tanned, thoroughbred legs slipping into view through the hip-high slit in her pale silk dress, which she parts, inviting his exploratory fingers. He knows full well that she is using him to stimulate herself for eventual pleasure in the hands of others, but he doesn't care. Since learning of his ruination, he has discovered that he cares for very little, nothing at all in fact, not even death – which is probably where he's heading – and certainly not the antics of his guests. Let them fall where they may. Lady Strongbow's thighs are just as smooth, and the moisture seeping between them just as sweet.

The Benedicts have already removed all their clothes, quickly and efficiently. For them, getting undressed is not an erotic act but merely a necessary prerequisite for engaging in good, healthy, deep-breathing athletic sex. Frau Benedict is sitting up on her knees facing the dancers on the balcony, her spine straight, her breathing deep and even, while Herr Benedict kneels behind her, gently massaging some thick aromatic oil into her parts, softening her up for later penetration with loving devotion, hardly even lifting his eyes to the dancers on the balcony. Still half dressed in only his shirt and underpants, having removed his trousers and socks, Lord Strongbow, deciding to apply himself to the job at hand, joins the Swiss couple, dipping his fingers into the oil and spreading it over Frau Benedict's small but lively breasts. Frau Benedict neither encourages nor discourages him. She is doubtless holding out for a male with a little more vigour, like Joe or Terry or the baron himself, to bring out the best in her breathing, but with the Dance of the Double-Dong to consider, she is not ruling anybody out just yet.

Mrs Watson has selected her favourite dildo, her BBC (Big Black Cock), both long and thick and cunningly curved. Keeping her skirt modestly covering them, she opens her knees and uses both surprisingly small chubby hands to slip the BBC into the cavernous spaces beneath. She jerks and her eyes go unfocused for a moment as the ebony length slips into place. She eases her haunches forward to lock it into position, then places both her hands on her knees and her eyelids flutter closed as if in profound meditation, holding still but for the faintest, almost imperceptible movement of her hips.

The action on the balcony is reaching a turning point. Blue Zither and Cherry Blossom have ganged up on Sun Petal, the smallest and most fragile, and have turned the dance into a ritual stalking, pulling pieces of clothing and adornment from her body. They have her trapped between them, and are closing in on her, her covering her breasts with her arms and staring in wide-eyed alarm at the audience, when Fraulein Zhenhua, always the Mistress of Ceremony, steps forward and raises a hand. The dancers freeze where they are. The Eastern music stops. The stars shout down into the stillness.

From the left of the balcony a pale figure materialises, a slender column of ivory emerging into the soft light that seeps from the lounge. This figure moves with a grace that makes the goose girls indeed look like a trio of clumsy geese; she does not dance as much as pour herself rhythmically through the air to unheard music. Zhenhua has outdone herself in creating a costume of absolute simplicity for this wonder, an off-white, short-sleeved frock which shifts around her body like a veil, translucent, with six ivory buttons down the front and a hint of lace around a hem floating just above the knee. The body momentarily outlined, revealed and concealed as she moves is both slender and voluptuous, ripe and glowing with youth, petite and perfectly proportioned; her face is small, almost elfin with high cheekbones, soft straight blonde hair to her shoulders and sly, almond-shaped eyes. With her simple, natural look, this vision of sensuality couldn't stand in greater contrast to the goose girls with their heavy make-up and elaborate costumes, looking more like overdressed dummies than ever, their movements stiff and vacuous compared to the sinuous approach of the interloper.

The audience reaction is immediate. Mrs Watson squirms on her cushion as if trying to grind herself through the floor; the blood rushes into her face. Herr Benedict stops breathing and stares, as does Frau Benedict with fascination and some alarm. Too busy staring to see what he is doing, Lord Strongbow starts rubbing oil into Herr Benedict's ear. Lady Strongbow seizes the baron's exploring hand and squeezes it so hard, her finely manicured nails bite into the flesh of his palm.

'Where did you find her?' she hisses.

'Keatown,' he says carelessly. Like the rest of them, he can't take his eyes off the girl, at the same time marvelling at her absolute command of everybody's attention.

'She's soooo spunky,' Lady Strongbow says.

'Orchid,' the baron breathes into her ear, taking full pleasure in the sound of the word.

The girl is an absolute natural, with all the easy grace of an animal in the wild. More than that, she has a glow, a luminosity around her, like a fragrant space. Maybe that is due to the cunning way Fraulein Zhenhua has applied make-up to make it look as if there is no make-up, and played off the olive nakedness of Orchid's bare arms and legs against the pearly white of her frock, but the baron is not concerned by questions of art and artifice, just the effect.

Lady Strongbow turns towards him and takes his arm. Both her knees press against his thigh. Her voice crackles in his ear.

'Let's have her.'

The baron knows full well what the good lady is suggesting with those three hoarse words. That they take Orchid for themselves. That they take the girl off into one of the bedrooms and make a meal of her, a long meal, just the two of them. Leave the rest of the guests to their devices.

As if to emphasise the nature of the deal, her fingers crawl towards his crotch. The dear baron has always been generous in sharing his dancing girls, but this Orchid is something else again. Lady Strongbow must have her. And what Lady Strongbow must have, she gets.

In that moment, the moment Orchid faces the audience and smiles a small ambiguous smile, like the Mona Lisa, like his Arya Tara, the baron arrives at an understanding. He wants the girl, yes, but he does not want to share her with the rapacious Lady Strongbow, or anybody else for that matter. Not only that, he doesn't just want to take her, but make her want him, for always, always and always. This is a new feeling for the baron, and he doesn't have a word for it. It is a dumb yearning, painful in its intensity. More painful than lust has ever been. And, most oddly from his point of view, this painful new feeling is not connected to his crotch – Lady Strongbow's fingers, having found their mark, are working to little effect – but rather stuck in his chest, cutting off his breath, as if his heart had grown too large for his ribcage.

Deal or no deal, he will take this girl, this woman, with him when he leaves in his Turboshaft 300, and she will come willingly, no collar required, on his arm, and they will both be radiant. That is not quite the deal they have come to, of course, but that is the way it will work out. Once she knows how he feels. His ruination is nothing compared to having this girl the way he wants to have her. There is a word for it, unfamiliar to his lips, but he finds himself shaping it in his throat nonetheless: wife.

The end of the world is on hold, as far as the baron is concerned.

The Arya Tara smiles at him from the other end of the universe. Ah! Ha! Big joke! And the joke's on him. Have another line of coke!

At that same moment, as Orchid's own Buddha smile is consuming the room, and the baron is having his epiphany, everybody becomes aware of a disturbance. It begins with frantic barking. Manny. The baron has locked Manny outside for the night as the mixed aromas of human group sex tend to excite and confuse him. He shouldn't be barking. He's too smart. From beyond the balcony, on the northern, upper side comes the sound of something heavy falling, and the next moment they're there, clambering over the northern wall where the balcony meets the side of the hill, sliding and tumbling onto the balcony itself.

The first is a portly Asian man dressed in a faded grey suit, carrying a battered briefcase hugged to his chest. He walks with short, staggering steps, his body heaving from side to side as if the briefcase weighed a ton. Behind him comes a huge bearded man with long matted black hair, dressed in farmer's dungarees and gumboots, absurdly gripping a tube of lipstick. Behind him comes an old Caucasian woman with white hair and a long, thin face, dressed in a tweedy, tailored suit. She is carrying a magazine which she swings up towards her face as if she were about to open it at some random page and read something. And behind them a skinny male teenager in holey jeans, and more come, and more, silent and blank-faced, pushing onto the balcony.

Manny attempts to harry them, barking all the while and looking to the baron for guidance. At the signal from his master, Manny would tear these interlopers to pieces. Dog instincts spliced with porcine cunning make a vicious combination.

The baron understands immediately what has happened. Some of the half-people have been pushed upward by the town's ragtag wall, and are now swarming through mansion territory. Obeying something like the law of the diffusion of gases, they tend to end up everywhere, even on his balcony, which admits only a narrow access on the northern side. The maths flashes through his mind even as he gets to his feet.

Orchid, Zhenhua and the goose girls make a run for the lounge, falling over the Benedicts and Lord Strongbow, falling over each other. It's already too late

Breach

Book Five

the Pentecostal flame

Rasputin wakes up on the cold grey stones of the church floor. He would like to have slept longer, and on the comparative comfort of his mattress, but God allows him little sleep these days, and less comfort.

He rises stiffly, like one from the grave, takes himself to a bucket of water and splashes it over his head and neck. The water is clean and cold and stings him awake. Being awake doesn't only mean facing the day to come but remembering the night before, remembering the things God showed him in the darkness of his hour. The conspiracy between Orchid and Orlap, the baron's evil influence over Orchid, the danger to the Baby as the demon baron reaches out his hand for him – and of course the temptation of Rasputin: how the devil showed him the way to Orchid's affections.

When Jesus suffered his temptation, the Devil offered him dominion over the earth and its kingdoms. All he has offered Rasputin is a way into the heart of one woman. His last picture of her, quietly snuggling up to Orlap at the party, still burns brightly in his brain. He thought then they were conspirators, and perhaps they are – lovers, the greatest conspirators of all.

He breakfasts on a couple of strips of venison jerky and cold water. Perhaps today might bring some relief. Perhaps today the Lord might spare him the agonies of the night before. Of course, those agonies are not entirely over. Jesus was able to bid the Devil be gone; for Rasputin it is not so simple. Bid the Devil be gone one moment, and he creeps back into your thoughts the next. Scream and shout at him, he won't just drop dead. The reverend told him once about a man, a writer, who threw an inkpot at the Devil. But even that was no use. The Devil retreats only to wait his moment. He knows when the time is right to strike. That is, in weak moments. All Rasputin has to do is think of Orchid – her smooth skin, the swell of her body under her clothes, her rich scent, her woman's eyes and her child's voice – and Satan is right back by his side with a grin on his face, ready to serve him. All this can be yours...

The last time he saw Orchid as one of the mokopuna, looking fresh and tomboyish, was the day the first two driftdead clambered up the northern side of Pine Point and he shared a conversation with her among the hushed pines. Since then she has become something mysterious and disturbing.

He thinks of the three days he spent in the presence of the Lord during the unholy storm that brought the driftdead in its wake. How simple it seemed then, in those transfigured moments! How straightforward it was going to be to face his demons and live in the Lord every waking moment, maybe even save Orchid from the evil clutches of the baron. The Lord touched him so that he would become the leader of his people. Things haven't worked out that way. If he is to be the spiritual leader of his people, it must occur naturally, as in the course of events, and as he proves himself, rather than declarations and crowns upon his head. It is pride and vanity to assume the mantle of saviour, he told the reverend. But if that mantle should fall upon him, so be it.

True, a soul here and there has perceived his God-touched state, but the mokopuna, where he hoped to begin his ministry, have proven infertile ground. He hoped to begin modestly, with the little girls they call the twins, Miranda and Witch Hunt, but Miranda has gone off to stay with the librarian and Witch Hunt avoids him, hiding away in the schoolhouse just across Beauty Parade, never showing herself to him or inviting any approaches. Rasputin has always imagined that, underneath it all, people hunger for salvation, but he finds that isn't true. People don't want salvation, which is like walking through fire; they want comfort, ease... forgetfulness. The last thing they want is to be tested, the most uncomfortable experience in the world. Like the little girl, they would rather hide from salvation.

Take Little Sanyo, for example. Where does his endless curiosity get him but into the most awkward and trivial places? Does God have a mother? he wants to know. Or, how can Rasputin prove that we all have a soul – that sort of thing. Lost, quite lost. Or Sad Toof, who says that if there were a compassionate God, he would remove the offending tooth. What God would ever permit a young soul to suffer such perpetual agonies of the gum, what sin has the doleful kid committed that would justify such trials? Rasputin is learning that just as God's grace might strike from behind, out of nowhere, unearned and undeserved, so might the withdrawal of that grace. And Sirocco? The pagan just smiles at him. A friendly enough smile, true, but there is no trace of salvation in it, and sometimes Rasputin wonders if the pagan is secretly laughing at him.

Doesn't it say in the Good Book that a prophet is never recognised by his own?

He finishes chewing his venison, which takes a long while to soften in his mouth, has a swig of water and goes to the door to look out at the world. It is so quiet the world outside could have ceased to exist. And no wonder, it is barely dawn. The sea looks almost black, right up to the horizon line in the east, behind which first light glows. As usual, he glances over at the school to see if Witch Hunt is around. It's a reflex action, as the little girl is most likely to be sound asleep at this hour.

Coming around the northern edge of the school building is a group of driftdead. Just the usual ragged collection of the damned. He is about to ignore them when something catches his eye.

A silver flame, like a fish hanging upside down in the air.

It is hovering above a woman – or rather a creature who was once a woman, ordinary-enough looking, a shopping bag in her hand – hovering a hand's width above her head. The flame is silvery and translucent, although he can see the sky behind it, and it seems to catch the silver of the sky and the clouds. The flame hovers but sways as it moves along with her, as if attached by an invisible cord.

She is not the only one. They all have them, every one, although not all are silver. He can see a couple in the distance, crossing Beauty Parade further up, and even from a distance he can see the flames quite clearly. They have a luminescence, soft and pale in the dawn, but distinct, like little jewels, each glowing with its own colour from gay yellows to sombre purples. Some sparkle, some glow, and some smoulder. Some appear to wink on and off like fireflies, fading and rising.

As the group crosses the road and comes closer, he can see that each flame, while of shifting colours and vividly mobile, has a distinctive overall hue that is different from any other. No two flames are the same.

And they are not flames. They only look like flames. As the party passes by, just uphill of the church, he gets a good look at them. The shape varies too, none exactly alike but each with a leaf or fishlike appearance. Some are more translucent than others, too. Some are almost opaque, dark with swirling colours, while others are so pale they can hardly be discerned.

God, who it seems has been waiting for Rasputin to arrive at just this moment, hits him from behind once more. These 'flames' belong to the spirit world. They are spirits, bodiless entities; they are… souls.

Souls.

Souls of the driftdead. Their souls have not quite left their bodies, but stay attached to them. Driven out by demonic forces, the soul exits the body but hangs on, clinging to the flesh it can't leave.

This is like last night, only a lot worse, he thinks. He has to face the implications. If the demonic force can be driven out, the driftdead soul can be reunited with the body, re-animate the body with life – and, like any other person, be capable of redemption. The black blood would flow again, re-oxygenate, just like Hera and the other Humanists imagine. It follows that it must be sacrilege to kill them. The Devil may have them in his hand, but the Lord has not given up on them, and by His grace their exiled souls hover near their bodies, perhaps waiting to become human once more. The possibility cannot be ruled out. Even if it smells like blasphemy.

It feels like heresy to think this, but what God has shown him is no less than the truth. And the truth, it is said, shall set you free.

We have been wrong about the driftdead all along, he thinks, with a dawning horror. Satan has not claimed their souls, merely their bodies; their souls ride in attendance. And we destroy those bodies carelessly, as if we were stepping on bugs. Cockroaches.

Without delay he tracks north, keeping well clear of the road where most of the driftdead getting through the barrier are concentrated. He arrives just east of the library and soon has a vantage point from which he can look out over the barrier to the hosts of driftdead beyond. With the first light of dawn still to directly touch them, the mass of dark bodies is a sea of dancing lights, sparkling more colours than there are names for.

The sight is breathtaking and beautiful, but lots of questions flood his mind. Since he has never seen this before, and nobody else has seen it, or presumably can see it, this is a revelation from God; God's greatest test yet.

God has granted Rasputin this singular vision.

Pinky and a couple of other men are working on the barrier just down a bit from where Rasputin is standing. A driftdead stumbles into Pinky, who casually slices off the man's head in two swift, well-practised strokes of a machete, Pinky's latest weapon of choice.

The spirit dances in the air like fish on the end of line, before disintegrating.

He is going to have to tell others what he sees. Imagine what people are going to say when he tells them they must stop killing the driftdead. How's he going to tell a town under siege that its attackers might be holy in the eyes of the Lord? Who is going to listen to such madness? And yet, tell them he must, say something he must, because the Lord would not have vouchsafed him such a vision for nothing. Those pale fires hovering above the driftdead are nothing less than the Holy Spirit, a spark from the Pentecostal fires that descended upon the Apostles after the death and Transfiguration of Jesus. He would purge the image from his mind if he could, and pretend that he never saw it. But the Lord knows he has seen it, and the Lord never forgets anything, candle or flame.

Rather than look upon him as the saviour, the people are more likely to treat him as a pariah. Thank you, Lord!

they never go home again

For Sirocco Cornet, the beginning of the end is heralded by the arrival of a strange young woman at the door.

When Gypsy opens the door, she is there, just standing there saying nothing. Gypsy and the young woman look at each other for a long time.

'Sister,' Gypsy says.

Sirocco remembers Sister. That was about the time Gypsy's mother floated away on a sea of cushions, not long after Gypsy found Sirocco wandering in the desert. He remembers a girl leaving the village in the space-age cab of a petrol tanker. It's the tanker he remembers best, a great machine, hinged in the middle, long and yellow, full of magic and madness and shouting metal. The front wheel was way taller than his shoulders. Music was coming from inside, swift, pounding and repetitive. Sister leapt into it, swinging a bag before her, an eager, grateful look on her face. She was saying goodbye to Keatown! The shiny seat pumped at her backside.

She had no words of goodbye, just a frozen wave of the hand.

Now she's standing at the door staring inside with the blank intensity of a blind person. Or a driftdead. She has long, luxurious black hair that hangs down over her shoulders. Hair like Gypsy's, only longer and tanglier, with rat's tails. Behind the hair her face is pale and empty. Her eyes slide over the room without much recognition. She is wearing ill-fitting clothing that bulks out around her.

Gypsy looks swiftly at Scale and Sirocco. The same thought flashes through the three heads. Driftdead. It's hard to mistake that look. But although the pausers may pause for a while, and move their heads back and forth, the driftdead don't stop to look into doorways unless you believe Cherrie Lamont. They don't stop for anything. And they never go home again.

Scale laughs. A stupid, nervous laugh. He immediately begins strutting up and down like a rooster.

Sister walks into the house and sits on the floor facing the door, which faces north, and from which she can see Sirocco's crab apple tree.

Scale walks around her, looking at her from all angles. He keeps turning his head from one side to the other as if his eyes were on the sides of his head, like a bird's.

'Welcome home,' Gypsy says, but there is not a lot of welcome in her voice. It is not at all clear to Sirocco that the girl is Gypsy's younger sister, although that's what she looks like. It crosses his mind that she might be Gypsy's daughter, but he can't quite line up their ages.

Sister doesn't move or say anything, just stares out the open door. It looks like she's waiting for something.

Scale and Gypsy look at each other.

'Jus' like that,' Scale says.

'With never a please or a thank you,' Gypsy says.

'Maybe she's not aware of us,' Sirocco says. 'I mean, properly aware.'

The implications of that hang in the air.

In his crib in the corner, where Sirocco sleeps, the Baby stirs and mutters in his own language. Slowly Sister turns her head and looks at the crib, then slowly back again to the door. In that action she looks very much like a pauser, the same mechanical head movement. Gypsy hands her a glass of water and she drinks it, steadily, until the glass is empty, and places it on the floor in front of her. The driftdead don't drink water either.

'Well,' says Gypsy.

'Well,' says Scale.

'Well,' says Sister. But Sirocco thinks she might have said 'Wow.'

Gypsy and Scale both talk at the same time, but Sister doesn't respond. It's not just that she fails to answer, she doesn't appear to hear the questions. She doesn't say anything until the end of the day, after having sat in the one place unmoving the whole time. Nobody is talking to her, just getting around doing their work, when Sister says in a loud, clear voice, 'It will soon be over.'

'Ha haaa,' the Baby shouts, his voice very loud.

'What did you say?' Gypsy says.

'Ha haaa,' the Baby shouts again, his voice very penetrating.

'What did you say?' Gypsy says, this time directly to Sister.

'It... will... soon... be... over.' Sister closes her eyes as if in sleep while still sitting upright facing the door.

'There are holes inna words,' Scale says.

When Scale says that, an idea blossoms in Sirocco's mind. Sister might be a recovered driftdead. Despite the bloodless walker, the hope that the driftdead might recover their humanity has never quite died, even though Hera and her adherents can give no rational account as to how that might come about. Throughout the defence, and the random slaughter of many hundreds of them in the name of the safety of Keatown, all of us have been haunted by Hera's question to everybody: what if they came back? Even the reverend, who is firmly of the opinion that the driftdead are a walking blasphemy marching towards the Gates of Hell to the siren call of the Devil, is not prepared to second-guess God. Only Pinky doesn't care, and is not haunted by anything. In fact, he's been heard to suggest that if all the driftdead suddenly became human again, they would be far more dangerous than in their zombie form.

However, if one were to recover, might she not act just as Sister is acting now, only half there, struggling to get back into the world? Sirocco thinks so, but he doesn't share his thought with Gypsy and Scale just yet. An idea as fresh and new as that, with the hope it implies, needs a little more consideration. Lizard taught him that impulsive actions can lead to disaster, which in the desert means death. The merest slip means death. It is not the foot that slips into the crevice, but the mind, Lizard warned him. And like the foot it can't be pulled out.

'What does she mean?' Gypsy says.

'Could be good,' Scale says.

'Could be bad,' Gypsy says.

'I'm a glass half-full personage,' Scale says.

'Like hell you are.'

'I have never been properly appreciated.' Scale brushes the fingernails of one hand against his black singlet as if it were a tuxedo and he were the finest dandy.

'It will soon be over. Does that sound like a glass half full to you?'

'I reckon. The drifters will go back to the wind.'

'Sounds more like a threat.'

'Sounds more like a promise.'

'What's she thinking? Turning up like this. Walking in the door without so much as a by-your-leave and sitting down? Expecting to be fed and looked after, I suppose.'

'I suppose,' Scale says, and gives a silly little giggle. 'Put her to work, that's the answer.'

'Does she look like she's able to work?'

'She c'n sweep up the fish scales.' This being the lowliest job in the fish shed.

'Dream on.' There is more than a touch of bitterness in Gypsy's voice. Life with Scale has not been all beer and skittles, not by a long shot. When Gypsy's mother died, Gypsy felt deserted, as if her mother floated away on a sea of cushions because she wanted to get away from her daughter, Keatown, and everything – but particularly Scale.

'So what are we going to do?' Gypsy says. She's got a voice she uses when she is trying to get Scale to take some sort of responsibility, and act, even if just for the moment, like the head of the house.

'Nothin'.'

'Just like that?'

'What would you do?'

Gypsy looks as if she has an idea but chooses not to share it. Instead she hands Sister a broom, her indefatigable broom. Sister examines it as if for blemishes. Then she closes her eyes and strokes it as if she were in deep communion with it.

'You see what I mean?' Gypsy says. There is a brittle edge in her voice unfamiliar to Sirocco.

Scale is contemplating Sister and the broom as if they were some rare landscape, perhaps, or some strange object that might yet find its place within the living history of inconsequence.

Gypsy squats in front of Sister, placing herself directly in the girl's line of vision. 'What will soon be over? This plague of walkers?'

Sister opens her mouth as if to answer, but nothing emerges except the water she has drunk, which dribbles down her front.

'That's just bloody wonderful,' Gypsy says. 'We're really on a roll around here.'

Scale's silence infuriates Gypsy, who snatches the broom and stands up. Scale steps back as if he's about to be attacked. 'There's your glass half full,' she says, 'vomited back at you.'

Scale continues his silence but the Baby gurgles in sympathy.

if you eat me, you'll die

Life in the Cornet household continues its erratic course as before, working around the woman sitting on the floor and the jars of Ock's hock Scale keeps producing and they both keep drinking. After that first pronouncement, Sister says nothing more, but there is an alertness to her that suggests a conscious mind. Gypsy might have picked up the same idea, as she begins to look askance at Sister, and tread a little warily around her.

Sister's muteness and her stillness create not only a sense of mystery, but of anticipation, fear even, especially after her one gnomic utterance. Her silent, upright form becomes emblematic in some way none of them can identify, like a statue of an unknown deity. She is difficult to ignore. She seems to give out a kind of energy, like a magnet, and while she doesn't move, everything else seems to move around her, and in relation to her.

Gypsy tries giving her food from our precious stock, and cool water from the water jar. She even offers her a mug of Och's Hock. Sister either refuses the food or eats abstractly, moving her jaw around as if that motion were unrelated to the food in her mouth. Gypsy gives up after a while as everything Sister takes in is regurgitated shortly after, hardly altered.

'She's got to be one of them,' Gypsy says to Sirocco. 'Just a different variety. Maybe more like this will come.'

'Could be,' Sirocco says. 'She's like a hybrid, half driftdead and half human.'

'Half full,' says Scale. 'She might get up in the nighty-night and murder us all in our sleepy-sleep.'

'She can start with you, Sunshine.'

They toast their glasses and drink. And giggle.

Certainly Sister's presence is not reassuring, and her silence not comfortable. Sometimes her hands move restlessly about her body as if she were trying to find something, like a packet of cigarettes or a wallet. When she gets up to go to the toilet, there is nothing of the remote, plodding of the driftdead in her step. Hers is lithe and forceful, of someone in full, lucid possession of themselves. It all adds to the mystery.

Sirocco remains convinced that Sister is a recovering driftdead, slowly reclaiming her humanity, but there is an opposite possibility, already suggested by Gypsy, that she has turned, but not totally, that she got halfway through the process which, for some unknown reason, suddenly stopped. That she is a half-turned. Or, the process is so slow it is still happening. A slow-motion turning that might complete itself before the end of the century.

There is not much evidence either way, so Sirocco decides to ask her. He waits until Scale and Gypsy are out of the house, and Witch Hunt is nowhere around, before approaching the sitting woman. He cannot be entirely sure that this is the same girl who leapt so eagerly into the cab of that petrol tanker and went off to find her life a few short years ago. He's not even sure that Scale and Gypsy are entirely convinced. He holds the Baby loosely in his arms as he sits beside Sister, facing the door as she is doing. The Baby has been fed and should be sinking quietly into sleep. There is the crab apple tree, still half buried in sand, a familiar and comforting shape. There is the smooth slope of the sand dune behind, blocking what was once a fair north view. As he sits down, a lone driftdead teenage girl, with hair in a retro-punk style, coasts down the dune at an angle, passing behind the crab apple tree.

'Do you think babies can turn into...' he gestures at the passing girl. He doesn't want to say it. The idea is too frightening. This is the first time it has occurred to him, but it will not be the last. He cuddles the sleepy Baby a little closer.

Sister doesn't answer but Sirocco imagines that she has heard and understood him, and proceeds on that basis. Once, in the desert, he'd spoken to a dog, and convinced the dog not to eat him. The dog didn't speak a word, or give any sign, but it understood. 'If you eat me, you'll die,' Sirocco told it, and the dog believed him, just as Sirocco had believed Lizard when Sirocco had been about to eat him.

'Did you come from the north? We all want to know what's happening up there. What's happening to the cities.'

'It will be over soon.'

Sirocco notes the light variation, the moving of 'soon' to the end of the sentence, and feels encouraged.

'What will be over?'

But the direct question is a mistake, apparently, as Sister clams up. Sirocco tries to think of the right way forward, but finds the task beyond him. They may as well both sit in silence. He suspects there is a key that will unlock her, some special code that will bring her back to the world, but finding it is beyond him.

The Baby speaks into that silence. It is one of his made-up, pretend sentences full of oogles and boogles, and gurgles and wurgles. And he laughs, as if he is fully aware that his pretend sentence makes no sense but doesn't care. What's a sentence? When you're a baby you can say whatever you like in any language you care to make up on the spot.

Sister turns her head and looks down at the Baby. It is a very deliberate movement.

'Meet Baby. We haven't named him yet. His mother didn't name him, but I'm going to have to. Akona told me that he needs a name for his sense of self. A word he associates with himself as a separate person.' Sirocco has some experience with this, especially with not having a real name. So what is he? A dry, desert wind?

Sister gently touches the Baby's face, and looks at Sirocco with a strange ardor, as if his is the first human face she has seen for a very long time.

'Soon. It will be over.'

'Very soon?'

She nods, 'Very soon.'

Sirocco, however, is unsure if she is affirming or merely repeating what he has said.

'Perhaps you are tired. Perhaps you have come a very long way.'

She continues to gaze at him as if she would memorise every feature of his face. 'A very long... way. I was walking...'

'Walking a long way,' Sirocco says, 'makes you tired.'

This time she touches his face. Her fingers are warm. 'I am not tired,' she says distinctly, as if sounding the words out to a baby.

'Perhaps you have a fever,' Sirocco says, noticing the faint line of sweat on her upper lip. But it is too late. Her mind has drifted from the conversation, and her attention is back on the crab apple tree.

Sirocco gets up, quite content. It wasn't much of a conversation, but it is a start. She even disputed him. Next time, he thinks, I will make more progress. He is more convinced than ever that she was once one of the driftdead and is clawing back to reality. That is his glass half full. Half fool.

Sirocco likes to get away from it all. He does his best to resume his old habit of getting up at dawn and slipping away from the house, more difficult when he has the Baby to take care of, but he manages it. He has taken up his stick and resumed his dialogue with the now sandy soil under the crab apple tree, the very spot where it all began, with the wind and the Rose Woman. The tree is gnarled and eternal, buried up to its waist in sand, the lower branches sticking up like independent saplings. It still bears some fruit, small, green and bitter, on its upper branches.

The canvas on which he has to draw his stars and circles, however, has changed. Around the half-buried tree the sand has formed waves, like a frozen ocean. Any moment, it seems, their motion might resume and the ocean continue to swirl around the tree. Here is a pattern that will never be complete, no matter how hard the wind may try. He has to draw on top of those waves, through the bumps and troughs, and not much of a wind is needed to obliterate his shapes, as they collapse and widen even as he draws. Dissipating circles and crumbling stars of dry sand.

But even out here he is not completely free from the influence of Sister. Looking back at the house, he becomes aware that Sister is watching him through the open doorway. Or at least appears to be watching him, although maybe she's just staring in his direction.

She wants to live, he thought. It's just that she's forgotten how. Forgotten how to run, dance, laugh.

She wants to talk.

She wants to come out and play.

a matter of milk

For Akona, rising at dawn and greeting the world has become a ritual. Not intentionally so, but from the sheer force of repetition. She likes to stand at the marae's highest point, face the sea, and have a little sing-song with the dawn, give thanks to the four directions for her turangawaewae, her own personal place to stand. Her being in that place, at that time, is affirmed – and with gratitude. There are times when the dawn light hitting her skin seems more like a miracle than a simple, ordinary, natural event. The arrival of the driftdead hasn't changed any of that for her.

'These things don't belong to the land,' she said to the Man in Black.

'Then they won't last,' he said, the first time he'd spoken in a long time. It is not that the Man in Black can't talk, rather he has nothing to say, mostly.

This particular morning, however, she wakes while it is still dark, wondering what has disturbed her. The sound of someone moving, perhaps. Or one of the goats gently bleating. Sometimes the Man in Black gets up early too, but he moves like a shadow and never disturbs her. Or maybe it's just her own mind, prying her awake. Grumbling to herself she gets up and dresses, remembering how once before she was pulled out of bed early and had to wander around the marae until she found what had woken her. A tree, in fact, that she had forgotten to water and was in a state of distress. Once she'd watered the tree, and it was happy, she was able to go back to sleep until dawn arrived. It is a hard time for trees, she reflects, but she doesn't feel anything like that now. Whatever has woken her up is something different.

She exits into the warm night, allowing her eyes to adjust to the soft light of a fading moon. Despite the warmth – it has been a long time now since the nights were properly chilled – there is something new in the air that brings goosebumps up on her arms. She looks up at the sky. The stars are where they should be, but pale and remote rather than alive and vibrant, as they can look on clear spring nights. There is an unfamiliar heaviness in the air, more like late summer rather than late spring. Something is on its way, coming up fast, but it is not what has woken her.

She visits the outbuildings first. In one of them Sad Toof will be asleep, and she hopes Little Sanyo. All along she has resisted becoming a mother to the mokopuna. Or even their grandmother. That is not her job. But as for offering them refuge, a place where they can sleep in safety, that is another matter. Although she has no children of her own, sadly enough she is starting to think she still believes that children are the most precious part of ourselves.

She doesn't look for the Man in Black as he prefers to sleep under the stars and beds himself down in any number of places. Thinking of him gives her a pang in the heart. She doesn't know how it has come about that she should be living with a man who is no more than a shadow and might speak two sentences a year.

She stands for a while in the garden. All seems well. The busy hush of night, she thinks. Spring is a hectic season. There is a particular spot ideal for planting a tree, and she briefly visits the spot, taking pleasure in imagining a tree growing there, a fruit tree perhaps or a native. Something small that will not overwhelm the garden. She has been waiting for a clear signal as to just what to plant. While she is standing there, she hears, quite distinctly this time, the quiet, mewing sound of a goat – Nanny if she is not mistaken.

The warmth of the night is giving way to the brief chill of dawn as she heads in the direction of the goats. The Man in Black has made a shed for them, with a yard to run in where they might be fed. Akona likes to let them roam around free, but she is always mindful of her own, and other gardens. As she approaches the goathouse, Nanny gives another of her mewing cries, sounding soft and imploring. It doesn't sound right.

When she enters the goat shed, she sees a figure hunched behind Nanny, and hears the soft hiss of milk into a jar. She remains silent watching and listening. The milker is no more than a shadow in the gloom of the shed. The milk hisses rhythmically into the jar. Akona begins to hum softly, realising it's 'Santa Lucia', sung by Hera at the sad fish-shed party.

Typhoid Mary jumps to her feet and faces Akona.

After a moment's silence, Akona says, 'You need milk?'

In the quickly growing light, Akona can see one full jar at Mary's feet and another half full.

'This is not the first time, is it?'

Perhaps because of the mildness of her tone, the tension lessens, but still Mary doesn't seem to know what to say. Akona might have expected her to have a story all made up for the occasion.

'What you are doing with the milk. Is it for yourself?'

'Why would I tell you?'

So she has a tongue. Akona says, 'The milk is for the Baby.'

Mary looks at her thoughtfully, squats back down and continues milking Nanny, filling the half-filled jar.

Akona makes no move. She has no wish to throw a scare into Nanny. Goats can be skittish, and a fright could dry up her milk. Both goats are restless enough as it is. She waits until the second jar is full and the lid screwed down securely.

'Why not come in broad daylight?'

'You ask a lot of questions.'

Akona examines the answer and decides that it is synthetic. A manufactured answer, something the girl might have heard in a movie or TV show. A slick, dummy answer.

'You could have asked.'

Mary tests the jar lids. 'Sure. You going to stop me from leaving?'

'Should I?'

'You going to call up the Man in Black so he can measure me for a coffin?' There's a sneer in Mary's voice, but a touch of fear too. Being the town's undertaker does have its own mystique. And there are few prepared to cross Akona, little old lady or not.

'I'm thinking about it.' She isn't, of course. The Man in Black wouldn't hurt a fly. He is far more comfortable manhandling the dead than the living. But Mary doesn't necessarily know that.

'You don't need to do that,' a voice from behind says.

It is Orchid. The town beauty is standing in the doorway behind Akona, her face obscured in shadow.

'I knew you were here,' Akona says.

Akona is not impressed by the town beauty, and never has been. There is something wrong with Orchid, even if Akona can't figure out what it is.

People tend to forget that Orchid is a Kensington, even if a black sheep of the family. Orchid's mother was Bob Kensington's niece. A Kensington marrying some handsome unknown drifter called Karl Fleet. Alice Kensington let the side down by marrying beneath her – and paid the price.

Orchid signals to Mary who, jars of milk in hand, moves around Akona to join her. Given the constricted space of the goat shed, getting around Akona is an awkward business, particularly as she does nothing to make it easier. As Mary squeezes past, Akona takes her by the shoulder and says in a low voice, 'Why do you always wear that handkerchief around your neck, Mary?'

'It's not a handkerchief, it's a scarf.'

'Let's see.' Akona takes the scarf and pulls it away from Mary's neck. It's too dark to see clearly, but there is a mark, or a scar. Mary jerks her head away. Akona can hear the girl's breathing, heavy and laboured, as if she had suddenly undertaken strenuous exercise.

'Fuck you,' Mary says.

'What's the milk for?' Akona says to Orchid, letting Mary move away. She has wondered about these girls. Not whether they are lovers, as Cherrie Lamont would romantically imagine, or Pinky make grubby innuendos, but as to who is really the power of the two. Since Mary stays in the background, Orchid appears to be the dominant one, but that doesn't follow.

'For the Baby,' Orchid says, and turns to go.

'How come?' Akona says.

She follows the two girls out into the fading starlight and the open air.

'Goats stink,' Mary says, flapping her hand under her nose as if she were some rich bitch.

'Why steal milk for the Baby? He gets plenty.'

'It's for later.'

'Ah.' Akona begins to understand. It is no secret that Orchid believes she will be the next baby-bearer, since she joined Hera in her confinement and served her in every way. That was before Mary appeared on the scene. But Orchid has no immediate prospect of becoming the baby-bearer any time soon, unless of course…

'The milk will spoil in a day or so.'

'I know,' Orchid says.

'So what will you do with it?'

'Put it in the freezer.' Her bored tone suggests she has something to hide. Annanda has freezers. Some of the nearby farmers have freezers, although not all of them are functional. Akona cannot, however, imagine Annanda allowing this without comment – or payment. Orchid is capable of charming some farmer into letting her use his freezer, but this scenario doesn't sound likely to Akona.

'Whose freezer?'

'A friend.'

'Why won't you tell me?'

'Because it's none of your business.'

'None of my business that the Baby might go hungry today?'

'There's plenty left,' Orchid says.

At that moment the sun edges above the horizon and its light is caught by a window up mansions somewhere. Maybe the Strongbows, or Fairweather. The light is bright red and blinks at her in its own Morse code.

'Don't come again,' Akona says, and without further word turns her back on the girls and walks away.

The dawn turns sad for Akona. That bright moment, when the day is full of hope, is darkened. Akona feels an intense bereavement, as if she has just lost somebody near and dear to her. According to the beliefs of her people, all things are composed of positive and negative forces. Dawn will face its dusk, good will dog evil at every step, bravery will vie with cowardice. To prevent these forces from destroying each other, and to check all 'wayward and provocative action,' as some would have it, is the duty of the guardians. Akona has already sensed that there is some kind of disorder among Te Kuwatawata, Hurumanu, and Taururangi, the guardians of Te Hono-i-wairua, the gathering place of the spirits of the dead, whether they come by the south wind, the west, the east, or north winds. It is from this disorder that the driftdead have emerged, she senses. All from the north.

Holding her bereavement in her heart as if it were a gift, she faces the north and tries to sense its shape and character. Traditionally, the north is the direction that represents the ancestors. She instinctively turns to the north when she sings her karakia, for often ancestors, in their feather cloaks or coats and tails, have been her only audience. She faces the south when, after singing, she seeks that far-off still point, the still centre of all things. There is only grief, flowing out of the north. She cannot sense the guardians of Hono-i-wairua. It is as if the caverns of the dead are emptied.

Nor can she sense any other poutiriao, those entrusted with the governance of the winds, the oceans, the sun and the moon. From them there is a great silence.

Only now can she understand the source of her bereavement. Those two girls and their conspiracies are lost, quite lost. The poutiriao charged with protecting young souls and guiding them to wisdom have withdrawn their services.

Her final understanding, however, is a bitter one, with the grit of the north wind in it. It's us, she thinks. We are the real guardians. And we have turned our back on our charges, just as I, in my righteousness, turned my back on Orchid and Mary.

It is we who have abandoned the world. No wonder it is now peopled with the driftdead.

Flay's suspicions

Flay fires the last of the industrial staples into the building paper, taking comfort from the solid thump of sharp steel into wood. Thwack! Thwack! Thwack! There is something very satisfying about that sound, and about the recoil of the staple gun against his arm. He takes a step back to admire his handiwork. Not too bad, if he says so himself. The paper is now nice and tight. The stuff is tougher than it looks too, with one side thick and black and the other, a different material, silver and shiny. Of course, he has to put the shiny side out because it's smooth and slick, which is just the way he wants it. The next step is to measure another sheet and attach it to the third pole, which he has dug into the strip of weedy land that borders the northern edge of his property.

'Hello! I thought you might like a cup of tea. You've been so terribly busy.'

It is Cherrie Lamont, and she is already grating on his nerves. She talks distinctly, enunciating every word like a character in a children's book. And she plays on her accent because she thinks it's charming, giving the word 'terribly' a very French twist. Flay suspects it's not real. He met plenty of Froggies in London, and none of them chirruped the way she does.

'Yeah, and I'm busy.' And, he thinks, I don't drink tea. The woman must be even dumber than she makes out not to have figured that.

'It's terribly exciting.'

'What is?' He tries not to eye the silly flouncy blouse she is wearing. Mutton dressed as lamb, he thinks sourly. What that makes him doesn't bear thinking about.

'This project of yours. I think it's going to work.'

'Do you now.' How fucking profound.

'I mean, it's not as if there is a lot of passing traffic, ha ha.'

This is exactly what he said to her the day before, without the 'ha ha'. Now she is parroting it back at him. She must think he's as stupid as she is.

'Can I help?'

'No thanks.' He's already tried that. He asked her to hold a sheet of building paper steady while he stapled it, but never again.

'Your tea's getting cold.'

'Yeah.' He doesn't know why he's being so polite to her. She came by yesterday and the day before that, asking all sorts of questions, and he was polite to her on those occasions too. He thought that if he was polite and indifferent she would go away, but there are other methods. If she were angling to get him into the sack... well, he's had dumber women than Cherrie Lamont, remarkable as that might seem. Some of them were so stupid they couldn't feel anything between their legs. So... he must be getting picky in his old age.

'You're terribly clever to think of this. I was telling the librarian, and some other women, and they were all terribly impressed. Everybody wants one!' And she caps this off with a giggle.

'There's nothing stopping them.' He can't help sounding like a grumpy old man. He is a grumpy old man, even when he's trying to be nice, and right now he's not trying to be nice.

'But not everybody has… your terrific skills.' 'Terrific' now getting the same tortured Frenchie sound as 'terrible.' The effect is far more terrible than terrific.

What she says is true enough, but he doesn't say so.

'Hold this end against this pole while I fix the other end.'

The pleased Cherrie Lamont jumps to obey.

'All you have to do is hold it in one place.' He makes it sound as if it will be difficult for her to do that, and so it is. This flibbertigibbet can hardly stand in one place. Mind you, there's a lot of it going around these days, people getting so jumpy they can hardly stand still, running from one thing to another as if the hounds of Hell are on their trail. Plodding pedestrians everywhere you look.

He fixes his end and goes down to fix hers. She crouches down and holds the bottom of the sheet while he fixes the top. He gets an unasked-for view down her front. She lets go of the sheet before he's ready and it flaps around until he too crouches down and fixes it. Now they are both crouched down, huddled together. She stinks of some kind of cheap and nasty French perfume. He doesn't find it that unpleasant. It's been a long time since he smelled any kind of perfume, and it's sort of touching that she has bothered at all. Once a floozy always a floozy, he thinks.

'It's done,' he announces, standing back to look at his handiwork.

'It's working,' she says rapturously.

He fires a few staples into the air.

What he has built is a crude wedge shape about as high as his shoulders, made of tough, shiny building paper and anchored to a forward pole. It acts like the bow of a ship against which the pedestrians break and are guided down either side and past Flay's Garage, sliding along the paper walls. The wedge is angled towards Highway 6, where the pedestrians are the thickest. This protects his petrol pumps and keeps stray pedestrians from wandering into his garage. Of course, it has the effect of closing the pumps off from road access, but, and here we go again, there's not much passing traffic these days. Ha ha.

It's a simple device but it works pretty well. He used the last of the cement to get the posts in; they aren't going anywhere. Any pedestrians bashing into the posts will just bounce back. The paper walls are not meant to be blundered into head-on, which the occasional driftdead does, or one might be jostled against it, and it won't last forever – but in the meantime it's just what the doctor ordered, and the meantime is all anybody's got.

As they stand there admiring it, one of the driftdead stops, goes into a kind of listening pose and swivels his head from side to side. Pausers, they call them, he thinks. He doesn't like them. There's something spooky about them, the way they seemed to be searching, scoping out the territory ahead. If they are going to be bloody pedestrians, the least they can do is keep walking. And this one does, after a time.

'Your tea is still there.'

'It'll be too cold now.' He keeps his tone good and surly in case Cherrie Lamont starts getting some fancy-pants ideas, but he is not displeased. His garage is pretty much a pedestrian-free zone, his pumps are protected, and he's got a bird on his arm for the first time in a long time. Even mutton doesn't look too bad, not when it's dressed as lamb.

He looks up and sees Annanda across the road, also admiring his construction. As Cherrie said, everybody will want one – but there is only so much building paper. Eat your heart out, pansy, he thinks, in a state suspiciously resembling happiness.

He's about to suggest that they go inside and raid his declining stash of cold beers, when he sees a familiar set of blonde dreadlocks briefly joining the driftdead along Highway 6. A moment later Orlap appears, a big fat smile on his face.

'I see you built a boat,' he says.

'Just call me Noah,' Flays says, but his good humour, if it ever was that, is fading fast. Captain Orlap is here for his diesel, and Flay doesn't want to sell it. Not even for that lovely gold bar. There must be more where that came from, he thinks.

They go inside but Flay doesn't get into his cold beers.

Buggered if he's going to give away a coldie to the conniving Nord.

Sooner or later, Flay's going to get to the bottom of all this, and then... and then we'll see.

do you see what I see?

The girl is in pauser mode. Gazers, some people call them.She stands, facing downhill, towards the southeast corner of the shed, her head turning back and forth. Little Sanyo has seen this kind but never had a chance to examine one closely. The movement reminds him of pictures he's seen of rows of clowns' heads at fairs and carnivals, moving back and forward, their mouths open, inviting people to put money in. Her mouth is not wide open, only partly so, but the movement of the head is repetitive and mechanical.

She looks more like a machine, he thinks, not for the first time. He's eliminated the idea that they are androids, because they have real flesh and blood and internal organs, even if these are not functioning. But perhaps some biological machine – the Frankenstein effect. Dead but animated. But that is not quite it. She reminds him of something else he can't quite put his finger on.

He grabs a stool from under the bench, sits as close to her as he can get and peers up into her face, remembering how last time he did this he thought he saw a glimmer of recognition, a glimmer of cognition, in her eyes, imagined or not. He has to resist the impulse to personalise them, to give them names and histories. If once human, then it follows that the driftdead surely do have names and histories, parents, friends, family, community – lives from which they have been ripped. The little girl might be his sister, the boy his brother, and it would be all too easy to start pretending things. If they were his friends, he could tell them all about his parents with their drugs, fast cars, fast money and fast deaths. In fact, a couple of times he's caught himself talking to her, and put a cork in it pretty damn quick. She is not his sister, or his friend; she is just a cipher. He doesn't like the idea that he might be assembling a personality for her, and the boy too, out of need and loneliness. Personalities they might once have had.

He's already admired the girl's high forehead and high cheekbones. Noticed her wide-spaced eyes, soft and brown. Looking at her, he thinks intensely of his parents, how sometimes they would talk about having another child, a brother or sister for their Little Sanyo. A sister would be ideal, they said. They might well have imagined a raven-haired girl just like this.

Along with all these foolish thoughts there comes an equally foolish hope that this pauser phase might indicate a recovery. Sirocco has told him his idea about his new sister, the one they call Sister, that she is a recovered driftdead, and the idea suddenly has enormous appeal to Little Sanyo. If one can recover, others can recover. Maybe there comes a moment when they start breathing again, putting oxygen into their blood, food into their cells. Warmth into their touch.

That all this is little more than a wild hope, he knows only too well, but that doesn't make any difference.

Shaking his head as if to clear it from all this stuff, he tries to focus on his observations, developing a line of thought just starting to emerge from the mess. Like the classic zombies of old, the driftdead will keep coming until their brains are blown out or their heads removed. That suggests nervous-system activity, perhaps of an electrical nature. Maybe, with the right electrical currents applied, it is possible to turn them off. Nobody has an explanation for the pausers, but, in terms of the speculations developing in Little Sanyo's mind, the pausers might be rebooting. That's what the girl looks like she is doing, forced to stop while the program driving her reboots. This would make the driftdead more like androids than real people, despite their human flesh. It might represent an eruption of the digital into the real world. These comic-book monsters have walked for so long that they have walked out of Marvel land right into Keatown.

'It will soon be over,' he says to her, remembering what Sister said to Sirocco. 'It will be over soon.' Or was it, 'It will all be over soon'? He repeats this phrase, with variations, thinking it may be a code of some kind that will unlock the girl's mind, but nothing happens. What would I do, he asks himself, if this were a TV series and I was the writer and had to come up with some new ideas for Season 5. Play the driftdead some music. That's what the heroes of Fringe would do. Find a piece of music suitably grand and imposing, like one of Beethoven's concertos, and it would unlock the minds of the driftdead. The great moment of awakening captured on camera. In fact, he thinks, the idea has already been used in Battlestar Galactica when the song 'All Along the Watchtower' is used to activate Cylons who think they are people. And again in Firefly, a series of notes is used to activate a girl into a weapon.

Irrationally, he somehow feels that if the hack masters of TV series have used an idea, it's unlikely to apply to the driftdead, despite the well-known prophetic power of science fiction. Once it's written and filmed it can't happen, because reality doesn't mimic fiction so precisely. More likely, any stimulus that switches them to pauser mode, or recovery mode (if there is one), is entirely internal, perhaps even random.

Discouraged, he rocks back on his stool. He could sit here until Hell freezes over, gazing into her once-pretty face, searching for a sign, for anything. Time to close down this little failure of an experiment. It would be a matter of sheer luck if he happened to be sitting here when she came out of pauser mode, back into full driftdead mode. There is no way of knowing how long she will stand like this, head turning vacantly back and forth. Some only pause for a few moments, others stay that way forever.

'Wouldn't it be nice,' he says aloud to the garage, to the tin walls, and to her, 'to see you change.'

As he says this, her head, swivelling in his direction, stops. Her vacant eyes are on his face. She is as still as a statue. He holds his breath. Her face comes alive with a series of rapid eye blinks. She sees him! Seize him! Her left hand begins to move up towards his face. She is going to touch him. She does, her hand brushes his face, but only to follow through the movement that has begun. He falls backwards off his stool, falling awkwardly, as she takes a step to match her arm movement. She is walking again.

She has rejoined the driftdead.

He has been granted his wish, to catch her at that moment of change – and how likely is that? To think a thing and have it happen immediately: what are the odds on that?

More importantly, in that moment when the booting-up was complete, just before she moved, he saw a human being in there. A real live person, just as he's imagined. A girl who might have been a sister. Or a friend.

And he can't shake the feeling that she'd been about to speak.

just the wind and nothing more

Something wakes Sirocco. Usually it's the Baby, but not this time.

He's been dreaming. While most have been deserted by their

dreams, Sirocco has been having some full-colour, wide-screen visions, often involving the desert and Lizard.

Not this time. This time he's been dreaming of the librarian, and his Book of Imaginary Sentences. His imaginary book has become a real book and is sitting proudly in the library between Sun Shuyan and Brando Skyhorse. The librarian takes his book off the shelf and opens it. Words fly up and spin about. The words are like little objects, all part of the living history of inconsequence. Lizard is there, hiding in the bookshelves. Just like Lizard to be lurking on top of a large book called The Living Desert.

The door to the library blows open and a chill wind enters the room. The librarian looks around in fright. 'Tis the wind and nothing more,' she says. Somewhere in the distance, a door bangs shut. The books whisper to themselves.

The librarian closes Sirocco's book and puts it back on the shelf as he opens his eyes. The Cornet living room is a bundle of shadows. The Baby is asleep. All is quiet. But there is a presence in the room, as if a person or animal has entered and is standing quietly out of sight. Sirocco looks around for something out of place. Except for Sister eerily asleep while sitting upright, there is nothing odd about the room. No unaccounted-for shapes.

But when he stands up the world totters around him. He feels giddy, as if he's standing on the edge of a vast space he could tumble into at any moment. When he lies down once more he can still feel it. It is not an entirely new feeling. He remembers it from the desert where it was part of his daily life. Desert vertigo, he called it, and assumed it was the result of hunger and thirst, or the juices of some of the desert plants he sucked to stay alive.

Maybe this is what if feels like to turn, he thinks.

At the same time he becomes aware that the silence is gone, the silence of the sky, the stillness of the air left over after the storm. He hears, in the distance, the chromatic shift of air through the pines on Pine Point, the dull thunder of waves on the beach. The Baby opens its eyes and looks full into his face. He's not gurgling or laughing or doing baby things, just lying still staring into Sirocco's face with eyes as wise as the world is old.

'It's a wind,' Sirocco whispers. 'The wind has returned.'

The Baby says something it his own language.

They both agree. This new wind is not the wind of storms, a wind that tears things down or breaks them up, a wind that turns the ocean sideways to the land. Nothing so grand. It is as unobtrusive as that first trickle of air that rubbed out Sirocco's circles and stars under the crab apple tree. But this is no infant wind. This is a cagey, wily wind, which maybe only he can feel, yet – and that makes him afraid.

It is the wind, rubbing up against his sleep, that has woken him. He didn't hear it, but he felt it. This is a wind you hear with your whole body, with every cell. It recognises no boundaries of the flesh. It is inside the body as much as outside.

I'm turning, he thinks again, this time with rising panic. This must be what it feels like to be taken by the wind.

The Baby waves his hand in the air as if he could touch it.

'You can feel it too,' Sirocco whispers.

The Baby whispers something back.

Sirocco wants to hug him so close the Baby would never have to feel that wind, the taste of it in his mouth, the rub of it against his tender skin.

On the bed Scale mutters and turns over. Gypsy makes a slurping sound.

Sirocco finds himself clutching the Baby close to his scrawny chest. It feels as if he has an extra, tiny heart beating inside his body.

He starts to cry. Tears on the wind, he thinks.

He's not accustomed to crying, as Lizard counselled against it. 'Tears waste your precious bodily fluids,' the reptile told him when he was sobbing into his loneliness. He got out of the habit of crying, but here he is, tears crawling down his face and onto Baby's arm like little glaucous insects. He mourns them, those little tears, as if they were some indissoluble part of himself that he is losing, not just salt and water. A part of himself never to be collected again, poured back into the jugs of his eyes and eased into the matchbox of his flesh.

Baby begins crying softly in sympathy.

Gypsy and Scale stir. They can feel it, even in their sleep, Sirocco thinks. The new wind, subtle and devious. He doesn't want to think of what it might bring.

Cold. The room has grown much colder very quickly. It's not a cold that belongs to the usual warmer-than-usual spring. It is an ancient cold, hiding in ice for a very long time. It feels more like a part of his dream than anything else. Nights in the desert could feel like this. He closes his eyes and tries to project himself back into the library. It was nice to see his book with real pages and a real cover. That doesn't work.

To distract himself, he tries to work on his book, with an eye to seeing where the librarian might fit in, but finds it hard to concentrate, to find the voice, hear the sentences rolling through his head the way he likes. You see, my mokopuna, you see... Suddenly he cannot recall a single conversation he had with Lizard, yet he and Lizard had spoken profoundly for many hours. But it is all there, in his imaginary book. He can find the page in his mind. The first conversation I had with Lizard was about eating him. I was very hungry, like the hungry caterpillar, and I wanted to eat him. Yes, that's right, but how does it go from there? Lizard said he wouldn't taste very good. Yes, but it would sound better in direct speech. Except he can't do it in direct speech because he can't remember Lizard actually saying those things in those exact words.

Thinking about the desert is not a good idea, for it reminds him of when, giddy with hunger, he could hardly stand under the tall sun. Chasing Lizard to try to eat him had kept Sirocco alive, but he feels too raw in his tears to start remembering all that, even for an imaginary book. On the other hand, it would be nice to have Lizard around right now, with this new wind starting to blow. If Lizard weren't able to give good advice, he might at least be able to make Sirocco laugh, that was always one of his great strengths.

One day, oh my mokopuna, I saw three suns in the sky instead of one. Lizard, in his great wisdom, suggested I take my stick and poke out the eyes of two of them, so they were blinded and couldn't see the earth. I laughed so hard that when I looked back up at the sky there were nine suns instead of three. When they met in the middle of the sky they would explode. Starting to sound better, but did it really happen that way, or happen at all? He can remember dancing on a hot rock, half mad, trying to poke out the eyes of the sun with a stick, all while Lizard urged him to conserve his energy.

Sirocco tries to visualise Lizard somewhere in the shadows of the room, conjure him into existence, but the images are as fleeting and without substance as his words. He is hiding, Sirocco thinks. One thing he is good at is hiding. Staying out of sight. Maybe he has his eyes closed and doesn't see the world anymore.

Sirocco closes his eyes in the hope of seeing Lizard there, perhaps against a painted desert backdrop where there is no wind to rub against the sand, or against sleep. But that doesn't happen. Instead, circles and stars explode and contract behind his eyeballs as if those suns really did meet in the centre of the sky and explode. These suns are more than just single burning orbs, they are universes, bubbling in and out of existence at vertiginous speed. He wants to turn over, to look the other way, but the Baby is right by his side. Mustn't smother Baby. He turns on his back, carefully, but that does not help much, as the bubbling universes turn with him. He is still facing them. He has to fight down nausea.

'It's the wind,' he whispers to Baby. 'It's giving me vertigo.'

The Baby stares at the seething cosmos inside Sirocco. Perhaps it can see inside to where the universes are bubbling away. Everything exists inside ourselves, Sirocco thinks, struggling for a foothold in thought that would make sense of all this. The universe is being. We are it. There is nothing outside being, even the driftdead.

As if to offer proof, the Baby puts out his hand, reaching for right inside Sirocco, right into his belly where the cosmos is seething. Inside, down the spiral of his navel, time is so speeded up that nothing exists discretely, as an object, but turns into a blur. As time approaches maximum velocity, things disappear completely, even the blur. It seems as if the Baby, seeing all that, seeing right through him, wants to reach his curious little hand, with its tiny chubby fingers, right into the centre of maximum velocity where the sum total of everything is zero.

Those chubby fingers, however, encounter Sirocco's skin, which becomes infinitely tender, even bruised, as if it has known remorse, and his blood inhabits territories he knows only by their smell. From the nothing comes the something, Akona said to him once.

'In the desert,' he whispers to Baby, 'I could see pools of blood at night. Moon mirages. In the day you see shimmering water, always in the distance; at night you see still dark pools of blood, always close.' He thinks for a moment, gently stroking Baby's head. 'You take no notice of them. That's the point.'

The Baby answers with his own imaginary words. He knows about shadows. He arrived recently from a shadow world himself. The Baby too is writing his imaginary book.

Sirocco screws his eyes shut but it doesn't help the nausea. He lies huddled in some trackless place, with the sour stench of rotting metal, the howling lament of tree stumps, the sprung rhythm of the pine cone, the fractal division of the sky. He is not spared any sensation. Even if he imagines himself to be a desert rock, ancient and worn, he can still feel the prickle of the earth, the insect bite of the sun, the claw of the moon and the tiny thorns of the stars. He is sliced apart and tuned into countless tiny coils or scrolls, each with its own harmonic.

This is how I really am, he thinks. I survived the desert, days of fever, I can survive this. Survival is something he is good at. Lizard showed him how.

'Tis the wind and nothing more, the librarian whispers.

As gently as I can, I disentangle Sirocco and the librarian, mindful of my limited powers, even as First Person Singular, to alter the course of events. There are things Sirocco has seen and felt that do not belong to the librarian's world, rather the world Sirocco came from, the world he calls the desert. Not only are these things beyond the librarian's experience, but beyond her capacity to experience, and might therefore be quite dangerous for her. It is the kind of danger she is not likely to anticipate when she sits down before her keyboard and the blue eye of her computer screen.

'Tis the wind and nothing more.

the screaming begins

When it happens, it happens suddenly, as if from nowhere.

After lying unmoving on the bed for many hours, his eyes open, octopus eyes that gleam in the half-light, fixed on Sister, Scale gets up and walks across the room on feather legs, as if his legs are back-to-front, to where Sister is sitting. He looks more like a stick insect than a human being as he approaches her, and there's a low growling at the back of his throat.

Before he can reach her, Gypsy is off the bed and halfway across the room, screeching like a mad woman. She throws herself at him, and for a moment the two of them wrestle, howling into each other's faces. Sister sits unmoving, like the shadow of a stone. Sirocco turns away. He doesn't want to watch the battle. Seeing Scale's gangly naked body, which looks like it was made with left-over limbs from a body factory, with bits of hair stuck on here and there, and Gypsy's body, lush as marble, scratching and beating at each other, makes Sirocco want to cover the Baby's eyes. But the Baby sees anyway. He's watching with enormous interest.

Unexpectedly, Sirocco thinks of Mary, her feral little face and weasel body. A bit like a desert creature herself. While he doesn't want to think about her any more than he wants to watch Scale and Gypsy fighting, it's hard to know where to put his mind, especially as he can hear them, their bodies clashing together like rocks in an avalanche.

'You're mad!' Scale shouts. 'Holes inna head!'

'You touch her, I'll kill you! I won't care. I'll kill you and drag you down to Hell myself.'

It isn't a friendly fight. Not one of those fights that might turn into a fast and furious lovemaking – that would have had Sirocco racing for the door. It is a bitter, dirty fight, as between two people who have hated each other for a very long time.

'Stop!'

Sister's voice is so loud it cuts through everything. She doesn't get up, just sits there looking from Scale to Gypsy.

'It will be over soon. I promise.'

'Promise?' Gypsy's face is a picture of contempt. 'How can you promise anything? You can't even talk.'

Sister seems stung, hurt even. 'I promise, I promise!'

Gypsy turns in contempt to face Scale. 'So! You would screw a half-wit, would you? Maybe join Pinky and rape some driftdead while you're at it.'

Scale visibly wilts. His whole body wilts. He hangs his head like a man in a noose. Sirocco guesses that pretty soon he'll be snivelling.

Sister stands up. Her shoulders are back and her chest is thrown forward proudly. She is not cowed. Unconsciously, Gypsy mirrors her posture. The two women stand, tall and proud, facing each other. Sister's mouth is working but she is struggling to make a single word. Language is a very distant thing for her.

'It's coming,' she says at long last.

'It's coming, you're going,' Gypsy says. 'Go pack your bags.'

'I promise it's coming. Soon.'

'Yes, yes, now get the hell out of here.'

'It's the muddle of the night,' Scale says in a small voice.

'Muddle you too. So what?'

'The stars are too big,' Scale says. He looks across at Sirocco as if he might have something to do with stars being so big.

He's feeling the wind, Sirocco thinks. He just doesn't realise it.

'She'll cope.' To Sister, she says, 'You understand me, don't you? You're out. You found the door once, you can find it again. If I have to throw you out, I will. I'll have no compunction. It's your fault, sitting there all day doing nothing. Sitting around like a ripe plum.'

'Not her fault,' Scale says. He's looking sadder with every passing moment.

'You'd defend her? Of course you would. Angling for another chance, are you?'

'The wind comes in,' Sister says. It seems she would say a lot more, but hesitates between a myriad alternatives. Her throat can't find words, not because there are none, but because there are too many. 'I am the last,' she finishes, as if she has just made a long speech and everything she said connected up.

'You can say that again. It won't all be over soon. It's over now. Get out!'

Sister obeys. She came with nothing and will leave with nothing. She'll walk out into the night and maybe we'll never see her again. All of them, even the Baby, watch her walk to the door. I'll have to follow her, Sirocco thinks. Maybe take her up to Akona. If she is a returned driftdead, she'll need help. He begins to wrap the Baby up for the front pack.

Without a backward look, Sister goes out the door.

With the door open, Sirocco can hear the new wind trying itself out on the world.

A moment later the screaming begins.

a fizzy fizzler

It has to be Sister, although they don't recognise her voice. It is drowned out by a vastly amplified sound, the sort of horrible squeal the fishing boats sometimes make as they scrape up against the wharf. It doesn't come from a human throat.

Gypsy stumbles to the door, pushing her way past Scale who's standing there with his mouth open.

'Get some bloody trousers on,' she says.

Sirocco, clutching the Baby, is right behind her. The Baby does a big, happy crap, but Sirocco can't worry about that right now. The moon is very bright. The sky and stars are hidden behind it. There is an unfamiliar chill in the air.

The first people Sirocco sees are Sister and Sad Toof and Little Sanyo standing on the top of the sand dune that has half buried the crab apple tree, looking seaward, their jaws hanging open, their eyes staring out of their faces, looking like decaying gargoyles on the roof of a forgotten temple. Whatever sounds should have been coming out of their mouths have long since fled.

Sirocco and Gypsy wade up the side of a dune to join them. Scale speeds past them, kicking up sand like a madman, the very picture of manic virility. 'Whale onna starboard bow!' he yells as he gets to the top. A grinding squeal from beyond the sand dune sounds like some monster answering him.

The Cornet household is not alone. Everybody comes out to look, even Flay and Annanda, and gather in ragged lines along the ridges of the sandscape that has now become their town to get a better view.

The bay is blotted out by a tall iceberg, an ice mountain large enough to stretch right across the bay from Pine Point to the wharf. The chill new wind, gently blowing from the south, is pushing the wall of ice up against Pine Point, making that agonised screeching that has brought them all out of sleep.

It sits so calmly, so in possession. So monstrously pure. And so impossibly tall, towering over Pine Point, the bay, the docks, the roundabout, Keatown itself, completely blocking the Pacific Ocean behind.

'Musta got blown here in the night,' someone says, which is sensible enough. But it doesn't feel that way. Its appearance seems sudden and magical, as if it had indeed popped up through 'holes inna ocean.'

In the foreground a few driftdead make their way south along the beach. It is business as usual for them, and there is the usual throng on Highway 6, but nobody takes any notice. All eyes are fixed on the iceberg that hangs over the town, vast, cool and clean, like some indifferent deity. Massive and overwhelming. Its cliffs are precipitous, its slopes sleek and impossibly pristine in the moonlight. And it sweats. Sheds purity. Water flows from its flanks that has not seen the light since the earth was young.

The smell of ancient ice is in the air.

And that deep, slow rocking, as if it would copulate with the land.

'How do we get out to fish?' Orlap is heard to comment.

Sirocco stares at it for so long it seems as if it were the land under his feet in gentle undulation, not that great imperturbable slab of ice. His vertigo from before has not completely gone; somehow his experience earlier is tied in with the arrival of this leviathan.

Standing there, staring at it, it seems impossible that life should go on in any normal way, but there is a town to rebuild and a barrier to maintain, as the mayor reminds them. And it won't matter that the fishermen can't fish for a few days, as they are still working on the The Merry Widow.

Getting on with the job has always been the mayor's philosophy, and he's not about to change it now. It's such a pity, he's overheard saying to Mavis, the iceberg would have made an amazing tourist attraction. Better than a brothel, even better than whales. To satisfy everybody's curiosity, the mayor suggests that, come dawn, Orlap and a couple of fishermen take a dinghy and check the 'berg' out. He likes to call it a berg because that makes it sound more like a friendly pet than the monstrous and unthinkable thing it really is. It's a smart idea. Put a couple of men on the ice and next thing you know somebody will be playing toboggans on the slippery slopes. Plant the flag. Make it our berg. How many towns can boast an ice mountain?

Dawn is painting the tip of the ice mountain with a creamy pink by the time the expedition is ready to set out. Big Bill himself plans on going, as if paying a visit to some passing potentate. In his own mind, going himself makes the visit to the berg official. There are some naysayers. Mavis thinks it's a stupid idea. 'What are you going to do when you get there? Plant a fucking flag?'

Which is exactly what Big Bill intends to do, except Keatown doesn't have a flag. Flay offers one of the oil company pennants that hang hopefully from his roof, but the mayor finally settles on an old Silver Fern rugby flag that Scale produces from his collection of rugby memorabilia. Flay provides a thin iron rod for the flag, a few tools, and the party is good to go.

There is a last-minute quibble over the gender balance of the rowboat crew. Orlap has to go, the mayor insists on going, Orlap wants another young fisherman, or Butch, to assist. Mother Smiley, however, whose newfound cheerfulness has not faded, suggests that a woman should go, herself for instance, or Akona, or maybe Gypsy.

'What kind of game are you trying to play?' Mavis asks her.

Mother Smiley brushes that one off with a smile. 'Why should the men have all the fun?' she asks sweetly. 'After all, fair's fair.'

Whether she's implying that Butch is not a real woman is not clear, but Butch gives her a dirty look just in case. The mayor, who doesn't give a toss one way or the other, readily agrees. Mavis immediately states that she won't be going, implying she would be the natural choice, which is not at all clear to anybody, particularly Mother Smiley. The vote goes to Gypsy, by popular acclamation. Gypsy doesn't like the idea of approaching the monster 'berg' any more than Mavis, but goes along, the women cheering as she steps onto the dinghy.

So Orlap and his merry crew set out to make a royal visit to the berg. To plant the Silver Fern. They watch the berg loom larger as they approach, and marvel at the huge caverns the milder water has carved in its mother bulk. Those on shore fall quiet as the dinghy is dwarfed by the ice.

They are not quite the first to touch its bulk. Some of the driftdead bob by, legs still churning. A few are washed up against the berg but can get no grip on the ice. Everybody claps as the tiny boat draws close to the leviathan. When they touch the ice, Orlap stands up upon the bow and raises his arms above his head, as if this were some great fish he has personally landed, a continent he and his brave mates have drawn up out of the ocean. The crowd clap louder and cheer. Sad Toof shakes his head in despair, 'They're all fools,' he says.

Getting the Silver Fern onto the ice is another matter. There is no way they can scale those walls without full mountaineering gear; crampons, ropes and pulleys. Orlap hacks futilely at the ice wall with a pick-axe Flay provided. 'They're gunna need a fucken drill,' Flay says. But Orlap doesn't figure that out as fast as Flay, and keeps hacking at the ice. Then he uses a heavy hammer, again courtesy of Flay, to drive the steel rod directly into the side of the ice. The rod slips and slides on the ice. Orlap sways and falls, the splash hardly heard on the beach. 'I told you so,' Sad Toof says. Orlap surfaces and Butch and Gypsy pull him on board while the mayor perches on the other gunwale to balance the weight. The dinghy wallows dangerously. Orlap is safely on board but he is empty-handed. The rod, the flag and hammer are gone. 'Silly fucker,' Flay says. 'Dumb-arse Viking.' He should've learned his lesson in London as far as the Nords were concerned: never lend the cunts anything.

Mavis is in full agreement with him. 'Well, that was a fizzy fizzler,' she says with some satisfaction. 'Hail the conquering fucking heroes. Mission accomplished!'

It is as the conquering heroes are returning, heads bowed in defeat, that everybody falls silent, aware of something new in the light movement of air. Little Sanyo, with his ears so finely attuned to silence, is the first to hear it. 'It's like a tightly stretched piece of wire vibrating,' he says. 'Only a very long piece.'

Then everybody can hear it, or at least hear something, but nobody describes it the same way. To Sirocco it sounds like someone playing the high notes of a flute in the far distance, on the edge of hearing.

'The iceberg is singing,' Witch Hunt says.

'From holes inna ice,' Scale says, jabbing at the sky with his finger as if he personally was poking those holes.

'I'm sick of your fucking holes,' Mavis says. 'You have a bee in your bonnet about them.' But there's no real spite in it. She can hear it too. It sounds unpleasantly like a child crying in the wind, and gives Mavis the willies. The sound of wailing babies has always given her the shudders, which is why she's never tried to have one herself.

'It could be the Elfie,' Witch Hunt says. This refers to a local legend, about a boy, wild and feral, who is said to live in the mountains and the foothills, who will never allow himself to be glimpsed by human beings. He is known, however, because in certain winds you can hear him play his flute, said to be a pipe with simple stops he made from a piece of mountain beech. As long as he remains unseen, he will never age, but remain like a Peter Pan forever playing his flute and bouncing the sounds off the icy slopes of the alps.

The librarian has traced the legend back about a hundred years before it peters out among several stories of children who were lost in the wild. Only Ock Arglin, the mountain moonshiner, claims to have actually heard the Elfie from close up, 'just the other side of the valley', and his testimony is as dubious as his brew. 'I thought angels were coming for me,' he told anybody who would listen.

'It's just the wind cutting the ice,' Sad Toof says, unimpressed. Maybe even those holes Scale was on about.

Sirocco feels comforted. Some things never change. How can it be that Sad Toof, with all his negativity, is suddenly a rock in a heaving flux of change? And he could be right, except he has it around the wrong way: more like ice cutting the wind. This creepy new wind was cutting across jagged edges, turning our visitor into a giant ice harp. Making a thin, keening sound. Nobody can be sure, as the sound seems to come from all around. It might just as well have been spirits in the air. Ock's angels coming for us all.

The librarian hears not one note but several, an arpeggio as crisp as new sunlight scaling icy slopes.

chapter and verse

The iceberg has been sitting in the bay for two days now, but Rasputin hardly cares about it, hardly glances at it as he leaves the church each day after a night of insomnia and austerity. Unlike some, who treat the berg as a sign or portent – although of what is not clear – or have already woven some kind of superstition around it, Rasputin refuses to see it as more than an oversized lump of ice, doubtless calved from the great ice shelves in the far south, where south turns into north again.

Truly, without the Lord, people fall so quickly into darkness and delusion! In this case, like anyone with any sense, Rasputin is happy to accept Little Sanyo's observation that since the great ice shelves to the south are melting and breaking up, it is not so surprising that their advance guard should appear in our coastal waters, or, by accident, wash up in one of our bays. All it takes is a bit of wind from the south. Straightforward enough, but it is amazing how people ignore the obvious and search for some hidden conspiracy or endlessly devious complexity. They would rather believe that the berg was suddenly deposited here by a contrary god, or towed by ten thousand rowers in a thousand canoes, than simply blown here by a convenient wind.

Some people don't have the sense God gave them, and ask what God means by the iceberg, as if it has to be a message from God. Something so massive has to be a portent. Eventually, the reverend says rather tartly that God put the iceberg there to test their faith, so they'd better stop asking questions. And they do. Mostly.

Rasputin's so busy, what with the soul-flames on the heads of the driftdead and the iceberg, having something other than Orchid to think about, that he gets a shock when he sees her approaching him as he stands, somewhat irresolutely, at the door of the church. For a moment she might have been just another thought of a particularly vivid kind, a hallucination even.

She's put a jacket on against the cool wind, but wears a girlish skirt with pleats. Her legs are smooth and shapely. He puts up a brief battle against looking at them, but his eyes know where they want to go. Her hair is straw-tousled, like a boy's, just as it was another lifetime ago on

Pine Point. She approaches him warily. He doesn't appreciate quite how rumpled and wild-eyed he looks.

'I would've seen the reverend, but...' she shrugs.

'The reverend... hasn't, isn't himself. Lately.' He can hardly stumble out a sentence.

'I reckon.'

'Why did you want to see him?'

She snuggles into her jacket and looks at her feet. He looks at them too. They are fine, slender feet. He wants to look somewhere else.

'How do you know when you're doing the right thing? I mean, how do you know? Do you ask God or something?'

'Uhhh...' The right thing. How does he know? Suddenly he doesn't know anything about anything.

They shuffle around in front of one another. The wind picks up; the iceberg thinly sings.

'It depends on what it is, and if it hurts people.'

'Is it always bad to hurt people?'

Rasputin doesn't know. Such a simple question and he doesn't know. She's looking right at him now, and he knows even less.

'Mostly, I reckon.'

'But not always.'

'Unless I know what you're talking about...' He scratches his elbow.

Because he doesn't know what else to do, he sits on the steps of the church and rubs his hand on the rough stone. There's a loud, harsh cry overhead from a seagull, floating towards the iceberg.

Orchid sits beside him, close enough for their knees to touch. She pulls something from her pocket and shows him, leaning towards him. He catches a scent, like wild thyme.

'This was my mother's. It's called a cameo.'

He sees an ivory-coloured face on a rose-coloured background. A little brooch.

'My mother got it from some old aunty. When I was young, I used to imagine it showed my mother's face. I thought I'd lost it.'

He keeps rubbing his hand on the rough stone. He'd rub the flesh right off.

'It's very pretty,' he says.

'Isn't it! My grandfather was Thomas Kensington, did you know? He married Prudence Dawson. Their daughter was Alice, my mother. She was a very gracious woman. She told me that the face on the cameo is Prudence, my grandmother. Do you think she looks like me?'

Rasputin is not sure. The cameo face looks serene and beautiful. She strokes it with her forefinger, tracing the outline of the face. He can smell the heat coming off her body and feel the silk of her voice in his ear.

Being this close to her is like being in a different medium, like stepping from cold air into warm water. Given time he might learn how to breathe, talk, move about, think straight in this new medium. Right now all he wants to do is reach out and touch her face the way she is touching the cameo. His body begins to shake, as if it were in a fever. Absurdly, he wants to dance. No, God wants him to dance. To come down off the steps of the church and swing about in the sand and the light like some heretical dervish.

He recalls his jealous suspicions at the party, while Hera was singing 'Santa Lucia'. There is no air of falsity and corruption about her now. He can't feel the shadow of the baron over her. All he feels is her trembling and her vulnerability.

'What happened to your mother?'

Orchid looks down at the step below. It takes Rasputin a moment to realise she is crying. He gets up and sits back down again. Tears are often the sign of a troubled conscience, the reverend once said, but it is hard to believe that it's so in this case, for he can hear nothing in her sobbing but an aching loss.

'Is this what you wanted to talk to the Reverend about?'

'Sort of. A mother shouldn't abandon her child. It's wrong.'

'Yes.' But it happens. The long emergency has seen lots of 'left behind' kids, like Little Sanyo, some left on the side of the road like an unwanted pet. 'Did your mother abandon you?'

'My mother? She was so proud of her Kensington blood, she was.'

'Is she dead?'

'Might as well be.'

'Does God answer your prayers?'

'God's gifts can be unexpected.'

The cameo lies in her open palm. She closes her fingers over it. 'The reverend just quoted chapter and verse. That's what he called it.' She laughs briefly. 'It was like going to see an oracle. Ask him a question, and you get a nice little verse to ponder.'

Rasputin laughs too. 'I'm not so good at chapter and verse. But we only ask the opinion of others when we suspect we are doing something wrong.'

'Would you kill somebody? If you had to?'

'That's not a fair question. If you have to do something, then there isn't a choice.'

'If you wanted something more than all the world, would you risk everything to get it?'

'That doesn't sound like a fair question either.'

At the same time, the question excites him. There is something more than all the world he wants, right now, and it feels as if he would risk his immortal soul to get it. To touch the cameo of her face.

'Nobody needs to die. That's the point.' There are still tears in her eyes, making them look large and glaucous.

The suspicions Rasputin has harboured that Orchid and Orlap are up to something surface once more, fuelled by her refusal to be explicit about what is bothering her. But none of this is the issue anymore; the issue is what he is about to do. The issue is the wind that shakes his body. His huge, trembling uncertainty.

'Rasputin, have you ever wondered what would happen if... I mean, what if... everybody deserted. What if we all turned into driftdead?'

'I don't like to imagine that.'

'Nobody would care then, would they?'

'I suppose not.' He doesn't like thinking about it.

'Even the Baby. Imagine the Baby...'

He tries not to. Those tiny feet trying to pedal south, those bright, alive eyes turning lustreless. He tries to close his eyes against that vision.

'It's only blind luck, isn't it, that we haven't turned yet? Or do you think God is condemning some and saving others, reaching out his hand here, but not there?'

He moves uncomfortably within his clothes. 'No,' he says. His voice is so hoarse he can hardly recognise it. He doesn't think God is like that, nor does he like blind luck. Is a blind god any more likely than one who can see?

'Any moment it could happen to you. To me... to the Baby.'

'Yes. That's how we live our lives now, under that constant threat.'

'Do we? Do we have to? Is that what's left for us?'

Rasputin can't answer these questions.

'Not me,' she says, standing up. Her tears have gone, leaving her eyes looking cold and glittery. 'I'm not going to stand for it a moment longer than I have to. Not a moment.'

'Is that why you came to me?'

'How do you mean?'

'Did you come to me just to bring yourself to this decision? To get all the worry out of the way?'

She smiles. It is the first since the conversation began, and it slips across her face, brief as a dream. 'I came here for chapter and verse,' she says.

Despite the numbness of his body, he takes her face in his hands. It rests there, between his palms, warm and living.

'Rasputin, what are you doing?' The way she says his name makes it sound like a caress.

'Looking at your face.'

'Haven't you looked enough?'

'No. Never. Eternity wouldn't be enough.'

'Take your hands away, now, please.'

'Why?'

'You can't leave them there forever.'

His hands drop to his sides, full of regrets. They loved the feel of her face.

'I'm sorry. I wanted so much to do that.'

'Don't be sorry. You have shown me something.'

'How?'

'You had to overcome your fear of me, didn't you, to do that, to touch me like that?'

'I shouldn't have done it.'

'Don't say that.' She puts a finger up to his lips. 'For a moment you overcame your doubts and fears and did what you most wanted to do, which was touch me. You had to bring yourself to that... point of resolution.'

'Yes, but...'

Again her finger touches his lips, sealing them tight. 'Don't you see? You have done exactly what I have to do. Show that kind of resolve.'

He's still looking at her. She can't stop him.

'That's better than chapter and verse,' she says.

the silent invasion

The new wind has a rather unpleasant edge to it, even though it has polished the air, made it sharp and clean, like the ice itself, and blown away the humidity and murk built up over many windless days. There's some activity down on the wharf, where work on the The Merry Widow continues despite the fishing fleet being trapped behind the iceberg. There is the usual trickle of driftdead making their way south along Highway 6, the tiny flames of their souls dancing on their heads. Rasputin tries to take no notice of them.

There is some activity at the barrier, however. A knot of people, the sound of shouting. He doesn't bother going down to the roundabout and along the road, but cuts straight across the slope, through a couple of properties and some empty land, and past the library, where he spots the librarian emerging from her cellar, blinking like a nocturnal animal in the pearly light. He joins her and they approach the barrier together. He suspects the librarian is an atheist, but it hardly seems to matter. He's beginning to wonder, quite blasphemously, if God himself is not an atheist.

They give each other anxious looks as they approach the defences.

There has been a serious breach in the barrier just north of the library. A segment of the bulwark has folded from the weight of the thronging driftdead; tin, wire and sharpened stakes are trampled underfoot as the crowd surges forward. Many of them are wounded by the spiky remains of the barrier, with gashes and holes in their bodies, but they take no notice. Pinky is there with his mates to pull the barrier back into place. A stripped-down version of a man is Pinky now; gaunt and bone. 'We can't hold them,' he shouts. 'Bring the guns!' The mayor rushes forward, with no guns, as if he alone might turn the tide, and stumbles. Pinky pulls him to his feet before he goes under. There is something wrong with Mayor Broonzy. He's waving his arms around and shouting as if he has a whole army to command. He's drunk, Rasputin realises with a shock.

It's Rasputin's last thought before he and the librarian are surrounded by driftdead. He is forced by their sheer numbers to retreat, and is immediately separated from the librarian. If he goes down he might never get up. All around him pale flames dance in attendance above their heads. They are translucent enough for him to see the sky behind. He knows these must be the souls of the afflicted because he can feel the holiness in them, the divine spark. Feeling a little like a doubting Thomas, he passes his hand through several of these bobbling flames and can feel for himself the tingle of divine energy. He can feel the Lord. The Lord is everywhere around him, even in the midst of the damned. The Lord has given him this true vision that he might understand, and through his understanding come closer to the Lord. As gently as he can, for he understands now that even the damnedest of the damned, even while marching to perdition, are precious in the eyes of God, and that violence against them is both sacrilegious and futile.

He has to tell the reverend. Keeping quiet about this up till now has been nothing but sheer cowardice. Let them revile him, hate him, stone him! He must speak out, not on his own behalf but on behalf of the truth itself. What good is he otherwise?

He feels a purposeful tug on his sleeve. It is the librarian, trying to pull him to safety. They make their way to a hillock a short distance uphill. The driftdead are flowing each side like a great river. It looks like a scene that should be full of the noise of battle and yet, but for the shouting of the few humans and the shuffle of the endless driftdead, there is an unnatural silence. Rasputin can even hear the cry of seagulls hovering over the wharf.

It is a silent invasion.

There are a few others clustered on the rise, having retreated from a last-minute defence of the barrier, among them Pinky, the mayor, Mavis, Orlap, Butch, Sirocco and the Baby. And the Reverend Stickman. He is standing beside Hera staring at the flood of the unholy dead – he still thinks of them as the Devil's pilgrims – going by. Perhaps Rasputin's news will not upset him. Perhaps he will be pleased. The idea that the driftdead carry their souls with them bobbing along behind the way a child might carry a balloon, could come as a relief. God is still in charge! At least, that's the way Rasputin plans to present it. The reverend might well grasp at the thought like a drowning man grasps a stick.

Rasputin takes his master's hand and gives it a squeeze. The initial flood of driftdead from the breach has now settled into a steady stream. Most flow either side of the little group, and the few that come front-on can be pushed aside easily enough, at least with constant effort. Pinky and Orlap guard Sirocco and the Baby.

'We'll make it to our place, the mayor's manor,' Mavis says, 'if we all hold hands.' She giggles.

Another drunk one. Only Ock Arglin gets drunk this time of the day. Rasputin looks at the reverend for enlightenment, but the reverend's gaze is far away.

'Of course we will!' the mayor declares. 'Who says we won't?'

'Not me,' Mavis says.

'It's the best idea,' Orlap says.

'No!' the rev says.

They all look at him, but he's not looking their way at all. He's looking towards the library. 'No,' he repeats.

Rasputin follows the direction of his gaze and sees Hera – and understands. It is not completely unexpected.

the great battle of his life

Growing thinner and more wan than ever, Hera has recently taken to walking up and down the straggling lines of driftdead along Highway 6, her eyes drawn towards them, as if she were searching for a remembered face. Invariably Reverend Stickman would be by her side, talking and gesticulating, pleading, preaching. It is the great battle of his life, and he doesn't even quite know why he has to fight it. Especially given that he knows he is bound to lose.

Unless the Lord intervenes.

He's exhorted her to heed the whisper of life within and not the shout of death without, to turn her face away from the Pilgrims of Satan, to not allow Satan to suck her soul from her body. Rather she must turn her face to God, hold fast to the love of God, for that is all we have left now – and hold fast to her body, especially that, for it too is an expression of the love of God. These are the best sermons of his life, sermons not based on Ecclesiastes, on the vanity of life and certainty of damnation, and the hellfires that dwell therein, but on the God of creation who becomes the God of Love, the God that redeems.

At first it seemed as if the ex-celeb, ex-Queen, ex-baby bearer was heeding the reverend's words. She would listen gravely to him, nod her head and stare deeply into him as if she had to see his very soul to know the truth of his words. And she did, Rasputin decides, see into his very soul, which, in all its agony, he revealed to her. It wasn't much but was all he had. As time went by, however, her nods grew shallower and her gaze more abstracted. She no longer looked into his soul but somewhere beyond it. The further she drifted away from him, the more he pleaded with her and exhorted her, tears of frustration streaking his face.

Rasputin could have told him what it was he was really feeling, and was on the verge of it several times, but God stayed his hand. Now is certainly not the time to remind him of his previous attitude to the mansion whore who gave herself airs, the very whore of Babylon herself, or ask him what he is feeling as he paces by her side. Or tell him about his own experience with Orchid, and how he reached out his hands to her. The last thing he wants is the collapse of the reverend's exhausted and delicately balanced mind. Seeing the truth might be the straw that breaks this camel's back, enough to consign the last shreds of his sanity to the hellfires of the heart.

That sanity is at stake now as the reverend sets off towards Hera, standing in the flow of driftdead, facing them, face as blank as theirs. 'No!' he shouts. His voice carries over the muted shuffling of the driftdead, but she doesn't appear to hear him. Rasputin follows as he rushes up to her, pushing aside the driftdead to keep up.

'Her eyes are not moving,' the reverend says. He waves his hand in front of her face. 'She's leaving the world.'

Rasputin grabs hold of his sleeve. 'You can't help her, master. Only God can help her now.'

'But I must! I must help her.' Briefly, he turns a haunted face to Rasputin.

'But he can, of course he can!' The mayor is waving a bottle in the air. 'I've got the cure!'

'The cure!' Mavis echoes.

'Don't do this,' Rasputin says, grabbing the reverend's sleeve.

Without looking at him, eyes fixed on Hera, the reverend shakes him off.

'I bet you've never seen a drunk driftdead!' Mavis shouts at them. 'Stay pissed, no risk!'

She and the mayor roar with laughter and throw their arms around each other.

'Why what?' The reverend is almost as far away from the world as Hera. Just as she can't tear herself away from the blur of figures in front of her, he can't tear himself away from her. I'll lose him too, Rasputin thinks with a sudden pang. Then where will I be?

'No more deserting, dumb-arses. Stay drunk, stay outa sight of the Devil, Rev! You can't go walkies if you're legless.' Mavis's laughter is a high-pitched shriek, as she pushes away some driftdead, shoving them hard enough that they bump into one another.

'Her soul is safe,' Rasputin shouts to his master with all the authority he can muster.

The reverend hears. 'What do you mean?'

'The Lord has her. He has all of us.'

'Not them!' The reverend shoves one with all his might, just the way Mavis did.

'Yes, even them! He has their souls in the palm of his hand. I've seen them.'

'No, no!' The reverend begins to babble. 'He has forsaken them. That is what they are, the forsaken of God. The Godforsaken.'

He grabs hold of Hera's arms with both hands, and plants his feet firmly in the earth, bracing himself for a final great wrestle with the Devil.

Mavis laughs her head off. She's never seen anything quite so funny. 'Give her a kiss, won't you! It works in fairy tales. She'll be your little lambkin forever.'

The mayor pushes his way to them, shoves the reverend to one side and lifts a bottle to Hera's mouth, forcing it between her teeth. Amber liquid flows down her chin. There's the acrid stench of Ock's hock in the air. 'Drink up, me lovely,' the mayor croons, 'and put a bit of ol' Ock's fire in your veins. It's got special ingredients that keep away the dead!'

'Climb on top of her, won't you,' Mavis says, grinning like a skull.

The reverend pushes the mayor away. 'Don't touch her, you son of Sodom!'

After a brief tussle, the mayor swings the bottle at the reverend's head. The reverend steps back to avoid it and the bottle hits Hera's shoulder with a thud. She hardly seems to register the blow. She does, however, register the sudden cry of the Baby. She turns in Sirocco's direction. Sirocco is not sure if she can see him or not.

'Stop it!' Rasputin commands, holding both arms in the air as if he holds sway over all things.

'Fuck off,' Mavis advises him. 'Who are you anyway? You're no saviour. You're just a jumped-up, punk kid, God-botherer, what would you fucking know?' She thrusts the bottle at him. 'Here, have a fucking drink, son,' she pinches Rasputin's cheek, 'then come and see your Aunty Mavis... she'll show you what it's all about!' To Big Bill, she says, 'Don't you think he's a pretty boy?'

The reverend shouts to Sirocco. 'The Baby! the Baby! the Baby – the Baby will save her! Bring him! Now! Oh God!' he buries his face in his hands.

Rasputin and Sirocco exchange a swift look. They both know it will do no good, but Sirocco moves in with the Baby anyway, Pinky and Orlap in attendance, shoving aside the driftdead.

'Show her the Baby,' the reverend commands Sirocco.

Sirocco holds the Baby up in front of the mute woman. Obligingly the baby reaches out towards her, gurgling and smiling. She takes no notice. The Baby tries to stick his fingers into her mouth.

'The Baby is not named,' the reverend babbles. 'That might make a difference. His innocence is not yet sanctified.' His stick-like figure sways in the wind, sweat stands out on his face like tiny beads. 'We must have a naming ceremony. Now. No child should grow up unnamed and unblessed.'

'That's true,' Rasputin says. 'All in good time.'

'Now,' the reverend says. 'It must be now or never. He can't touch her soul until he is blessed by baptism.'

Hera takes no notice.

'If the Baby were christened she'd feel differently,' the reverend says, looking wildly around. 'Bring me some water and I will christen him. Now.'

'You have lost her, master,' Rasputin says, amazed at the sadness in his voice.

'Give her the Baby,' the reverend says to Sirocco, in a broken, desperate voice. 'Let her feel him in her arms. He will make her feel human again. I'll christen him in her arms. Get me some water! For the love of God, some water! Rasputin, where are you?'

Rasputin gives a tiny shake of his head. Already he can see it taking tentative shape, the slender, translucent flame forming above her head. He is watching the birth of a driftdead, the soul leaving the body. The bodiless flame forming above. The emptiness below.

'Then give the Baby to me.' The reverend reaches out for the Baby.

Sirocco clutches the Baby close. Orlap steps forward, his eyes on the Baby.

'Heathen! Give him to me! Let me have him before you sacrifice him to that infernal lizard!' The reverend tries to snatch the Baby. Sirocco pulls away. Rasputin grabs his master with both hands and squeezes tight. The feeling hardly registers on the reverend's demented face. Orlap comes up on the other side of Sirocco. 'I can take the Baby if you want,' he says evenly. 'Keep him safe.'

'No thanks,' Sirocco says. The Baby looks with mild interest at Orlap.

'Will somebody give the good reverend a drink!' the mayor says to one of the passing driftdead.

'Time will name the child,' Hera says. Her voice is very remote, as if she is talking to them from another planet. 'His name is... time...'

The reverend hands her the Baby's shawl, his face bleeding with joy. 'The time is now, for that joyful union...' His arms are open to receive her, but she's already gone.

The Baby's shawl in hand, she joins the slipstream of the driftdead, not looking back.

Soon nobody can spot her among them. She is just another anonymous, bobbing figure.

The reverend faces them like a naked man. 'I loved her,' he says.

Nobody says anything.

the endgame is played above

With the collapse of the barrier and Hera's desertion, the town's morale takes a distinct downward turn. There was something special about her, a true celeb. Everybody agrees that she knew she was going, and that she handed the Baby on as soon as she became aware of it. Foresight and courage are added to her other virtues.

Some quiet tears are shed, but not for long; Keatown of the driftdead is no place for tears. With her loss comes the realisation that Hera was the heart of the town, its summer rose, even though not everybody saw it that way at the time.

After Hera's departure, for reasons she can't fully understand, the librarian's attitude towards Miranda softens. With her blonde curls and pretty face, Miranda might be Hera's daughter rather than Jolene's, but it is something more than that. It is something to do with beauty, and the survival of beauty in the world. It seems to the librarian that ugly things survive in this world over beautiful things, as if ugliness has some kind of competitive advantage. There are some things almost too beautiful for this world, and which only touch us in their passing.

Keen to catch that thought on the wing, she writes, It's harder for the pretty ones, sometimes. And stops. That is not the thought she wanted to catch! It's a different thought. Instead of writing one thing, she's written another. That's the thing about writing, it's too easy to get it wrong, just a little bit wrong even, and, having got it wrong, it's too easy to stop. For, along with stops come doubts. After all, she has just written a commonplace observation, trite even, rather than the elusive idea she wants to express. That slip from beauty into prettiness is an all too common one. Even sentences can be subject to it.

It would be better to cross out that sentence – when in doubt, throw it out! Except it raises certain unrelated issues. The librarian herself has never been one of the 'pretty ones', let alone beautiful, which she counts as a blessing, for being young and pretty seems a lot of hard work. All that striving and flouncing around to little purpose; the librarian had a good opportunity to observe it all when she was young, and to be grateful not to be a part of it. The bliss of being able to sit to one side with a book! To feel quietly superior to one's prettier peers, ha!

None of this is fit for the Chronicles of Keatown of course, or has much to do with the town's reaction to Hera's desertion. Even Hera's detractors are shocked and saddened, as if having just realised what they have lost. Grandmother Gaunt has gone uncharacteristically quiet. The reverend is inconsolable.

Melissa Tonguestone, who might well have been counted as pretty before terror took its toll on her face, finally decides it is time for her and her suicide group to take action. It's embarrassing, having a suicide group that stays alive just to talk about it. Hera's desertion is just the trigger Melissa needs, not that there was any love lost between them. Encouraged by the reverend's agitation, Melissa developed an intense jealousy of Hera. So easy in her beauty, it made Melissa uncomfortable to witness it, as if there was something obscene about the woman's very existence. Her desertion, however, does not come as a relief. It's death coming one step closer, that's all it is.

She convinces a local farmer, whose wife has deserted, and who has a heavy-duty Four Wheel Drive, to join her suicide club, to load up the Explorer and head south across the desert. Better to die an anonymous death on the road in the middle of nowhere than in Keatown besieged by zombies. They made a death pact that if any one of them turned, the survivors would shoot that person, then each other. It is like suicide by rolling a dice: throw a double six and they all die. But if they don't throw a double six, and none of them turns, they just might make it across the desert.

Nobody turns up to bid them farewell as they set out at dawn, intending to drive all day without stopping. Margo, however, arrives at the last minute to try to talk Melissa out of the whole idea. Life, she says, is too precious to throw away. Those two have disagreed on just about everything, and nothing much has changed. Who then would have expected Margo to have a tear in her eye as she watched the car with its little band of desperadoes disappear into the south.

This all passes through the librarian's mind as she dithers, her hands hovering above the keyboard, her eyes fixed on the last sentence she has written: It's harder for the pretty ones, sometimes. She was thinking of Miranda when she wrote the words, but now they remind her of Ellen Johnson, whose nine daughters to Peter Johnson were each prettier than the last, according to the legends of the day. The triumphant Ellen managed to marry each one of them off to local gentry, or what passed for gentry in the colonies – grocers, tailors, farmers, traders. God-fearing men with a cash flow and a decent shot at respectability.

Sometimes she tries to imagine what that woman was like – her courage and determination. There is one late photograph of her and her nine daughters, taken around 1900. They are posed in a semi-circle, with that awareness of posterity you see in colonists' relationship with the camera. The famous Johnson beauties would be described at the time as 'handsome' and 'buxom' and 'comely' – good pioneering, baby-bearing stock, looking at ease and relaxed. Young women confident of their charms.

Looking at these photos makes the librarian feel guilty.

What use is her admiration for Ellen's sterling qualities if she doesn't aspire to them herself? What would Ellen have done with Miranda? Dressed her in hand-me-downs, gashed knees and a smudged face notwithstanding. Fed her, clothed her, kissed her goodnight, said a prayer, made the girl feel, even if for a brief moment, wanted and loved. The librarian can't emulate that, since all she really cares about are her books, and her Chronicles, which must increase each day by a certain amount or she grows fretful. Caring for a child the way Ellen Johnson must have is a new and not particularly welcome idea. The librarian has put a lot of time and effort into avoiding entanglements of this kind. Her work has required her absolute commitment.

However, these women needed all the advantages they had, she writes. Then she deletes it. Worse and worse, from commonplace to cliché in one slip. Having the girl Miranda sitting in the corner doesn't help. How can she write properly with someone else in the room? Especially someone whose presence is charged with a mute appeal. Every so often she ushers the girl from her writing room, gently but firmly she would hope, and sets her up in the library with a book. But back she would creep, like a shadow, like a dog with a domestic heart, into a corner of the writing room once more. It is all she seems to ask, just to be here with the librarian, yet it is more than the librarian can grant, at least when she's at work on her Chronicles. When she's in the library itself, checking out her books and dusting them off, she has no problem. She even likes it when the girl sits quietly and reads, just as the librarian herself used to do. A quiet reader makes for a happy book.

Perhaps the worst of it is that Miranda's presence reminds the librarian of what is going on outside. Since her spade attack on the young driftdead female, the librarian has been reluctant to leave her fastness. Staying above ground long enough to see the breach in defences, the flood of driftdead and the desertion of Hera was enough, more than enough. The town is doomed. Keatown is history. Her Chronicles will come to an end, here, down in this bunker, as the endgame is played above. If only Ellen Johnson could have seen this moment.

After a time she gets up from the keyboard, powers down the blue eye and goes upstairs to make some cocoa for Miranda. Cocoa with powdered milk and sugar. What could be nicer? When she returns Miranda is sitting in the children's section holding a picture book upside down. The smell of the cocoa revives her, and she takes it shyly but eagerly, holding it in both hands.

'Thank you,' she says in a small voice.

After a moment, the librarian gets up and returns to her writing room.

I breathe a sigh of relief. Feels like another crisis has been weathered.

Mr Flay does not look his best with his mouth hanging open

Flay and Annanda stand at the supermarket window and watch the solid mass of driftdead passing by. The passing parade that goes on forever. Flay can remember seeing crowds like that packing into a stadium for a football game or rock concert. Couldn't get a vehicle through that lot, not without making a hell of a mess – which brings him to the matter at hand: the devious schemes of Orlap the Viking and his faithful companion Butch.

Annanda makes a melancholy gesture towards the driftdead. 'So many, so many, and not a single customer. I must lock my door, and you, my friend, must see to your barricade.'

'It won't last.' From here he can see the hammering his clever device is taking. Sooner or later the building paper will give, and that'll be it.

Annanda says, 'That is the fate of all things. If we look inside ourselves we may witness the birth and death of suns. The only question is, does it rob us of courage or inspire it?'

The pumps will go next, Flay thinks. Game over for Flay's gas. What a bitter fate, to be overrun by pedestrians! The last of old-time petrolheads, walked on like a piece of dogshit.

'These Rakshasa are not immortal, Mr Flay. They too will pass. When I lie awake at night and listen to them go by, it is like hearing the wind in the grass.'

If either of the two men are afraid to watch the driftdead, they give no outward sign of it. Unlike most, they don't avert their eyes. Perhaps that is because Flay would never in a million years turn into a pedestrian – give me a break! – and Annanda would draw upon the strength of Hanuman himself to avoid becoming one with the Rakshasa. They are united in this, if little else. That this feeling of invulnerability is an illusion certainly occurs to Annanda, but he isn't bothered. Surely it is the Lords of Illusion who rule now anyway.

'He still wants the diesel,' Flay says abruptly. Enough of this wind-in-the-grass business. He's had enough of that kind of candyfloss from the Lamont woman, his piece of fluff!

'Ah,' Annanda's fingers make spidery movements in the air.

It strikes Flay that he does it deliberately, camping it up just to annoy the homophobe petrolhead, to wind him up. Well fuck him! 'Yeah, 'ah' is right. Apparently the The Merry Widow is good to go.' He resists the temptation to waggle his fingers in the air.

'Ah, a happy moment for the town.'

'If you say so. I'm not big on fish myself. But there's a whacking great berg slap in the middle of the bay, how's he gonna get in and out, I ask him, and he waves his hand around and says, it can be navigated. It can be fucking navigated.'

'Hanuman could do it. He can lift mountains, look!'

Flay looks at a picture of a skinny guy with a monkey snout dressed like a pansy carrying a mountain like a waiter carrying a cake.

'So we take him at his word?'

'We don't have to. We have an informant,' Annanda speaks very softly, as if about seriously intimate matters, and gestures through the window.

Flay is amazed to see Butch pushing through the driftdead to arrive at the supermarket door. Annanda lets her in and closes the door quickly behind her.

Butch regards Flay with open hostility. 'You didn't tell me the bloody fan-belt was going to be here,' she says to Annanda, 'I'd've brought my shotgun.'

With great dignity, as if at some official occasion, Annanda says, 'Mr Flay needs to know. Conscience and common sense dictate...' He breaks off, apparently suffering a sudden loss of words. All of those many, many things that conscience and common sense dictate!

'Why should he care?' Butch says, ignoring Flay who is standing right in front of her, and talking to Annanda. 'He'll have his gold bar for his diesel. Deal done.'

'Of course... but the wider circumstances... I've thought of Mr Flay, you sir, as a public-spirited man.'

'It's his diesel, I guess,' Butch says with a twisted grin. 'It's a pity actually. I would love to have seen the look on his face when he found out. I was looking forward to that.'

'Found out what? And I am here. You don't have to talk about me like I'm not here.' Flay hates the whine he hears in his voice.

Jesus, a pansy and a dyke! The way they talk to each other reminds him of the way kids at school would pinch his lunch and throw it back and forward to each other over his head. That all stopped when, inspired by something he'd seen on the box, he removed a couple of fingernails with a pair of pliers. Handy things, pliers, he discovered. Pity he doesn't have a pair of right now.

Butch's grin has become a positive leer. She's determined to make a meal out of this, one way or another. 'You're going to deliver the diesel to the wharf in a tank, right?'

'He's paid for it. And I get the tank back afterwards.'

'Right. Then what happens to it?'

'They use my fucking mobile pump to fill up The Frilly Fuck or whatever.' Flay doesn't have to pretend to be getting steamed up. Any more of this argy-bargy and he'll blow a head gasket for real.

'That's where you're wrong, Flywheel! As soon as your back's turned, Cap'n Orlap loads the drums onto Mr Annanda's truck and takes the back road up mansions! And you, Flywheel, don't even get your tank back!' This final detail sends her into fits of tobacco-phlegmy laughter that ends with the inevitable cough and hack.

Whatever the look might have been on Flay's face, Butch certainly gets her money's worth, and Annanda looks politely away. 'Let me get this straight. He on-sells the diesel – who's buying?'

'The Baron Fairweather.'

'Fuck my brown dog.'

'You could say that, but what happened to the duck?'

'What?' Flay feels as if his head is being unscrewed. Maybe he should have kept away from the skunk. 'The only reason... He wants it for his helicopter.'

'Quick thinking, Flywheel! Keep this up, and you'll have it all worked out by Christmas.'

'And Orlap gets a whole heap of gold bars,' he says.

'Think again, Mr Camshaft.'

'This is the perfidious part,' Annanda puts in. He has not been enjoying the painful spectacle of Flay's awakening, preferring to look down at the floor. Mr Flay does not look his best with his mouth hanging open.

Flay gets it in the end. It all falls into place. 'He's buying his passage out. He doesn't give a shit about the gold bars.'

'Bingo! His place on the chopper! Diesel for a weasel.'

'So why tell us?' Flay figures he already knows, but it might be nice to be on the other end of the tormenting this time.

'He needs me, a partner in crime, but then he is going to ditch me. Double cross me. I really thought there was a place on the chopper for me.'

'More fool you,' Flay says sourly, but there's no bile in it.

Butch readily agrees. 'But no longer.'

'The question now becoming,' Annanda says, 'what is our right course of action?'

'I've got a few ideas,' Flay says grimly.

you can never go home again

After the desertion of Hera, most of the survivors retreat to the mayor's place for more of Ock's cure. The heart has gone out of the town, Sirocco senses. Some kind of critical mass has been lost; too many have turned. Keatown, my beloved Keatown, feels deserted despite the driftdead everywhere. Too many empty houses, too many doors left open and banging. Some of these houses, especially those with doors facing north, have filled up with milling driftdead who blunder inside and can't find their way out. Gardens are trampled, trellises and fences and garden sheds destroyed, everything pulverised into the sand. In bulk and en masse, the driftdead create a swath of destruction from Pine Point to the western turn-off.

One or two places, like the mayor's, bordered to the north and west by a thick macrocarpa hedge, the library, which is mostly underground and easily barricaded, and the marae, perched on the promontory, remain relatively unscathed. Sirocco does not follow the others to the mayor's place. Instead he turns south, instinctively perhaps, heading for home, for the Cornet's house. In his mind's eye he sees it the way it was, filled with wonderful improbabilities, like its colourful inhabitants. He sees Gypsy sashaying around the lounge to the winding beat of Arabic reggae, Scale fooling about pretending to poke holes in the walls, improbably bright sunlight coming in through the windows, the ageless crab apple tree with its gnarled branches and bitter wisdom offering protection to a runt who might sit beneath it and draw shapes in the dirt.

The time he has spent in the Cornet's house, from the day he arrived as a wide-eyed blinking creature from the desert to this very moment, trudging through a new, undulating landscape, appears in his mind like a bright, tropical fruit. And when he opens that fruit it is full of laughter and shouting. A piece of time can appear like that, in the round, a teardrop of time, like the smooth, translucent pieces of glass that make up the necklace Scale playfully placed on the deer's antlers. The tastes are of home, warm oats, condensed milk, crab apple jelly – and of course fish. Scale seldom returned from the fish shed without something for the pot. In his mind's eye it will always be that way, full of quickness and silliness and magic.

He knows that it is not going to be like that, cannot be like that, but at the same time he is impelled at least partly by that vision.

Meanwhile the day is changing. The sky has lowered, and turned leaden. In the sullen twilight, it is hard to tell what time of day it is. Even as he becomes aware of it, the chill brought by the arrival of the iceberg deepens. The world is a dull, pearly grey, the light seemingly coming from all directions. Only the iceberg still glows with daylight, as if lit from within. It looks spooky, Sirocco thinks. Big and spooky, towering over everything, so tall its peak almost touches the low-lying sky. Plodding along with the driftdead, in the same direction, is unnerving enough without the touch of the berg's cold heart. It is too easy to feel just a part of the crowd, to imagine walking forever. Forever a part of, yet isolated from, those around him. He trudges on, holding the Baby close, ignoring the other walkers, wondering where Witch Hunt has got to. Right now it would be nice to have the company of his pesky little shadow. Witch Hunt knows how to be brave in the face of big, scary things.

The slope of the dune, which offers some protection from the occasional driftdead, is no defence against the horde, as Sirocco finds. When he gets to the top of the dune, the first thing he sees is the besieged crab apple tree still half buried in sand, now with its branches broken and torn by constant jostling. He gives it a little pat as he goes past.

The house itself is sturdy enough and has sustained no major damage, although one window is broken and a driftdead man has stuck his head through the frame and remained that way, trying to push the rest of his body through. Sirocco ignores him and goes up towards the door. There are driftdead everywhere, and he wonders if he's imagining that they are thicker around the house, as if clustered around their own memories, and he recalls what Cherrie Lamont said.

He pushes his way to the door, knocks and calls out. The Baby calls out too.

Scale meets them at the door. Black T-shirt on back-to-front, baggy trousers tied with a bootlace. Behind him Sister sits in her accustomed spot. She looks up at Sirocco tranquilly.

'Where's Gypsy?' Sirocco says, already afraid of the answer.

'You took her.'

'What? No...' Sirocco moves to go inside, but Scale blocks his way.

'From the desert, bad dreams come. All your fault.'

'My fault?'

Scale snaps his fingers, 'You bring it on.'

Having a conversation with Scale is a bit like trying to land a particularly tricky fish, one which knows when to jump and when to dive. And when to run.

'Where is she?'

Scale snaps his fingers again, close to Sirocco's ear. The sounds reverberate through his head. If the snapping finger were a word it would be 'gone.'

'Did she turn?'

'Suddenly sudden. The bad dreams come. She step into the air.' He lifts one knee to demonstrate. 'She step through the air.' Snaps his fingers again.

'Where?'

Tears appear on Scale's face, through holes in his eyes. 'She was cha cha cha and then she was...' he waves his hands in front of his eyes, and makes his eyes go cross-eyed. 'You took her. Into the air. I seen you.'

Gypsy. It seems impossible. The woman who saved him from the desert, who brought him to a place where there is a cool spring and a mattress in the corner of a large room filled with all kinds of bits and pieces, the nature and possible histories of which fill his book, the Book of Imaginary Sentences. Gypsy is in that book too, with her wild, dark gypsy hair. She is a big part of that large room. If Sirocco has loved anyone in Keatown, it has been Gypsy, he realises.

Maybe Scale feels the same; he looks miserable enough. There is no bounce in his feet. All those holes everywhere are now in his hostile stare.

'I don't remember the last time I was with her,' Sirocco lies, while searching for a defining moment. A moment he wants to remember. The tropical fruit moment. The teardrop moment. There is none. Only parts of her. Her hair, her full bosom, her broad, man-like shoulders. And only fragments of action. Her laughing. Her slapping Scale's face. Her full-sail dancing. Where is she in all these leftover bits and pieces?

Half the town's gone now, he thinks. Soon there'll be nothing left but a cluster of drunks at the mayor's place.

'Me neither,' Scale says. He draws a circle in the air to illustrate the emptiness of his memory. Questions about the sequence of events tend to confuse Scale. In his head everything is happening at once. He has a poor grasp of before and after at the best of times, which these are not.

He's not making any sense, as he has just said he saw her before she...steps into the air? That made less sense. Even for Scale.

'I have to come in,' Sirocco says. Scale steps aside.

The house looks the same, only darker, colder and emptier. The vital spark has gone. The upper body of the driftdead half-way through the window wriggles around like some live wall trophy, to go with the antlers and the pelt of the tarn hiding a hole in the wall. Sister sits, a solemn totem. She gives no sign she can hear them.

'I'll go soon,' Scale says, following him inside.

'Go where?'

'Through th' air. Jus' like Gypsy. Y' lift your leg up, like this, and you put your leg through to th' other side. Easy.' He makes it look as easy as putting on a pair of pants with one hand while looking in the other direction. It doesn't sound like turning to Sirocco, but something happened, Gypsy has gone. Her absence is palpable.

'You. You did this.' He points an accusing finger at Sirocco.

'Did what?'

The accusing finger draws another circle, 'Everything.'

Sirocco shakes his head. Scale's original dislike of him shows nakedly on his face. 'It started t' change when you came.'

'What did?'

'Everything.' Scale draws another circle. Back to the beginning again.

Perhaps his arrival here upset some delicate balance between Scale and Gypsy, some inner equilibrium that kept the relationship going.

'You bring Gypsy back,' Scale says. 'Go into th' desert and bring her back.' He speaks distinctly, as if to an idiot. 'Right now.'

'How do you know she went to the desert?'

'Through holes inna air,' Scale says vaguely. 'Inna hair.' His resentment, all that was holding his thoughts together, has dissipated, leaving his thoughts to wander off on their own like lost sheep.

Sirocco feels a bit the same. There is nothing for him here except a few nappies and a small supply of milk. He fossicks around, trying to ignore Scale, who's watching him as he would a dog about to give chase to a rabbit. He finds a few tins of baby formula Gypsy must have put aside. Seeing them gives Sirocco a pang. Gypsy didn't ever bargain on a baby in the house, but kept her eye out for him nevertheless. Nearby the driftdead wriggles uselessly in the window frame.

Sirocco feels displaced, as if he were a teenager leaving home. Except the house is no longer a home but just a house half filled with junk, a house that feels empty despite the junk. Cold and empty. Scale seems like little more than a talking, gesticulating shop mannequin, Sister a cipher. Sirocco can imagine that when he leaves, Scale will fall silent, perhaps even stop moving, like Sister, and become nothing more than another object in his own museum of inconsequence, and slowly, like everything else, gather dust.

'She didn' take her magic mirror,' Scale says. 'That's what she shoulda taken.'

At the mention of the mirror Sister looks up.

'What mirror?'

'Her mother gave her that mirror, which came from her mother.' Tears start in the corners of his eyes. He wipes them with his singlet.

'The oval one.' Sirocco has seen it a couple of times, but never noticed it to be so important. Certainly not magic. Gypsy kept it away in her own dressing room, as it is known, off the main lounge.

Scale draws an oval in the air and peers into it as if at his own image. 'You take it.'

'What for?'

Scale moves behind the oval he has drawn in the air and observes Sirocco through it. A look of great cunning has appeared on his face. Perhaps this is the face he's just seen in his imaginary mirror. 'T' give it t' her, of course. You took her. You know where she is. I seen you.' He chants this last bit, like a child who's caught someone out, someone doing something bad.

Sirocco can't argue with this madness; he doesn't have the energy to spend. All he wants to do is get out, get out of this cold house and away from Scale, away from the driftdead hanging half-way through the window.

'Okay!' He holds his hands up in surrender. 'I'll take it, but you know I'll never see her.'

Scale grins in triumph and points to Gypsy's room. He's like a conjurer now, pulling mirrors out of hats, conjuring up rooms.

Sirocco hesitates. He doesn't want to go off on some fool's errand, sent by the confused Scale, although he might just to humour the man. On the other hand, Scale thinks he's up to something, and that's interesting enough in itself.

At the same time Sirocco feels a debt of obligation to the departed Gypsy, to her memory. She always claimed she went into the desert because of a dream in which a lizard came to her and told her she had to make a journey south. Lizard sent Gypsy out into the desert to save Sirocco's skinny ass. In some crazy way, Scale is right to resent him.

'It won't be long,' Sister says to Sirocco. 'Very soon now.'

'Okay,' Sirocco says, unconvinced. Sirocco tends to avoid mirrors. They remind him too much of desert mirages, shimmering images that recede as you approach.

'I never thought she'd go,' Scale says with sudden lucidity, gesturing to the room where the emptiness speaks for itself. 'Without a word. She wus always the one t' have the last word.'

the memory room

With a touch of superstitious dread, Sirocco pushes open the door. Gypsy never allowed anybody into this room, and Sirocco has only seen it a couple of times from the doorway. These glimpses gave him the impression that the room was for all of Gypsy's personal stuff, her family stuff, mainly. This was her memory room, where she could trace some of the stages of her life and her Roma roots. Although Gypsy has gone, the memories are still here, lying around stagnant. Sirocco pokes around among them only reluctantly.

Scale doesn't follow him. From some obscure impulse, Sirocco closes the door behind him. It is a small room, perhaps originally designed as a single bedroom. There's a window looking west with a view to the shuffling driftdead and the mountains in the background. His first impression is of clothes, clothes spilling out of drawers, scarves hanging everywhere of the brightest colours: skirts, saris, frocks, blouses, belts, undergarments with lace and flowers. There is more here than she ever wore. It looks as if at one time everything had been neatly packed into the drawers and hung in an orderly row in the wardrobe; now there is stuff everywhere, as if she'd gone through everything in haste, looking for something perhaps.

Among the clothes are other items, bits of jewellery, bangles, headbands, some bottles of perfume. A wonderful new list for his Book of Imaginary Sentences. Sirocco can remember her getting that perfume. Little Sanyo found it on South Beach, a nice little wooden case with several bottles set in blue velvet. Little Sanyo gave it to

Gypsy in return for the privilege of being able to sleep under the Cornet house and not having to hide. It was nice and spacious under the Cornets' house – until the storm, that is.

Some of the items, like a battered old button accordion and a patchwork baby blanket, don't look valuable or even useful, just family heirlooms. The baby blanket gives Sirocco pause. Perhaps this was Gypsy's own, although it is hard to imagine the indomitable Gypsy as a baby. There's a shelf with a fancy set of cups and saucers, celebrated for their thinness and delicacy. She put them in here to keep them out of harm's way, that is Scale's way, Scale not being that great with thin, delicate things.

Sirocco sets the Baby down on the handy baby blanket with a silver shoehorn of Gypsy's to play with. The Baby is quite happy lying there, kicking and gurgling and waving the shoehorn like a little monarch waving a sceptre. Sirocco's reluctant to search through Gypsy's things, feeling guilty, like a thief come to rifle through the sad possessions of the dead. He doesn't have to. He finds the mirror sitting on her dresser, facing him, as if she put it out for him. A heavy, oval, hand-mirror with a mother-of-pearl backing and leaf-shaped handle. Sirocco knows little about it other than it being, Gypsy once said, part of a twin hairbrush and mirror set belonging to her grandmother, but the hairbrush had long since gone walkabout.

Sitting beside the mirror, neatly stacked, are several photographs, also looking as if they have been placed there for him to find. He shuffles through them with the thought that he might be in one of them. Most are of Gypsy in another time and place, far from Keatown: Gypsy as a little girl standing under a huge spiny palm tree with a big fat passenger jet in the sky behind; Gypsy as a brooding teenager dressed severely in black surrounded by men in grey suits; Gypsy at a dance on the arm of a man; Gypsy playing the maracas; Gypsy with another man Sirocco hesitates to identify as Scale, since the man is smartly dressed and handsome... The mysteries of a life lived in another time, another place.

He picks the mirror up by its leaf-shaped wooden handle, surprised at the weight of it, the glass thick and solid. Every inch a family heirloom. He doesn't like the back-to-front mirage world of a mirror. He looked at writing in a mirror once and decided that it was returning a false image by turning the world around.

He begins by examining the back of the mirror, where the mother-of-pearl gleams eternally fresh in the tired gloom of the room, as if sparkling at the bottom of the sea. The polished paua has been inlaid in the wood so perfectly the joins are smooth. The mirror is made from a single, carved piece of wood.

He turns it over and sees what he's intended to see.

The oldest man in Keatown

His own face.

For a long moment he can't believe what he is seeing. The idea that this is some terrible joke of Lizard's passes through his mind. A trick mirror. Very funny. Gypsy's magic mirror, ha ha. Scale's cunning little trap, now sprung. Ha ha.

What he is looking at is not the face of a boy, even a runty boy, but the face of an old man, as ancient as rock: scarred skin, crevices deep with time, like a desert landscape. Rheumy eyes fixed within dark sockets. Wispy grey and silver hair whirling around a half-bald dome. A face that looks as if it has been formed by countless years of wind and erosion, out there in the desert. How long did he spend wandering in circles?

He must be the oldest man in Keatown.

The runt is no kid, just an old man who's forgotten time. An old man who runs with a bunch of kids. Or a very ancient monkey who scratched his life away on the sand under the crab apple tree for several hundred years. Now he understands a lot of things, like the deference some of the mokopuna show him, like the gleeful mockery of Pinky – and why Hera might have chosen him to be the baby-bearer.

He looks carefully to make sure he is not mistaken, that he is not looking at a child after all, albeit a wizened one. A wizened child who shot straight to old age with nothing in between but the trackless wastes of a desert. Age, they called him when Gypsy brought him in from the desert, Age short for Ageless. He didn't like the name so he changed it to Sirocco, the name of a haunted wind.

The face in the mirror blushes to its roots, and he lets out a groan bigger than his runty body can hold. He buries his face in the mirror, but the glass is cold and unyielding.

Fool! Fool! Sitting under the crab apple tree playing in the dirt, pretending he was a child.

He closes his eyes and sees imploding circles and exploding stars, and the face, the face he's been trying to draw in the sand – for how long now? He's afraid to open his eyes. With eyes closed tightly shut, he can believe, for a moment or two, that the image is merely a cruel hallucination, a momentary shape in the mind. But when he opens his eyes, the same face stares back. The face of a deluded old man, pale with shock.

There's no fool like an old fool, so they say.

And nobody said anything to him. The mokopuna – they just took him for granted. They pretended along with him until it wasn't pretence any more, it was just the way things are.

'Okay, joke's over,' he says to the absent lizard. 'You can let me die now.' Let me float away into the universe, the vast sidereal movement of driftstars. Lizard, I am so tired. All along, that's what I've been feeling – all that vertigo, all those cliffs of fall, the endless desert of memory... just tiredness.

a conversation with a fantasmosaurus

In the mirror, behind the old man's face, over Sirocco's right shoulder, stands a reptile, as huge as he was once small. Larger than a crocodile. Some Fantasmosaurus, about the size of a Stegosaurus. Luminous and iridescent. He could always do that. Just appear out of nowhere. It's camouflage and stillness that does it. You can't beat a creature that hardly has to blink.

'So here we are again,' the lumbering beast says. Behind him, a familiar landscape. Barren heat-baked mountains. Stony slopes and desiccated tussock. Heat reverberating from one side of the sky to the other. A distant hazy horizon.

Sirocco shivers. It's all there, in his memory.

'Lizard?' He can hardly credit that this magnificent creature is that slithery little reptile he first noticed out of the corner of his eye passing like a shadow from one rock to another.

'Still slow on the uptake, I see,' Lizard booms.

Sirocco is silent. Gypsy's room, and all her stuff press in on him. In the desert he and the tiny, quick-witted Lizard would have their conversations under a wide-open sky replete with stars. It was all so different that for a moment he doubts that the booming creature in the mirror really is Lizard.

'Why come back? I'd almost forgotten you?'

'Don't lie. You hadn't forgotten me. I am a part of you.'

'Why appear in a mirror?'

'I don't think you would want to see me in my full manifestation right now. I have no wish to harm you.'

'Why are you so enormous?'

'It was fun being small and slithery, but all good things come to an end.'

Attracted by the smell of baby shit, a heavy, fat blowfly does a lazy arc around Sirocco and passes over the half sleeping Baby, a preliminary reconnaissance. Lizard watches it with lazy eyes. 'You have become very comfortable.' He gestures to Hera's room. 'The baby-bearer! King of the town! Centre of all the fuss. You have forgotten the nights when you had to lie down under the spider stars, naked as this babe here.'

'It seems I have forgotten a lot of things. A lot of years, for starters.'

'Years go by like the whispering sands.'

'Why didn't you tell me I was old?'

'Old?' Lizard's great, mottled throat throbbed. 'I'm a prehistoric beast. You're just a child! I've got several millennia under my belt.' Bulbous, heavily lidded eyes watch him, like a very ancient drunk who hasn't moved from his bar stool in a thousand years.

'All this time I thought I was just a kid.'

'No you didn't. You didn't think at all. You didn't stop to wonder.'

'You let me carry on, deluded...'

'Me? You can't blame me. You never stopped to take a good long look at yourself. Then you would have seen. The truth is always only a glance away.'

'But the shame!' Only Hera refused to treat him like the runty kid he thought he was.

'We all have our cross to bear. I thought I was just a lizard sitting on a rock.'

Having completed its reconnaissance, the fly returns for another fly-by, moving at full speed, passing between Sirocco and the mirror he is holding up. In the mirror, Lizard moves a little closer to the glass.

Sirocco bats uselessly at the fly. 'You could have given me a clue.'

'Am I responsible for the quick, hot thoughts of you mammals? What do you think I am?'

'I thought you were my friend, my guide, my light in dark places.' Sirocco can taste the bitterness. It is in his mouth. Most people, when they get old, can at least say that they have lived a life. They have a life to look back on, memories to shuffle.

'How can I show you something you can't see? You can't teach a wild cat to see colours. You'd only doubt me, that's the way mammals are, all skitter-brained. Little doubting creatures with darting thoughts. When you came to Keatown, you had the opportunity to see for yourself. Then I would be home and free. But no. You refused to look. Skitter-brained, as I said.'

'It must have been very tiresome for you.'

'You've no idea. Having to lurk under rocks to hide from hawks, keeping company with rabbits, having to show up before you fuck up. Saving your life, little things like that. On and on it goes.'

'Then why are you here now? To gloat?'

'We have a communication problem, which is why I'm here, brought out of retirement as it were. I was quite happy hanging out with the skinks, although they are lesser creatures.'

'So what's our problem?'

The fly returns, more confident this time, and does a lazy but noisy orbit around Sirocco's head.

'I hate flies,' Lizard says, his eyes following its path.

'But you eat them.'

'An evil necessity, Sonny Jim. Nothing more.'

'So why are you here?

Ponderously, Lizard says, 'We have now reached the interesting stage where I can't tell you anything you don't already know. I've taken you as far as I can myself go. I am after all a desert creature. I have reached my horizon,' he points to the mirror, 'the rest is up to you.'

'So you turn tail at the crucial moment?'

'All moments are crucial. I tried to teach you that, but your deafness resounded through the whole universe. Embarrassing.'

'I hate you Lizard, for deceiving me.'

'After everything I have done for you! Guided you beneath a foreign sun, kept watch in the shadows, appeared to Gypsy in a dream and told her where to find you – now that wasn't easy! I guided you to water, to what to eat, how to hide from the big birds...'

Sirocco remembers them now, the big noisy birds. Clattering birds. Vultures with mechanical wings.

'...You didn't want them to see you because they spat fire. You ran away into your Book of Imaginary Sentences. So what happens? I get you a real sweet set-up here in Keatown with a good family, that's what happens. And what do you do? You forget who you are, you wander around in a daze with a bunch of kids – and you get yourself a baby!'

'Not exactly a sweet set-up. Sleeping on the floor on an old mattress.'

'Is there anything wrong with the mattress?'

'Not exactly, although it smells a bit, and it's a bit cramped with the Baby now.'

'Best I could do at short notice, Sonny Jim. Good enough for a desert rat. Who are you to complain? I remember a time you were grateful to have a patch of sand to sleep on instead of stones. Now my duty is done. I'm up the road and round the bend.'

He sounds horribly delighted.

'What am I going to do with the Baby?'

'Ah yes, birds sing only of their eggs, and mammals coddle their young, even let them suck nutriments from their bodies.' He shudders delicately, one eye on the fly that does another pass over the mirror. 'Look at us reptiles, we know how to handle that side of things. Once they're hatched they're dispatched, none of this suckling and nursing. Messy business. And some mammals even eat their young, you know, if they're given a chance – what could be more gross than that?'

Sirocco is about to retort that humans don't eat their young, but thinks twice. Arguing with Lizard is futile.

'I can't have a rational conversation with you.'

'You don't have to. This is a fairy tale. It needs a simple moral. Like, a fool and his money are soon parted. Have you heard that one? Watch out for your baby, mammal.'

'What should I do?'

'Tut-tut. Aren't we a little old for that now? Always running to me. I am not your mother. I'm not even real, remember? I'm just a manifestation of the powers of the earth. We worked all this out long ago, in the desert, but you've forgotten. Your vulnerable mammalian brain has probably already started to degenerate.'

What a ray of light in the dark this reptile is! He may be big and lumbering but his tongue is as sharp as ever. His words are to remind Sirocco of his debt of gratitude to Lizard. Once Sirocco found that he had walked in a giant circle, and when he rejoined his trail he sat down and despaired, which is when Lizard came and told him to walk at right-angles to the scorpion sun, to its upraised tail. That was the day he found water, just a damp patch in the ground, but when he dug a little water oozed into the hole. He lived beside that hole for many years apparently, under the spider stars and the scorpion sun. Until Lizard returned, in fact, with tales of rain in the north and east. A magic spring, and water that ran down to the ocean. Sirocco had never seen the ocean, only mirages, so he assumed at first that Lizard was talking about a vast mirage.

'At least you haven't forgotten everything.' The fly comes by again, passing at terrific speed. Lizard, in all his granite dignity, ignores it.

'Am I walking in circles now? Am I still in the desert?'

'What do you see out there?'

'Sand, and ghostly humans who are only half there. Mirage people.'

'There's your answer.'

'I'm on my own.' That feeling had a taste too. Something deep down and empty.

'You always have been. That's the funny part.' Lizard tries to laugh but he's not very good at it, not being physiologically designed for it. That's one thing Sirocco has over him.

'I liked you better when you were little. You were good company. And you were very mortal. Remember, we had our first talk when I was going to eat you. You talked me out of it.'

'Oh, I remember. It was a moment of great danger. One moment you are alive, slithering over a rock, the next you are staring death in the face.'

Perversely ignoring the nice stinky baby on the floor, the fly returns to Sirocco. Lizard's tongue slips to the front of his mouth. The fly arcs lower. Lizard, the quintessence of stillness, moves once. An amazingly long tongue snips forth straight through the mirror and snaps the fly out of the air.

'I hate flies,' Lizard says, as the fly vanishes back through the mirror and into his mouth.

The Baby, who's been happily wriggling around on the floor playing with the shoehorn, begins to cry softly. With a practiced sweep Sirocco scoops the Baby up with his free hand, the other still holding the damn and damning mirror.

Sirocco makes the mistake of taking another look at his face. His old man's face, grown pitted and bulbous. Behind it, Lizard's body begins to distort, to turn into a shapeless mass. The Baby reaches out and grips the handle with surprising strength. The mirror swings in his direction, and Baby sees himself for the first time ever.

Baby, meet Baby.

Like Sirocco, he struggles to understand what he is seeing. His eyes grow huge and wondering, the way they do when they look up at the wheel of the night sky. He gazes into the depths of his own eyes, screws up his face, gurgles and laughs. He laughs so hard he craps his pants, and that makes it even funnier.

It makes a nice contrast, Sirocco thinks. The baby laughing and crapping at the sight of his face, me crying and holding my water at the sight of mine.

He goes to say something to Lizard but Lizard has vanished. Just like the fly.

Gone for good this time.

the dismantling of Sister

Sister sits in her cage of light. She goes to grasp the bars, but her hands pass right through. Since she cannot take the world apart, she is left only with herself. Fastidiously, the light unpicks her skin. She scratches at it, as if there were mould growing on her. She picks at the scabs of shadow.

Both Sirocco and Scale witness it. If they hadn't, they would never have believed it. They stand together in that large room filled with the living history of inconsequence and watch like helpless spectators – or voyeurs.

Sirocco almost misses it. Once he has the accursed mirror, he has no reason to linger, quite the opposite. Even if he doesn't know exactly where he's going, he wants to leave the house at a run. No longer does it feel like the refuge Lizard had in mind for him, rather the house of his shame. Everywhere he looks he can see only his own past folly, how he would watch Gypsy and wonder if he would ever marry such a woman. It is not so much that he pretended he was a child, just that he didn't ask the right questions, didn't look in the right places. Now he understands Scale's suspicion and hostility, and Gypsy's on-off maternal attention. Gypsy was indulging him, while Scale was trying not to. When he came in from the desert, he must have been like a child, having all his memories swallowed up by the lizard sky, his mind picked clean. He had forgotten how to be a man, and had to learn how to be a child again.

He can't bear to feel such shame before a person like Scale, himself the most shameful of men. He can barely look at him. Scale, however, barely glances at Sirocco, and certainly doesn't register any change in him. He's too busy staring at Sister, who appears to be coming alive. Rather than sitting still as a statue, she is looking about with full awareness, particularly focusing on her own body, touching herself where the light falls as if to make sure she is intact under her knee-length smock, while flexing her arms and legs.

She is fascinated by her hands, her left hand in particular. She turns it back and forth before her, making the fingers chase each other, the little finger first and the others following after. She opens and closes her fist with the same inordinate interest. From fist to fan and fan to fist, her eyes widen as her fist opens and narrows as it closes. With the right hand she takes her left hand and places it on the floor as if it were a creature she has picked up and wants to return to its natural element.

The left hand lies there, face down, without moving. She watches it warily.

Sirocco and Scale watch it too, caught up in the same spell. Some drama is unfolding here. Yet it is a perfectly ordinary hand: small, well proportioned, slender.

Then it moves. Just a little at first. Just a twitch. The fingers bend – and pull. They attempt to drag the hand along. But the hand is attached to her arm, which in turn is attached to her body. Yet rather than draw it back, she attempts to block it with the right hand, making a wall out of her right arm. The left hand is not impressed, and proceeds to climb over the right, its movement spider-like. Finally, she jerks her left hand back. With some struggle, she places it in her lap and laces the fingers of both hands together. For a moment the two hands sit quietly, but soon a struggle begins, with the left hand trying to pull free. It looks comical, one hand fighting with the other, but neither Sirocco nor Scale laugh.

It's not funny either when, having finally pulled free and clawed its way across her hip to the floor, the left hand has to suffer a beating from the right. She doesn't hold back. She whacks away at herself as if pounding in a nail. She grunts but does not cry out.

The beating stops abruptly, right hand in mid-air, left hand bruised and battered on the floor. Something else is happening. Her bare right foot, on which she's partially sitting, is starting to bend and flex at the ankle. And, even as the battered left hand begins to show signs of life, the toes of the right foot begin to scratch at the sandy floor, making a rodent noise. The big toe digs deepest, attempting to pull the whole foot along. But the foot is attached to her leg which in turn is attached to her torso. Once more however, she attempts the futile manoeuvre she used with her left hand, blocking the progress of the right foot by putting her left leg in front. She can do this without too much contortion, but her left hand, now recovered, is also attempting to set off on its own. Her hand seems to be the worst problem, as the powerful wrist muscles are almost strong enough to drag her along.

Her left hand and her right foot are turning while the rest of her is trying to stay put. Scale and Sirocco realise this at the same time. Scale looks wildly around as if for a weapon. There is nothing nearby but the broom that ran out of faith. Scale and Sirocco look at each other, but find no help there either. The house seems deathly quiet, except for the muffled thumping of the driftdead halfway through the window.

Sister, who also seems to grasp the situation, looks around and begins to drag herself towards the hardwood table, the one with the tendency to accumulate objects. Half her body wants to go one way, half the other, but her will is stronger, and her left leg and right arm slowly win the battle. Her right foot can gain little traction on the floor, not enough to resist the power of her entire left leg, which she uses to push herself along. At the same time she tries to hold up her left hand where it can do no more than clutch at the air. She looks like a broken, wind-up doll still trying to go through the motions.

When she gets to the table, she manages to hook her right arm around one of the legs and hold on tight. In the struggle she jostles the table and the iron birdcage falls to the floor beside her. It was designed to look like the skeleton of a bird, with the ribs forming the bars of the cage. A perfect size for the black Barbie doll at present in residence. The head of the cage is solid metal, with the beak a nasty, sharp protrusion. After a moment's calculation she lets go of the table leg, seizes the iron bird, and proceeds to break each finger on her left hand by smashing the bird down on them, using the solid back of the head rather than the beak. Inside the black Barbie flops around stiffly. One by one the shattered fingers go still, or wave feebly, until only the thumb is left, thumping at the floor to no effect; this, she spares.

With her left hand out of action, it seems, at least momentarily, she has won the battle. There is a brief lull.

'Rope.' Scale says, again looking around. 'We c'n tie her.'

'Yes,' Sirocco says.

But neither makes any move. They know it won't make any difference.

The struggle quickly resumes. Her whole left arm is working now, trying to lever her along by the elbow, the hand dangling uselessly. That is matched by the right leg, which gains mobility from the knee down. She fights to remain seated as she raises the birdcage above her head and smashes it down on her knee. It takes two blows to do the job. She is grunting and sobbing as she turns her attention from her bloodied knee to her left arm, dropping the birdcage to seize her left arm with her right hand and to twist it around and up until the bone snaps. A definitive sound.

Now that her right leg and left arm are incapacitated, she once more gains the ascendency in the battle against her traitorous body. She takes a brief rest, lying shuddering on the floor, still in her cage of light.

'It'll be over soon,' Scale says to her in a gentle voice. He kneels beside her and tries to make her head a little more comfortable. His actions are careful and tender.

A few moments later it is over. First she loses control over her left leg. She's going to have to smash that one too, at the knee. With both legs smashed she won't be going very far. She goes to pick up the iron bird but her last loyal limb, her right hand, begins to twitch and jerk. A spasm runs through her body as if she has been hit with a bolt of electricity. The iron bird jumps about, and falls to the floor. There's a soft sound as Barbie's head hits the cage.

Sister falls on her back, her shattered body convulsing as her head and torso resist the pull of her two good limbs. She fights to the very last, trying to dig the back of her head into the floor, her shoulders squeezing, as if they could gain traction on the smooth wooden floor. A few moments after that, her shoulders fall limp before starting to work in the other direction. Now only her head is left, uselessly arched backward.

Slowly but surely she is being dragged along. Dragged south, inch by inch, but she is still in there, her head. You can see her in her eyes, now totally trapped in the birdcage of her body.

'We can't leave her like this,' Scale says soberly.

Sirocco agrees. But neither of them knows what to do.

Sister screams.

the boy who isn't there

Little Sanyo approaches the barn for the last time with the sense that he has failed. His original intention, to capture some driftdead and study them, and learn all sorts of amazing things about them, has not come to fruition the way he hoped. In fact, if he looks at it coolly, he has learned nothing, at least nothing everybody else has not learned in some other way. Cutting one up got him exactly nowhere, as Pinky has been spilling driftdead guts all over the barricade. No secrets there.

He has studied the girl for signs of consciousness, but except for a couple of ambiguous moments, he has learned only that the driftdead show fewer signs of cognition than your traditional zombies, who have to at least be aware of humans to chase after them. The driftdead are not chasing anything. They may have a dream they are following but it is not of this world. For a moment he thought he saw a spark in her eyes, but he probably made that up out of the desire to discover something. In fact, he has discovered nothing.

He has been wasting his time.

It's time, he has decided, to close down his little experiment. In itself, that too doesn't quite make sense, since he could have just not come back, left the boy chained to the bench and the girl bumping up and down against the south wall. The old guy rotting on the bench. But he finds himself returning to unchain the boy and open the main doors to let the girl out. There are no rational reasons for these actions, since he has no evidence that it matters one way or the other to the driftdead themselves, any more than it matters to a twig in a stream whether it is bobbing along freely, snagged on a branch or washed into a stagnant pool.

He feels obscurely guilty about the whole exercise, which is perhaps the real reason for his return. He took these three driftdead and tried to experiment upon them. He saw them purely as objects to be studied and experimented upon. Despite this, they are somehow not objects, and his return to the scene of his rather unsavoury defeat is evidence enough of that. The way in which they are not objects is something his mind does not want to approach, not yet, for, at face value at least, it makes no sense, and Little Sanyo is not accustomed to doing things for no reason.

He pauses as he approaches the barn. Last time he left the north-facing side door open to see if the girl might find her way out given enough time. He also wonders if he might not catch another one or two, who might blunder though the side door by accident. It is not on their main route, but with the collapse of the barricade there are enough around.

As he approaches the door he finds himself still bothered by his own motives, and the unsatisfactory nature of the whole business. He's a beachcomber, but even he understands that there has been something not quite right about this whole, secretive experiment, as if he has in some way become Dr Death for these three driftdead. And that is quite absurd. They have no awareness of him and are, after all, already dead. However unproductive his efforts have been, it is silly to see him as some kind of sadist, some mad kiddy scientist from Dr Who.

If my efforts had paid off, he thinks, I would feel differently. Everything would have been worth it, and I would be feeling proud of myself. Everybody would clap and admire me for my enterprise, my genius. My discoveries would help defeat the driftdead. I would be a hero.

That has not happened, and what he sensing is the bitter taste of defeat, of failure. That's what he doesn't want to face, and that's what draws him back.

Understanding these things makes him feel very adult. Like a real scientist.

As he gets close to the door he can hear the random thumping of the girl as she bumps up against the south wall. Still going. The only unanswered question with her is, how long would she keep going before she wound down, or turned off, or whatever. Longer than Little Sanyo has to hang around and find out. Maybe she could just go on and on forever; he doesn't have time to find out.

Inside, it takes his eyes a moment or two to adjust to the gloom, and the stink of the old man's rotting flesh, which is normal enough. At first he can't register what it is that's changed, just the shock of realising that something is terribly wrong. The girl is still bumping along as expected, the old man is still lying half cut up on the bench rotting happily, no surprises there. The difference is...

... the boy has gone. That's the very impossible thing. Little Sanyo has the presence of mind to open the main, eastward-facing door to get some light into the back of the barn before carefully examining the bench to which he handcuffed the boy. His first thought is that the boy somehow pulled himself free. An examination of the cuffs soon scotches that theory. They are completely intact, still locked. He'd anchored the cuffs to the vice with the dog chain, and that hasn't gone anywhere. The chain is still wrapped around the vice, the cuffs dangling uselessly at the other end of the chain. He'd placed the key on the shelf above the bench where it was not readily visible, and it was still there. Or was replaced exactly where he left it.

To all appearances, the boy has just vanished from inside his cuffs.

Or somebody came along, unlocked the cuffs, let the boy loose, and locked the empty cuffs afterwards. That's almost as hard to believe as the boy just vanishing into thin air. It's possible that someone could let the boy loose, just to confuse him, one of the mokopuna perhaps. But as he runs through the mokopuna in his mind, that seems less likely. Perhaps one of the townsfolk happened by. That is possible, but doesn't explain why whoever it was, the mystery person, would let the boy loose and not release the girl. Or let the boy loose in the first place.

Suddenly the barn seems very cold and dreary. The driftdead are a mystery but at least they can be studied, even if the results are disappointing. The absence of the boy, however, can't be studied, as there is nothing to study, no trail to follow, no clues left behind. Just a gap, a place where thought and speculation stop, where the mind can find no traction. No place for an adult, rational being like himself.

Without further delay he guides the girl to the open doors, and gently lets her rejoin her kind. She shows no relief or gratitude. She simply moves off as if she has never been held up. For a useless moment he watches her. How nice it would have been to establish communication! Now the garage is empty but for strips of flesh from the old man and his decaying carcass.

Despite the mystery, about which he can do nothing, he is happy now to walk away, to put this whole incident in the past, to never think of it again, in fact.

Just walk away.

a brave little girl steps forth

A very frightened little girl sits at a desk in her abandoned classroom and tries not to look at the passing driftdead. She looks like a kid who has forgotten to go home after school has finished. She's not afraid of the driftdead anymore. Well... a little bit, perhaps, especially when she remembers the large woman in a nurse's uniform bearing down on her out of the storm. The spookiest thing about them is their silence, as if they were all holding onto some deep, dark secret. It is the secret that is the scary part.

Her classroom has a south-facing door, so few driftdead come in, and the ones that do take no notice of her and soon blunder out again.

Although... she thought she saw one of them, a stern man, looking at her, actually seeing her.

She's not too frightened because she has her own theory as to who the driftdead are. They are like her, people without homes, and they are all going in the one direction because that's where their homes are. They have been away a long time, and their families miss them, or worse, have forgotten about them. When they get there, to their homes, they will all become normal again, and have children that they tuck up in bed at night.

It's simple. The driftdead are going home.

It's a pity she can't go home, but her mother took to Ock's cure a long time ago; Witch Hunt became homeless in her own home long before the masses of homeless appeared. This tatty classroom is the best she can do. She can sit here and play school to her heart's content, imagine that the librarian is there reading her Little House on the Prairie.

Only a few days or so ago, she could have run to Miranda's place where Jolene would have let her sleep on a mattress beside the warm body of her friend. Her once and only friend. There's no use dwelling on that! Miranda is not any kind of friend anymore, and Jolene has joined the party at the mayor's as far as Witch Hunt knows. What makes it all worse is that now that Miranda has moved in with the librarian, that possible refuge is closed to Witch Hunt, although sometimes she likes to imagine Miranda and her sitting together holding hands and listening to the librarian reading. Miranda has the softest hands! Only a day or so ago she might have slipped across to the Cornet place to sit with Sister, keeping her company, or trail around after Sirocco and the Baby – she likes to do that. But the Cornet place is no fun anymore, and the big room is starting to look neglected. The clutter of found objects is beginning to grow cobwebs.

Right now, she doesn't even know where Sirocco is. They were separated when the barrier gave way. The driftdead, flowing through in a solid stream, are now everywhere, herds of them; a little girl could get trampled underfoot just running from the school to the roundabout.

Witch Hunt goes to the door of her classroom and looks out, aware of the growls of hunger in her stomach. She thinks of oats and raisins with nice thick cream on top, which makes her stomach growl even louder.

Across the road, she can see the open door of the church where

Rasputin spends his nights. No much food there. Just last night she saw him at the doorway looking dark and pale and quite scary, as if he'd spent the night fighting ghosts. She wonders if people have forgotten how to eat.

She hid so he couldn't see her, because his eyes are the scariest part of him. His God eyes. According to the reverend, nobody can hide from God – but at least she can hide from Rasputin.

There's no sign of him now which is some relief, but there are plenty of driftdead, millions of them. All she can see are the backs of them as they flow around the schoolhouse, two streams that have mingled by the time they reach Beauty Parade. She's not quite so scared of them when they are all walking away like that. It's a comfort to know that they never look back. A couple of them, however, a man in a soldier's uniform carrying a pen, another behind him quite naked carrying a toothbrush, have stumbled onto the covered walkway that provides access to the classrooms. The naked man looks like he's half asleep and heading for a bathroom.

Witch Hunt steps back to let them pass, trying to stop her heart from beating too fast. She hides from them even though she knows they are not trying to find her.

Little Sanyo once told her that if she could make her heart beat slower, she wouldn't feel so afraid, but he didn't explain clearly how to do that. He'd just talked about the great silence of the sky and the heartbeat of the sun, and that didn't help much. She holds her breath, which Little Sanyo said didn't help, telling herself that the men will not come into her room because that would mean turning north, and the driftdead never turn north, not unless they are trapped. Sure enough, the men go down the steps into the playground and plod towards the rusting swings and slides.

She steps outside again, hunger ratting her belly. She's going to have to go somewhere. And eat. The best place is probably the marae. Sad Toof might be there, and Akona won't turn Witch Hunt away. Sad Toof likes the marae, the Man in Black in particular. He told Witch Hunt once that when he grew up he wanted to be just like the Man in Black – tall, silent and mysterious. But that's Sad Toof for you. Witch Hunt is not so keen on the Man in Black. Sometimes he gives her funny looks, as if measuring her up for a coffin. She's not so sure about Akona, either. She believes that Akona can put spells on things, and people too. Miranda once told her that Akona had put a spell on the Man in Black, which is why he never speaks, and Cherrie Lamont says that the old woman put a magic spell on her garden to keep the driftdead away. 'I heard her with my own ears,' she said. 'She was chanting and holding out her arms.' Witch Hunt is not sure if this is true, but it's better to be on the safe side. Adults are unpredictable creatures at the best of times, witches more so than ordinary people. Akona may seem like a nice person, she's hardly Baba Yaga of the iron teeth, but that means nothing.

Food will be there, however. She could brave the Man in Black and the witch for the sake of food, if it were not that the marae lies a distance to the south, a good walk for a little girl with no company but the driftdead. A lonely walk.

The mayor's place is closer, and there will be all sorts of food. There are many legends about stashes of chocolate and muesli bars, bottles of soft drink and fruit juice. Even cake. She believes these legends because the mayor is fat and greedy. It is just like him to have all sorts of goodies hidden away. And while the horrible Mavis might gnash her teeth and curse like Baba Yaga, she is no witch. There will be lots of people too, and she's at least as lonely as she is hungry. Even drunk people are people.

There is a big problem with that, however, a very big problem for a little girl wanting to get there. The mayor's place lies north, which means Witch Hunt will have to walk against the streams of driftdead, into the face of them all. Huge creatures with oblivious faces bearing down on her, trampling her underfoot, uncaring. If only somebody were with her! Sirocco with the desert eyes, the dreary Sad Toof, even Rasputin with the God eyes.

She looks across at the church but there is no activity. Only driftdead.

Her stomach utters a loud groan.

A brave little girl steps forth.

a melancholy sepulchre of mewling voices

When Big Bill's grand barricade is breached, the librarian shuts off both the outer and inner doors to the library, closing her and Miranda in, at least until the initial surge of invaders has subsided – if it does. The outer courtyard, where the librarian hacked the driftdead girl with the spade, is now packed with them milling about, trying to find a way around the building. Over it, under it, any way.

She shudders to think of the library packed with them.

As she shuts the door, she notices that there are more children among the driftdead than before. Vacant-faced adults are one thing, but zombie children are a dreadful sight, at least for the librarian, who has lovingly guided many a child to the joys of reading. It's in her professional blood to have a proprietorial attitude to children, the readers of tomorrow. To nurture their young minds. Cultivate their tender moral sensibilities. To teach children how to read is to teach them how to apprehend their world, for to learn to read is to learn to orientate oneself in reality. That, she has always firmly believed. Witch Hunt is not the only one who remembers the librarian reading Little House on the Prairie to a class full of dreaming children.

However, closing off the library for what seems like a final time, threatens her identity as a librarian. She doesn't know what she is anymore, or why she's there. She has tried giving Miranda books, and the girl dutifully opens them and turns the pages, but they are both merely going through the motions, her pretending to be a librarian, Miranda the eager reader. Once she discovered Miranda biting a book as if she could hurt it or infect it.

A library that can't open becomes a crypt, its librarian a ghost. Even its many books, each one a testament to hope, are muffled. All those authors, she thinks, who thought they were adding to the body of human knowledge and experience, were deluded optimists. There is no body of human knowledge, no accumulation of wisdom, no passing on of experience; there are just fleeting individuals who remember some things and forget others – and take nothing with them when they go except their memories, and those memories are then lost to the world.

She wonders if books, like gods and mortals, can die. Perhaps Miranda could bite one to death. As she walks along the shelves, ostensibly looking for something to interest Miranda, she resists the idea. When Nietzsche said that God was dead, she imagined he meant that God, the cultural concept, was dead, not the actual God behind it all, if such a being had ever existed. A book can't die, she thinks. It can be destroyed, but as long as it remains, it's more like a seed. It might lie buried for years before being watered back to life by the bright gaze of an eager reader. She holds on to that idea because it's a nice one, and she even tells Miranda, who nods and smiles blankly. Her library, she tells herself, is like a seed bank. All it needs are the right conditions and the seeds will sprout again, and words will do their song and dance upon the page.

It's a nice idea, but there's not much comfort in it for the librarian. It comes uncomfortably close to the mayor's helicopter fantasy, his firm faith in a return of prosperity. There is no longer any comfort to be found in the library. It is a tomb of words. A melancholy sepulchre of mewling voices.

She has to ask herself, what is the point of continuing with the Chronicles, putting all that loving care into the shaping of the sentences, only to consign the book to the tomb of words when it is all done? She has dedicated her life to her Chronicles. They are the one element in her life that makes sense, a carefully constructed sense, what's more.

If the Chronicles are to be consigned to oblivion before they are even finished, why finish them at all? All that fascination, that momentum of mind – going nowhere. All this writing is no more than a ritual of faith. All those words are heading for nothing more than an apartment in the city of death. All these books on her shelves are nothing more than tombstones for lost worlds. It is too late for them now. And all the new ones come running along, all bright and shiny and full of hope, only to find that the party's already over. They keep coming, even when they know the party's over. Her Chronicles will be among them, just another book, a few scratchings in the sand already corroding in the zombie wind. Better perhaps that it remain unfinished, for in its incompleteness it will remain full of promise and possibility; once complete, it will be just another book on another shelf in a library at world's end.

The solemn books, with their eroded voices, are suffocating her. Her home among the books has become a cul-de-sac. She can't open a book without feeling nauseous. All those words crawling across the page are just like trailing lines of driftdead. Driftwords. Sitting among these august tomes it is easy to believe that this great weight of words is leading to something, something stupendous and final; that all these words do, in the end, spell it out, make it plain, sum it up and finally make sense of it all. Easy to believe in a conclusion, something definitive and final.

Language is never at rest, I have to remind her.

Her writing annex she has come to hate most of all. A tiny room the Vintner probably used to do his accounts. All it contains, other than the desk, is a square eye the size of a large handkerchief: the malevolent blue eye of the computer, her old friend and adversary. The game is played this way: she sits and stares at the eye and it stares back at her. Occasionally she blinks and occasionally it flickers. She knows that the flicker is not a good sign, the blue eye needs no nictitating membrane, and that deep in the heart of the machine, in its motherboard, some tiny component is disintegrating, some dot of solder cracking, but she pushes that knowledge aside. It's the best blue eye the Vintner's money could buy. And the electricity supply is no patch-in job. She has fortified cables jacking right in to the main mansions' line. She's cased the computer in plastic to keep any possibility of sand away from it.

Somewhere in that blue, enfolded in eternity, floats her Chronicles of Keatown, her would-be book, if there were publishers left to publish. Since, unlike a book, it might flicker out of existence at any moment, she has a pile of printed paper in her drawer. A pile of printed paper is no more than a gesture towards a book, an intention; and besides, since Annanda has run out of typing paper, she has found herself ripping out the end pages of some of the lesser library books to keep going. She is confident that the authors would understand her predicament, and would probably do the same in her position.

She doesn't want to open that drawer and review that pile of paper, an activity that used to give her some pleasure – not right now, maybe never. Her hands hover over the keys with nowhere to go. Her fingers wait for the command to strike, but no command comes. She thinks of the pioneer woman, Ellen Johnson, founder of Keatown, and tries to evoke that woman's indomitable spirit, the spirit of the Chronicles, she realises, but she can't find it. The facts of the woman's life lie before her, but they add up to nothing more than what they are; they do not overleap themselves into some stupendous existence. There is merely toil and the habit of dedication.

What she does take from her drawer, however, is an old photograph with a precious image. She doesn't take it out very often, not anymore, fearful that each time she looks at it, a little of its magic will be used up. So she will take it out and, without even looking at it, caress it with her thumb, drawing energy and inspiration from the memory. Somehow this photograph is her stake in the world, the world beyond the Chronicles, beyond me even. It is part of her inner life beyond my reach.

Miranda has now crept in behind her and is standing quietly in the doorway watching her. Miranda likes watching the librarian when she's writing, loves the way her fingers do their tap dance on the keys, and the way she murmurs in her throat as the words take shape, as if she were talking to a lover.

The photograph Miranda has seen before, but never the image. A man, she fantasises. A tall, strong, handsome man, like the one in the book she's holding, the one that silly twerp Witch Hunt used to like so much about some goody-good girls living on a prairie and meeting Indians and getting sick. Miranda likes to hold the book because she knows how upset twerpy-face would be if she knew, but it remains clutched, forgotten in her hand, as she creeps up a little closer to the librarian, determined to catch a look at the precious photograph at long last. She is sure the librarian has some secret sorrow, some lost lover in the past.

The librarian has been kind to her, in a remote sort of way, feeding her and letting her sleep in the lobby, but she has made it clear that she is not going to play at being Miranda's mother, which suits Miranda well enough – she's had enough of mothers for a while. Jolene doesn't want to be her mother either. Not anymore. Nobody does. It was better when she could sleep out in the lobby, and could see the courtyard and the stars, but now that the librarian has closed all that off, she has to sleep inside, which is not so nice. She can go outside if she likes, but there are so many of those spooky people out there, and spooky kids now too. She can't hear them inside, but sometimes she thinks she can, a dull shuffle inside her head when she wants to sleep.

The librarian remains seated, lost in thought, fingers still hovering over the keys. Every so often her fingers jerk and words, like little black ants, creep across the blue eye. But no sooner are they written than the librarian hits the delete key and all the little ants are eaten up, from the last back to the first. She is so self-absorbed she doesn't notice the little girl creeping up behind her. Miranda can see the photograph more clearly now. It is quite small, with scalloped edges, but the frustration is, she can't see the image because the librarian's big fat thumb is covering it.

'Ah,' the librarian says. Letting the photo fall to the desk, her fingers begin to jab at the keys, fast this time, the little ant words not creeping steadily across the page but scattering at a furious pace, as if someone has poked a stick into the anthill behind the screen. And they keep pouring out, faster than the delete key can gobble them up.

Finally, finally! Miranda can catch an unimpeded look at the photograph. There is not much to look at. A darkened background.

Trees or something. And what was once a face, or might have been a face by the shape of it. But the librarian's thumb has done its work, and through so much devotion has almost wiped the image clean. All that is left are arms and a torso. The head and neck have been rubbed to a ghostly luminosity, almost invisibility, as if the subject's head had turned into light.

Miranda closes her eyes against the image but can still see it. Shoulders and a spray of light. She begins a slow retreat, suddenly very afraid the librarian will spin about in her chair and see her. Nobody likes their secrets uncovered. Miranda takes a few steps backward. Then another few steps. Then she turns and

In the Halls of the Mountain King

Book Six

a prisoner of my own creation

Party at the mayor's!

Everyone not heading south is invited. In fact, attendance is mandatory.

The word quickly spreads among the survivors. Many, like Hera, desert when the barrier is breached, as if some barricade within themselves also collapses, and nobody wants to be alone when being alone means being among the driftdead, waiting with dread for the evil hour to arrive. There is a comfort in being with others in such circumstances, a spurious sense of safety in numbers. Get wasted and talk loud enough and fear retreats, temporarily, into the shadows.

For that very reason, as soon as Miranda deserts, the librarian decides to go to the party, although she is no drinker and certainly not a believer in Ock's cure. It is unhealthy to remain cowering underground with the driftdead tramping above. Entombed with her books, however – she can see the sense in that. She doesn't need the First Person Singular to tell her.

'The computer went down today,' she says, speaking aloud, hoping perhaps that I might hear. 'It took half an hour to boot up. I'm sure it's the motherboard.'

Such a resonant expression. Without the motherboard, the hard drive is an orphan, a pile of code without a home. Her life's work, her Chronicles of Keatown is becoming a pile of words without a virtual space in which to take form.

She's still writing, scribbling away with a pen on the end pages of books. She's starting at A (Arnold, Atwood, Asimov,) and has calculated that it might take her a year or more to get to Z (Zelazny, Zukoufsky...). Hopefully, that would get her close to the end of the history of Ellen Johnson and her nine beautiful daughters. She doesn't want to stop now because she is increasingly entranced by the fairy-tale elements of this real colonial history. A brave and resolute mother risks the high seas to come to a godforsaken land, a windswept piece of hillside and wild coast that wasn't even a settlement yet, to move in with the rocks and the seals, with nine beauteous daughters who are destined to be courted by burghers, farmers and remittance men who come from far and wide for the privilege. Most of the daughters move away to places wide and far with their husbands, and the history of Keatown moves on, but it seems to the librarian that the spirit of Ellen Johnson hovers over the town, now more than ever. That spirit has soaked up the essence and flavour of the mountain and the sky: you will endure, the spirit is saying. That is what you do.

Yes, the librarian thinks, I will endure. But is it worth it? Endurance for its own sake has never much appealed to her.

She hardly dares look to her own situation for an answer. Here she is, incarcerated in her own library with a driftdead girl she once knew as a living human being, and now somehow can't release. All she has to do is take Miranda by the hand, lead her to the door and gently expel her, but she can't bring herself to do it. To do it would be to admit something she doesn't want to admit. So she pushes the matter right out of her mind, and the driftdead Miranda stays, banging up and down against the south wall where the biographies are kept. At one point Winston Churchill falls from a shelf above onto her head, but she doesn't notice.

I'm in no position to help her, even though she sends her prayers to me and blames me for everything that's happened. She doesn't appreciate that we're in the same boat. She, however, is a prisoner of her sentiment, while I am a prisoner of my creation; I can't release her any more than she can release Miranda, even though she has at times begged me to do so.

Over these last days she has become convinced that she is a fictional character living inside a book, maybe Sirocco's Book of Imaginary Sentences. In this book the First Person Singular is supreme, easily able to fend off any Third Person pretenders, she figures. And she, the librarian, is no more than one of those pretenders.

'I'm not much of a character,' she tells me. 'It would be easy for you to write me out altogether. After all, I don't do much. I don't have a character arc or anything fancy like that to justify my fictional existence. I just hang around in the library, writing and fretting.'

She's mostly wrong. I hesitate to tell her that I have already considered that option. However, it wouldn't be as easy to write her out as she thinks. She may not do much, but she has a certain stubborn insistence. You might call it endurance. She permeates everything. Besides, she allows me to keep my distance from events in Keatown, past and present – and that is the key to my survival.

Much of her hand-wringing has been over the problem of Miranda.

It is something she has been dreading, the first of the mokopuna to desert. She had come to believe that perhaps the mokopuna are magically immune to turning. Most of the town gone, but not a single mokopuna. She'd allowed herself to imagine the mokopuna carrying on unscathed to renew the town, keep Keatown alive. She hardly asks herself why it is so imperative that Keatown should not die, not vanish under sand dunes and off the map. Intelligent as she is, she doesn't fully grasp that since, in her Chronicles of Keatown, she has invented the Keatown she writes about, she has a creator's investment in her own creation. She can't make the distinction between the real Keatown and the Keatown that emerges from her pages, the reconstructed lives of Ellen Johnson, Peter Johnson who lived in the shadows, and their successfully married daughters.

It is a shock, therefore, when Miranda turns. The librarian doesn't see what happened. Only afterwards, when she comes out of the tiny writing room and finds Miranda bumping repeatedly up against the southern wall of the library does she understand. She watches the girl-who-is-no-longer-a-girl, and cries. There is nothing else to do. She keeps remembering when she came to came to Keatown as a young woman, a school-teacher with classes full of little sweet-faced girls like Miranda. She keeps bumping up against that same memory over and over, just the way the driftdead-Miranda is bumping against the south wall. This repeated, mechanical movement of mind frightens her, and she has to consciously wrench herself out of it the way a dreamer might wrench herself out of a nightmare.

She is no longer that young woman, so full of love for her sweet-faced children. She traded that in for a library and sweet-faced words. Words written and words yet to be written.

On the other hand she doesn't have the heart to put Miranda out. All she does now, when she's not filling in the end pages of her library books with her scribbling, is watch the shell of Miranda banging up against her world, waiting for her to die or do what driftdead do instead of dying. Do they ever lie down and give up? There is an empty curiosity in her observations. Will Miranda stop moving, eventually? Will she rot and stink the place out? Will she rot before she stops moving or afterwards?

It is perverse not to put the girl outside, to let her join her kind in their vacant march, but the librarian's got used to having her around. At first she is afraid that keeping the girl in would amount to cruel treatment, but Miranda is no bird trapped in a windowless room. It doesn't make any difference to her where she is. Yes, she keeps banging up against the south wall in a curious little circular path she follows, but feels no frustration and shows no anxiety at being trapped. With no will, no volition, there is no desire and therefore no frustration, no thwarted desire.

There are times, however, when she becomes uneasy about keeping Miranda around, almost like a pet, talking to her the way people do with pets. As if the driftdead girl were some kind of company. 'I'll put her out eventually,' she tells the library. Her motives are obscure. 'It doesn't seem fair,' is all she will say if pressed on the matter. There may be a touch of superstition in it. If she keeps Miranda in the library, the rest of the mokopuna may not be infected. Some vague nonsense like that.

I have to cultivate and cajole her, soothe and stroke her, treat her more like a lover, perhaps. She is not a machine to be switched on like a computer. She is to be encouraged and brought alive, if she is to do her best. I let her know, however, that it is time she faced the world once more. Anything less is cowardice. That's what I tell her anyway.

Keatown is facing another day, why isn't she?

I tell her, 'It's an abdication, that's what it is. A dereliction of duty.'

That is hardly soothing and stroking her, but, like her, I get impatient. She may not have turned but she has deserted nevertheless. Keeping company with the driftdead is the next best thing to deserting. It's easy enough to dream of a time when you were younger and the world looked different, when there was frost on the ground in the winter and fire in the blood instead of dust. You can always stay stuck in a memory loop between the shelves and the bookends. You can always turn to the mythical First Person Singular and appeal to be released from your lowly third-person subjective status into the generality of the driftdead, the 'they' and the 'them'. The grey murmuring. The mass shuffle.

Mechanically, she dusts the book shelves and clears away the silverfish, grey as ink, that slip in and out of time, eroding paper and cardboard, but her heart is not in it – she is just going through the motions. It is as if the books themselves have turned, turned into driftbooks whose voices are a distant and receding murmur, and who have left behind these meaningless shells of words. All very morbid, she realises, being locked up in a tomb with a dead person who won't lie down and lots of decaying books. It's all very Edgar Allan Poe-ish, she thinks, trying to jolly herself out of it. Find some literary references to hold onto. But she doesn't care. Even the allusion to Poe doesn't cheer her up.

There's only one thing for her to do, unless she wants to suffocate. She opens the door wide, lets the day in and Miranda out. She watches as her pretty little blonde head goes bobbing off into the distance. The day is dark with cloud, and the little girl's hair glows like a patch of wheat at dawn. Tears are hot on the librarian's cheek.

Despite the overcast day, real light now enters the library through the open doors. All those silverfish making a run for it. All those books, suddenly conscious of their dust. The shadows pale. She comes out of the library, quite unsteady, and looks around at the teeming driftdead.

All she can do is blink.

party central

The driftdead now have the town, trampling everywhere, collapsing fences, filling up houses, especially those with doors and windows facing north, in some cases busting the houses apart from sheer weight of numbers. Orlap has abandoned his efforts to refloat The Wanderer and joined the party. However, he announces to everybody, to ragged clapping and cheering, that he still intends to take The Merry Widow out to test the waters for fish. He speculates that the iceberg will have brought with it many interesting fish, drawn along in the wake of its cooler waters. Some suspect, and Mavis openly suggests, that Orlap, Butch and a select little crew that would probably include that sly little minx Orchid and her pock-faced sidekick, will set sail and never come back. It can't be this way everywhere, people reason. Sail far enough north, or south, there'd be no more driftdead.

Under the mayor's semi-incoherent directions, Pinky and his crew cannibalise the old bulwark to reinforce the natural defence provided by the thick macrocarpa hedge that defends the mayor's place to the north. In view of what Flay achieved with a few posts and some building paper, the mayor designs a defence not aimed at blocking the progress of the driftdead, a failed policy, but deflecting them, mostly downhill and eastward. They have plenty of material to work with, and it's not long before party central is sitting pretty snug and safe, like a rock in a river, driftdead streaming around it.

Ock's hock, reputed to have a secret ingredient that will protect the imbiber from the peril of desertion, flows freely at party central, although Ock won't reveal what the secret ingredient is, making veiled references to mysterious mountain herbs – and after Hera's desertion, something of a watershed moment for the town, the survivors of Keatown are ready to grasp at any straws. Even though they must know, as the reverend keeps pointing out to them, that Ock's so-called secret ingredient is merely raw alcohol, and offers no more protection than a brief forgetfulness, the denizens of Keatown turn eagerly to the 'cure'.

To keep the party rolling, the mayor keeps raiding his own secret storeroom, producing all kinds of goodies from smoked ham to barrels of brandy. This is the mayor's fabled secret stash, real after all. Who would have guessed that the fanciful rumours were true? Well, everybody, apparently. Everybody who sits at the very last party at the end of the world eating meringues and fancy chocolates, or swigging expensive bottles of cognac. Oh yes, they knew all along that Big Bill was hiding the goods. But they forgive him.

Mavis is furious with Big Bill for all this uncalled-for generosity, and berates him in suitable language, but Big Bill doesn't care. His own fine liquor is sitting well on his gut, and he has a Smiley sister on each arm, Jolene and Mother Smiley, who are dividing him up between them, much to his satisfaction. Mavis has developed the fine art of spitting on the floor in front of them.

The aim of the last party at the end of the world is to extinguish itself in general oblivion, but the road to oblivion can be as long and as rocky as any other road. And despite everyone's avowed enthusiasm for alcoholic poisoning, the mind will cling to consciousness until the last possible moment. Perhaps it's the febrile atmosphere, the desperation, the adrenalin, but the harder they seek oblivion, the further away it seems to get.

If you're going to die, best die on the road

Not everybody at the party is getting drunk. Some have better things to do. Like Flay, who's in bed with his scrubber having a little party of his own. And there, beside him, is Cherrie Lamont, more willing than able perhaps, but Flay isn't complaining. It's been a long time since he had any kind of scrubber in bed with him, and the feeling... well, the feeling is rather nice. As it turns out she's not too bad once she stops talking, and just a little skunk-weed makes her nicely incoherent.

Perhaps all this indulgence has made him lazy and careless, because when he wakes from a light, pleasant doze and the smell of cheap imitation French perfume to the sound of a truck starting up, he knows he's been shafted. He immediately recognises the sound of his own truck, his Bedford RL, the beast that never dies, all loaded up with diesel for delivery to the wharf tomorrow, and he's out of the bed reaching for his shotgun before his brain has kicked into action, mumbling and snarling. Why didn't he remove the distributor cap last night? he keeps asking himself as he lurches for the door. He might have known there would be some last-minute trickery. That fucking Viking has over-reached himself this time.

Too late. His truck is in first gear and rolling before he can clear the doorway, and in second gear and halfway down the road before he can get a clear shot. He doesn't take it. There's no use in blasting away at his own truck. He has been finessed, that's the simple fact of it. Outsmarted. He is so astonished by this that he wonders if Cherrie Lamont has been in on it all the time, sent to distract and lull him, which is just crazy given that all her deceptions are hopelessly transparent.

He stands in the middle of Highway 6, pedestrians all around him, watching the tail lights of his own RL disappearing into the distance. Easy enough to hotwire the old RL, if you know how. This is not how it is supposed to go. Flay's bold plan is to wait until Orlap has reloaded the diesel onto Annanda's Isuzu, which Butch said was Orlap's plan, accost him, beat him senseless, throw him into the harbour, and drive the truck himself up to the high and mighty baron and do a little horse trading of his own. Mr High and Mighty may find the price of diesel has gone up. A damn fine plan it was too. Positively elegant. Butch liked it because it made her laugh. Of course the fairy grocer turned his nose up at it, but in the end he came around. Flay guesses that it was curiosity that got the better of him; couldn't resist getting a close-up peek at one of the mansions, could he? He did plead for softer treatment for Orlap, to which Flay replied that that was a matter best sorted out between his tyre-iron and Orlap's head.

Now that little fantasy is down the toilet. Unless...

He pushes on as fast as he can to Annanda's supermarket and hammers on the door. Annanda is right there.

'Get your truck,' Flay says.

'I think pursuit may be futile,' Annanda says regretfully, opening the door for him.

'Get your fucking truck!' Flay has no time for argy-bargy. He taps the barrel of the shotgun against the fairy's chest. His RL would be slow with that load on. The Isuzu should catch up with it quickly enough, especially when they turned off into the hills. The mountain road is no race track.

Annanda throws his hands up in surrender. 'Yes, Mr Flay. We shall go in hot pursuit. But first...' he gestures discreetly.

Flay looks down. He is stark naked, standing there in front of the fairy.

Annanda quickly throws some clothes at him as they hurry through to the back of the supermarket. Some pinkish shirt and designer slacks. Girly-man clothes. Flay's got them on by the time Annanda has started the Isuzu. He feels like a fool, and must certainly look like one, but at least he's doing something. As he sinks into the passenger seat, he clutches his shotgun till his knuckles go white. All this humiliation will be answered. Somebody will pay. And pay dearly.

As soon as they hit Highway 6, their way is blocked by the packed crowds of pedestrians. Annanda noses the Isuzu gently out onto the highway.

'It'll take us a month of Sundays this way,' Flay snarls. 'Just run 'em down. You can be sure Captain Orlap won't care.' My RL will be a bloody mess, he thinks. Orlap won't be sparing the old Bedford.

'It wasn't Orlap, Mr Flay,' Annanda says, making no effort to speed up, just puttering along at the same speed as the driftdead in front of him. 'It was first mate Butch. I saw her.'

'What's she playing at? I thought she was with us, keen to take the Nord down a peg or two. Keen to see him floating in the harbour.'

'That is correct. She was outraged that he would try to use her to make his escape, leave her here with no recourse...'

'Then what's got into her?' But Flay thinks he knows. His own plan, which was to steal the diesel back from Orlap and take it up to the baron to do a little horse trading of his own, obviously appealed to Butch. So she thought she'd steal a march and get in first. Maybe harbouring her own hopes for buying her way onto that chopper. That chocker chopper. And, if they continue to creep along the road at this pace, she'll be up, up and away before they get to the turnoff.

Flay sticks his shotgun into Annanda's ribs. 'Either you drive or I drive,' he says. He might have guessed Butch would have the know-how to hot wire the Bedford, being smarter than the Nord.

'You drive,' Annanda says. 'I have no stomach for running the Rakshasa down.'

'They're only pedestrians,' Flay says. 'Wouldn't want t' muss ya hair, eh?'

They waste a few more precious moments as Flay takes the wheel. He takes a moment to wipe his sweaty, oily hands on Annanda's pink shirt. Annanda pretends not to notice.

'You know,' Annanda says, 'This must be the Butch acting alone, without her Captain's knowledge, I mean.'

'More than likely.'

'You know,' Annanda says again, as the Isuzu begins to push and bash at the plodding driftdead, 'You have been handsomely compensated for your diesel, Mr Flay. The captain paid in advance for the use of my truck, which he has not used, for whatever reason... I am in receipt of the gold. As you are, I'm sure.'

'Get on with it.'

'You could say that what he does with the diesel, having paid for it, is his own business.'

'You could say that. Or you could shut up and let me drive this piece of shit.'

'And yet...'Annanda goes on thoughtfully, 'although you have been paid in excess, in gold bars in fact, you still feel as if you have been ripped off. Don't you find that curious, Mr Flay?'

As if in answer, Flay speeds up, swerving and smashing into the driftdead. Soon he finds a trail of broken driftdead and bloody corpses from the Bedford ahead.

'Don't kill us, Mr Flay.'

If you're going to die, best die on the road with your hands on the steering wheel and your foot on the accelerator, Flay thinks. And gets on with the job.

the night to be felt

Akona wakes after an uneasy nap. The party holds no attractions for her. Keatown's last desperate stand at the mayor's place is just that. It makes her sad to see the town dying, but the land will still be there, under their feet. The town will go, the driftdead will eventually pass, but the land will still be there.

And behind the land stands Te Kore, the Nothingness from which Te Po nui, the Great Night, emerged.

Te Po nui
Te Po roa
Te Po uriuri
Te Po kerekere
Te Po tiwha
Te Po tangotango
Te Po te kitea...

The words roll off her tongue as she gets to her feet. Such are the varieties of night. The Great Night, the Long Night, the Dark Night, the intensely Dark Night, the Gloom-laden night, the Night to be Felt, the Night Unseen... This is the great darkness before creation, the nothingness from which something emerged, and it comforts her to evoke it now, for it is the very womb of creation, that from which all things emerge and to which all return. Those they call the driftdead are marching straight into that Great Night, that Long Night, like a people gagged and blindfolded, but the living will follow their trail eventually. Te Kore never ended. It will be there long after the earth has passed.

The big-throated shag has closed its beak with a snap.

What has woken her, however, is a dream not easily put to rest. She often dreams of figures she identifies as her ancestors, her tūpuna, but she understands that they exist within her as much as without. Her ancestor Nōpera was with her in her dream, trying to tell her something. It was to do with Wai-O-Tapu, the spring. And there was an animal which drank from the waters of Wai-O-Tapu. Nōpera's words were lost in the rush of water.

Those who claim that the ancestors exist in the imagination rather than residing in some cavern under the sea do not understand that the dead are held within the imagination of the earth, not just their own. Her imagination is a fleeting thing, like the trackless path of a butterfly, but the imagination of the earth is as slow and as deep as the Gloom-laden night itself. As is her dream.

Slowly she becomes aware of somebody standing in the room. A figure standing in the doorway. Behind it the sky is intensely grey. She identifies the figure by its stillness.

'If you've come to say goodbye, you've chosen a bad time.'

'I must,' The Man in Black says.

Akona understands; she really does. It's time for the Man in Black to return to his own land, find his own tūrangawaewae in a place far to the west, beyond the mountains. If he doesn't take this journey, he will be swept away in the flood of the half-dead, trapped between here and the afterlife. They cannot cross over. They cannot find the entrance to the world below. Surely Kuwatawata, guardian of the entrance, has hidden it from them, barred them from the solace of the dark embrace of Hine-nui-te-pō, Great Woman of the Night.

'The banded rail disappears fast,' she can't help but murmur as she gets to her feet, feeling her age in her bones. It is not fair on him. He is only doing what he has to do, going where he has to go. But of course she is going to feel abandoned. Like losing my shadow, she thinks, trying to remember who it was, some little mokopuna, who lost his shadow and had to have it sewn back on.

He inclines his head in acknowledgement, and does not attempt to answer her. There's nothing he can say and they both know that.

'I had a dream, just now. I dreamt of my ancestor, Ellen Johnson, the indomitable one. She was an old lady, in my dream, sitting in a drawing room with lots of English things around. The librarian told me once what that room would have looked like. Like the fancy piano brought from London and hauled miles over rough roads to her colonial mansion. Like the bone-thin china tea set. When I came into the room the old lady stood up, and I saw she was carrying a baby, a baby as brown as she was white. I curtseyed before her in the style of the English upper classes – they did teach me how to do that when I was a kid, you know – and she handed me the baby. There was no ceremony. It was unexpected. I woke up straight away.' She doesn't say anything about Nōpera, or Wai-O-Tapu, and the animal that drank from that cool spring. Those images are too diffuse.

The Man in Black smiles. His teeth are very white in the grey light. 'I'm glad.'

'About what?'

'The gift.'

'Ah...' To have such a dream might signify the blessing of an ancestor. But her heart does not feel any of the gladness a blessing might bring.

He steps backward out of the doorway, but still he is in shadow.

She follows him. 'Why is it so dark?'

His silhouetted figure gestures towards the sky. From one cave into a bigger cave, is what it feels like to step outside. The larger cave of the sky, as swollen as a pregnant belly. It looks so close she could touch it. The warmth of the earth is being sucked into it.

'I'll walk with you as far as Wai-O-Tapu.' She hesitates to say more. He will continue on, following a half-forgotten trail through the mountains. She has no clear idea of what she's going to do when she gets to Wai-O-Tapu Spring, but doesn't worry about that. She'll know when she gets there.

The Man in Black has already packed his flax kit.

'A white heron flies once,' she says.

the fool folds his hands, and eats his own flesh

Not everybody at the party is drunk, or out to get drunk. It amuses the librarian, who's had a tipple herself – just for show of course – to see the reverend and his acolyte Rasputin huddled in the corner deep in disputation about the vexed issue of the relationship between body and spirit. She makes a point of getting close enough, and staying invisible enough, to listen to their conversation. At one time there would have been at least four or five of the faithful, or semi-faithful, crowding around to listen or take part, but since Melissa Tonguestone took her little suicide party into the oblivion of the desert, and since Mother Smiley and Jolene have given themselves over to the demon drink and the lusts of the flesh, true believers are a bit thin on the ground.

Seeing them there huddled in sober conversation reminds the librarian of the solemn Johnson family Bible, with its teetotaller pledge signed by all members of the family, even the maid. And there they are, the inheritors, just two of them. Neither of them have smiles on their faces. The reverend knows that normally churches fill up when mysterious or disastrous events occur, and blames himself fully for the scattering of the faithful in this case. Nothing to smile about. It is his loss of nerve, his emotional collapse with the desertion of Hera, his horrified realisation that he loved the woman he reviled as the Whore of Babylon, that has brought this about. Now, except for Rasputin, he is alone with his God, stripped of everything – even his faith. Little wonder he has been abandoned by his little flock, those who remain, that is.

He is so busy blaming himself, a time-consuming activity, that he doesn't perceive what Rasputin perceives, if dimly; namely that the nature of the driftdead themselves does not inspire faith but rather destroys it. As the wretched pagan baby-bearer said to him, when you look at the driftdead you don't see God. What you see, what you feel, is the total absence of God. Who wants to cleave unto a God like that, a God that can withdraw his grace so absolutely and arbitrarily? A God that offers neither protection nor solace. It is almost as if God himself has turned and joined the senseless march south. A driftgod. The people can't believe in a god like that. Such a God is too terrible, even for one as staunch as the reverend.

For Rasputin it is different. He knows that, however it appears, God has not deserted the driftdead, but is gently sustaining their souls while their bodies are given over to mindlessness. Thus they are spared perdition. He wants to convey this to the reverend, but to do so he will have to tell him what he can see, describe those frail-looking flames that dance on the heads of the driftdead. The reverend will be upset. Why didn't God vouchsafe him such a vision, for the relief of his soul? He might even doubt Rasputin's word, suspecting that his all too loyal acolyte has imagined it, or even made it up, to make his mentor feel better about the world, to draw him out of the Slough of Despond.

'You must keep the faith,' Rasputin is saying to Rev Stickman. He keeps repeating it, like a prayer or a penance. 'You are the one who told me that the Lord would test every nerve and fibre, didn't you tell me that?' He wants to go on, and tell the reverend that he too has been tested nerve and fibre, and he did what the reverend didn't do, which was to reach out to someone and touch them with the hands of love. And there was no sin, only God in it. God in the hands that touched, and the face that was touched, and the movement that was the touching. God in all of it. The sin only was a stain in the mind, imagined rather than real.

Stony faced, the reverend nods. He's not going to show his feelings here, among a bunch of reeling drunks. Ock Arglin himself is there in person dishing out his hock cup by cup. He looks like a gnome, a troll, a preternatural creature born out of the mountain itself, and every time he catches the reverend's eye gives a devilish wink. He's the only one in town whose business is thriving, not because he believes in the cure but because he likes drinking, and does so solely in order to get drunk. 'Can't see the point in drinking otherwise,' he says. He and the mayor stand around the hock barrel burbling at each other. It sounds as if their words have already passed over into driftdead land. Garble garble garble.

'Don't patronise me,' the reverend says in a voice low and testy. 'And don't talk to me about faith. We've lost half the town. More. The demon fear is among us now.' He speaks in a flat monotone. He points to the mayor who is pouring drinks for the Smiley Sisters who are bouncing their chests in response.

'The fool folds his hands, and eats his own flesh.'

Rasputin can't help noticing how caved in his old master's face looks, as if it had long ago been bashed in. Although he's trying to stand straight he still manages to look hunched over. What he is saying is the truth, however. Rasputin's witnessed it himself: sudden mass desertions, three or four or five at a time.

'Despair too is a kind of vanity.' Rasputin doesn't know if this is true, or if Ecclesiastes says it, but it sounds right. He takes a deep breath, 'Besides, we don't know for sure that these souls have been damned by God.'

'I can see what is in front of my eyes. The dead walking to Hell.'

'People say that God works in many mysterious ways, but they won't allow him to be mysterious. How can any mortal man pretend to know who God has saved and who he has condemned?' Or what salvation even means, Rasputin thinks.

He thinks of his conversation with Orchid. Who can claim that God has condemned Orchid, when all she had really done is suffer? She came to him, perhaps for absolution, and he had taken her face in her hands and wanted to kiss her. Chapter and verse! Here is the chapter: kiss! And here is the verse: kiss!

'Who can pretend to know what God wants and doesn't want? That's vanity for sure. Faith in adversity, that's the message of the Book of Job. Faith! even in the face of the cruellest absurdity.'

As he says these words, Rasputin looks up in time to see Orchid and Orlap enter the party. They both look around as if expecting to find somebody. Orchid's eyes slide over him without interest. His brave pitch for faith in the face of absurdity twists in his gut. He knows that Orlap and Orchid coming in at the same time means nothing, should mean nothing – their simultaneous arrival might be mere coincidence – but his jealousy says something different. His jealousy sees a secret love affair in every casual gesture, every glance. Logic and common sense have no power over this monster. Even God seems put to the test.

After all, she told him nothing but that there was something to be told. How can there be any absolution without a full confession?

'I'm not Job! He was set up by God and the Devil as a test of their powers. It was a power play. A put-up job. They conspired, god to god. They gambled on a man's soul as upon the roll of a dice or the fall of a card. It was bluff and call-my-bluff. They tortured him to see who would win. I don't want to believe in a God like that anymore. Was it worth it? To put one man's soul in jeopardy to prove the Devil wrong? I don't think so. What's God got to prove?'

Rasputin can hardly contain his sorrow. To see such a giant in the faith totter, lose his nerve. 'God knew Job's will. The strength of Job's faith. For God, it was a sure bet.'

They don't sit together, he notices. Orlap goes off and joins a group of drinking men; Orchid sits quietly on her own until Mary joins her. Mary, appearing out of nowhere, as she does. Jealousy even finds this deliberate splitting up suspicious. The way Orlap turns his back on her is a little too emphatic, perhaps, as is her looking everywhere but at him.

'I know, I know!' the reverend is trying to keep his voice down. 'But God tortured Job, like he's torturing me.'

'If you carry on like this, you know what will happen, don't you?'

'What?'

'You will desert, turn into one of them. You'll go the same way as Hera. Is that what you want?'

'Maybe it is. Deep down, maybe that's what I want. Abdication.' He wants to abdicate but he can't. God won't let him.

At that moment God intervenes in the conversation. Rasputin opens his mouth to blurt out what he can see on the heads of the driftdead, when God puts some different words in his mouth.

'What's your name?'

'What?'

'We call you reverend, and some call you the Stickman. Apparently, before God found you, you were a master of the billiard cue.'

'I know, I know...'

'But what's your name? The mayor is Bill. Even Sad Toof has a real name. Johnny or something like that. And Witch Hunt is...'

'Yes, yes.'

'In fact everybody has a real name – except Sirocco. He can't remember his because he lost it in the desert. Gypsy had to give him one.' That gets him thinking about Sirocco in the desert in a new light, but there's no time to follow that thought up.

'I prefer people to just call me reverend.'

'Yes, I know. But you must have a real name.'

The reverend is oddly reticent about it. 'What's it to anybody?'

'It's something to me. When I'm talking to somebody, I like to use their name. Reverend is your role, your title, not your name.'

The reverend is uncomfortable with this. He looks around the room as if for some other topic of conversation.

'When did somebody last use your name when talking to you?'

'I've put all that behind me. Everything. Even my name. I gave it all to God. I came to Keatown with nothing.'

'Well, now God wants you to have it back. You're in need of it.'

'It'll only remind me of things. Things I left at the gate. Vanities all of them. Strait is the gate, narrow is the way. You're talking about the old me. I don't want the old me back.'

'You need a name. Just like the Baby. If you don't have one, you must take a new one. And you should be christened with that new name. Then you will be a new person. Without a name you aren't a person, not properly.'

The reverend looks at him with sudden suspicion. 'Is God telling you these things? I've never heard you talk like this.' What he means is, talk to him like this. Rasputin is usually too respectful to challenge his mentor in such a way.

'God is telling me these things. Because he wants you to live. The Slough of Despond is a trap. God has shown me that your way out is to take a name, if not your old one, a new self, renewed in the Lord. I can baptise you.'

The reverend hangs his head as one in shame although truly, Rasputin thinks, he has nothing to feel shame for. Sometimes the guiltless take the burden while the guilty walk free, free and confident in their self-righteousness. He feels like taking this frail man's face in his hands and lifting his face up to Heaven, so the light might shine upon it. The last thing he needs is for the reverend to break down in front of everybody and start blubbering.

They stand there for a long moment while the hell-bent drinkers carry on around them, oblivious to the drama. Orlap is laughing with the men, but he is not drinking, Rasputin notices. He's only pretending to drink, lifting the glass up to his mouth but not taking anything in. Not only is he pretending to drink, he's pretending to laugh; he's pretending everything. It's not jealousy making this up, Rasputin thinks. What I'm seeing is for real. And when Orchid came to see me it was because she wanted to tell me something, which in the end she couldn't tell me.

'I'll do it,' the reverend says at last, 'because I know you speak the truth. God has touched you. I saw that after your first night in the church. I will take a name. I will be baptised with this new name. And you must do it. Then I'll know the blessing comes from God, and is a true blessing and therefore a true name.'

'I'll do it,' Rasputin says, his voice trembling. 'We'll go up to the Spring.'

'There is one thing.'

'What?' Rasputin is suspicious. The reverend looks as if he's making a deal, and you don't make deals with God.

'The Baby. He must take a name too. You must convince the lizard worshiper to baptise him along with me. We will both take names.'

'I'll do my best. To convince him I mean. But he is the baby-bearer, for better or worse.'

The reverend nods glumly, but Rasputin can see that some strength has come into his body. His spine is straighter. The prospect of baptism has cheered him up.

There's a burst of drunken laughter from the corner where the mayor is cracking a keg of brandy. The one he's been saving for a rainy day. Something's set them off. Rasputin closes his eyes and allows the voices to lift into the general blather, and says a quick prayer for his blighted people. He remembers a passage in which Jesus likens his love for his hometown to a hen's love for its chickens, that desire to bring them all under her wing, and finds that he can understand it. All these lost ones! Would that he really were the redeemer and could shed their despair for them.

'Why didn't we do this in the first place?' the mayor fumes at Ock Arglin, at anybody who would listen. His famous bulwark, which bled the energy and resources of the town, was a strategic error. While there are not enough resources in the town to protect every house with a lovely smooth-walled wedge, they might have thought in terms of creating funnels and corridors to regulate the flow, rather than trying to block it off. Still, hindsight is a great thing!

With his place well protected, plenty of the cure on hand, and with the choppers doubtless on their way to save the town, the mayor feels pretty good. There is light at the end of the tunnel! Things are looking up! The tide is turning! Like that famous bird whose name he can't remember that rises up from the ashes, Keatown will live again. All everybody has to do, he reasons, is to stay drunk and wait it out. Either the choppers will come or the driftdead will stop coming. After all, it stands to reason, they can't keep coming on and on forever.

He faces his picture of Queen Elizabeth and raises his glass in a stiff salute. Everybody laughs as if he is making a joke. The Smiley Sisters laugh louder than any one. Mavis makes a harsh sound, like a crow cawing. Kark kark. Belatedly he notes that some wag has drawn a thin Salvador Dali moustache on the radiant Queen. How childish, he thinks with irritation. Small things amuse small minds.

'The heart of the wise is in the house of mourning; but the heart of fools is in the house of mirth,' the reverend says.

Rasputin offers up a sigh of relief. It's now or never, for telling the reverend about the souls of the driftdead.

With a quick glance at Orchid, who is deep in some secretive conversation with Mary, he opens his mouth to speak – but again God intervenes.

I'm going to desert, so goodbye and God bless you all!

The last party at the end of the world could hardly proceed without incident, but it is the antics of the sober Reverend Stickman that first bring everybody together in something like a collective glee.

It all begins sombrely enough when Pinky comes in from checking the defences, looking badly shaken up. Days of warfare and defeat at the hands of the implacable driftdead have taken their toll on the young punk. His sadism and aggression have morphed into something else – a formidable grimness of spirit. Towards the end, just before the bulwark gave way, he appealed to the mayor to break out the weapons they'd salvaged from the Humvee and go down in a blaze of glory, taking out as many of the mindless horrors as they could. The mayor resisted. It was a waste of ammo, he said. It seems he has been holding the weapons in reserve, but for what, nobody knows. However, facing down a determined Pinky is not a pleasant experience.

Nobody has worked more constantly at such close quarters with the driftdead as Pinky. Even the staunchest of his mates can't take his pace. His attitude has changed over the long hours of battle from contempt to horror. A horror so deep he can't root it out no matter how many he destroys. 'They are not many, they are one,' he keeps saying, and only the reverend seems to know what he is talking about. 'My name is legion,' the reverend intones. The more he hacks them to pieces the more they multiply. It is as if they are reassembling themselves behind his back into a single creature. There is no killing it; there is no victory. And that is where the horror begins for Pinky. All the driftdead coalesce into one nightmarish figure whose face and body are forever changing but forever staying the same, and which cannot be killed.

Nobody takes much notice when he walks inside looking for a drink. He chats to a few mates and they drift outside. A few others trickle after them, and soon everybody has gathered outside, to the south of the mayor's property, numbly watching the two streams of driftdead merge. It takes everybody a moment to realise why most of the Driftdead appear to have shrunk, with a few giants walking among them.

'Children,' the reverend says in a hushed voice. 'They're just children.'

And mostly they are. Children in nightgowns, children clutching teddies, children all dressed up for a birthday party, Halloween children, naked children, children in uniforms with forgotten insignias, children with pony tails, children with their socks pulled up to their knees, children of every shape, size, colour and cast. All clutching something. But there are still some adults, towering above them like Goliaths, striding indifferently through them.

Everybody just watches them.

'Midget zombies,' Mavis says, grinning at her own wit. She's brought her glass with her and raises a lone toast to the midget zombies.

Rasputin stands loyally beside his master. The reverend is shaking hard enough to rattle his bones. Before this interruption, Rasputin was about to raise the issue of the souls of the driftdead. He can see them, the tiny souls of the driftkids, so translucent they can hardly be discerned, hovering above their little stumbling bodies. Be ye as little children, Rasputin thinks, but doesn't voice the thought. In this context it seems blasphemous. The great mystery of who or what the driftdead are strikes Rasputin with redoubled force. To what extent their actions are willed is still a mystery. On the other hand they don't 'drift', which suggests aimlessness. They are more like machines, with no intent, no desire, no will, merely a function.

Even the children. In children, the mechanical nature of the driftdead is laid bare. Children should be laughing, jumping, running and playing, not trudging along like stiff-jointed puppets.

'Let us pray,' the reverend intones, dropping his head to his chest, but nobody does, not even Rasputin. Everybody just stares at the driftkids, forgetting all about the danger of turning. Hundreds of kids. Thousands. And through a town, largely childless. The childless women who remain watch the kids with haunted eyes. Among them is Margo, who looks more haunted than any of them. Since her friend and adversary, Mellissa Tonguestone, left town with the suicide club, Margot has attached herself to Grandmother Gaunt, this way hoping to get closer to Sirocco and the Baby. Now she stands stricken in a sea of children nobody can claim, looking about her helplessly.

'Let us pray,' the reverend intones, louder than before. 'For the souls of these little ones lost to God.' But he doesn't pray himself. Instead, with tears flowing down his cheeks, he steps gently among them, arms outstretched. 'Suffer the little children to come unto me,' he cries.

Margo and another woman join him, hungry for children, trying to scoop them up into their arms. To grab one or two or three. None of the driftkids are interested. The reverend wanders lost among the children. He's trying to bless them but his mouth can't form the words.

'Get him out of there,' the mayor shouts, ordering imaginary troops into battle. 'He's not drunk. Someone get the fool drunk!'

Even as he speaks, Margo, a toddler clutched in her arms, turns, face emptying of expression, and, still holding the squirming toddler, begins to walk south. The woman who had joined her calls, but only once.

Nobody runs to try to save her. We've all learned.

In the silence that follows, Pinky laughs. He sounds like the grim reaper on the killing floor.

'I'm going to go too, with these children of God,' the reverend announces to everybody, taking hold of a passing child's hand. 'I'm going to desert, so goodbye and God bless you all! You have Rasputin to guide you now.'

He faces the librarian. His eyes blaze up like a couple of suns going nova. 'Write a true report of me,' he commands. The librarian nods her head, keeping a straight face.

He does his best. He tries to join the driftdead kids. He imitates them, matches his speed to theirs, plods along in the same mindless fashion under a leaden sky, face set, expressionless, but nobody is deceived, least of all himself. 'Get that fool out of there,' the mayor shouts, but he may as well not have bothered. The reverend falls to his knees and slams his fists on the ground.

'Rejected by God,' he screams as the driftkids bump into him and around him. 'And rejected by the Devil too.'

Nobody laughs, not even Pinky. Only the librarian will, later, in the privacy of the library, have a bit of a giggle.

Rasputin quietly gives thanks.

Then something quite unexpected happens. Pinky wades through the driftkids, ignoring them, until he gets to the reverend, who's a huddle of misery curled up on the ground. He puts his hand on the reverend's shoulder and gently draws him into a sitting position. The reverend looks across at us, all staring at him, his expression unreadable.

He will be all right. He'll pull through. He's tougher than he thinks he is.

Sad Toof and the tooth fairy

As Sirocco steps away from the Cornet house it begins to snow.

The leaden sky has broken apart and turned into tiny flakes, like ash, drifting gently, spinning and shifting in the still air – soft but insistent. He watches the flakes as they slide out of the sky. Looking up at them from beneath, they look dark, seemingly weightless, yet float inexorably down. Little stars drifting out of the great circle of the sky. They seem as light as gossamer. Already there's a crisp outline on the dunes around the house. A curious ivory light infuses everything. The driftdead seem to slow down, as if impeded by this new medium, but Sirocco does not trust the impression. It is like a side effect of the dull, muffled silence of the falling snow.

Sitting by the crab apple tree, under the protection of its spiny branches, are three figures, one tall and gangly, the other two small. Already the snow is beginning to settle on their shoulders. Sad Toof, Little Sanyo and Witch Hunt. Waiting for him, it seems. The last of the mokopuna, he thinks.

The crab apple tree is unfamiliar now with its first halo of snow. Its branches are tense with springy strength, tough green leaves still hold on; tiny crab apples cluster, hopeful of a change of fortune. Sad Toof stands up and the others follow suit. Sad Toof is reflexively gripping his jaw.

They knew all along, Sirocco thinks. They knew and they never said anything. At least he knows why they followed him around. Or perhaps they knew and forgot because they didn't care. And still don't. He's certainly not going to say anything. What happened was between him and Gypsy's oval mirror, and will stay that way.

The Baby comes to life and reaches out for the snowflakes as they float past. Like most things he reaches for, stars, mountains, clouds, faces, he can never grasp them. That is like trying to grasp an image in a 3D film. When a cold flake hits his fingers he tries determinedly to grip it and bring it to his mouth. Sirocco loosens the front-pack so the Baby can turn more easily, making sure his little woollen bonnet is secure over his bright red ears, pink as flowers. Soon, after some struggling with his legs, the Baby is facing forward, both arms outstretched to the falling snow, urging Sirocco along.

'I'm going to the marae,' he says. He is ashamed to look at them. All this time he has been a fool, such a fool. He stops and shakes a little snow off the crab apple tree.

'Nobody up there,' Sad Toof says. 'Empty.'

Nobody up there. It seems incomprehensible that Akona would turn. Or the mysterious Man in Black. Surely Akona, with her roots deep in the land, would be last to go. But then, he felt that way about Gypsy. Like all of them, he wonders briefly when the scourge will start taking out the mokopuna. The odds mount with every passing moment.

'I've got a supply of milk at the mayor's,' he says. Better than that, the mayor has a well-kitted-out laundry where he can wash a couple of the Baby's dirty nappies. The baby brigade has somehow melted away. Where is Grandmother Gaunt when he needs her?

'They're all drunk,' Sad Toof says.

'Yes,' Witch Hunt says, reaching for the Baby, having him clutch her finger instead of a piece of snow. Solemnly she adds, 'They're all drinking reindeer piss.'

Little Sanyo laughs. 'That's a good one. Who told you that?'

'Ock Arglin.'

'He's getting himself confused with Santa Claus,' Sad Toof says, pulling hard on his jaw. His face twists into a familiar rictus of pain.

'Let's go,' Sirocco says, abruptly turning away from them. Their banter disturbs him. They are, after all, children. He wonders how it was possible for him to imagine he was one of them. Perhaps it was the instinct for camouflage. Lizard taught him the value of taking on the colouration of things around him. Or perhaps, during those many years in the desert, his psyche got worn right back down to its childish nub. He didn't pretend to be one of them. He was one of them. Now, no longer. Now, he knew.

Sirocco concentrates on putting one foot in front of the other, heading north. The snow is heavy and already the world around him is turning into the same dull, pearly grey as the sky. The driftdead kids trudge towards him, as indifferent to the snow as to everything else. They look quite stoic, as if they were heading to a party where the soft drinks and cakes will make it all worth it. The sand is shifting under the weight of the snow, and some of them sink to their knees, even their waists, with every step, but it doesn't bother them how fast they move. One toddler disappears entirely. But she must have hit something solid beneath, for a few moments later she re-emerges, clawing her way through the sludgy sand, not bothering to flick the muck out of her face.

The soft silent snow muffles, isolates and generalises everything even more than the sand does, turning the forms of the world into pregnant suggestions, sketches, which, as more snow falls, become more abstract. Like a fine rim of moss it grows, and seems to eat into the shape beneath. Along with everything else, voices too are muffled and isolated, as if each person were speaking in a sound-proofed room.

He is dimly aware of the conversation behind him. Little Sanyo explaining that snow might look light and fluffy but can be so heavy it will snap concrete, or even steel. And Sad Toof commenting that probably the girders would collapse and smash up Annanda's supermarket. He seems to relish the idea.

There's a silence after that, before a sudden exclamation from Sad Toof. A cross between a gasp and a shout. It's such a strange noise everybody stops and turns to him. He has his hands up to his mouth. His eyes are wide and staring. He brings one hand down from his mouth and opens up his fist.

There it is, a shattered enamel stump and deep black root; he stares at it without comprehension.

'It's my tooth,' he says, unbelieving. His other hand is probing his jaw.

'Let's have a look,' Witch Hunt says.

He holds it down for her to see.

'Did it hurt, coming out?'

Sad Toof shakes his head. 'It just came out.' One moment he is stumbling along with the others nursing his sad tooth, the next moment it is in his hand. Quite at a loss, he stares at it. Here it is, his pain, the very shape of it, lying in his palm in all its grotesquery.

'Let's have a look in your mouth,' Little Sanyo says.

Sad Toof obliges. He seems eager to have the reality of this confirmed, as if the tooth in his hand could be lying. He pulls his lower lip down, exposing that part of the gum where his sad tooth once reigned.

'It looks dark in there,' Witch Hunt says.

'I can see it!' Little Sanyo jumps up and down with excitement.

Where that proud, stubborn tombstone soared alone, ruling the pyorrhea-ridden gums around it, there is now a yawning gap. Nothing all the way down to the bone.

'There's no pain,' Sad Toof says. He can't believe it. Not yet. He is waiting for it to return. It always does. If there is one thing that Sad Toof has learned in his short life it is that relief is temporary. 'All my life. Go to bed with it at night, wake up with it in the mornin''. Already there is a touch of bereavement in his voice. He has something new to feel sad about – the loss of his sad tooth. He is already beginning to mourn the tooth as if he's been deprived of a loved one. There is a gap where his identity used to be. An absence instead of an abscess. He's still Sad Toof, he just doesn't have the tooth to back it up. And sadness, without the underpinning of pain, doesn't quite have the same gravitas.

Akona meets Irawaru

Akona and the Man in Black make their way uphill, following the path of the Wai-O-Tapu River. It is still snowing, and the murky weather has contracted distances. Right now, she would love nothing more than to rest her eyes on Irirangi, its cool, ethereal peak, its pristine slopes.

She will accompany him to the Wai-O-Tapu Spring, and he will continue on from there, following an old walking trail that will take him through the mountains. For all her age and reputed wisdom, she is as bad as anybody else at saying goodbye. When he departs, the Man in Black will take a little of the wairua, the soul, of the marae with him, and she can't hide that from her heart. She is a tribe of one, which is no tribe at all. The ancestors are all very well, but no substitute for a family. When she is gone, the marae will fill up with ghosts. Until the day when the children of the land return, and the air fills up with the smell of baked kumara and the happy sound of playing children. Which is about as likely, she muses, as the return of the mayor's helicopters. As it is, each step brings her closer to the moment when they must part ways.

The stones beneath her feet are as grey as the air around her. The only flash of colour is the red scarf she has around her neck. The Man in Black, walking a few paces in front of her, is no more than a moving outline, the suggestion of a man, no more than a trick of the eye.

When that moving shadow falls still, she stops too. He doesn't say anything, so she is quiet also. The silence around them thickens. As soft as a shadow herself, she moves up to join him. Standing in the snow on the path ahead of them is a dog, but unlike any dog she has ever seen. He is not quite the right shape for a dog, and there is something undoglike in his stance and focus. The Man in Black makes no move to keep walking. He is studying the dog-thing carefully from under lowered eyes.

'Ka whakakurītia e Māui a Irawaru,' she says softly. Irawaru, a man, was turned into a dog by Māui, the trickster god.

'He understands human speech,' the Man in Black says.

'Ah but only English,' she says.

He grins. 'This one can kill. In English.'

'He has the wairua of a pig,' she says.

'The eyes of an octopus,' he says.

'And the cunning of a man,' she says.

Keeping their eyes lowered so as not to confront the animal, they continue to study it, and the dog-thing studies them in return.

'A mansion monster,' she says. 'I've heard of such creatures. He's a bit far from home, isn't he?' Actually, she already knows who this beast belongs to. She has never seen him before, but she has felt his eyes upon her from the rocks and hills around. He is Brian Fairweather's creature, sent out to spy on the land and bring reports back to his master on the state of his master's domains, in particular the Wai-O-Tapu Spring.

She suspects that Fairweather knows all about her visits to her ancestral territory, and that he even bought the property for an outrageous price, certainly one the greedy Bob Kensington couldn't refuse, because he knew what an outrage and violation it was. He did it, not because he needed the land for any purpose, but because it was sacred, not sacred to her in particular, but to somebody. It would amuse him to demonstrate his indifference, contempt even, for the very notion of the sacred. Like anything else, the sacred can be bought and sold – and destroyed at the whim of an owner.

She steps forward, lifts her eyes up to meet the creature's, and says, 'Go home! Go home now.'

The creature's eyes are an uncanny pink, like a pig's, but the pupil is a horizontal slit, like an octopus. He makes no move to obey her, or react to what she is saying. A moment later he gives two sharp barks, as if signalling somebody or something in the distance.

'We could go around it,' The Man in Black says. It's a good idea. At this spot it would be easy enough to leave the track and give it a wide berth.

They don't have to. As if perfectly aware of their conversation, the dog-thing moves aside in a clear signal that they might proceed. They move on, and pass warily. It falls in behind them, pacing them at a distance not quite comfortable. They cross paths with several driftdead, most of them children, but the dog-thing takes no notice.

Soon they are approaching the rocky outcrop where she saw her first driftdead, a man she mistook for her grandfather Lawrence crossing Makurutanga at an awkward spot. The roar of the Wai-O-Tapu Spring comes from ahead of them as from the throat of a taniwha. A massive and fierce but friendly taniwha, with its tail buried deep within the mountains. The dog follows them, but with one eye on the swiftly moving Makurutanga.

The snow is thinning and beginning to lift as they approach the spring. A landscape of black, white and gray opens up around them. The surface of the spring is dark, almost like ice except for the quiver on the surface and the rush of sound. She follows the Man in Black up a little beyond the spring where they stop and take their leave.

He takes her by the shoulders and they gently rub noses.

'Te toka tu moana,' she says. And that is what he has always been. A rock standing in the ocean.

The tears are going cold on her face by the time she turns back to the spring. She'll need to wash them off in the uprush of fresh water. More than that, she's going to need to get right in, to wash her whole body which, she suddenly feels, is tainted.

The dog-thing is still there as if waiting for her, sitting at a respectful distance from the spring. There is nothing particularly aggressive in its stance. It is merely watching.

'Stay your distance then,' she says to it, confident that it can understand her.

She feels oddly abashed, taking off her clothes in front of the dog-thing. It is unnerving. 'Why don't you leave me to have my dip in private?' she says, but the dog-thing simply continues to look at her, quite happy it seems.

It's a good thing Cherrie Lamont is not here to see the mad old woman go naked into the cold waters of Wai-O-Tapu, flakes of sky still falling into her hand. Not such a bad way to go mad, she thinks, slipping into the water. The cold numbs her body but wakes up her sleeping mind. She remembers her dream, Ellen Johnson and the brown baby. Nōpera and the spring. I'm alone now, she thinks as she sinks under the water. At the edges of the spring she can do that. Deeper in, the upthrust of the water from below would push her back up into the air. Beneath her feet the ground quivers. The crystal cold water froths and bubbles around her.

I could die right here and now, she thinks with great clarity. Let the cold warm me. Die, right at the source, the Wai-O-Tapu. Tempting, but she can't die with that infernal dog-thing watching her. It would be nice to think that it really is Irawaru, still in his dog form. No, rather it is a result of gene splicing with a pinch of dark magic thrown in. Whatever it is, she doesn't want to die in front of it. It is not a fit witness. She hates the image that creeps into her mind of the dog-thing pulling her body from the spring and feeding on it. Her old flesh is not worth much, but surely more than that.

She surfaces, her body on fire with the cold, her mind as lucid as the full moon.

The dog thing is sitting closer, closer to her bundle of clothes. It is watching her with its tongue hanging out like a normal dog.

'So, Irawaru, that's why you're here, not to kill me, or guard me, or watch over my clothes, but to shame me into staying alive. Well, it worked. I'm still alive.'

In the distance, the sound of a motor, working hard. A truck.

She pulls herself out of the water. 'So what is it the tīpuna want of me?' The ancestors are never at rest; they always want something.

a survivor's cunning

Because he is not tall enough, Sirocco has to stand on a box to comfortably use the old concrete tubs in the mayor's bathroom to wash out the Baby's nappies. Just one of the inconveniences of being a runt, old or young makes no difference. A runt is still a runt. On his way to the mayor's, he's had plenty of time to reflect on the thought that his diminutive size has made it easier for all the big people, of whatever age, to treat him like a child, especially since he was not much better than a slobbering baby when Gypsy brought him in. There have been times when he has believed that he was born in Keatown, and that Gypsy and Scale are his real parents, because his time in the desert seems more like a dream, or an elaborate fantasy created for the sake of his Book of Imaginary Sentences, than a life lived.

He is using a large cake of rough, grainy sand soap that must be a hundred years old, scrubbing the nappies against the side of the tub. He keeps glancing at the Baby who is lying on the floor nearby, kicking his arms and waving his legs. Little Sanyo has told him that fit, grown men can't keep up the kicking and waving that a baby does. Being a baby is hard work. Sirocco's back is to the door into the main room, where the party is in full blast, and he's just starting to feel vulnerable when the alcoholic roar increases in volume momentarily. Someone has come into the room and shut the door again.

'Hi.'

'Hi.'

Sirocco keeps scrubbing, glancing at Mary's pocked-marked face, weaselly and secretive. And the grey silk scarf around her neck. Typhoid Mary they call her, always staying out of sight, never coming into focus. Never allowing herself to come into focus. Mary of many mysteries.

'I've got a question for you, Age.' She is sitting on the edge of the mayor's bath, with its old iron claw-feet, one leg crossed over the other like a posing model. She has a small but expensive looking shoulder-bag draped over her left shoulder. Dressed in her usual dowdy rags, with tatty dungarees that Scale might have worn, her pose looks incongruous, even mocking.

Sirocco stops scrubbing. He wonders why Mary would use his half-forgotten nickname. 'Then ask it.'

Staying brusque is the best thing he can do. There is something of the desert animal in this girl too, her feral face and snake body, lithe and twisty. A survivor's cunning. And something else she reveals to no one, except perhaps Orchid. She is stronger than I am, Sirocco realises, as she steps closer to him and places her hand on the box he is standing on, as if to hold it steady. She's got it over me, more powerful in every respect. He has to be very careful. He is vulnerable on that box too, her hand so casually close to his legs. He doesn't trust her. He doesn't trust the box. He doesn't trust his legs to hold him up. She is smiling at him as if they are sharing some wicked secret.

Letting the nappy slide into the tub, Sirocco steps down off the box. He may be shorter than she is, and probably no faster, but at least he has his runty dignity.

'If we could take the Baby to a safer place, would you let him go?'

'We?'

'Orchid and I.'

'Why not ask me herself? She's just out there.'

'Because I'm asking first.'

'Why not take me as well?'

'There's a chopper. But there's only so much room.'

'I don't weigh much. I can fold away into a corner.'

Mary fidgets with her scarf. Her eyes slide around the room and come to rest on the Baby, still doing his kicking and stretching exercises on the floor.

'What are you hiding under that scarf? A scar? A birthmark?'

'It's none of your business.'

'Did you try to cut your throat... or did someone else try?'

'Don't change the subject.'

'So answer me first.' There's a time to hold your ground, Lizard once said, and a time to run. This feels like a time to hold his ground. Whatever shame he might have to bear, he's not going to let it put him at a disadvantage. She's far too dangerous.

She puts her hand on Sirocco's shoulder, like a buddy. 'Let's not kid ourselves, Age. Keatown is fucked. There's no future here, not for anybody, and specially not for him.' She gestures to the Baby with her other hand.

'There never was.' Sirocco eases his shoulder out from under her hand.

'The town's finished. We can just huddle here and die, or wait until we turn. What will happen to the Baby if you turn?'

She is right, but Sirocco isn't about to say so.

'Who are you, Mary? I mean, who are you really? I know Orchid. She's a local. She's got a father somewhere around here, if he hasn't turned. There are people here, like Akona, who remember her being born. But you, you just appeared out of nowhere when Hera got pregnant. Nobody knew you, nobody had ever seen you before.'

'I'm not the one that matters, Age. I'm just a stray cat that Hera fed. Like you, Keatown found me, that's all.' She points again to the Baby. 'He's the one that matters, and getting him out of this hellhole.'

'And who's going to do that?'

'The Baron Fairweather. He's in love with Orchid. And she won't leave without the Baby.'

'Why?'

Mary drops her sophisticated pose. She looks around the laundry as if there were some other way out than through the door, back into the last party at the end of the world.

'Because she's his mother.'

Sirocco says nothing. He gets back up on the box and looks into the tub at the half-cleaned nappy. He turns on the cold tap and watches the water sluicing the nappy clean.

'Think about it, Age.'

'I am.'

Orchid went into confinement with Hera, that's all he knew. And a very pregnant Hera would be seen going to and from the Sunshine Supermarket. He doesn't know who attended the birth, but someone would have to know about this.

'Akona,' he says.

'She didn't attend the birth.'

'So who delivered the Baby?'

'Hera did.' She says it very calmly, as if it is the most natural thing in the world.

'And nobody knows this.'

'Nobody. Almost.'

'But you're telling me.'

'Because I want you to know. I want you to feel good about handing the Baby over to Orchid for a better life. Orchid has worked hard for this, pretending to let the baron entrap her, taking stupid dancing lessons, enticing the baron to fall in love with her, even dancing at one of his revolting sex parties. It was all for the Baby, for getting him away from Keatown.'

'So Hera walked about with a pillow under her smock?'

'That's right.'

'But why did Orchid...?'

'Think, lizard boy, think! Orchid was underage...'

'The Baby's father...'

'Now you're thinking. But don't ask. I can't tell you. Only Orchid can do that.'

'Hera was protecting her...'

'That's right?'

'So why didn't Hera give the Baby to Orchid?' He remembers their meeting on Pine Point, the strained conversation.

'We'll never know, will we? But now you have the opportunity to make good. To do right by the Baby and his mother.'

I'm sure Hera had her reasons, Sirocco thinks, as he moves quickly off the box and towards the Baby. He takes one of the clean nappies left, folds it in a triangle and slips it underneath the Baby who's busy chewing on his own hand as if it doesn't belong to him.

'How does the baron know a safe place? Is any place safe now?'

Sirocco wonders if the real Baron Fairweather is anything like the evil genius Rasputin believes him to be. People seldom live up to exalted expectations.

'He knows. He's in contact with important people all around the world.'

'Of course he is.'

'So you'll do it? Let Orchid take the Baby?' She sounds as if she doesn't quite believe it.

'What's in it for me?'

This should be good.

Mary takes her time. She puts on a little show. She resumes her sitting pose on the edge of the bath, slides her right leg over her left. Out of her shoulder bag she produces a fancy gold packet of cigarettes and a gold lighter. She elaborately lights the cigarette and blows the smoke into the air. A single smoke ring hovers, a diaphanous blue halo. Nobody's seen cigarettes like that in Keatown since the beginning of the Long Emergency, something Annanda finds himself explaining over and over again to twitchy customers, some of whom don't believe in the Long Emergency and think that Annanda is holding out on them.

'The baron thought of that. He'll hand over his mansion and everything in it, including many years' worth of supplies, good water and secure electricity, to you, Age. Think of that!'

Sirocco does.

'And, the baron will leave behind two of his special girls to be your servants, your slaves if you want. Think of it! Your own servants, both beautiful girls, to do your bidding.' She flashes the gold packet of cigarettes as if it were collateral, or some token of the baron's largesse. Perhaps the baron could leave behind his Aladdin's lamp too. Sirocco flips the edges of the nappy expertly around the Baby's hips and secures it deftly with Annanda's undersized pins. The Baby gurgles appreciatively.

Mary is reading him closely, watching his every twitch. 'You're pretty good at that,' she says admiringly. Between her slim fingers, the cigarette burns brightly.

'Okay, maybe you don't want servants, or even the mansion, it doesn't matter. The baron's not trying to buy you. The real thing is to do right by the Baby.'

Sirocco stops doing things and frankly studies the person in front of him, making no bones about his inspection, wondering how she has succeeded in staying hidden for so long, hidden behind Orchid's pretty face. The librarian once told him that if life was anything like fiction, then all you had to do was find out what your person of interest wanted most in the world and you had the key to understanding their every action. It is not clear, however, that life is like fiction in that regard, no clearer than who Mary is and what she wants from the situation. Perhaps getting hold of the Baby was her price for a place on the chopper.

'Let's say,' Sirocco says, 'that I don't want the two servants. Let's say, that I want you. You stay behind, Orchid takes the Baby.'

This should be even better.

Mary is quiet. Between her fingers, the cigarette twitches. A piece of ash falls. There is the sound of breaking glass and shouts of laughter from the party.

'Is that really what you want, Age, or are you just saying that? To test me.'

'Test you? I don't know.' His voice sounds querulous and lonely, even to his own ears. 'Here's a test. You want to do the right thing? You stay behind while Orchid and I take the Baby on the chopper.'

Mary giggles. Her right leg quivers. 'You and Orchid? Ha, ha.'

Sirocco tries to ignore the hurt and keep going. 'That's not what I mean. I mean that Orchid accepts me as nanny instead of you. It would make sense. I'm experienced with him now. You can have the mansion and the two servant girls.'

She slides her right leg up so that she can rest her right hand on her knee, and ostentatiously waves the overworked cigarette with the other. 'Now you are being silly, Age – and silly boys get punished.' She jabs the air with the cigarette, creating two instant smoke rings.

'I'm not a boy.'

'You are. A very silly boy. What do you think you are?'

For a moment Sirocco doubts everything. His vision of the old man in the mirror, his conversation with Lizard, his memories of the desert. All this suddenly seems no more real than if he made it up for his Book of Imaginary Sentences. He's just a confused kid living in his fantasy world. Except the Baby, lying on the floor, starting to think about his next feed, is no fantasy. Nor is Mary's power to make him doubt himself, assault his identity, attack his most vulnerable point.

'You mean Orchid wouldn't do that for the Baby? Leave you behind?'

Mary stubs the cigarette out on the side of the bath, pushing it hard enough to squash it flat. 'Are you a virgin, Age? No much going in the desert, I imagine.' She slides off the side of the bath and approaches him. He doesn't dare look at her, afraid of the snake fire in her eyes... more powerful in every respect. She strokes his face with the back of her hand. He smells tobacco. Tears spring to the surface of his skin where her fingers have been.

I'm not going to win this, he thinks with great clarity. She is too strong. If I carry on this way, I will lose, and lose the Baby. She'll take the Baby and walk out of here and that will be that.

'You think about me, don't you? I know you do.'

'You don't think I'd give the Baby up for...'

'No, no, no. No. This is something quite different. I want to.'

And he sees that is true.

She really does want to do it, not out of any real attraction for him, that would hardly be possible, but rather out of an urge to debase herself, for it is in that debasement she will find her pleasure. She's not afraid to do it with the runt, the homunculus, as Pinky has called him.

Sirocco shudders. It's not that he doesn't want to. Like a couple of animals on the floor of the bathroom. Anything is possible. He could take pleasure in her debasement too, and in his own debasement, for by debasing herself she debases him and he, in turn, debases himself. General debasement all around. Welcome to the world of the baron. Sirocco begins to understand how the Baron Fairweather works, how he leverages off moral collapse.

She steps closer until she is right up against him. She has a heady scent, like a tropical flower, completely unexpected. It opens up pathways in his body he has forgotten or never knew. He can't meet her grey snake eyes so he stares at the floor. It isn't a terribly clean floor. If he stares at it long enough maybe she'll go away.

Behind him the door opens, he can tell by the sudden increase in the alcoholic roar from the rest of the house. He turns around as the door closes.

Orchid is standing there.

Hera's worst dreams

She looks so angelic, standing still in the gloom of the dreary laundry. She is wearing a simple, modest white frock that glows among all the greys, and her bare arms look slim and brown against it.

Mary steps away from Sirocco, but not before her hand has lingered on his cheek. A little promise, a little tease, a little threat.

Sirocco takes the opportunity to quickly pick the Baby up from the floor and restore him to his front pack. But Baby doesn't want to go into the front pack. He squirms around so he can look at Orchid. He reaches out for her as if she were the moon.

'I'm very sorry,' she says to Sirocco with a brilliant smile. 'I didn't ask Mary to do this. She has told you, has she?'

'Yes.' The Baby is kicking against the front pack, reluctant to go in.

'It's true.' Orchid comes into the centre of the room. She looks a bit like the fairy at the top of the Cornets' Christmas tree, the way she radiates. 'Hera covered for me.'

Sirocco tried to imagine it.

'They were watching Hera, not me. Trying to find out who the father was. That was the game.' For a moment she looks quite proud of the deception.

'Why do it?'

Her brilliant smile fades. 'My dad would have killed me. He threatened to. He said if I ever got pregnant he would cut me open and take the baby out.' She laughs, hard and jagged.

'Who is the father?'

'I can't tell you. I swore a solemn promise.' She bites her lower lip.

'Will he be going with you, in the baron's chopper?'

A darkness comes over Orchid's face. She looks down at the none too clean floor.

'I hope so.'

'Why would Hera do such a thing?'

Orchid's mood grows darker. She won't look at Sirocco.

'Because the same thing happened to her. When she was young.'

The Baby is finally in the front pack, but not happy about it. Sirocco takes the neglected washed nappy and wrings it out. He hangs it on a towel rack and gets ready to leave. He's had enough of the soapy gloom of the laundry.

Orchid sits on the edge of the bath, exactly where Mary sat, but what a different picture she makes. Her head is lowered, her knees and feet are pressed together, her arms cup her knees. She doesn't look the least bit self-confident any more.

When she looks up her eyes are glaucous. 'I stuffed everything up, right from the start... even Hera turned against me... nobody knows...'

'Knows what?' Sirocco edges towards the door, aware of Mary's beady eyes on him.

'Hera hated the baron. Something he did a long time ago. The reason for her coming to Keatown. We had a huge fight about me going up there. That's why she gave the Baby to you. She stopped trusting me. She went back on her word...' Orchid goes to bite on her fingernails, and stops herself.

'And now you want me to make good.'

She wipes incipient tears from her cheek and stands up, her face burning and the set of her mouth determined.

'I am his mother, Sirocco.' She gives the Baby a look that would have broken the heart of any creature except a scaly, cold-blooded lizard who always finds mammalian child-bearing a messy and somewhat revolting business. And for a moment Sirocco becomes that cold-blooded lizard unmoved by the flush of human drama.

'She was trying to protect the Baby.'

Orchid hangs her head in shame. 'Just like I am now,' she says in a small voice.

'It was me Hera really hated,' Mary says. She has lit another cigarette and is lounging against the wall like a TV crime-show streetwalker. 'She always loved you, her deadly little flower. Remember? Killed her in the end, didn't it? Broke her big wide heart.'

'Don't say that.' Orchid can't manage more than a whisper. 'You can't know that. People turn…'

'You don't know the half of it, Age. Sweet waterworks here can lie even while she's telling the truth. The real reason Hera took her in is because Hera could no longer have a child herself, which is what she'd always wanted, right, little flower? So tell Ageless why Hera couldn't have a child. Go on. Tell him.'

Orchid sways her head from side to side like an animal being beaten.

'Tell him what the baron did to her. With a knife.'

Sirocco wraps his arms around the Baby. They are not very long arms but they manage to get right around.

'Go on, sweetie pants, tell him!'

Snarling, Orchid turns on Mary. 'Fuck you. Just fuck you in the face.'

'Woah!' Mary turns to Sirocco as if to say, see what I've got to put up with.

To Orchid, Mary says, 'It was never going to wash anyway. Ageless here would never have gone for it.'

Sirocco takes a quiet step towards the door, another two or three quick steps and he could be out. Only curiosity holds him back.

'The baron won't be on that helicopter,' Orchid says, her voice as cold as death. Zhenhua knows of safe places to go.'

'So this Zhenhua person will kill the baron?'

The two girls look at each other.

'Mistress Zhenhua doesn't kill if she can avoid it.' There is pride, mixed in with regret in Mary's tone. And something else Sirocco can't catch.

'Would you take me on the chopper and leave Mary behind?' Sirocco asks Orchid.

Orchid is on her feet and approaching Sirocco. 'Sweet baby, sweet baby,'she coos. Then her voice changes. It is no longer hers, but deep and croaky. 'Give him to me. Now! Now!'

Sirocco is too afraid to turn his back on her and take those last steps to the door, so he retreats a step, still facing her.

Orchid shudders as if she were shedding a skin. Her face grows mottled and ugly. Her fingers hook into claws. 'I'll kill everybody,' the deep croaky voice says.

And it's gone. Pretty Orchid is back in front of him again, but ruined by tears which shine in the half-light. 'You want to cling on to him. I understand. He is such a sweetie... Now it's time for him to come to me, his mother...' She reaches out. Her arm seems to extend much further than an ordinary arm.

Mary gives a screeching laugh.

Sirocco slips through the door and back into the last party at the end of the world.

just a little pricking

The party has deteriorated, despite the best efforts of a carousing few to keep up the illusion that everything's still going at full swing. There are a group of still-upright citizens standing around Ock Arglin and his stack of hock, carrying on some semblance of a conversation. Ock can drink the whole town under the table and still be thirsty. Orlap and his fishermen are among them, talking and laughing extra loud to make up for flagging energies and thinning numbers.

Ock's conversation consists mainly of a jumble of common sayings and homilies, little bits of wisdom that he has, over the years, learned how to parrot. 'You pays your money and you takes your chance,' he is saying sanctimoniously to Orlap. Orlap has a glass in one hand and a smile fixed on his face, but he is distracted by the sight of Sirocco slipping out of the laundry door, Orchid and Mary following. Ock decides it's time for a toast. There's nothing like a toast to boost a flagging party.

Raise your glasses! 'Among friends,' he announces, 'there is never enough booze.' There is a ragged cheer and raised glasses.

Big Bill is beyond cheering. He has taken his mission to get drunk seriously, and may be one of the few people in the room who actually believes in Ock's cure. Our mayor is slumped on his favourite easy chair, underneath his poster of the radiantly young Queen Elizabeth II holding aloft the beacon of empire. But Broonzy doesn't look as happy as he should, given that his house is safe and he's too pissed to get up and stagger south. Maybe he is just starting to figure out that staying at home and drinking himself to death in order to keep the driftdead out of his head isn't such a good prospect after all.

Right now he's bemused by some row going on among the women. Something to do with him. Mavis is bitching at Jolene who's bitching back and sticking out her tongue like a little kid. Mavis is in a tense, vicious mood. Sharp and brittle as broken glass.

Grandmother Gaunt and Mother Smiley are trying to keep them apart, but are not doing much good, being as drunk as the combatants.

'Fuck you!' Mavis screams at Jolene. 'You fucken put your dirty little hand down his pants, that's what you did. I saw you.'

'He didn't seem to mind,' Jolene sneers. Grandmother Gaunt and Mother Smiley forget their mission as peacemakers and sneer along with her. All men are pretty much the same as far as Grandmother Gaunt can see; stick a hand down their pants and you have men where you want them.

'I'll kill you. Easy as. Quick as look at you.' Mavis pulls a skinny knife never designed for chopping vegetables from her clothing. She's as fast as a street fighter. Her red hair flares around her face, her freckles glow like hot embers on her pale skin. The knife's already in the air when she suddenly loses interest. Her arm drops. In the middle of a murderous thrust, she turns. Just walks away, still holding the knife, heading south.

The whole room falls silent.

The same thought hits everybody at once. Drunk, and still she deserted!

The mayor, semi-comatose, is just conscious enough to mutter, 'Not drunk enough.'

No one believes him.

'I'll drink to that,' Ock Arglin says. His voice is as empty as his glass is full. He doesn't believe it either.

Into the sudden silence of the room the Baby lets forth a great wail.

A moment later Witch Hunt starts screaming.

'The Baby! The Baby! They're stealing the Baby!'

Rasputin witnesses it. The look Orchid gives Orlap when the three emerge from the laundry is enough to alert him. His jealousy has allowed him to see what nobody else has noticed. Hours of covert observation have paid off. He has not imagined a conspiracy between these two. There is a conspiracy – to take the Baby from Sirocco. Orlap has made a deal with the devil. Not because he is evil, but because he is a fool, and takes the lure of evil at face value.

It is too late to warn Sirocco, which Rasputin would most certainly do. The lizard whisperer is preferable by far to the eater of souls up mansions. Witch Hunt and Sad Toof approach Sirocco, Sad Toof being dragged along by Witch Hunt, who is on the edge of panic. She throws Rasputin a desperate look. Sad Toof is quite distracted, following along tamely, looking around as if he has lost something. Mary comes up behind Sirocco and is in the act of unhitching his front pack from his shoulders when Sirocco turns, quick as a lizard himself, to face her.

'No you don't,' he says. He speaks loudly, at least for his piping little voice, but none of the dedicated drunks take any notice.

'Talking time is over,' Mary says. Her hand goes to her scarf.

A squealing Witch Hunt throws herself at Mary, wrapping her arms around Mary's legs and bringing her down in a tackle. That draws the attention of a few drunks. From his station at the hock barrel, Ock Arglin claps. There's a few laughs. A bit of a show. Not much of one but better than nothing.

But as soon as Sirocco has swung around to meet Mary, Orlap moves briskly in behind him, no sign of drunkenness, and slips the straps of the front pack off his shoulders. Struggling to keep the Baby steady, Sirocco turns to face the new threat. Sirocco and Orlap face each other. Sirocco's arms wrap fiercely around the Baby.

'You must give him over now,' Orlap says in a slow, grave voice, as if carving the words in the air.

'The Baby! The Baby!' Sirocco screams, jumping up and down. The Baby giggles with delight. The drunks are entertained. The runt looks pretty absurd jumping up and down red in the face. He looks like a leprechaun, Ock Arglin observes. Grandmother Gaunt makes a rush for the group, braking only when she sees that Orlap is armed with a thin knife used for gutting fish.

'It's not right,' Sirocco says to Orlap.

'You know it is,' Orlap says in that same sepulchral tone. A man with a sad duty to perform, sad news to impart.

'Yes Sirocco,' Orchid says, coming up and standing beside Orlap. 'You know now. We've had our chat.' Her voice is calm and slippery.

'Yes,' says Orlap. 'Ignorance is no excuse now.'

Sirocco falters, Rasputin can't understand it. The lizard worshiper may be many things, but a coward is not among them.

Gaunt, panting hard, looks from Sirocco to Orchid and back again. 'What does he know?' she demands of Orlap.

'Never you mind, Granny,' Mary says. 'Go home and eat your oats.'

Sirocco keeps a firm grip on the Baby. 'I only know half of the truth.'
'The other half is standing right in front of you,' Orchid says.

'What the hell?' says Gaunt, looking around as if everybody knows something she doesn't but damn well should.

The reverend is staring at Orchid, shocked and horrified. 'I was wrong about Hera,' he says, mostly to himself. 'Wrong, and so righteous! Vanity, vanity!' He faces Rasputin as he would an accuser. 'I was the first to pick up a stone.'

Mary and Witch Hunt are still struggling. The determined little girl has a hold on Mary's scarf and won't let go. Mary beats and kicks her but still she won't let go. No stranger to beatings, Witch Hunt closes her eyes and tightens her grip. Even death won't loosen that grip. Mary has a stark choice: choke to death or lose the scarf. That grey, none-too-clean silk scarf, seemingly made to look as inconspicuous as possible, is suddenly the centre of attention. It has even registered with the drunks that something extraordinary is going on. The mayor is awake and doing battle with his eyelids to follow the action.

After a few moments of incredulity, Mary spins on her feet, ducking like a rock-and-roll dancer to free herself of the scarf before she chokes to death.

For the first time her bare neck is exposed. A strip of mottled, dark blue circles her throat and up under her hair. For a moment the librarian thinks it is a birthmark.

'What is that?' Gaunt says. Her voice has collapsed into a whisper.

'It's the mark of the beast,' the reverend says.

Mary laughs, loud and mocking. 'Pleased to meet you, reverend,' she says.

'What are they talking about?' Gaunt looks around the room for someone she can direct the question to.

'The mark of the collar,' Orchid says, her voice small and quiet in the silent room.

'I've heard about this,' Gaunt says, gripping Mother Smiley's arm for support, 'but I never thought I'd live to see it.'

'See what?' The mayor is on his feet, and his eyes are almost able to stay open on their own.

'Slavery,' Gaunt says.

'There are special collars with little needles in them,' Orchid says, giggling.

'You hardly feel it,' Mary says. 'Just a little prickling.' She grins at Witch Hunt as she says this.

'Then you wear it forever,' Orchid says. 'The collar can be removed but not the mark.'

Gaunt moans and buries her face in her hands. Is it worth it, she wonders, to live so long and see so much?

Witch Hunt quietly hides herself behind Sad Toof.

The mayor waves his arms about importantly, looking for an opportunity to take command. Like Gaunt, he too has heard stories, dark talk he has dismissed as tall tales and exaggerated rumour, like the genetically engineered dog with three heads. The stuff of myth. Of course, he doesn't like to appear as ignorant as he really is. He likes to think of himself as a man of the world, knowledgeable in the ways of human depravity.

'Who is your master?' It is just starting to occur to the mayor, whose brain is working only sludgily, that Mary has been on a mission all this time. That she infiltrated the mokopuna for a purpose. Big Bill has never had any time for the doings of the mokopuna, now he sees his mistake.

'The slave masters. A special club, you could call it. They own people. Some slave masters own hundred of slaves.' Mary's voice is touched with pride.

'Oh, Jesus,' Gaunt moans.

Mary defiantly holds her ground as Big Bill approaches her and stares closely at the mark. He sees that the tattooed strip has a pattern, wide and narrow stripes like a bar code. It is a bar code, he thinks, kicking his brain into action. Anyone with the right scanner would instantly know her ownership history.

'The baron,' He says. It's a foregone conclusion in his mind.

Mary sneers. 'He's nothing,' she says. 'He's less than nothing.'

'Zhenhua, his personal assistant,' Orchid says. 'She's...'

'She's my mistress,' Mary says, standing tall and arching her neck proudly so that the mark of the collar, in all its glory, can be seen by all. 'I serve her and no one else.'

'I'll drink to that,' Och Arglin says, his voice as hollow as an empty wine barrel. And he does.

'Get thee gone!' the reverend says with a flash of his old fire. His stupidity has made him angry. 'Hera,' he says, his voice cracking. He couldn't have been more wrong about the woman.

As the librarian later learns, Mary's parents deserted her when she was five. Parents did that sort of thing at the beginning of the Long Emergency, abandon their children – and even eat them. Novelists wrote books about it. Zhenhua bought her on the net before the exodus, and kept her hidden in Keatown away from the eyes of the baron. She was Zhenhua's secret agent.

'It is an honour to be offered the collar,' Mary says, still arching her neck. 'Hera turned it down. Refused the honour. That's when Mistress Zhenhua kicked her out.' Mary's voice is full of contempt, 'She didn't deserve it, that's the truth. You have to earn your collar. Instead she slunk down here, to Keatown!' Mary directs every word at the reverend, stabbing him with her voice. He rocks backward on his feet like a man receiving blows, but holds upright under the assault. He will answer to God, not this lesser demon!

'Why're you here?' The mayor demands. He has won the battle of the eyelids and now fights to get on top of the slur in his voice. He puts the question to Mary but his eyes slide across to Orchid and Orlap. Slowly, very slowly, it is beginning to sink in.

Orlap steps up to him, pulling Orchid along by the hand. 'We have come to claim our baby. I am the father. We now want to take him to safety.'

'Lies!' the reverend screams. He's gone into a frenzy, his whole body shaking. 'The Baby, unchristened and unnamed, will wear the witch's collar! The mark of the beast will be upon him, and he will be bartered in the marketplace of souls.'

Rasputin is in no position to pacify his master, although it is a little easier for him; he saw it coming. Nevertheless, he just stares open-mouthed at Orchid. All this time... living this lie... pretending to be indifferent to Orlap... pretending that Hera was the mother... giving him a smile or two, a little gentle encouragement to keep him deluded... He should be as furious as the reverend but he is not; he is merely sick. If this is love, he doesn't have the stomach for it.

It is in that moment, while everybody is standing around open mouthed, even Ock Arglin whose mouth mostly opens only when his elbow bends, that Mary makes her move. She jumps Sirocco from behind, appearing to thump him lightly on the ribs as she mounts him. Sirocco, who feels only a slight pricking in his side, turns, trying to prevent himself from falling on the Baby, and, as he falls, Mary jumps off him, scoops up the Baby, front-pack and all, and makes a run for the door. A moment later she is through the door and gone. Out into the slipstream of the driftdead.

Witch Hunt starts screaming.

Orlap briskly salutes the mayor before he and Orchid follow Mary.

Sirocco leaps up onto a table, where, for once, he stands above everybody. He no longer cares about his silly little piping lad's voice, or his walnut old-age face, or his runty body. He points to the door. 'Save the Baby!' he shouts.

The reverend comes up and stands by his side. 'Save the Baby!' he thunders.

The mayor gets the idea.

And another, even better idea.

sheer drops and brief showdowns

When Flay and Annanda catch up with Butch, there is a brief battle on the road before Butch gives up. That part of the road has sheer drops on one side as it winds around the first rocky outcrop at the southern end of mansion city. All Flay has to do is blast on the Isuzu's tinny horn a couple of times and make threatening movements towards the RL's tail end. Not that he'd bash into the back of his own Bedford, but Butch doesn't know that. A little bit of crazy tailgating does the trick.

Meek as a lamb, she pulls up as close to the hillside as she can.

Butch is shaken. There's no fight in her.

'I'd rather battle a storm at sea in a piddling little fishing boat than drive that truck along these roads,' she says.

'Don't blame ya,' Flay says magnanimously. 'There's an art to driving the old girl when you've a heavy load on. She can get a sway on, if you know what I mean.'

'Fuck that.'

'Count yourself lucky you weren't driving that piece of shit.' He points at Annanda's Isuzu. 'Good thing you didn't try to get the diesel up here on the back of that.'

Annanda stands patiently through this interchange. He'd sent more prayers to Rama coming up here with Flay at the wheel than in his whole life.

'I see you're nicely dressed for the occasion,' Butch says, trying to gain back a bit of ground.

Flay curses. He has forgotten his pansy outfit. His pink shirt has tiny sequins down the front and his slacks narrow at the ankles. Christ!

'You can sit on the back,' Flay says, making ready to swing up into the RT, on the driver's side of course.

'Not me, Cap'n Fancy Pants. I'm up on the bridge where it's all nice and cosy.' She winks at Annanda who is still waiting patiently.

'So what wus the big plan? You and that grinning idiot? I thought you were ditching him.'

'Orlap has to get the girl and the Baby up here. So he gives me the job of hauling the diesel. That's the kind of fool he thinks I am. But it suited my purpose, didn't it?' She looks slyly at Flay.

'You mean they're goin' to snatch the Baby, take 'im by force?' That amuses Flay, imagining how pissed-off the runt will be. Ever since he became the baby-bearer, he's done nothing but walk around putting on airs, playing king of the castle.

'That's the plan.'

Annanda shakes his head in sorrow.

The three of them squeeze into the front of the RL, with Annanda in the middle, Flay grumbling as he makes sure he has plenty of elbow room for some hard driving. If he could imagine Hell, it might consist of being confined in a small space with a poofter and a dyke. That would sure take the fun out of jerking off.

drunks and guns

Big Bill steps up beside the reverend. He loves it when church and state can stand side by side, at one in righteousness. Prayers and guns, a satisfying mix. A laser light has cut through the fog in his brain. He stands up and thrusts out his chest, ignoring the twinge in his back as he does so.

'They've stolen the Baby!' he bellows.

Everybody shuts up and stares at him. Some, still catching up with what has happened, blink at him like sleepy owls.

Nobody would ever accuse Big Bill of being a revolutionary, or a man who has wasted his life being envious of the rich. Not at all. He's fed off the rich. It is the rich who will one day return in their choppers bringing the cargo, bringing the good times... But as soon as he saw those boxes of weapons in the back of the upturned Humvee... he knew... he knew he would never waste a single bullet on the driftdead, who are too dead to appreciate a good bullet.

He steadies himself for the last political speech he will make, his last rallying cry. His mind is clear, even if his body is a little uncooperative. 'Traitors in our midst have stolen the Baby. What for?' He stops to clear his throat and find the right rhetorical tone. 'To take up mansions, where else?'

There is a murmur of drunken agreement. That much is clear to everybody by now.

'Where he'll be sold to the highest bidder, that's what.' The murmur of drunken agreement turns, as it so easily does, into a murmur of drunken anger.

'They tried to pretend that the baron is not behind this, but we know about him, don't we?'

The drunks, who know nothing about the baron other than his name, cry out in agreement. The baron! The baron! Conspiracy! At the same time there is confusion. Orlap, the father? Orchid, the mother? How could that be? Grandmother Gaunt has collapsed into a sitting position on the floor and is staring aghast at anyone who will meet her eye. Sirocco is jumping up and down on the table. 'Let's go, let's go!' he's shouting, but hardly anyone is taking any notice. Go where? Some have already forgotten. Ock is pouring again.

One of the fishermen, Celif, captain of the third boat, Thor's Hammer, says, 'Butch is in on this too. They have stolen the diesel and have sold it to the baron. The Merry Widow will never put to sea.'

'How do you know this?' the mayor asks with huge indignation. Something happening right under his very nose and he didn't know? How is that possible? Ah, the conspirators kept their plots well hidden.

'Butch told me. She's stolen Flay's RT and is taking the back road.'

'The whole town's been had,' the mayor shouts.

People shout back at him and at each other.

'Fairweather will have a chopper,' Celif says.

'Of course he will!' It is all falling into place for the mayor now. 'I want that chopper,' he says. 'I want it so bad it hurts.'

'And he has gold. Lots of ingots. Orlap's got some. He paid Orlap well.'

'I bet he did,' the mayor says.

'Let's go get'um,' someone shouts. 'Whad're we fuckin' around here for?'

It's not quite clear if this enthusiast wants to go after the gold or the traitors or the Baby, but it doesn't matter. Action! That's what they crave. The time for sitting around waiting to turn is over.

Sirocco jumps off the table and runs for the door. He's had enough talking. With every moment that passes, the Baby gets further and further away. Lizard would tell him to be quick or dead, if Lizard were here.

Ock Arglin holds up a glass full to the brim and toasts Sirocco as he rushes past. The old drunk's face is shining as if he has just had a vision of the genie in the bottle. 'The guns! Break out the guns!' he cries.

This is exactly the cue Big Bill has been waiting for. 'Then let's just do it!' His favourite political slogan.

Everybody cheers as Big Bill crashes into his storeroom and starts dragging out the guns. The lids of the steel trunks are thrown back on dark, cosmolined automatic weapons. Military grade. For a moment they all hold back, but only for a moment. Pinky, who has just found a new purpose in life, takes the role of the man handing out the weapons and the ammo.

The reverend misses his moment. He steps forward to warn them of disaster, but it is unlikely they would have cared; disaster means nothing to them now. The worst has already happened. Drunk and armed! There is general glee.

Many of the men, fishermen and farmers, are surprisingly adept with the weapons. Even Grandmother Gaunt is grimly competent. She doesn't have to pretend outrage. And being kept in the dark all this time is a good portion of it. She's ready to start shooting.

Big Bill has some qualms when he sees such weapons in the hands of the Smiley Sisters, the drunk Smiley Sisters, but there is no time for qualms. He does, however, snatch a weapon from Little Sanyo, who has almost taken it to pieces already. 'No guns for the mokopuna,' he proclaims.

Shortly afterwards the mayor leaves at the head of a well-armed, well-oiled rabble, no more than forty souls in all – the last of the inhabitants of Keatown.

'No shooting till we get there,' General Big Bill commands.

If Keatown is going to go down, then let it go down fighting – and he'll go down with it.

That chopper will never leave the ground. Unless he's on it.

He'll make sure of that.

a shift of allegiances

Akona dresses quickly, ignoring the stare of the dog-thing.

Now that it has stopped snowing, except for the occasional flake, the air has become a mix of cool and warm currents. Pretty soon the snow will begin to melt. Already it has a wet, shiny look, like ice.

The waters of the Wai-O-Tapu have done their work, and she feels fresh, if not exactly born again. Someone once tried to explain to her that the effect came from all the minerals the spring water drew from the deepest earth, but Akona holds her judgement, as she likes to do with such explanations. People have all sorts of ready answers for things, some simple, some elaborate, some just plain stupid, and she has learned over the years to put less weight on the explanation and more on the experience itself. The water makes her body tingle through to her bones. It wakes her up from Te Po-te-kitea, the Blind Night. That's all she needs to know.

Instead of setting off back down to the marae, she continues upward along the trail the Man in Black would have taken, heading towards the ridge along which the back road runs, and which approaches the mansions from the south. She's not prompted by much but the desire to keep climbing. Beyond the back road there's another ridge from which she will be able to view not only the whole of Keatown, but get a clear look at Mt Irirangi, and the remoter peaks of the Alps behind.

As often happens when she approaches this spot, she remembers how easy it was as a child to talk to Mahuika, goddess of fire, and be guided by her warmth in the cold ways of the world. As the years passed Mahuika faded and her visits became rarer until finally disappearing in the sweats of adolescence. It is always interesting, she thinks, to note the way memory attaches itself to places. The place where she can remember Mahuika is the place where the goddess resides.

These are peaceful thoughts, lit by the hope that since she is at the other end of her life Mahuika might come to her again. It would be fitting. A happy completion. But that is merely a fantasy, like Sad Toof's tooth fairy who would one day appear and conjure the rotten tooth out of his mouth. Mahuika is under no obligation to an old woman with her memories shaped in pearl.

As she approaches the road, she's chagrined to find the dog-thing still tracking her at a discreet distance, backtracking here and there, but not allowing her out of its sight for more than a moment. Not stalking her but accompanying her, like an ordinary domestic dog, its interest not so much predatory as proprietary.

She waits until it catches up with her. It sits and watches her at just the right safe distance. He, she has to remind herself. The dog-thing is most certainly male, but feels more like an it than a he. She squats down to be at the creature's height. Both dogs and children appreciate that gesture, she's found. She locates his uncanny pink gaze, uncanny because those eyes see right to the back of her head. The creature is capable of great violence. Even at this distance it could slice open the artery in her neck in a second, she does not doubt. It was bred to do such things. Doubtless prowling its territory sniffing out intruders when it found her.

'Are you going to keep following me?'

The creature pants happily.

'I don't pick up stray dogs.'

The creature looks sadly at the ground, suddenly appearing very dog-like.

Akona grins. Perhaps this Frankendog has a sense of humour.

'Well, you poor misshapen soul, I don't know what your name is, but I am going to name you Irawaru. Irawaru was once a man, a man who displeased the demi-god Maui, who turned him into a dog.'

Irawaru stands up and throws out his chest. His nose points upwards towards the sky.

'You like the name, eh? Good for you.' This Irawaru is a gift from the tīpuna, she thinks. An unlikely guardian.

'Why me?' she asks Irawaru, as if he might answer.

He just grins at her. It could mean anything. It could mean that he will tear her to pieces the moment she turns her back on him. Now that would be a fate!

Despite, or perhaps because of, the magical nature of the universe, she has never been comfortable with the notion of special destinies or fate, and she's too old for that kind of nonsense now. Her destiny is no more than what happens to her and what her actions bring about. It's just a fancy word for having to live a life through memory, and make choices at every turn, even when the world turns slippery. We like to think that our actions make some kind of sense, and are rooted somewhere in the will of the gods. All that is largely imaginary, more comforting than true... But this Irawaru...

This Irawaru is something else. The way he turned up just when she reached Wai-O-Tapu Spring, just when the Man in Black was about to take his leave forever. Trained in loyalty and obedience, yet he attached himself to her immediately. A gift from Wai-O-Tapu is a gift from the life source, and not hers to refuse, fate or no fate.

She shrugs and gets back to her feet, groaning a little as she does so. Damn the gods and their caprices, their precious destinies, their signs and signals. 'Okay big boy, you can quit posing now.'

Irawaru is still standing with his nose in the air, but it's not pride. He's pointing to the sky, which is starting to change colour. Mauves and purples and indigos float across the deep in veils. Striations of colour. A vivid green koru unfolds against the background of the Milky Way.

Irawaru looks up at her inquisitively. He is not afraid, as an ordinary dog might be.

'Aurora Australis, the Southern Lights,' she says. She hasn't seen anything like this since she was a child. The Aurora Australis is seldom seen this far north, at least not such a dramatic display and never, as far as she knows, in the afternoon. It needs a clear sky at night, she thinks.

A flash of colour catches her eye. She looks back down to Keatown to see the iceberg glowing with the colours of the sky, like an enormous pulsing crystal in the middle of the bay. All around her the snow faintly reflects the same shifting colours. The world has gone from grey monochrome to smudgy, swirling bands of colour, lit by bursts of unlikely light, lime green and turquoise.

'Hello Mahuika,' she says to the sky. 'I was just thinking about you.' And here she is, trailing her multicoloured cloak across the bend of the sky.

Out of the snowy silence comes the familiar sound of a truck, labouring hard as it climbs the steep zig-zags of the back road, and she is reminded that she heard the sound earlier. Now it is close.

Irawaru goes into alert mode. The hair on his spine bristles as he moves between her and the road. He is not graceful, as she understands the term, but he is lithe and fast, which is all he needs to be.

A truck comes into view, looking black in the hanging lights of the sky, but Akona recognises Flay's RL.

The truck pulls over as the driver recognises her. She silences Irawaru with a gesture.

'Would you like a lift, granny?' A grinning Flay leans out the window.

Flay in a gay mood! 'We wouldn't want to be late. Party at the baron's place!'

Irawaru growls, lifts his lips to reveal a set of shining canines and fixes Flay with an eerie, wide-eyed octopus stare.

'Holy shit!'

Beside him, Annanda sends a quiet prayer to the spirit of Hanuman, another genetically spliced being, demi-god with an ape's face, human feet, and the strength to lift mountains. Why should he balk at a mongrel demon whose eyes suddenly flash human?

'What is it?' Akona asks Irawaru, just as if he were a normal human being.

'Somethin' wrong with my face,' Flay says with self-conscious laugh, 'tell me somethin' I don't know.'

Truth is, he's not just self-conscious; he's terrified. He's heard all the tales about monsters, dogs that smell like fish and who have poison in their teeth, and dismissed them all with the flourish of his spanner. Tales to frighten kids. You don't need to pay big dollars for security if every bugger is terrified of the place, treats it like Dracula's Castle. Put the word around. Very clever. Even multibillionaires don't like to pay big dollars unless they have to. He had it all worked out. Until now. Up until this moment, there wasn't much that couldn't be fixed with a good grease and oil change. Now staring into the glassy eyes of a monster dog, he's been stripped down to the bone, right to the marrow, by the monster's scrutiny. He's hit with a terror he's never known before. Here is a predator's scrutiny, amped by a cool intelligence which apprehends him completely. If he even thinks too hard about the shotgun at his side, he will be dog meat, he has no doubt of that.

He slams the gear lever into first and just about tears the pistons out of the engine getting the fuck away from there. Soon there is nothing to be seen of the RT but dust and small stones.

Akona laughs. 'That put an end to that,' she says.

Irawaru can't laugh, he can't even grin and make it look less than evil, but there is no mistaking his insouciant stare in the other direction.

A moment later he is nosing his way between an upright pair of rocks she'd always called the Two Sisters, looking back at her.

Akona grumbles as Irawaru leads her along a path that skirts the front of the mansions, doubtless tramping over people's private property. Up mansions, it is all private property. Of course, at one time Nōpera's people roamed up and over this ridge without giving it a second thought. It was their stamping ground. Then along came people like the Kensingtons who thought they could buy the sky with a blanket. And if they couldn't buy it, they could steal it. And sell it to the highest bidder.

When Irawaru leads her through a forest of concrete and steel pillars to a shadowy cave, she recognises the place, dry and dead as it is. The cave Okewa, which means rain-bearing clouds. The name suggests that the cave is like a hole in dark clouds. It might have looked like that once, looking up from below, before the celebs came and built their eyries.

By accident or design, the massive earthworks have formed something of a protective shell over the cave opening, a spacious concrete veranda. The cave is big enough to hold a whole council of elders. It was a vantage point, even then. 'From the cave of Okewa you can see halfway to the North Star,' her grandmother would say.

Irawaru sniffs around. He seems to have lost his purpose.

'What am I doing here?' she asks, but the dog-thing is busy finding a way around some timber that had been used to make a rough covering for the cave entrance.

'I'd forgotten all about this place,' she says. That is sad enough in itself. Like the cave, her memory has been boarded up. She helps Irawaru by pulling aside some of the timber, working with a certain grim satisfaction. Let the spirits out!

At the same time she feels a bit foolish. Irawaru might have come here on some fool's errand of his own. Who knows how the creature's mind works? And what's the use of opening up the cave to nothing but concrete clouds?

In a few moments Irawaru has found his way through and she follows, making a big enough hole for some light to filter in.

There's nothing much in the gloomy interior of the cave. Just cool rock and shadows. But it doesn't feel stagnant, like a dying stream. Or the memories of a riverbed. There is something alive here, but she's not sure what that means. A memory can feel alive too, come alive in the moment of remembering.

Deeper in, and Irawaru begins to dig around in the dust and sand. The floor here is quite soft. There are indentations, as if people have been sitting on that spot quite recently. Maybe Irawaru is just showing her his territory, the places he comes to piss.

'Wait a minute,' Akona puts her hand gently on the creature's shoulder, but it's too late. Something has been uncovered. She can't see in this light. The walls of the cave seem to have receded, making it bigger. 'I didn't come here to get spooked,' she says.

Irawaru looks up at her with his saucer eyes.

'I'm not sure about you,' she says.

She kneels and clears the stone and sand away from the emerging object – a box. An intricately carved wooden box. The design on the lid is of a sailing ship in full sail, as if before a strong wind.

Irawaru sniffs at it.

'You couldn't have known this was here,' she says.

But why not? He might have sniffed it out with his genetically enhanced nose.

The lid fits snugly, but it is not locked and easily opens. Inside there is a package made of fabric soaked in beeswax. Carefully, she undoes the package. It protects a letter, more like a legal document. Keeping it in its beeswax cover, she takes it to the mouth of the cave and out onto the path where there is just enough light for her to see what it is.

It is the will of Peter Johnson, Ellen Johnson's shadowy husband. A few yellowing sheets of paper.

She's always imagined him as a solemn man in white and black Puritan dress. A stern man with a strict work ethic, it was said. Late in life, he managed to join his wife in the colonies but had unflaggingly sent Ellen and his daughters money, every penny he could scrape together after a week of honest labour. Twenty years of absolute loyalty to his family. Twenty years of thinking only of others before his heart gave out while carrying a sack of very ordinary potatoes.

> It is my will and testament that the Spring known to the Maori as Wai-O-Tapu is to be gifted to Nōpera and his descendants in perpetuity. At all costs, the Spring, and the land around it, should not fall into the hands of the godless Kensingtons. My wife Ellen is a woman of good heart, and always thinks the best of others, even those who bear her ill will. What my good wife does not understand is that her true friends are not those of her own race. I never approved of our daughter Beatrice's marriage to Alfred Kensington, a venal man. Her true friends are the family of Nōpera, the native people who have long known and loved this land. Ellen and our daughter Charlotte need to stand with Nōpera and his people against ungodly and unchristian greed...

Fine sentiments from a Puritan gentleman. Laudable, in fact, to find virtue in a heathen above his own kind. But useless to her now. Worthless pieces of paper fluttering in her hand. Nobody cares what a man long dead wanted, least of all the baron. Bob Kensington would just laugh. So, the point of all this? Just more salt in the wound. More salt in the wounds of history. The goddess having a little joke on a silly old woman, silly enough to follow a demon creature like Irawaru. Perhaps she should take these pieces of paper and front up to the baron and wave them under his nose. The man was unlikely to be impressed, but it would be something. It would be a reminder that human beings cannot own the land, and never have. Only in their dreams. They can no more own the land than a bird can own the sky it flies through. All they can do is drive their stick in the ground and strut about, build mansions with helipads designed for quick getaways. When the baron makes his quick getaway, his claim on the land will be about as meaningful as Peter Johnson's will.

At the same time the thought of confronting the baron appeals to her. The man is supposed to be intelligent, perhaps intelligent enough to appreciate the thought that he had never owned Wai-O-Tapu or the land around it in the first place. Never owned the land his precious mansion was built on.

Carefully she refolds Peter Johnson's last will and testament and puts it back inside its waxed fabric envelope.

Perhaps it is time for a one-woman occupation. A one-woman sit-in. She wouldn't be alone. All the tīpuna would be with her. Even Ellen Johnson, she fancies. They would all come in from their years to be with her. Together they would reassert the ancient right of the Nōpera family to the land, to the use of the land.

'What do you think?' she says to Irawaru. 'Shall we take over this place? Fill it up with the ancestors until the invaders depart?'

Irawaru appears to laugh. Which is impossible.

'Okay. Now show me the way to the evil man.'

In her heart of hearts, Akona does not believe in evil men, or women for that matter. There are silly, deluded, frightened, even cruel men – self-serving and base – but she finds no evil in nature, only in the troubled dreams of man. Bob Kensington, for example, was not acting out of some supernatural evil when he sold the spring to the baron, merely venal and malicious, and with a sense of entitlement that is an uncomfortable mirror of her own. These things are what happens when a dog pisses on the wrong side of the tree.

Irawaru leads the way.

the double tap, twice

Baron (Brainbox) Fairweather stands astride his balcony looking down at the pathetic remnants of the town below for what may very well be the last time – at least he hopes so. The glistening colours of the Southern Lights cast the town in a brief, romantic glow, except the colours are not right. The sea should not look black but silver, the sandy edge of the bay should not be electric blue, the bare strip that is Highway 6 has no right to be deep purple. People pay good money for substances that make the world look like this, the baron has done so himself, but here it comes for free, courtesy of geophysics.

The baron doesn't care. The place can go out in a blaze of glory as far as he's concerned. Calls have been put through. Arrangements have been made. Forces marshalled, and put in motion. The fuel he needs for his Turboshaft 300, with its latest design coaxial-drive diesel engine, will be here directly. Already he can hear the sound of a truck in the distance, grinding along in low gear. Should be here in twenty minutes, ten minutes to fuel up – he could be out of here in half an hour.

The missing piece is Orchid and the Baby. They should be on their way, if all has gone according to plan. He's spent most of the day sitting in front of Arya Tara with her eternal Mona Lisa smile, trying to deal with the feeling that he is riding the wave of some larger, unseen algorithm, something undreamt of even in his maths. If only he could penetrate Arya Tara's bronze imperturbability he would know the truth, see the future beyond mere Elliott wave projections and the tidal wash of hormones through his blood.

Over and over, while sitting there like a dummy hardly moving a muscle, he has tried to tell himself that all he cares about is what the Baby is worth, not in terms of cash, that is irrelevant now, but leverage, insurance that he will be a member of the top .000001 percent who survive and potentially profit from a disaster of even this magnitude. Bringing a gift like Orchid and the Baby to the table would seal just about any deal he wanted to make with anybody on the planet. They are human assets, he told Arya Tara, but she didn't believe him. She saw right into the truth of his heart. His loneliness and greed.

If it weren't for the Baby, and Orchid's insistence that they take him, the baron could have Orchid beside him right now and ready to leave as soon as he has fuelled up. Apparently some runt in Keatown has the Baby and won't give him up. Orchid rushed back down there to buy him off with riches enough to choke on. Failing that, she and the weasel girl Mary would snatch the Baby and run. He offered to send Jo down with an Uzi SMG, a good solid Israeli weapon, to ease the argument. Maths is all very well for high finance, but some issues are best settled in other ways. A quick chat with an Uzi has solved many a problem. But Orchid refused.

'We don't want a bloodbath,' she said.

He wasn't sure he agreed. To leave Keatown awash in blood and flames would be fitting, satisfying in some deeper sense. Of course there was always the switch that would signal the destruction of the spring and an end to Keatown's water supply. His doomsday device.

His eyes fix on the coloured iceberg, which looks like a gaudy popsicle that has been in some kid's mouth for too long. A nice finishing touch. Uneasy tides have jostled the berg closer to shore, threatening the wharf and the newly restored fish shed; another little push and it would disdainfully reduce them to an untidy pile of sticks and tinsel. To the north, the ingenious bulwark - and he had to admire the inhabitants for their industry and perseverance - is now almost completely destroyed. They expended themselves in that effort for nothing. The half-people are not content to flow through the gaps created but continue to pile up behind those sturdier remaining defences. Now they are everywhere, climbing through fences and trampling over gardens. The baron grins, pleased to think that when he goes, there will be nothing left of Keatown. He'll take the best of it with him.

He takes a good long look at this balcony too, where he's spent so many hours watching the ocean and cooking maths in his head. He'll always remember it like this, however, in its strangest moment, gaudy sky above, dark blood-stains on the balcony below. It took them much sweat and blood to reclaim those few square metres of concrete during the driftdead attack, as he calls it. Joe used a sledgehammer on the ledge that allowed the half-people access, while the baron and Zhenhua broke out the Uzis and proceeded to pump bullets into the milling bodies until there was nothing left upright. Zhenhua and the goose girls then dragged the bodies to the south edge of the balcony and heaved them over. They needed Joe's help to get poor Mrs Watson, or what was left of her, up onto the wall and over the balcony.

So they won the Battle of the Balcony, such as it was, only to now abandon it.

Reflexively he puts his right hand down by his side to stroke Manny's head, but the dog is not there. Since the arrival of the driftdead, Manny has been out a lot, roving around, but not only that – he's been acting a little strange, whining and not settling, and every so often he sits and looks at the baron with prickly eyes. The baron wonders, not for the first time, just how stable Manny's genetic mix is. Because he is one of a kind, no one knows exactly how his mind, his limited awareness of who and what he is, will change over time.

Lady Strongbow joins him on the balcony. She's another issue but hardly one of a kind. On the night of the abortive orgy, she refused to go home with Lord Strongbow, and hasn't been home since, sleeping in one of the empty guest rooms below. 'I'm leaving that milksop cuckold,' she told the baron at the time. 'I can't bear him a moment longer.' She shuddered. 'For God's sake send him one of those goose girls. He'll slobber over her and forget about me.'

The baron has not, however, sent Lord Strongbow a goose girl. Though they hold no further interest for him, he's damned if he's going to give one away to appease Lord Strongbow. Or rather, Lady Strongbow. And he's damned if he's going to take orders from this woman, who seems to be making an awful lot of assumptions.

'It's Orchid, isn't it?' she says. The girl seems to weave a spell over everybody who comes her way. Like a snake, she hypnotises.

Unless she, Lady Strongbow, is angling for a ride on the chopper. He's tried to keep the details of that as secret as he can, but the signs of preparation are obvious. No luck, girl. The chopper is chocker.

'I'm haunted by her,' Lady Strongbow says. 'I can't stop thinking about her. That dance. The way she moved. I can't sleep.'

When the baron looks at her, he sees a wilted flower in a vase. Very wilted. Even the goose girls look like springtime in the apple orchard compared to Lady Strongbow.

'When are we going to see her next?'

'She's got stuff to do in Keatown.'

'It's to do with that baby down there, isn't it?' There is a touch of wistfulness in her voice.

He makes a decision. He moves off the balcony and back into the lounge, Lady Strongbow trailing along behind him.

They have cleaned up as best as possible after the attack, but his state-of-the-art computer has been crumpled beyond repair, windows smashed, furniture cut up by bullets, gouges in the wall, blood on the carpet – the place looks like a war zone. Even Arya Tara received a wound, one bullet carving a long groove in her leg. He regrets leaving her behind with nothing to do but preside over an empty room for as long as the room remains, or the mountain beneath remains. Solid bronze might even outlast the mountain. No doubt she would get the last laugh. He would like to have a final chat with her, about his emotional immaturity, his infantile sexuality, his stalled spiritual path and general ruination, but there is no time for pleasant conversation, even with the enlightened one. Time is short for the fleshed.

As he passes her he trails his fingers along the length of her wounded brass leg, along the gouge mark, enjoying the coolness of the touch. He goes to the annex at the back of the room, fishes out a key and opens a metal box. Lady Strongbow stands in the doorway behind him. He turns his back on her so she can't see what he is doing. No point in alarming her. He takes out his gas-operated semi-automatic pistol Mark XIX Desert Eagle, checks to make sure the clip is full and slips it into his inside jacket pocket. Another solid Israeli weapon.

'No chance of you leaving her with me, is there?' Lady Strongbow says. 'You'll tire of her soon enough, you know. You tire of them all in the end. Just take the baby and run. Think of what he might be worth.'

'I want to show you something,' he says, leading the way to the back door he and Joe secured against the invasion, down a set of steps to the second floor. He goes straight to the bathroom and Lady Strongbow follows.

'What are we doing? Taking a shower together?' Her voice is playful.

'Something like that.'

He steps onto the shower area where the concrete floor slopes gently to an outlet. Not just one but three shower heads, positioned for maximum saturation, separate controls for each. She follows him.

'Do you want me to take off my clothes?'

'It doesn't matter,' he says, taking out the Desert Eagle and shooting her. Once in the heart and once in the forehead. The double tap, the pros call it. As the blood begins to flow he turns on the shower and pink water swirls towards the outlet. Nice clean body for Joe to dispose of later.

He leaves the water running and heads for the door. 'Enjoy your shower,' he says.

He goes straight to Zhenhua's room a couple of doors along from the bathroom. He's not concerned that she will have heard the shots, not with the way he built these walls. But Zhenhua's not here, just as he hoped. Down on the third floor with the goose girls, no doubt, telling them what they can and can't take with them.

Zhenua's office is a model of minimalism. She could have chosen any size or shape or luxury, but instead designed a small, almost poky room, walled off against the magnificent landscape as if she deliberately didn't want to see it. The wall in front of her computer, which could have had a window looking out over the most expensive view in history, was blank. Just a touch of grey in the white wall.

Her single concession to decoration is several Japanese prints in subdued water colour depicting erotic encounters in gardens and courtyards. These he ignores as he activates her computer screen. A box appears, written in Mandarin, no doubt asking for a password. From his pocket he takes a device no bigger than a memory stick and slots it into Zhenhua's USB port. A little invention of his own. The computer shuts down and proceeds to reboot, this time through his device, neatly by-passing Zhenhua's not inconsiderable firewalls. The handy little device also does a search-and-destroy operation on any other code-protects Zhenhua might have installed, until all her computer's files are open to the baron's scrutiny.

It only takes seconds to find what he's looking for, and to use his celebrated brainbox to scan-read the material and find the pattern, that hidden, anomalous algorithm he'd seen in the cold equations of ruination. And it takes him even less time to work out the implications.

Zhenhua has been ripping him off, right royally. Taking him left, right and centre, working in collaboration with her friend Yum Yum. Both of them. It's so typical it's pathetic. The rich and powerful betrayed by their most trusted is a very ancient story. And he thought it would never happen to him.

It started in earnest when most of the rich shits took to their choppers, and the so-called Long Emergency began. Which has never been an emergency for someone as rich as the baron – until now. Now the brainbox has been outbrained. Outboxed and outfoxed. Zhenhua and Yum Yum have profited handsomely from his ruination. Just as he, of course, has profited from the ruination of others in the past. Numbers tend to do that, eat each other up as fast as they replicate. Which doesn't matter as long as they replicate faster than they eat each other up. Much easier to print money when you don't actually have to print it.

She's there now standing behind him, watching him access her files. He's always known when she is in a room with him, no matter how silent her entry. She has an unmistakable physical presence. He turns to face her, thinking of how she has played him all along, played on his sexual infantilism, corrupting him, making sure he never married, keeping him where she wants him. Much more thorough than a simple rip-off, this is a carefully constructed set-up, years in the making, taking the raw elements of his personality and constructing the kind of monster she needs to feather her own nest.

He is what she has made him.

The massive scale of it staggers him. But things have changed. Now he knows, and not only that, now he stands on the threshold of a new life, a life with Orchid and a baby. A wife. He can think it now without flinching. A family. Wife and family. A home instead of a house.

'So you found out?' she says.

Oh, she's a cool one all right. A picture of studied indifference.

'Yes.'

'Well,' she shrugs, 'I don't suppose it matters now.' Implying that the same driftmaths that ruined him will ruin her too, that the creeping spread of the chaos of numbers would already be eating into her investments and hedge funds and all the other hidey-holes she found for the stolen money. Very clever. She's sure to be hedged every which way, sure to have stitched it up tighter than a Victorian maiden's corset.

To cap it all off, he's supposed to just let it all go by. Forget about how she set him up and ripped him off. Because he's too weak to do anything about it, she's made sure of that. While appearing to support him, she's been weakening him, wearing away at him.

She pushes past him to her computer and closes down the files he has been viewing, snaps shut the lid of the laptop with a decisive flick. She is quite calm, just busy thinking things through. She doesn't care that he has discovered her crime, and is brazen enough to carry on as before as if nothing has happened, as if everything were the same and they were still an unstoppable team. Except now, subtly, she is in charge. He the donkey, she the rider.

For a moment he toys with the idea of doing it in the chopper. Deal with the matter from a great height. Joe would do the honours. The world must look very different five thousand feet up without a parachute, with nobody to hear you scream. There's pleasure to be taken in the thought of it, but alas, delightful as the prospect may be, he can't afford to indulge it this time around. She is simply too dangerous and deceitful.

'Okay,' he says, pulls out his Desert Eagle and shoots her, twice. The old double tap.

She has time for one quick look of total shock before she goes down.

The baron steps around her body and heads for the stairs looking for Joe, already thinking about Orchid. It might well have been a mistake to allow Orchid and her pocked-face friend to return to Keatown to get the Baby, to let Orchid out of his sight at all. But no leaving without the Baby, that's her bottom line.

He should have sent Joe with her to speed things up. It's not too late.

He's back up in the lounge when he hears the clatter of small arms fire. Joe is out on the balcony pumping bullets into the night.

'We're under attack,' he says to Arya Tara.

Sure enough, bullets are returning, coming back out of the night, chipping at the concrete of the balcony or slamming into the wall.

Without delay he heads for the holding bay he calls the hangar, where his helicopter hangs out. It serves as a garage, where it might be maintained and serviced. The first thing he sees is the red switch that will trigger the explosives that will destroy the Spring. He's about to do so when the thought occurs that it might be a useful bargaining chip. He thinks about it as he activates the roof door and the hydraulic lift that carries the chopper to the roof. It all goes smoothly, the roof opening as the chopper rises. Even if the electricity died and the lift stopped he would not be alarmed. If the worst ever came to the worst, he could raise the lift manually, by an old-fashioned turning of a wheel. When he installed this set-up he had no intention of being trapped in his own magnificence.

Instead of flicking the tempting red switch, he takes a moment to re-route the trigger through his hand-held. Now he can do it anywhere, at any time, no physical switch-flipping required. It would be quite spectacular to watch from the helicopter, as he was flying away.

What he can do, however, is activate his high-tech security system for the house before his final retreat to the roof. Anyone crazy enough to try to enter the house from below would have a surprise or two waiting for them. Via his hand-held he can monitor all the cameras in the house and see who's on their way up. If Orchid comes up this way he will soon know.

the first person invisible

Sirocco is wounded. He is bleeding from the side. During the scuffle at the Mayor's, Mary managed to stab him without anybody noticing, even himself. Just that slight pricking in the ribs. No more than half a finger's worth of blade, if that; not much, but enough to kill him if he keeps bleeding. Lizard taught him that you can't run away from bleeding. Your blood will follow you wherever you go until it finds your corpse; at least that's the way the scavengers will see it. The only way to deal with it is to staunch the flow.

He loses precious seconds as he does just that. The wound is superficial, but the bleeding is profuse. He finds a wall that protects him from the north, and he's ripping up his shirt to try to bandage the wound when the librarian turns up with a large piece of surgical plaster and slaps it right over the wound.

'You can't die,' Sirocco says. He is feeling light-headed from the loss of blood and loss of the Baby.

'I'm pretty sure I can,' the librarian says. 'And turn, too. Why should I be immune?'

'You're not allowed to,' Sirocco says, feeling the patch on his side. There is no blood seeping at the edges. He looks up and sees the colours drizzling down the darkening sky. 'Then there would be no one left to bear witness to it all. Your Chronicles of Keatown...'

'You have your own book,' the librarian says quickly. She is unwilling to talk about her Chronicles, or even admit them into the conversation, it seems.

'But mine is just an imaginary book. I'm its sole reader.' And I'm not an easy reader to satisfy, he thinks, mindful of all the changes he has made.

'That doesn't matter, it still has real words, remember? Even an imaginary book has real words. And real books have imaginary words.'

'An imaginary book for an imaginary life.' The wall behind him is cold and hard and concrete at his back; nothing imaginary about that, or the driftdead that surge around them.

'Then I'd have to say the same of my Chronicles of Keatown. An imaginary book about an imaginary town.'

'You're just saying that to make me feel better because I'm dying.

Yours is a real book about a real place. A place that has a name, that's on a map, that you can find if you stay on Highway 6.'

'The differences are not as great as you imagine, believe me.'

'My book is nothing but circles and stars, like a child would draw in the sand...' Sirocco's eye wanders across the sky. Pity he is not the child he thought he was; plenty of circles and stars up there, all ringed in pale fire. The wound is seeping again, but he doesn't tell her that. He covers it up with his shirt. His blood is drawing maps on his shirt, but he doesn't know the territory.

'And you're not allowed to die either, Sirocco. We can't have that. Bleeding to death out here surrounded by driftdead, what would Lizard think?'

'He wouldn't be surprised. He expected me to come to a sticky end. He'd say I didn't keep my wits about me.'

He could die here just like Gypsy's mother, float away on clouds of cushions, in his case imaginary cushions, like Aladdin on his magic carpet, smoothly over the bobbing heads of the driftdead.

'Well, don't prove him right.'

'Okay.' Sirocco tries to get to his feet. He's having trouble finding his centre of gravity. It's not just the loss of blood, but the weight on his chest where the Baby nestled is gone.

'He's gone, you know,' Sirocco says, taking a tentative step.

'You can get him back.'

'I don't mean the Baby, I mean Lizard. I saw him just recently. He showed me my true face. Then he told me he was leaving, and I believe him. He's had enough of this world. He's going back to his desert. He was only ever in this world on sufferance.'

There was the rattle of small arms from nearby. A shout from Pinky.

'They're getting ahead of us, can you walk?'

Sirocco tries it out. 'I feel like a moonwalker. Thanks for saving my life.'

Sirocco may be pleased, but I am furious. 'How often are you going to put patches on Sirocco's life?' I ask her. 'How long are you going to jolly him along with all sorts of silly nonsense?' As I expected, she doesn't know what to answer. She hates it when I intervene like this, and so do I. I'm not like Sirocco's Lizard who will pop in and out of the story as he pleases, or like Rasputin's god always trying to pull the strings from behind the scenes. I am the First Person Invisible, and prefer to keep it that way. Intervening in her narrative is the last thing on my mind.

'Certain rules apply here,' I tell her. 'If Sirocco is going to die, you can't stop him, not with any kind of patch. He can't escape his plot.'

'We'll see,' she says.

She likes to live her life as if it were a book, a fictional world in which life's verities are only provisional, and even the dying might be patched back into life by a piece of hopeful prose. It's sad, really.

'By prolonging his life, you are just prolonging his agony,' I tell her. 'And that's cruelty. A writer doesn't take a Hippocratic oath. Mary stabbed him fair and square. It's not your job to redress the great moral imbalance of the world.'

Every time I make this little speech, it seems harder to get the point across. As if, almost imperceptibly, she is drifting away from me.

This time she gets morose, her voice dark, 'Sirocco is one person in this shitty little town who is capable of realising who he is, what he is. After all, that vague background and the desert and everything is a dead giveaway. He may be on the verge of putting the pattern together. Bringing the circles and stars into one universe.'

'That's not your fault,' I say sharply. 'That's no excuse for bending the rules.'

'You're a great one to talk,' she says as she moves away, Sirocco by her side. I don't know what she means by that, but I do know that everything depends on her staying a reliable narrator, so that this history can be honestly told.

'Just because you're the First Person doesn't mean that you're king of the castle.' She shouts this, back over her shoulder. It's clear now that she never approved of me in the first place, and why should she?

It's lonely sometimes, being the First Person.

councils of war

Together the librarian and Sirocco move upward towards the sound of shouting voices, she letting him lean on her arm. Big Bill is shouting instructions. Pinky is taking pot shots at the sloping eastern wall of the baron's mansion. There is nothing to hit but the wall itself, much to Pinky's frustration, but letting off a few rounds keeps him juicing. He's encouraged by the fact that somebody up there is returning his fire, since a few bullets from above splatter wide of their position.

Sirocco doesn't quite know how it happens, but Witch Hunt is by his side again, holding his hand. It's not hard for her to know how Sirocco must be feeling, but she promises him that together they will get the Baby back. The other mokopuna are nearby. There's Sad Toof, still sad at the loss of his sad tooth, shambling along with his head down, hardly paying attention. And Little Sanyo, who has managed, despite the mayor's prohibition, to get his hands on a weapon, an automatic pistol by the look of it. Even Rasputin is there, having somehow become separated from his master.

Sirocco turns to say something to the librarian but she has melted away. That's just like her. At first he thought she was shy, but now he understands otherwise. She is a historian, and is apparently answerable to a mysterious First Person who is always worried she will contaminate her story. She wants to tell the story, not become part of it, and Sirocco can understand that well enough, except that it's not really possible. Life doesn't work that way. It's all a big mutual contamination. She couldn't just let him die like a dog in the shadow of a broken wall, the driftdead flowing by each side. That's the way life works. He's surprised that the librarian, given all her wisdom, hasn't realised this yet. The wall she imagines that separates her from those she writes about is no more real than the barricade the town built to keep out the driftdead. She should understand that by now too, and that she and her subjects have become inextricably intertwined.

They catch up with the war party which has paused at Stag Point. The closer they have come to the mansions, the more the difficult the assault looks.

Big Bill holds a council of war with Pinky and a few others who have kept up.

'These places are built like bloody medieval castles,' he says. 'There's no attacking from below.'

'There are steps coming down,' Celif says. 'They come from different mansions. They connect with Beauty Parade, and with the Back Road at the top. Orlap would come this way when he brought fish up for the baron, or the Benedicts.'

The fishermen are all for a direct rush up the paths. Orlap's betrayal has bitten deep into their mood.

'Orlap and Orchid would know these paths, we don't,' Big Bill says, thoroughly annoyed at himself for not knowing the lay of the land himself.

'We could still take one of the paths, creep up on the bastards.' Pinky is all for a rush too. The rounds he's loosed off at the bulwark above have given him the taste for it. The return rounds have sharpened that taste. At last, an enemy that fights back.

Everybody strung out single file on an unknown steep, rocky path, drunk and angry in the aurora-lit dark, doesn't strike Big Bill as a propitious vision. He pats Pinky on the shoulder. A tower of strength is Pinky. 'Let's skirt to the south and gather on the back road,' Big Bill says. At least that way they would be able to march on the baron en masse and directly to his rooftop helipad, even if they did lose a little time doing it.

'I know how to get to Back Road from here,' Little Sanyo says.

Big Bill doesn't doubt it. The nosy little bugger has roamed all over the place, spying.

'Lead on!'

The last thing he wants is to lose momentum. Leadership, that's what is needed right now.

If the glass isn't full, it's empty.

the rescue party

Sirocco is about to follow Little Sanyo when he feels a tug on his arm. It is Witch Hunt.

'I know where they took the Baby,' the little girl says, wiping the dirty blonde hair out of her eyes. 'Not to the road.'

'We'd better hurry.'

'There's a back way up through the house.'

Witch Hunt leads him along a path that skirts below the outer walls of several mansions. These outer walls have turned into one long continuous wall that serves as a buttress for the lawns and buildings above. Huge wooden pillars and great blocks of reinforced steel have been built into the rock to support the structures above. The path snakes along in front of all these earthworks, before disappearing between two pillars, great tree trunks with banded steel at intervals.

'How did you know about this path?'

'I didn't. I can smell the Baby. I always know where he is. I can follow his scent in the air, you know.'

'No, I didn't know.'

She leads him to a dark, cave-like area. As his eyes adjust he sees two luminous orbs, like UFOs, hanging in the dark. I'm losing blood, he thinks, pushing in against the wound on his side. It will be chariots next. The orbs flame yellow, then blue. They resolve into eyes. Beneath the eyes there are teeth.

'Quiet, Irawaru,' a familiar voice says. 'Don't frighten the little girl... and the wounded man.'

'What are you doing here?' Sirocco says, staring at Irawaru. There were beasts like this in the desert who were much feared by vulnerable creatures like lizards. Genetic experiments like this pretend-dog, experiments gone wrong, and the beasts dumped in the desert to evolve or die. Invariably the latter. Not this one, by the look of it.

Akona points to a tunnel that goes deeper into the rock.

'They went that way. I'm surprised they didn't try to steal Nanny.'

Witch Hunt pulls him on.

'Don't leave it too long,' Akona says. 'Find a quiet place to die. That's what Lizard would do. Your time has come.'

'You're right,' Sirocco says as he follows Witch Hunt, leaving Akona in the shadows. But he doesn't really believe it. He is losing blood but he isn't dying. Surely he would know if he were dying. In the desert he often bled to the point of lightheadedness from cuts and gashes, but he always recovered. This bleeding will slow down and stop, just as it did then, not in the gloom of rock, but under a sweltering sky.

'We're close now,' Witch Hunt says. 'They've slowed down.'

'Why?'

'The baron will have booby-trapped the house. Mary will try to disable it.'

'Mary must be very smart.'

'Zhenhua would've showed her.'

'How do you know? You sound very sure.'

'I heard them talking. I can hear them, follow their voices in the air, you know.'

'No, I didn't know.'

A few moments later they catch up with the little party. Mary is running a piece of card around the crack in a closed door.

'Well,' she says, seeing them first. 'Here comes the rescue party.'

Orchid doesn't deign to turn around. She just holds the Baby firmly and stares straight ahead. Orlap gives Sirocco a big, sickly grin, like a host who has forgotten his manners.

'That's a brave little warrior you have there, desert man. When she grows up she will be a great leader of her people. If she grows up.' Mary shows her teeth. 'And if there are any people.'

Witch Hunt shows her teeth back.

The door clicks open and a bell begins to hammer the air. Orlap blows it out of the ceiling with a blast from his rifle, an old .303 he keeps on board. He didn't have it at the mayor's place, so he must have hidden it outside somewhere, where he could collect it on the way up here, Sirocco decides. It has all been carefully planned.

The Baby begins to cry. Since the Baby rarely cries, the sound is unexpected and poignant.

'The fucking bell set him off,' Mary says.

She steps through the doorway and waves her hands around in the air. 'Zhenhua should be up there to let us in. Something's gone wrong.'

'The baron won't want to kill us,' Orchid says.

'We gotta get to the service lift. It'll take us straight to the roof.'

All this is part of a plan, Sirocco realises. Not the baron's but Zhenhua's, and it probably involves killing the baron and seizing the helicopter. Sirocco's prepared to do anything he can, right up to his last breath, to make sure the Baby is not on that helicopter.

'We can still get up there, can't we?' Orchid says, rocking the Baby who doesn't stop crying. 'He won't leave without us.'

I would say all bets are off the table, Sirocco thinks, but keeps quiet.

'Where the hell is Zhenhua?' Mary says.

we don't want any trouble

Sad Toof explains it all to Rasputin, the only person who will listen despite being preoccupied with the problem of convincing the reverend that the driftdead still have souls.

'It's all t' do with pain,' Sad Toof says patiently. He's something of an expert on pain, he feels.

They are hurrying along with the others, following Little Sanyo's lead up through the steps and trails that criss-cross the scrubby slopes below the mansions. The war party has fallen quiet, except for a low rumble of talk and still-angry muttering.

'I alwuz thought that th' toof was the problem,' Sad Toof says. He taps his jaw significantly, right on the spot where the absent tooth once reigned. He thought that if the tooth went away, he would feel differently about the world. It hasn't turned out that way. 'There's a phantom toof, still there, like th' old one never went away.' He taps harder at his jaw, but this pain goes deeper than any bone. The phantom tooth can never be pulled, the pain never uprooted. 'I wish I had me old toof back.' He looks at Rasputin, bewildered.

'You have to believe in something more than just your pain,' Rasputin says. A tiredness is creeping up on him, a world weariness. It can't go on like this forever, he thinks. Even God... but he doesn't finish the thought.

'I bet God could do it,' Sad Toof says. In that moment he sees God as a great dentist in the sky, drill poised to bore right down into his soul. It makes him shudder to think of it.

'Among all the teef in the world, my toof was the one,' he says.

The party ahead has come to a halt. They have entered a property, the sudden, unexpected sweep of a lawn, a large and well-kept lawn. For a moment it subdues the rabble. Two people wearing identical dressing-gowns stand facing them, both tall and blonde and athletic looking. Both are breathing deeply. The Benedicts. The mayor knows them by reputation. From what he's heard they didn't spend much money, even in the heyday of the mansions, because they believed they could live just by breathing the air. How anybody so crazy could get so rich is something Big Bill can't and will never understand – his imagination doesn't stretch that far.

Right now, the Benedicts look scared, which is no surprise given that a small army of drunks have turned up on their lawn, waving vicious looking military-style weapons. They are facing the emergency by breathing as deeply as possible. They are unarmed, not believing in weaponry of any kind; health is their business and guns are very unhealthy.

After a brief word with Little Sanyo, Big Bill steps forward and summons a polite tone. He can afford to be gracious, since he's the one holding the guns. He has no particular beef with these people. Why, they may turn out to be neighbours one day, if he can't get himself on that chopper.

'We just want to cross your property to get to the Back Road. Our little guide here,' he points to Little Sanyo, 'has led us to the bottom of your property, I mean the front...' Fuck it, now isn't the time to get tongue-tied. Fuck Ock's hock and Mavis's cocaine.

'We don't want any trouble,' Herr Benedict says. They'd come a long way to this remote eyrie to enjoy trouble-free fresh air.

'We're chasing fugitives. The baron is attempting to steal a baby from the town. Our baby.'

Frau Benedict looks interested. 'You have a baby?' Frau Benedict is too healthy to have a baby herself, and therefore takes a healthy interest in other people's babies. She turns to her husband, 'Why didn't anyone tell me there was a baby?' Her husband doesn't know. Right now he's having trouble with his breathing. Fear is very bad for your breathing.

Frau Benedict fishes in the pocket of her dressing gown as she approaches the mayor. 'When you see your baby, give him this.' She hands the mayor something. He has to rearrange the weapon in his hands to take it. It is a food bar of some kind, wrapped in non-plastic plastic.

'Ah... I don't think... he's... eating solids yet. He hasn't got any teeth.' The mayor feels pretty stupid right now, but what can he do? The mad woman is staring at him fixedly, shaking the food-bar under his nose.

'It is not for eating, but sucking. Like rusks.'

'Rusks?' Big Bill is lost. His war party is milling around uncertainly while this woman talks about rusks. Herr Benedict pats randomly at his pockets as if he too might have something to offer the restless natives.

'For the Baby's gums.'

Christ! Big Bill snatches the rusk or whatever it is out of the woman's hand. 'We have to keep moving,' he says loudly. There is a murmur of assent.

Big Bill pushes on up the hill. The Benedicts stand to one side and watch them go past. As Pinky goes past he flourishes his weapon and grins evilly at Frau Benedict, who immediately begins to hyperventilate.

no flies on Flay

Because much of the house is set into the mountain, the roof itself is almost level with the nearest ridge, along which the Back Road winds, serving the mansions, until terminating at a ramp which leads up to the baron's roof and helipad. It is along this road that Flay now drives his beloved Bedford RL. The gates that mark the end of the service road, and entrance to the baron's rooftop helipad, are in sight. There're more pedestrians around too. Somehow they have found their way up here and are thickening up along the road.

Beside him, Annanda keeps shifting about uneasily. He doesn't like being squeezed in between Flay and Butch. He feels his soul beginning to wither. Butch holds on to the passenger side door handle as if she were about to make a jump for it.

Flay understands that it isn't the diesel or the gold he's here for; it's the chopper. That is the real prize. No diesel no chopper. Something like that. He doesn't have a plan.

Neither does the mayor. The baron's back gate is still some distance off when Flay and company run into the raiding party, milling about on the road like a bunch of idiots. Some stand back and clap as Flay drives through them, grinning at the fools out his side window, noting, however, the military hardware everywhere. It doesn't take him long to put two and two together. Others wave their guns threateningly at him. These are the smart ones who have figured out that he might double-cross them all.

The flustered mayor tries to wave him down but Flay drives right around him. As far as Flay's concerned, the raiding party is just a nuisance. A side issue. The real drama would begin when he got inside the gates.

He doesn't get too far from the raiding party when he has to slam on the brakes, throwing his passengers forward. Standing in front of them is a dishevelled-looking man in a white shirt hanging loose, not much else on except a pair of polka-dot underpants, waving some pea-shooter in Flay's direction. A bloody drunk toff, if Flay is not mistaken. He's familiar with the type. Inherited wealth. More money than sense.

Flay winds down the window and sticks his head out. He takes the man in, from mussed hair to scuffed slippers. What a wet!

'Where do you think you're going?' the man demands.

'Who do I have th' pleasure of talkin' to, then?'

'I'm Lord Strongbow, and you are on a private road.'

'Am I? It was a public road just back there.'

'Where are you going?'

'I'm makin' a delivery, is what I'm doin.'

'Perhaps not.'

Flay is quiet for a bit. It's been a while since he ran into a toff. Plenty of toffs in London, where you might expect to find them, usually wearing suits. The polka dot undies are a new one for Flay but who is he to talk with his ridiculous pink shirt and natty slacks?

Strongbow peers into the RT at Annanda and Butch. 'Who are all these people?'

'Respectable citizens of Keatown.'

'What business do they have up here?'

'Their own business, I would say.'

'You're taking diesel to Fairweather, aren't you?'

'Never heard of him.'

'I'll pay double what he paid you to dump the fuel on the side of the road.'

'Now that'd be a waste.'

'He'll just fly out of here and piss on us as he passes.'

'What's it to you?'

Strongbow doesn't answer, but such a bitter look comes over his face, Flay decides it has to be about a woman.

Flay curses. Another random factor. 'You can kill him as many times as you like,' he says. 'But I got plans for this diesel.'

He must have sounded too boastful, because the toff caught his meaning immediately.

'You'll never do it.'

'Well... it's nice to chat,' Flay says, 'but I need to drive on and you're standing in the middle of the road, if you catch my drift, squire.'

'I do. And I'm not moving.'

'Okay, Squire,' Flay says, sounding world weary. He gets out of the cab and faces Lord Strongbow. 'Let's talk this over, mano a mano, shotgun to shotgun.'

It's a short conversation.

dead still is alive

Reluctantly, the baron discards his Desert Special for a straightforward MTAR-21 (X-95), simply known as the Tavor. You can't beat a twelve-hundred-rounds-per-minute, open-bolt, blowback-operated submachine gun when it comes to bringing a rabble under control – and there is a rabble at the gate, an armed rabble what's more. With Terry dead, he's pretty thin on the ground in terms of forces, but he quickly deploys what he has.

That's ten rounds per second. A three-second spread would place thirty rounds.

Overcoming his reluctance, he arms the goose girls, who are searching for some kind of purpose in life now that their mistress and mentor is dead. He's surprised to find they are familiar with the Uzis, surprised to learn that Zhenhua trained them in more than just dancing and the fine art of whoring. He places the platinum blonde Sun Petal, the least competent, on the balcony and in the lounge, where she can command the lower reaches of the mansion. No invading force is likely to come up that way but you never know with a rabble. Sun Petal can also watch the upper side, where the driftdead that stray this high will come from, and an invading force might seek entrance.

The red-haired Cherry Blossom, and Blue Zither, he takes with him to the roof and the helipad. The chopper gleams black and businesslike in the darkening evening, a little tubby with its extra fuel tanks. Joe approaches him from the shadow of the helicopter. 'They're here,' Joe says.

The baron flips the switch on the arc lights, flooding the area with a hard, bright light.

Five figures appear behind Joe. The service lift to one side of the helipad is their most likely route, he figures. All part of Zhenhua's little plot, no doubt.

The baron resists the urge to rush over to Orchid. He stands very still and lets her approach him. She does, with Mary and Orlap half a pace behind. Behind them, hanging back, is a runty little man with a wizened face and a pint-sized girl with straggly hair.

'I'd like you to meet the Baby,' Orchid says, turning around so that the baron can see the Baby's face. He is lying in the front pack with his eyes closed. As the baron dutifully peers in at him, the Baby opens his eyes and meets the baron's inquisitive look with one of his own. Then he laughs. It's a gurgly sound but there's no mistaking it. The baron can hardly deal with his awkwardness; he has no experience in saying hello to babies. Not that he has any objection to them, in principle.

'He thinks I'm funny.'

'He likes you,' Orchid says.

Orlap nods, 'He is very happy.' Orlap enounces every word, as if he were just learning English. He keeps glancing at the Tarvor, and the Uzis in the hands of the goose girls, and Joe, so wide across the shoulders that the Uzi looks like a toy in his hands.

'Where is the diesel?' the baron asks Orlap.

'It comes.'

'Where's Zhenhua?' Mary asks.

'She's gone. You're her creature, aren't you?'

'Gone?'

'Dead and gone to heaven.' He had been intending to lie, tell her that her mistress had turned into a walker, but he is beyond lying now. He hasn't got to where he is by feeling ashamed before others, especially slaves. Once he'd been a bashful geek. Lashings of money and a craven appetite soon fixed that.

'You killed her,' the pocked-marked one said in a flat voice.

He doesn't bother answering. He's not accountable to her. He sees her directly for the first time, the urchin figure of her. And the runty little guy, he notices, is trying to stop a bleed on his left side.

The baron has pretty much worked out where the elusive one fits. She is no longer wearing her scarf and the mark of the collar is plain. It looks dark, like the path of a noose. Much becomes clear to the baron. Zhenhua would have betrayed him at the last moment. Killed him or left him here to rot while she took Orchid, the Baby and her slave girl. Even Orlap wouldn't have made it, probably. Zhenua would have completed her own cold equations.

To Mary, the runty guy says in a high reedy voice, 'Once he gets you up in that chopper, up high enough, he'll push you out. Without a parachute. You'll take the long dive. Have you ever tried to swim in the air?'

'You're dying, aren't you, Age? That's why you're talking funny. Actually, I thought you'd be dead by now. You should be. Maybe you are. It's hard to tell these days. We shouldn't be having this conversation. After all, I should know.' Mary pats her hip where the knife that went into Sirocco's side pertly sits.

'You know I'm speaking the truth. You were Zhenhua's, not his. He can never trust you,' Sirocco turns to the baron, 'can you, Baron Fairweather? Tell her yourself.'

'Okay,' says the baron and, from the hip, fires a quick burst at Zhenhua's slave. Unaccountably, at the last minute, he pulls the shot to one side, putting a couple of slugs in her ribcage to the lower right instead of her stomach.

Mary goes down without a sound. It is Orchid who screams.

The runty one saves what's left of his life by standing dead still. Like any desert lizard he knows that it is movement that catches the eye and triggers the trigger finger.

Dead still is alive.

Right on cue, the sound of a truck grinding up the ramp. Orlap grins like a magician who's just completed a magic trick.

The baron gestures for Joe to open the gate.

'We have other visitors.'

'Then show them some hospitality.'

Joe doesn't look happy. 'They're armed to the teeth.'

'Take out the fat guy and a few others. The rest will turn tail.'

'They can smell the gold.'

'Then give it to them,' he gestures to the service lift. 'Get the forklift and bring up a pallet.

That'll take Joe ten minutes. Twenty minutes, and he could be out of here. Of course, he won't be taking everybody who thinks they're coming, not by a long shot. There's a reckoning yet to come. The cold equations of distance divided by weight divided by available fuel. Those are the sort of equations the Brainbox can eat for breakfast. He knows exactly how far his generosity can carry him, to the last mile.

He goes to the gate, which is made of tree trunks to give it a vaguely medieval look, and to suggest its strength. He could suffer a siege behind this gate, but doesn't intend to.

He peers through one of the peek holes built into the gate. He sees an ancient Bedford truck. Then a deeply creviced face on top of a pink shirt.

'Special delivery for the gov'nor.'

I should kill this man the first chance I get, the baron thinks. He knows the type. The phony subservience, the sarcasm, the low cunning. Seen it all before. A viper if ever there was one.

'Who're those people coming up behind you?'

'Dunno. Probably come to see you off. Wave and cheer as you chopper away into the sunset. You lettin' me in? You want the diesel? Or shall I give it to Lord Strongbow, one of your neighbours, I gather. He's keen to get his hands on the diesel too. He wants to piss it away on the side of the road. Funny fella!'

The baron would prefer to leave the truck at the gate and fill the chopper from there, but there are too many technical problems, like having a hose long enough, for example. If he brings the chopper to the gate, complications could ensue. The mob might try to storm the place.

He opens the gate and the RL surges confidently forward.

Little Sanyo battles a mansion

When Little Sanyo sees Flay's truck disappear between the baron's log gates, he decides on a bold course of action.

There have to be other ways into the house, and he's just the kid to find them. Air ducts, service corridors, secret passages, escape holes.

The mayor, the reverend, the Smiley Sisters, Grandmother Gaunt, Pinky and the rest of the riff-raff from the party are milling about not knowing what to do next. The ramp is the only way onto the roof. A wall follows the edge of the roof all the way around, cutting off any line of sight – or access.

The raiding party is effectively stymied, but only a few of the hottest heads want to follow Little Sanyo. Among them are Celib and Pinky.

Rasputin decides to stay with his mentor, and Sad Toof opts to stay with him.

'It's not the same without Sirocco,' he says.

'Maybe Sirocco is alive in there,' Little Sanyo says. 'Maybe he will rescue the Baby after all.'

'No,' Sad Toof says. 'Mary, she stabbed him with a dagger. I seed it with me own eyes.'

'Let's get on with it,' Pinky says. He's carrying enough guns for a small army: pistols sticking out of his belt all around. A belt of grenades over his shoulder, along with spare racks of ammo for his machine gun, he looks like a nightmare terrorist.

'That's what I'm talking about,' Little Sanyo says, eagerly leading his band around the rock and towards the lower parts of the building. He has no idea where he's going but his snooper's instinct tells him that there will be back entrances, even secret ones, which are the best, if you can find them.

It wouldn't be quite fair to say that for Little Sanyo all this is just a great big adventure, the best in his whole life, but it would come close. It is not that there are treasures inside the building far beyond any little beachcomber's dreams, although he looks forward to discovering them; it is, as it always is with him, the fun of doing it. More than once he's thought about breaking into the mansions, but tales of weird guard dogs and booby traps have kept him away.

His snooper instinct does not let him down. He finds a small, sealed entrance among a jumble of rocks. There is no mechanism or lock on the outside, suggesting that this is an emergency exit, not designed for entering.

'I'll fix the bastard,' Pinky says. 'Stand back.'

That's what they do while Pinky blasts away at the door with a heavy pistol, a .45, Little Sanyo figures. The shots sound dull and pitiful in the face of all that rock, but they do the job, and soon Pinky is able to put his foot through the door. There are more shots, this time from inside the house, and Pinky stumbles backwards, dropping his pistol.

'The fucking house shoots back,' he says.

'Booby traps.' Little Sanyo says.

'Fuck me,' Pinky says, 'I'm dying. Shot by a bloody house.'

The others crowd around to see. It looks bad, is the general consensus.

'It's a good thing we don't turn into those fucking driftdead when we die, like with real zombies, the ones that eat you. They can infect you with one bite.' Pinky was beginning to shake. Deep shudders from the inside.

'They're not like those kinds of zombies, the one's in the movies,' Little Sanyo says. 'The driftdead don't seem to get hungry at all.'

'But they are,' Pinky says, lying down because he can't stand up. 'They want to turn us.' Blood bubbles from his mouth.

Little Sanyo thinks of his useless experiments in the barn. The idea that the driftdead want something other than just to march south, interests him. Even at this late stage, he can't keep his curiosity at bay.

'How do you know?'

'Dunno. I'm tired. I can hear them thinking. Pushing thoughts at me.'

Celib nods, 'I have heard other stories like this,' he says. The big fisherman kneels and cradles Pinky in his arms. He rocks gently back and forward.

'What kind of thoughts?'

Pinky is getting sleepy. His pistol slips from his hand. His head falls on Celib's shoulder.'No words... no mind...'

'Anti-thoughts,' Little Sanyo says.

'Drift-thoughts,' Pinky says.

His eyes wander towards the sky, and stay there.

simplifying the odds

The baron watches carefully as the battered old Bedford pulls through the front gate, making suitably groaning noises. The driver does not simply pull up, however, but does a three-point turn so that the vehicle is facing the gate instead of away from it. Only then does he switch the motor off. Looks to the baron as if he's planning to make a quick getaway.

Then people begin to pile out. There's an Indian in paisley, and the driver with a face like a grease pit and clothes like a poofter. Then there's Strongbow, dressed in little more than a dirty white shirt and polka-dot undies, who's apparently hitched a ride on the back and is now standing beside a dykey-looking woman with a sailor's cap.

'What's this, a gay pride parade?'

'Where's my wife, Fairweather?'

'Died and gone to the great slut-wife gangbang in the sky.'

Lord Strongbow is dressed so absurdly, the poor man's legs looking skinny and pale and hairless in the harsh light. Like the bones of a snowman. Less absurd is the rifle he's carrying.

'Where's my wife, Fairweather?' He says it in the same tone of voice as before, as if he's asking for the first time.

'Chasing butterflies. You need to look after her better.'

'She was here just a while ago, I know. I made a point of knowing.'

'Maybe she ran off with my dog. Manny's missing too. And I thought he preferred Sun Petal, but there you go!'

The baron believes that Strongbow is far too weak-kneed to bring doom upon himself for the sake of revenge, like some TV drama hero he once played. And for what? The honour of his wife? Now that is a laugh. It's hard to take a cuckold seriously when he's standing before you ready to die for his dignity in his polka-dot undies. The baron is wrong. In the end folly wins out over cowardice.

The spasm of fury on his face makes him easy to read. The baron is able to cut him down before he can get his rifle's nose out of the dirt. Strongbow always was a little slow on the uptake. It's a bit far for a double tap, but a quick round into his belly does the trick. With a bullet every 0.05 seconds zipping from the Tavor, a second or two makes a hell of a mess out of soft squishy places.

Probably out of panic, the dyke makes a grab for Strongbow's rifle as he falls. That's a mistake. It puts her in the play. He pumps a couple of seconds into her too.

Simplifying the odds, that's what it's all about.

Flay pretends to take no notice of the trigger-happy bastard. Psychos with guns. Y' have t' be very careful. He deliberately puts his shotgun down as he focuses on uncoiling the hose for the diesel transfer. He can feel the psycho's eyes on him, drilling into his head, trying to unpick him. Good luck with that, psycho.

But he has a clearer idea for the chopper, now he's seen it with his very own eyes. While he's pumping diesel he can work out how to get his arse into the driver's seat, so tantalisingly near. Can he operate it? If it's a fucking motor, he can operate it. On the ground, in the air, in the water, under the water, it's all the bloody same. He was born out of a crankshaft covered in engine grease, of course he can bloody operate it. Then he'll be the one flying high. He'll be the one sitting pretty. No point going back to town to open up Flay's Garage. Flay's Garage is history.

Some people, when nervous or afraid, have to talk. Silly babbling talk. Annanda is one of those, and the casual murder of two people right before his eyes gets him going.

'I usually find,' he says in a conversational voice, 'that a little deep breathing, pranayama, is helpful in these situations. I have never followed the yogic path myself, but I do know of the value of a little pranayama to calm the mind and steady the spirit.'

The baron turns to Orlap. 'Who's this fool? Is he part of the deal? Have you thrown him in with the tank of gas?'

If the Nord gets the joke, which is unlikely, he doesn't laugh. Instead he makes sweeping gestures with his hands. 'He's nothing,' Orlap says with a certain grandeur, like a king making a decree.

'Which is less than something,' the baron says, readying the Tavor for another quick spread. For some unaccountable reason, his head is starting to fill with maths, a beautiful sweet flow. Now is not the time!

'Hold on there, squire.' Flay decides it's time to be firm with the psycho. He holds no great affection for the fairy, but if the psycho's not checked and the killing goes on, Flay might very well wind up on the wrong side of a spread himself.

He levels his shotgun at the tank of diesel, at the tap where a blast would do the most damage. 'Let's just do this easy and peaceful. No need to go killing innocent bystanders.'

'My sentiments exactly,' Annanda says. 'Reasonableness is our best weapon, and that is the outcome of a steady respiration.'

'Then you have to shut him up,' the baron says to Flay. 'I've got neighbours who talk like him. Nutcases.'

'Fair enough,' Flay says as if they were two reasonable men agreeing on reasonable things. He turns to Annanda. 'Shut the fuck up.'

Whatever Annanda is about to say dies fast.

Flay does not think this is the time to make a little speech about how the diesel belongs to the community, rather than rich cunts with their helipads, and how Orlap betrayed that community. You don't negotiate with a psycho, or try to appeal to their better side. They don't have a better side. You shut the fuck up and make your plans.

The baron turns his attention to Orchid and the Baby. He gestures with the Tavor. 'Quick, into the chopper.'

But Orchid doesn't move. She is staring at him, wide-eyed. 'You shot Mary.'

'Into the chopper.'

'Mary is my friend.'

'No she isn't.'

'We were all in this together.'

'Were you now.'

'Together, to make a better life for the Baby.'

'You and Mary and Zhenhua.' He takes a step towards Orchid. A small step towards togetherness.

Orlap takes a step forward to match the baron's. 'Now we all can make a better life for the Baby.' His grin is big and brave.

The baron looks him up and down. He points to the heavy backpack Orlap is carrying. 'What's that?'

'Goat's milk. For the Baby.'

For a moment the baron is nonplussed. It hadn't struck him that the Baby would have to drink and eat, piss and crap, just like the rest of them.

So this shaggy sea captain has brought him the diesel, arranged safe passage for Orchid and the Baby, and brought the goat's milk as well. Can't be quite as stupid as he makes out.

'Throw the backpack into the chopper, Mr Atlas. We've got to be on our way.' He notices that the grease monkey has made short work of hooking the diesel up to the Turboshaft's auxiliary tanks. The fuel is pissing in even while they speak. He also notices that the runty man who's wounded, and is resting in the lee of the elevator housing, is watching his every move. Although he's not doing anything, the little man's scrutiny makes the baron uncomfortable. There is no warmth or human glow in the dying runt's steady observation, just cold lizard eyes.

'I'm good. I wear it just fine.' Orlap holds his hands up as if being offered an unwanted drink at a party.

'I don't think you understand,' the baron says, flicking his hand over his forehead to clear away the maths, which just keeps coming back. He has been finding that a lot lately; people slow on the uptake, mistaking his friendly chatter for good intentions. It is as if his brain were starting to work at a turbo-charged rate, as it does when he is doing maths. People just get left behind. He, the brainbox, is at the spearhead of these events and plans to stay that way. One jump ahead of all the other monkeys.

Orchid, however, seems to follow his purpose quite clearly. Her eyes are still glassy with shock, but she's not deceived.

'He's the Baby's father,' she says.

One again even turbo-brain is nonplussed. The general idea of 'a baby' sounded like a good one, but just as it didn't strike him that of course the Baby would need food, he hasn't given a thought to its parentage.

'Izat so,' he says.

'Izat so,' the Baby says.

'Not part of the plan,' he says.

'Argle goodle bardle blubber,' the Baby says.

Orchid is crying but the Baby is not. The Baby is looking up at the baron with those all-seeing eyes. Orchid will get the hang of it, the baron thinks. She'll come around. She won't have any choice.

He hears the rumble of the service lift, which will be Joe bringing up the gold, and he hears Orchid say, 'I am the mother.'

Orlap steps forward, ready to make a speech, and the baron shoots him. Twice. One for the forehead, one for the heart – well, actually, the stomach in this case. Orlap dies on his feet and collapses onto the slushy ground like a sack of stones. His blood seeps darkly into the slushy concrete floor.

'Now I'm the Baby's father. I'm adopting him.'

'Oh so,' the Baby says, and stares at the baron. Meeting the Baby's scrutiny, the baron is shocked to find himself looking into the eyes of Arya Tara, into the eyes of the cosmos itself. Suddenly, it is as if the heavens unfasten, and the trickle of maths through his brain becomes a waterfall. Through the baby eyes of Arya Tara he sees it – God's algorithm, the mathematical description of everything. He staggers to one side, trying to keep his feet.

Orchid collapses on the ground beside Orlap as if kicked from behind. A deep, hoarse wail comes from her throat.

'Woah!' Flay steps closer to the chopper while seeming to step back from the psycho. He sees his chance, and it's coming up fast.

piss on your socks!

It doesn't take too long for Little Sanyo to figure out how to disarm the machine gun that killed Pinky. He takes Pinky's jacket, puts it over Pinky's rifle and waves it back and forth in front of the door. The machine gun stutters away until it either runs out of ammo or jams, reducing Pinky's jacket to tatters.

Celib and the others are reluctant to follow him in. There's no more drunken crowing or clowning around. It's one thing to blast open a door, another to enter the cavernous spaces of the fabled mansion, full of unknown perils. It's not just the prospect of further booby traps that alarms the men, it's more like a superstitious dread. All the tales that have been told of this place, and the other mansions, have created a purely fabulous world in the minds of the men. A fantasy realm where demi-gods and supernatural creatures reign.

Little Sanyo is the only one apparently not affected by this atmosphere of awe and dread. He skips on down the narrow corridor, chattering excitedly. 'We have to go up,' he says. 'Look for a lift, or staircase.'

None of the men likes the idea of getting into a lift. As Celib puts it, most of the men are sailors who work under an open sky, with no great love of confined spaces. Little Sanyo, culvert crawler, doesn't care. Shortly, however, they find a side door leading to a staircase. With no lighting activated, the stairwell is sunk in gloom. It's like a gothic castle at twilight. The men look at each other nervously and murmur.

'We go up,' Little Sanyo says cheerfully.

The men grip their weapons and follow him. They arrive at a landing without incident. Some of the men are relieved. Some are even starting to look a little excited. It isn't the loot so much anymore, or even the Baby, but the pleasure of violation that has them in its grip.

The rich wizard's abode, wide open to them, the stealthy invaders.

They have just started on the next step when a thick, heavy gas begins to filter down from above. The men cough. By a freakish coincidence, the little genius recognises it as mustard gas, lung-rotting and lethal. And he knows what the men in the Great War did to survive a mustard gas attack.

'Piss on your socks!' he shouts as he does just that. 'Then put it over your nose.' There is no time for him to explain that the ammonia in their piss will neutralise the mustard gas, to some extent anyway, but the men soon get the idea with varying rates of success. Peeing under these circumstances is difficult. Finally, with their socks or scarves or shirts over their mouths they run, back down the stairs, mustard gas billowing down after them.

Little Sanyo, however, moves in the opposite direction, upward, and finds he quickly moves beyond the gas, which has been emitted from holes in the stairwell wall. He waits for a while to see if the men will return, but they don't. Too spooked, he decides with some amusement. Little Sanyo, on the other hand, is having the most exciting time of his life. He has to pit his wits against a house which fights. They could make a movie of him and it would be the most exciting movie; he'd certainly watch a movie like that.

At the next landing there is a door, and he has to decide whether to continue upwards or open the door. He opens the door, just for a peek, and luck is with him. On the wall there is some kind of control panel. He approaches it warily, and removes the outside casing with his knife. Circuitry! A small part of the brain of the mansion.

He takes his time. He's careful in his study of the control panel. He doesn't touch anything.

After a long pause, he knows what he has to do.

a controlling demon

Outside the back gate to the Fairweather mansion, Rasputin stands with the Mayor's raiding party getting whiter and colder. The northern lights have gone, and the last afternoon light has given way to evening. The moon mixes a dull pearly light from the clouds, and a gentle snow is falling once more. Little flurries that blow this way and that as the wind keeps changing its mind.

The walls protecting the Fairweather mansion are back lit from from the glare of arc lights behind. They can hear Flay's Bedford still running, and muffled human voices.

There are more driftdead up here on the back road than Rasputin expected to find, not making their way down the hillside towards the town and Highway 6, but negotiating the ridges and mountain trails. Maybe the Alps themselves are riddled with them. It makes Rasputin dizzy to think of the whole country from coast to coast crawling with them. Around him the driftkids carry on their never-ending journey, like kids at a party playing zombies. Their tiny souls flare above their heads, like miniature candle flames, the trick kind that start up again with a crackle when you snuff them out. God will take care of them, Rasputin thinks; their little souls will never be snuffed out. They will always quietly crackle back into life when Satan's not looking.

Behind him stand the reverend and the librarian. The three of them make a little cluster of the sober. The raiding party is running out of momentum, but nobody is talking about going home. Most want to follow Little Sanyo's lead and find another way into the mansion. Ock Arglin passes among them with a cup of cheer, which most gladly accept, but the moment of high drunkenness has passed. They wipe the snow from their faces, clutch their weapons and stare at the gate.

'You can't know,' the reverend is saying. 'There is no way you can be sure of this beyond doubt.'

'But I know what I see. Like little candles everywhere, all of different colours, like oil on water, every single candle different from every other. The soul of each one dancing in attendance, like wild flowers in the meadow.'

But the old believer is having a hard time believing. He turns to the librarian. 'Do you see these little flames dancing in attendance, on the heads of the driftdead?'

'No. But reverend, Rasputin may still see them.'

'He may, but nobody else sees them.' He looks sceptically at some passing driftdead. 'Still, it is a very comforting thought.' He addresses the librarian, 'Any loyal acolyte might try to relieve his master's tormented brain with such a pleasant little fantasy.'

Rasputin's having none of that. 'I serve you by serving the truth, Master. I don't hold stuff back from you.' Rasputin is starting to feel cold. Not the cold that comes down from the sky, or up from the earth, but from inside, from the very marrow of his bones. This is what the withdrawal of God's grace from the world must feel like, he thinks. This is what disbelief feels like. As cold as clay. As empty as a starless sky.

'You believe so, but there is not a shred of truth or honesty left in the world. We've squandered it. Now there is nothing left but lies. Behind one lie there is another, and so it goes.'

'I know what I see.'

'Reverend!' the mayor shouts. 'Can you ask God to open up these gates for us?'

The men murmur in agreement. It's about time God did something for them. They're standing around with their guns in their hands and nothing moving to shoot at.

'That Asian kid was going to open them, that was the plan. Something must've happened.'

The reverend takes no notice. He is following a line of thought and won't let it go. He bends over Rasputin, his voice a low hiss. 'But what do you see? Really? Little flames dancing attendance like flowers in the meadow? Or malicious demons feeding on the life-force of their prey?' The reverend laughs, a series of hisses. 'What if each pretty little flame is a controlling demon, like a parasite, draining the soul energy from the helpless driftdead, taking them over, marching them off to Hell?'

Rasputin's inner cold intensifies. That's what death must feel like, creeping up from behind. The chaos of milling men fades to nothing as he is hit by what his master is saying. All Rasputin can do is see – but what is he seeing? The reverend's explanation has the same explanatory power as his own in terms of understanding the soul flames, but has the added advantage of offering at least a partial explanation for the driftdead themselves. They are the husks left over after their parasite has emptied them. If they felt anything, it would be like the godless cold creeping out of his bones.

And yet, when he first saw them, outside the church that day, he knew immediately what they were. They didn't look like demons. Or is that the whole point, the mockery of deception?

'Why me? And only me?'

'Don't fool yourself. No messiah can arise in a world like this. There are no foundations for it. Truth and belief. How quickly we lost those things! A messiah would just be another fool. A bigger fool.'

Rasputin has no answer. If the reverend will place no faith in his understanding, what can Rasputin say?

He becomes aware of the librarian, listening intently to the conversation. He wants to talk to her about the reverend's spiritual state. Perhaps somewhere in the library there is a recipe, a secret potion that will free the reverend from his nihilistic blackness.

They are distracted, however, by action at the gate.

The gates are opening. A hard light is spilling out.

how many bars of gold does it take to build a pie in the sky?

What the raiding party see is not Little Sanyo letting them in, but a very big man driving a forklift, and depositing a pallet of gold outside the gate, on the edge of the ramp. The gold is stacked up like firewood to dry, several layers of gold bars, four, no, five deep, nine layers – there are heads working faster than the brainbox calculating forty-five gold bars in all.

Forty-five.

Joe steps back in a deliberate gesture, and nods at the gold.

It's all theirs. And spread on top of the gold, like hundreds -and- thousands on a birthday cake, are various jewels, diamonds and rubies.

But nobody moves, not at first. Everybody stands around looking at it.

'Must be a trick,' someone says. This idea has a few supporters. It's iron painted gold. It's a bomb.

'It's not a trick. It's something worse than a trick,' the Rev Stickman says.

'Enough for one each,' a voice says.

'Enough to rebuild a town,' the mayor says.

'These are Mammon droppings,' the reverend says. 'His followers worship his excrement.'

'It's only worth what somebody will give you for it,' somebody else murmurs, and there is general agreement on that too. How can it be that they are staring at the largest pile of gold ever dreamt of and still feel short-changed? It puzzles them. The baron is trying to buy them off. There is something contemptuous in the way the gold has been dumped unceremoniously at their feet, the way Joe gestured to it. They are being fobbed off.

If the baron doesn't care about his gold anymore, why should they?

These are paradoxes for which their minds are not well equipped. It makes them angry. They wave their guns around. They try to see around Joe, and catch a glimpse of a flaming redhead with an Uzi, and Flay's truck.

It's the dressing of rubies and diamonds on top that gets to the Smiley Sisters, the first to approach the treasure. Soon they are fondling the precious stones and saying 'ooh, aah' at each other.

'We have to figure out a strategy,' the mayor says, exerting the authority of his bulk over the gold. 'They still have the Baby, remember.'

'The Baby! The Baby!' a few of them say, but the enthusiasm is not catching. Many have given up on the Baby. Perhaps each one of them is wondering if they are really prepared to die for the Baby, or for the loot stashed away behind those walls, the fabled treasures of Baron Brian (Brainbox) Fairweather. Perhaps they are asking themselves what the use of such treasures would be in a world where the driftdead reigned, in a world where they could only take one thing with them, the thing they happened to be carrying, even if that thing was quite meaningless or something they hated.

'I bet there's plenty more inside,' somebody says. No disagreement there.

'Then,' says Big Bill with great emphasis, 'our best strategy is just to sit here and wait until the baron has departed, and the whole mansion will fall into our hands like a ripe plum. We can live like kings.' This is Big Bill fronting up to his defining moment like a man, a man as somewhat sober as he is somewhat drunk.

It is hard to disagree with his logic, but nobody likes it. They want to shoot at something. There is a frustrated murmur. Not one of them believes that they will ever live like a king.

A skinny figure in a black singlet steps right around the gold as if it were a mere obstacle. He walks across the invisible line that separates the inside from the outside. It is Scale, carrying a yard broom loosely in his arms, as if it were a weapon. He goes right up to Joe, and taps the broom on its long handle.

'This is a shotgun, single-barrelled, probably a four-ten by the looks of it, but you might call it a yard broom if you want.'

'Izat right?' The big Polynesian says, looking interested. He gestures to the weapon he is holding. 'This is a Kalashnikov, but you can call it an AK-47 if you want. Lotsa bullets come outa hole in the barrel.'

'How many?'

'Six-hundred per minute, cyclic rate of fire.'

'Ten per second,' Scale says.

'Smart. A smart bantam we have here. Watch this.'

Joe makes the Kalashnikov go clicketty-snap, stands back and starts pumping bullets into a cluster of driftkids making hard work of the snow outside the gate. In the dull air it sounds like a whole lot of sticks breaking. One of the kids, carrying a small, grey plastic knife, folds over in the snow as if he were tired. On the ground he keeps crawling. Joe keeps firing, six-hundred rounds a minute. It takes a lot of bullets to bring down a driftdead unless you blow their heads off, which is Flay's specialty. You more or less have to tear them to pieces. But that's okay, Joe has plenty of bullets.

At the end of a solid minute's firing the area around is piled up with corpses. They look like ordinary dead kids.

A cold grey silence follows.

The snow continues to sift down, eddied here and there by gentle puffs of wind.

'I can't think that fast,' Scale says.

'You don't have to,' the Polynesian says, reaching out for the broom which has begun to sway back and forward.

'Let me try that,' Scale says, reaching for the Kalashnikov. 'It looks pretty easy.'

Suddenly he's grappling with the big bodyguard, holding onto the Kalashnikov with all his strength. Joe swings him around as if he were a kid holding onto a stick. It looks comical but it isn't.

'Hey!' Some of the men yell and rush in to help Scale. With Scale still clinging to the weapon, Joe unloads a spread into the approaching men. Then everybody's shooting. There are cries of rage and pain. Rasputin pulls the reverend down with him behind a large rock standing to one side of the ramp. The librarian is already huddled there. From what he can see, Joe and Scale are down, and the shooter doing the most damage is a girl with red hair. Both the Smiley Sisters go down, covered in the baron's jewellery.

The carnage goes on for a few more moments until everybody is either dead or well hidden.

The librarian buries her face in her hands. 'It's not supposed to turn out this way,' she says to the reverend, who fervently agrees. Nothing turns out the way it is supposed to. God is in his Heaven, but it's showtime on earth.

how the First Person disavows the librarian

I can barely contain my anguish. All these people dead or dying. I am furious with the librarian and her sudden unhistorical views. There is no 'supposed to' in history, just what happens and the reasons for it. There are alternative histories at every turn, but only one real history, the one that is lived. Does she really think she has control of these events? As the First Person, I have a feeling that one day these random and senseless deaths will come back to haunt me.

It seems the librarian hasn't learned anything from the Sirocco experience. It would be nice to put a patch over the slaughter, that's what she's thinking. Over and over again she thinks she can change all this. She'd put a patch over me too if she could. She never approved of having a First Person in the first place. You need to stay out of my history, she said, and of course I agreed. I was more than happy to be an invisible presence, until events themselves brought me out of the shadows.

Sadly, after all this time and our long association, I have to disassociate myself from the librarian. After a long, simmering hostility, it has finally come to this. I fear that she will never complete her Chronicles of Keatown. I fear that it is already compromised. The footprints of the driftdead are all over it. Truly, she has lost her way.

But even at this last moment, I hesitate. Turning my back on her is more easily said than done. It's like a god turning her back on her chosen people. Perhaps she did invent me, but I in turn have invented her. We have bootstrapped ourselves into some kind of existence, and here we are, huddled behind a rock, trying to keep out of the carnage. She, and the Stickman too, struggling with their absent deities, huddled together. Abandoned.

She's waiting for me to give her a pep talk, but it's gone too far for that.

Up until now, she has carried out her duties with an almost fanatical faithfulness, just as much a slave to my words as Mary was to Zhenhua. The collar she wears may leave no needle marks on her throat, but it stings just the same. No matter how hard she may tear at it with bloodied fingernails, she can never remove it. To abandon her now may seem churlish, even cruel, but she cannot be permitted to rewrite history according to her own presuppositions. She is not the first historian to attempt to turn the tables on history, only to find the tables turned back again.

As for me, I try to pretend that I am not helpless in all this, that I can step in and by command strengthen her resolve and clean up the mess. It doesn't work that way either. I wear her collar just as she wears mine.

get in the chopper!

Orchid rises from the dead body of Orlap like a woman who has spent all of her life in a dream. She was young when the dream began, little more than a girl, now she is old, with a lifetime of disillusionment to bear. In her youth she loved and hoped; in old age she buries her dead.

'I see that the stories I've heard are true,' she says, rising from Orlap's body as if she were his ghost. Through all this, she has depended on him and he has never deserted her. He stood by her when she decided to pretend that the Baby was Hera's. He kept silent about being the Baby's father, even when he was bursting with pride. Now she was on her own.

'Good. So get in the chopper,' the baron says. He's struggling to get the words out through the cascades of maths.

'You never were going to take Orlap, or Mary, were you?'

'Hardly room. Now, get in the chopper.'

With the gates open, driftdead have begun to filter onto the rooftop. Many of them are children. Orchid imagines the Baby's tiny limbs trying to paddle south. They have seen toddlers, barely able to totter along. Some have claimed to see crawlers, children not old enough to even walk.

'Why should it be different anywhere else?' Orchid says, her voice thick in her throat. She looks around for other options. There's not much going. Sirocco and Mary lie dying in the shadow of the service lift. Witch Hunt is with them, holding Sirocco's hand. Flay is fiddling with the hose. Blue Zither is watching their every move, while the red-haired Cherry Blossom has gone to join the bodyguard at the gate. Annanda is hiding behind the truck.

'I've changed my mind,' Orchid says, moving away from the

helicopter.

The Tavor swings around to point at the Baby's head. The Baby, who appears to be following everything very carefully, calmly considers the business end of the Tavor. He reaches out for it.

As Orchid backs off, the Baby grabs the barrel of the Tavor and tries to pull it into his mouth.

'He wants it,' the baron says. All he has to do is pull the trigger. So easy. Simplify the odds, eliminate complications, do the maths.

Orchid says. 'If you kill the Baby, you'll have to kill me.'

'That's starting to look like an option,' the baron says. But he's getting that tearing feeling in his chest when he looks at Orchid. Pain in unaccustomed places.

'Oh so?' the Baby says to the Tavor.

'I have the maths' he says to the Baby.

'Quaddle bubble, quiddle goo-ga zang zang,' The Baby says.

'That's right.' Even the pain in his heart won't stop the maths. Even killing the baby wouldn't do it.

The Baby sticks his tongue into the barrel of the Tavor.

All the baron wants is Orchid. For a few moments the maths recedes and his vision clears. The roar of numbers fades to a murmur, a distant celestial choir. He comes to staring at the Baby. The accursed Baby, coming between them. He'd throw the Baby to the wolves if he had to. She can always have another baby. His baby. A clean slate always looks tempting.

A sudden loud bark, short and sharp, brings him around. The world, suddenly fluid, flows into place, everything oozing into its accustomed position, and he finds himself confronting a familiar face. Thrust close up to his. Large glassy eyes and gleaming canines.

'Manny,' he says with relief. 'It's about time...'

But there is something wrong with Manny. The hair on his back is bristling, his lips peeling in a silent snarl. What's strange is that the baron is on the receiving end of this treatment. He can't understand this simple thing. Manny, about to tear out his throat.

A moment later he hears the song. Not just any old song, but 'Sing a Song of Sixpence' which his mother used to sing before he became a baron or a brainbox. And not just that song, but his mother's voice, not quite in tune. 'The king is in his counting house, counting out his money. The Queen is in the parlour, eating bread and honey...' the words are hardly enunciated, more like a humming, but the voice cannot be mistaken... 'the maid is in the garden, hanging out the clothes, when along comes a blackbird and pecks off her nose.'

It's not his mother singing but a little old lady with a brown face, like a baby's but full of lines. His first thought is that the old baby-faced woman has bewitched Manny, but soon sees how absurd that is. Manny is genetically designed to have one master. You don't bewitch Manny; he doesn't have the neural pathways for it. And he doesn't switch allegiances.

His second thought is that he has been spooked if not bewitched himself. There is no way the old woman could have known about that song, or the baron's mother who used to sing it. And how it gave him his great love of maths, turning his head into a counting house.

'Manny,' he says again, the Tavor moving away from the Baby's head towards Manny.

'You can call him Irawaru,' the old woman says, 'or is the word too slippery for your tongue? It means one who has been turned into a beast by a god.'

'His name is Manny,' the baron says. 'That's his birth name.'

'He no longer recognises it. Just as this land no longer recognises you.'

There is something wrong with the Brainbox's brain. People are talking, but their words seem to fly off in all directions. Not like the clean lines of maths once more swelling in his brain. The celestial chorus is growing louder; he can hardly hear his own voice.

'All right, Granny, but can you talk some sense into the Baby's mother and get her into the chopper.' These are normal human words; they sound okay to him, but what does he know about it? Almost as soon as the words leave his mouth they become senseless. Only the numbers make sense. Four and twenty blackbirds baked in a pie.

'The Baby's mother?' the old woman seems to forget that the baron is there. She stares at Orchid and the Baby, her face slowly going grey. She doesn't seem to be very fast on the uptake.

He speaks slowly and carefully, as if talking to a brain-damaged person. 'I can take her and the Baby and get them out of here. There are safe places.' He's not sure if this is true, but it sounds right. There must be safe places. Places he can quietly focus on the maths he needs to do.

'The Baby's mother?' the woman repeats. 'How is that possible?'

The baron concludes that she is a simpleton. How she got Manny away from him hardly seems to matter anymore.

The baron makes up his mind. Baby or no Baby, Orchid will get into the helicopter now or he'll shoot them both. As soon as he stops simplifying the odds, they multiply and turn against him. Like Manny. He'll have to shoot Manny too. The simple old woman hardly matters, nor do a few extra rounds.

God's algorithm

At that crucial moment, when there is action to be taken and people to be shot, the baron has an extraordinary vision. A sudden ruckus at the gate distracts his attention, and he looks up to see, beyond Joe and the gate, a driftdead man, an old man, maybe in his late sixties, with a craggy face, a prominent Roman nose, and long silver hair, wandering along the roof edge. This one doesn't seem so fixed on having to go south with every step, and his movements are quite casual – that is until the baron sees him. As soon as the baron notices him, the old man stops and turns his head in the baron's direction. There is an uncanny moment, an awareness that connects them. He is able to see himself through the driftdead's eyes, and sees an infantile man, somewhat overweight, with a big shaved head, waving his gun around. How ridiculous, he thinks, back behind his own eyes again, still looking at the old man. The old man, with a peculiar gesture, like a magician about to make something disappear, begins to disintegrate. He falls to pieces, and the pieces fall to pieces; atom by atom he falls away, returns to nothingness; the slow crumble of the flesh along his arms – bones turned to a whisper, the skull to a brief burst of static electricity. Yet he doesn't stop looking at the baron, not until he has nothing left to look with. Finally, the old man vanishes completely, nothing remains but a momentary sheen of wizard-grey hair.

He has melted back into the air.

The 'brainbox' understands; he's watched the maths of the creature's body unravel, taking the flesh with it. The maths tells him that the driftdead are hasty, improvised creatures with no life of their own, built by multiplying fractals and taken apart the same way. Not randomly, but unpacked in the reverse order to the way they were constructed.

The numbers give with one hand and take away with the other.

He has never ceased to be astonished that the total energy balance of the universe adds up to naught. He's done the maths himself and knows it's true. And when the pie was opened the birds began to sing. That makes the universe, and everything in it, an illusion, technically speaking. Everything cancels everything else out.

The universe therefore has to borrow energy to exist, and that energy has to be paid back. It's a debt problem; it always is. The driftdead are no different. They have to borrow the energy from some quantum dimension in order to exist, and at some point that energy has to be paid back to balance the equation. And when it's all paid back there is nothing left. It all has to add up to naught. Nix. Nada. So the driftdead run out of algorithm and disappear. Vanish piece by piece as the energy balance is restored.

Maths flashes through his head like storm bursts. As a young, idealistic mathematician, he dreamed of a final equation, the master algorithm that would unlock not just the secret of the stars, but the space behind the stars, the very mystery of creation. God's Algorithm, he jokingly called it. All he had done, with his famous 'five-sided' equation, besides astound the mathematical world, was to unlock the vaults at the Federal Reserve and every central bank around the world. He mistook that for success, how could he not when there was money raining out of the sky? But he hadn't cracked it, God's Algorithm, or only the tiniest part. Staring at that disintegrating old man, he feels close to it again, that master algorithm. More maths flows through his head, a steady stream of equations, all heading in the one direction, a mathematical 'south.' The lineaments of an understanding begin to appear, and time begins to slow down.

The look of horror on the old woman's face as she confronts Orchid takes a millennia to form. Manny is closing his jaws on thin air, but slowly, slow enough for many lifetimes to come and go. Time has become vertical. All the hours of his life are stacked up on his eyelids as God's algorithm unpicks linearity.

He sinks down onto the floor and begins scratching numbers with the tavor.

something for the pain

The dying Sirocco and Mary get a ringside seat from which to observe these last-minute, panic-stricken manoeuvrings. They are lying down with their backs propped up against the wall of the service lift. Witch Hunt is with them. She wants to help keep them cheerful while they die. They see the baron freeze, as some people do before they turn, but the baron doesn't turn. He's staring at something in the distance.

'I'm bleeding out from the same place that you are,' Mary says with a little laugh. 'Maybe the same vein. Wouldn't that be a giggle.'

'We need something for the pain.' Sirocco can feel his own now. A dull ache that keeps turning duller. He's starting to feel giddy from loss of blood. It is a familiar feeling, almost a friend. In the desert he was often giddy from hunger.

'I could find something,' Witch Hunt says. 'The librarian might have...'

'I suppose you think this is poetic justice,' Mary says, her voice thick and heavy. 'Me killing you and now bleeding out myself. From the same place.'

'No,' Sirocco says calmly, 'It just happened, that's all. I don't see any kind of justice. Or retribution. It's what you learn in the desert. Things happen. Really fast. You don't burden yourself with too much explanation. It slows you down. You learn to keep up.'

'It's easy to get sorrowful,' Witch Hunt says.

'I might have liked you,' Mary says to Sirocco, 'if I hadn't killed you. I mean, if we both weren't dying.' She tries to laugh.

'Or maybe not. Both of us dying creates the illusion of some kind of commonality, some kind of bond. A shared experience. We could sit here imagining that we might have been friends, maybe even that we were friends. Talk about all the fun things we did together.'

'Jesus, you're a hard bastard.' She pushes her hand in against the pain. 'No pledging eternal friendship as we go out the back door?'

'What would be the use?'

'You are a fucking hard bastard. That's why I could have liked you.'

'I met a hedgehog in the desert once, and I liked it. I liked it for all the reasons people hate hedgehogs. Because it stank, because it made snuffling noises at night, because putting my hand on it was an unpleasant experience. And yet it hung around. In the end I had to eat it.'

'Poor hedgie!' Witch Hunt says. 'I hope you asked its permission first. It's okay if you ask its permission.'

'He was happy he could keep me alive.'

'Have you ever been in love with anybody, Age?' Mary runs a hand over her stubbly hair, streaking it red.

'Gypsy, maybe. I loved to watch her, just doing stuff around the house. Especially dancing to her Arabic music. Did you know she could do a real belly dance? That's hard to do, you know.'

'I loved Gypsy too,' Witch Hunt says.

Mary says, 'For me, it was Zhenhua. A slave always loves her mistress, but it went beyond that with Zhenhua. I proved how much I would suffer for her, how far I would go for her. No humiliation was too great. I would betray Orchid. I would have thrown the Baby on the fire if she desired it.'

'That's horrible!' Witch Hunt says. 'I bet you wouldn't.'

Mary's voice has taken on a feverish, sing-song quality. 'Zhenhua understood pain. She was the Mistress of Pain. The baron came to her for pain and he didn't even know it, she did it so well.' She points to the circle around her throat. 'Do you know how painful that was? Day and night, and the nights are much worse. A ring of fire around your throat. That's when you learn about love.'

'You did betray Orchid,' Sirocco says, and Witch Hunt nods in furious agreement.

'Orchid is a milksop. She looks very mysterious and everything but she's dumber than a fence post, when you boil it down. She goes this way or that, whichever way the wind blows. You can talk her into anything. Zhenhua and I would have had that Baby out of her hands in no time.'

'I've had one guiding principle, Age. Loyalty. Absolute obedience to Zhenhua. My every move is shaped by her will. Do you have a guiding principle?'

'Far stars.'

'What?'

'Far stars are the ones that don't move,' he says.

The world flickers for a moment, like an old movie at the end of its reel. A driftdead girl dressed in white pauses at the gate, head to one side, seemingly staring in at Sirocco. He stares back. The ground slopes up from nowhere. The gate recedes to the horizon.

the bravest thing

Something strange has happened to the baron. First he sinks to the ground and scratches on the floor with his weapon, murmuring to himself. Then he is on his feet wandering about, waving his weapon in the air. Maths is pouring from his mouth into the world. It is creating the world. Creating patterns and order along the lines of God's algorithm.

The action on the rooftop is suspended as everybody stops to watch the Baron, who looks around at them all, laughing. Ten dimensional maths is really so funny. Since most of the equations that make up the Great Equation are time reversible, all time has become absurd. Why isn't everybody laughing? Time is like a beachball.

'I've found it,' he says to the old lady with the brown skin.

But the old lady doesn't look like she cares. All she is focused on is Orchid and the Baby. His Orchid. Her baby. There is a dead man lying at their feet.

'And I've been taken for a fool,' she says.

"ÜIôAôAiÞ ° aiÜçAi Þ," The Baron says. It is all true and nobody can take it away from him.

Witch Hunt seizes the moment and makes a dash for the helicopter. Orchid knows what to do; she doesn't think twice but thrusts the Baby into Witch Hunt's hands. A deep, broken voice comes from her chest. 'Run!'

This is the bravest thing Witch Hunt has ever seen anybody do, but she doesn't stop to say so. The Baby in her arms, Witch Hunt flees.

The baron doesn't appear to see Witch Hunt running off with a baby-sized bundle. When he sees the pretty girl standing by the helicopter, facing him bravely, he hardly recognises her. Dark hair in soft waves, pale skin, lightly freckled across her nose, blazing green eyes with straight, dark eyebrows. A small face with finely honed cheekbones, a faint dimple in her chin, and rich, curved lips. But there is nothing ethereal about this girl. Inside her there lies a creature of the earth, dark and strong. A beast that would tear him to pieces if he came too close.

Surely he knew this girl a long time ago, when love was possible and heartbreak only a glance away. In a universe of quantum chances, he would get into the chopper with her and fly away to paradise. And that isn't just a fond dream. Paradise exists. It's there in the maths. It is a whole dimension in itself, governed by its own inspired equations. But that is not this universe, the one with the glaring lights and dead people walking around everywhere. That too suffers from its own inevitable contingency.

All around him the world is returning to its constituent numbers. Irawaru is at his side, not as a dog is to its master, but as a guard is to a prisoner, but none of that matters.

Far off, above the melee, he hears the mocking cry of the kea. Kea! Kea! Kea! But he doesn't care. The derision of the world no longer touches him.

There's chaos at the gate. It looks like Joe is down. Cherry Blossom is emptying her magazine into a melee of screaming people, but the beauty and elegance of God's Algorithm has struck the baron blind. That the world is only coming through in waves should frighten him, but it doesn't. The waves are only maths and he can ride those waves, surf the numbers to the ends of the universe and back.

There's a scream from his helicopter. It's Blue Zither pounding on the back of the grease-monkey who's climbing into the pilot's seat. With everybody distracted, and the psycho away with the fairies, Flay has seen his opportunity and seized it. First he grabs the blue girl's weapon. He doesn't like to fight with a floozy, but there it is. By the time the baron gets there, the grease-monkey is in control of the chopper and Blue Zither is lying on the ground with red blood on her blue hair. Orchid is also on the ground, the body of the dead man in her arms. She looks up at the baron but appears not to see him.

The grease-monkey grins at the baron from behind the pilot's door window. The baron could soon turn that grin into something else, something with lots of blood, but he has a better idea. He sits on the floor and begins to draw in the dust. The maths flowing through his head is too voluminous to write down, at least for the moment, but it does have a shape. All he needs to do is capture that shape, and the maths will more or less do itself.

When he gets to wherever he's going, he'll need a couple of computers and access to data on quantum dispersal, but in the meantime, the dusty floor and his finger will have to do. As he draws his shape, the maths flows in and around it. God's Algorithm is a thing of great beauty. He's aware that the runty little man dying over by the service lift is watching him closely. He seems to be trying to say something.

Whatever it is, it's lost in the clatter of the helicopter as it rises unsteadily into the air, and his emerging shape in the dust is scattered by the wind from the screaming rotors. He doesn't care. He doesn't have to go anywhere anyway. He's already there.

He seeks out a dustier piece of floor.

the death of a petrolhead

Flay's reign of terror in the sky above the baron's mansion is brief and spectacular. The machine sways this way and that as the mechanic tries various controls. It almost crashes. It spins around like a top. The real trouble starts when Flay discovers the two machine guns mounted above the wheels on either side. His first random burst picks across the roof and out the gate, smashing into the gold, and nearly kills the mayor.

Big Bill doesn't know who is in the chopper, or why they can't seem to fly it, but he does know that if the baron or anybody else tries to get away, the raiding party has enough hardware to bring it down. What's left of the raiding party. Before somebody took her down, the crazy girl with the red hair heaped up the bodies around the gold where they still lie, like human offerings to an indifferent god.

He steps forward with his own weapon and begins firing at the chopper, although strategically it makes no sense. He'd counselled his troops to let the chopper go, so the rest of them could take over the mansion. That was before the shooting started. Before Scale, now dead, lying across Joe, also dead, began their silly argument, and the crazy red-haired girl, also dead, started shooting.

Now everybody is shooting at the chopper, which swings in their direction, with more purpose this time, and a further line of machine gun bullets marches over the baron's roof, ripping into several of the shooters and wounding the mayor.

The Reverend Stickman steps out from behind the rock that has been sheltering him, and walks towards the unsteady helicopter. 'Vanity of vanities, saith the Preacher,' he proclaims, apparently aiming to pluck the aircraft out of the sky. 'Your country lies desolate, your cities are burned with fire; in your very presence aliens devour your land; it is desolate, as overthrown by aliens.'

He is rewarded with another burst of machine gun fire. Fifty-calibre shells rip and tear up the air and earth around him, stitching patterns in the snow, yet death blithely, almost delicately, passes him by. For a moment or two the chopper vanishes. Rasputin, hiding with the librarian, enjoys the sudden silence. Flakes of snow slide by, each in their own dream. The moon slips in and out of cloud. The reverend, his head bent, stands among piles of the dead, lost to the world; the driftdead dead and the human dead, one and the same.

Then Flay discovers the missiles. The first one he hits by accident, and it whizzes off down towards Keatown. The second is more carefully placed. He succeeds in hovering, just below roof level, and getting one away through the balcony and into the lounge. When it blows it takes half the roof with it.

Satisfied, and now with better control of the craft – it's a piece of piss once you learn how – he gains some height, ready to make a getaway... but not as much height as he'd like. A quick look at the dials tells him the story. His precious diesel is dribbling away. The fuel line must have been hit in the attack from below. He can fly away, but he can't get very far. All that fuss for that extra tank of gas. Another four or five hundred miles. Now pissing out all over the hillside.

Flay is not big on irony, but you have to laugh. There's one sure way to get them laughing on the other side of their faces. He grips the controls and sets his course for the already battered rooftop below.

Should make a nice little explosion. Finish the job.

The last of the petrolheads goes up in a ball of exploding hydrocarbons.

the goose dance

Little Sanyo finds himself walking down a hushed hallway in bare feet on a thick, spongy carpet as warm as slippers on his feet. To his left there are doors which open into bedrooms, each with a view overlooking the ocean.

Since disabling the building's defences, at least those he could access, he has been wandering like a little child through an Aladdin's cave of wonders, paying little attention to anything else. Treasures everywhere, whole rooms full of treasures. It feels as if he has walked into his parents' dream home, their dream life, their heaven. He has the uncanny sense that at any moment they might appear, high as kites just as he remembers them, and will rush forward to hug and kiss him and tell him how much they have missed him, being dead all this time. 'Welcome home,' they will say to him. 'Look, you can live in a world where all your dreams come true and you don't have to sleep in culverts or under people's houses anymore,' they will say, and he will cry and be happy. Prince Sanyo!

All this is his now! A mansion has washed up on his beach.

There are storerooms filled with provisions, enough to last for years. There are foods here he didn't even know existed, like powdered greens and dehydrated superfoods with strange ingredients from foreign lands. He can't stop anywhere for too long, however, as there is far too much to explore. He can always return, he tells himself after filling his pockets with some chocolate and muesli bars. The whole house belongs to Prince Sanyo now.

As he prowls through the bedrooms, he thinks of the tale of Goldilocks, how she looked over all the beds, the too large and the too soft, until she found one that was just right for her. That's what he's doing now, sizing up the beds and the bedrooms, imagining himself in occupation. One bedroom, on a corner with a huge window overlooking the town and the coastline, draws his attention. He can imagine, when the sun is up, how light and airy this room must be. The smells in the air suggest that this is a woman's room, and sure enough he finds a whole lot of women's clothes in the wardrobe.

Perhaps that's the same smartly dressed woman he finds on the floor above, lying dead in what is obviously an office, a wide-eyed look of surprise on her face. He finds another dead woman in the shower, this one hardly dressed at all. He tries not to take too much notice of these bodies. He remembers the fish he found on the beach, how dead it was, how quickly the gulls scooped out its eyes, how soon its tent of flesh collapsed. He's lived long enough to learn that all dead things are pretty much the same, and not really that interesting. Death soon trivialises the flesh, fish or fowl; he doesn't linger over the details.

He finds gold. Stack and stacks of ingots, but he doesn't find them as fascinating as he might have thought, except perhaps for their unblemished smoothness. You don't find stuff like this on a beach, where time and the elements have scratched the face off everything. It's fun to try to lift them, more than one at a time, because they are so heavy, but otherwise they don't do much. Stealing them, even one of them, is hardly an option given their weight. Besides, he's stealing the whole house, isn't he? The ingots are his by default.

He finds a stash of weapons potentially much more interesting, but there is no time to examine this treasure trove. He doesn't really care about shooting things, but the precision mechanisms fascinate him. More to look at later.

On the top floor he finds himself in a huge room that occupies the whole floor. It takes him a moment to absorb it all. He's never seen a room this big with so many windows in his short life, nor has he imagined one. There are two frightening pictures on the wall of men who are so naked their skin looks peeled away. He doesn't want to look at them. More interesting is a realistic, life-sized metal statue of a woman lying on her side, one hand propping up her head, watching him. She is bedecked in beads and wears a clinging dress. There is a nasty gouge along one leg which he touches, tentatively.

'I see you have found Arya Tara.'

The voice is a girl's and comes from the set of glass doors that lead to the balcony. The girl is standing by the door, an Uzi crooked comfortably in her arms. She has the blondest hair and the darkest eyebrows he has ever seen. And her lips are pink.

'That's a funny name.'

The girl watches him for a moment, the Uzi swinging this way and that.

'Do I have to kill you?' she asks, and purses her pink lips nervously.

'Do you?'

'Are you invading the house? I'm supposed to kill any invaders. Somebody was firing at the wall just before.'

'I'm just having a look around.'

'Are you looting?'

'I don't think so.'

He demonstrates that his pockets are empty, except for a few chocolates. Just a curious kid wandering around, is all he is.

From the open doors that lead to the balcony, they can hear the rattle of small arms from the roof. The Uzi swings in his direction. 'Who are you? What's your name?' The girl looks nonplussed. This in not exactly the invader she imagined. He's not even armed. He looks more like somebody's geeky little brother than anything else. And he doesn't look the least bit like doing any invading.

'I'm Little Sanyo. Who are you?'

'I'm Sun Petal.'

'That's a funny name.'

'So's yours.'

'Your hair is very white.'

'I know. It's called ash-blonde. Or platinum blonde.' There's a touch of pride in her voice. She shakes it a little so it moves around on her shoulders.

As she approaches, Uzi still at the ready, he sees that she is older than she looks, even though she is very pretty. At least, not as pretty as Orchid, but pretty enough. Her dark eyebrows make her face look strong. Even fierce. But her lips are soft and pouty and her eyes are a gentle blue.

'Please don't point that gun at me. I don't like guns, except to take them apart.'

'Okay.' She decides there is no danger from such a harmless little boy, puts her rifle aside and sits down beside him on a low backless seat placed in front of Arya Tara.

'The master often comes and sits here, right where we are sitting.'

'Why? There are more comfortable seats.'

'He talks to her,' Sun Petal gestures to the statue.

'Why would he do that?'

She shrugs. 'No one else to talk to, except Mistress Zhenhua. But now he's killed her.'

'Why?'

'Because she betrayed him.'

They sit silent for a while staring at Arya Tara, who is after all their excuse for sitting there in the first place. Arya Tara looks if she is enjoying a very private joke of her own.

'Do you have parents?' she asks.

'I used to. They died.'

'Oh.'

'What about yours?'

'They sold me.'

'To the baron?'

'To Zhenhua. She paid top dollar, I heard.'

'Oh.'

'Yeah, oh.'

'That sucks.'

She shrugs. 'It could've been worse.'

'You said Zhenhua's dead.'

'She ripped off the baron.'

'Then you are free. You have no owner.'

Sun Petal looks down at her Uzi. 'I'm the baron's now.'

'How come?'

'He won me, along with the rest of Zhenhua's stuff, when he killed her.'

'That sucks too.'

She doesn't like him saying that. She shakes her head to and fro.

'What do you do up here all day long?'

'I'm a dancer,' she says with a touch of world-weary pride that makes her seem very adult to him at that moment. 'And Zhenhua has been training us for a black belt in wushu, her own family-based style called Hung Gar.'

It all sounds very impressive to Little Sanyo, who listens quite awestruck.

'She says that the Hung Gar style goes back thousands of years in her country.'

Looking at the bronze statue of Arya Tara, Little Sanyo can well believe it. The bronze statue looks like it goes back thousands of years also. What a little flea he is, compared to these grand things. 'Does that mean you are a ninja?'

She smiles ruefully. 'I wish! I'm not as good at it as the other two girls, that's Blue Zither and Cherry Blossom. Zhenhua says I'm too clumsy.' There is a touch of sadness in her voice. 'It's the same with the dancing. We're called the goose girls, you know, because we dance like geese, or at least I do. I'm not half as good as that new girl, Orchid.'

Little Sanyo doesn't know what to say to these confidences. He can't pretend to know anything about the world she comes from, its joys or sorrows. It's all a big mystery to him.

'What about you? What do you do all day?'

'Me? I'm a beachcomber.'

'What's that?'

'I go along beaches looking for things washed up by the tides. Useful things, sometimes precious things. Once I found a note in a bottle.'

'What did it say?'

'Help.'

Sun Petal giggles. Suddenly she doesn't seem so adult any more. 'Do you want to see me do my goose dance? Zhenhua says I'm quite good at that one.'

'Okay.'

She puts down the gun, gets up and adopts a posture with one elbow out. 'I'm supposed to be a goose pretending I have a broken wing so I can lead the hunters away from my nest.'

She demonstrates, leaning to one side and waddling in a clumsy circle, lifting one leg up every step.

Little Sanyo claps. 'That's a pretty good goose dance,' he admits.

She grins with pleasure. 'It's not as easy as it looks.'

They can hear the sounds of war outside. There are screams and shouts and the sound of a helicopter taking off, but it is all so muted it might be happening on another continent.

'I had tinnitus once,' he says.

'What's that?'

'Ringing in the ears. It's like a constant pitch inside your head.'

'What happened to it?'

'It went away.'

'That's funny.'

'Yes it is.'

They run out of things to say. Little Sanyo very much wants to find new things to talk about. He feels like he's made two new friends in one go: Sun Petal and Arya Tara. Sun Petal may not be the brightest in the class, but she is fun. The bronze statue is not much of a talker, but a pretty deep thinker.

He could sit and talk with them forever.

heavier than a mountain, lighter than a feather

Arya Tara is heavier than a mountain and lighter than a feather. While she is made of a dense amalgam of heavy metals, her essence is of air. She was formed by molten bronze that made her much heavier than the cold cast method used for lesser statues, yet her consciousness was formed from the flare of stars.

Time means very little to Arya Tara. She was never born because she always was and has been and will be, and even the ending of time itself won't end her. She gave birth to time not the other way around; death has no sting for her. She is not, however, unmoved by time-bound life, life that flickers and dies on her skin, life that comes to partake in her consciousness only to die after a hasty moment of terrified awareness.

She has only compassion for the brief creatures who fashioned this image of her in molten metal; somehow they have grasped her sensual beauty and her unknowability, her mystery. Awareness is not confined to these tight molecular bonds of bronze, any more than it is confined to the mushy brains of the image makers. They partake in her but don't know it, foolishly believing that they are the source of their own consciousness, and because of that their compassion has no room to grow. Unfulfilled, they die just the same.

With great gentleness she cups the fevered minds of those who come close to her. She sees that the man who comes to sit by her each day as he tunes into the divine murmur of mathematics craves eternity, wants to live forever, not understanding that eternity is not about living forever, but about endlessness. Endlessness in all directions. Only now is he beginning to understand.

Little does he know, or indeed the two creatures that sit before her now know, that Arya Tara is the conqueror of dreams, the dealer of death to phantasms. Mara, the great god of false appearances, the magician of illusions, once plagued her mind with images of great beauty and with armies of terror. But Arya Tara soon learned that Mara's images could pass through her quite harmlessly, despite the density of her fabric. The only power they had was that which she gave them. Once perceived as what they were, they disappeared, vanished into thin air leaving nothing but a faint trace in memory. Sometimes they took the form of handsome young men, or women of great seductive power, or marching armies of slaves or demons.

The smile that has, over many eons, etched itself into her metal face, giving a shiver of mystery and delight to anyone who sees it, formed in the instant she understood that Mara was powerless, and all the false worlds created by Mara were without substance. In comprehending that, she is free of all that might distract her, detract from her substance, free to allow her consciousness to range through all the dimensions of existence at will.

Out of this great freedom, compassion arises; to see creation in all its splendour is to weep. Creation is saturated with her tears; within those oceans, worlds come and go. The intensity of her love makes her body glow as if it has been polished by a thousand devoted spirits. The two young people sitting in front of her are blinded by it. They feel the force of it without understanding it. It lifts them up outside of their bodies so that they hover in the air above their bodies, just like the soul-flames of the driftdead in Rasputin's vision.

In that moment Little Sanyo sees something terrifying. It has the face of Flay, a demented Flay, his face contorted into a rictus of fury. He is holding something in mechanical hands – a missile, cold and sleek. He is holding it like a spear about to be thrown. At its tip it holds the brightness of suns. Little Sanyo says something to Sun Petal who nods, takes his hand and rushes him to the exit door.

A moment later they are gone and Arya Tara is left alone in the oversized living room with its Frances Bacon nudes and a view to die for. The moments before the missile arrives are as an eternity to Arya Tara; she has had an eon to contemplate them. She doesn't need the packed chains of matter that make up the bronze of her body. Her body is little more than a locus, a momentary whirlpool made up of whispering sounds and fleeting histories. An image and nothing more, a fractal creation of coherent light.

The missile comes through the open front doors almost lazily, floats across the room and strikes Arya Tara direct. Much of its energy is taken up reducing her to a few crusty pieces of slag, much of the rest of the energy is absorbed by the thick bunker walls the baron built. The force of the blast blows away the back door to the room and sends its dragon breath down the stairwell, but Little Sanyo and Sun Petal have long gone.

For Arya Tara, little has changed. The forced disintegration of her atomic structure is no occasion for grief or regret. Others will sense her presence and make images of her, multitudinous images, masks of creation, but her boundlessness will never be bound, nor her nature caught in the net of the human mind.

the shadow beast

Annanda looks up into the sky. The aurora might have gone, but it has left a polished sheen on the sky. There was nothing like that in India. Sometimes people spoke of lights that ran across the ground before a thunderstorm, but nothing like a coloured sky. As a child he'd had a book on the life of Krishna, and it had contained pictures showing a blue man and skies of many colours. Death, he'd learned then, might be known many times. Krishna had been reborn so many times death just made him laugh. Shiva juggles death on one of his several arms. It may be a part of life, but it is still death. All around him there are dead people, most of whom he once knew, their lives nothing more than flashing foxfire.

He's wandered out the gate, thinking he'll walk back down the road to pick up his truck. He doesn't know what he'll do then, but he's in the hands of Rama now.

He can't believe his eyes when he sees his dear friend Suneal trudging along slowly with the driftdead. He doesn't pause to ask how this is possible, with Suneal two oceans and a world away, but he knows what he sees, despite the dark and the paling moon. He can't be mistaken. There can only be one Suneal.

He does appreciate that people often think they see friends and relatives among the driftdead, maybe because of the neutral masks of the driftdead faces. This is different. This is Suneal. He has that same walk, with the little feminine twist of the hips his friends would tease him about so mercilessly. The same slight lean to the left, as if he were about to turn a corner.

Annanda emerges from the shadow of the mansion wall, the safer, downhill side, further from the gate. He has no problem being a coward when the bullets begin to fly. A sensible man runs for cover. Once guns take over, they tend to stay the course until everybody is dead. Mostly everybody.

He keeps a wary eye on the gate as he joins the driftdead throng.

Annanda is not sad, despite all the death and destruction. He may mourn the town but not fall into despair. The forces hostile to life itself will never triumph; the gods are too big to fall. Creation cannot be undone.

As he turns his back on the mansion, he is aware that he is also turning his back on the world. Not to become a Rakshasa, but a sadhu. In his tradition, many Brahman men when they reach retirement age, just like his grandfather, leave their jobs, their homes and their loved ones to set off on the road for a life of religious devotion, carrying no more than a tiny swag, and living off the charity of others. Not that Annanda could become a real sadhu in this empty land, nor does he have a family to leave behind, but the impulse is there. Made stronger by the notion that he might share a small part of the endless road with his old friend.

Once more he remembers his grandfather, on the eve of his setting out, counselling the young Annanda, 'The world may be made for us, but we are not always made for the world.'

What a fool I have been in my life, he thinks. Even now he feels nostalgic for his shiny supermarket with its snazzy sign and empty shelves – what can you do with such a man? Abandon him to his folly, is all. But it hardly matters now; the life of a wise man and a fool weigh equally in the eyes of the gods.

He quickens his pace, hoping to catch up with Suneal and confess what a fool he has been. All those years apart when they could have been together. For a dreadful moment he loses sight of him among the crunch of shifting shoulders and merging backs, some of which seem to disintegrate as soon as he shifts his focus. It's probably a night mirage, but for a moment he feels part of a single giant beast, a great shadow beast crawling across the land, crawling towards dawn. It is a relief to see Suneal's familiar back once more. This time he makes no mistake and overtakes his friend. For a while they trudge along together, Annanda matching Suneal's pace until they are in step, like soldiers marching.

'The first thing I must do is apologise, dear friend,' he enthuses. He would like to hug Suneal, but of course his friend can't stop walking because he is part of the great shadow beast, and it is the beast that is walking. The best he can do is match Suneal's pace in a friendly fashion, and chat away as they used to. 'It was never about the money, you know. That would make it very trivial, hardly worth a story. It's all about the money, they say, but it never is. It's mostly about fear. Look at the money-baron; it wasn't about the money to him, it was about numbers.'

'And look at this mansion we are passing like ships in the night. It belongs to these Swiss people. For them it wasn't about money, but about fresh air. Imagine, all that money for a breath of air! For me, it was a shiny dream at the end of the world, and you were always part of that dream, goodness yes, but the world ended before the dream. That's the consequence of living day-by-day, dollar-by-dollar, breath-by-breath. And here we are again, after all these years – isn't it strange? The gods catch us out in our lives. Catch us with our pants down, ha ha. But I'm just a simple trader, a hustler from the back streets of Mumbai where dreams are cheaper than friends and fear is never far away. So, still I'm trading. Trying to trade my wretched past for an unlikely future, talking to you as I would talk to Rama, wanting no more than to set the world to rights, return to the past and kiss your dear eyes.'

It's not the same when Suneal can't chat back, for the great shadow beast is a silent one. He has to do the chatting for both of them, which becomes a strain after a while. All those years, what can he say about them? Whenever he falls silent, the greater silence of the shadow beast makes itself felt. It's a good thing he's with Suneal, otherwise he might get spooked by that greater silence, by the rustle of clothes and the shuffle of feet. His real worry is what will happen when he has to sleep. Then Suneal will get ahead of him, so far ahead Annanda might never find him again. Perhaps if he just catches naps he can keep up, stay with his dear friend. Nothing else matters.

Of course, he will run out of things to say, eventually, but that doesn't matter too much either, since he can just say the same things again in a different way, or even the same way, it's not going to matter to Suneal. Besides, some things are worth saying more than once, because their truth makes them joyful, just as some memories will never wear out, even if you'd like them to. Like that silly little hotel in Bangalore where they lived for a week like careless students and ordered every dish on the menu, and were finally ejected by an indignant proprietor. Remembering it now makes him smile. This is a memory he can live with. With others it's not so easy, like the day he left to travel the continent and two seas. The memories you can't live with are the ones that haunt you every day.

And when he gets tired of the sound of his own voice, the stolid silence of the driftdead can be soothing. They have no more deals to make, no more hustles to run, no more hunger gnawing at their days the way it gnawed at his childhood – and Suneal's too. They would joke that they both crawled out of the same Petri dish of flies, famine and favours. Annanda crawled as far away from that Petri dish as possible, and here he is, in this strange land, up on a mountain road, talking to his friend who might well have just pulled himself out of his grave.

'Don't listen to me,' he advises Suneal, trying to stare into his friend's face, trying to make eye contact. 'I appreciate your austerity, your silence. Our Lord Rama is, after all, the lord of self-control. The lord of calm. I was the one always running off at the mouth, getting excited over silly things. That's how we got together at the beginning, remember? Me talking and you listening. You were such a shy listener! And I was such a bold talker, so full of myself! When I was trying to teach you how to make a sale I told you - remember? - to keep talking as long as the customer hangs around undecided. People don't want to part with their money! Real people I mean, not those celebs. You have to talk people around. Which is what I did with you, ha ha!'

Later, when the boot was on the other foot, so to speak, Suneal did the talking and it was the bold Annanda who became the shy listener. But that's all history now.

Happiness, in this human world, is always underwritten by melancholy. This, Annanda has discovered, is a general rule. It's to do with time. Since everything becomes history, mere thoughts in Rama's brain, everything can be mourned. Even at the height of the boom years in Keatown when the Celebs ruled Beauty Parade, and the air was filled with laughter, melancholy was not entirely banished, merely pushed into the shadows where the passing days lurked. With Suneal it was different. It was joy unalloyed, untainted by past or future. No messy deals or trade-offs. The whispers of the world were but straws in the wind when they laughed. Melancholy was just a romantic word.

He can remember those things now, and feel the joy once more. True, the driftdead Suneal isn't aware of Annanda's existence, at least not on the surface, but that doesn't worry Annanda. Suneal will know, at some level he will know. Hanuman will whisper it into his ear, the inner ear that can still hear. And he will love, with the inner heart that still loves. He will know and he will take comfort. And one day he will come out of it. He will emerge, as from a cocoon, and be his old self again. He will embrace Annanda with the joy of seeing him and they will never part again, not in this world or any other.

With the spirit of Hanuman in them, they will make their way in the new world, whatever it might look like. It is all in the hands of Lord Rama, even the very next step.

He knows he is indulging in his old habit of painting rosy pictures of the future. That was all very well when he actually had a future, but the road he is on now doesn't lead to any future, rosy or otherwise. These pilgrims of silence are not going anywhere. The world is just their treadmill.

Annanda has no fear of turning, but there is a growing comfort to be had being with them, a part of the great shadow beast, moving in the same direction, letting his feet find their path. All around him the driftdead are doing the same thing. In some ways he feels he belongs here.

Monkey laughs at the idea but Suneal doesn't.

Very quickly Keatown drops away behind.

Soon it will be no more than a memory.

He looks up from his feet to say something to Suneal and finds that Suneal is gone, simply vanished into thin air, and he is walking beside a complete stranger, talking to a complete stranger, acting as if that stranger were Suneal. Very embarrassing.

Still, he realises, it makes no difference if his companion is Suneal or not. In the world of the shadow beast it is all the same.

Already he can't remember his friend's face.

out of the hat

The arrival of dawn finds the librarian in search of the First Person – she who must be obeyed. She can't believe that the First Person would ever renounce her. Such a thing is inconceivable. With every step, every word, the First Person has always been with her. More often than not an invisible presence, perhaps, but a presence nevertheless. Without the First Person there would be no Chronicles of Keatown, she's convinced of that.

Without the First Person, there is no writing.

She's come all this way just to arrive at her aloneness. How can that be?

She wants her revelation, just like the others, and she believes I can provide it. She thinks I can pull it out of the hat at the end and, like the magician, flourish it about as to an audience of credulous children. She doesn't see why not. After all, everybody else has received some reward. Unlike her, their journey has not been for nothing. A few crumbs do sometimes fall from fate's table. It's not exactly a lolly scramble, but it's something.

Sitting in front of her keyboard, where she feels most comfortable, but not writing, she counts off the blessings received by those she has written about. She has marshalled all her points, lined them all up like soldiers for me to inspect. Her resentments are to the fore. I think she wants me to feel guilty.

Take Sirocco. He dies, true enough, but he gets to see his real face in the mirror. That's something. He hates it, but at least he gets to see it before he dies. He dies in a state of truth; he will return to the desert. She's jealous of him for that. After all, he was just a desert rat, with an imaginary book, while she has laboured long and hard at her Chronicles. Doesn't she too deserve a little truth and reconciliation?

Take Witch Hunt. The least of them all, and she ends up as baby bearer, the greatest honour. She couldn't feel more proud.

Even Sad Toof loses his tooth in the end, which is a nice resolution for him no matter how much he moans and groans. Saved by the tooth fairy. Three cheers for Sad Tooth! He gets to live a pain-free life. There is no tooth fairy for the librarian.

Then Annanda finds Suneal. He gets to walk into the sunrise chatting to the old friend he left behind. How touching that they should find each other after all this time and distance. She doesn't begrudge Annanda his happiness, far from it. It just makes her feel lonely and used up.

Little Sanyo gets to fall in love, and is miraculously saved by a sacred image in bronze. Nothing could be sweeter than that. She suspects that the first person had something of a soft spot for Little Sanyo, who should have died in that missile blast. The librarian can't ask for anything as extraordinary and exalted as that. Love and Salvation! But surely she's entitled to a little compensation.

Take Flay, next up. He gets to go out in a blaze of glory. He couldn't have asked for more.

Rasputin's god grants him a true vision of the driftdead.

The poor Reverend Stickman is granted the agony of love, even if too late.

Akona makes a new friend, and reclaims the land of her ancestors.

To make matters worse, the evil baron gets let off the hook and is rewarded for his evil with a vision of God's Algorithm, even if he has to turn into a simpleton to do it. How disgusting is that? He should at least have died an agonising death and been sent to hell in brackets. Still, the First Person giveth and the First Person taketh away.

Mary gets to flout her collar before getting her comeuppance, the Mayor dies on a platter of gold, even the bloody dog is transformed... The librarian has used up all her fingers now, but there is one missing. A phantom finger. Orchid. There is a hole where Orchid's ending should be. Last the librarian saw of her, she was standing by the helicopter just as Flay was knocking out Blue Zither, having just handed the Baby to the nimble Witch Hunt. What happened to her? Where did she go?

This reminds the librarian of other holes in the narrative, such as how Sirocco ended up with the Baby, but this is not one she can patch. As she sees it, the responsibility is wholly on the first person. She points her finger right at me.

All the effort she's put into her narrative seems wasted now that the driftdead have trampled over everything.

Still brooding on the injustice of it all, she gets up and wanders into the library, her strength and solace. Hush hush! Here be books. The mind cannot be quietened so easily. What does she get? she asks me. Where is she when the goodies are being given out at the end? The good guys get the rewards and the bad guys get their comeuppance; that is the way it's always been. That doesn't change just because the world goes mad.

She looks around the library. Everything looks very familiar. A familiar silence reigns. All the authors are in their proper places. Hush hush! Here be order, the stately unfolding of the alphabet.

No one comes to the library and leaves empty-handed. That's the rule. Everybody has a chance to find their First Person.

In her little writing room her blue eye springs into life all by itself. It has done that before, jerking itself out of sleep mode. Power surges probably. It blinks a couple of times, like a call to action. Is that all? she asks me. Is that all I get? More work? More words on the crawl to the end of the line.

Is that it? More sleepless nights? Days on the chain gang.

I don't answer her. It may seem cruel, but it's better that way. She thinks I have omniscient powers, but what she doesn't appreciate is that I am little more than a distraction as far as she's concerned. I know her but she can never know me. There's nothing I can do to change things and make everything the way she wants, force events to conform to the images she forms in her mind. She thinks I can send the driftdead back to the north, and the winds back to their four directions, and all the other things she would like to see that would right the wrongs of the world and put all the upturned furniture on its feet in alphabetical order.

Here she is, between Highway 6 and nowhere. With no recourse.

She sits at the keyboard once more. The blue eye is alert. There's nothing else to do but face the job. The job ahead. Word work. She can do it; it's what she does. She doesn't need me, not the way she thinks she does. I guess she knows that once she starts writing, I can never be that far away.

She knows where to find me, you might say.

Her fingers hover over the keys.

Coda

from The Book of Imaginary Sentences, written
by the ghost of Sirocco

the survivors

The keas are back. Little flocks of them. They keep crying out the town's name, as if they could raise the town back to life with their voices alone.

If you joined them, took to the sky, hovered on the lower slopes of Mt Irirangi and looked back towards the east coast, you might spy a group of people making their way slowly along the walking trail that leads up from the coast to the Wai-O-Tapu Spring, following the course of the Wai-O-Tapu River. They would look so tiny you could hardly make them out.

The survivors, they call themselves. The ones left over, Sad Toof says, as if they were somehow surplus to requirements, ingredients left over after a cake has gone in the oven. He makes it sound like a sad thing. A good story would have no leftovers. Everybody would be accounted for and ticked off, the bodies all laid out neatly for inspection.

There are pitifully few survivors, and I'm not one of them. I'm here in spirit only, you could say, ha ha. I am a self-appointed First Person, narrator by default, Sirocco in absentia, here only to witness the naming of the Baby. After that, the dispensation that allows me to stay here will be withdrawn; I will return to the desert and there'll be nothing left but the wind whining through the tussock on the foothills.

It's a little amusing to hear them talk about me from time to time.

Witch Hunt can't sense me, but nor can she quite believe I'm dead. Sad Toof feels the same way.

'He might have gone back to the desert,' Sad Toof says. 'I think Lizard will come and fetch him soon.'

I'd like to be able to tell them that that's not likely to happen, as Lizard has already said his goodbyes and I don't think there's much he can tell me about the desert I will soon be entering.

Come a little closer and you will soon see the remarkable little girl that leads the party. She has the Baby slung across her back, a spear in her hand, and by her side trots a mutant dog creature. They both move with a coordinated confidence. And so they might! Witch Hunt is the proud new Baby-bearer, and with the fearsome Frankenbeast by her side, Witch Hunt has become not just Baby-bearer but undisputed leader of the survivors.

Ostensibly, the spear is for any unexpected driftdead, but its real purpose is to signify her power. When she takes her spear and speaks, everybody listens.

No one is quite sure what happened to Orchid. She was never found after Flay's missiles put an abrupt end to the action on the Fairweather mansion roof. They assume she was killed in the blast but Witch Hunt secretly believes that Orchid died of broken dreams.

Behind the proud Baby-bearer and her preternatural guard comes Sad Toof, with the Blue Zither and her Uzi. Her hair is not really blue, and has grown into quite an ordinary brown colour. She was only knocked out by Flay when he stole the helicopter, joined the mokopuna and can make even the Baby laugh with her impersonations of others, particularly Sad Toof. Sad Toof of course doesn't laugh, but he is impressed nonetheless. He's already a little in love with her and dotes upon her every word. Witch Hunt has suggested quietly to her that she should get pregnant as soon as possible. That really makes her laugh.

Behind these two lovebirds comes Little Sanyo and Sun Petal, not quite love birds but getting there. They are doing most of the scavenging in the mansions and have found all kinds of treasures and interesting stuff. They found a teddy-bear with sapphire eyes, a fancy curved sword that might have been from the Crusades, and a lump of molten bronze about the size of a fist Little Sanyo swears to be the last remains of Arya Tara. They have both been living in Baron Fairweather's mansion, in the lower reaches away from the damage, and have spent many days picking their way through the wreckage of the main room and other interesting places. They have placed the piece of bronze on a table and have fun seeing all kinds of different shapes within. Little Sayno swears the lump keeps changing shape. 'It might look like a piece of metal,' he says, 'but it is really a cloud.'

No one except Sun Petal believes him.

Behind these two scavengers come Rasputin and a new boy they call Fortune. Nobody is quite sure who he is or where he came from, but one morning Rasputin found a small boy sitting some distance from the marae, watching them. He wasn't making much of an effort to hide. Irawaru had already spotted him and was sitting at a discreet distance when Rasputin approached the boy. He seemed more bewildered than afraid.

No one was sure if he was a driftdead or not, but they gave him some food which he ate, although mechanically, and only after staring at it for a long time. So far he's only spoken one word, fortune, which immediately became his name.

Rasputin has speculated that Fortune was once a driftkid whose soul re-entered his body and one day he woke up to find himself alive. Everybody wondered if that could happen, and Fortune is the proof that it can. Like rays of light shining through dark clouds, God's grace touches here and there, he says. Sad Toof is sceptical of the idea, and the notion of salvation in general. The kid could just as well be an urchin who travelled with the driftdead but was not one of them. Someone who just got pulled along. Or he could be the phantom pipe player sometimes heard in the hills.

Whatever the truth might be, the little boy is quickly becoming a part of the mokopuna. When he saw the stores in the ruins of the baron's mansion his eyes grew as huge as Irawaru's. And he's not the only stray kid out there. There are others who haven't yet had the courage to show themselves, but who are just waiting the chance. Soon, I think, Witch Hunt will order Blue Zither and Fortune to go out and bring them in. Maybe they are driftdead coming back to life, finding themselves once more subject to cold and hunger. Maybe they are refugees fleeing the driftdead. The survivors will find out, but I will be gone by then. Very soon, in fact.

Fortune has quickly attached himself to Rasputin, and follows him around wherever he goes. Rasputin is still a dark horse, a loner, but since he dropped the Saviour of Mankind business, he's turned out to be pretty okay. It seems that without the reverend around, God stopped bothering the boy and he felt better for it. His big revelation was to realise that he is nothing special, not singled out by some malicious deity for extraordinary tortures or some exalted fate but just an ordinary kid, a bit shy and sometimes able to see things other people can't. Like the souls dancing on the heads of the driftdead. No one else can see them but we all pretty much believe that they're there, because since he dropped all the God stuff and became ordinary he's much more believable. He doesn't preach at all, just talks about ordinary things, and Witch Hunt has had to talk him into doing some religious duties, like saying a prayer over the graves of the mayor and the others mowed down by the mad mechanic.

Witch Hunt likes him much better without his big god-smile. Once she came across him at Stag Point praying. She was impressed by the way he was wrapped up in the sinewy arms of his god.

Without thought, she dropped down beside him and joined him in that quiet, intense moment. Rasputin looked at her in sheer surprise. As far as he knew she didn't believe in anything, but sometimes spoke wistfully of Sirocco and Lizard. She didn't care about who might believe what. They were both just a couple of ignorant souls down on their knees before a sky larger than all the dreams of mankind, in a world deserted except for the dead who drift past on their way to nowhere.

Now that he's just an ordinary boy again Rasputin's fate is no longer readable or ordained. Without God there to orchestrate a happy ending, Rasputin is happy enough to take his chances with the rest of them from day to day with no guarantees. He has to live with the same uncertainty everybody does, unmarked by any god for a special destiny. Actually, he told Witch Hunt, the new uncertainty is no more uncomfortable than his god's certainty, a relief even. Now that's something that I, ghost or not, would like to understand better than I do. I'd always thought that those who live in the promises of their god are pretty much home and hosed as far as salvation goes.

Behind Rasputin and Fortune come the last surviving adults, Akona and the childlike baron. He's hardly the baron anymore, still less an adult. He's more like a big baby. He sits all day with his stick, rocking back and forward, doing maths in the sand. He seems to prefer the sand, even to the paper and pencil Sad Toof gave him to play with. Perhaps there is something visceral about the sand that makes the maths real, as if the sand were the true element out of which the numbers emerge. It makes me think of where all this started, me drawing circles and stars in the sand. The first wind arriving to mess it up.

Sometimes I look over his shoulder and I can see those circles and stars in his equations. The patterns I was searching for with my scratchings in the sand, the baron has completed. The baron is coming along to the Baby's naming on sufferance. He'd rather not go anywhere, but Witch Hunt decides he can't be left alone on the marae. He scuttles crablike behind Akona as if she were his mother, whimpering if she gets too far ahead. Every so often he tries to squat and dig his fingers into the ground where all his numbers are buried, but Akona keeps him moving.

All the other adults are accounted for – except the librarian. She has disappeared and nobody knows what has happened to her. Nobody saw anything. She has either left or locked herself in the library with the First Person. I don't believe she would ever willingly desert her post, or abandon her writing. After all, she has spent most of her life labouring away at her precious Chronicles of Keatown, and her love for Keatown has never been in doubt. Our witness and historian.

Some kind of superstitious dread has kept everybody from going to the library and opening it up. Little Sanyo checked it out. The library was locked and nobody wanted to force the door. They didn't want to find her dead, or turned, or anything like that. Compelled by his curiosity, Little Sanyo will eventually do it, but that hasn't happened yet.

Rasputin, who was the last to see her outside the gate to the baron's rooftop before Flay's missile hit, said she was devastated by the massacre and had a big argument with the First Person. That sounds bad. We know that, for the librarian, the First Person is, if not exactly a god, then a superior presence with much greater authority than herself, and that relations between them were not always easy. Everybody is answerable to somebody, Rasputin says.

I'd like to talk to the librarian about my book. The Book of Imaginary Sentences. Sometimes I get frightened. Driftwords, that's all they are; look at them too hard and they disappear in a puff of smoke. I know that she's felt the same way at times. There's a story in everything, she once said. See that rusting tractor in that paddock. There's a story to that tractor. I was very impressed by that. I'm sure her Chronicles must be wonderful. It's hard to write a book, even an imaginary one. And even harder being a ghost. She could tell me what to do, how to find the stories inside things instead of just writing lists. I mean, I have a list of things that require sentences, real sentences, in order to be properly imaginary. I don't understand this, but I'm sure the librarian would. And these sentences, I can't even be sure if they exist in the present or the past. If I don't know such simple things, how can my book be any kind of book? I'm sure the librarian could sort out this hopeless confusion. Also, it is easier for me to imagine an imaginary reader than to imagine a real one. Easier because an imaginary reader will do just what I want them to do, and see what I want them to see, and clap their hands whenever I hold up a sign that says, clap now. Real readers will not be half so co-operative, I'm sure, and the librarian could tell me more about them, having seen lots of them popping in and out of the library. She must be an expert in them by now.

I can't wait to talk to her all about it and get myself sorted out.

All the other adults are dead or turned, even the reverend, who died of grief shortly after the cataclysmic events at the baron's mansion. He just lay down and gave up his soul. Rasputin couldn't save him. Nothing could. I don't think even the appearance of God himself in person would have changed his mind. He was not ill, just too heartsick to keep living. He'd seen enough. He'd had enough. He'd looked right through the human heart to the other side of vanity, and there wasn't much left of him after that. Just a few tatters. In the end, his god had mercy on him.

Big Bill bled to death, alone, within an arm's reach of the gold that would be the basis of a new prosperity for Keatown. Odd little detail, at the moment he died, and his body relaxed, some chocolates wrapped in gold foil fell out of his pocket.

Flay's missile took care of all the rest. Although, Sad Tooth believes he has heard drunken singing coming from the mountains that can only be Ock Arglin, too tough to kill.

Behind Akona and the baron come the last of the party, the two goats, Lucifer and Nanny. They follow along, keeping a watchful eye on everything as they go, Irawaru in particular. As with the baron, Akona had been reluctant to leave them behind. Unlike the baron, they are too precious to be allowed out of sight.

The only remaining celebs, the Benedicts, take no notice of them. Perhaps it is all that fresh air and tantric sex, but this vigorous pair haven't turned. In fact, their lives have hardly changed at all.

Despite Flay's missile, the baron's food cellars are largely intact. As it turns out, the place was built like a bunker with fortified walls at every level. Maybe the baron knew the day would come. Here, at the end of the world, in the depths of the Long Emergency, the survivors sit in the lap of luxury, years' worth of supplies all around them. And there are other mansions, too, some similarly stocked. It feels odd to sit in the ruins of the town and feed on caviar, bamboo shoots and the finest Mediterranean olives, but they soon get over that.

the dead don't dream

The survivors are quite familiar with the section of the track they are now walking. It has become the preferred route to the mansions, being a somewhat gentler slope than the steep steps at the top of Beauty

Parade. Although, except for Little Sanyo and Sun Petal, they prefer to live on the marae, they spend a lot of time up mansions looting food, and anything else they need.

As this little party makes its way up the river, they encounter a few driftdead but take no notice of them.

The ranks of these zombified invaders have thinned considerably, to the point where they have once more become little more than a nuisance. The baron's vision of the old man disintegrating has been repeated many times since. The driftdead, or at least some of them, are literally vanishing into thin air. Little Sanyo tells everybody the story of what happened to the boy he had chained up in the barn, how he just vanished. Maybe they will all vanish.

But some do not, and are still just plodding south, adults and children, as if nothing has changed. Sometimes it looks as if whole families are on the move, but that is an illusion, a coincidence of movement.

There are still others, however, whose tendency to stop and notice the world around them, peer into windows and so on, has also increased. In them, the overriding desire to go south has lessened. They are the biggest nuisances, as they tend to crowd around doorways, or cluster where people are. These seem to be haunted by their memories of humanity, perhaps of the lives they once led. Akona found one in her house sitting at the table as if waiting for a meal to be delivered. Sad Toof saw another trying to open the door of Flay's abandoned alfie, repeating the same motions over and over again. Rasputin found one lying in his bed staring at the ceiling.

In this last phase, just as the driftdead appear to be fading, a new mystery has opened up. Now many of the silent invaders are dressed in all kinds of period costumes, as if they are off to a dress-up party, or as if they have just walked through some time portal. One was dressed like a king, with a crown upon his head and a jewel-encrusted sceptre in his hand. He walked along grandly, as if through throngs of admirers.

The survivors are starting to dream once more, another sign the plague is on the decline. I envy them this more than anything else. The dead don't dream, for there is no night in this realm fit for dreaming.

The survivors hardly noticed that their dreams had stopped until they started again. Blue Zither is the first to have reported a dream. She was back in the mansions during the invasion of the driftdead, fighting for some elbow room, pushing and clawing. Others also have reported dreaming of packed rooms or hemmed-in spaces. People everywhere. Strangers clamouring to get into their dreams. Sad Toof dreamed that he created a huge hall inside the iceberg, a great cave of ice to accommodate them all. Witch Hunt dreamed that she was the empress of a vast empire, and that Irawaru, her consort, had been turned back into man, a very handsome prince. Her dreams had casts of thousands toiling beneath a warming sky.

'We have all been a little driftdead,' Rasputin commented. 'If losing your dreams is the first step towards turning, we all took that first step.'

'Now we have to dream for all of them driftdead,' Sad Toof said. 'It's not fair.'

the cloak of rage

After they have passed the first now meaningless Private Property sign, Witch Hunt calls a halt and they rest in the shade of some beech trees. The heat of the day has built up quickly, and the Baby feels heavy on her back. Akona bathes her feet in the cool water. The baron stares at the river as if he has never seen moving water before. He tries to touch it, as if it were something solid. Irawaru laps up water in great gulps. Sad Toof grumbles about the heat. Blue Zither lies down in the river, clothes and all.

Akona seems quite placid. She has cleared the area from there to the spring of the explosives the baron placed everywhere. Irawaru led her to them. He knew exactly where they were placed. She has every reason to feel some satisfaction, having secured the spring, but that is not exactly what she is feeling. In fact, what she is feeling is something of a mystery, even to me, reminding me that even I, in this situation, have limited powers. This self-appointed First Person can't know everything.

In point of fact, being a ghost narrator is working out pretty well for me, so far. It's working out okay for the Book of Imaginary Sentences too. I've got lots of real words by now. It's rather fitting, I think. Only the words are real, the rest is smoke and mirrors, as they say. Pipe dreams. Being a ghost narrator has some advantages. I can pretty much be anywhere at any time with nobody seeing me. The perfect fly on the wall. Except Akona. Akona can see me, mostly. Or rather, sense my spectral presence.

When that happens, she is able to cloak herself in a way that prevents me from knowing what she's thinking. All I can do now, for example, is watch her kick her feet in the water, and the striations of reflected light from the river on her face. Her expression is unreadable; her thoughts are carefully hidden from my scrutiny.

This is not the Akona I know, or at least the one I knew when I was alive. Like everyone else, she had her private places, but nothing so dark it must hide from everything, even a ghost.

Come to think of it, she hasn't been her old self since the battle of the mansion. Something is eating away at her. That's the expression. I should be able to see it, but I can't. After those momentous events, Akona fell largely silent, like the Man in Black. She speaks only when spoken to, and then as briefly as possible. The others have taken this silence for wisdom, but I can see that it isn't that. There is purity in wisdom that makes for beauty. Akona has the air of one who has renounced beauty.

All this time she has been preparing herself for something, something too horrible to even contemplate, and I don't know what it is. Grimly, she has gone about her duties, clearing away the explosives, getting Witch Hunt and Baby established at the marae, transferring Irawaru's allegiance from herself to the Baby-bearer. This last was the most difficult of all. Irawaru obeyed, but everybody could see his sadness. She has carried out these activities with the air of someone ticking items off a list.

And now the last item. The naming of the Baby.

Perhaps she is simply impatient to be gone, to follow the Man in Black along the trail of her ancestors to the Western Land beyond the mountain, impatient to shake the dust of Keatown from her heels – but I don't think that's it. She is a person of this place, an expression of it; she is not anxious to be gone, or to travel too far from the place of her ancestors.

All that I can sense is that she is building herself up to some momentous act, something that will change the world forever. Something she won't even let the spirits see.

I'm not the only aspect from the spirit realm attending these events. I keep catching fragments, bits of memory, momentary awarenesses coming and going; names and histories and emotions. A moment of hope, a moment of hatred; a birth and a murder. To ascribe identity to these remnants is fanciful. Here, nothing stays still even for a moment.

It's all remains and residues, lees and leftovers, all mixed up and flying around. There is no gravity of the flesh to hold all those bits and bobs together. But here and there something forms that might be called a presence. Usually in forms around some powerful emotion or intent.

I can feel them around me, but I can't see anything because there is nothing to see.

There's a warrior figure that can only be Nōpera Kāmaka. And a queenliness that smells of carbolic soap that makes me think of Ellen Johnson. And there is another I know to be Alfred Kensington from the tender feeling he had for his wife, Beatrice Johnson, daughter of Ellen. I am momentarily swamped in his love for her, and his determination to leave their family rich in lands.

This is no peaceful procession of ancestors turning up to witness the naming of the Baby, but a confused swirl of disturbed emotions. All is not well here in the afterlife, if that's what this is. I can hear sounds of conflict, the clash of arms, the cries of the dying, the screams of women and children. The world in all its bloody history is swirling all around us.

At the centre of all this Akona sits placidly, dangling her feet in the river, planning whatever it is she is planning. She is not just at the centre of it. It is all inside her. Akona is changing, slowly turning into something else, the shape of which I cannot see.

She is the first on her feet after the break. She tugs at the baron's arm to get him moving. He's now trying to inscribe his equations on the moving water.

naming the baby

From the Wai-O-Tapu Spring hardly anything can be seen of the mansions except for the nearest, a series of domes like a moon base a comfortable distance away.

There is nothing around but rocks and sky.

Its energy undimmed, water surges from the Wai-O-Tapu. They can all feel the power of it under their feet.

'What are we gonna call him?' Sad Toof wants to know.

Everybody looks at everybody else, and then at Akona. A few names have been bandied about, even my own. That's a silly idea. It was never my real name. I lost my real name somewhere back in the desert.

Besides, who'd want to name a child after an errant wind?

Everybody looks to Akona, for while Witch Hunt is the Baby-bearer, no one doubts that the surviving village elder should name the Baby. It is her privilege. Her moment.

But now that the moment has arrived, Akona hesitates. It's as if she is caught in two contrary winds. She looks over at Witch Hunt. I wonder if I am the only one able to see her trembling. Not an ordinary leaf-in-the-wind trembling, but a deep-seated ambivalence. Whatever it is, it will soon be visible to me. No one else seems to notice anything amiss.

There is no protocol for this moment. Nobody really knows what to do. At the same time, the moment is so ceremonial everything takes on a ritualistic aspect. Everybody watches with a suitable solemnity as Witch Hunt slides the Baby off her shoulders and out of the backpack.

The Baby rises to the occasion by perking up and looking about alertly. When he sees Irawaru he grins delightedly and waves his arms about. A moment later he is distracted by the spring. He becomes fascinated with the up-thrusting water. His eyes are magnetised by it.

Witch Hunt briefly holds the Baby to her chest, and hands him over to Akona without hesitation. After the battle of the mansions, everybody expected Akona to become the new Baby-bearer; that seemed the most natural thing to happen. No one knows exactly why she passed the role over to the 'liddlist of the liddle', except that she was getting ready to leave. As she has been silent on the issue, as on so much else, the matter has never been cleared up.

Now, as the Baby passes from Witch Hunt's hands into Akona's, I get a sudden glimpse of something entirely different, as if at that moment Akona has become one of the driftdead.

'No, no!' I scream, but as the old saying goes, you can't scream if you don't have a mouth. And even if I could, they wouldn't hear me. Nobody would hear me but the desert hawk. I may be the self-appointed First Person but nobody knows I'm here. I can't change anything. Not even in this imaginary book. I can understand now what the librarian's First Person was trying to tell her.

Akona holds the Baby in the crook of her arm. There he is, once the hope of Keatown. There he is, the inheritor. Gently she rocks him back and forth. The oldest and the youngest of Keatown, for a moment a single being. The Baby looks up at her and his eyes grow as huge as Irawaru's. He can see what I can see, but he is not frightened. He is fascinated. Suddenly Akona is as interesting as the rushing water of the Makurutanga. Perhaps he doesn't understand enough to be frightened. Since one of the living, even a baby with no real words to describe it, can see it, my own impression is confirmed. I can help the Baby out. I can find my own imaginary words for what we are both seeing.

Which is, Akona has turned.

Not into a driftdead, but something far less benign, as if the driftdead were just the first wave, and the second wave was this, the eclipse of the soul, mostly invisible to others but transforming its victim into his or her own shadow self.

And here she is, the shadow Akona, in the flesh. It would have been better if she had turned in the normal way and trudged south. We wouldn't be here, at this moment, with me so helpless, as this Akona thing nods to the four directions and steps towards the water, the Baby still resting in the crook of her arm.

I go to each one of them and try to tug at their minds. Witch Hunt, Sad Toof, Blue Zither, Fortune – and last of all Rasputin. If anybody other than the Baby and me could see it, it would be the god boy. Rasputin is no stranger to darkness, or eclipses of the soul. But he can't see it. None of them can. He's thinking about the naming of the Baby, running lots of names through his mind like a roll call of the unborn. He looks at Akona and sees what he expects to see, a familiar figure.

Then Irawaru sees it. Strangely, he turns his head up to the sky and snarls, as if at all that immensity. Now three of us can see it, three who cannot speak. I'm walled right off. I can see everything as if through glass. In vain do I beat on the glass. I'm only a momentary creation myself, a brief flare of luminosity as I see and understand.

No! No!

Finally I grasp the moment I witnessed as I lay dying from Mary's stab wound: Akona, stumbling when she learned that Orchid was the Baby's mother as if she'd been hit in the heart. That was the moment, the moment she turned. The moment her eyes went dead.

It had been carefully hidden from her, the fact that Orchid was the mother, for very good reasons. Orchid's mother, Alice, was Jack Kensington's sister. And Jack Kensington was Bob Kensington's father.

The Kensingtons would inherit what was left of Keatown. The nothing and the everything: the storm-wrecked land, the burnt-out sky. The Kensingtons would inherit the earth.

When she saw that, she turned. The dying Sirocco witnessed that moment. She knew what she had to do. Like a driftdead, she could have only one purpose, one aim.

And here it is, the moment. There is death in her hands. She steps into the water, the Baby still cradled in one arm. She doesn't feel the cold, just the sinewy movement of water against her legs.

'What are we going to call him?' Witch Hunt says, an edge of nervousness in her voice.

Akona knows, but she is not going to say it out loud.

There will be no name.

The Baby will go into the water. He will go under the water. But he will not come back. Not alive. Not if she holds to her grim intent. They will never stop her in time.

A baby's life hangs from such a thin thread, doesn't it?

But the real terror of this turning is that she is not a zombie. She is still there, inside the shadow, a morally responsible being. She can stop it. In fact only she can stop it. But only if she wants to, and she hardly wants to. She stoops over and lowers the Baby.

As the Baby enters the water he gives a thin wail, echoed on the bank by the goats.

Witch Hunt makes a rush for the water, Irawaru at her side. They know it's too late, but there's nothing else to do. It's up to Akona now. Everything hangs in the balance.

As the Baby goes under the water, Akona's mouth stumbles for a blessing. Her tongue reaches for a name.

The words are a long way off.

End

Also by Mike Johnson

Novels
Lethal Dose
Zombie in a Spacesuit
Hold My Teeth While I Teach You to Dance
Travesty
Counterpart
Stench
Dumbshow
Antibody Positive
Lear: The Shakespeare Company Plays Lear at Babylon

Shorter Fiction
Confessions of a Cockroach/Headstone
Back in the Day: Tales of NZ's Own Paradise Island
Foreigners

Poetry
The Raising Light Trilogy
Ladder With No Rungs, Illustrated by Leila Lees
Two Lines and a Garden, Illustrated by Leila Lees
To Beatrice: Where We Crossed the Line
Vertical Harp: The Selected Poems of Li He
Treasure Hunt
Standing Wave
From a Woman in Mt Eden Prison & Drawing Lessons
The Palanquin Ropes

Non-Fiction
Angel of Compassion

Children's Fiction
Flippity Fluppity Flop, Illustrated by Daniela Gast
Kenni and the Roof Slide, Illustrated by Jennifer Rackham
Taniwha. Illustrated by Jennifer Rackham

Mike Johnson, fiction writer and poet, is recognised as one of New Zealand's leading, innovative writers. He lives on Waiheke Island and has taught creative writing at AUT University and the University of Auckland. In 2002 he received The University of Auckland's Literary Fellowship, having been Literary Fellow at Canterbury University in 1987. His first novel, Lear, the Shakespeare Company Plays Lear at Babylon was short listed for the New Zealand Book Awards in 1986, his novel Dumb Show won the Buckland Memorial Award for Literary Excellence in 1995, and he won the Frances Kean Award his short story, 'Magic Strings' in 1999. His first book of poetry, The Palanquin Ropes, (1983) was co-winner of the John Cowie Reed Memorial Competition. His non-fiction, Angel of Compassion, was shortlisted for the Ashton Whyle Award in 2014, and a poem from Vertical Harp, The selected poems of Li He (2006) has been anthologised in the Essential New Zealand Poems: Facing the Empty Page (Random House, 2015).

Mike Johnson is the author of twenty-six books including nine books of poetry, three of shorter fiction, one non fiction, three children's books, and ten novels.

www.ingramcontent.com/pod-product-compliance
Lightning Source LLC
Chambersburg PA
CBHW032110110726
47902CB00003B/531